THE EAST BERLIN SERIES
Omnibus Edition

'A compelling re-imagining of East Germany's peaceful revolution in 1989—exploring what might have been. As Europe grapples with the consequences of austerity, this novel poses questions both about the lost chances of 1989, and about how we organise our society—questions that are becoming more relevant with each passing day.'

Fiona Rintoul, author of *The Leipzig Affair*

'An authentic atmosphere of tension and uncertainty ... The brilliance of *Stealing the Future* lies in the honest portrayal of a young country and its idealistic inhabitants struggling to keep alive their dream of freedom, justice and equality in the face of international and domestic opposition.'

Jo Lateu, *New Internationalist*

'Creates the perfect atmosphere that existed around the fall of the wall: the sense of hope dashed by the awful reality of reunification.'

Peter Thompson, *The Guardian*

'An intriguing and gripping page-turner of a thriller—believable and exciting. More than that, though, it's an exploration of power—political, economic and electric power; and what it might be like, day to day, to put our ideals and hopes for self-determination into practice.'

Clare Cochrane, *Peace News*

ALSO BY MAX HERTZBERG

The East Berlin Series
Stealing The Future (2015)
Thoughts Are Free (2016)
Spectre At The Feast (2017)

Reim Series
Stasi Vice (2018)
Operation Oskar (2019)
Berlin Centre (2019)
Baltic Approach (2020)
Rostock Connection (2021)

Other Fiction
Cold Island (2018)

Non-fiction
with Seeds For Change
How To Set Up A Workers' Co-op (2012)
A Consensus Handbook (2013)

After the experience of the East German political upheaval in 1989/90, Max Hertzberg became a Stasi files researcher. Since then, he has been a book seller and a social change trainer before writing his debut novel, Stealing The Future (2015).

Visit the author's website for background information on the GDR, guides to walking tours around the East Berlin in which many of his books are set and to sign up to his newsletter.

www.maxhertzberg.co.uk

THE EAST BERLIN SERIES
Omnibus Edition

Max Hertzberg

Stealing The Future
Thoughts Are Free
Spectre At The Feast

WOLF PRESS

P 1 2 3 4 5 6 7 8 9 10

Omnibus edition published 2021
ISBN: 978-1-9131251-4-1 (paperback)
ISBN: 978-1-9131250-7-3 (epub)

Stealing The Future first published in 2015
ISBN: 978-0-9933247-0-3 (paperback)
ISBN: 978-0-9933247-1-0 (epub)

Thoughts Are Free first published in 2016
ISBN: 978-0-9933247-2-7 (paperback),
ISBN: 978-0-9933247-3-4 (epub)

Spectre At The Feast first published in 2017
ISBN: 978-0-9933247-4-1 (paperback),
ISBN: 978-0-9933247-5-8 (epub)
This edition and previous editions published by Wolf Press.
www.wolfpress.co.uk

Wolf Press, 22 Hartley Crescent, LS6 2LL

Set in 11 on 12½pt Libertinus Serif

Stealing the Future
Book I of the East Berlin Series

The German Democratic Republic
showing the situation of West Berlin and West Silesia

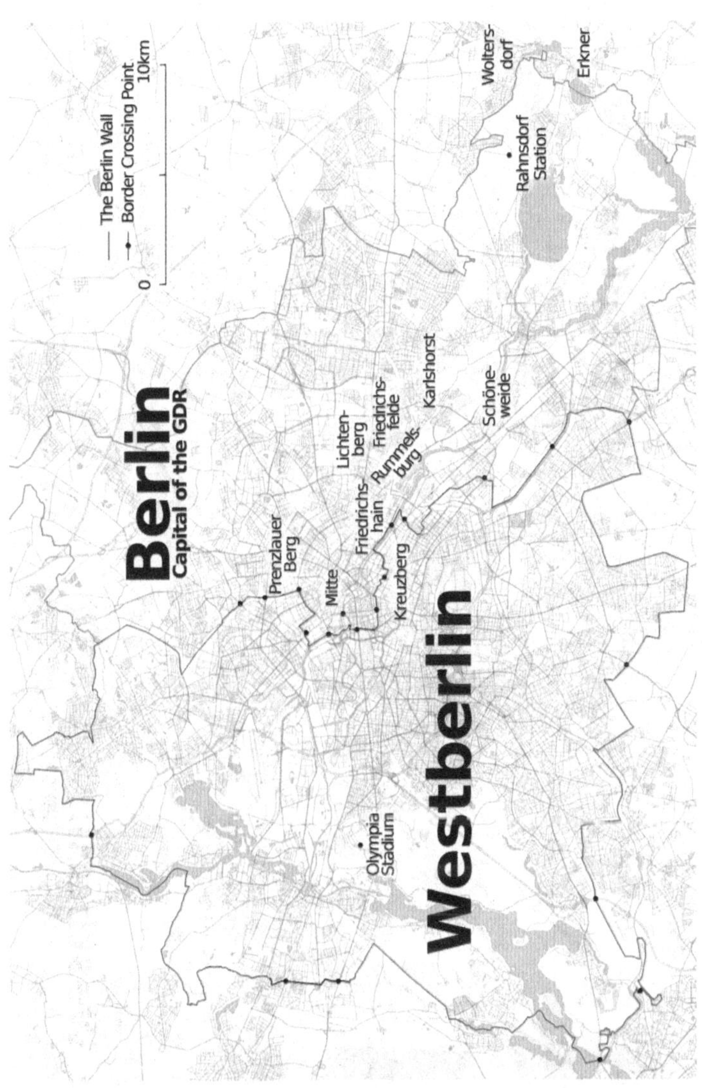

Berlin
showing West Berlin and
Berlin, Capital of the GDR

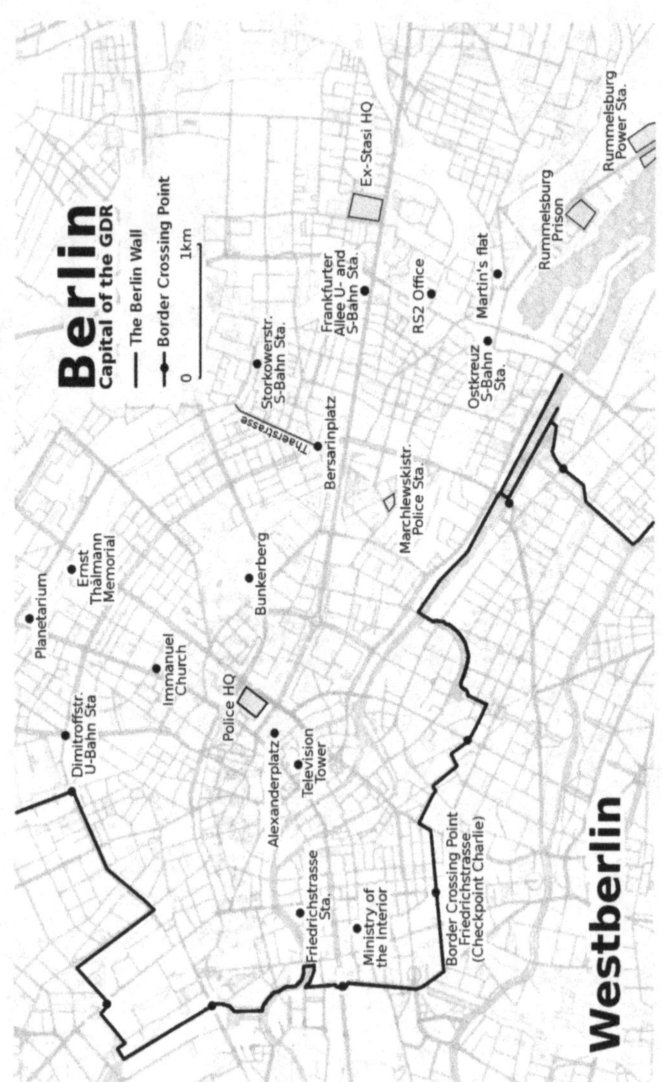

Central Berlin

DAY 1
Wednesday
22nd September 1993

13:07

Sunshine and darkness march across my path, the car diving through bands of light and shade. My eyes struggle to adjust to the glare flickering through trees lining the road, but after a few kilometres of peering through the dusty windscreen I make out a pair of petrol pumps, a prefab hut. The Trabant rumbles across the concrete slabs, and the attendant appears, wiping hands on overalls.

"What have you got?" hoping for anything.

"It's not good, whatever it is—even thicker than heating oil," he rubs his face with an oil-spotted rag, looking away, up the road, out of the sandy town. "It'll work. I cut it with grain schnapps—you'll get home."

I turn away, gesturing with a cigarette by way of an excuse, and wander to the side of the road. Lighting up, I watch him lift the bonnet and fill the tank from a canister, still talking about the fuel. The radio in the car chatters to itself: ... *protests continue throughout the Soviet Union after President Gorbachev was impeached yesterday. It's not yet clear whether Gorbachev is under house arrest, but reports indicate he is negotiating with both the army and the KGB.*

I could go back to the car, turn a knob, silence the newsreader. But turning my own thoughts off will be much harder. I'm tired, *dead tired.*

Not the best turn of phrase.

The image of the body on the rails hangs before me in the blue-grey haze of the cigarette. The head crushed, the feet crushed.

Not crushed, no ... I need a better description. I tap ash off my cigarette.

Smeared.

There was nothing left to indicate the shape of the head or feet: bone, flesh and brains smeared along the rails and around the heavy steel wheels. The smell of blood might have been there, merging with sand and hot metal.

Above the torn body a steel lattice work, thirty storeys high, half a kilometre long. Its sheer size giving it a gravity that dragged my attention towards it—I hadn't known where to look: the body, or the mining machine.

Rusty girders merged with the dusty air over the exposed coal seam. My mind, silted with sand and blood, refused to take in the impossibility of what my eyes were seeing. I could only look from one to the other. Corpse. Machine. Corpse again. Both just too far from everyday life experience: I had no reference points, no context to help me understand them.

I force myself back to the present, the practicalities of the case. Breathing in smoke, breathing out questions.

Who was the person this body used to be? Local cops were working on that—papers pulled from the victim's pockets identified him as the politician Hans Maier. Fingerprints would confirm his identity. Maier had always made a big thing about his persecution in the 'eighties by the Stasi: there'd be files, prints would be on some record, somewhere.

But why was a politician dead on the tracks? And why had the local West Silesian police called their Saxon colleagues in? Considering the pressure we were facing from West Germany over the Silesian question, the whole situation is nothing short of alarming.

Thinking things through, I feel my shoulders and neck tighten. I feel lost. Out of my depth. And above all, bloody scared.

Back in Berlin by early afternoon, I went straight to the office in Lichtenberg.

As I entered, the smells of the building—polished lino, *Optal* disinfectant and the warm earthiness of brown coal smoke—sharpened my concentration, helped me ready myself for what was coming. Up the stairs, past the discreet sign marked *RS2*, and through the door.

"Bärbel, can you get everyone together—my office?"

"Give me a minute or two."

Into the toilets, sluicing my face in rusty water, then a glance in the foxed mirror. I still looked tired, but was at least a little calmer. I'm at home here, I told the stranger in the mirror. He said it right back, so he must have been me.

What I've found out, what I fear, perhaps I can pass it on to the rest of the team—let them deal with it. The stranger in the mirror looked furtive, then guilty. That's not the way we do it any more he seemed to be saying. And he was right. Still, once I'd told my colleagues it would become a shared responsibility.

"A problem shared ..." I said to the mirror.

We usually met in my office, it was the biggest room on the floor, but it was dark, the net curtains dusty, hiding more of the light than they needed to. Using the moments before my colleagues arrived, I fished out a piece of paper that had only been written on one side, and a stub of pencil from the chaos that lived on and around my desk. I made brief notes about what I'd seen.

I'd just finished the short list when Klaus came in, smoking one of his cigars. He said nothing, but went over to the corner, lowering himself on to the most out of the way chair, putting his feet on another. Erika followed, grimacing at the smoke already hanging in the air, waving her hands in front of her face, but looking towards me.

"How's it going? You don't look so good-"

"In a moment, let the others get here first."

"There's only us three here today: Dieter's away, and Laura is at the Ministry. But here's Bärbel."

The secretary sat down in the corner, a pad of paper on her knee, pencil poised to take shorthand minutes.

"Klaus? Can you put that cigar out—I can't think with that stink."

Klaus shrugged, nipped the cigar and laid it gently in the ashtray. "What's up?" he asked.

"I didn't want to wait till the meeting tomorrow. I want to know what you think of this one. Have you got enough time right now?"

"You'd know if you hadn't missed the morning meeting." Erika, somewhere between disapproving and sympathetic.

"OK, let's get started."

Erika and Klaus were looking at me now, curious, concerned. Klaus slumped in his chair, Erika sat forward, her hands in her lap, eyes searching my face. I needed to learn to hide my impatience.

"I've been on the road since just after midnight. I've been to West Silesia and back," The way I said it, it sounded like I'd been all the way to Siberia, not West Silesia, just a few hours south of Berlin.

Erika's eyes widened slightly, her hands moved a fraction on her lap.

"Are we even allowed into West Silesia at the moment?" asked Klaus, studying his fingertips, acting nonchalant. But I could see the tenseness around his mouth.

"Probably not. I got a call from the Ministry of the Interior, so I didn't ask, just went.

"I don't know how the Ministry got hold of it, I guess the Saxon police were trying to pass the buck upwards. It was near Weisswasser. A body: the politician Maier. The big fish in the WSB," the *Westschlesischer Bund*—the West Silesian League, the party behind the move to split West Silesia from the rest of the GDR, our East German state. The WSB wanted West Silesia to become a West German enclave, like West Berlin, deep in our territory.

"What were the Saxon police doing there?" asked Klaus.

"Not sure. I'd like to know that too. I guess the local West Silesian cops just panicked, called their ex-colleagues. West Silesia haven't got the forensic set up, and all the records are still in Dresden, so they rely on the Saxons for technical support anyway.

"The body was found on the tracks those open cast mining machines run along." I didn't say it, but his body hadn't been found until the whole thing had run over him. Dozens of wheels dragging him along. "Identity papers were found on the body, they're checking his prints to confirm. We should know more in the morning."

Klaus looked tense, exhaling audibly. I felt exactly the same way. If the body was Maier's then we'd have a problem. The Silesians might accuse the GDR government of doing it, the West Germans would know how to use that as leverage—and the kind of leverage the West Germans were after was the kind that would make us give up West Silesia.

"I still don't get why they're so interested in Silesia."

The West Germans were pumping money and technical support into the Region. They were clearly still annoyed that three years ago we had held a referendum and voted not to be taken over by them. The whole world had expected us to gratefully allow ourselves to be swallowed up by our cousins in the West, but instead, we decided to remain independent. To remain the German Democratic Republic. To continue the social experiment we'd started the autumn before.

"We may be about to find out what their interest is. This whole thing scares me—the Ministry asked me to go and check it out, which means they suspect foreign interference. And we'd better hope it's the West Germans, because it isn't going to be the Poles, and that just leaves the Russians."

Erika picked up on my agitation. "Do we even have the experience to deal with this one?" She was watching me, a frown creasing her face. "There's something else bothering you too, isn't there?"

"I don't know, a gut feeling. But that body. It was awful," I didn't continue, but my thoughts ran on.

That place, barren, empty. Just dust and industrial equipment. Part of the moon, an immense rocket launcher collapsed across a sandy pit that stretched to the horizon. Underneath that immense machinery, underneath the rusted steel and the wheels, a dead man: broken, fragile, pitiful. Maybe I was just tired, but it had really got to me.

"You're right, this could have waited till tomorrow morning," I tailed off, feeling pathetic.

"No," Klaus sat up. "You're right to tell us. Might be a big one, might be coincidence. Why don't you tell us how far you've got, then go home and catch up on some sleep?"

"Not much to tell, I have some film of the crime scene." I took the small camera out of my pocket, and tossed it on the mess of my desk. "He was probably killed elsewhere and the body laid out on the rails." Other than that, just questions: why Maier? Why now? Why were the Saxon cops there? "The senior officer present, *Unterleutnant der Kriminalpolizei* Schadowski was very reasonable. First of all he didn't want to talk to me, but when I showed him my RS pass he was all 'Herr comrade *Oberleutnant*'. I guess these silly titles they gave us can be useful." The other two grinned, glad of a chance to break the tension; even in these times of change, official pieces of paper and officer status bought influence.

"There's so many more questions, but I can't work it all out. Too tired. Sorry, it's not much to show for a day's trip."

"Thanks Martin. If you want to go home I'll take the film up to the police technical support offices for a quick turn-around. Klaus and I will have a think about what else we need to work out. Let's check the photos and sort everything else out at the meeting tomorrow."

I looked at the other two, wishing I could follow their suggestion. I didn't feel up to these all night missions any more, they belonged to another time, a younger time. Perhaps a more idealistic time.

"No, I've been asked to report directly to the Minister. I should have gone straight there, but I wanted to talk to you first."

I got up and went to the door. Bärbel had already left the room, I could see her through the doorway, sitting at her desk. She'd put her notes in front of her and was reaching for the phone. Before I could leave, Klaus stopped me.

"Wait, one last question: who sent you down there?"

"The Ministry. It was the night duty officer."

Klaus nodded, his eyes unfocussed, far away, deep in thought. Erika and I watched him for a moment before I turned again and left.

16:31

I left the Trabant where it stood and walked to the station for the S-Bahn train. I'd spent enough of the day cooped up in the small car, and I enjoy getting the S-Bahn: once close to the centre of town, the train runs along a viaduct, giving a chance to look down on Berlin from on high, peer through first floor windows as you trundle past. My favourite bit is going between the museums—classical buildings between Marx-Engels-Platz and Friedrichstrasse—the pockmarked rendering of the Bode Museum's outside walls contrasted well with glimpses of exhibits beyond the windows.

Once past the museum I waited by the doors until we entered Friedrichstrasse station. Pulling on the handle, I heaved the heavy sliding door open and stepped off the still moving train. Down onto the platform, a slight skip to keep my balance. Moving with the crowd out into the open, I followed the street then crossed Unter den Linden. The Soviet Embassy stood huge before me, red flags hanging limp in still air. Down the side of the Aeroflot offices, and round the back to where the Mauerstrasse started.

The first building on the left was also imposing, but in a more antique style than the monumental Soviet mission behind me. From either side of the door a trio of flags hung: red and black flags flanking the new GDR flag, a black, red and gold German tricolour sporting the *Swords to Ploughshares* emblem of the opposition. All over the country variations of this flag were to be seen: the round crest often replaced by something else: black stars, red stars, sometimes even a black A in a circle, or a hole where the old communist hammer and compass had simply been cut out.

Next to the main door a graffito had been chalked on the wall: *Where there is authority there is no freedom*, I nodded at the sentiment, as I entered the building.

Showing my pass to the policeman standing guard on the door I went straight up the wide staircase to the first floor. The smells were the same as at my offices in Lichtenberg—*Sigella*, *Optal* and brown coal—but the lino here wasn't worn into brown patches, and the stairs and banisters were polished stone.

I told the secretary I was here to see the Minister about the body in West Silesia, and without looking up from her typewriter she gestured me to the row of chairs against the wall.

Instead of sitting down I took an empty glass from the table in the corner and wandered off to find a tap. I didn't hurry back, but stood in the corridor, enjoying the majesty of the staircase and the light shining through the stained windows. Behind me I heard the door to the Minister's office open. I turned to see him shaking hands with a man carrying a briefcase and wearing a light green suit, well cut from slightly shiny material. The suit obviously came from the West, as did the wearer.

I made no attempt to be discreet, remaining where I stood, watching as the visitor headed downstairs. He showed a certain confidence, suggesting he was no stranger here.

"Martin, you'd better come in." The Minister stood for a moment, adjusting the cuffs of his shirt peeking beyond his suit jacket sleeve.

"Have you come to see me?" Behind his large desk, the Minister was at home, confident.

"I've just returned from West Silesia. The night duty officer sent me down to have a look at Maier's body, said I should report directly to you on my return."

I wasn't certain the Minister already knew about Maier's death, but it was reasonable to assume he had been briefed by now.

"Mmm ... yes, it was you they sent down," he mumbled, more to himself than me.

"I'm sorry?"

"Do you have a report for me? Just hand it in to the secretary." He leafed through the papers in front of him, then looked up, slightly irritated that I was still there.

"As I said, I came straight here. I haven't had time to write anything, I thought you might want to a verbal report immediately."

"Yes, that's very kind of you. Well, you'd better let me have it, I suppose, since you're here now."

He nodded absently as I told him what had happened in the mine. I left out my reactions to the size of the conveyors and excavators, the helplessness of the broken body. I kept it all businesslike. At the end of the account he nodded once more, and asked me to let him have the written report by the end of the next day.

"And Martin? No need to worry about this, it's all in hand. What I mean is, there's no need to prioritise it over your other work. We can handle the liaison with the Saxon police and the Round Table sub-committee."

Without looking at me, the Minister returned to his papers, and I returned the half-full glass to the secretary.

The Minister's attitude perplexed me—but I also felt drained, happy not to think about Maier. After all, the Minister himself had told me not to worry.

We went way back, the Minister and I. It's not like we were close or anything, but still, must be more than ten years. Benno was his name, not that any of us called him that any more. We used to call him Benno or Pastor Hartmann, but nowadays we generally just called him 'the Minister'.

He used to be the vicar at one of the churches which gave shelter to opposition groups, a safe place to meet. But he had been more than that—he took part in some of the demonstrations and events that activists organised. Some said he only took part in actions if he was guaranteed exposure by Western journalists, and that he'd soon disappear once the cops showed up. There were often snide rumours and jokes circulating about him in opposition circles, usually when he was mentioned in one of the West Berlin papers. I didn't pay much attention at the time, but did notice that when the revolution really got going in November 1989 he very quickly managed to get a place on the Central Round Table that had begun by advising the government, and soon became a part of the government.

Most of us involved in the opposition movements at that time were working flat out, organising demonstrations, creating news-sheets and leaflets, helping new people to get involved, showing them how to design and print their leaflets and set up their groups. We didn't have time to sit down and negotiate with the Communist Party about how to run the state. But a few people—some who had been very involved in protest and resistance over the years, others merely on the fringes—started working with the Party. Most of them now occupied leading positions in what central government was left. A lot of power had been devolved down to the local level, but a few state functions remained stubbornly centralised: foreign affairs, customs and border controls, taxation and policing, in which somehow I had become a minor cog.

It was the end of the working day, the sun was hanging low in the sky, just visible over the top of the buildings opposite. I decided to walk down Mauerstrasse to get the underground line that would take me to Prenzlauer Berg. I hadn't been up there for a while, and I fancied a quick beer in a small bar, something different from the workers' pubs in my native Lichtenberg.

As I went down the steps onto the platform, I could feel the warm air being pushed out of the tunnel by an oncoming train, the same smell of hot metal and oil as this morning in the mine pit. I hopped on, finding a seat on the long bench along the side of the carriage, feeling slightly nauseous, lost in my thoughts of that sandy, dusty hell.

It took a few stops for me to become aware of my surroundings again. Lots of people boarded at Alexanderplatz, and I amused myself by playing Spot The Westerner. The number of Western tourists had increased dramatically in the last couple of years, and it looked like I wasn't the only person heading up to Prenzlauer Berg in search of a cool bar.

The train laboured up the steep ramp out of the underground and onto an elevated section of track, stopping almost immediately at Dimitroffstrasse station. I got off and crossed Schönhauser Allee, then took a few turns at random, pausing to read the neighbourhood Round Table's noticeboard. They'd provided a short summary of decisions at the top, with references to the relevant parts of the latest minutes posted below.

Sometimes it felt like our whole lives were being taken over by meetings, and even if you weren't at a meeting, the chances were somebody would expect you to know what had been talked about in it. At the end of a long day at work I didn't have the time or patience to read about the proceedings of every relevant meeting.

I turned away from the noticeboard, not bothering to read the notes, and still wanting a beer. It was too early for the clubs to open, but I hoped to find a drink somewhere not too far away. After a few hundred metres I stopped in front of a tenement block draped in flags and graffiti. Even by the standards of East Berlin this building was in a bad state. Balconies had fallen off or been untidily removed, and on the pavement lay mounds of bricks and dusty rendering. It looked to be one of the abandoned and derelict flats that had been squatted at the start of the revolution. Curious, I went into the entrance, and saw a crowd of punks drinking in the yard. Two of them were setting up a ladder below a broken light, stopping every so often to gulp down a mouthful of beer. When the ladder was in place, one climbed up while the other fed him electric cable. On the other side of the yard I could see the door to the cellars in the side wing, the word BAR crudely smeared in red paint. A few steps led down into a damp corridor. A bodged rack held leaflets, all jumbled up, and off to the side a door lay across two trestles with a crate of beer on it. Above the improvised table a slogan was daubed in the same red paint: *People who talk about revolution without understanding what is subversive about love, and what is positive in the refusal of constraints, such people have a corpse in their mouth.* Quite a mouthful, corpse or no, a typical sound bite from the Situationists. Something to ponder on while I had a drink.

Next to the crate of beer was a jam jar with a slit in the lid. I dropped a Mark in and took a bottle, looking around for a bottle opener. There was none, but a young woman appeared next to me, her head shaved at the sides, the remaining hair forming a drooping mohican, painted with washed-out red food colouring. She smiled at me, grabbed the beer out of my hand, and took the top off with her teeth.

"Nice trick."

"You gonna get me one then?"

Another Mark in the jam jar, and the punk took a bottle out of the crate, opening that one too with her teeth, then tapping my beer with her own.

"*Prosit!*" She smiled, looking slightly coy under her ragged hair, poor teeth giving her mouth a lopsided look.

"*Prosit!*"

I tipped my bottle, allowing the beer to trickle down my throat, and let out a sigh.

"Hard day?"

"Like you wouldn't believe. What's happening here?"

She mustered me as if trying to work out whether I was a cop. I must have passed.

"We're holding a talk on energy use in the GDR; you know, the energy crisis, pollution, brown coal. For the demo on Saturday. We're holding more talks on the theme too, every night next week in different squats and bars." She was enthusiastic, stumbling over her words, keen to impress me.

"Demo?"

The punk moved over to the leaflet rack and pulled out a tatty flier. Badly mimeographed, a line drawing of a power station spewing out clouds of smoke which made up the word DEMO. Underneath that: *For a sensible energy policy—in East and West. Alexanderplatz, Saturday 25th September, 14.00.* On the back was a mass of text, originally typewritten, but hardly legible after its journey through the smudgy copier. I read it over while I swilled my beer.

"Thanks," I said, screwing the scrap of paper into my pocket.

"You coming then?"

"The demonstration? You know, I might just be there."

Not sure why I said that, maybe it was because of the impression the open-cast coal mine had made on me. Whatever my reasons, it seemed to please the punk. She smiled at me again, and I stuck my hand out.

"I'm Martin Grobe."

"Karo," she said, shaking my hand.

I'd nearly reached the door when she called out.

"Hey, Martin!"

I turned back.

"Cheers for the beer!"

I gave her my best smile.

DAY 2
Thursday
23rd September 1993

... at 8 o'clock on Thursday the twenty-third of September, this is the news on Radio DDR I.

Moscow: *The Second Crisis of the Union in the USSR has deepened after President Gorbachev called elections for both Soviet Parliaments. Delegates of the dissolved Soviet of the Republics refused to leave the parliament building despite water and electricity supplies being cut off.*

Berlin: *The Ministry for Foreign Affairs has lodged a formal complaint with the West German Mission in Berlin concerning the supply of military hardware to the breakaway Region of West Silesia. So far neither the West German Mission nor the Inner-German Ministry in Bonn have replied. The Central Round Table will hold a press conference at the Palace of the Republic later.*

And now for the water levels and draughts on the inland waterways ...

08:07

I had the coffee ready when the others came into my office for the morning meeting, there were only four of us, plus Bärbel, who, as usual, sat in the corner without a word, pencil in hand. We shook hands with each other as we sat down and I turned the radio off.

I looked over to Laura. "Did the others fill you in on what happened yesterday?"

"It sounds quite horrible—are you OK?"

I nodded towards the package marked with a police stamp that Erika was holding. "Yes, I caught up on some sleep last night. But I'm not looking forward to seeing those photos."

We passed the pictures round. For all their gruesome detail, they told us little; they just showed the body of Hans Maier, head and feet crushed, legs ripped and stained with blood and oil.

"I asked Dresden to forward Maier's police and Stasi files," said Erika. "They arrived with the overnight courier. I've only had a quick look—but it was enough. See for yourselves." She put another package on the table.

"These are the photostats of the files the police have managed to pull so far." Erika looked at the top sheet, which had a letterhead reading *LdVP Sachsen*. "We've got copies of his F 16, F 22, a Disciplinary File and his I 210—his written declaration of commitment. That's all they could come up with at short notice—they said they'd carry on looking."

I sifted through the pieces of paper. Apart from the declaration, none of them actually had any markings on them to indicate which was which. I glanced through the handwritten document, the usual pompous phrasing: *On the basis of my Marxist-Leninist convictions, I, Johannes Friedrich Maier swear to collaborate with the Ministry for State Security in order to secure and strengthen the GDR …*

"Of course, we should look in the central archive in Ruschestrasse, but for the time being, this is what we have: the F 16 file has the person's real name. The reference number is in the top right-hand corner," continued Laura.

I looked at the file. Johannes Friedrich Maier, along with the various addresses he'd been registered at during the last twenty years. The reference number began with a Roman numeral.

"What was HA XVIII?"

"That was the MfS department monitoring industry," said Laura. "It makes sense—Maier always claimed to be a victim of the Stasi, but at the time he was a big fish in the *BMK Kohle und Energie*—the combine that did all the building work at power stations. He was in the main offices in Hoyerswerda for several years."

The next file card didn't mention Maier by name—it just had his reference number stamped in the corner. His codename: MILCHMÄDCHEN, date of birth, first contact in 1964 by HA I/12. The most interesting entry on this card was the field marked "IM-

Category/Offence". The entry here simply stated 'IM'—*Inoffizieller Mitarbeiter*, informal collaborator. This, along with the written declaration told us that he'd worked as an informant for the Stasi, and it looked like he'd been recruited in 1964.

"What was Maier doing in 1964?" I wondered aloud.

"Looks like he was doing his military service," answered Laura. "I put together a summary of his activities yesterday."

"You have been busy!"

A grunt from the other side of the table was Klaus's first contribution of the morning. I looked up.

"Yeah, these two got excited about doing something interesting," he gestured towards Erika and Laura.

"Well, it's good to get a head start, you never know what we'll be saddled with next," from Erika.

I could understand her irritation—Klaus rarely said very much, so when he did, it came across as an important announcement. Light-hearted criticism from him could sometimes feel like a serious accusation.

Klaus fell back into silence, and Erika and Laura busied themselves with flicking through the papers.

The final photostat must be the Disciplinary File. It had Maier's details, including his full name rather than his codename. The file was dated summer 1988, and scanning through the text I could see that Maier had been reprimanded for having an inappropriate relationship with another asset, and had been told to end the affair. There was no further information.

"I've never seen one of these before—why has Maier got one?" I asked.

"It's interesting, I thought they were only used for Stasi full-timers, not for informants. But Maier was just an IM, not a paid officer— looks a bit strange. If we had the VSH card then we could double check, but they didn't send it. Maybe it got lost." The answer came from Laura, who had become something of a Stasi files expert.

"None of this seems to help though, does it? Half the files are missing, and the ones we do have don't really tell us anything." Klaus was studying the cobwebs up in the corners near the ceiling, probably in an attempt to avoid Erika's indignant glare.

"I guess all this doesn't really matter anyway. The Minister asked me to write up a report on my trip to Silesia and to leave it at that," I looked around at the others, all staring at me.

"He told you to drop it?" asked Laura.

"Yeah, said I'm not to worry about it."

"Wait a moment," Klaus suddenly leaned forward, like he had a point to make. "Did he actually tell you to stop working the Maier case?"

"No ... not in so many words. But he definitely meant it."

"So, what did he say?"

"That I shouldn't worry about it, erm ... and not to prioritise the report, even though he also said he wants it by the end of today."

"OK, so, we can carry on working on it. After all he didn't tell Martin to drop it-"

Erika held up her hand, palm outwards, as if to stop the flow of the conversation.

"It's clear he meant we should leave it. Presumably someone else is working on it and we shouldn't just go against him like that. And anyway, what's the point?"

Klaus shrugged, sitting back in his chair again and crossing his legs. We all sat looking at each other, slurping coffee from our mugs. All except Bärbel who was still taking shorthand notes.

"Now that I think about it ..." I started, wondering whether I was saying the right thing. "He seemed sort of, shifty. Like he was unhappy that I was involved, he couldn't wait to get rid of me."

"Doesn't have to mean anything. Probably a bit stressed or busy. I think it's safe to assume the case is being dealt with, no doubt by another RS department. Klaus—do you really think we should carry on looking into Maier's death?" Laura asked in a matter of fact way.

She saw herself as the grounded and rational one in the office, and she wasn't wrong about that. She wasn't just seen as being a little bossy, she also had an obvious need to keep busy, and see others around her being kept busy too—I think this led her to chivvy us along, make sure we were doing our work, that our meetings didn't go off-topic and down sidelines. It could be annoying, but on the whole I think we appreciated having her around—she kept us on our toes.

"No, not really. It just all piqued my interest—it all sounds a little far fetched. But no, I think you're right," Klaus looked down, fiddling with one of his evil cigars.

"OK, so shall we leave it there then?" Still the voice of reason, Laura was looking around at us, checking that each of us agreed. "Right, so that's that. What else have we got on the agenda today?"

After the meeting I decided to write up the report on my trip to Weisswasser, get it out of the way so that I could concentrate on the stuff I ought to be doing.

It didn't take too long, after all there wasn't much to say: I went to West Silesia, I saw a body and a mining machine, the police seemed to be taking care of everything, so I came home. I didn't bother mentioning that my RS2 team had been looking at Maier's Stasi files —it didn't seem relevant, particularly since we weren't actually going to do anything with that information.

I finished the last page and pulled it out of the typewriter, putting the top sheet with the others in a file to take to the Ministry. The two carbon copies went in another pair of files, one to keep here, the other for the central RS archives.

I sat back in my chair and peered through the dusty net curtains. It was a nice day out there, the sun was shining, the sky blue. Shame to be cooped up in the office, I thought, much better to be outside.

10:23

I handed my report to the secretary, I could have sent it in the internal post, but I had enjoyed the trip to the Ministry. I was about to leave when she did that thing with her hand again, the disdainful wave towards the chairs. I waited while she decided whether she was going to tell me what she wanted.

"Wait. The *Staatssekretär's* assistant wishes to speak to you."

The secretary handed my report back to me, and I took both the file and a chair, like a good little boy. So Gisela Demnitz, the assistant to the senior civil servant at the Ministry, wanted to see me. She was the person I usually dealt with, the one with the responsibility for the peripheral agencies in the Ministry of the Interior.

I wasn't kept waiting—a buzzer on the secretary's phone soon sounded, and she informed me that Frau Demnitz was ready to receive me. I walked along the corridor and went into Frau Demnitz's office after a polite knock. She was sitting behind her desk, a standard woodchip number, with grey steel legs.

"Herr Grobe," she said, as she stood up to shake my hand. She and I were still on formal terms, perhaps because she'd always worked for the Ministry and valued the traditional protocols of government.

I sat down in the chair opposite her, the desk between us. Frau Demnitz fiddled with some papers, peering through the horn-rimmed glasses perched on the end of her nose. Finally, she looked up and addressed me.

"Herr Grobe, I understand that you have received information from the police officer responsible for the Maier investigation in Dresden. I can only assume that you requested this information while in personal and contiguous contact with the *Unterleutnant* Schadowski yesterday, and I am certain there is no need to remind you that the Minister explicitly stated that there is no need for any further involvement on your part. The Minister has in fact asked me to inform you," here she looked at her notes, presumably in an effort to get what she was about to say exactly right, "that the investigation is in hand." Demnitz paused before starting her next sentence, long enough to give me a chance to appreciate the Minister's words.

"Additionally, the Minister wishes to instruct you to take on the role of liaison between this Ministry and the Four Powers. In its wisdom the Central Round Table," Demnitz broke off to give what I'm sure was a disparaging sniff, "advised that such a task should be carried out by this Ministry. Your instructions are to provide the formal framework for contact between the German Democratic Republic and the military missions of the Soviet Union, the Republic of France, the United States of America and the United Kingdom. You will begin this afternoon. A meeting has been agreed in principle with Major Sokolovski of the Soviet Army Western Group of Troops in Karlshorst. I would be obliged if you could contact his office to confirm the time and communicate the details of your appointment with this office."

Frau Demnitz handed a file to me, and I gave her my report in return. Before I'd made it to the door, I was called back.

"Herr Grobe," and this time it was definitely a sniff, "while I am sure we appreciate the fact that you have prepared this report within a notably short frame of time, I would nevertheless request that you provide a more comprehensive account. If you would be so kind?"

11:58

Coming through the door to the RS2 offices I could see that Bärbel was not there, and that the post had been delivered—it was in a pile on the secretary's desk. I shuffled through the letters and parcels, but there was only one for me: a fat letter from Dresden, *LdVP Sachsen* stamped in the top left corner. The Saxon police. Perhaps this was the information from Dresden that Demnitz had been so excited about? It did make me wonder how she'd known about the letter even before it arrived, but the obvious answer was probably the right one: Second Lieutenant Schadowski had been on the phone with someone from the Ministry.

I went into my office, tearing open the envelope and poking my hand into it. The cover letter included an inventory identifying the contents of Maier's pockets when his body was found. None of it looked familiar, even though I had probably seen it while I was down there. But at the time I must have asked for the list to be sent to me at the office, because otherwise it would have bypassed me and gone straight to the Ministry.

A second sheet informed me that fingerprints had been taken from some scraps of paper (copies enclosed) found in Maier's pockets. These fingerprints had been identified as belonging to Chris Fremdiswalde, DOB: 17.09.1973, place of birth: Löbau, currently registered as living in Thaerstrasse in Berlin-Friedrichshain. He had been arrested in 1987 for theft at his school in Hoyerswerda, and a photo of Chris at the time of his arrest was included. There was no explanation why the police had bothered to compare his fingerprints with those on the papers in Maier's pockets, but there must be some close connection otherwise they couldn't have come up with the fingerprint match so quickly.

The other items in the envelope didn't look particularly interesting.

There was no diary, only a few scraps of paper that looked like shopping lists. Except one, which had a date, the 25th September, along with the time 14.00, and a name: Alex. Looking at the note, I pulled out the crumpled leaflet that Karo the punk had given me the night before: *For a sensible energy policy—in East and West. Alexanderplatz, Saturday 25th September, 14.00.*

I stared at both pieces of paper for a while. Why would Maier be interested in a demo here in Berlin? True, he'd been involved in the mining business, but that was three years ago, before the revolution, before he'd become involved in politics and the business of Silesian devolution.

I shovelled the bits of paper back into the envelope and tossed it on to the pile that I called my in-tray. Time for some proper work. But before that I had an appointment to confirm with the Russians.

15:12

Fortunately my meeting with the Russian liaison officer was in Berlin-Karlshorst. It could have been worse—I might have had to find my way to the Soviet Army headquarters in Wünsdorf, thirty kilometres south of the city.

I parked the office Trabant near the S-Bahn station, and wandering through Karlshorst to arrive at the grey steel gate sporting a red star. One of the guards posted in front checked my pass and ushered me in, the gate clashing shut behind me. I was in a small paved yard, Soviet soldiers in dress uniform and fatigues hastened between the main building and various side wings. No-one paid any attention to me, and not quite sure where to go I just headed for the main entrance.

Behind the tall wooden doors the hall was both large and high, with expansive bay windows at the back, and a wide staircase to my right. Soldiers bustled around, looking both purposeful and efficient, clacking their boots over the polished parquet. Not even sure who to ask for—had Frau Demnitz mentioned a name?—I stood just inside the doorway, and flicked through the file I'd been given. It contained nothing but the addresses and telephone numbers of the Berlin headquarters for each of the Four Powers, each on a separate sheet.

When I looked up I noticed that a soldier wearing fatigues and a cap was standing right next to me. He spoke in Russian, and although I tried to work out what he was saying, I really hadn't a clue. He held his hand out, pointing to some chairs just to the side of the stairs, before he too moved purposefully off. I watched him march away, and as he went past an open doorway another Russian caught my attention. It was the eye patch that did it—hardly a discreet fashion accessory. And now I looked more closely at this man, I noticed the blue flashes on the collar and the blue stripe on his shoulder boards: KGB. Now that I was looking at him I could see that he too was mustering me with his only eye. A curt flick of his head, acknowledging my existence, then he moved further back into the room, beyond my line of sight.

I hadn't quite got to the chairs when someone else spoke to me, this time in German.

"Lieutenant Grobe! Very pleased to meet you. I am Major Mikhail Vassilovich Sokolovski. No relation."

I didn't understand who he might not be related to, and didn't like to ask for fear of causing offence. But the major in front of me spoke in smooth and clear German, which was also a good way to describe his appearance. Dress uniform, red flashes, very neat. Several rows of medals did his chest proud, indeed the medals would have looked cramped on a narrower chest. He held his hand out for me to take, a huge paw of a hand that could easily crush mine, but thankfully didn't. The major pointed the way upstairs, arms gesticulating the whole while, underscoring the small talk he was using to show off his flawless German, but I was far too busy looking around me to pay much attention to what he was saying, something about a cultural event at the embassy.

I'd never been in a Russian military base before, and it was not at all how I'd imagined it. Outside rigidly controlled 'cultural events' the population of the GDR had been kept well away from the Russian brothers. To us, the Russians were different: alien, and at the very least, disconcerting. Even after nearly three years of revolution I found it hard to believe I was standing here in the Soviet Military Berlin HQ. But it all felt rather informal, I could see through open doors how soldiers and uniformed secretaries were shouting down phones, taking down dictation, typing away at noisy old mechanical typewriters, and all the while the endless stream of people moving around, carrying papers, boxes, radio sets, furniture—anything you could imagine. Nobody bothered to salute the major as we went past.

We reached an office with a view over a large parade ground surrounded by red flags. The major gestured that I should take a seat while he closed the door. Turning to a filing cabinet he took two glasses and a bottle of vodka from the top drawer. He set the glasses up on his desk and filled them to the brim before handing me one.

"Before we start, a toast. I propose we drink to the architect and inspiration of the colossal historic victories of the Soviet people; the banner, pride and hope of all progressive humanity. To the great leader and the teacher of my country and yours: *da zdravstvuyet* Joseph Vissarionovich Stalin!"

My glass tipped in shock as I listened to his words, recognising the style from a time not too long past. The major laughed loudly at my reaction.

"No, my friend, times are different now! A small joke is allowed between friends, no? But perhaps you had better make the toast?"

Still not quite sure what to make of this man who looked so formal, yet started our first meeting with a joke about Stalin, I stood up, glass in right hand, looked him in the eye, and tried my best:

"In these uncertain times let us drink to continued and fraternal co-operation between our peoples!"

Again, the loud laugh, and Sokolovski tipped back his glass, swallowing the vodka in one go. I nervously followed his example.

"Good, very good, *tovarishch*," he said. "My colleagues might at this point recharge the glasses, and make another toast. They find it amusing that you Germans, so very exact and proper in all you do, are unable to get beyond even the tenth toast without falling over. And I? I consider myself open to the civilising influences of your culture, so instead I give you the bottle, and we shall meet again. We shall talk about whatever it is people higher up tell us we need to talk about, and have many more toasts."

He shook my hand, opened the door and ushered me back out into the busy chaos beyond.

This was pretty perplexing, but I considered that I had made contact and that, at least so far, I had neither questions nor reports for my Russian liaison. All in all, the major was right: we were finished for now. At least it meant I could go back to the office and get on with writing up that report.

I wandered out of the building and to the gate, the sentries merely nodding as they let me back out into the street. Arriving back at the car I looked at the bottle in my hand. Deciding I'd had enough vodka for one day, I opened the bonnet, took the cap off the petrol tank and poured the Russian alcohol in.

DAY 3
Friday
24th September 1993

__Moscow__: For the first time since the crisis began, large numbers of KGB forces have been seen on the streets of Moscow. The KGB issued a statement stating that troops have been mobilised to assist militia and internal forces in their efforts to keep public order in the Soviet capital. It remains unclear whether or not they support President Gorbachev who remains under house arrest in the Crimea.

08:11

A nice short morning meeting today, which suited me; I was anxious about the backlog of work building up on my desk. We all had ongoing projects we were working on, and there was no need to divvy up any further work. The others thought it unfair that I had been ticked off by Frau Demnitz, which made me feel a bit better, and they were surprised about the liaison task I had been given.

"She asked you to do liaison by yourself, or did she mean we should take on the task jointly?" Erika asked.

"Just me. But as far as I'm concerned we can share it. Sounds boring, really. Anyway, I've already been to see my Russian counterpart, it was ... He toasted Stalin, then laughed at me and threw me out." My description garnered a chuckle from my colleagues although I could see they thought I was exaggerating.

There had been nothing to decide in the meeting today, but even when there was, we rarely voted. Most decisions in the *Republikschutz* departments were taken in the small teams working on any particular topic, but if we thought a case might have an impact on any other team we would check in with them first. Here in RS2 we generally talked any issues through until we found a way forward that worked for everyone involved. It used to be quite a frustrating process, but with time, as we got to know each other, to understand how each of our colleagues ticked, it all became both easier and quicker. Knowing each other's quirks and interests—along with Laura's help in making sure that we didn't talk for hours about something that didn't matter—meant that we'd become quite efficient in our decision-making.

I was just making a start on a report about my visit to Karlshorst when the phone rang. It was the Minister's secretary informing me that a meeting had been set up for this afternoon with Major Clarie at the British Army offices in the Olympic Stadium. It looked like the Minister wanted me kept busy for the next few days.

After the phone call I found it hard to concentrate on writing the report, but if I was to be in West Berlin this afternoon then I didn't have enough time to get involved in any of the other pieces of work waiting for me either. I found myself looking again at the package the Saxon police had sent me, I was particularly intrigued by the slip of paper with tomorrow's date on it. Alex, 14.00—perhaps Maier had been planning to meet someone called Alex on Saturday afternoon, but I wasn't convinced. It just had to be the Energy Demo.

Thinking about it—the demo, with its focus on brown coal; the site where the body was found; Maier's own past in the brown coal mining industry—I couldn't get rid of the feeling that there were too many coincidences. I shook my head, trying to rid myself of questions. I wasn't the one investigating the murder. Not only did I not have any part to play in the investigation, I had been warned off by Frau Demnitz from the Ministry. And on top of that, I'd agreed with my own colleagues not to pursue the case any further.

I caught the tram heading down to Rummelsburg, finding a seat as we creaked round the corner and under the railway tracks. Brown coal was a seam running through this case, and even if I wasn't actually involved in the investigation why shouldn't I express an interest in a matter that was clearly a potential security issue for our Republic?

I could see the twin chimneys of the Rummelsburg coal power station beckoning from way down the road; but they were much further away than they seemed—it was several more stops before the tram finally arrived at the main gates.

I showed my pass to the works guard and asked to speak to the director. A short wait, then I was met by a guy in a suit who took me to a high Art Deco building with a façade of reddish-brown bricks. Everything about it was narrow, its ten storeys were tall and lean, as were the windows that stretched from marble floors to soaring ceilings.

We tapped our way across the marble to the stairs. On the next floor the walls were covered in glassy green tiles, the floors with well polished red lino. I was ushered into an office, where another suit sat behind a dark antique desk. The suit rose and took my hand, beckoning me to sit down.

"How can I help you?"

Good question. I'd come on a whim, unprepared: I wasn't too sure myself what I was doing here. Curiosity perhaps? A desire to see with my own eyes another part of the workings of the brown coal industry? A hope that mere proximity would help my brain make some connections? But curiosity, a desire to follow up on a hunch— those weren't reasons I could admit to.

"The *Republikschutz* is interested in the impact the West Silesian crisis might have on the electricity supply in the Republic," I ad libbed.

"It's already having an effect." The director sat back, crossing his hands over his expansive belly, I'd clearly hit on a favourite topic of his. "Most of the power produced in the Silesian Boxberg power station is used in the south of the Republic: Saxony, Thuringia. Up here we get coal from the mines south of Spremberg, most of them also in West Silesia. They've been dropping hints about setting a 'market price' for the coal that they send to us. As I've already informed the Ministry for Coal and Energy, in the case of West Silesia seceding from the GDR we would lose over half of our national coal reserves, and half of our generating capacity to boot. We are already importing some coal from Poland, but that would have to increase—our Welzow field doesn't have enough capacity to feed the Schwarze Pumpe power station, and the West-Elbe fields are still supplying Espenhain and what's left of the chemical industry," the director continued, his mellifluous voice outlining technical details and statistics that were far beyond my ability to understand, never mind remember. The gist of it was that most of our coal reserves and a huge amount of electricity generating capacity were in West Silesia, and therefore at risk.

After a few more minutes of this shop talk I interrupted: "But if West Silesia became independent then they'd have too much generating capacity for their own use—surely they'd be happy to sell it on to us?"

"You'd think so, but there is talk of an extra-high voltage transmission line running from West Silesia to West Germany, presumably in order to export the electricity to the Western markets."

West Germany wasn't suffering from a shortfall in energy supply, so why would they be interested in importing power from West Silesia? Except, of course, to make life difficult for us.

12:33

Deciding not to go back to the office I went home. Arriving at the flat I could see a note on the door, just like the old days before I had a phone. A neighbour had taken a call for me, and left a message on the notepad hanging from the door frame. 'Katrin called, please phone back'.

I turned the key in the door and opened up. Going in, I crossed a beam of sunlight, making the spotlit dust in the air dance in my wake. Putting the still warm bread rolls I'd just bought on the table, I went to the stove to boil water for coffee.

Standing in the kitchen, looking out of the window and enjoying the warm, yeasty smell of the rolls, I watched an S-Bahn train squeal around the curved tracks below. Its dull red and dark grey paintwork swallowed the low sunlight, the passengers behind the smeared windows barely visible, a shadow puppet show. The train passed, and the weeds between the tracks waved their goodbyes. Turning around I stared at the telephone that had just started ringing.

"Grobe."

"Papa! It's me."

"Katrin, is anything wrong?"

"Oh nothing much, listen—has the post arrived yet? No, never mind, I've got a cancelled lecture, thought it would be good to see you. Besides, I've got something to talk to you about. You got the day off work?"

"I've got a few hours free. Why?"

"Do you want to come out here? I'll buy you coffee."

I'd planned to go to bed for a short nap before I had to meet the British major, but I knew I'd probably end up lying there, staring at the ceiling, thinking. And even if I did manage to nod off then I wouldn't sleep well tonight and would be grumpy all day tomorrow. No, better to get out and about, enjoy a bit of time off. I turned off the stove and headed back out the door. I hadn't seen Katrin for a couple of weeks, and I was heading over to West Berlin anyway: the Olympia complex, where I was to meet the British liaison officer, was in the British sector.

I didn't go to the Western part of the city very often, there wasn't much for me there. The heady days after the Wall had opened were long gone, we knew we could have bananas whenever we wanted them, and we knew we couldn't afford them. We knew that the people who populated the other half of our city were mostly better fed, better dressed and better housed, but they weren't as happy as we were. Looking around at my fellow East Berliners you could be forgiven for disagreeing—we were a dour bunch. But we had something the people in the West had never had. They had experienced dictators, as had we, and they now had a stable democracy—which we had never had. But they scrawled a cross on a piece of paper every few years, and let the politicians do what they pleased. Their bodies had never surged with the adrenaline and endorphins that come from the power of revolution. We may be the poor cousins on this side of the Wall, but when it came to living life, we were rich.

Changing trains at Friedrichstrasse station was nothing like it used to be. Nowadays it was as simple as changing platforms. Not so long ago —so recently we could still measure the time in months—the short distance to the trains to the West couldn't be bridged by a few steps down a corridor and up some stairs to the platform. In those days it took years to get the piece of paper that allowed you to pass the border controls. Years of tears, and usually a one way ticket. In those days most of those who left on the westbound train could never return.

As the S-Bahn whined along the viaduct I looked down at the Wall that still drew the boundaries of this double city. The barbed wire and fences were gone, and the first line of the Wall—whitewashed concrete slabs marking the eastern edge of the border defences—was being dismantled. Behind that there were rows of potatoes, beans and other vegetables growing around the watchtowers and fence posts. The outer wall, facing West, was being maintained while the nation debated what to do with it. It was permeable now, we could pass through a number of new border crossings, but trucks and vans from the West weren't welcome. After the Wall opened in November '89, West Berliners had started coming over to the East, buying up subsidised products and taking them back to sell on the street markets. This quickly led to shortages in the capital, some claimed it was a deliberate attempt by West Germany to destabilise the GDR even further—as if that were possible in those days when the Communist state was already teetering, pushed by a population hungry for change.

So for the time being the Wall stayed, an economic barrier that gave us space to breathe and grow into the country we wanted to be, whatever we might turn out to be.

★

A few stops later I got off the train and, following the instructions Katrin had given me on the phone, I made my way to the café.

Tables and chairs were set out on the pavement in front, all populated by young people in their young clothes, wearing their young faces. Katrin was inside. We hugged. This was a new thing, at home people mostly just shook hands when they met up, but Katrin had started hugging me after she moved to the West. I sat down at her table, and she pushed a cassette across the wooden surface. I put my hand over it and drew it towards me.

"What's with all these tapes? I mean, it's not that I don't appreciate them, in fact I'm rather enjoying them. But, well, why?"

Katrin was sipping a hot chocolate, I nursed a black coffee, no sugar. I could see how my daughter noticed the way I deliberately sat with my back to the tray of pastries on the counter, and I think she knew how hard it was for me to ignore their sweet, sticky call. I couldn't afford one, yet still hoped that Katrin wouldn't offer to buy me one either.

"Promise you won't go off on one?" Katrin, nervous, looked at me. I wondered what was coming as I constructed a lopsided smile (the one Katrin called my Zen-face), and nodded.

"It's just, after mum … well you had your hands full. With me, queuing for food, cooking, working in the factory. And after all that you'd go out, some meeting in some crypt, some church hall, or your friends would come round, and you'd turn the radio on loud and hold whispered conversations around the kitchen table. But you weren't listening to the music. You never had time for music, even though I know you love music. West music, East music, the lot."

This made me think. *The old days.* Strangely, life was simple and straightforward, then. A tug of nostalgia came from somewhere deep in my chest, setting my thoughts on a tangent: *did I miss those days?* I hoped I still had my Zen smile stapled to my face, but just by looking at Katrin I could see that it had slipped a little.

"I had the blues: Engerling, Cäsar, Bodag … it's just, after that Udo Ludendorff guy did that song about the train to Pankow, and why can't he do a gig in our Workers' and Peasants' State … it was so unreal. Patronising. *Westmusik.*"

"Lindenberg."

The smile must have gone by now, the Zen-face turned into a question-mark.

"Udo Lindenberg. That was the guy's name. And he just didn't get it. How could he, a Wessi? But that's just it. You listened to the West Berlin radio station RIAS, and heard the shit stuff. Anyway, Lindenberg was one of the few to respond to Freya Klier's appeal for help in '88."

I had to admit, that was true. When the singer-songwriter Stephan Krawczyk was arrested along with several others for trying to join a demonstration on Rosa Luxemburg day, his wife Freya Klier, who'd already been released, went on Western TV to appeal for support for him and the other interned activists. Lindenberg was one of the few Westerners to put pressure on the Communist government to let them go.

"But the *Puhdys*?" Katrin would never let go of what she considered my poor musical choices. "Have you still got that album, *Das Buch*? God, it's dire!" She pulled a face, then changed tack. "No, the point is. You were doing all that stuff for me, for us, for all of us here in the Republic, I mean, over there," a gesture, through the window, vaguely eastwards, and I wondered whether this was the point to break in, defend the Puhdys, but I'm glad I didn't, because:

"And here I am, I'm at uni, meeting all these people, finding out about all these things, hearing all this music. And I feel you missed out, and, yeah, I know, music isn't such a big thing, but it kind of is too." Another pause, then: "So, these tapes. They're my way of saying thanks."

I wasn't sure where to look. I'm not good at public emotion; too many years of not wanting to give the state a way into my life, not wanting to give the Stasi a clue to my weaknesses. But I could feel a tear beginning to pool in my right eye.

"Thank you too," I managed, blinking rapidly and looking away from my daughter.

Katrin smiled. Genuine, not frustrated. A little nervous still, experience telling her to keep something back.

"But, is it your Republic, still?" I asked, without thinking. Now I was sort of looking at my daughter. "I mean, here you are in West Berlin, with all your new friends, your new clothes, your new money.

Your West student's grant from the West German government ..." A pause, what I've just said sinking in. "No, I'm sorry, I didn't mean it that way. It came out wrong. Sorry. I meant, when are you coming home?"

But that, too, was the wrong thing to say.

"Papa, I'm just at the other end of the city! You can come out here any time you want!" But, seeing my face, she stopped. It wasn't about the physical distance. It was about the symbolism. The Wall is still there, no matter how many holes we'd punched in it. She was in the West, I was in the East. Same city, different countries.

"Papa," she said slowly, "maybe I should have come back that winter. Things were changing, but all I could think about was that the system had broken you. I didn't want to go the same way. I wanted to study, but they wouldn't let me. You know all this."

Her face pointed at the table, but her eyes turned upwards, checking how I'd react. I think my face had gone hard, immobile—the calm look I'd been trying to keep up had definitely gone. Katrin was drawing circles with her fingertips on the dark wood, as if the Zen that had slipped off my face had landed on the table in front of us, a pool of viscosity she could dab her fingers in. It was obvious to us both that we were each thinking of the day she left. The furtive goodbyes, nothing said aloud in case the Stasi were listening. The knowledge that once she crossed the border into Czechoslovakia, on the way to Hungary, and from there to the West, once that first frontier had been crossed there would be no return. We would probably never see each other again. I remembered the desperation, the claustrophobia that had driven her away. I remembered my feelings that day: crushed, hurt, betrayed. *Don't shed any tears for them* they told us, ordered us, on the TV and radio. Don't shed any tears for those who couldn't stay in this stagnant land. But I still cry when I remember that awful day four years ago. And I know Katrin does, too.

"Do we have to do this every time, Papa? We always do it."

I could hear the frustration, the pain, the anger in her words. And I could feel answering emotions rising up inside myself too. It was the state she was angry at, that old GDR, run by pensioners. Stalinists. But she was angry at me, too. The daughter of a known dissident had not been allowed to stay on at school after 16, not to do her exams at 18, nor go on to university. She'd never said it aloud, but that was all my fault. It was my choice to do the things I'd done, and she had been made to pay for it.

Are families always like this, rubbing each other up the wrong way, accusing each other without words, the past a ghost that is always present? Having the same arguments again and again, hurting each other in the same places time after time? We always said, and left unsaid, the same things. Katrin was the only family I had left, I didn't want this.

"It's just, some of us are trying, Katrin. Some of us *stayed*," there was an emphasis on the word, as if I had pushed my emotions into those letters before forcing them out of my mouth. "We pushed the *Bonzen* out, we kept the West out, and we're making a real, independent, democratic state. Probably the first in the world! You know this! You know we need people. Young people. We need people like you, Katrin! You can study at the Humboldt University in the East. We lost tens of thousands of young people that autumn. You should have stayed. We need you."

I should have kept my mouth shut, I knew it as soon as I'd said the words, I knew it before I'd even said those words. At times like this, I feel like I'm my own angel, hovering overhead, watching, seeing everything, my own face, her face, hearing my own words. The angel could see how I'd just taken a bite out of my own daughter. I see it, but I always seem powerless to stop the mess I'm making.

"*Stayed?* Like you? And what are you doing now?" Her words were sharp with barbs. "What's your contribution to the glorious revolution? Get off your fucking high horse. You, you spy! That's what you are, creeping around, look you even have a sad trenchcoat! A spy, no better than the fucking Stasi!"

This had to hurt. The angel watched my face become hard, my eyes glazing as I absorbed the shock.

"You don't mean that."

"Well, it's true, isn't it? They got rid of the Stasi, and they realised they still needed it, so they asked the sheep to put on wolf's clothing, didn't they? The Minister of the Interior himself, good old Benno, he was the one who asked you! Didn't he?"

"No! You know that's not how it was. How it is. You know!"

"So if it's not true, tell me what exactly you do? I mean, I have no real idea what my own Papa does!"

"You do know, I'm with the RS."

"Yeah, but I mean, it's just another of those weird acronyms, combinations of letters that could hide anything! Tell me, tell me what it is you do? What have you been working on this week, yesterday, today?"

I could have told her about the Russian major, made her laugh about the Stalin toast and my summary dismissal from his presence, but my mind was stuck on the Maier case. I recalled that feeling of fear that I'd experienced on the way back from West Silesia. It was a fear that I hadn't had to feel for a few years—I used to know it so well, this extra sense. I'd almost anticipated it, welcomed it. An old friend. You knew where you were with that fear. It was from the days when we didn't know whether the Stasi were listening, whether the Stasi were watching, whether the Stasi were coming to get us. It reminded me why I was doing those things back then. Daring to disagree, to find out about things the state didn't want us to know. But nowadays it just made me feel sick.

"It's ... it's confidential. I can't tell you. Sorry," it sounded lame, even to me, even without my angel's ears listening to the words. But I couldn't share this with Katrin. She was safe now. Here, in West Berlin.

"You know what, it's all rubbish. All shit. You and your new society, based on *trust and openness and honesty*," this last bit in a different voice, sarcastic. "And there you are, in your secret job, doing secret things for the secretaries in the secret ministry!"

I just sat there, head sagging, face inches from the table.

"Shit. I've gotta go. I've got a lecture in half an hour."

I didn't look up as Katrin stood up, put her coat on, gestured to the waiter and paid. She was watching at me, I could tell, even though I was still hunched over the table, shoulders rounded inside the trench coat. Without another word she turned, and left the café, swiftly negotiating the chairs and tables, away from where I was still slumped, fingertips just brushing the cassette on the table.

I nudged the cassette round to read what was on the label. It said simply: *Thanks*, with a smiling acid face drawn next to the word. Sliding the tape off the table and into my pocket, I moved towards the door. Nowhere near as elegant as my daughter in completing this manoeuvre, bumping into tables and the backs of chairs, drawing questioning looks from the chattering students. I was no longer at home in a young persons' café—when did that happen? Or was it my clothes, my hairstyle, my smell, identifying me as from the East? I made it to the door in one piece, and hoping to slip out without causing any further scenes, I pulled the door open. Too hard: it slammed against the coat stand behind it, and I stumbled out, not looking back to see what the students thought of my awkward exit.

There, to one side of the door, stood Katrin.

"Katrin! Oh-"

"It's OK, I'm going already."

"No! I mean, please. Wait. You're right. I should share more. Open up a bit. One more chance?"

Katrin hesitated, a vague smile peering through her tears. She looked towards the bus stop, back at me. Maybe she did have a lecture to go to.

"OK, do you want to go back in?"

"No, it's true what I just said, it's confidential. I shouldn't be telling you, so I definitely shouldn't be talking about it in a café in the middle of West Berlin!"

Katrin smiled. A grin that reminded me of her mother when we first met, before the care and the worry crept into our relationship.

"Let's walk a bit, here, this way. And you can tell me why you're so cagey these days."

She took my arm, and steered me down a side street, as if I were an old man needing to be helped home after getting lost. It must have presented a strange sight: an attractive young woman, in trendy, Western clothes walking arm in arm with a bulky, grey headed man clad in cheap, synthetic-mix clothing. But I guess everyone in West Berlin has relatives in the East, so maybe it was normal.

We turned another corner, tall buildings—delicate in yellows and creams, stucco patterns and reliefs gracing the façades—looked down on us.

"I'm sorry about before. I shouldn't have made fun about your coat

—I mean, it's not like you were the only one in a beige trenchcoat hanging around there." A few more steps, another street, cross to the other side while I wonder where she'd seen another Ossi, then: "You know, I will come back. I am coming back."

I looked at her, waiting for her to continue, not wanting to break in on what I hoped she was going to tell me. She'd never before spoken to me about her plans for the future. Not since she'd left.

"But I'm enjoying being here, at the *Freie Universität,* being in West Berlin. It feels like, after all the years of, of ..." she was struggling to find the words: *"suffocation,* I can finally ... unfold. I know that amazing things are happening, over there, back home," again the vague eastwards gesture. "And I want to be part of that. I will be. But this is *me*-time. Does that make sense?"

It made a lot of sense, and I wondered if I were younger, would I be doing what she was, or would I be in the midst of this new society we were building in the East? I was thinking of the endless meetings with the other residents in my tenement block. If I were in my twenties, would I want to sit there and plan everything from the communal kitchen garden to insulation measures? Maybe the answer was yes. There were some younger people in my block and while I could see that they sometimes switched off (usually when Frau Priepert from upstairs was talking about noise levels or cleaning rotas for the communal areas), they were actually really engaged. Without them we wouldn't have the bike workshop in the cellar, without them we wouldn't have links with the farm on the edge of the city—the farm that brought us food. Last week when I got home they were hanging off ropes, repairing the rendering on the side of the building —it looked dangerous, the work slapdash and piecemeal, but watching them, I felt a sense of pride. And the building desperately needed the attention after years of neglect.

While my mind was wandering, Katrin had continued talking. She was telling me about her course, the other students. I tried to keep up, but I had somehow become fixated on the bike workshop. I made a mental note to take my old bike there and get it sorted out before the weather turned too cold to cycle.

"But you shouldn't think you can get away with it that easily," grinned Katrin. "Tell me all your secrets!"

I often had a strong feeling with people who knew me well, particularly ones who cared about me, that my face simply betrayed those thoughts I wasn't even consciously thinking. Like now, I guess I had been hoping Katrin would be sidetracked by her stories of student life, and that I wouldn't have to tell her about West Silesia and the dead politician. Had she read that on my face? Was that the reason for the sudden change of subject?

"Well, I had to go down to West Silesia. It's all kicking off down there."

"Yeah, tell me about it! A student in my seminar group is from Görlitz, she says they have guards on the Silesian borders now. They're wearing West Silesian uniforms, but are actually BGS." *Bundesgrenzschutz*—West German paramilitary border police.

I was surprised Katrin had heard about this, I'd only heard the rumour last week. So far we weren't clear whether the West Germans had actually put their own troops on the Silesian borders, or whether they were just providing training and military hardware. Either way it was a confrontational move, an incursion on our sovereignty—West Silesia was still, officially, part of the GDR.

"So, I go down there, because there's a dead politician, probably murdered-"

"Who?" Katrin interrupted, attracted, as so many are, by the hideousness of violence.

"I shouldn't say," but the look on her face, how could I hold back? "Maier. That slick one. But don't tell anyone!"

Katrin had gone quiet. Her keen curiosity had been shed the moment I said the name.

"Fuck!" she said quietly, almost whispering.

"Yeah. Things are going to get interesting now."

"Do you know who did it yet?"

"No, not yet. But the Saxon cops are involved, so it won't just be the Silesians dealing with it themselves."

West Silesia was small, very small, and just didn't have the resources to deal with a difficult case. Or alternatively, I reckoned the investigation, if left to the Silesians, would come up with whatever result best suited the politics of the day.

Katrin seemed distracted, she looked at me. "Thanks, Papa. Thanks for talking. But I have to go—that lecture. You can find your way back to the station?"

"Hang on, you wanted to talk to me about something?"

"Oh! I need to go, we'll talk about it another time!"

15:22

I wandered around a bit more after Katrin left, stopping at a Currywurst stand to get a drink. I stood by the booth, enjoying the weak sunlight, but not enjoying the weak coffee in the cardboard cup. I was next to a crossroads regulated by traffic lights, and every couple of minutes a shrieking, roaring stream of motorised metal hurtled across the junction, first from one side, then the other. It was loud and smelly, and made me appreciate the fact that there were so few cars on the road in East Berlin. A couple of years ago, we probably had as much traffic as here, although the cars were neither as large nor as shiny. But the collapse of the Eastern European trading bloc, Comecon, in January 1990 meant we were now paying market prices for the Russian oil we imported. The price of petrol and diesel had shot up, and on top of that it was rationed, the lion's share going to industry and agriculture.

There were attempts to find other fuel sources, using feed maize and sugar beet, but we needed the land to produce food for ourselves and to earn hard currency through export. Fuel for personal transport just wasn't a priority.

Raising the sour coffee to my lips I smiled—it was ironic, just a few years ago our tiny plastic cars with their two-stroke engines symbolised freedom. Now we had real freedom, political freedom, and we didn't have cars. Or, at least not the fuel to put in them. I wondered if there was an inverse relationship between freedom and the number of cars. If there was, then I had to feel sorry for the people here in West Berlin.

Upon reaching the dregs of both coffee and ruminations on transport and freedom I set off again, looking for an underground station.

★

Exiting at Olympia I asked around until I found the British base on the Olympic stadium site. A guard wearing fatigues, rifle slung over his soldier, examined my RS pass and told me to present myself at the gatehouse beyond. A second check, this time of both my RS pass and my identity papers, then I was asked to wait. After a few moments a sergeant came to fetch me, asking me, in English, to follow him. We crossed a grassy courtyard and entered a red-brick single storey building. It looked fairly new, no more than 10 years old, and all the paint work was fresh, but somehow the overall impression was of shabbiness. Inside the building the ceilings were low, and the walls unplastered, the brickwork covered only by glossy grey-green paint. A wooden door with a frosted glass window stood partly open, and the sergeant knocked, then saluted to whoever was in the room.

"Mr. Grobe here to see you, sir," he reported, not pronouncing the final E in my name.

"Very good, show him in, will you? Thank you."

The sergeant gestured towards the open door, muttering something which could have been 'Sir', then headed back outside. I went into the room to find a major sitting behind a large desk, head bent over paperwork, pen in hand, poised perhaps to sign or correct. He looked up as I shuffled in, a vague smile playing at the corner of his lips.

"Martin! Welcome, Tom Clarie, Tom or Clarie to friends, but never both. Defence Intelligence Staff, yes, quite, really ought to be SIS that receives you, one would think. But somehow we get the honour—this is your first visit, I understand? Well, yes, welcome!"

He'd spoken in German, and was now getting up, his fatigues rustling as he pushed his chair back and extended his right hand, damp and limp. I took it, saying my name and feeling foolish about it because he was clearly already in possession of that basic fact.

"Please, please sit down. A cup of tea and a biscuit, perhaps?" his finger hovered over an intercom system on his desk, and he slowly, almost reluctantly moved it away when I shook my head. My stomach was unhappy about the cardboard coffee I'd had less than an hour ago, and it certainly didn't like the thought of some over-brewed tea made with a tea bag. And definitely not with milk in it. But I was intrigued by being offered just one biscuit, and wondered what kind it might be.

"I'm very pleased to meet you. I gather you are my counterpart from the other side? Quite odd, we used to deal with the chaps from your Ministry for Foreign Affairs, but actually you're from the Interior Ministry, aren't you? Well, the world changes, as we've so clearly seen these last few years, what, old boy?"

I really didn't know what to say, this chap seemed to be straight from the Babelsberg film studios. His German was perfect, but with a deliberate English accent: an oversized plum in his throat. Although his fair hair and blue eyes made him look more Prussian than British, his language was that of an officer and a gentleman. Fortunately Major Tom (as I had already christened him in my head) ploughed on, neither waiting for nor expecting a response.

"Now do forgive me, but I'm actually frightfully under prepared—not something that you would expect from a British intelligence officer, eh? But we got a call from your office first thing this morning—they seemed awfully keen to get us chaps to meet up a.s.a.bloody-p. if you see what I mean. So, all things said and done, I've been caught on the hop. Just reading through my notes from the last liaison meeting, actually, but perhaps you have something for me?"

Major Tom peered at me over gold rimmed spectacles, as if hoping I'd have answers that had eluded him throughout his career as an intelligence officer.

"Er ... no. I gather that this is more of a social call, so we can get acquainted," I improvised, not understanding why the Minister felt it so urgent that I meet the Russians and the British.

"Ah! Splendid, splendid. Very civilised, actually. So there's nothing in particular you feel we have to talk about? Splendid."

He glanced around the office as if to find something to talk to me about. My eyes followed his, and settled on the bookshelves. Several shelves held weighty tomes on economic theory, everything from Mill to Marx, by way of Keynes, Locke, Smith, Friedman and Proudhon.

"You're interested in economic theory?"

"Why, yes, actually. Are you a fellow economist? Not strictly in my job description, but a firm economic understanding is essential in this post, I find. Take your country, very interesting. Sadly I don't receive intelligence reports on economic affairs, and what one reads in the newspapers over here is pure propaganda, not worth wrapping your fish and chips in it, as far as I'm concerned. But tell me, is your government not going to privatise industry? Surely you need the capital investment?"

"Actually it looks like things are going the other way: most workplaces are mutualised, sometimes formally by agreement, but often just because of the impact the Works Councils are having."

"Oh, really?" the major interjected politely, but without enthusiasm.

"Many of the larger factories and organisations still have a hierarchical structure, but the Councils are involved at every level of decision-making, they represent the workers." I persevered. "That means everyone can be involved in every decision, whether that's to do with production or work conditions. I think it's inevitably going to lead to some kind of syndicate system—as people get more confident, and more aware of the kinds of decisions that need to be taken, and why. We're all getting more involved in running our own workplaces."

"But that's not going to sort out questions such as what needs to be produced, and in what quantities," Clarie was more interested now, warming to the debate. "The Communist planned economy failed, so you need some other way to make those decisions."

"Yes. The Marxist-Leninists were arrogant, thought they knew best. But the capitalist systems of the West aren't any more efficient—look at how resources were wasted in the boom years of railway building in your country, or the redundancy and waste prevalent in the West German healthcare system. And capitalism isn't efficient in allocating resources either—isn't it immoral, having both poor people and rich people in the same economy? In the GDR that's simply unconstitutional. Our economy is structured from below—by the people, just like everything else in our country. We need to get the balance right—between what we *can* produce and what we *need* to produce, and like everything else in our society that's taking a lot of negotiation. Think of it as central facilitation rather than central planning."

"But that's impossible—surely one of the reasons that the planned economy system failed was because it's impossible to calculate all the factors!"

"Maybe, but it doesn't have to be perfect, just better than the alternatives. And let's face it, Adam Smith and his followers haven't done such a great job of it either," I gestured towards the *Wealth of Nations* on the bookshelf. "There's no perfect information to allow supply and demand levels to be correctly recognised, the whole system skews supply towards those with the greatest access to means of payment, rather than those with the greatest need. And we're not starting from scratch, pretty much everybody in my country has an understanding of what is broken in the economy, where there are shortages or gluts in production. We need to build on that, find new ways of sharing information on production and to make decisions together on the larger economic issues."

"Shades of Hertzka, if you ask me," Clarie paused long enough to look pleased with himself. "But it's rather naïve to expect everyone to become an economic expert."

"Why not? Every household already makes economic decisions. I think we need to experiment with how best to share economic information, honest information, and trust that people will behave in more rational and fair ways—whether they're deciding what to buy, or what they should be producing in their workplace."

"Seems a bit optimistic to me, if you don't mind me saying, old chap."

"Perhaps, but I think it's got a better chance of working in a society that is already making those links—being involved and making decisions together at home and work."

Clarie just grunted, I'd lost his interest. His eyes wandered the bookshelves again. I could tell he was unconvinced by what I was saying, but I didn't mind. After all, just a few years ago anyone dreaming about a grassroots revolution in our country would have been called a fantasist. It was all a big experiment, and it probably wouldn't work too well—but as I'd said, to justify itself it only had to be marginally better than the alternatives.

Finally, the major's eyes returned to the desk in front of him, and he shuffled together the papers he had been looking at when I came in. Picking them up, and slapping the sides of the bundle of papers against the desk to square them off, he casually waved them at me.

"Minutes. Presumably you've read them, have you? Your predecessor, our meetings, I mean?"

"No, I was only tasked with liaison yesterday, the paperwork hasn't caught up with me yet." In fact, until now I hadn't even thought that I ought to ask for the minutes of previous meetings.

"Well, I'm sure you know the ropes already, no need to tell you about it all? Basically you and I will stay in touch, any problems with the MLM or BRIXMIS, you know? And we'll see each other on the 7th as well, along with the others."

The 7th of October, Republic Day, when we celebrate the founding of the GDR. It used to be a day of official marches past the Communist Party leadership, since the revolution it had become a 24-hour street party. But now it sounded like I'd be wearing a tie and jacket and getting bored at some formal function in the Palace of the Republic.

"Of course old Mikhail Vassilovich will be there too, you know from SERB?"

It took me a moment to work out that he meant Sokolovski, but SERB? (not to mention MLM and BRIXMIS!) I was out of my depth, and annoyed with the Minister and Demnitz for dropping me into this without even a proper briefing.

"Naturally, we won't talk about anything that matters, like the small problem you folks are having down in West Silesia," Major Tom's face took on a cunning cast, "Unless, of course, you actually feel we may have something to contribute?"

"That's a very kind offer, and we may take you up on it." I considered for a moment, then: "Is there anything you feel might be of use?"

"Well, of course, these things are usually quid pro quo, old chap! But, since we're new friends: I do sometimes wonder what would happen if our old friends the Russians, and your old friends the West Germans got together, perhaps with a little help from those chaps who used to run the Stasi ..."

Major Tom winked at me, then pressed a button on his intercom system.

"Sergeant, could you bring one of the specials in? Thank you." Turning his attention back to me, the major continued: "In recognition of our new relationship, and the hope that it will be a long and fruitful one, ah-"

A brief knock, and the door opened. The major got to his feet and took a bottle from the hands of someone standing just outside.

"Here we are, yes. Fruitful. Quite."

Another bottle of alcohol, this time whisky. The label said *Talisker, 20 years*. Whatever that meant.

I was already feeling ignorant and ungracious, arriving empty-handed and not knowing anything about what I was meant to be doing here. I had the feeling that if I stayed much longer my ignorance could only become more obvious, so I made my excuses, shook the major's hand again (which he didn't seem to be expecting, becoming flustered and red-faced), and exited, bottle in hand.

18:36

Three trains and a short walk later I was back in my corner of Berlin, between Friedrichshain and Lichtenberg. Walking down the middle of the cobbled street in the last light of the day. My mind was still in the West, with Katrin and Major Tom. What did he mean when he talked about the Stasi, the West Germans and the Russians getting together? Did he have any useful information, or just empty words? It didn't make any sense to me—the Stasi had been disbanded three and a half years ago, and why would the West Germans want to work with the Russians? I couldn't think of any way of finding out, short of asking Major Sokolovski.

Round the final corner, and there was my building, one of the last of the old tenement blocks, standing proud against the sea of new-build flats that had washed down from Lichtenberg. Heaving open the solid wooden door, I went through the hallway without thinking; trying to switch off and glad to be home, working out what music to put on the record player, what I could be bothered cooking for dinner. David Bowie on the stereo with some sausage and beer sounded about right; *Ashes to Ashes* would fit the bill, I thought of the lyrics, and had to giggle at the idea of the terribly English Major Tom on drugs.

As I reached the bottom of the stairs, I caught sight of the row of metal boxes, just out of the corner of my eye. It was enough to make me hesitate. And the hesitation was enough to make me turn back and look in my letterbox. There wouldn't be anything in there for me, and if there was, it would be a bill. I poked my fingers through the slit, exploring, checking for a letter. The tip of my index finger brushed paper, something scraping my fingernail, another rough surface pushing against the pad of the finger: I had two letters. Between index and ring finger I fished out the first letter: West Berlin postmark, West German stamp. Handwriting unfamiliar. Fingers of the right hand pushed back in through the slit, this one a little more difficult—a small package of some kind—requiring more care and effort to manoeuvre it through the narrow slit. I recognised it before I even had it out of the letterbox—another of Katrin's tapes. I smiled as I held it in my hands, looking forward to another musical journey courtesy of my favourite and only daughter.

The other letter was intriguing though—who, other than Katrin, would write to me from the Western half of this ghost town? Absent-mindedly climbing the stairs, I looked at the address of the sender, up in the top left-hand corner of the envelope. A postbox number in the West Berlin postal district 61—was that Kreuzberg, over towards Schöneberg? Letting myself into the flat, I dumped my bag and the letters in the hall, went into the kitchen and put a pan of water on to boil, then went back and picked up my mail. I opened Katrin's package first. A cassette, marked *Seduction*, and just a slip of paper with the words: "Don't be cross! K." scribbled on it.

Turning my attention to the other letter, I ripped open the brown envelope. Inside was another envelope, addressed to: *Chiffre* "Alone in the East", c/o Zitty Stadtmagazin. There was no stamp on this second envelope, and "Alone in the East" was written in English. I turned the envelope over in my hands before opening it: cream coloured, expensive cartridge paper, the kind we so rarely saw here in the East. A faint smell of Western scent came off the thick ribbed paper, heavy musk, mingled with lavender and the lighter notes of rose. No name, but an address, also in Kreuzberg in West Berlin, was written on the back of the envelope. I opened it up and unfolded a single sheet in the same thick, creamy cartridge paper as the envelope. The scent was even stronger now, feminine, but not light.

Dear "Alone in the East,"

I was touched by your lines in the lonely hearts column. Perhaps you'd like to meet? I'm 39, no children, looking for adventure and a fresh start in these exciting times. I enjoy cooking, going for walks in the forests around Berlin. I'm looking for someone to read me beautiful books, enjoy the bronzes and reds of autumn, and watch the sun go down over the river. Sounds like we're made for each other.

Hope to meet soon,

Yours affectionately,

Annette Ruhle

Katrin! She'd only gone and put a lonely hearts ad in a magazine! And a West Berlin magazine at that! I stormed to the telephone and dialled my daughter's number. Down the line I could hear her phone purring, but nobody picked up. She'd still be at her lectures.

Slamming the receiver down in its cradle I turned round, looking out of the window. The sun was setting, and although the sun itself was already out of sight, the little corner of sky that I could see was turning pink and purple, as if it had been beaten up. My lips curled upwards as I realised what a stupid simile my mind had delivered, and I looked at Annette's letter again.

Katrin meant well, I conceded to myself, as my ire died down, and, well, perhaps I could meet up with this Annette? Yet I couldn't imagine that someone who could afford such expensive writing paper would be interested in an Ossi with no access to convertible currency. I held the paper up to the light and admired the watermark, noticing the writing—clear, regular, well-formed letters, slanting slightly forwards, written with a decent fountain pen. The scent made its way again to whichever parts of the brain were responsible for smelling, and registered as pleasant, interesting. Yes, even sexy.

Perhaps ... Should I write back? I knew I wouldn't, but the thought amused me. Looking at the letter again, I turned it over—there was the address again, the same as on the envelope, and under that, a telephone number. What did I have to lose?

I read the short letter again, went through to the hall, put the letter on the table next to the phone, lifted the receiver, and dialled.

After the phone call I went back into my living room, sitting down in my favourite chair. I thought about Annette and the strange week I'd just had. I was glad it was Friday—it would be at least Monday before the Minister could give me any new tasks.

But in the meantime I could do with a drink. I thought of the whisky Major Tom had given me, and getting up with a sigh, I fetched a glass from the kitchen, putting Bettina Wegner on the record player as I went past. Sinking back into the chair, pouring myself a measure, I toasted the living room at large: *"Drushba!"*

To friendship.

DAY 4
Saturday
25th September 1993

Berlin: A demonstration has been called for this afternoon in the capital of the GDR. The protest has been called by several basis groups, including the Umweltbibliothek *and* Grüne Liga *with the support of the Central Round Table. Speakers from both the GDR and West Berlin are expected to talk about the impact the Silesian crisis will have on electricity supplies.*

09:26

Saturday. A day of rest, of enjoyment—even in this hard-working little Republic of ours. But I went into the office this morning to write the report on my trip to West Silesia; it was a dull morning, overcast, the window spotted with rain—I wasn't missing anything outside. Opening the outer door to the office I could see a light burning. Erika was at her desk.

"Morning, Erika—you here again?" I propped myself in her doorway, looking at the pile of papers she had in front of her.

"Speak for yourself! You planning on doing a bit of *Subbotnik* too?"

"I've got some catching up to do—I hardly managed to do any proper work this week, I still have to write this report."

"I was looking for you yesterday afternoon—wanted to ask you about something I'm working on."

"The Minister's secretary phoned, she told me to visit the British."

"That's odd," Erika paused to wonder. "How did it go?"

"Oh, same as with the Russian—he didn't have much to say. I

wasn't really sure why I was there. But the British liaison officer and I did have a chat about economics, well, to be honest, I had a bit of a rant and he was polite enough to listen. He compared what we're doing with something he called 'Hertzka'."

"I think he meant Theodor Hertzka, an economist who wrote a novel about a utopia—it had ten principles, including free association, profit sharing and democratic control. A bit like the small workers' co-ops that are being set up here, except Hertzka was terribly patriarchal and imperialist."

I looked at Erika in surprise, maybe she should be the one liaising with Major Tom, they'd chat about economic history.

"The thing is, after this chat about economics he said something strange, I can't work it out. Something about the Russians, the Stasi and the West Germans being behind the problems in Silesia. He didn't drop much more than a hint, then changed the topic before I could ask anything."

"Do you think he knows anything, or is he just playing games?" Erika looked out of the window. The clouds were breaking up, and the rain was easing off. "I've been thinking more about Maier. Maybe you and Klaus were right, maybe there is something fishy about the whole thing. Do you still feel the same way?"

"You could say that. I mean, first of all I get sent down to West Silesia, then the Minister is determined to distract me and keep me off the case. Now we've got some British officer dropping hints about an international conspiracy. If I thought the Minister had someone working on it, that'd be fine, I'd get back to my usual work. But instead of telling me that another department is looking into it, he just comes up with ways to distract me. I mean setting Frau Demnitz on me, and this liaison stuff, it doesn't make sense to ask me to do it: I can't speak Russian, and my English is nearly as bad. Klaus speaks both languages, and both you and Laura are way more diplomatic and clear communicators than I'll ever be—any of you would do the job far better than I can."

"Did the British guy say anything else?"

"Not much, just that hint about the Russians, the Stasi and the West Germans. I guess it could have been a joke."

"Not a joking matter. Actually quite scary—which reminds me, I was thinking of going to the big demonstration this afternoon—feels apposite, thought it might help clear things up in my mind. You fancy joining me?"

"I got a message from the Saxon police yesterday." I told her about the scrap of paper with today's date and Fremdiswalde's prints all over it.

"Didn't you think to tell us about this?"

"We agreed we weren't going to do anything about Maier, so I just put it to one side and forgot about it."

Erika pulled a face. "Right, I'm definitely going to the Alex this afternoon. You coming?" Erika had her legs crossed, one foot tapping the air. Excitement, if I knew her at all.

"Mmm, love to, but I'm meeting someone ..."

I must have blushed or stuttered. Whatever I did wrong, Erika picked up on it.

"Really? Who?"

"Oh, nobody, really. Sort of a date."

"A date? Great! That should take your mind off work for a bit. Who is it? Where are you meeting her?" Erika's eyes were shining, it made me wonder why she was suddenly so interested in my private life.

"She's from West Berlin, said she was coming over for the demo and suggested we meet up there."

"You're taking her to the demo? What kind of date is that?"

I headed to my office, thinking about Erika. She and I were very different, but out of all my immediate colleagues, I liked her the best. As with all of us here at the *Republikschutz*, she was from the ranks of the old opposition, chosen for our scepticism of the security services and our experience of being on the receiving end of the Stasi's tactics. I hadn't had much to do with Erika in the old days, before 1989 we'd seen each other at various gatherings, and maybe a couple of times on some of the bigger protests, but she'd been active in one of the women's groups so we'd never had the chance to work together on anything. That was a shame, because I enjoyed her company. She was easily flustered, took her time thinking things through, but was dependable and thorough, both qualities I appreciated.

Sitting down at my desk I stuffed some paper into a typewriter, winding it through until the top of the page was in the right position, then started typing. I left out Major Tom's hints and the Saxon police reports, just describing, in laboriously overblown detail, my trip to West Silesia and my impressions and initial conclusions. I made the usual two carbon copies for our own records, then took it in to Erika.

"Here, have a look at this. I've still kept it basic, but padded it out with useless detail. What do you think?"

"Yeah," said Erika, frowning in concentration as she read through the report for a second time. "Makes sense to me, keep it simple. The Minister knows that you've been getting reports from the police in Saxony, but probably won't appreciate hearing what conclusions you've drawn from them. You've got to get it to him by the end of Monday? In that case we should check in with the others at the next meeting. There'll still be time to change it if needs be."

It seemed a little overcautious to me, but I shrugged agreement and put the report and the carbons in an envelope and left it on my desk for Monday.

Back home I put water on to boil and stepped into the shower. Like most people living in pre-war buildings I didn't have a bathroom, just a shared toilet on the half-landing. The only place to have a wash was at the kitchen sink, so I'd rigged up a shower cubicle in the kitchen. It worked well enough, but it did take up a lot of space.

I was quite excited about meeting Annette and wanted to look my best for her. I couldn't remember when I'd last had a proper date, but it was certainly years ago. After a quick wash I got out of the shower and poured the boiling water into the sink for a shave. Looking at myself in the mirror, I smiled. No longer a spring chicken, but plenty of life in me yet. I was looking forward to getting to know her, even if our first date was a demo. Perhaps we'd go for a coffee afterwards ... My mind wandered, taking in all the possibilities the afternoon might bring. What would she look like? She sounded nice on the phone. Self-assured, perhaps a little bossy, taking control of the conversation early on. Typical Wessi. But it felt good to have someone directing the conversation—a little businesslike perhaps, but if it had been left to me I would have stuttered and stammered and said ridiculous things. Yeah, it felt like it might be a good one.

Nervous about being late, I arrived at Alexanderplatz far too early. We'd agreed to meet at a quarter to two under the World Clock. With a half-laugh Annette had said that it was a romantic thing to do, and I didn't disagree. But here I was, half an hour early, wandering around the square, killing time.

The cops weren't exactly out in force, just a couple of small groups at either end of the square to keep an eye on things. A makeshift stage had been set up near the *Centrum* department store, and Western media teams were positioning their microphones on the speaker's stand. It was nearly a quarter-to when I realised that I'd forgotten to buy a *Berliner Zeitung* newspaper—I was to hold the *Berliner Zeitung*, and Annette was to have a copy of the West Berlin *taz*. That way, even if there were lots of people under the clock, we could still recognise each other. I struggled down into the underground station, swimming against the mass of people crowding up the steps to the square for the demo; along the long pedestrian tunnels, pushed to the side, pressed against the underwater-green tiles lining the walls. I managed to get through to the kiosk, then back up and out into the square. This time going with the tide, but slowly, too slowly.

I dashed across to the clock, paper clasped under my arm, peering through the scrum that was gathering. There! A tall woman, reddish blonde hair tied back in a pony tail, holding a folded *taz* in front of her, the red print of the title contrasting with her light coat. I paused for a moment, watching her scan the crowds, and feeling a smile climb onto my lips, then I dived through a gap.

"Hi—you've got a *taz*!"

She laughed, "Yes, I'm Annette. And you have a *Berliner Zeitung*, so you must be Martin."

She had an infectious smile, broad, welcoming, splitting her face almost in two and showing strong teeth. It was impossible not to smile with her. She had laughter lines in the corners of her green eyes, between them a nose that was slightly bent to the left as if she'd been a boxer in a previous life. She hooked her arm through mine, her long fingers tickling the inside of my elbow.

"Shall we get close enough to hear what the speakers have to say?"

Without waiting for an answer, she set off towards the stage, pulling me along in her wake. I lost the *Berliner Zeitung* along the way, but I noticed that she kept a firm grip on her *taz*. There was a good crowd of people already, many holding banners and placards—the Watt-eater goblin from the 1950s energy conservation campaign was a favoured motif, along with other messages encouraging a reduction in energy use.

"Why did you suggest the demo?" I asked, not particularly interested, being too busy looking at her smiling face and shining eyes, but feeling that it might come across as rude if I stared too much and talked too little.

"Well, it's something I'm interested in—in West Berlin we get our electricity from you, but air pollution and water pollution are an international problem. Just because there's still a border it doesn't mean that the pollution stops at the Wall, or that we have no responsibility for it. Besides, I do part-time research for the AL, and energy is my area."

Annette worked for the AL, the *Alternative Liste*, the West Berlin branch of the Green Party, and currently a coalition partner in the West Berlin Senate. In the past they'd been very supportive of the GDR opposition, but had been less keen to help out since we turned down the offer of merging with West Germany in early 1990, although parts of the party still maintained close contact with the Round Tables.

The first speaker had stood up, standing by the lectern. I recognised her—she was part of the *Arche* network, now working with *Grüne Liga*, and had long been involved in researching alternatives to the lignite brown coal used for electricity generation. She started her speech by summarising how, since the early 1980s, the GDR had electrified train lines and converted most power plants to make more use of the domestically mined brown coal in preference to oil imported from the Soviet Union and the non-socialist economies. The speaker then went on to talk about the current use of brown coal.

"321 million tonnes of brown coal were used in 1985. By 1990 this had been reduced to 260 million, and we're on course to go below 200 million tonnes by 1997. But the open cast mines are swallowing whole villages, are even now gnawing at the edges of Leipzig—and they aren't our only problem. In 1989 our power stations produced nearly two mega-tonnes of sulphur dioxide, but we can cut this by a third within two years if we fit sulphur filters. We are overhauling our brown coal power stations to double their efficiency. Conversion of power stations to combined heat and power stations is already providing yet more savings.

"It all sounds positive, particularly when we add the following facts: rationing of fuel for personal transport decreased transport related smog by nearly 60% this summer; cutting the military has reduced overall energy demand by a further 15%; and increased recycling and re-use decreases the embodied energy of products in circulation.

"Nevertheless, the fact is we are still using open-cast brown coal, with its high sulphur and salt content. Our electrical appliances and machinery—at home and in industry—use on average 20% more energy than those conforming to international standards. At current rates it will take another 20 years to replace these.

"But we don't have 20 years!

"Today the speakers will address the problems of acid rain killing our forests, smog in our cities, sulphates and iron in our water and the impact open cast mining is having on our landscape. Last, but certainly not least, we'll talk about the fact that if West Silesia secedes from the GDR we will lose nearly half of our brown coal reserves, threatening our energy supply."

As promised there followed a series of speeches that were both illuminating and depressing. The final speaker, an academic from the Humboldt University, spoke of the impact the loss of the Silesian coal fields would have on the GDR economy. Imports of brown coal from the Czech Republic and Poland would be required until production at our other coal fields could be increased. He remarked that efficiency savings and the building of renewable energy sources such as wind turbines on the Baltic coast will take time to realise, and if West Silesian secession happens before these measures are in place, the GDR would inevitably be bankrupted.

He didn't need to spell out what that would mean: the end of our social experiment, followed by unification with West Germany.

Just as in 1989, events were moving so fast we didn't feel we could keep up. In those days we didn't have time to dream or strategise, only to react, we'd been caught up in a whirlwind of enthusiasm and energy. But this time it felt like we may not even have time to react.

The first speaker took the microphone again in a bid to give the event an upbeat ending.

"Just a few years ago we came on to the streets to protest against an undemocratic and centralised government—a government that was incapable of listening to us, the people. Once again, we are here in the name of the people. But now we are in a time of change. Now *we* hold the power. Now it's up to us." The speaker waited until the cheers died down, the cries of *Wir sind das Volk!* slowly ebbing away as she held up her hands, asking to be allowed to continue.

"The time when we trusted the Party—or anyone else—to take the decisions for us has gone!"

Again a roar of applause and cheers. I looked at Annette, she was cheering with the rest of us, even though she was just a visitor to our revolution. But maybe she felt that she could help us with our work?

"With or without West Silesia, we can't rely on dirty fuel. Brown coal has to stay in the ground! We can't afford to switch the nuclear power stations back on. Uranium has to stay in the ground! We can't afford to use this much energy. We must use less—we have to stand our ground!" She spoke in waves, ebbing and flowing, peaking each time she said the word *ground*, the crowd's cheers and cries the sound of surf crashing on the beach.

"Go back to your neighbourhoods, back to your workplaces. Talk to your neighbours and colleagues. Discuss what you've heard today. We need plans to reduce our consumption. We need plans for more efficient energy use. We need plans to improve and replace high energy input machinery. This isn't the first time we've had to deal with difficult questions. As a nation we are talking, sharing and discussing difficult topics: the Wall, our constitution-"

She clearly had more to say, but a young woman had gained the stage and was talking to the speaker. It was Karo, the punk I'd shared a beer with on Wednesday. After a brief discussion, the speaker passed over the microphone. Karo took it, and stood, looking out at us, nervous, the arm holding the mike shaking. Her eyes scanned the crowd as if searching for someone she knew, then she started talking.

"My name is Karo, erm, I'm from the *Thaeri,* a squat in Friedrichshain. I've just come back from the Czech Republic. I've been working with a group of people fighting the new nuclear power station at Temelin. They're called the Energy Brigades, and they're brilliant! They've been going round their neighbourhoods and villages, helping people install insulation in their houses and flats. And they've helped out with improving people's heating systems in their homes. It sounds boring, but they've halved domestic energy use! Their aim is to save so much energy that there won't be any need to build the new nuclear power station. And," she gestured to the side of the stage where a couple more punks were watching, they reluctantly came up and joined her next to the microphone stand. "These two comrades have come up from Bohemia to show us how to do it. On Monday morning we're going to the Friedrichshain Round Table to negotiate a budget to set up some energy brigades here in Berlin."

Karo wasn't proposing anything new, but her enthusiasm was infectious, and she earned herself a round of applause.

"Do you know her?" Annette asked.

"I had a drink with her a few days ago. Why?"

"Oh, you were just looking proud," Annette was showing her smile again, teasing me.

"You know what? I am proud. Not just of Karo, but of all these young people. Where would we be without their energy and enthusiasm?"

"You're not so old yourself, and Katrin said you're still pretty enthusiastic."

"Katrin? You know Katrin?"

Annette's smile turned off for a moment, her arms hung by her side and her eyes lowered.

"I promised her I wouldn't tell you. She helped out at the *Alternative Liste* over the summer, and she told me about you. I liked what I heard. I bumped into her the other day, and she said you'd put an ad in the lonely hearts column in *Zitty,* so I thought why not? She encouraged me, said we'd be perfect together."

Katrin! She was going to get an earful when I got hold of her!

"Well, I'm glad my daughter has taste," I squeaked, and I'm sure that I blushed.

Annette treated me to her special smile, put her arm through mine again.

"Shall we go and get a coffee? This looks like it might go on for a while."

I looked up at the stage, and I could see that a line of people wanting to take the mike had formed. I nodded. A coffee with Annette sounded just right.

We walked under the train tracks and over to the television tower, a tall stick of asparagus standing in the centre of East Berlin. The lift—a small metal cube operated by a uniformed attendant—clunked and clicked up the tower, making Annette visibly nervous.

"Does it always shake and make such noises?" she asked in a low whisper, worried about offending the attendant.

"Probably. Haven't been up here for years."

We reached the revolving Telecafé level, and waited for the *Dispatcher* to place us, eventually being directed to a table next to the window. It was still cloudy, making the city far below us appear dull, overshadowed. But the line of the Wall was clearly visible—follow the Unter den Linden as far as the Brandenburg Gate, the Wall stretched out either side, then doubled back east, embracing the old centre before heading off into the hazy gloom. Annette stared past the Red *Rathaus*, over to Kreuzberg on the other side of the Wall, south of where we sat, but to our minds, West.

"It's strange. I mean look, I live, what, two kilometres? Not far from here. Closer than you do." Her eyes flicked to the south-east, towards Lichtenberg, and I had a brief sense of unease that this woman who I'd known for less than two hours knew where I lived.

"But," she continued, "we still live in two completely separate worlds. Different societies, at least. Just a few years ago I was glad to be living in the West. Then in 1989 and 1990 I wanted to be back here, with you all. Now I wonder whether it might not just be best if you joined us, if we became one Germany again. That way you wouldn't sit shivering at home, starving."

Her eyes sought mine out, genuinely curious, and seemingly unaware how hurtful her words were.

"I saw you just now, down there, cheering with the rest of us. Don't you feel this, this ... power we have, as a people? Is that not worth shivering and starving for?" I could feel my arms moving around, gesticulating, taking in Berlin that lay at our feet.

"But is it really, or are you just being idealistic? It's not going to work, is it? Really?" Again her words stabbed at me, and I wondered whether it was my pride or my hope that she was wounding.

"I think it will, if we're given the chance. But what did you mean? When you said *back here*?"

"I was born here. My parents came over here in the '50s. Full of hope. They wanted to help build the better Germany. Idealism, it was, a sense of duty. Just like Bert Brecht and Maxie Wander and all the others who came here to take part in the great experiment."

"But your parents left? They didn't stay, and nor did you?"

"No. We went over to West Berlin when I was still little. Just before they built the Wall. My parents said it was all a sham, they couldn't be part of it any more. A power game run by Moscow and the Communists. And now I wonder whether this is just a rerun of those first, naïve years. I wonder whether my parents would come back again if they could?" She was still looking out at Kreuzberg. The revolving bulb in the tower, the restaurant we were sitting in, had turned further and she had to look back over her shoulder.

"Where are they now?" I asked.

"Dead. Both of them. I think they died of broken hearts, broken dreams. My dad had a heart attack, and my mum went soon after."

"I'm sorry. But you know what? I think they'd see the differences this time." Why is it always so hard to find the right words when people talk of death? I avoided her eyes, preferring to watch the toy trains running into and out of the station two hundred metres below. The green and black carriages of the long distance services, and the ivory and red of the local S-Bahn, stopping to pick up passengers.

"Would they?" She was looking at me now, intensely. Staring into my eyes, as if she could find hope there. "Has that much changed? You still have the same propaganda, the same exhortations to work hard, to go without for the good of the country."

"I think it is different. I think your parents were right back then. At that time it was all a sham, it was all about control and blindly following a broken ideology, no matter the cost. But we're doing it differently this time round. There's no ideology, other than listening to each other, working together. There's no leadership of the Party, no dictatorship of one class over another. The days when the Party was always right, they've gone for good."

"So how's it different? Because from where I'm standing it doesn't seem all that different." She was still looking deep into my eyes, searching for answers, perhaps hoping I could persuade her.

"Well, look at the way we work now, and live together."

"Ah, yes! The famous collective decision-making process! You should see the stories about that in our newspapers!" She laughed, but I didn't find it funny. For me it was all deadly serious.

"Well, it's not easy. But if we can build our society on the basis of active participation, where everyone has a part to play in deciding about the things they're involved in, that's got to be better, hasn't it?"

She saw how earnest I was, suppressed the smile on her lips and changed the subject.

"What is it you do again? Katrin mentioned something about diplomacy."

"Well, that's a small part of it. I'm in a team that keeps an eye open for anything, or anyone, who is trying to undermine what we're doing here."

"And what do you do when you find something out?" Annette was looking sceptical now, call it paranoia if you will, but I was sure she was thinking *Stasi*.

"We're not the police, and we don't have the power to prosecute—that's one thing we learnt—we don't want to be like the Stasi," I said. "We tell the people who are affected, make sure they're aware of the problem. So, for example, we suspect that investors are coming over from West Berlin, trying to persuade people to vote to allow their flats to be privatised. Presumably these Westerners see some way to buy in and make a profit."

"So, what do you do when you find this happening?"

"We work out what's going on then if there's a problem we'll go to a residents' meeting, and tell them what the Westerners are up to. If we suspect anything illegal then we'll pass it on to the police."

"And this is really happening? Why isn't there a law about it?"

"We're having to change our whole legal system: it's a massive job, it's going to take time. Some of our law dates back to the nineteenth century—even the Party didn't get round to updating the whole legal system, even though they had 40 years! We have to look at each law, see whether it's democratic. And anyway, we're just not used to all these capitalist tricks; our laws are so full of loopholes that anyone who's out to make a fast buck can practically do what they want."

Annette looked thoughtful. "I see. I hadn't thought about it that way. We're so used to people trying to sell us stuff and rip us off we don't even notice it any more. What else have you had to deal with?"

I didn't want to talk about what I had been thinking about so much over the last few days, so I told her a story about how confused we were about pyramid schemes when they first cropped up. We'd needed to get an expert in from the West to help us get our heads round them.

Annette laughed, showing her teeth again, the laugh subsiding into a big smile. It was impossible not to laugh with her, even though I suspected she was laughing at our naïvety.

"And what's happening in West Silesia? It's never out of the news, but I'm not sure I understand it at all."

"I don't really know what's gone wrong there. We're hearing lots of rumours, the West Silesian Round Table is saying the administration there has sidelined them."

"I read about that in the paper, but I didn't understand it, I mean, I'm not even sure I understand what a Round Table is."

"It's just another way for people's views to be represented, parallel to the Regional and national parliaments. Each Round Table and Works Council sends delegates to the next level up. They're there to keep an eye on what the elected representatives are doing, provide a sounding board, and a way of passing information and ideas to and from the grassroots."

"But that's really complicated! And what are you going to do if your Round Table tells you something you don't like about your *Volkskammer* representative?"

"It's simple. If anything goes wrong, say our representatives aren't keeping to agreements, or aren't checking in with us on important or controversial stuff—we can require them to come to a meeting, or even recall them and elect somebody else."

Annette had to think about this for a while, then: "OK, I can see that's better than what we have in the West, but it is really complex, isn't it? And do people actually care what's happening?"

"Yeah, they do. Since 1989, people have been really engaged. And it's not like the parliaments are doing their thing and nobody knows or cares what's going on. The issues get debated in the Works Councils and in the neighbourhood Round Tables. And that gets passed on to the Round Table delegates who are working with the elected representatives.

"But I think the biggest change is how we're distributing decisions and resources as far down the chain as possible. So the national *Volkskammer* parliament and the administration in Berlin aren't even responsible for that much any more—mostly foreign affairs, tidying up the legal system, debating constitutional changes, stuff like that. Things that matter on a day-to-day basis, like transport and food, are decided on a Regional, District or even Neighbourhood level."

Annette smiled at me, and her eyes danced, sparkling with amusement: "I'm sorry, this is meant to be a date, and here I am, asking you all these boring questions."

"You know, it's kind of nice to talk to someone who isn't involved. At work, at home all we talk about are details, but you and I are talking about the bigger picture—the structural stuff. I don't get to think about that too much," I smiled back.

"But there's something else that I'm curious about: Katrin says you like the Puhdys?"

I grimaced. I'd definitely be having words with my daughter.

Day 5
Sunday
26th September 1993

Görlitz: It has been confirmed that the body found in Nochten open cast mine last Wednesday is that of Johannes Maier, the Party Secretary of the West Silesian League, the WSB. There has been speculation about the whereabouts of Maier since he failed to speak at a WSB rally on Thursday evening. A spokesperson for the West German Interior Ministry described his death as 'concerning'. Meanwhile, in West Silesia, the Regional parliament will vote on a WSB sponsored directive dissolving formal links between the Round Tables and the Region's political structures. The West Silesian Round Table has announced a protest rally later today in the capital Görlitz.

09:25

I woke in a positive mood—the date with Annette had gone well, and it was nice to feel that the future might hold something more than just work and meetings. I decided to allow myself a lie in, staying in bed, reading a book and drinking *Mocca-fix*, soundtrack courtesy of Panta Rhei and Engerling.

Just before midday the phone rang, so I levered myself out of bed and went to answer it, wearing only socks and an old pullover.

"Grobe," there was no answer. I tried again, "Hello?"

A couple of clicks then the line was dead. Nothing surprising there, the telephone system had been overstretched for years and had never worked particularly well. Still, it was good that I was up, it was time to head over to the weekly neighbourhood potluck. Every Sunday afternoon, residents of the block would bring a dish and meet up in the *Kulturbund* rooms next door. It gave us a chance to have a chat about any issues without making a meeting out of it. The idea was that if we could sort things out face to face then petty grievances and requests wouldn't need to be discussed formally at the block plenary. It was also a chance to get to know each other, spend a bit of time building trust and friendship.

I usually enjoyed these get-togethers, despite not being a particularly gregarious person—the food was generally good, and if we hung around for long enough, sooner or later the Skat playing cards and *Kornschnaps* would make an appearance. Unfortunately, I was quite often working, even on a Sunday afternoon, or too knackered to be bothered to show up. It was nice to be able to attend, not just in a good mood, but with enough energy to look forward to the event.

I arrived with a bowl of potato salad. There would probably be at least two or three other bowls of potato salad there, but I had leftover potatoes already, and it seemed the simplest and quickest dish to prepare. Besides, you can't go far wrong with potato salad.

Margrit from upstairs was talking with the old ladies from the ground floor. I greeted Margrit with a hug, and the ladies with a handshake. They cooed over me for a bit, telling me how they hadn't seen me for ages. I asked after their cats, not actually interested, but knowing that the cats provided these ladies with their main distraction between the potlucks. After a few minutes the ladies started swapping knitting pattern tips, forgetting that I was standing there. I felt my social duty had been adequately fulfilled and went back to Margrit who was deep in conversation with Dirk from the top floor. Dirk seemed unusually friendly, in a good mood, slightly hyper.

"Hey Martin, your Bärbel's coming along today," Margrit turned, including me in the discussion.

"Who? Do you mean my secretary from work?"

"I'm not *your* secretary, Martin, as you know—I'm the departmental secretary." This from Bärbel, who had just come in through the side door.

I didn't really know Bärbel, despite having seen her nearly every day for months. She didn't actively take part in meetings at work, she'd sit quietly in the corner and take notes, pretty much invisible to us all once we were involved in discussing work rotas and cases. I hadn't really reflected on this strange relationship before, and it made me feel a bit uncomfortable now I encountered Bärbel in an informal setting.

"Hi Bärbel, of course. That's what I meant. Departmental ... good to see you."

She gave me a tight smile, and turned to Dirk, giving him a hug, and offering Margrit her hand when Dirk introduced the two. Dirk then ushered her towards the side table, offering her an *Apfelschorle* while already mixing apple juice and sparkling mineral water. I could hear him explaining that the apples were from trees along the nearby railway embankment. He was trying to impress her, and she looked like she was prepared to be impressed, or at least pretend to be.

I turned back to Margrit, who had been quietly observing me as I watched Bärbel and Dirk, an amused twinkle in her eyes. I had always rather liked Margrit's eyes. One was hazel-green, the other blue, although I was never one hundred percent certain that they were always the same colour. I often found myself wondering what eye colour had been entered on her identity card. Her hair was frequently dyed, a dark red or black which really showed her eyes up even more.

"Nice shoes," I said, looking down at the brown tooled leather.

"Yes, my aunt sent them from the West. You don't really know her, do you?" she asked, looking towards Bärbel who was smiling over her glass of *Apfelschorle* at Dirk.

"No, I guess not. Is it that obvious?"

"Mmm," Margrit murmured, nodding absent-mindedly. "But she'd like to get to know you."

I watched Bärbel, now giving Dirk a lot of attention, nodding and smiling coquettishly at whatever he was saying. I'd never noticed Bärbel showing any interest in me, and there was certainly no evidence of it now.

"Nah, don't think so, I mean look at how she's flirting with Dirk."

Margrit didn't say anything, just looked at me with those remarkable eyes of hers. She was good at this, making me feel uncomfortable, and I was relieved when five or six more residents crashed through the front doors, carrying trays and plates and bottles. I saw Eli, Robert, Steffen and a few others milling around and laughing too much to make identification from this end of the room easy. They had obviously been drinking, probably been in the park or the small bit of grass in the yard at the rear of the building by the washing lines. They were in good spirits, and hungry. Without much ado the plates were first stacked on the table, then doled out and everyone dived into the food. Pea soup, soljanka, roulade, red cabbage, a leaf salad, potato salad (only one today, apart from mine), a couple of loaves of dark rye bread and even some bread rolls from the day before, rock hard inside, the crust shrivelled, anaemic and rubbery.

We tucked in, conversation dying down for a few minutes while we tried out the various dishes. There weren't too many of us today, so we fitted around one table. The young families of the building weren't represented at all.

"They're at the *Pionierpalast*," said Frau Lehne, one of the cat ladies. "There's some event going on, little Steffen was so excited about it."

Frau Lehne was interrupted by the door opening, and a tall, thin man, with longish curly hair and dirty blue denim work-clothes came in. He looked around the table, and, his eyes directed somewhere above our heads, put his hands behind his back, as if about to recite a poem.

"Good day, comrades. And a good appetite. How does it work here? I mean, with the food?"

He had a Thuringian accent, and looked hungry, slightly desperate. Dirk stood up, and gestured towards the table with the serving dishes.

"Are you hungry, brother? Join us, we have food."

The man looked hopeful, but avoided looking either at us or the food, even at Dirk, who was now well within his field of vision.

Dirk crossed to the table where the food was laid out, and cast about, wondering whether to serve the man's food on a plate, or find some disposable receptacle for the man to take with him.

Around the table, people exchanged embarrassed looks, unsure how to react, when Bärbel suddenly piped up.

"But a contribution towards the costs would be appreciated!"

This was unexpected, Bärbel was as much a visitor as this man, and as far as I knew she hadn't brought a dish, nor vegetables or any other kind of contribution. At Bärbel's pronouncement Dirk dithered even more, he had been about to take a plate to serve the food on, but now looked around the table uncertainly. The stranger's face had hardly changed—he seemed unsurprised by Bärbel's interjection. He still looked hopeful, but the desperation around his eyes was now unmistakable.

More looks were exchanged around the table, the old ladies looked slightly shocked, but I couldn't tell whether it was by the man's begging or Bärbel's protest. All conversation had ceased, everyone was looking shifty, uncomfortable.

"Of course you should eat, brother," said Margrit, finally breaking the awkward atmosphere that had settled over us. She gestured at Dirk: *give the stranger some food.*

At this the man moved towards Dirk, pulling an army mess tin out of his bag. Dirk filled it with soljanka, with some of my potato salad on the side, placing one of the dry bread rolls on the top, so that it soaked up the sloppy stew. Within seconds the beggar had left, murmuring thanks, and wishing us a pleasant Sunday.

When the door swung shut behind him, there was a moment's silence. Margrit broke it.

"If people are hungry, we feed them. We have to—the revolution doesn't stop at that door," she gestured towards the door through which the stranger had just disappeared.

There were murmurs of agreement from around the table, but Bärbel wasn't cowed by the strength of Margrit's statement.

"But we can't feed everyone. We're still struggling to find enough food for ourselves. And this guy, I mean, if he was part of a work collective then they'd see that he got food, even if he didn't have money."

Most foodstuffs were still subsidised, at least the staples were, meaning that anyone who was in work, or receiving an old age or disability pension could afford to both eat and pay their rent.

"So this guy," Bärbel continued, "he can't be working. He's probably going round begging food from different neighbourhoods and projects. It's not socially acceptable, it's selfish and profiteering behaviour."

"If someone is hungry, we feed them. I don't care where they come from. We don't know why that man's not working, or even whether or not he's working," one of the young men who lived on the floor above me joined in.

Dirk sat down again. He still seemed uncomfortable, but looked up and began to speak.

"I've seen that guy before. He was at our works canteen a few weeks ago."

He spoke slowly, deliberately, but gave no indication about what he thought about the man who had been begging.

"I agree with your guest," Eli chimed in, looking at Dirk. "Food isn't free. It might be one day, but at the moment we pay for it, we work for it, and we don't have much money, none of us do."

"I've seen him before as well," said Robert. He'd been looking thoughtful the whole time. "He was at our factory too. He was asking around for work, but the co-ordinator turned him down, sent him packing. Apparently he was in the Firm—the co-ordinator recognised him, he said he was one of the guards at Hohenschönhausen prison."

This gave us all food for thought, and there was silence for a while. Bärbel broke that silence.

"So he should go to the Reconciliation Commission. We set up procedures for this, we all know the score. Confess, apologise, work out how to make amends, ask a neighbourhood to take you in."

Things weren't quite as straightforward as this, and Bärbel knew it. I wondered why she was being so hard on the man. The Reconciliation Commission wasn't uncontroversial. It wasn't even universally accepted in this little Republic of ours. There were plenty of people wanting revenge, not reconciliation, and there were plenty from the ex-security services who felt hard done by. The whole thing was a huge mess, and I for one was worried it may get worse before it got better.

"But he's human. We've all done things we're ashamed of," Dirk spoke again, looking pensive. That surprised me, not just because I'd had the impression he was trying to impress Bärbel, and by disagreeing with her he was probably ruining any chances he had, but also because I knew that Dirk had been in the Stasi prison in

Hohenschönhausen, and in Cottbus as well.

"We have to move beyond this, otherwise we've got no chance of succeeding in this revolution of ours." Again, Dirk had surprised me. I hadn't heard him talk about the revolution before at all. He had gained the attention of the Stasi not for opposing the State in any real political sense, but for *Republikflucht*—trying to flee the GDR across the Iron Curtain. Nevertheless, he had clearly suffered badly at the hands of the Stasi. We had all seen, but not mentioned, how he limped during cold or wet spells.

"It's like 1945 again. We can't just give out Persil certificates, granting clean vest status—these people are dirty. Some of them are downright evil!" Frau Lehne said, cupping her hand behind one ear in order to better follow the discussion.

Another surprise. I had never heard Frau Lehne talk politics either.

"But we can't send them to concentration camps—we can't fill the Stasi jails with Stasi agents. It's a cycle, a cycle of malice, of violence and fear. And it's up to us, it's our responsibility to break it," Dirk was less hesitant now, more sure of his position.

The discussion had slowed; this was an old argument, yet one that still had no answer. It was something that we all had to deal with, one way or another. Too many people had been victims of the Stasi, or working for the Stasi, or informing for the Stasi. Many of the informants were unaware that what they said was going into the Stasi files, and now those files had been rescued from destruction and opened up it was proving virtually impossible to tell who had deliberately informed, of their own free will, who had been blackmailed, and who was innocent of any wrongdoing, despite being named in the files as an informer.

"The Commission may not be fit for purpose, but what else do we have?" asked Margrit. "We have to deal with this. We can't just chuck these people out of the country, send them to the West. We need to clean this shit up by ourselves. We need the skills and the workforce. We can't afford to lose another few hundred thousand people."

The GDR had suffered badly from the exodus of disenchanted citizens in 1989. So many people had left the country, fleeing through Prague and Hungary, and then directly over the border to West Germany once the controls had been relaxed that November. Many had come back, but not all, and the ones who hadn't come back were generally those with specialised skills, such as doctors and engineers —the ones who could find well paid work in the capitalist West. A lot of these sent back money, either to friends and family, or directly to the Round Tables, and this helped to replace some of the financial support that had formerly been provided by West Germany. But Margrit was right, we needed skills and bodies as well as hard currency. We couldn't afford to exclude thousands from the workforce.

"It's got to be up to each neighbourhood, each workplace to work out what they can accept, who they can accept. These people have to be reintegrated into society. If we don't do that then we will be creating a fifth column within our Republic," Dirk again. He was still sounding confident of his case, but looked unsure what we'd think of what he had to say.

"They are already a fifth column!" spat Frau Lehne. I looked at her, trying to work out how old she was, whether she'd already been through a similar process in 1945 when the Communists had imprisoned a few of the Nazi bigwigs and lots of the small fry, but gave the middle ranks new positions in the brave new world the Stalinists were building in this corner of Germany. I wondered whether she had had any run-ins with the Stasi. I found it hard to believe that this cat-loving old lady would be of any interest to even the most paranoid secret police. But I hadn't known her before autumn 1989, and even if I had, we certainly wouldn't have talked politics in those days.

Bärbel ignored this latest digression, and came back to the problem of food: "Look, this apple juice," she held up the glass of juice that Dirk had poured for her. "It was you who looked after these trees. Pruned them. Kept an eye on them. It was you who collected the harvest, pressed the juice." She looked around at us all, making sure we knew we were the ones she was talking about. "There are food shortages. We're struggling to grow enough food to feed the country. We're using little corners of our city to grow fruit trees and bushes and to plant cabbages. 'From each according to their ability': that hasn't changed, we still need everyone to join in, to help out. And if we have people just wandering around, begging for food from hard-working communities, well, the whole system collapses."

Bärbel sat back, looking at her fruit juice.

"I don't think I disagree with anything anyone has said," I decided to weigh in. It felt like the conversation was about to start going round in circles. "Bärbel's right, we're all working hard to ensure that everyone has enough to eat, and it's fair to expect that everyone should do their bit. But we have a humanist duty to ensure that people don't go hungry. That humanism is why we are still independent. We weren't seduced by the promises the West Germans made. I don't have to tell you what we all signed: the Statement *For Our Country*. We remember what we signed: 'peace, social justice, freedom of movement'. Our material and moral values. Those weren't just words, where they? We believed in them. And I think we still do. And if someone hungry walks through that door, that's our challenge. He was in the Stasi? So what! He's still hungry, and we need to deal with that first, regardless of whether or not he was in the Firm. Right now, he's a hungry human, and we have food for him."

Silence. I wondered whether I'd put a lid on the discussion. That hadn't been my intention, but it seemed to have been the effect. I got up and went over to the jugs of apple juice, giving people a bit of space to restart the conversation if they wanted to. When I got back to the table, the old ladies were talking about the queues at the Konsum co-op shop. Dirk and Bärbel were sitting stiffly next to each other, not talking to each other, nor to anyone else. Dirk gave the impression he was thinking about something, Bärbel was looking a little defiant. I sat back down next to Margrit, who also looked pensive. She looked up as I sank into the chair.

"Did I just shut that discussion down?" I asked her.

She shook her head and gave my hand a squeeze. "It's just hard," she said. "You know that better than any of us. You spoke of challenges, and there's so many of them, they're wearing us down. In the old days we could just get on with our lives. We'd moan at home, but we'd go to work, take part in some stupid meetings. You know how it was, just say some set piece—you could practically say the same thing every time, something ideologically correct, maybe a quote from Lenin," a far away, almost nostalgic smile crossed Margrit's face, then she looked back at me. "But we didn't have to think. Work, meetings, queuing up for whatever we needed, family life. But now we're having to think, we're having to work harder than ever. We're not used to it, and it hurts."

She was right, in some ways we had it easy in the old days. So long as you didn't do anything stupid—like apply for an exit visa or make a fuss about whatever you disagreed with—if you kept your head down then you didn't have to worry about anything. You got wages, that covered food and accommodation, with enough to put aside for holidays. The old men in the *Politbüro* did the thinking and the worrying for us. I wondered whether people realised what they were signing up to when they said they wanted the GDR to remain independent.

"Do they have to do all this thinking in the West?" I asked.

"I don't think they do. They're scared, but they don't even realise it, because they don't think. They have other worries."

I nodded, my thoughts turning to my daughter in West Berlin. They certainly didn't lack when it came to things to buy. More food than they could possibly eat, more consumer goods than anyone could possibly want. But nobody looked particularly happy. Everyone looked well-fed, glowing almost, but tired. And worried.

I took in the people around the table, everyone was a bit grey, a little shabby. And tired too. But it was a different kind of tired than that to be seen on the streets of West Berlin. Over there, it was a sort of emotional exhaustion. Here it was a physical exhaustion, combined with an air of determination.

"Do you think we're more determined? Compared to over there?"

Margrit nodded slowly, thinking it through.

"Yes. If we weren't, if we hadn't been, we would have given up. Sold our values in return for an easy life, agreed to a take-over by West Germany. I don't think it was fear that stopped us from accepting the West German offer, I think it was determination." She paused again, lost in thought for a moment. "I think you were right, just now, when you mentioned the Statement. I think that wasn't just the moment when the old government became irrelevant, it was the moment when Chancellor Kohl's plans for us became irrelevant too. It lost him his re-election in West Germany, and gave us a sense of ownership over our own country, our own destinies."

In November 1989 the largest independent demonstration in the history of the GDR had taken place, on Alexanderplatz in Berlin. It was there that the *For Our Country* Statement had been read out by the author Stefan Heym, a statement calling for an independent GDR, coming out against unification with West Germany. At the time it had felt like an irrelevant call—the Wall hadn't even opened yet, we were still creating the spaces to feel free in, getting used to our new-found power. This was the first non-Party organised mass demonstration in the GDR. From that point on the Party was irrelevant, we had become ungovernable.

It was such an atmosphere, hundreds of thousands of us marching, independently, but together. The banners and placards—spontaneous, witty, joyful. We were the people, and we knew it. When I look back on that day now, I know that was when it all started—a determination to learn the lessons of history, to put our experiences to good use: *bleibe im Lande und wehre dich täglich!* Stay here, resist every day! That's when we knew we'd won.

And anyway, who was thinking of a merger with that other German state? Perhaps the hundreds of thousands already heading West?

But that was when the West German Chancellor Helmut Kohl chose to unveil his 10 Point Plan for the re-unification of Germany. His poor timing cost him the goodwill of the East German people, made them suspicious of all that the West had to offer: nothing less than a takeover of the GDR project, a full merging into a Western way of life.

A few days later, Egon Krenz, the newly appointed leader of the Communist Party, and de-facto ruler of the GDR added his signature to the already long list beneath the *For Our Country* Statement, an act of breath-taking self-servitude, an attempt to stay on the train of the revolution: the Communist Party was grabbing at every straw in sight.

Rumours began to circulate that Krenz's move was the first part of an attempt to wrest power back from the people, and a general strike was called. From that moment on, everyone, absolutely everybody knew the GDR government had become practically irrelevant. Even the Communist Party realised it, and they offered a share of power to the opposition: the decisions were being made in the Round Tables now. The government institutions at every level—from factory floor and local council upwards—were relegated to carrying out the will of the people.

Since then, virtually the entire resident population of the GDR had signed the Statement, calling for a socialist alternative to capitalist West Germany. It was a call for the whole country to reflect on shared anti-fascist and humanist ideals, and to take a conscious decision on a joint future. It was the starting point for a new constitution, a new political system, a new GDR. The Central Round Table wrote the new constitution in just four months, trying to keep up with the revolution happening just beyond their meeting room's doors.

"Can you imagine such a statement being signed by even a simple majority of people in West Germany?" asked Margrit. "That's what sets us apart from them. We share something. We agree that a better society is worth working for. There is still truth in the old saying: 'united we stand'."

What she was saying was by no means new. You could hear the same words, more or less, being said throughout our country. The repetition of these simple, even simplistic ideas gave us hope, resilience. We comforted, bullied, accused and supported each other with such phrases. They replaced the slogans of the dictatorship of the Communist Party. The Marxism-Leninism of yesterday was dead. Our only ideology was independence.

"Being an anarchist is a heavy burden."

I looked up, surprised. I'd never heard Margrit use the A-word before. From her face I could see she was trying the word out, putting a name to the feelings of justice, respect and mutual aid that filled her.

"A heavy, but a wonderful burden!" she smiled.

Her eyes shone as she looked around at our neighbours, chatting and arguing and plotting at the table.

After getting back from the get-together with my neighbours I pottered around the flat, playing at tidying while the fast guitars and heavy beat of Monokel kept time. I managed to get the dishes done, but left the pans soaking in water. I wiped down the cooker and the other surfaces in the kitchen, then brushed all the dust on the floor into the corner, a job for later. By the time the five nice boys from Monokel had got as far as *Bye Bye Lübben City* I'd already decided there was no need to exaggerate the whole tidying up business.

I'd enjoyed the chat this afternoon with Margrit. Since the revolution started, most people had developed an urge to talk about all the secret thoughts they'd locked up in their souls for so long. But it wasn't the case for everyone: the cautious, the timid, and those who had lived long. I guess if you've experienced first the Nazis, then the Soviet Occupation, followed by the Leadership of the Party you might be a bit reticent about opening up. But it felt like we were growing into our dialogue, learning to talk to each other. I think it's the small things, like this afternoon, that get us to open up: Dirk, Frau Lehne, and Margrit—each had surprised me, I'd learnt a bit more about them. It gave me a sense of belonging.

By now I'd completely given up on the idea of cleaning the flat, and I was just settling down in my favourite chair, a slight sense of guilt troubling me: I ought to cook some proper food. I hadn't been eating particularly healthily recently—too many bread rolls, too many potatoes and lentils. In fact, I was getting a bit bored with lentils, but the farm that supplied my house collective was experimenting with sources of protein that required less oil-based fertilisers and imported animal feed. This year was all about trying out various lentil varieties. Still, I'd had a decent selection of food this afternoon, and not just potato salad, so it wouldn't matter too much if I didn't make myself a proper dinner.

A knock at the door saved me from any further thoughts of cooking, it was Nikolai, a colleague from another division of RS.

"Nik! Long time! You coming in?"

"Beer?" he replied, closing his fist around an imaginary bottle and bringing it to his lips in a mime of drinking.

"Beer? Yeah, beer's good. Let's go!"

I took the needle off the record, and followed Nik down the stairs. It was practically dark already, a cold and damp night, the rain falling lightly but persistently. Behind us a Trabant started up and whirred past, tires whooshing over the wet cobbles, its red rear lights glistening and fracturing in the wet air before leaving us behind in dusky gloom. The sharp, oily tang of its exhaust cut the warm scent of the brown coal smoke. Winter was on its way.

At the bar on the corner you had to give the door a good shove to get it open. Nik tried, then gave up, looking at me expectantly, as if I might have a key or perhaps a jemmy in my pocket. I reached past him, braced my feet against the wet granite doorstep and gave the handle a sharp push. The warped wood of the door scratched across the threshold, the cracked yellow glass rattling. Behind the door was a heavy velvet curtain. Years ago it might have been deep red, but now it was a greyish pink, and it reeked of cigarette smoke and stale beer. Once we'd fought our way past the sticky curtain, things didn't really improve at all. We were in a dusty, dim room, a bar ran down the wall to the right of where we stood. Oblong tables, set in perfect geometric order, ranked through the remaining space, and the chairs were strewn fairly randomly around them.

"Evening," said Nikolai to the man behind the bar, holding up two fingers.

The barman, Jens, nodded and topped up two glasses that were waiting on the bar, already half full. Nik picked a table away from the habitual drinkers staring glumly into their evaporating beer. After sitting down and stretching his long legs to the side of the table, nudging another chair out of the way in the process, Nik started rooting around in his jacket pocket, eventually pulling out a damp paper packet of Russian cigarettes. He offered me one, even though he knew I hated the acrid sharpness of the black tobacco. In an attempt at diverting my irritation at Nik's cigarettes, I mused for a moment on the politics of being polite around people who smoked anti-social brands of tobacco. But Nik had another kind of politeness on his mind.

"See these?" He gestured with an unlit cigarette towards the packet. I couldn't see the point of nodding or making any affirmative noises, so just waited.

"You know where I got them? A Russian. Captain he is," Nik had this maddening habit of first posing a question, then answering it himself, which was one reason why I preferred to remain quiet when he asked anything. Stay quiet and let him get on with it in his own way and his own time.

Don't get me wrong, I liked the guy, I just avoided him enough to not get too pissed off with his conversational quirks, or his cigarettes.

"This captain-" he started, but broke off again as Jens came over with the beers.

The barman carefully placed the beers on the stained *Sprelacart* surface, slowly straightened up, stroking his palms down the dirty apron he was wearing then very deliberately shook hands with me and Nik.

"Food?" enquired Jens brusquely, his face the whole time immobile, expressionless.

"What's on tonight?" asked Nik, showing hardly any more enthusiasm than the barman.

"Soljanka. Lentil soljanka."

"Lentil soljanka?" I tried to keep the resigned incredulity out of my voice; the same farm that supplied my building obviously made deliveries to Jens' bar. I nodded to Jens, and after a pause, so did Nik.

Jens shrugged, and went back to the bar.

"Where was I?" Nik cast around with his still unlit cigarette, trying to regain the thread of his thoughts.

"The Russian. A captain. Was it Dmitri?" I sipped at my thin beer.

"Yes, dear Dmitri. That was it. The Russian captain. Do you know him?"

"No," I shrugged, "but you've mentioned him before."

"He's one of the good ones. Well, we met up again this week. I'm still not sure how much his commander knows about all of this. Poor Dmitri is either in line for a promotion or a one way trip to Novosibirsk. Where is Novosibirsk, anyway? Is that the one I mean?" Nik looked pensive for a whole second or two, before continuing. "Well maybe they're the same thing in the Glorious Soviet Army," he spoke the words in capitals, in the way we all had, ever since the glorious Red Army marched into town, back in 1945.

"Yeah, maybe promotion and Novosibirsk is the same thing, nowadays, in the Soviet ranks and cadres," I chipped in, hoping to get the conversation moving. Nik ignored my contribution, and continued along the path his thoughts were taking him.

"So there we are in the middle of some woods on the edge of Berlin. Well the Wuhlheide, you know, next to the Russian tank barracks, but you get the picture. There we are, trying to avoid the columns of Young Pioneers and Thälmann Pioneers in their red and blue scarves, marching around as if 1989 never happened. Do they still own that Pioneer Palace there in the woods? No, they don't do they? Been taken over by the Berlin *Magistrat*, hasn't it?"

Nik trailed off again, looking thoughtful and finally lighting his acrid, and now rather mangled cigarette. Blowing out his first puff, the dark smoke assaulted his nostrils, his nose and eyes crinkling involuntarily.

"So Dmitri and I, in the woods, with all these red-sock kids. He's telling me that something is up, that the Moscow cadre has turned up. They're all over the show in Karlshorst and Wünsdorf, and they're only taking orders over a direct Moscow radio link. KGB: that's what Dmitri reckons. And he should know. But if it *is* KGB, then there's only one reason why they'd be here in Berlin. OK, maybe two."

So this was why Nik was here. He'd heard worrying things and wanted to give me a heads up. Maybe he was right to worry. The Russians were always playing politics—officers would turn up out of the blue and start bossing the troops around—but if large numbers of KGB turned up unannounced at the main HQ of the Soviet Western Group of Troops—that had to be significant, particularly if they weren't talking to any of the KGB officers that were permanently stationed here.

"Did he have any idea about whether they're after us or the Western Allies?"

"No. Dmitri's in well over his head. He's not found anything out, or if he has he's too scared to pass it on."

The timing was vexing—why now with a coup attempt underway in Moscow?—it was bound to make everyone a bit jumpy. If the KGB were planning some high level operation in Berlin, it would inevitably lead to serious diplomatic pressure from the American,

British and French forces based in West Berlin. And any pressure would probably be directed at us—safer to kick the mangy East German cat than the still powerful Russian bear. The four post-war allies still jointly held nominal control over the whole of Berlin, both Eastern and Western Sectors, and that had never been a comfortable fact for any of the governments of the GDR. Strictly speaking, under international law the GDR did not even have sovereignty over its own capital city. That was fine while we sheltered under the protecting hand of the Soviet Union, but now that particular empire was collapsing, and we were going our own way—against the wishes of both East and West—the problem of sovereignty was becoming very significant. The only comforting factor in this mess was that West Berlin was in the same boat. Any moves to destabilise our country using the uncertain legal status of our capital would affect West Berlin too, something the West Germans would want to avoid. Not to mention the Western Allies, who no doubt still appreciated being able to keep tabs on us courtesy of their listening post deep in the heart of our little rogue Republic. They would want to keep an eye on us, make sure our little social experiment didn't prove infectious to other countries in the eastern half of Europe, or anywhere else for that matter.

On the other hand, if the KGB had for some reason drawn up plans against us it could be much, much worse. The Russians weren't too happy about the way we were heading, but they were a lot more relaxed about it than the Americans, the British, the West Germans, not to mention the ever suspicious French.

I was still chewing on this thought when Nik pulled a crumpled envelope from his pocket and passed it to me. Yellowish, thin paper, Russian. It was sealed, and there was no name or address written on it.

"From Dmitri," was all Nik had to say about it.

I put the envelope in my pocket for later, wondered whether to ask Nik about it, then decided he would have already told me more if there were more to say. So I brought the conversation back to the new KGB contingent.

"They might just be in town because of the negotiations around the demilitarisation of Berlin and the GDR?"

"Yeah, they might," Nik drew thoughtfully on his dark cigarette, which was burning unevenly down one side, glowing strands of tobacco were floating down to the table. "And my name might be Erich Honecker."

He was right, a peaceful and honourable KGB mission in our town was about as credible as me sitting in a dingy bar with the former leader of the Communist Party.

"These days I'm feeling more like Erich Mielke than Erich Honecker," I sighed, referring to the general who had been in charge of the Stasi for over 30 years.

Nik looked dubious. "Why's that?"

"Oh, nothing really. Just feels like I spend my time creeping around in shadows, spying on people. This isn't what we worked for years to achieve."

"What's brought this on?"

I told him about what my daughter had said a couple of days before, how she'd called me a spy, no better than the Stasi. Nik was quiet for a moment, and to his credit he didn't try to theorise about Katrin's motives.

"OK. I know what you mean. It's sometimes ... sometimes uncomfortable, isn't it? But we're nothing like the Stasi. Nothing at all. We're worlds apart. Honourable."

"But that's what the Stasi said too, 'we're honourable'. I mean Mielke, right at the end: 'I'm a humanist, I love all people—I did it for you', wasn't that what he said?"

Nik didn't answer immediately. He was looking at the dark smoke curling upwards from the side of his cigarette. I could tell this was a subject that had been bothering him too.

"Oh yes, yes. I know what you mean. But the Minister said ..."

"The fucking Minister!" I broke in, "Yes! I've heard it. Exceptional circumstances, social experiment under threat, blah blah blah," I was speaking in a low hiss, but I could tell that the anger in my words was affecting Nik, who was still staring at the smoke.

"And there's stuff happening," I continued. "Like West Silesia, like Moscow, like what your Dmitri's been telling you about. So maybe the Minister *is* right. But at the same time ... Oh—I don't know! I just feel uneasy. It's like we're crossing a line, and I'm not actually sure exactly where that line is! Or what that line even means. I just know I'm not happy about it."

Now Nik was looking at me instead of his cigarette. His intense face probably mirrored my own.

"Listen Martin—you, me, thousands of others. We worked hard over the years. At the end we were hundreds of thousands, even millions. And each one of us risked our jobs, our homes, our freedom, even our families. All to stand up and say what we believed in.

"Me, you, all of us in RS, even the Minister. All of us. And we know about solidarity. We helped each other out in the old days. OK, we didn't expect the Autumn Revolution. Fine, it took us as much by surprise as it did the Party *Bonzen*. But we kept going, we never stopped. The *Bonzen* tried to jump on our bandwagon. The people threw them off again. The West Germans tried to pinch the wheels off our wagon. But we fought them off with sheer bloody determination. And I'll tell you this now: no bastard Russian or American is going to stop us. Because if they want to stop this ... this piece of humanity that we're creating, this Grassroots Democratic Republic that we're piecing together with our own blood, sweat and tears, if they're stealing our future, Martin, we won't let them." His voice lowered, almost a growl: "*We. Won't. Fucking. Let. Them*! The Russians stole our past. If they get hold of our future, then all we have left is the present. And that's not enough. It's got to feel worth it. All that work, the fear, the worries. All this hard work now. What else have we got left to fight for, if not the future?"

I hadn't experienced this side of Nik before, passionate, determined, caring. But he was right. I looked at him, face lowered over the table, the cigarette burning down between the fingers of his left hand, loosely hanging over the edge. He looked tired, as if it were only his spirit that kept him going. Once we'd had an intoxicating sense of empowerment and optimism, but now there was no longer any fizz. The giddy roller coaster of events in autumn 1989 and spring 1990 had given way to lots of talking, lots of arguing, too much hard work. OK, maybe I no longer felt the heat of the revolution coming off every single person I met on the street. But there was still a sense of can-do. The whole country was rebuilding itself. The economy was getting back on its feet after years of stagnation and alienation in the workforce. People were coming together to organise and run their own workplaces, their own living spaces. Yes, Nik was right, nobody could take this away from us. Not without a fight.

"But you're right, of course," Nik had lifted his head, and was studying the smoke from his cigarette again, his voice almost back to normal. "You're right," he repeated. "There's a line. There has to be. We can't cross that line. If it ever gets critical, meltdown stage, with the Russians, or anyone else for that matter, we have to go public. We can't leave it up to the Minister."

It was good to know that Nik was having doubts about the Minister too, that I wasn't alone with my vague worries.

"But how?" I knew the answer, but wanted to hear Nik say it.

"The Round Tables. We'd get word to them, get them to spread the news in their areas, so that everyone hears about what's happening."

It was a simple idea. But I wasn't sure how easy it would be in practice. The Round Tables were only as strong as their members—they were made up of representatives of local Neighbourhood and Works Councils—ordinary people. Some were savvy, others inexperienced in dealing with difficult situations, never mind real crises. Some were dominant, seeking power, most wanted to share power, find solutions together. But direct democracy is only ever a step away from dictatorship: it only takes one determined bastard to spoil it for all of us. Just one of us crosses that line and we'll be back to where we started.

"Maybe it's us who are stealing the future," I said.

"Then we better fucking hope we get away with it," Nik was growling again, "because this is the only chance we're ever going to get." He looked over to Jens, holding up two fingers, and then pointing at me and himself. Another beer and a glass of *Kornschnaps* each were on their way, and, thankfully, would probably get here before the lentil soljanka.

DAY 6
Monday
27th September 1993

***Görlitz**: Yesterday, over ten thousand people took part in a demonstration in support of reinstating direct representation structures in West Silesia. The demonstration was called by the Regional Round Table. Meanwhile, the West German Federal Ministry of Inner-German Relations has described the death of the WSB politician Maier as 'alarming'. West Silesian police investigating the death are being assisted by officers from Saxony.*
***Moscow**: The Russian Orthodox church has offered to mediate between the Soviet President Gorbachev and Boris Yeltsin, President of the Russian Federation. Yeltsin is believed to support the Soviet of the Republics' attempts to impeach Gorbachev, who is still under house arrest in the Crimea.*

06:55

I was lying in bed, nursing my hangover, trying to persuade myself there was no need to go to the office today. I needed water, but water was two whole rooms and two narrow doorways away, and I knew that if I moved, the ball bearing currently pressing against the inside of my skull would go rattling all the way down to my legs, taking all my soft organs with it. My stomach was already unsteady—it really didn't need an oversized steel marble passing through it. On the whole I felt it was just fine to suffer in bed.

The telephone had other ideas. Still a relative novelty, it had only been installed after I started working for the Ministry—and this was my first encounter with a ringing phone whilst suffering the early stages of a hangover.

So far I really wasn't pleased with the experience.

I moved, more to shut it up than out of any sense of duty. The ball bearing kindly stayed up high, pressing against my skull, but upsetting my sense of balance. Two smaller ball bearings materialised somewhere in the lower body, but still being slightly drunk from my meeting with Nik, I couldn't work out exactly where. I stumbled, crawled and lurched towards the screeching phone in the hall.

"Yeah?" I didn't even answer with my name, not sure I'd manage to pronounce it.

"Oh Martin! It's you! How lovely to speak to you again!"

It was a soft voice, a northern accent, from somewhere along the coast. Warm, inviting. Flirtatious even. And youthful, lively. Despite the pitiful state I was in, I straightened my back, attempting to project a positive image down the phone line, even though I still had no idea who was on the other end. The result wasn't pretty—I slid down the wall, my head feeling like there was riveting work going on inside it. Perhaps someone was busy closing up the hole left behind by the lobotomy I had doubtless acquired the night before.

"Martin, are you OK?" The sensitive voice again, warm. A cuddle on a winter's day sort of warm. I wished I was in a better position to appreciate it.

"Eurch. Long night," I managed.

"Oh, really sorry, dear Martin—I've caught you at a bad time! Look, it's not important, I'll call again later."

This person was causing me to visit new tortures on my brain. I pushed some energy into my shrunken grey cells, asking them to come up with a name to match this gentle voice that seemed to like exclamation marks rather a lot. Come on, a name, any name to fit this voice!

"But I'm glad I caught you, speak later!"

"Evelyn ..." I said, but too slow. Evelyn had taken her voice and gone.

Feeling strangely better after these painful efforts, I allowed my desiccated tongue to feel its way round the corners and curves of her name: *Evelyn.*

I said it again.

Since I'd already got as far as the hall, I decided my bed was now just as far away as the kitchen, where the mirage of taps beckoned.

Glass of water in hand, sip, swallow, grimace as the ball bearing banged around my head. Try the soundscape of Evelyn's name out loud again. The thought of her made me smile, which did something awful to my facial musculature. Grimace again.

Trying not to move my mouth, I concentrated on the magic lantern show inside my mind. Individual scenes flickered past my internal eye, Overexposed and crumpled by frequent handling and time, some details in clear focus, others just a suggestive shading. Evelyn's blue dress the first time we met. Her smile, her penetrating but soft blue eyes, her pointed chin.

It had been an outing to the State Opera, on the Unter den Linden, my work-brigade from the factory plus husbands and wives. It had been during the interval when I first saw her, holding a tray of drinks for the Party *Bonzen* sitting upstairs. I could see her from the bottom of the stairs where we'd been hemmed in by the crowd. She glanced my way, and that's when I noticed her eyes, framed by a blonde bob, her dress matching their exact, impossible hue. Katrin's mother noticed me staring up the stairs and followed my gaze to the young woman. She gave her one of those disapproving, assessing and thoughtful looks that wives and girlfriends seem to reserve for women who might sleep with their men.

I took the cue from my wife's reaction and sheepishly turned away. Knowing me, I probably blushed, even though there had been absolutely nothing significant in the fact that I had noticed Evelyn.

Actually, had it not been for the way my wife had assessed the situation and my embarrassment, I probably wouldn't even have recognised the woman the next time I saw her. It was winter: I remember I was picking my way across the snowy yard in front of the factory, trudging through the wet sawdust put down over the grey snow when I noticed her at the gatehouse talking to the works security. She glanced towards me as I passed, and waved me over. I changed direction to see what she wanted, still not sure who was beckoning to me. Concentrating so much on not slipping in the slush, I didn't pay any attention to the figures at the gate.

When I got close enough, I looked up and saw her eyes. The woman from the opera house. She was wearing a red parka—she must have dyed it somehow, because I hadn't seen one in that colour before, even though it was obviously made here in the GDR. The bright colour lent the cheap fabric an elegance it didn't deserve. Under the parka she had on a brown woollen skirt or dress, woollen stockings and decent brown boots, stained by the snow.

"How nice to see you again! It's all right comrade, this Gentleman will see me to the BPO offices." She said the word Gentleman in English: *Tschändlmann*, and even though I had no idea how the word ought to be pronounced, the soft G, the feel of the word rolling over the high T and the low M and N gave her such an air of charm and grace that confused the surly security guard, and he let her go with me.

"So it's the Works Party Organisation you're needing?" I asked, using the familiar form of you, as if we were both Party comrades or close friends, but I was neither. Even as I said it I realised my mistake, and blushed. I hoped she would put my red face down to the cold wind scouring the open space, but then realised that she too had used the familiar form, *du*, when she'd greeted me just now. By this time we were halfway across the yard, and the security guard was still standing there, staring after us. He shouldn't have given this woman access without a reliable chaperone, and I certainly wasn't counted as reliable.

"Thank you for saving me from waiting in this cold," she said, still using the familiar *du*, "I believe that guard wasn't even going to let me into the gatehouse: the brute would have made me wait out here!" She threw a deprecative look backwards. "And may I ask you your name? I'm Evelyn," she held her hand out before adding her surname: "Hagenow."

"Martin, Martin Grobe. Pleased to meet you."

I showed her my right hand, hardened and dirty from the workshop. She looked at the hand, raised an eyebrow, bit her bottom lip, then gave me a broad grin while she firmly took hold of my dirty paw. Taken together, all of these actions were enough to make me blush again.

"Where do you work?"

"Over in building B4, in the assembly hall," I gestured with my chin, so that I wouldn't have to look at her while my blushes subsided.

"Well I do hope to meet you again! It's a shame—we're like ships passing in the night!"

"Well, Evelyn, your ship is brightly lit," I heard myself say. As the words fell out of my mouth, my neck and cheeks reddened yet again. Even by my poor standards, that was a clumsy attempt at flirting. In my embarrassment I turned brusquely away, mumbling a short *Tschüss*. But I still caught Evelyn's answer a split-second later.

"How sweet! Well, I look forward to seeing you again, Martin!"

After Katrin's mother had gone, Evelyn showed up again. She just appeared in the church crypt where we held our meetings, quickly integrating herself in the group, bringing supplies of paper, stationary and even a newish typewriter. On one occasion she managed to get access to an Ormig copier—not at all easy in those days when all reproduction and printing was strictly controlled by the state.

Despite our semi-flirtatious early acquaintance, nothing had ever happened between us. No doubt she was as charming and attractive as ever, but I was stressed and exhausted—working all day, queueing up outside shops every lunch break to buy enough food to feed myself and the young Katrin. At home, I was cooking, cleaning, trying to sort out coal deliveries in the winter. The daily grind of life in a broken economy was tedious and tiring. A dirty, dusty and depressing business, even without a child to look after, not to mention my involvement in the group that met in the crypt.

And I was still hurting with my wife's absence. I doubt I would have noticed if Evelyn had danced for me, naked, on the rickety tables of the cold church hall.

Yet here she was again. Evelyn. I have no idea how she got hold of my number, or what she wanted. I hadn't seen her for about five years—I think she disappeared after the mass arrests in the wake of the Rosa Luxemburg demonstration in January 1988. It was a depressing time, we were all disheartened, and a lot of people dropped out.

Since then, I'd seen pretty much everyone from the old group at irregular intervals, but Evelyn never came into my life again. I hadn't really noticed it until now, even though I'd heard all sorts of rumours: she'd moved south, to Saxony, or to West Berlin, perhaps even to the Federal Republic. But now she was phoning me up.

Despite my hangover, the lingering memory of Evelyn's voice made the whole day seem a little brighter.

07:13

Now that I was on my feet and had a litre of tap water inside me I decided to keep moving. A painkiller, swigged down with strong coffee, and I began to feel like I could possibly function again. As the throbbing in my head eased, a feeling of disquiet grew in my belly. I was excited about Annette, and all the promise, the possibilities and hopes that she represented, but suddenly Evelyn was on the scene again. Evelyn belonged to another time, a very different time: the old days.

By now I was back in my bedroom. I picked out my trousers from the heap of clothes in the corner, held them up and sniffed the crotch. They'd do for another day at least. Pulling them on, I did them up, then looked at myself in the mirror. Grey skin, large pores. Bags under the eyes. I pulled in my paunch, trying to persuade myself that I looked OK for my age, and stood there, studying the reflection. Then I let my shoulders drop, and my tummy sag, pushing my hands into my pockets. My left hand crumpled some paper. Rough, scratchy. Soviet paper. I pulled out the envelope Nik had given me, and ripped it open. It was empty. Pushing my forefinger in, I poked around. No, completely empty.

Squeezing it open, I peered inside. There was faint writing in there, lightly written with a soft pencil. I tore the envelope and folded it open to read the words: *Tue. 17.00h Woltersdorf Lock.*

Was all this really necessary? I had no idea, but I wasn't exactly reassured by the thought that a KGB captain felt a need for such discreet messages. Would I meet him? Again, no idea. I decided that was a question that could wait a bit longer, at least until I was feeling a bit more human. For now, it was enough to get to the office.

★

It was a cold, clear morning, golden sunshine feeling its way uncertainly over the rooftops, leaving the deep streets in dank shade. I walked unsteadily, meandering along the pavement. Stopping only at the baker's to fill my shopping bag with bread rolls, I made my way to the offices.

The stairs nearly finished me off, and I stood on the landing for a moment, getting my breath back before opening the door and going in.

Bärbel was already at her desk, and she gave me a slight nod. I wasn't sure whether to say anything about what had happened at the potluck, and decided it might be simpler to keep quiet. Bärbel seemed to see things the same way—by the time I'd pondered this minor problem of social etiquette, standing in the middle of the front office, she had inserted several pieces of paper and carbon sheets into her typewriter and had begun pecking away. More than anything else, the hammering of the keys drove me into my office. I shut the door, knowing I'd only have a few minutes of peace before the others came in for the morning meeting, and I sat down with a heavy sigh. Feet up on the desk, move some paperwork out of the way: the report on Maier's death, due at the Ministry this afternoon, and currently minus any references to both the British major's curious comments and the police report from Saxony.

I tossed the papers back onto the desk just as Erika and Laura came in, talking about the demo on Saturday. Klaus followed, thankfully without a cigar, holding instead a cucumber in one hand and a stack of plates clutched to his chest. Bärbel brought up the rear, holding a pot of coffee.

"You look like you've been up all night! Was it that Wessi?" Erika's opening shot.

I didn't bother to reply, just groaned, and carefully moved my feet off the desk and onto the floor. The others didn't comment, Klaus just clattered the plates onto my desk, placing the cucumber on top before going to his usual chair in the corner, Bärbel was already sitting, pencil poised over paper, and Laura deposited a tub of *Marella* margarine and a jar of home-made lentil spread before moving a chair fussily into position and sitting down, back as straight as a Prussian general's. They all sat there, staring expectantly at me.

"What?"

"It's your turn to facilitate," Klaus said. "But if you don't feel up to it then I can take over." He didn't smile, just chewed on one corner of his moustache while looking at Laura's chair leg.

I nodded while rummaging around in my drawer for another painkiller, then swallowed the pill. I put my bag of bread rolls on the table, and there was a moment of minor chaos as everyone scrambled for a plate and a roll. Everyone except me, I didn't feel hungry.

"Right, so what's on the agenda today?" Klaus asked.

"I could do with a second opinion on this fascist case I'm working on," Erika mumbled around a mouthful of bread and cucumber.

"Nothing new from me,"—Laura.

"More on Maier, and I wanted to ask you about this report for the Minister," I contributed. "Oh, and I should tell you about Major Tom."

We started with my points, and I described my visit to West Berlin. My colleagues were suitably amused by my account, perhaps I even did an impression of the British major for them, despite the hangover.

"Did the Englishman not give you any more hints?" Klaus wanted to know.

"No, and I'm not even sure he meant it seriously, either. Maybe he was just pulling my leg. Who knows?"

Nobody had any more questions, so I moved on to the Maier case. I told them that I'd completed a fuller report and was going to head off to the Mauerstrasse at midday to hand it in. I was just about to explain about the evidence that had come from the Saxon cops when Laura jumped up.

"A wasp!"

We watched the wasp lazily checking out the corners of the office, flying in and out of the folds of the dusty net curtains. Laura was standing by the door, anxiously following the wasp's progress. It was unexpected, seeing Laura like this—her behaviour didn't chime with the image I had of her—she clearly wanted nothing more than to get far away from this flying insect.

"Is that it, can I go?" she asked, eyes still fixed on the wasp.

We all murmured assent, and Bärbel and Klaus followed Laura out, while Erika climbed up onto my desk, a piece of paper in one hand and an empty coffee cup in the other.

"Can I ask you about this case I'm working?" she asked. "I wanted to talk to you about it on Saturday, but we got sidetracked."

"Yeah, no problem. Your place or mine?"

"Let's go over to mine, I have the paperwork there," Erika leaned out of the window and released the wasp from the cup. It flew off in the chill breeze as if nothing had happened.

I grabbed my coffee, and we went over to Erika's office. It was much smaller than mine, but lighter—she'd taken down the net curtains and cleaned the window.

"The police have been watching a nest of fascists at the other end of Lichtenberg," she began, opening a file on her desk, and flicking through the papers, looking for something.

There was nothing new about Nazis in Lichtenberg, the GDR had always had problems with fascists and neo-Nazis, but until 1989 the Party simply pretended they didn't exist, going so far as to persecute anti-fascist groups that tried to do something about the problem. Now the fascists were taking advantage of the freedoms we'd fought for in order to spread their poison.

"They opened up a squat last year, and first of all it was used as a base for the usual stuff—getting pissed, listening to violent music, going out to beat up foreigners and punks. But then, six months ago something changed. Things seemed to quieten down. No more late nights, no more blood on the pavement outside. Men in suits are going in and out, rather than just young lads in bomber jackets and para-boots."

She showed me a photo, big men with shaved skulls in wide, shiny suits, bull necks with the edges of prison tattoos peeping over collars.

"The police got someone to talk. He said there's a proper office there now, with a telephone and even a fax machine. There's boxes and boxes of propaganda, piled high, everywhere in the squat. Leaflets, newspapers, West German flags. And this."

She pushed another photograph towards me. Large placards were piled up on a wooden pallet, maybe a few hundred of them. In bold letters, black, red and gold, they read *Wir sind ein Volk!* We are one people—the battle cry of those who wanted unification with West Germany—just one word different from our motto: *Wir sind das Volk!*, but so different in meaning, aspirations and politics.

"So where's all this coming from?" I asked Erika.

"We don't know, and that's why the police asked us to get involved. It certainly looks like a political-ideological diversion: they think there are links with the West German *Republikaner*, and possibly the West-CDU."

The *Reps* were a West German far-right party, the CDU on the other hand was a mainstream centre-right party, represented in both East and West. They had held power in West Germany under Chancellor Kohl—at least until he failed to persuade us to join his free-market paradise, at which point he was unceremoniously voted out of office by the West German voters.

"They've seen a few of the *Rep* big shots visit the squat. As for the West-CDU, no concrete evidence so far, I think it's just based on those rumours of co-operation between the *Reps* and the CDU during the Autumn Revolution."

We know that the *Reps* came over in force during the first stages of our revolution, back in autumn '89, distributing West German flags and placards, trying to get the public mood to swing in favour of unification. We were almost certain that the campaign had been paid for by the West German CDU. Now it looked like they could be preparing a second attempt at counter-revolution.

"So what do you need me for?"

"Just wanted to check in with you. You see, the police don't know whether it's money or the materials that are being brought into the country, so they've given the customs authorities the registration numbers of all known fascists' vehicles, West and East, and they'll be checked on the borders. They're looking at the bank accounts of fascists over here for any suspicious transfers from the West."

I nodded, and sighed. "Sounds like the kind of thing they used to do to us, doesn't it?"

Erika nodded too. "But back then they didn't do that to the fascists, which is why we're having such a problem with them now."

I considered what Erika had told me. It all seemed sensible, legal, and considering the stakes, proportionate.

"Sounds OK to me. Could it be one for the 96-15 debate?"

"Yeah," she replied, "that's what I was thinking. I just wanted to get a second opinion on it—might be a useful example, provided we embargo it until the investigation yields some results."

Paragraph 96, section 15 of the 1990 Constitution allows the government to set up a counter-espionage service—my own outfit, the *Republikschutz* was just a stop-gap, crewed by amateurs. One of the many national discussions we were having in this Republic was whether we needed a professional intelligence service. People were justifiably sceptical of any kind of secret service—to many people they were just an excuse for macho, militaristic games of James Bond, and I couldn't disagree. For the time being the RS had only an accountability and advisory role, and no actual police powers to investigate, arrest or prosecute anyone. Whatever the nation decided to do, this case was a perfect example of how real the threat of foreign interference might be. If this fascist squat really was part of a bigger scheme to undermine the revolution, financed by the West, then a competent foreign intelligence body could have given us earlier notice that something was up, and it would have been able to trace the money trail inside West Germany.

"Thanks for working on this, it doesn't look like fun." I smiled encouragingly at Erika, who pulled a face at me.

Back in my office I pulled out the case that I was working on before I was sent down to West Silesia—the speculation in housing stock that I had told Annette about. I'd hardly opened it when the phone rang. It was the Minister's secretary. Half expecting her to send me on some wild goose chase, maybe to the French garrison in Tegel in West Berlin, I was surprised when she ordered me to go to Ruschestrasse—the old Stasi headquarters—to fetch some files. She said they'd be waiting for me, all I had to do was pick them up from the porter. Files for Maier and Fremdiswalde, she said.

I put the phone down without saying goodbye, I wasn't happy about being told to play messenger boy. I'd had the feeling right from the start that the Minister was playing games with me, power games. That's not the way it was meant to work any more. I sat there for a moment, feeling peeved, then picked up the phone again.

A couple of minutes later I had the latest from Schadowski, the police officer in charge of the Murder Investigation Commission in Dresden. They'd found evidence of a struggle near the site where the body had been discovered, along with two pairs of footprints leading there, but only one set going away again. Even though it had never been considered a serious possibility, suicide had now been firmly crossed off the list. Schadowski had also attempted to interview some senior WSB members, trying to establish Maier's movements in the days before he was murdered, but he'd been warned off. The policeman had sounded resigned at this development, as if familiar with the situation from a time not too long past.

The news I had just received from Schadowski didn't help improve my mood, and I picked up the Maier report I'd written for the Minister and banged my way out of the office. Once outside though, the cool air eased my thick head, and I had calmed down by the time I had walked as far as the concrete tower blocks which start just this side of the Frankfurter Allee. I crossed the Allee at the traffic lights by the underground station and started up the slight incline of Ruschestrasse, going past the faded graffito *Freedom for my files!* next to the main entrance.

I showed the guard my RS pass, and went into the large courtyard of the old Stasi headquarters. Concrete tower blocks surrounded the whole complex, making it impossible to see in from the outside. Opposite me was the main building where Erich Mielke, the general in charge of the Stasi, had once had his offices. I headed over the yard and went in, asking the porter if a package was waiting for me.

"Here you are, comrade *Oberleutnant*, ready and waiting for you."

I took the large envelope and signed the receipt she thrust over the counter.

I didn't look at the envelope until I was in the U-Bahn. It was standard A4 size, made of rough, grey paper with high wood-content. Not particularly fat, and most interestingly, not even sealed. To me that was as good as an invitation.

I pulled out the files. Maier's first: not much in there, the F 16 and F 22 index cards I'd already seen copies of, and a few sheets of paper listing his career at the Stasi, starting in 1964 when he began informing on his fellow recruits in a Border Troops regiment. It looked like he stayed in touch with the Stasi once he'd finished military service, reporting on colleagues all the way through his work life: starting in a factory, candidature of the Party, full Party membership, conferences. All the people he'd reported on were of course hidden behind codenames, but whoever they were, there were a fair few of them.

It was neither particularly interesting, nor particularly unusual. There were tens of thousands of these ordinary IMs, everyday informants for the Stasi, watching everyday people do everyday things. There were no citations or medals mentioned, no particular rewards or criticisms, all very middle of the road.

We were pulling in to Alexanderplatz station now, and I changed on to the underground line to Otto-Grotewohl-Strasse. Once seated, I flicked through Fremdiswalde's file, pausing to take a look at his mugshot. It was probably taken a few years ago—the longish hair and wide collars told me that much, but it showed a frightened young man with his life ahead of him.

The train squealed around the tight curves, making flashes of light scratch across the inside of my still tender skull as I read the forms and reports. Again, nothing interesting—Fremdiswalde was known under the codename WERTHER and was listed as an offender, not an IM, and the details matched those the Saxon police had given me.

I put all the papers back in the envelope, and put that in my bag, next to the report I'd written for the Minister. Maybe the answer to Maier's death wasn't in the past. Perhaps it was a straightforward murder, a criminal action, rather than a political one. If that were the case then there was no job for me or for RS here—only for the police.

11:34

I got off at the final stop, and walked up Mauerstrasse to the Ministry. A sand-beige coloured Wartburg Kombi was parked opposite with a couple of goons sat in it. They looked bored, as if they'd been waiting a while—probably chauffeuring some *Bonze* around, poor sods. I ignored their stares and went into the Ministry and up to the first floor. This time I wasn't kept waiting, but ushered straight in to see the Minister.

"Ah! Martin!" The Minister rose to shake my hand, then gestured over to the armchairs grouped around a coffee table.

I made my way to the informal seating cluster while the Minister pressed a button on his desk and ordered coffee to be brought. He joined me, slowly lowering himself into the chair with a sigh.

"Martin, I wanted to apologise for my behaviour last Wednesday. You wouldn't believe how busy it is round here at the moment—ah, coffee! Yes, just put it down there please—right, where were we? Yes, I've got the Round Table breathing down my neck about the Maier death, demanding I come to their meetings at all hours of the day and night, asking awkward questions, making demands. As if I haven't got enough on my plate! I told them: 'As Minister of the Interior I am responsible for security matters, and the police are investigating the case.' But why, they ask me, are RS involved?" He paused, and looked at me meaningfully.

"But why are we involved?" I asked straight back.

"Well, the duty officer that night must have become confused. Made assumptions. And he decided it might be a matter for RS. Presumably you were on call that night? So you got sent down. Unfortunate mistake. But you have that report I asked for, thank you. And the files from Ruschestrasse?"

I handed over the grey envelope and the file with my report in. He put my report on the table then absent-mindedly flicked the open flap of the envelope while I sipped my coffee. Too hot, I blew gently on it, trying to cool it down.

"Strictly speaking, that's the end of your involvement now, but since you've been dragged into this sad business already, I thought you might want to take part in a little jaunt tomorrow. As an observer, if you will. It'll be tied up in the morning." He leaned forward conspiratorially, then, in a loud whisper: "We've identified the murderer, here in Berlin. A lovers' tiff, apparently."

The Minister leaned back again, and gave another sigh. Satisfied.

"Tomorrow morning at 0600 hours, *Volkspolizeidirektion* 52—that's Marchlewskistrasse police station to you and me. Ask for *Hauptmann* Weber. You'll be there at the arrest, you'll be my eyes and ears, so make sure there are no loose ends. We want it all done and dusted. No mistakes." Again he gave me that odd look.

I was surprised: the murderer must have been identified in the last few minutes—Schadowski hadn't mentioned they were close to focussing on a firm suspect when I spoke to him.

"Officially you'll be there in your accountability rôle, make sure things are done according to the book. You know how sensitive the situation is with the WSB right now.

"Right," he continued brusquely, before I had a chance to ask any questions. "The other thing I wanted to talk to you about is the national debate on the inner-German border." He stared up at the corner of the ceiling, elbows on his desk, steepling his fingers. "The Central Round Table and the *Volkskammer* are scheduling the national debate, getting all the materials together for people to think about and discuss. The usual drill. The Ministry for Foreign Trade is dealing with customs and trade, the Ministry for Family and Social Affairs is dealing with the social questions, and we have to come up with a summary of the security aspects of the border and the Berlin Wall. I'd like you to take that on, come up with a structure for the report, and a quick overview of positive and negative impacts. Make a start on collecting data and statistics, see which way the evidence is pointing. You can liaise directly with the Round Table Committee for Internal Affairs, but keep me posted.

"And finally ..." the Minister got up and moved over to his desk, rifling through some papers in a tray. He grunted, and came back with a form. "Here you are, this is for you."

I took the page, turning it round to read it. It was a confirmation of my promotion to the rank of captain, signed this morning by the Minister.

"*Hauptmann* Grobe!" The Minister said, with an oily voice. Until that day I'd never been sure what was actually meant by 'oily voice'—but this was definitely oily. A tone that called hair pomade to mind: slick, greasy, and shiny.

"We decided your new roles necessitated a higher rank. Take the paperwork along to the secretariat and they'll issue you with a new pass and a chit for the extra pips for your dress uniform."

The promotion to captain didn't really mean anything to me personally, except for the increase in pay and pension entitlements. In fact, it was rather embarrassing. I'd never worn my dress uniform, and I had no intention of changing that particular habit. Apart from that, my promotion meant that I now held the senior rank in the office—until now we had all been at the same level, and that had suited our way of working. But there were other messages here, too many to keep track of. I wasn't keeping up—I needed to find a quiet corner and have a think, but the Minister kept on talking.

"Why don't you organise a little party? Celebrate with your colleagues, I'm sure we'll be able to pick up the tab."

The Minister had stayed on his feet, and he held out his hand for me to take.

"And remember, the rank of captain is a very real privilege—and privileges bring responsibilities," the Minister peered at me in a way that he probably thought significant. "Let me know when it happens, your party, and I'll do my best to come along," he said, as he steered me to the door. "Congratulations, again!"

I was standing back in the corridor, and the Minister had disappeared behind his closed door.

12:57

Straight back to the office to try to clear some of the backlog that had been piling up since last Thursday, not to mention this new task the Minister had given me. Strictly speaking, I ought to wait before starting work on it—we'd sort out who should take it on at tomorrow's morning meeting. Nevertheless, I started looking through the paperwork—I liked this kind of thing, it felt worthwhile. A series of structured debates were to be organised throughout the country, information materials provided—available at town halls and community centres, summaries printed in newspapers—all to encourage people to think about the various aspects of the question, 'what should we do about the Wall?' The results from neighbourhood meetings would be fed back through the Round Table system, and using that, the *Volkskammer* would work out one or more questions for the referendum, to be held sometime in spring. It was a lot of work, and it was essential that the information materials were clearly written, and above all, fair to all sides of the argument. I didn't object to the task being given to us, quite the contrary, but it really didn't fall within our scope. However, since we didn't have a clear remit we often got saddled with the tasks nobody else in the Ministry wanted.

I went out to the front office and added a note to the agenda for tomorrow's meeting, then came back into my room, pulling the file on housing speculation out of the pile of papers breeding on my desk. Opening it up and flicking through the pages I found I couldn't concentrate. My mind kept returning to the Minister—his behaviour really niggled. I sat back with a sigh, and tried to put my finger on what was bothering me.

First of all, Wednesday, he seemed pissed off that I'd been to see Maier's body in West Silesia, and he clearly wasn't comfortable with me working the case: "No need to prioritise it," he'd said. Not exactly warning me off, but nervous, trying to divert me with lots of extra duties—the liaison with the Russians and the British, which he'd somehow hastily organised, making sure my time was taken up for most of Thursday and Friday. Now more work, this report on the Wall—thinking about it again, it struck me that the Minister had said "I want *you* to take it on," using the singular *du*, not the plural *ihr*. He hadn't asked me to bring it back to RS2 for us to work on collectively, he wanted *me* to get tied up with the research. But what about the arrest tomorrow, and the promotion? I guess the promotion was meant as a carrot, behave myself and I'll do all right. By ordering me to be present at the arrest, he could show me that everything was being taken care of. In his words: all done and dusted.

The person that was to be arrested tomorrow morning is here in Berlin, according to the Minister. I had no idea who it was, the Minister hadn't seen fit to let me in on that particular secret. That brought another train of thought to mind—the West Silesian crisis had been brewing for months now, and had serious security implications for the Republic. Yet, as far as I knew, no-one from any of the RS units had been involved in keeping an eye on things, despite the fact that this falls exactly within our area of responsibility. Here we were, scuttling around, checking out minor criminal cases, such as unscrupulous Westerners trying to cash in on our naïvety, when the elephant in the room was the West Silesian League and their plans to bankrupt the whole country.

I considered what had been happening in West Silesia, the unexpected rise of the West Silesian League, coming from nowhere, yet somehow well resourced, producing good quality leaflets and posters and able to get them widely distributed. The apparent ease with which they succeeded in gaining autonomy from Saxony, setting up their own Regional government in a very short space of time. Then suddenly there was talk of secession from the GDR itself, joining the West Germans under article 23 of their Basic Law. An agreement had been signed with West Germany to allow the transit of goods between West Germany and West Silesia, without any inspection by our customs officers. And we were hearing rumours of military hardware and even military personnel being brought from West Germany into Silesia. But when I begin to take an interest in all of this—albeit only tangentially—the Minister suddenly takes it upon himself to distract me.

Back to the Minister, no matter what I thought about, my mind always returned to Benno Hartmann. If I was right, that he was gently warning me off the Maier case—then why? And even if I was wrong, why hadn't he assigned either us or our colleagues in the other RS branches to take a close look at the West Silesian crisis? Even if he hadn't done so before, now would be the time—Maier's death was sensitive.

The only conclusion I could come up with was that the Minister knew it was being taken care of by someone else. But who? We didn't have any other central organ responsible for security—the criminal police departments were all focussing on local and regional criminality, and the Stasi had been disbanded over three and a half years ago. Was there a new, secret security operation I hadn't heard about? That hardly seemed plausible.

My thoughts were interrupted by the shrill demands of the phone.

"Grobe," I said into the receiver.

No response. They didn't hang up, there was just no-one saying anything. I could hear the faint rumble of traffic in the background, but no voice, not even breathing.

"Hello, hello! Can you hear me?"

Now they hung up. Just a soft click, then the dialling tone. If it was important, they'd phone back. A mental shrug, and I got up to make some coffee. Enough thinking, time to get down to some work.

It's a wonderful thing about being in love that you seem to glow. It's not like I'd fallen in love with Annette from West Berlin or anything, certainly not yet. But I had a second date with her, and I was looking forward to her company—she'd made a very positive impression on me, and I hoped I had on her too. In fact, I hadn't felt this positive about a relationship since Katrin's mother. I suppose Evelyn had always been there, a vague and unconfirmed possibility floating on the horizon, static charge deflecting the light around the idea of her. But she'd been gone for a long time too.

When I met Annette at Friedrichstrasse station and we walked along the Spree, arm in arm, we had that lovers' glow around us. I could tell because people smiled at us as we went past. This is Berlin, people never smile. But there they were, basking in our luminescence. We weren't the only ones glowing—on the other side of the road a couple stood in a doorway, locked in a kiss; on our side of the road a man stopped in front of us, his arms widespread, forming a roadblock. I was puzzled by this for a moment, until a woman sped past us, riding her bike on the pavement, head down, legs pumping, pretending to show determination to mow down any obstruction. With a squeal of brakes she stopped, and man, woman and bike collapsed into a heap of giggles. An older woman went past, holding a toddler by the hand. The kid was shooting pigeons with his forefinger, cocking back his thumb before each blast.

"Leave them alone Mario, the pigeons are our comrades too!"

Annette and I grinned at each other.

"That's what I like about this place—even the birds are your equals!" She joked.

"The state and every citizen has the duty to protect the natural environment as the foundation of life for present and future generations."

Annette just looked at me as if I'd gone mad.

"It's in our constitution. Saving the pigeons is the constitutional duty of all citizens of the GDR. Visitors too."

"Ah, a lawyer as well, I see! And I suppose you know which paragraph and section it is?"

I did, but I also didn't want to appear too geeky, so I just gave her a hug, which somehow turned into a kiss. A brief one, lips touching, then moving away, shocked by the electricity discharged between us. We looked at each other in surprise and delight, still in each other's arms, until I got embarrassed and moved away slightly. Annette took the hint, and we carried on walking, this time holding hands. We'd reached the Monbijou bridge, and the setting sun glinted off the Bode Museum. It was a bright evening, and the autumn leaves on the trees in the park were glowing pink in the dying light.

"Have we got any plans for this evening?" I asked.

I had some ideas of my own, but I thought that Annette would too, so I wanted to check in with her. She smiled, her toothy grin making me laugh.

"Yes, you'll love this, Martin, a bit of cutting edge multimedia entertainment."

"What's multimedia?" I asked. I must have looked sceptical because she laughed at me, grabbing my hand and running through the park.

"Come on, we can get the tram from here—where's the stop?"

We got to the tram stop, and she looked around, unsure which side of the road to stand on.

"Where are we going?"

"Prenzlauer Allee."

The number 71 rolled in, headed for Heinersdorf, and we jumped on. I stamped tickets for both of us, and we sat down as the orange Tatra shuddered and keened over the points into Rosenthaler Strasse. We sat near the back, and could see people getting on and off. In silly voices Annette made up conversations for the other passengers, trying to make her words match the movement of their lips. She wasn't saying anything particularly funny, but the childishness of it, and the lingering excitement of our brief kiss gave the situation an enjoyable levity. I felt like I was sitting in a bubble of light, even though outside the tram windows the town was turning dark, the street lights were winking on and the tram itself was ill lit by underpowered and dirty bulbs.

As the Immanuel Church loomed out of the dusk, Annette jumped up.

"This is our stop, here we go!"

We jumped down the steps of the tram, and went into one of the side streets.

"How was your day?" she asked, "I'm sorry, I should have asked hours ago, but I was so pleased to see you that I forgot my manners!"

"Crazy. Really weird. And stressful."

"Do you want to talk about it?" Annette sounded concerned, but had slowed down, and was peering at each house in turn, trying to find the numbers in the dusk.

"Something rotten in the State of West Silesia," I mumbled.

Annette had found what she was looking for, and I don't think she heard me. She heaved open the heavy door and ushered me into the hallway and up the stairs. It was a normal house, grey-brown rendering, grey-brown lino on the stairs, and that ubiquitous smell of floor polish, brown coal and cabbage. We stopped on the second floor and read a note pinned to the frame of a door: *Event in the cellar!*

Back down the stairs we went, looking for the entrance to the cellar: a stunted door, cowering beneath the staircase. It was wedged open, and we could hear distorted music coming from below.

We made our way down the steps, feeling our way with our heels in the darkness. The steps felt gritty underfoot, as did the floor of the cellar when we got there. Heads bent to avoid the pipes crossing the low ceiling, we stumbled through the grey darkness—there wasn't much light here, the flicker of a film projector showing us the way to the back of a small crowd where we settled on cushions on the floor. Before us Fritz Lang's *Metropolis* was playing against the wall, and in front of that a young man wearing dark clothes and sunglasses sat on a wooden beer crate, hunched over a guitar. His long hair obscured his face and fingers as he plucked the strings, his feet were stretched out, and before them an array of pedals. As I watched, his right foot darted out and tapped a pedal, then again just a few seconds later. The reverberating guitar chord was joined by another one an octave lower, and both stretched on while Lang's fantasy world was built on the wall behind.

The chords continued reverberating, joined by another one whenever the foot tapped a pedal. Without warning, a scratchy voice, a Saxon accent, began talking slowly. The measured, reverent tones suggested poetry, and it took me a couple of lines before I disentangled the words from his mangled vowels: Dante's *Inferno*. I shared a quick look with Annette, who was biting her fingers in an effort not to giggle.

I couldn't tell you how long it went on for—Dante's words had a lulling effect, and the music wasn't actually that bad, drawing me in, taking my mind off the events of the day.

"The contrast provided by the decayed context in tandem with the superior cultural experience provides a dramatic frame of reference suited to ..." began Annette as soon as we'd escaped. One of her silly voices, Saxon this time, same as the performer.

We laughed, and I pointed out that the interchangeability of both nouns and adjectives made her assessment as meaningless as a speech by the Party leadership on May day.

"A bit experimental for my taste, but, I don't know, there was a sense of preparation, practice and ability that won my respect," was my contribution, said in a low voice, for I knew I was talking bollocks, and there were still quite a few people on the streets. It embarrassed me to think that these strangers might overhear.

This made Annette laugh again, and she told me that it was I who was taking it all too seriously.

"What was that place anyway?" I wanted to know.

"A squat. An Ossi one, which is why the culture was so good!"

"Do you know many squatters?"

"Yeah, used to live in a squat myself, in Kreuzberg. Ancient history, but I still know a few people in the scene. I know some of the squatters who came over in '90, down in Friedrichshain, and through them I've met a few of the squatters up here in Prenzlauer Berg too."

Shortly after the Wall opened, a stream of squatters came in from West Berlin. Feeling the pinch from hardline police tactics over there, full of youthful arrogance and convinced that they were the ones to show us in the East how to do this revolution thing properly. A series of squats were opened up, the Wessis mostly concentrated round Friedrichshain, the Easterners taking over derelict buildings in Prenzlauer Berg, and, to an extent, in Mitte and Friedrichshain too. Unsurprisingly, the two scenes didn't mix too well—even though they had a squatters' Round Table, and the West-squats were all twinned with the East-squats. You didn't find many Easterners wanting to live in a Wessi-squat. I didn't blame them, the Wessi-squats sounded quite stressful. They tended to annoy their neighbours more with raucous parties and fly-tipping, and I'd heard that they had all sorts of alternative-living experiments going on—toilet doors being considered bourgeois, for example. Exclusive use of underwear, too.

The Ossi-squats seemed much more civilised to me—sure, they annoyed their neighbours too, with loud parties, graffiti art and flags, not to mention the below average awareness of hygiene and orderliness—but they were, on the whole, well integrated with their neighbourhoods, providing support and labour to whoever needed it, whether it was doing the shopping or taking empty bottles to the SERO for the elderly, or carrying out structural repairs to one of the many semi-derelict buildings.

But despite all that, it looked like they couldn't put on a decent cultural event.

"Do you know anywhere round here? A bar? A place to go dancing?" Annette wanted more of me, and I wasn't exactly ready to go to bed yet either.

"I'm sorry, I should have said before ... I've got a really stupidly early start in the morning—I can't stop out too long."

Her face fell, but a smile sprang back into position before I had time to respond.

"That's a shame, but never mind—Monday's not really the day to go dancing, is it? What's happening in the morning?"

"I've got to be there when the police make an arrest. Nothing particularly exciting-"

Annette patted my arm, reassuring me that it was OK.

We walked back to the tram stop, it was still rather early, and I hoped that Annette wouldn't think I was giving her the brush off, but if we went to a bar or something now, who knew what might happen between us. That was a really nice thought, but I wasn't sure I was ready for it yet.

We sat on the tram, silent, but still holding hands. When we got off, I walked her back to Friedrichstrasse Station and we said our goodbyes with a hug, and another brief kiss. This time it wasn't so unexpected, it didn't give us an electric shock like before. Even so, I still found myself responding, leaning in for another kiss, but Annette had moved away. I opened my eyes, she was already halfway down the steps to the U-Bahn.

"Bye Martin—thank you for the lovely evening!" She blew me a kiss, and was gone.

Day 7

Tuesday
28th September 1993

Moscow: The Soviet President Mikhail Gorbachev is no longer under house arrest. The news comes as Internal Military units, under the command of the Soviet Interior Ministry, move against the barricades erected by the KGB around the parliament building, which was occupied last week by members of the dissolved Soviet of the Republics. President Gorbachev is returning to Moscow to take command of the Internal Military, but it is unclear how he can survive the crisis without the support of the KGB.

Görlitz: The West Silesian government has ended the co-operation between Silesian and Saxon police in the matter of the investigation into the death of the WSB politician, Johannes Maier. The West Silesian Interior Minister, Jakob Schröter, stated last night that his police force is competent to run the murder inquiry without what he referred to as: 'outside interference'. As yet, there has been no official response to the offer of assistance made yesterday by the West German Federal Criminal Police Agency.

05:54

I showed my pass to the policeman sitting at the front desk and asked for Captain Weber. Instead of an answer, I got a finger, pointing me to the stairs.

This was my first time in Marchlewskistrasse police station, and I was curious. Apprehensive too. The cops from this station had a reputation: the hard lads of the Berlin police force, more than willing to take matters into their own hands. They were the ones who made sure suspects stumbled down stairs and walked into fists. Before the revolution, a friend of mine had his flat turned over by Marchlewskistrasse officers. No reason, no excuse given, and despite the fact that he lived in Prenzlauer Berg, a long way off their beat.

Up the granite steps, hand trailing the steel balustrade. The corridor at the top was busy—mostly cops in uniform, toting plastic shields and helmets, heading towards a pair of doors. I followed them into a large room. Red, black and state flags adorning one wall, opposite a notice board covered with press and magazine clippings, declarations and hand written headings: the brigade's wall newspaper. The police officers were falling into ranks, facing their commanding officer, who was conferring with a woman in mufti. The officer was a captain: that'd be my man. I waited for him to finish talking to the woman, then went to introduce myself.

"Grobe. The Minister requested my presence during this arrest."

"Weber. Take a seat," he shook my hand firmly but briefly, then turned away.

I looked around for a chair, the only ones available were against the back wall, by the wall newspaper. I remained standing but moved a little to one side, next to the doorway.

Silence fell, the cops faced their captain. Shields resting on the floor, held steady with the left hand, helmets clipped to belts, right hands pressed against legs, fingers parallel to trouser seams. All very correct and commendable, if a little intimidating to a civilian such as myself.

"Comrades, your task is to effect the arrest of a suspect. Intelligence provided by the ABV officer of the area indicates that the suspect is presently in the squatted building on Thaerstrasse.

"Disembarkation on Mühsamstrasse begins at X minus 7, mustering on Bersarinstrasse at a point 100 metres north of Bersarinplatz at X minus 3. At time X, Squad B will effect entry and secure the front of the building. Squad C will effect entry to buildings to the rear, on Bersarinstrasse," here Weber walked over to a detailed map, pinned to the wall next to a blackboard. "They will secure access to and from the rear of the squat. Squad C will follow Squad A and will provide support in locating and detaining the suspect who is using the flat on the second floor, right-hand side."

The captain paused, then walked back to the front of the ranked policemen. "Remember, this is a squat. We should be prepared for disrespectful behaviour, up to and including violence. Use of reasonable force in self-defence is acceptable."

A murmur rose from the assembly, the men at the back digging elbows into their neighbour's sides and grinning. The captain waited, face immobile, then pointed towards me.

"First Lieutenant Grobe from the *Republikschutz* will be coming along to observe the operation. Take note of his appearance—since he has chosen not to come in uniform you will need to be able to tell him apart from our clients."

Given the reputation of these bulls, the captain's order was disquieting. Thirty faces looked my way, assessing me, but giving no clue to what they thought. I decided that this was not the time to tell the captain that I'd been promoted, that I was now his equal in rank. But it might be judicious to let him know before zero hour, and if I could, somehow to give the impression that I had the ear of the Minister.

"Right, men! Time X is at ..." Weber looked at his watch, comparing it to the clock on the wall above the door, "0635. Embark immediately, transport is waiting in the yard. Dismiss!"

The cops filed out, talking in excited whispers, clearly relishing the prospect of raiding the squat.

"You can come with me, no need to go on a truck," with a brisk half-smile Weber strode out of the room, the squad parting to let him through, with me in his wake.

"Why don't you wait in the yard, we'll be taking the Volga. I'm just going to pick up the paperwork."

I made my way down the stairs, surrounded by cops telling each other stories of previous raids, pumping each other up, preparing for violence. The Minister hadn't bothered mentioning the fact that the arrest was to take place in a squat. He hadn't told me who we were supposed to arrest either. Presumably the snatch squad, Squad A, had been briefed on his identity before I got here.

Around me, the cops were talking as if 1989 had never happened, I could overhear snippets of conversation:

We'll show these arseholes!

They'll wish they'd been gassed when we've finished with them!

If any of them tries to resist … just let them try!

And here I was, on their side of the barricades. I was part of the system now, alongside these men who took pleasure in violence and who hated anyone who didn't fit into the meat-veg-and-potatoes, wife-and-two-kids model of how they felt life ought to be.

Weber had come out into the yard now, holding a clipboard. All of his men were sitting on the back of the W50 trucks, the engines growling as they waited for the signal to depart. A driver held the front passenger door of a black Volga car open for Weber, and before getting in he nodded to the nearest truck driver. With a roar and billowing exhausts, the trucks moved out of the yard and on to the street. I got in the back of the car, and we followed the convoy.

It was a short drive to Frankfurter Allee, the convoy heading up Strasse der Pariser Kommune rather than going by the more direct route via Frankfurter Tor, presumably to avoid alerting the squat on Thaerstrasse by driving past on the way to the rendezvous. It was all going according to plan: park on Mühsamstrasse, cops sprinting along to the junction and forming into three squads, one squad entering a couple of buildings on that street, the other two running around the corner into the Thaerstrasse.

Weber remained in the front seat, and I sat behind him, watching the uniforms disappear into the early morning gloom.

"We'll wait here a moment, let the dust settle," said Weber, half turning towards me.

I pushed my door open and got out.

"Grobe! Wait here!" Weber wasn't playing nice guy any more, he was half out of the car before he'd finished speaking.

"I have my orders," I told him, moving away.

"I order you to stay here," Weber's face was turning dangerously red.

"Fuck you, I'm a captain, too!" I shouted back over my shoulder as I broke into a jog.

I ran across the road, skipping over the tram tracks and holding my hand up to ward off the sparse traffic. Round the corner, into the Thaerstrasse. A small knot of cops stood around a doorway a bit further up the road. I shouldered my way through, getting an elbow in the kidneys for my efforts, although none of them seriously tried to stop me. Past a heavy wooden door, the lock smashed, and into the hall. Up the stairs: second floor right, Weber had said. I was going up as fast as I could, feeling the pain in my left kidney, but not responding to it, concentrating on getting up those stairs, blocking out the shouts and the screams around me.

A helmeted policeman, wooden truncheon ready in his hand, was standing at the entrance to the flat. He was peering in through the open door when I reached the top of the stairs, but he must have heard my laboured breathing, turning to face me. I held my palm out and moved past, into the flat. There were two doors in front of me, and the corridor bent round to the right. Both doors were open—one room empty except for a cop swiping his truncheon at a shelf of LPs. In the other room two bulls were shouting at a form huddled in a sleeping bag on a mattress. One bent down, pulling the sleeping bag from the bottom end, the other grabbing an arm that had come into sight. Between them they pulled the slim figure off the bed, screaming at her to kneel down, face the wall, hands behind the head. Only when she had complied did the cops turn to me, a satisfied grin on each of their faces as they stood either side of the naked woman.

"Is this who we're looking for?" I asked them.

They smirked at each other before one of them answered.

"No, it's not," then, as an afterthought, "Comrade *Unterleutnant.*"

I looked at the young woman, slim, not too tall, broad mohican, vaguely coloured red: Karo.

"You two—out! Now!"

The cops glanced at each other and shrugged, one looked down—devouring the image of Karo, naked and shivering on her knees, breasts lifted by her raised arms, nipples and goose pimples standing out in cold and fear—then gently trailed his truncheon over Karo's chest, deliberately catching a nipple, then up, over her shoulders as he moved out of the room.

As soon as the two cops had moved away, Karo turned to see who was in the room with her, hands still clasped behind her head. I could see the fear in her eyes give way to bewilderment, soon hardening to hate.

"It's you," she spat. "Wanker!"

I didn't say anything. What was there to say? I just turned and closed the door behind me, moving further into the flat. Shelves ran the length of the corridor, the contents lying smashed on the floor. More shouting ahead. Doorway left: bathroom, empty—looking untidy, but so far untouched by fist or truncheon. Doorway right: kitchen. Young man, also naked, lying on his belly on the floor, four cops: the pair from the first room stood by and looked on as their colleagues did the work. One had a boot on the boy's head, pressing it hard into the bare wooden boards. The last cop had a knee on the boy's lower back and was shouting directly into his ear.

"Where is he, you shitty communist? Speak up, can't hear you! Where the fuck is he?"

The kid was hysterical, shouting and crying, snot and blood running from his nose.

"Silence!" I shouted, in my best parade ground voice. It worked. The only sounds now were the background crashing and screaming from the rest of the house, and the snivelling of the figure on the floor.

The four cops looked at me, expectantly. It was obvious they didn't appreciate my interruption, but I hoped they would appreciate my rank.

"Is this the suspect?"

The four shuffled a bit, looking down at the mess of humanity lying on the floor. They shook their heads like naughty schoolchildren accused of stealing apples.

"Right, get out. Now. Leave this flat, now!" I grabbed one by the arm, the one with the most braid on his shoulder boards. *Oberwachtmeister*, I want all the residents gathered in the backyard. No need for further searches of the premises, just get the people together. Out there. Now."

"Yes, Comrade First Lieutenant!" he snarled, jerking his arm free.

"Move! Oh, and *Oberwachtmeister*? You'll address me as Captain."

The cop didn't look back, just moved down the corridor at a fast pace, already bawling orders. He stopped, shuffled around in the mess on the floor with his boot, then stooped and picked up some papers. He turned, and came back to where I was standing.

"Herr *Oberwachtmeister*," I deliberately didn't call him comrade. "What's the name of the person we're looking for?"

"Fremdiswalde, Comrade Captain."

I'd been too slow. Of course Fremdiswalde was registered at this address—I'd even seen it in his files. And there was obviously some connection between Fremdiswalde and Maier—Fremdiswalde had been to school in Hoyerswerda, which is where Maier was based before the revolution. Then there were the fingerprints on the papers from Maier's pockets. What had the Minister said? *A lovers' tiff.*

"Dismiss!"

Before he turned, he pressed the bundle of papers into my hand. Without looking, I rolled them up and put them in my jacket pocket, then turned my attention to the boy on the floor. His nose was still dripping, but the snivelling had turned into a heavy panting. I looked round the kitchen, found a paper bag with some dried bread crusts in it. Tipping them out I held it to the boy's mouth until his breathing calmed, being careful to avoid the blood and snot. Finally, he turned himself onto his back. A look of fear, then hostility crept into his eyes, the same hard look that I'd just been given by Karo.

"What's your name?"

There was no answer. It didn't feel like I was going to get far with my questioning, but I tried again anyway.

"Where's Fremdiswalde?"

The kid's face screwed itself into a grimace, and he spat blood onto the floor. He was sitting up now, leaning against a kitchen cupboard.

"Gone. Not here. You won't find him here."

"When did he go?"

"Cleared out last night, in a bit of a hurry. He's gone."

I left him to it, and went back down the corridor. The final door was open again, Karo was crouched down in the corner, now wearing a pair of jeans and a pullover. She looked up at me as I came in.

"Do you know where Fremdiswalde is?"

No answer.

"Come on Karo, this is important, he's wanted for murder!"

"Scum!" she spat.

"I think you've overstepped your authority, Herr Grobe," said a voice behind me. Captain Weber had caught up with me.

He was standing on the threshold of the flat, not quite inside. With two quick strides I was out of Karo's room, one more and I was in Weber's face. He stood his ground for a moment, then stepped back. I moved forward, taking care to remain in his personal space, pulling the door of the flat shut behind me. It didn't close properly, it had been kicked in, but it was now at least more shut than open. Pushing past Weber, I went down the stairs, looking out the back door into the yard as I reached the bottom. About a dozen punks were standing against the back wall, hands behind their heads, legs spread wide apart, some were naked, none had enough clothes on for the early morning chill. I considered going out there, issuing more orders in an attempt to improve the situation for the squatters, but a glance over my shoulder told me that Weber was on his way down.

I'd done all I could, and I'd definitely outstayed my welcome.

07:13

The number 13 tram was rattling down the hill as I reached the corner, and I sprinted over the road to catch it. The morning rush was just over—the early shift at the factories along the river would already be at their machines, the kids sitting at their desks and shopworkers opening up—so I had a choice of which seat to slump into.

When I got off at Marktstrasse, I swayed for a moment, uncertain which direction my feet should take me. I ought to go to the office, report back at the morning meeting. But my flat was closer, and the thought of a dark room and a cup of coffee was too comforting. Time to go home.

I put the pan of water on the hob as soon as I got in, and stared out of the window as I waited for it to boil. Clouds of steam brought me back, and I hurriedly spooned some ground coffee into a mug, pouring water over it. The round smell of coffee rose to my nostrils, familiar, comforting. I absently stirred the grounds floating on the top as I went through to the living room, and sank into my chair, putting the coffee on the floor by my feet. The curtains were open, but the sun was low and hazy so I didn't need to get up and close them.

The doorbell woke me. I put my hands on the chair arms and pushed myself up, pulling my feet back as I did so and knocking over the mug of cold coffee in the process.

"Shit!"

The doorbell rang again: loud, long and insistent. I left the coffee, and went to the door, opening it.

"Katrin!"

"Papa! What's happened? Have you been drinking?"

"What time is it?"

"It's about eleven. You have been drinking, haven't you?"

I trailed back to the living room, picked up the cup, then went to get a cloth from the kitchen. No harm done, just a bit of coffee on the wooden floor. I wiped it up, aware of Katrin moving around the kitchen, making more coffee.

"Are you OK, Papa?" she called through the doorway.

"Yeah, yeah. Fine. All the better for seeing you."

She grinned, but it was true: a couple of hours sleep, and the smiling face of my daughter—that's what good medicine is all about.

"So what's up? You look awful."

I thought about our last conversation, and the chat I'd had the other night with Nik, so when I took the coffee-saturated cloth back to the kitchen, I told her about my morning. The edited version, no need to go into the gory details.

"The guy you were looking for wasn't even there? So this whole raid was for nothing, barging in on people while they're asleep, shouting at them-"

"Yes-"

"It's no better than the bad old days, is it?" Katrin was on a roll.

"It wasn't my idea, and anyway, these things happen in the West too, don't they?"

Katrin softened, "Suppose so. Still doesn't make it right. Anyway, how do you know this guy is the one you want?"

"I don't. That's just what I was told, by the Minister."

"What? No evidence, just his word. Do you believe him?"

"Of course. I'm sure it's all right." Why was I defending him? "But to what do I owe the pleasure?" I asked, trying to change the subject.

Katrin blushed, then, mischievously: "How are you getting on with Annette?"

I grinned back. "I ought to be cross with you—interfering in my life like that! But, it was … interesting."

"Mm-hm?"

"Yeah, we seem to get on well. It's been nice. It was good to think about something different for a while. I doubt anything will happen."

"But you've met her twice already—of course something might happen!" Then, more quietly: "Thanks for not being pissed off with me."

"Well, like I said, I ought to be. But it's good to know someone cares enough to do something like that."

"I thought you'd blow a gasket—that's why I wanted to warn you about her last Friday, but then we didn't get round to it. And to be honest I hadn't expected Annette to respond so quickly to the advert. In fact, she'd spotted it even before I told her about you. But she's great, I really like her—she'll be good for you."

"I don't know if it'll get that far. And just because I'm not too annoyed with you doesn't mean you can carry on interfering in my life!"

"Yeah—sorry," Katrin did at least manage to look a little contrite. "But I hate to think of life passing you by."

"It isn't. And it's not as if there have never been any others, you know?"

Her eyes widened: "I didn't know—I never noticed."

"No, you wouldn't have—it was after you went. I was here, alone, it was a crazy time, that autumn. Everyone had so much energy, we were all so frantic, busy, tired, excited … things happened."

"But nothing lasted? I mean, was there anything serious?"

"No, nothing lasted. It was like … nothing could ever come close to what I had with her." I didn't say her name, I rarely do, but we both knew who I meant. "When the cuddling ended, when whoever it was had left, or when I came home again afterwards … that was it. Then I'd feel so alone. More than before. You hold someone, and you feel safe. Your thoughts are quiet, you can feel your heart beating. For a change it's not hurting. But then afterwards I knew I was by myself, and it just hurt all the more."

I'd never had this kind of conversation with my daughter before. In the time since Katrin left, she had grown up. The few short weeks between her going and the Wall opening, when we got to see each other again—those weeks had changed her. She was no longer my little girl, but an adult. Our relationship was being redefined, we were still working out how to communicate with each other, these two new people. I liked talking with her as a grown-up, as an equal.

"What was it like, y'know. When Mum ..." Katrin didn't finish the sentence.

"It was ..." I looked at her, my mouth spelt the word: *terrible*, but my breath wasn't strong enough to say it. Her eyes glanced off mine, sliding down to the table, her hands cupping the mug of coffee, her face wreathed in the rising steam. My own eyes slipped down to the table too. My hands were mirroring Katrin's, cupping my own mug of coffee. "Just ..."

Silence overtook us.

"I was so young. I don't know if I was too young to remember, or just blocked it out somehow," she whispered.

My lips shaped that word again. *Terrible*. My mind wandered back to those awful days. I don't think about it too much now, it still hurts. But I couldn't forget that time, even if I wanted to. How could I forget how, in the morning, I'd get up, functioning without being. I'd put a pan of water on to boil and go to wake up Katrin, make sure she got out of bed and dressed. I'd take her halfway to the school where she'd meet up with friends. We would hardly exchange a word, both lost in our individual battles for survival. I must have been a grim sight in those days. I wasn't sleeping. Wasn't eating. Just tired, running on empty.

After dropping Katrin off I should have gone to work. But I didn't. I don't know how long that phase lasted: days, maybe weeks. I couldn't be around people. Instead of getting on the tram to the factory, I'd head back to the flat. As soon as Katrin was out of sight I could feel tears drip down my cheeks, gathering in the corners between nose and upper lip. I'd stumble along, head bowed so that passers-by, hurrying to work or waiting at the tram stop in the grey, slushy snow wouldn't see my tears. Letting myself back into the flat, the tears would flow freely. I hated Katrin's mum. Loved her. I missed her so much, and felt betrayed by her absence. I was imploding with the weight of the love I still felt for her, that I could no longer give her. The years we would no longer share. The times we'd no longer laugh together, argue together, make love together. She was no longer there to hug, so I'd beat the walls with my bare fists. I had to feel a different pain. The bloody knuckles gave me a physical pain that I could deal with.

It wasn't long before I'd open another bottle of schnapps. It would dull the pain in the knuckles but not the agony of my corroding soul. It didn't stop me from thinking either. All the times together, the three of us. All the good times, all the fights. All the times when we had enough to be happy, and the times when we struggled to keep our little family going. I'd stare out of the window, the snow flying past, landing in dark heaps on the road, blocking the pavements. The flat would steadily cool as the morning's ration of coal burned up, the wind would whine while I sat and shivered, making not a sound. I'd used up all the chances this life was going to give me. There was nothing left, no other reason to continue the struggle. Except Katrin. For her I'd sober up, light the stove again, wash the coal dust off my hands, wash the tears off my face, wash the blood off the wall, try to make things OK for when she got back from school.

"I'm sorry Katrin, it must have been really hard for you. I did my best, but I know it wasn't enough. It must have been really hard for you." I was still looking at my hands, clasped around the mug, the fine tracing of scars, picked out by coal dust under the skin of the knuckles. I'd slid off into the past, my mind tracing the contours of years-old pain. I looked up at Katrin. On the other side of the kitchen table a cold mug sat in front of an empty chair.

A tune wavered through the open door from the living room. Low and reedy, sonorous. Familiar. My heart stopped, the whole world froze in a moment of ecstasy and anguish, the notes summoning an imprint of memory that immediately faded at the edges, leaving the silhouette of the woman I had lost.

I followed the traces of vibrating air into the hall. Katrin was standing in the living room, her back to me, swaying with the music she was playing.

I stood in the doorway for a moment, washed by the sounds. "That was your mum's."

The music stopped, and Katrin turned around, holding the alto recorder in both hands.

"Of course ... you knew that," I added.

Katrin smiled, a gentle figure, solid and real, taking the place of a memory. She carefully put the instrument back on the bookshelf, taking her time to line it up with the pattern of dust that outlined its home.

"I didn't know you'd learned to play," I said to her back. She stepped towards me.

"Yes," she looked up into my face, her mother's eyes gazing at me. "It's one of the few things I remember about her. A friend is teaching me to play." She came closer, and with her index finger stroked a tear off my cheek. She put her arms around me, ignoring my stiffness. "Isn't it time to move on, Papa?"

"What do you mean?"

"It's been years. You don't need to stay here, all alone. Life can offer more than this." She let go of me, took a step back, and tried to look me in the eye.

"I've got my work. And you." I looked at the recorder on the shelf. Easier to look anywhere than at my daughter. I wanted to tell her that my heart is just too big, I can't let go, can't just forget. There was no way to prise that pain out of my chest.

I continued staring at the recorder, the dusty shelf, the books, as Katrin picked up her coat, patted my arm, kissed my wet cheek and left.

13:23

I sat at home for another hour or so, not doing much, just trying to motivate myself to get on with the day. Finally, I put my coat on and went to the office. When I arrived, only Bärbel and Klaus were there.

"Laura and Erika have gone over to RS1 to talk about the Nazi nest," Klaus told me.

"Who's handling it at the RS1 end of things?"

"Nik's co-ordinating it. In fact, RS1 have been doing most of the work on it. What are you up to now?"

"Dunno. Thought I'd better come in, though. Guess I've got a load of stuff I could be getting on with."

I told Klaus about the raid, leaving nothing out. He was clearly shocked, but didn't say anything for a while, just sat there, smoking a cigar. Finally, he stirred.

"Wasn't the state prosecutor there? Or independent witnesses?"

"No, there was no need because it wasn't a search, just an arrest. But you can be sure they had a good look around while they smashed the place up."

"You kind of hoped those days were gone, didn't you? But here we are, three years in, and the cops are still bastards."

"Still the same people wearing the same uniform. I guess it's naïve to think things can change that fast," I said.

Klaus nodded, and chewed on his cigar for a bit.

"Maybe we need to think about taking this to the Round Table. We could suggest some kind of oversight body to be present whenever things are controversial or might get violent."

I didn't disagree with Klaus, just didn't want to think about it right now, so I cut him off.

"Yeah, sounds good, but let's talk about it with the others."

He jotted down a few notes on his notepad, then looked up as my phone rang. I was already on my way to the toilet, so I asked him to answer it for me.

"Who was it?" I asked when I got back.

"No-one there," he shrugged. "Bad line. Look, I've got to go to my old workplace, get some employment records stamped for the tax office. Why don't you come with me—it doesn't look like you're going to get much done here."

Erika and Laura had taken the Trabant, but a police patrol car was parked next to a colourful sign advertising a neighbourhood meeting. I admired the vehicle's green and white two-tone paint job, blue lights and loudspeakers on the roof. Klaus jangled the keys before unlocking the doors.

"How did you get hold of this?"

"You know the Wartburg we have?"

"The one that never works?"

"The only one we have, yes. Well, the cops were down here last week, when you were tootling around in Silesia. They just wanted to drop off some paperwork or something. They drove straight into the back of the Wartburg. Laura gave them a right talking to, so they towed the car away and a police mechanic is going to sort it out. Meanwhile, we get to use this mean, green machine," Klaus grinned.

We got in, and headed off towards Schöneweide. If I'd been in better condition I would have been tempted to play around with the lights and the sirens, but as it was we just sat there in silence while Klaus filled the car with cigar fumes.

We drove down Wilhelminenhofstrasse. On the left the usual soot stained brown-grey flats with shops on the ground floor. To our right ran railway tracks, a diesel locomotive, stationary, engine hammering out greasy smoke. Attached to it, a train, a long line of empty flat-bed wagons.

"Transformer works," said Klaus, nodding towards the factory beyond the goods train. It too was stained and sooty, but behind all the dirt were yellow bricks, and an elaborate industrial Gothic design. It must have been beautiful once.

"Just a bit further down—that's the cable works, KWO. Designed by the same architect for Emil Rathenau last century. And that, on the corner at the end is the TV factory, where I ended up working in '89."

I nodded, concentrating on the road ahead. The tyres rumbled over broken concrete flags that lined the tram tracks we were following.

"There's the main gate, over there. Can you see somewhere safe to park?"

On the left, the road broadened out as a side road entered, making a triangle with a pedestrian island in it. As we slowed down to park I saw someone come out of the factory gates opposite. He turned to go to the tram stop, and as he came closer I realised who it was.

"Stop the car! There's Fremdiswalde, it's him!"

Klaus braked to a sharp stop, and before I'd a chance to get out, he was already gone, leaving the door swinging open. I ran after him, catching sight of Fremdiswalde heading back into the cable factory. Klaus was at the factory gates before I was even halfway across the railway tracks, but someone jumped out from the gatehouse, tackling him round the legs. He crunched into the side of the gatepost, tangled up with a security guard. I took a short detour to avoid the mêlée, hurdling the slack chain hanging across the vehicle entrance.

"He went left!" shouted Klaus from behind me and I veered round that way, leaving Klaus to rain a string of curses on the guard who'd grabbed him. Ahead of me I could see dozens and dozens of cable drums in the lee of the factory wall. Next to the drums, covered in chalk, and dusted in soot, men were winding up a cable as thick as my forearm. To my right there was a three-storey building, built in the same yellow brick as the transformer works down the road. A door led into this building, and I was about to go in when I noticed that the men in chalk and soot were looking further down the way, towards a block set at right angles to this one. Taking the hint, I turned the corner of the long high building just as a door at the foot of a stairwell slammed shut. In through the door, I saw another to my right heading onto the ground floor, and a staircase snaking upwards. Brown art deco tiles covered the walls to elbow height, climbing steadily up with the stairs. They were greasy, threads of soot lining the grain. The steps were concrete, with steel runners, and although not steep, they were high. I ran up, following the echoing footsteps. Sometime around the third or fourth landing I lost track of how many levels I'd gone up, just concentrating on the pounding steps echoing from above. My heart ready to pop, my head banging, I'd already tripped over once, catching my right knee on a steel edge. Why was I doing this to myself? I wasn't a cop—I couldn't even arrest this guy if I did catch up with him! Some part of my brain kept feeding me reasons to stop, but still I continued up this nightmare of a staircase.

The crash of a heavy steel door falling into its frame: Fremdiswalde had exited the stairwell. It didn't sound too close, so I passed the next floor and carried on upwards. A large number 6 was painted on the wall where the staircase ended. The steel doors were to the right. I aimed for them, trying to shoulder them open, pulling down the handle as I hit the brown metal. A dull impact, a sharp pain. Ignoring shoulder and knee, I tried it the other way, pulling the door open, leveraging my weight against my heels. Behind the door the light was dim, the air filled with desultory dripping. What light there was came from the cracked skylights, but they hadn't been cleaned for decades.

Shadows danced in the corners. As I stood there letting my eyes adjust, some of the shadows materialised into workbenches, others into machinery, and, at the other end of a long room, a human shape. It was turned towards me, as far as I could see, and swaying. I stood there, trying to work it out, my eyes struggling in the grey light.

As my surroundings come into focus, I realised that the workshop was a lot longer than I thought: the figure wasn't swaying, but running down the length of the floor, jumping across gaps in the floorboards, and dodging drips from above. I didn't fancy following him, and while I dithered, the door behind me slammed. This was nearly too much for me, my knee and shoulder were killing me, my lungs were stretched thin enough to rip. I swivelled around to see Klaus, face red, panting. I pointed towards the fleeing figure, now nearly at the far end, and Klaus set off, jumping from one stable-looking part of the floor to another.

Meanwhile, I tried to use my head. I could go down a level, head Fremdiswalde off at the next staircase along. I turned back to the door, headed down to the floor below, and went in, turning left onto a corridor that was twice as long as the workshop above.

As I sprinted past office doors and frosted glass panels, a scream reverberated down the corridor, but there was no-one in sight, no sign who had made this sound, and nothing to suggest that anyone else was in the building: nobody came to their door to look out into the corridor.

I stopped, and over my own gasping I could hear a whimpering, a loud ticking and Klaus swearing. He didn't sound hurt, so it must have been Fremdiswalde who had screamed.

I picked up the pace again, skidding on the polished lino as I turned into a wider part of the corridor. Our fugitive was on the floor, holding his leg, face contorted in agony. Klaus stood above him, looking down, obviously unsure what he should be doing.

"What happened?"

Klaus gestured towards the paternoster lift clicking its way past an opening in the wall—coffin-sized boxes attached to an endless loop of chain running from the top floor to the basement and back again. You get in a box on one floor, and jump out when you've reached the floor you want. The lift doesn't stop, just goes round in an endless, slow loop.

"He ran down the stairs and jumped to get on the lift. He tripped, missed it—trapped his left leg. I had to pull him out," he shrugged. "But it looks like you've got your man after all."

I nodded, bent double, trying to get my breath back. When I straightened up, Klaus was examining Fremdiswalde's leg.

"You'll be all right, Sonny Jim. No blood, no broken bones. You'll probably have a whopper of a bruise in the morning."

Fremdiswalde didn't seem impressed, he was still on the floor groaning.

"Why don't you find a phone and call the cops, I'll stay here with him. Make sure he doesn't leg it again," said Klaus, repressing a grin as he took a cigar out of his pocket.

17:06

It took some time for the bulls to show up and take Fremdiswalde into custody. I considered going with him, make sure he'd be treated right, but guessed that I probably wouldn't be of much use. Besides, I had a mysterious appointment with Dmitri. Woltersdorf Lock, he'd said. I knew it was somewhere on the eastern edge of Berlin, but wasn't quite sure where, so I'd looked it up.

Strange place. Get the S-Bahn to Rahnsdorf, a station in the middle of the forests around Köpenick, then change to a tram that went through the woods to a little village just outside the city limits.

Klaus gave me a lift to the nearest S-Bahn station and the tram was waiting when I got off the train, so I climbed aboard, pushing my ticket into the stamping machine and pressing on the handle to punch a hole. I sat down at the back, thinking about the tram ride with Annette last night.

Only one other person got on, a middle-aged man in a long brown overcoat and a trilby. He sat down in the front seat without looking around, content to stare out of the window, watching the people milling around the entrance to the S-Bahn station.

With a jerk the tram moved off, it was a rattly old Gothawagen. After a few metres it left the road and swerved into the trees, grumbling over track joints, jolting and shaking the whole while. I wanted to have a think, try to process the day so far, but the lurching tram made it hard to do anything but look out of the window. After about a kilometre of trees the tram banged over a set of points, the track looping around an abandoned hut.

The man sitting near the front seemed to take this as a cue, knocking on the driver's window—a knock like a policeman's hard triple-rap. The driver clicked open the door, and the man leaned in, saying a few words. The tram was rattling too much for me to make out any of the short conversation, but the man seemed happy. With large, confident strides he came down the carriage, pulling open the rear door.

"You, this is your stop. Out, now!" The tram had slowed a bit, it was going about walking pace. "Quick, out here, go down that path and you'll be met!"

He spoke with a Slavic accent, and I think it was this combined with his confidence that made me follow his orders. I jumped down, my right knee almost giving way as I landed on the forest floor, the tram door slamming shut behind me as it hastened off, leaving the forest and disappearing round a bend.

I looked around me. Nothing but trees, tram rails, the hut about fifty metres behind me and a forest track going off into the gloom. I followed the path, back the way I'd come, past the abandoned hut.

"Grobe!"

I looked around. No-one to be seen.

"Grobe!"

A closer look, the voice had come from the other side of the tracks. I stepped over them, and found myself face to face with a Russian NCO. She didn't say anything more, just beckoned me to follow. At this point I wasn't seeing many alternatives, so I followed her into the forest, until, on a wider track, we came upon a Soviet Army UAZ jeep, well disguised in its olive drab.

Beside the passenger door stood a man wearing fatigues and an eye patch. A military haircut, skin thin as parchment, shiny and without any wrinkles—somehow it gave him a youthful look, even though he was about my age—it was the KGB officer who had been watching me the other day at the Karlshorst HQ. Without smiling, he held out his hand.

"Dmitri Alexandrovich."

I took his hand, but didn't reply.

"You must forgive me these little games, but you were being followed. Here, take these, put them on. We don't have much time."

He handed me a Soviet Army greatcoat and cap, and held the back door of the UAZ open for me. I shrugged into the coat, put the forage cap on, and climbed in. My guide got into the driver's seat, and Dmitri climbed in beside her.

The jeep made easy work of the rough logging track, and the three of us sat in silence as we sped through the woods. Anyone we passed would only see a Soviet vehicle with three Russian soldiers in it—with the cap and coat I would be unrecognisable.

We must have been on the go for about twenty minutes before we stopped. At first, we had stuck to forest tracks, but then we crossed a railway line and sped through the centre of the small town of Erkner. After that I lost track, but now we'd stopped in a clearing.

The NCO ran round the front of the jeep, holding Dmitri's door open for him. I climbed out under my own steam, hurrying to catch up with Dmitri, who was already heading down a narrow path. The NCO remained behind, sitting behind the wheel, eyes straight ahead, not looking towards me or her officer.

I caught up with Dmitri, who had stopped and was waiting for me.

"Once again, apologies, my friend, for the silly games. But I have to be careful." His one good eye assessed me; "And so do you, it seems."

"Why? Was I being followed? Is it because of you?"

"Maybe. But I think it is fair to assume that you grew a tail some time ago, and not just today." He'd started walking again, and I fell into step beside him. "After all, you are looking into the Maier affair. Think back. You know how this is done: remember! Think!"

Dmitri was right. I hadn't noticed, maybe I hadn't wanted to notice, but there had been clues. The Trabant that started up and drove off when Nik and I came out of my house on the way to the bar on Sunday. The couple kissing in a doorway, too many people on the quiet, residential streets near the squat last night, all heading the same way as us.

"You may be right," I admitted.

"Yes. Think, observe. They will not just be following where you go, but also following what you do. The Maier case is very interesting to a lot of people."

"Is it related to what you told Nik about the KGB team from Moscow?"

"Martin, listen. You do not know if you can trust me. You do not know me. But I know you. I know your files, I know what you've done, what you do now, the way you think. So I can talk to you, but you? Do you listen to me? That is what you must decide. Trust no-one. Only the people closest to you, and do not trust even them with anything."

I laughed. It was too absurd, all too dramatic. I'd been given a secret note, practically been thrown off a moving tram, then abducted in a Soviet jeep and taken to a secret location. All to be told not to trust anyone.

Dmitri didn't respond, he just carried on walking. I watched him for a moment, considering whether to go back to the jeep, demand to be returned to civilisation. Dmitri was right: I should trust no-one. Nevertheless, I needed to know more. I caught up him Dmitri again.

"OK, let's play it your way Dmitri Alexandrovich. What's your interest in Maier?"

We'd reached a lake, and Dmitri stared at it for a while before answering. It wasn't a huge lake, but big enough to take a rowing boat out on. We were surrounded by dark forest and no sounds could be heard, not even birds.

"I do not know, Martin. I wish I did. But the West Silesian problem ties in with the KGB and what is happening in Moscow right now. So that makes it my problem too."

"But you're KGB, surely you know what's going on?"

"Not my area, but I'm trying to find out. And now this detachment from Moscow ... I cannot use the normal channels. No *drushba* with these officers from the Third Directorate. No drinks and shared secrets," Dmitri sighed, and turned away from the water, his eye pointing towards me again. "And you know even less, but perhaps we can help each other, I think.

"So, in the KGB," he continued in his low, slow voice, the Slavic accent hardly affecting his German pronunciation, "there are two factions. There are those who say the time is not yet right, we should support Gorbachev because with him we have the best chance of keeping USSR together. But there are many more who say, it is now, it is time to remove Gorbachev, to move ahead with plans."

"Gorbachev will survive, won't he? And what plans?"

Dmitri considered his answer for a moment.

"Maybe he won't survive. It all depends on my colleagues in Moscow, whether the right people support him. It's difficult to say what will happen. We have the same problem as you. Agents have been put into key decision-making positions throughout the government—it's their job to keep control of power, whichever way it goes. At the moment it looks like the power will be in the economy, rather than the Party apparatus. If Gorbachev doesn't survive then Yeltsin will take over. He will sell off land and industry, and my colleagues will be there with the cash, waiting to buy it all."

"And if Gorbachev stays?"

"If he stays then his attempts to roll out perestroika will meet further resistance and more coup attempts. The problem is, Gorbachev doesn't understand economics. He's not in control of his perestroika any more."

"But if Gorbachev doesn't survive, how can we? We depend on Gorbachev to protect us from the West."

"That is why I am talking to you. Your little experiment here in the GDR depends on what happens to old Mikhail Sergeyevich Gorbachev." Dmitri looked at the lake for a moment, then stooped to pick up a small stone. He threw it into the water.

"See those ripples? The circles get larger and larger the further away from the centre they are. Gorbachev is at the centre—a small, insignificant pebble, and the GDR is a long way away from him. By the time the ripples get to you they make big circles, they seem quite significant. By the time they get to Bonn or London or Washington those ripples are part of a huge wash of water moving outwards from Moscow. It's his reputation that is saving you, making the West think twice about taking over."

"Do you mean that if Gorbachev stops making ripples-"

"I'm not sure what I mean," Dmitri was still staring out at the water. The ripples were flattening, growing fainter and fainter. "Perhaps only that you shouldn't rely on Gorbachev. He has troubles of his own, and if you ask me, he'd be glad to be rid of what he sees as an unnecessary burden. I think he gave up on you years ago."

We stood together like that, Dmitri lost in his own world, while I thought about his words.

"You mentioned that the KGB has officers in place in the Soviet government—are they here too? Is that the plan?"

I had the Russian's attention now. He gazed at me with his one good eye, a look of mild surprise crossing his features.

"You don't know? Mmm, I keep forgetting—you receive no briefing in these matters, you RS officers are just amateurs."

I tried not to feel nettled by what Dmitri said—after all, he wasn't wrong. I concentrated instead on what he was saying.

"But I know your minister has been informed of the situation, I had hoped that information would be passed down. No, the KGB isn't involved any more, we left it all to the Stasi to run, even though the plan was developed by one of our officers based in Dresden, and the Stasi set it up with our help.

"About six or seven years ago the Stasi began to put officers— *Offiziere im besonderen Einsatz*, OibE—into strategic political and industrial positions. At a meeting of all the Socialist secret services in June 1989—Egon Krenz represented the GDR—an overall policy was agreed. If the economy begins to fail, or the political situation changes dramatically, these officers will be in place to steer decisions and policy. Their aim is to remain in control of the country no matter what happens. In Moscow, they are waiting and ready, we call them the Oligarchs—a few men with a lot of power. In other countries the officers weren't activated, but here in the GDR? Who knows? I think the general strike in November 1989 was too much of a surprise, maybe Mischa Wolf didn't get the signal out in time. If they're still in position then they're still dangerous, they could take over at any time, and nobody would even notice until it was too late."

This was all news to me. It sounded like a conspiracy theory, but Dmitri seemed serious, and most importantly, believable. Markus Wolf—who liked to accentuate his Russian connections by calling himself Mischa—was until 1987 the head of the head of the HVA: the part of the Stasi responsible for foreign operations. He'd since fled to the West. Egon Krenz, the crown prince of the Party with a reputation as a hardliner had also gone West. Did they still have control of these OibE agents?

"What would make them activate? Are there any triggers other than this signal from Wolf?"

"Could be anything," Dmitri tossed another stone into the lake and watched the ripples until they lapped at his boots. "I think it would have to be some kind of major crisis. You've decentralised so much of your decision-making; that will make it hard for them to exert so much influence. But if there were a major crisis then they could engineer the re-centralisation of power structures, a state of emergency perhaps—that would give them back control, allow a taskforce to take power."

"And would they organise such a crisis? Is that what they're doing in West Silesia?"

"Precisely," Dmitri looked up, pleased with his pupil.

"So West Silesia is like a test run, to see how easy it is to sideline the Round Tables? And at the same time they can destabilise the whole of the Republic, setting the scene for a bigger crisis? But haven't they gone a bit too far? I mean, by involving the West Germans? Surely that's not part of a KGB or an OibE plan?"

"Yes." Dmitri was staring over the water again, thinking, "I doubt the Western involvement was part of the plan. But now the West Germans are on the scene they'll be turning the situation to their own advantage. Something went wrong, somebody went off the rails, is my guess. Perhaps that's why some of the KGB are here at the moment, perhaps they've been sent by Moscow to sort out the mess."

"Why are you telling me this? These are your colleagues."

"As I said, some of us think the time is not yet right. We do not want the Oligarchs to control our country. Or yours." His tone of voice changed, the rolling R and the alien vowels of his Slavic accent became more pronounced.

"For over 70 years we've made it our business to take people's dreams, to make them our own, then crush them without mercy. We told the world we were paradise, created and maintained by the iron discipline of the workers and peasants. We exported our revolutions, invited others to share our utopia at the barrel of a gun. We have failed. Our revolution was already doomed before the Kronstadt

Mutiny. The reforms are failing too. If Gorbachev loses his gamble then it is over for us. It will be your turn to carry the flag."

I didn't know how to react. When a KGB officer is this lyrical and this critical you have to pinch yourself, check you're still awake.

"You're a socialist?"

"Something like that. Perhaps something stuck, from school or *Komsomol*," Dmitri answered. "I think the same happened to you, no?"

"Perhaps. Perhaps you're right, Dmitri Alexandrovich."

We turned away from the lake and walked on through the woods in silence, only the cracking of the twigs underfoot measuring time.

20:24

It was dark by the time we drove back into Berlin, this time by road rather than along rough forest tracks. They dropped me a few hundred metres from the S-Bahn station in Grünau.

I got off the train at Ostkreuz half an hour later and wandered home, still trying to assimilate everything that had happened that afternoon. Dmitri was uncanny, the way he never smiled, how he seemed to know me and my feelings better than I did myself. Then there was the fact he had told me so much, yet, when I thought about it later, turned out to be thin stuff—so little of it was concrete or useful. Nor had he given me any actual advice, any indicators as to how I should proceed. Except to be careful, and to trust no-one.

"Thanks a bunch, Dmitri Alexandrovich," I muttered to myself, walking down the street. As I passed the bakery I glanced into the darkened window, using it as a mirror, checking to see if I was being followed. I couldn't see anyone, but that didn't have to mean much— they knew where I lived, they didn't have to accompany me to my door.

Trust no-one. Only the people closest to you, and do not trust even them with anything—Dmitri's words swirled around my head, but I had to trust someone, it would be good to talk through the events of the last few days, throw ideas around, try to get some perspective on what was happening, and what we should do about it.

Right now, though, I needed a drink and an early night. I stumbled up the stairs, and was standing outside my flat door, fumbling with the key when I noticed I had a new message on the notepad: *In the bar, come and find me when you get back, Nik.*

The idea of enduring a conversation with Nik didn't exactly re-energise me, but at least he was someone I could trust. Probably. At least he'd be a start.

I pushed open the heavy door of Jens' bar, and parted the stiff curtain, looking for Nik. He was sitting at the same table as last time. When I went over, he didn't notice me coming until I was at his shoulder, holding out my hand.

"Christ, I was expecting you hours ago! How did it go?" he asked.

"He's a bit cryptic, isn't he?"

"Yeah, he is too. But he's an interesting fellow," Nik laughed.

I nodded, thinking that *interesting* didn't do Dmitri justice.

"What did he tell you? Or shouldn't I ask, just say if I should shut up," Nik was looking into his beer, waiting for me to tell him to mind his own business.

"You know, honestly, I don't know. I'm knackered—it's been the longest day I've had since 1989. I need to think about what he told me, try to get it straight in my head. He was telling me about what's happening in Moscow, and how it might affect us. He talked about some very scary things." Nik was nodding, encouraging me to carry on. "But he was very clear that I needed to be careful who I talk to about the Maier case."

"Yes, you mentioned you'd been down to Weisswasser to see the body. But you're not still involved, are you?"

"Officially, not really. We arrested the suspect today, but I'm not actually working on it—we're not the police after all."

"You make it sound like you'd like to be on the case still?" He watched me nod before continuing. "I feel better knowing you're looking into it because somebody needs to. One of us—not an apparatchik—it should be somebody who cares. But you're not doing this by yourself? You shouldn't be—your work team should be with you on this."

"I'm really not sure we can do much about it."

"Look, you're working with good people. They care. If I were you,

I'd get them more involved. And Martin? You can rely on me. Whenever you need me—just shout."

He was earnest, pretty much the same as on Sunday night, but livelier, more animated. I nodded agreement and made my excuses, heading back onto the dark street. A quick look both ways, nobody in sight. Back into my own house, up the stairs and into my armchair.

Just as I was making myself comfortable the phone rang. I was beginning to regret having a phone at home, it only ever seemed to ring when I wanted to have a bit of peace and quiet. I picked up, wondering whether it would be another dropped call, and sure enough, all I heard was a couple of clicks and a vague hissing. I was just about to hang up again when finally a voice came from the receiver.

"Martin! Martin? Is that you?" It was Evelyn.

"Evelyn, yes, it's me—sorry I couldn't speak to you yesterday, I was in a bit of a state."

"Oh, poor you! I hope you're OK? But Martin, I'm so glad I've finally caught up with you—I'm so excited. A friend who works in the Ministry of the Interior gave me your number, I hope you don't mind, but it's been so long!"

"Evelyn, it's good to hear from you, where have you been all these years? What are you doing these days?"

"Oh, you know, just scraping by, doing the usual—I'm working at the Kosmos cinema at the moment, so let me know if you need free tickets! What are you up to? Oh, listen, talking on the phone isn't any fun—why don't we meet up? I mean right now—we could go to the cinema right now! That would be so much fun, do say yes, dear Martin, it's been so long!"

I was completely knackered, and wanted nothing more than to doze in my own chair. But Evelyn's enthusiasm was infectious, and she was right—it had been so long. Why not? A film didn't sound too strenuous, and I was curious about what had happened to Evelyn since I last saw her.

Half an hour later I was standing on Karl-Marx-Allee, in front of the Kosmos, waiting for Evelyn. Behind me lights beckoned warmly through the glass façade of the cinema, but I was shivering in the late September evening. After twenty minutes I was ready to give up and go to the tram stop when I saw Evelyn in the glow of the foyer, waving at me.

"Silly you! I thought you'd never see me," she grinned at me, not at all bothered about being late. "We'll have to go straight in, it's about to start." Evelyn was simply and elegantly dressed, as ever, and looked exactly the same as I remembered her—the years had taken no toll.

We went through the foyer, and past the ticket collector—Evelyn didn't bother with tickets, she just beamed at him as we entered the auditorium. The trailers were playing, and we slid into the back row, the ranks of white seats before us a dusky grey in the gloom.

"It's *Paul and Paula*—have you seen it before?" Evelyn whispered in my ear, her breath tickling, making me twitch. I hadn't seen *The Legend of Paul and Paula* for years, I probably saw it last with Katrin sitting between her mum and me on the couch at home. Because of its fairy tale escapism and its rejection of the rigid cultural demands of Socialist Realism it had been a popular film in the 1970s. But it had been banished to late night television and finally dropped after both the main actors went into exile in the West. Since the revolution the film had become popular again, a trend for nostalgia and an appreciation of the film's celebration of love made it a favourite among young people.

It's an enjoyable film, not demanding much attention or thought from its viewers, and the easy pace of the unfolding story suited my mood perfectly. We'd already got to the bit when Paul unexpectedly comes to Paula in the middle of the night, and is surprised that she has prepared a feast for him. The scene, playing on her prescience and his confusion, is touching, and I smiled at the memories it brought back.

It was at this point that Evelyn decided to slip her hand into mine. I froze, caught between the two-dimensional memories of a long dead past, and the heat making its way up my arm. I slowly melted into the warmth of the body beside me, and my fingers threaded through Evelyn's as we tightened our clasp. We explored each other's hands, tracing outlines of fingers and palms, our heads moved towards each other until they were resting together. Things didn't go any further, we just sat in a warm fuzziness as the story played towards its tragic conclusion on the screen before us.

After the film we sat in the foyer, Evelyn sipping a glass of *Rotkäppchen* sparkling wine while I confined myself to water. I was tired, and the memory of yesterday's hangover was still too fresh to ignore. We chatted about the film and the cinema, and how Katrin's *Jugendweihe* ceremony had been held here at the Kosmos.

"Do you remember: *Are you prepared?*" laughed Evelyn.

"Yes, and then they had to swear to defend socialism, and to be led by the revolutionary Party!" I added, but Evelyn didn't find that bit nearly as funny as I did.

She looked away, and there was silence for a second or two until suddenly she turned back to me, her eyes fixed on mine. "Martin, let's go, right now! Let's just go to mine," she laid a hand on my knee, and tipped her face down so that she could look up at me through her eyelashes. "Martin, it's been too long, say you'll come!"

I sat there stiffly, looking at her, not knowing what to say or do. I could still feel the outline of her hand in mine, and that had awakened a need for human warmth that I had all but forgotten. The idea of holding Evelyn in my arms, sharing her bed, feeling close to her, to anyone—it was almost overwhelming. But I was tired, so tired. I could feel every muscle in my arm as I lifted Evelyn's hand off my knee and placed it on the armrest of her chair.

"I'm sorry Evelyn, you've no idea how much I'd like to, but I think it would be better if I just went."

Evelyn lifted her chin, and looked at me directly again. As an equal this time, not attempting to pull me in with her charm. Her eyes flickered, and I couldn't tell whether what I read there was hurt, scorn or cold indifference.

DAY 8
Wednesday
29th September 1993

Moscow: Hostilities continued on the streets of Moscow last night as Interior Ministry forces clashed with the KGB. So far, the conflict has been focussed on the city centre, but there are fears that it may spread to residential areas.

Görlitz: Further marches in support of the Round Table were held in many towns across West Silesia last night. An estimated ten thousand people participated in the latest protest in the capital, Görlitz. The marchers have called for a full re-integration of the Round Tables at all levels of government in the Region. The West Silesian League condemned the marches, denouncing them as 'incendiary attempts by foreign agents to interfere in the internal affairs of West Silesia'.

08:15

I was hoping the day could only get better now I'd made it to the office in time for the team meeting. It had been a crap morning—I felt guilty about Evelyn, the alarm clock went off half an hour late, and I was clean out of coffee, even though I'm pretty sure I bought a fresh packet the previous week. In the end I'd settled for a lukewarm cup of *Presto* instant coffee, it didn't taste particularly nice, and it certainly didn't give me the jolt I needed to start the day. At least it got me to the office.

The sun was shining through my window, I had a steaming mug in my hand and my colleagues were with me. They all looked pretty sympathetic—I assumed Klaus had told them about yesterday's raid on the squat—nevertheless, once the meeting got underway, Laura had a go at me about not sticking to agreements.

"I know we agreed on Friday that I'd write the report, hand it in, then walk away from it. But we got some more information from Saxony, and I think it's fair to say we all had doubts, even last week." I picked up the envelope from the Saxon police, passing it to Laura on my right. "I would have told you at the meeting on Monday but the wasp thing happened."

Laura subsided visibly at the mention of the wasp, but soon rallied. "Tell us what you mean, Martin."

"Well, I did a report for the Minister, but I left out the new information from Saxony. I wasn't sure whether that was the right thing to do, and to be honest I'm not sure why I didn't put it in either. In the end it didn't matter, he knew about it anyway. Basically, the whole thing is weird, it doesn't add up at all." I started listing all the things that had happened this last week that I was unhappy about, ticking the points off on my fingers as I went. When I got to the last finger I tapped it on the table, pausing for a moment: "Finally, when he orders me to witness an arrest, he looks like some fat cat, satisfied that he's tied up all the loose ends, and then gives me a promotion. I got the distinct feeling he was trying to buy me off, and if that's the case, maybe we should ask ourselves why."

There was silence in the room, everyone looking at me, weighing up my words. For some reason I hadn't told them about Dmitri. I didn't have any good reason not to, in fact I should have told them— we were a team, we were meant to be working together. But it just didn't feel like the right moment.

"Martin's been under a lot of strain this last week, maybe he didn't handle it as well as he could, but I think we might have done more to support him too. And if Martin has a strong feeling about this then we should listen to what he has to say."

I was thankful for Erika's contribution, but knew what would come next.

"What do you think we should be doing, Martin?" asked Klaus.

"I think we should be careful not to rock the boat at this stage: if I'm wrong about this then there's no need for all of us to be making trouble for ourselves. But I'd like to interview Fremdiswalde. I don't think he murdered Maier."

"Martin! Why can't you leave that to the police? Surely that's their job!" said Laura.

"What are we here for if we're not trying to spot dangers to our society? So strictly speaking, interviewing Fremdiswalde isn't part of our job, but it doesn't mean we shouldn't take an interest! We didn't ask ourselves whether it was our job when we shut down the Stasi! That was the police's job, and they weren't doing it, so we turned up mob handed and took over the Stasi offices. Remember that? You were there too!"

"OK, OK, you two! Play nicely!" interrupted Klaus, leaning forward to attract our attention, "I know that last Thursday I was all for following it up, but I think Laura's made a good point: it's just not our job. Martin—those were different times, we don't work in those ways now."

"I'm not sure. I think Martin may have a point." Erika leaned forward as well. "We can't just sit back and let the state expand again, taking over responsibility for all areas of our lives. As RS, criminal investigation is outside our remit—but we're also citizens, and we have a responsibility towards our country. I think we should support Martin, give him another couple of days to see what comes up with. We can just try to keep it unofficial, try to minimise any fallout."

I smiled a 'thank you' at her, while Klaus and Laura shared a glance before nodding reluctant agreement.

We ran through the rest of the meeting, no surprises, nothing particularly exciting. I told them the Minister had asked me to prepare the security report for the Wall debate. We agreed to leave it a couple of days before deciding who should take that task on, give me enough space to nose around the Maier case.

The others filed out of my office, and I pulled the telephone towards me, poking around my desk for the letter from the Saxon police. Finding it, I punched in the number and asked for Schadowski. A couple of minutes' conversation, and I had all I needed: the police *Unterleutnant* had confirmed that the working theory was that Maier was having an affair with the much younger Fremdiswalde, who was now the chief suspect. Maier had broken off the affair, and

Fremdiswalde had lost it, killing Maier during a final liaison at the edge of the coal mine, then dragging the body down to where work was taking place. The Saxon police had prepared a report, and were sending someone up to interview Fremdiswalde tomorrow morning. I asked Schadowski to send me a copy of the report.

"One other thing, comrade *Hauptmann*," continued Schadowski, "I thought you should know: I've been ordered to report any contact with RS to the Ministry of the Interior."

I thanked Schadowski, and hung up. His final words were hardly reassuring. Why the hell should I not talk to the Saxon police, and who exactly at the Ministry was keeping tabs on me?

12:37

Sitting on the S-Bahn on the way to the Ministry I thought about last night. On the way home after the cinema I'd felt physical regret: it would have been so nice to cuddle up to someone in bed, to lie spooning another warm body. And there was a feeling that after all these years—years of being aware of that flirtatious tingle whenever we saw each other—something was inevitable. I couldn't shake the feeling that by avoiding the inevitability of Evelyn, I had somehow cheated fate, and fate would come looking for revenge.

But this morning I just had a sense of vague guilt. I felt guilty for refusing Evelyn, even though it wasn't something that I'd actually wanted; guilty that I hadn't thought once about Annette last night, even though being with her didn't just feel good—it felt like we had a future.

I swept my thoughts to one side as I got off the train at Friedrichstrasse, and my mind turned to work matters. I'd had a phone call, been asked to report to the Ministry by some minor civil servant, so here I was. As I turned into the Mauerstrasse I saw the same goons that had been sitting there yesterday, today they were in a dark blue Lada. Feeling their stares I pointedly ignored them, and went up the steps into the building.

I reported to the Minister's secretary, expecting to be directed to Frau Demnitz again, but instead of which I was told to go upstairs to one of the tiny offices where the worker bees administered paperwork. I was seen by a young man in a brown suit with no tie. He sat behind a desk that filled the space between the walls so fully that I wondered how he got out from behind it at the end of the day. His window looked over the courtyard below, but faced south, so I couldn't see much more of him than a dark shape silhouetted against the bright sunlight.

"Captain Grobe, you have been asked here today because it has come to our attention that you have not surrendered for correct processing the paperwork attendant on your promotion." This guy had obviously been taking lessons from Frau Demnitz, and I wondered how long I'd be kept here, listening to bureaucratic declamations.

I concentrated on the blue sky behind his left shoulder, developing an absurd interest in a fluffy cloud, high up in the sky, that was making a slow journey across the window. I watched as it crossed from left to right.

When I next tuned into what the drone was blethering on about, he'd moved on to the responsibilities of higher rank. I wished now that I had paid more attention, because if I understood what I was hearing, this suit here was actually threatening me. Of course, he made use of the various bureaucratic stock phrases, but the gist of it was that if I didn't pull my socks up, start behaving like a captain and do what I was told to do instead of phoning Dresden at every opportunity, well, what? Unfortunately I'd missed the bit where the implicit threats might have been outlined. I was vaguely curious, but didn't want to give him the satisfaction of asking him to repeat the juicy bits.

The civil servant hadn't even begun to wind down when I stood up. As I left I asked him over my shoulder whether he had finished, but didn't bother hanging around for an answer. I closed the door on him and wondered whether to just go back to Lichtenberg without dealing with all the promotion crap. But I thought that since I was here anyway, I might as well go and sort out the paperwork—if I didn't, they'd just haul me back again tomorrow. And then the next day, and so on until I sorted out the bureaucracy.

I took the back stairs down to the ground floor and found the secretariat. The front desk wasn't occupied, and all the other staff were busy typing away, steadfastly ignoring me. I looked around the room while I waited, the sound of typewriter keys and the pinging carriage bells echoed round the bare room. In the corner a dusty cheese plant was about to give up the fight for life, and next to it a door stood slightly ajar. Not enough to see through the gap, but over the clackety-clack of the typewriters, and the more regular chatter of the telex, a woman's voice spilled out of the room beyond. I couldn't make out what was being said, but I could hear the accent: gentle, Mecklenburg, quite a high voice. I'd heard it recently, very recently. But when?

"Can I help, comrade?" The secretary whose job it was to deal with enquiries had returned to her post.

I handed her the Minister's commission papers, still staring at the door. The secretary drew a new pass out of a locked drawer, along with a form. She stamped the form, then handed that and the pass to me, along with some more papers for me to scribble my signature on.

"Comrade Captain—your new papers and a requisition slip for the dress uniform. You can get that at the *Präsidium*."

I took the papers without looking, I was staring at that door, the one with the sign, *Archiv* on it, thinking about the voice coming from behind it, because now I'd recognised it. The context had thrown me, but I knew whose voice it was. But the question was: what was Evelyn doing here, at the Ministry?

13:57

When I came out of the station at Ostkreuz, the first thing I saw, on the corner of Simplonstrasse and Sonntagstrasse, was a dark blue Lada. The same two goons sat there, watching people come out of the station. They hadn't seen me yet—I'd stopped just under the shadow of the overhead track—and hesitating only for a moment, I turned around, crossing the tracks by the bridge and heading for the exit on the other side of the station. As I came down the steps off the pedestrian bridge I could see the tram number 82 just go round its turning loop. A quick sprint, and I caught it as it was about to leave.

I have an unfortunate character defect. At least, the Marxist-Leninists were always telling me that it was a defect, but I keep hoping that in these new times it may be seen as a positive trait. Whenever someone tells me to do something, I develop a strong urge to do the exact opposite—particularly if what they're telling me to do seems unreasonable. And that's probably why, a few minutes later, I found myself in front of Rummelsburg prison.

I went to the administrative block beside the main gate and, after identifying myself, asked to see Fremdiswalde's belongings. A guard took me to an office on the first floor where he barked an order at a secretary. She disappeared for a while before coming back with a grey archive box containing a grubby handkerchief, a small bottle of *Aminat* shampoo, a red penknife, a black and white cotton Arabic scarf, a partly squashed *Fetzer* chocolate bar, a KWO works pass, an empty *Forum* cigarette packet, twenty Marks plus small change, a set of keys and an envelope with Fremdiswalde's name on it. The envelope was addressed to a flat in Berlin-Friedrichsfelde.

"Is that it?"

"Yes, sir. Accused 264721 had no further items on his person at the time of arrest."

I took the keys and the envelope, put them in my pocket, and signed the receipt the protesting secretary was waving at me.

I waited as the grey pressed steel gate, five meters high, ground open until there was a gap just wide enough for me to slip through. A prison guard in grey uniform and peaked cap sat in a metal sentry box, staring at me, no smile or acknowledgement touching his face. I stood in a non-space, a space that didn't exist—neither the outside world, nor the prison—the gate rattled shut again behind me. Looking at the steel plates of the second gate ahead of me, waiting for them to open, I ignored the guard and the watchtower above. In my mind I was elsewhere, or rather, in another time.

The last time I'd been through these gates I was lying in the back of a truck, police boots resting on my head, neck, back and legs. So often I find myself having to forcefully remind myself of the changes this country has gone through. Just a few years, but already I take so many of our new freedoms for granted, feel resentful of the burdens we have willingly taken upon ourselves as individuals and as a society. In the old days we were expected to go to meetings and official demonstrations, but to be there in body only. Now we demanded of ourselves that we give our whole presence to meetings. *No revolution without participation* read the clumsy slogan daubed on walls throughout our Republic. No matter how inconvenient it may be, active participation is our guarantee that no longer will people be thrown into prison for daring to think for themselves. And, as I reminded myself, active participation was the reason I was here now.

The clang of the gate opening again behind me shook me out of my thoughts. Another guard came in, gesturing back through the gate to the outside world.

"Accused 264721 is on police remand in Block B," he announced.

I followed the guard back out through the gate onto the Rummelsburger Hauptstrasse and around to the left, to another set of buildings outside the prison walls. We went through another grey gate, this time a mere two metres high, but with iron spikes along the top, and then past a long row of garages to a red-brick building. Once inside we passed through several locked gates, some backed with reinforced safety glass, and down the stairs into the cellar.

"Wait," I said to the guard. "How long have you been here?"

The guard and I looked at each other. It was difficult to read his face or thoughts, the peak of his cap was pulled low to hide his eyebrows, hide his expressions. He was about the same age as me, perhaps he had been there when I was last dragged into this prison? Perhaps he recognised me. But he must have dealt with hundreds, thousands of politicals in his time. He knew that someone like me must have been somewhere like this at some point in the not too distant past. He continued to return my stare.

"Fifteen years," he said, just when I'd given up on getting an answer.

So he had been here when I was bundled through those gates. I ran through a short catalogue of all the injustices, the indignities, the physical and mental cruelty I had experienced and seen here. What are we going to do with people like him? Our new way of doing things requires respect for each other, but how could I respect him? Inside myself I could feel the desire for revenge gnawing away.

The guard marched off, opening another barred gate to a long corridor, expecting me to follow. A quiet *fuck you* directed at his back, and I decided, for the moment, to put it all to one side. I wasn't here to reopen old wounds, but to talk to Chris Fremdiswalde, see if I could bolster my doubts with some information, some real evidence. I entered a corridor lit by dull bulbs, cells lined one wall.

Fremdiswalde was in one of these cells, barely two metres wide and not quite as deep. A rough wooden bench was attached to the back wall, and the front of the cell was made up of bars. The tiger cages. I'd heard of these remand cells from friends who had been arrested and held here by the police. Although there was a bench, you weren't allowed to lie down during the day, and even sitting on it was discouraged by the guards. Maybe that was why Fremdiswalde was hunched up against the wall, hardly noticing me and the guard standing on the other side of the bars.

"Stand back! Announce yourself!" the guard barked.

But Fremidswalde didn't even flinch. He was nursing his right hand, his left eye was so swollen it had almost sealed itself shut. He was putting most of his weight on his right leg.

"Chris?" I said gently, trying to attract his attention while I moved between the guard and the bars.

Still no reaction. Chris remained hunched against the wall. The guard, standing slightly behind me, shifted, leaning back against the brickwork.

"Chris?" I tried again, "Chris, my name is Martin Grobe. I'm from the *Republikschutz*. I need to ask you a few questions about Hans Maier. Did you know Maier?"

Still no reaction.

"What was your relationship with Maier? Did you work with him? Were you friends?"

Nothing, not even a slight movement.

"Chris, you do know that Hans Maier is dead? I've seen his body myself."

I thought that Fremdiswalde still hadn't reacted, but then I caught the shine of tears gathering in his eyes. I looked over my shoulder to the guard.

"Get this man a cup of water."

The guard shifted his gaze from Fremdiswalde to me, his eyes hard underneath his visored cap, a satisfied set to his mouth.

"It is forbidden to leave accused persons in the presence of civilians," he smirked.

I drew myself up to my full height, turning to face the man directly, and with the hardest voice I could manage: "What is your name?"

"Nagel."

"*Unterwachtmeister* Nagel—go and get some water for this prisoner. Now!"

The guard hesitated for a moment, considering his options, then: "*Jawohl*, Comrade Captain!" before marching off down the corridor.

I waited until he had turned the corner before looking at Fremdiswalde again.

"Chris, you've got to tell me. I'm the only one who can help you in here."

I wasn't holding out much hope for an answer, but then, shaking with sobs, his eyes moved to meet mine.

"I can't," he stammered. "They'll kill me–"

"Who? Who will kill you?"

But by now the guard was coming back, pacing along the corridor, and Fremdiswalde was sliding down the wall. I waited long enough to make sure that he got his water, then left. There seemed little point in asking any more questions. Fremdiswalde was already half-scared to death.

They let me out through the front gate, and with a deep sigh I found myself back in the real world, on the Rummelsburger Hauptstrasse. In the middle of the road the tram tracks stretched off in both directions. No traffic, no parked vehicles, nobody to be seen. No tail. I looked again to my right, towards the twin chimneys of the power station, I couldn't see them over the top of the prison wall, although the white plume from one of the tall chimneys, hung motionless in the blue sky, pointing north towards Lichtenberg. Turning left, I followed the wall of the police compound, trying to find the end of the prison complex.

Where the wall of the cells turned away from the road there was a gap, then the army barracks began. I walked as far as the gate, and showing my RS papers I passed the guard and walked through the military base, down to the river.

The camp was practically empty. Compulsory military service had been ended, professional soldiers had been drafted into the factories—only the disarmament corps and the *Grenzer*, the Border Police, still used the site. At the jetty a launch was casting off, about to patrol the border between Kreuzberg and Friedrichshain, on the lookout for smugglers crossing the river between West and East Berlin. I watched the launch steadily make way down the Rummelsburg Lake to the River Spree, the new GDR flag fluttering at its stern. Ahead of them, beyond the prison, barges and lighters were moored along the bank, all empty, all waiting to fetch the next load of Silesian brown coal for the power station. Some of the barges were dead or dying, slowly collapsing into the water, timbers rotting, water stains seeping up the lifeless sides. A sapling had rooted in a wheelhouse, and was growing directly up to the sky, but it looked like it was growing sideways out of the listing vessel. It was a clear day, the sun hanging fairly low over the *Kulturpark* hiding in the woods of the Plänterwald off to the left. The bright light shaded the trees in their autumnal livery: more yellows and golds, fewer reds and bronzes now, hardly any greens.

I sat on a bollard, looking out over the water, watching autumn emerge, trying to let the lapping water wash away the fear, the anger, the shock that I had felt in that prison. I felt somehow powerless in the face of that institution.

Accompanied by the sound of the water licking the bank I could feel how my own fears from the past were gradually separating out from how appalled I felt at Chris's treatment. No matter what Chris might have done, there was no way he should be abused like that.

In our enthusiasm for building a different society had we neglected the question of criminality and punishment? It couldn't be denied that we were concentrating more on economic survival and changing the everyday lives of the majority of the population. Beyond an amnesty for political prisoners we'd hardly spared a thought for all those left behind in the cells. It was understandable, we couldn't deal with everything at once, we'd actually come a long way in less than three years. But seeing Chris just now ... Were things still really still that bad? Had nothing changed? Or had Chris for some reason been given special treatment? I hadn't seen any other prisoners, Chris was being held alone in the underground cells so I had no way of comparing their welfare with his.

I left the waterside and walked back to the main road. On the way I pulled Fremdiswalde's keys and envelope out of my pocket. The envelope was empty—the police had probably kept whatever letter had been in it. I didn't recognise the address—it wasn't his registered address at the *Thaeri* squat, nor was it any of the earlier addresses listed in his Stasi files, although they'd be a few years out of date by now. The keys were normal, a mortice key and a four sided key, together on a ring. Looked like the keys to a flat.

A tram and a bus later and I was in Friedrichsfelde. I could have taken the scenic route, tried to shake off anyone that might be following me. But I guessed it was pretty obvious that I was still taking an interest in Fremdiswalde, and I was sure the prison would have already passed on word of my visit. Nevertheless, I looked around as the bus belched off. I couldn't see anyone, I was there all by myself.

It didn't feel like Berlin, not the Berlin I knew. Low rise houses, plenty of gardens, some of the side streets unmade, just beaten sand marked by car and bike tracks. Turning into a side street I could see that the residents had blocked it off, making raised beds to grow vegetables on what had been the roadway. A sign, decorated with rainbow swirls, read *Colour from below*, a huge pile of pumpkins jostled for space on a mound of compost, and colourful peppers, cucumbers, herbs and flowers populated the surrounding beds.

The house I was looking for was three storeys high, and had two front doors. I tried the mortice key in the lock of the nearest door, but the door was already unlocked, so the key stopped after half a twist. Good to know I was on the right track, though. I went up the stairs, checking the names on each door as I went. Up two flights, and past a toilet on the half-landing, and there he was: Ch. Fremdiswalde. I let myself in using the four sided key and halted just inside, quietly closing the door behind me. No sound. Just that dead feeling you get from an empty flat. Stale cigarette smoke, and another smell over the top of that. I sniffed, trying to identify it, similar to the cigarette smoke, but vaguer, sharper.

It wasn't a big flat: a tiny hall, just a couple of paces long, a small press, and behind that a bedsit with a kitchen-niche taking up the wall opposite the window. I stood in the middle of the bed-sitting room and looked around me. What was I looking for? I decided to give the place a brief once over, then do a second, more thorough search.

There wasn't much here, a few clothes, a pile of newspapers on the table. No books, no posters or pictures decorating the walls. The kitchen area looked like it had only been used for making tea and coffee, mouldy coffee grains were to be found in a few mugs, but no crumbs or food wrappers.

On my second sweep, I started with the table in the corner: lots of notes, scribbled, scratched out, pretty much illegible. Newspapers, piled up. I flicked through them, in each one articles had been cut out. I checked the dates: all from the last few days, the earlier ones had holes in the front pages, more recent papers were cut up inside, the cut-outs smaller each day. He'd cut out the reports about Maier's death, but where were they? I looked in the steel bin by the side of his desk, here they were, mixed up with letters, written on expensive Western paper, partially burned. And that was my unidentified smell: burnt paper. Whoever did this must have been in a rush, just throwing a match in the bin rather than feeding each page to the flames. Soot marks streaked up the inside of the grey steel bucket, but here and there legible bits remained: *My dearest Chri ...* was on one charred remnant, another corner of a letter: *Görlitz, d. 13 Juli 1993—* the date and place written at the top of a letter. And here again on another fragment: *Your ever loving Hansi.* I found an envelope, and carefully filled it with the scraps of paper, the ones that still had some handwriting on. When I got back to the office I'd compare them with Maier's handwritten statement from his recruitment as a Stasi IM.

I surveyed the room, poking into corners, feeling under socks, patting down pullovers. But it was hopeless, I didn't know what I was looking for, I'd probably found the most useful stuff already.

From Friedrichsfelde I decided to return home. My team had given me two days to come up with something concrete, and so far I was a day in with nothing significant to show for it. Sitting on the underground train, rattling through the darkness, my mind raced through all the material it had been collecting since last Wednesday. I looked at the reflections of other passengers in the dark window. The tunnel wall speeding past was just a few centimetres away yet invisible, more felt than seen.

When I got to my flat I rolled out some left-over wallpaper on the table, anchoring it with a shoe at one end and the English major's bottle of whisky at the other. Looking at the expanse of paper before me I started a mind map of everything I could possibly connect to the case: Maier's involvement with West Germany, Fremdiswalde as Maier's killer, the brown coal industry, the Minister's extraordinary behaviour, the KGB detachment that had arrived from Moscow, Major Tom's cryptic hints, Dmitri's conspiracy theory of a Stasi taskforce centred around an experienced and well-trained OibE. And finally, the question: *Hansi (signed love letter) = Hans Maier?*

But why was Fremdiswalde so scared? Who did he think would kill him if he talked? The guards? Maier's colleagues in the WSB? Or Dmitri's taskforce of Stasi ghosts?

I looked at the branch that concerned the Minister and added a few more notes. Why was the Minister behaving so oddly? Tying me up in work, keeping tabs on me? Who had been following me? Were they connected to the Ministry—after all, I'd first seen those thugs in the car outside the Ministry on the Mauerstrasse. Or was I just being paranoid, fed by Dmitri's conspiracy theories?

I looked at the untidy diagram I'd scrawled and I wasn't particularly impressed with my own efforts. But even this had to be better than just reacting. The whole of this last week I'd been a mere chess piece, being moved around the board by the Minister, the police, the prison service, a KGB officer and even my own daughter.

But I had to be honest with myself, I wasn't getting anywhere. I wasn't uncovering clues or putting together a theory about the whole case. I looked at each of the points I'd jotted down—searching for anything I could pull on to make the whole thing unravel; some aspect I could check out, some lead to follow. There wasn't anything. The police investigation into Maier's death was closed to me—that was the responsibility of Schadowski and his team in Dresden. And I couldn't imagine simply marching up to the Minister to demand he tell me what the hell he was up to.

The only gap I could see, the only point where I could find any room for manoeuvre was Dmitri's conspiracy theory. If I wanted to accept Dmitri's ideas then I should check them out first. But I had no realistic chance of confirming whether there were actually any Stasi sleepers posted at the Ministry and finding out why the KGB had sent a detachment from Moscow was even less likely.

The only thing I could check was whether I was in fact being followed or not. This morning I'd nearly told my colleagues about my suspicions, but in the end I'd kept it to myself. Was I really certain I was being tailed? The Lada at Ostkreuz station had brought back bad memories, but were they really there for me? I couldn't shake the idea that I was just being paranoid, encouraged by Dmitri.

Enough questions; time for a test.

17:06

"Thanks, Nik, I'm glad you could help."

Nik didn't say anything, he was too busy peering over the top of a book, making a mental note of a battered old Citroën parked about twenty metres up the other side of Karl-Marx-Allee.

"I'd say it feels like the good old days," Nik replied eventually, "except it's not, is it? In those days we knew why we were doing it. But now? Shouldn't we have got past all this bullshit?"

I waited for Nik to answer his own question, but for once he didn't seem inclined to do so. He closed the book, and slotted it back into the gap on the shelf, stepping away from the plate glass window to join me in the shadows at the back of the bookshop.

"You spotted the green Citroën? I didn't see any others, but they could just be driving around the block, waiting for you to go out again." He looked me up and down—beige raincoat, slouch-hat, "I see why you wanted me to wear my coat and hat. So that's your plan. How long do you need to get rid of them for?"

"We should swap hats, yours is a bit different," I answered. For the rest, we matched up pretty well: similar size, age and build, same vintage raincoats. If Nik kept his head down he could easily be mistaken for me.

"I don't actually need any time—it's enough for the moment to know whether or not I'm being watched, and if so, how serious they are about it. Just take them round the corner—unless you feel like leading them on a tour of Berlin, in which case: be my guest!"

Nik chuckled, pulled out a newspaper, unfolding it as he stepped out the door on to the street. He walked off, head buried in the paper. I stood by the window and waited to see what would happen. The Citroën drove off, did a U-turn further up, then slowed down just past the bookshop, picking up a grey woman wearing an anorak and carrying a shopping bag. I leaned out of the shop and watched as the Citroën turned off around the corner, following Nik.

20:32

I couldn't get comfortable sitting at home. The roll of wallpaper was still spread out on the table. I stood up and looked at it, shaking my head. So now I'd confirmed that I was being followed. What next? If I was honest, I wasn't actually me that much further.

I picked up the whisky bottle and the wallpaper rolled itself up, slowly at first, then gaining enough momentum to knock the shoe onto the floor before sliding down after it. Pouring myself a measure of scotch, I stood by the window, looking down at the shadowy S-Bahn tracks below. I was too restless to stand here drinking whisky, waiting for trains to pass. I put my jacket on and left the flat.

I walked around the streets near my house, no destination in mind, no purpose to my journey. Just movement. A block or two away there's a site where a house had collapsed. It was, I thought, a sort of representation of what has happened to our country. For 40 years the Communists had simply ignored the need to maintain buildings all over the GDR, all their hopes, dreams and money had gone into building prefabricated concrete flats. By the 1980s the pre-war housing stock was literally crumbling: whole streets like the Mainzer Strasse, whole quarters like Prenzlauer Berg, even whole towns like Meissen and Görlitz were falling into rubble. This tenement block here in my neighbourhood had given up the fight against gravity by the end of 1989, and the neighbours had shifted the debris, putting huge timber beams into place to shore up their buildings on either

150

side, then turning the empty space into a park. A play area for the kids at the front, a rose garden with seating at the back.

The garden was unlit, the orange semi-darkness of street lamps not quite penetrating as far as what had once been the back yard. I wandered the narrow, curved paths between the rose-beds for a while, imagining rather than seeing the dark green and brown of the mottled leaves. Reaching one of the sturdy wooden props against the side of the house next to the park I turned to go back. A figure was standing on the empty street, but from the silhouette I couldn't tell whether they were looking towards me or away. As I watched, the shadow slipped away along the street. It was time for me to be getting home too, I was feeling the cold.

I left the park and turned back, heading home. I could never understand why the streets were so empty in the evenings—thousands of people lived in this neighbourhood, the lights in all the windows were some kind of proof of their existence. But once people had come home from work, once the shops were shut, the only signs of life came from the old-fashioned pubs on the corners. I turned onto another road, the pavements here were narrow, hemmed in by concrete street lights and parked cars. A man, tall, wide, wearing raincoat and tweed hat was heading in my direction. As he came close I drew aside, standing on the kerb to give him enough room to pass. But he must have felt that I wasn't giving him enough space because he shouldered me into the gutter as he passed. I spun as I stumbled onto the cobbled road, trying to keep myself from falling. By the time I'd found my balance again, he'd disappeared around a corner.

In my agitation the minor incident affected me more than it should have. A drunk, weaving his way home, nothing more. But it made me question my own ability to gauge distance, trajectory, movement. I was beginning to question my own judgement.

I was just walking up the stairs to my flat when my neighbour Margrit came down.

"Hi Martin! I'm glad I bumped into you—the Neighbourhood Round Table has just told us that our allocation of paint has come in. I've called a house meeting to decide what colour we want. Can you manage the weekend?"

This was good news, for years our country had been drowning in greys and browns, the Communists never seemed to plan for the production of bright paint, and it was only now, after three years, that we were in a position to start livening up our towns and cities with splashes of colour. It didn't really improve the standard of accommodation, but it would make us feel better about the places we lived in.

Pleased as I was by this piece of minor good news, I wasn't in the mood to have a chat in the stairwell about it. I told Margrit that Sunday would be fine by me, and was about to carry on up to my flat.

"Are you doing anything now? I thought we could have dinner together, or a drink later?" Margrit asked.

"I don't know, it's been a heavy week. I was planning on having an early night."

"Why? What's been happening?"

Until that moment I'd felt pleased that Margrit was taking an interest, but now the dark cloak of mistrust cast its shade again: why did everyone want to know what was going on at work? Could she know I was interested in Maier's death? I tried to clear my head, this was crazy; I was becoming paranoid.

"Sorry Margrit, just too tired to be good company tonight. Maybe next week?"

I carried on up the stairs, reproaching myself for being unfriendly and too wary, the whole time hearing Dmitri's voice playing in a loop: *Trust no-one!*

As I opened the door to my flat the telephone started ringing.

"Grobe?" I said into the receiver.

"Martin! It's me!" Evelyn. The last person I wanted on the end of the phone right now. "Martin, I wanted to apologise for dragging you out last night! It was very naughty of me to do that, but I hope you'll give me another chance?"

Completely lacking in the energy required for decent conversation I just grunted. I wasn't sure what to say, and I distrusted my ability to navigate the difficult emotional waters around Evelyn.

"Why don't we have a proper date, maybe next week, or what

about the weekend? Oh, that would be lovely! Say you will, Martin—you have to because I've had the worst day ever!"

My ears pricked up at this, I knew that Evelyn had been in the Ministry this morning, in the archives. I'd thought about it on and off all day, but could come up with no reason why she should have been there.

"I spent the *whole* day following the District Secretary of the *Kulturbund* around the cinema. He wants to put art on the walls of the auditorium! Imagine that, Martin! 'It's a cinema!' I told him-"

"I'm sorry Evelyn, I have to go—I'm meeting someone. I'll phone you back." I put the phone down on her, and stood in the hall, looking at the grey apparatus, wondering why I'd been so pleased to get one in the first place.

Dmitri's voice was still echoing around my skull.

Day 9

Thursday
30th September 1993

Görlitz: Boxberg power station in West Silesia is to be privatised. A spokesperson for the West Silesian League announced this morning that the power station and all coal fields in the Region are to be transferred to a Trust Company while proposals from the international markets are solicited. The Berlin Ministry for Coal and Energy said they have not been consulted on the plans.

Moscow: Clashes between KGB and Interior Ministry troops have continued throughout the night. Reports of fighting have also been received from the capitals of other Soviet Republics, including Kiev, Minsk and Tbilisi.

08:12

Morning meeting, again. Normally they were a gentle preamble to ease us into the workday—the only one working hard at these meetings was Bärbel, who kept the minutes. The rest of us used it as a chance to have a second breakfast, make contact with each other and keep up to date on what was happening in our lives, inside and outside of work.

But I wasn't looking forward to it today. Once again I'd got out of the wrong side of bed—my alarm clock had gone off late again, even though I could swear I'd reset it. The weather was foul, and felt even worse after the last few days of sunshine. But to cap it all, I couldn't find my shoes—I'd ended up splashing through the rain and puddles in an old pair with cracked soles.

All this rather put me on edge, and made me worry that Laura might criticise me again—it wasn't much of a fear, I know, but I had wet feet and hadn't any coffee inside me.

As it was, things didn't turn out too badly. I wouldn't say the meeting was harmonious, but everyone listened while I reported back on yesterday's events. Laura kept her peace, and Klaus snorted when I got to the bit about Nik helping me to spot my tail. I had their attention now.

"You need to tread carefully, Martin. Somebody out there isn't happy about you sniffing around," was the response from Klaus.

"I think they've been following me all week, even before I was actively looking into the Maier case. They're just keeping an eye on me, I'm not in any personal danger."

They were sceptical about my reassurances, and, thinking about the state Chris Fremdiswalde was in, I wasn't particularly convinced myself. But they didn't make any more of a fuss, agreeing to my suggestion that I try to interview Chris again.

We finished up and Erika asked Bärbel to go and fetch more coffee from the *Konsum* shop in the next street, then suggested I go over to her office with her.

"Are you OK?" she asked once we'd got there.

"Yeah, fine. It's all a bit surreal, and I can't shake the feeling that I'm wasting everyone's time. But then I remember how Chris Fremdiswalde has been really badly beaten. It's like nothing has changed. When you go inside those prison walls, it's like you've stepped back in time."

"Have we changed anything at all about the prison system?" she replied, thinking aloud. "We've broken down the walls of the prison-state that we lived in, but we haven't touched the walls of the physical prisons. Why aren't we coming up with other ways to see justice done?"

Since my visit to Rummelsburg yesterday I'd been asking myself much the same question. Murder and other violent crime was still being committed—and prison was the traditional remedy for such ills. But even if most prisoners weren't treated as badly as Chris had been, it was still inhuman to simply lock people up. Where were the second chances, the opportunities to make good any damage done, the option of living a life?

"I think this is something we should talk to the Round Table about
—we're part of the Ministry of the Interior, so in a sense this is our
area. Let's find out what's changes there have been since 1989 and
how we can get more involved. I mean, we're already involved—
we've got some responsibility: Chris is there because we found him." I
noted that Erika had said *we*, accepting collective responsibility for
his capture. "And he's not the only one we've dealt with that has
ended up in jail. We need to be coming up with alternatives to the
current system."

"OK, let's talk to the others about it."

Erika nodded and tapped her pencil against a pad of paper for a
while. Finally, she turned her attention back to me:

"But Martin, what I wanted to talk to you about—I've been
thinking about what you said about the Minister. Let's imagine, just
for the moment, that Maier was negotiating with West Germany
about coal and electricity. And if that's the case then maybe he also
negotiated delivery of money, arms and BGS troops too? What if the
Minister is involved in Maier's murder—because he wanted to stop all
this from happening? He could be trying to protect the GDR?"

Erika's face was flushed, she was quite excited about her theory. It
wasn't an impossible scenario that she painted, it just seemed very
improbable. But then again, I couldn't think of a reasonable
explanation for what was going on.

Sidling out of Erika's office, I could see Bärbel had returned from
the shop, a packet of coffee lay on her desk next to the typewriter.
Erika's office was behind Bärbel's desk, so she didn't see me in the
doorway—her eyes were fixed on the door to my office, over the other
side of the reception area. She had the telephone receiver cupped in
her hand and was talking quietly into it:

"Yes, he said he was going to the prison again ... I can confirm
that," she said softly before putting the phone down.

"Bärbel, who were you talking to?"

Startled, she twisted around to look at me.

"Bärbel, tell me—who were you talking to on the phone?"

"Martin, I was talking to a friend about dinner—as if it has
anything to do with you!"

How sure was I that I'd heard her right? And even if I had, she could have been talking about anyone—it didn't have to be me. I stood there looking at Bärbel, she just shrugged and turned her back on me, shifting files around her desk. The more I thought about it, the more uncertain I became—I couldn't shake the feeling that I was misjudging everything at the moment.

I went into my office and phoned the director at the power plant. "You mentioned plans for high voltage power line from Silesia to West Germany—do you know who was negotiating the deal?" I asked.

"Didn't I mention it? Until last week that would have been Hans Maier, you know, the guy who was found dead in the mine."

14:12

Here I was again, for the second day running: Rummelsburg prison. I checked in at the guardhouse by the gate, and was asked to wait. After a few minutes, a prison officer marched up to me.

"I'm to take the Comrade Captain to the director's office," he reported, as if he were talking about someone who wasn't present.

Before I had a chance to reply, he did a smart about-turn, and headed back the way he'd come. I followed him to the red brick administration block, up some steps into the hall, then up more steps to the first floor. He knocked at the director's office, and we entered.

"I regret to inform you, Comrade Captain, that Accused 264721 was found dead in his cell an hour ago," said the director without looking up. He was a tall man, wearing civilian clothes and a narrow, clipped moustache. He didn't bother rising from his chair to greet me, merely extended a hand over his paperwork.

"I'm sorry you've had a wasted journey," he added distractedly.

"How was he killed?"

"Not killed, Comrade Captain. Suicide. Now if you'll excuse me-"

"I want to see his body."

Finally, the director looked up from his forms, if only to give me a faintly surprised but indignant look.

"Very well, if you wish." He gestured at the guard to take me away.

The guard and I headed through the main gates and into the main body of the prison, through a further gate in the fence that ran across the centre of the site, under a mesh of steam and heating pipes and past the huge three-storey cell blocks and modern concrete buildings. Finally, we came to a more human sized red-brick house, with a low concrete wing added to the right of it. A plaque by the entrance marked it as *Haus 8, Prison Hospital Wing.*

The cellar served as a basic morgue, and that's where I found Chris Fremdiswalde on a steel table. His left knee was still noticeably swollen under his trouser leg, and some fresh bruising could be seen around his right eye and cheek. He was wearing only the standard issue blue jogging trousers and socks, and two long, parallel welts could be seen running diagonally across his left breast.

"How did this happen?" I asked the nervous orderly who was hovering near the table like a geriatric bat. But I needn't have asked, the reason for Chris's death was obvious to anyone who cared to take a look at the body. Tongue protruding from blue lips, red marks around the neck, eyes bulging and bloodshot.

"He was found just over an hour ago, when they came to take his breakfast tray away. He'd hung himself from the bars, using his tracksuit top."

I stared at the orderly until he turned to take a form from the desk. It was the custody record, an entry had been made late last night advising that force had been necessary to subdue Accused 264721. That was it, nothing else.

"Tell the director I want a report on Citizen Fremdiswalde's death, on my desk by tomorrow morning," I snapped at the guard, and marched out of the hospital wing, letting him follow me for a change.

I stood at the tram-stop in the rain. Water was leaking through my shoes, but in my anger and agitation at Chris's death I hardly noticed the dampness.

I hadn't expected this. Chris had been frightened yesterday, but I hadn't taken his fear seriously enough. If I'd listened to him, maybe I could have done something, got him out of there. He'd still be alive.

I turned my back on the biting wind that blew down the Rummelsburger Hauptstrasse, hunching my shoulders against the cold and burrowing my hands deeper into my jacket pockets. The fingers of my right hand closed around a thick wad of papers, and I pulled them out. That cop had handed them to me during the raid on Tuesday. I unrolled the bundle, and looked at the first page. It was Chris's Stasi files. I'd seen them before, there wasn't anything useful in there. I flicked through the papers, then looked more closely at the first sheet. It listed Fremdiswalde as an IM working for the Stasi—that was different from what I'd read in the files we'd been sent.

I shuffled through the pages again, rain spotting the paper, wind ruffling the edges. What I read didn't make much sense; too densely wrapped in Stasi jargon and codenames for the groups, handlers and operational processes. But from what I understood, Fremdiswalde had been recruited after being detained for stealing at school—they'd signed him up when he was still a kid, under the codename WERTHER. The Stasi seemed to have had him reporting on youth subculture groups until late 1988, when he was given the new codename FELD and used in operations against individual targets. His handler was named as IMF MILCHMÄDCHEN, which was Maier's codename.

So Maier had been handling Fremdiswalde. That was a turn up for the books, although perhaps not too much of a surprise, considering the close contact between the two men. Reading between the lines I could see that Maier was also in charge of several other IMs—the name TRAKTOR had come up a lot in the final months before the Wall opened.

TRAKTOR WAS first mentioned in a handwritten note in the margin: DÄ GOTTFRIED. Meaning *Decknamenänderung,* change of codename— his previous handle had been GOTTFRIED.

I paused in my reading, following a thread of memory. I'd seen that codename before, I'd noticed it because Gottfried was Bishop Forck's first name—until recently the Protestant bishop of Berlin-Brandenburg—and that particular codename had cropped up several times in the file the Stasi had kept on me. Maybe I needed to pull the file on GOTTFRIED/TRAKTOR, see how significant he or she was, and why they'd cropped up in my own files.

At that point the tram rattled up, and I climbed aboard. I folded Chris's papers into a pocket and wiped away the condensation on the window. It had stopped raining, and the grey cloud was lifting. My eyes drifted down from the sky to the road running either side of the tram tracks.

To our right I noticed a brown Trabant spluttering along next to us. I was too high up to see who was inside, but I didn't like the way the car kept pace with the tram. The watchers had picked up my scent again.

I thought fast: the next stop was Rummelsburg S-Bahn station, if I got off there then I had two choices—get on a train, or run through the station to the other side. The tram stopped and I climbed down the steps, crossing the road behind the little grey car, passing between the row of workshops and huts that lined the entrance to the station. I didn't look back, but I could hear the tram move off while the cyclical whining of the Trabant's engine remained at a constant pitch, telling me the car was still stationary.

In the station tunnel, I turned the corner, ignoring the steps that led up to the platform, continuing instead through to the Nöldnerstrasse exit on the far side. A moment's hesitation as a train rumbled in overhead, and then I ran out on to the street and turned right. I'd intended to hide round the back of the church further up the road, but as soon as I made it out of the station I could see that it was too far away. But a scrubby patch of grass and several mature trees were right next to the entrance and I quickly slid behind the damp trunk of a large chestnut.

Footsteps and panting grew nearer, and peeking round the bole of my tree I could see a small, bald man run out of the station. He leaned forward, supporting his hands on his thighs, while he took a few deep breaths. Standing up straight again, he made for the phone box next to the station entrance, speaking into the receiver for a few moments.

The Trabant whined up, having taken the long way round by the road. It splashed up next to the phone box, and the small man got in, the car starting up and driving past as I edged around the tree trunk to stay out of sight.

The Trabant would be cruising around, looking for me, so I decided to avoid going directly to my flat, instead catching the bus to Lichtenberg station, before changing onto the underground for one stop, as far as Magdalenenstrasse. I walked into the old Stasi complex and asked the porter for the GOTTFRIED, TRAKTOR and FELD files. He returned after about five minutes.

"I'm sorry, Comrade Captain, the overview file for FELD has been signed out to the Ministry of the Interior, and I can't find files for either TRAKTOR or GOTTFRIED."

"Are there no library copies in the registry?" I asked.

The porter shook his head. "If you could tell us which departments and district they were registered in then I could have the F 77 lists checked, but it might take a few weeks."

"No need."

I left the Stasi headquarters. FELD's background files would presumably be the same as Chris's personal copy that had been found during the raid on the *Thaeri* squat and was now safely in my pocket. Far more interesting was the fact that the library copies of the GOTTFRIED-TRAKTOR overview files were missing. The library copies of files should never leave the archives—that way they couldn't be misplaced or lost, and there would always be a copy available. Had they been shredded in the last days of the Stasi, or removed more recently?

Maybe if I checked the references to GOTTFRIED in my own Stasi files I could gain some context, with a bit of luck perhaps even work out who it was.

15:19

I walked straight back to my flat, keeping half an eye open for the brown Trabant, but the only vehicles I saw were on the Frankfurter Allee, and there were very few people on the streets. A couple of *babushkas* carrying shopping bags, a few kids on the way home from school, if I was still being followed then whoever was doing it was good for me to spot.

I was halfway home when I heard the door to a tenement block open just as I went past. I glanced into the hallway, and there stood Laura, waving me in. A quick look up and down the street: empty. I joined my colleague, and she allowed the heavy door to swing shut behind us.

"Martin, they're waiting for you—some plainclothes cops came by and asked for you, and now they're sitting in a car outside the office.

They said you sexually assaulted a girl. During the raid on the squat," Laura glared at me, accusing me, waiting for an answer.

"What-" I started, but was cut off by her.

"Well? Did you?"

"Shit! Shit-shit-shit!" I hit the wall with the palm of my hand. Laura took a step back, her face hard.

Things were moving much faster than I'd expected. "Laura—now this is important. When they came to the office, where was everyone, how did they react?"

"Martin, what does that matter? We want you to come to a meeting, tell us what happened. And we want to know the name of the young woman so that we can talk to her too-"

"For fuck's sake!" I was almost shouting. "This is a fucking set-up! Do you really think I'd assault someone? Do you? Come on, it's classic Stasi tactics! Did those cops show any ID? Or did you just take their word for it?"

"You know what? I'm not interested in your excuses, come with me and we'll talk it through—you need to tell us everything that happened during the raid."

I could just shove Laura out of the way, keep moving, keep following the lead I'd found. But instead I tried to swallow my anger —I needed my colleagues, and I needed Laura to believe that I hadn't done anything wrong—it mattered to me what she thought of me. Another deep breath, pushing down my sense of urgency. I tried to get through to Laura again.

"Look, Laura: they killed Chris Fremdiswalde—he's dead," I looked into Laura's shocked face and pushed on. "And as for that assault story, it's classic attrition tactics. Just think about it: it's text book— you know how it works! I'm being followed, they've been in my flat, stealing my coffee, changing my alarm clock, trying to mess with my head. And all those phone calls with no-one on the other end of the line, and now this. It all makes sense, they're trying to make me doubt my own sanity! They're turning you against me, isolating me. Come, on Laura, we've seen all of this too many times!" I was getting agitated again, yet another deep breath, trying to calm down. "Those men that came—they're involved in the Maier case, they're probably not even cops. What did they look like—think back, remember the old days when they used to follow us, that's what those men looked like, isn't it? They had *that* look, didn't they? Laura?"

Laura nodded hesitantly, her arms crossed in front of her. She took another step back, and her eyes flicked upwards, away from my face. She wasn't happy. I'd taken control of the conversation, was putting her under pressure. I'd shocked her with the news of Chris's death, and that had given me a way to reach her.

"Come with me, we're going to meet somewhere away from the office, you'll have a chance to explain it to us, and then we'll work out what to do. Together." So she hadn't taken in what I was telling her, she was still trying to steer me back to the accusation of assault.

"Laura, I can't. They're on the lookout for me, and they probably followed you here. There's not much time, it's a matter of hours—they know I'm on to them, they'll be cleaning up, covering their traces. I think that's why they killed Chris. Laura, I need your help, I can't do this by myself. So just tell me: what was everyone doing when those men came to the office?"

Laura bit her lip, thinking, wondering whether to give me the benefit of the doubt. I could see the thoughts circling through her mind—the serious accusation competing with the picture she had of me, the trust she had in me. I could imagine her thinking about the Stasi, not wanting to admit they were still around, were still doing this kind of thing.

"And this, whatever it is you're doing right now, it's really urgent?" she asked.

I nodded.

"And when you've sorted this out then you'll answer our questions about the accusation?"

I swallowed the indignation as it welled up again—how they could still play us off against one another! I nodded, agreeing to what she wanted.

"OK. I was in the front office doing some photocopying—they talked to me first-"

"So where was Bärbel? Why didn't they talk to her first?"

"Well, the photocopier is right by the front door ... No, that's it—Bärbel went to the toilet just as they came in."

"She got up when she saw them coming?"

"Really, Martin! Does it matt-"

"Yes! Come on, tell me!"

Laura hesitated, her eyes closed, concentrating.

"A moment after, yes. The door to the stairwell was open, she may have seen them coming up the stairs."

"And the others?"

"They came out of their offices just as the cops went. I think they heard our voices, realised something was up."

"How did they react?"

"Shocked, I think. Erika sat down, Klaus looked grim."

"And Bärbel, how did she react when she came back from the toilet?"

"I didn't say anything to her, but she was there when I spoke to the others, she must have overheard everything. She ... she just carried on typing."

I paced up and down the tenement hallway, trying to process the information, fitting it in, slotting it this way and that like a jigsaw piece.

"Laura, get back to the office—have you got your personal Stasi files there? Really it's mine I need, but they're at home. So get your-"

"No they're not—you photocopied them at the office, then left them in the copier. I put them on your desk and watched how over time you piled more and more paperwork on top of them."

"You are a star! Get them for me. Get your own too, ask Erika and Klaus for theirs. Look through for someone called either GOTTFRIED or TRAKTOR. They're both the same person, and we need to work out who it is. Then meet me on the Grosser Bunkerberg in the Friedrichshain park at half past six. Bring the other two, but not Bärbel—don't let her know anything. Watch out for any tails. And call my daughter—tell her to get in touch with Annette. I need to meet Annette on the spooky bridge at eight. Katrin will know what I mean, just tell her it's important—that I need her help."

"And what are you going to do?"

"I'm going to the police headquarters," I told her.

Going to the police *Präsidium* on Keibelstrasse near Alexanderplatz was a bit of a gamble. I couldn't be sure the men who had come for me weren't actually cops, but even if they were, I suspected they wouldn't have put out an alert for me yet. And even if they had, who would expect me to head straight into the lion's den?

I felt nervous crossing Alexanderplatz, there were always police officers hanging around on the square, keeping an eye on the tourists and the punks. They didn't take any notice of me as I went to the payphone at the edge of the square. It was a Glasnost phone—no booth, just a rain hood over the payphone, wide open to any eavesdropping passers-by. But that was fine by me—I wasn't planning on saying anything.

I put a couple of 20 Pfennig coins in the slot, watching as two red lights lit up on the payphone, then I dialled the number for the KGB headquarters in Karlshorst.

"*Da,*" came the voice at the other end.

I didn't answer, just kept an eye on my watch. 10 seconds, then hang up. Redial, hang up after 30 seconds. I'd done the same from a payphone near Ostkreuz before I got the S-Bahn up to Alex. I'd laughed at Dmitri when he told me the procedure just the other day; but now he knew that I needed to see him urgently. A crash meeting.

No problems getting into the police headquarters, I just had show my pass at the gatehouse. I took the stairs to the basement of the equipment house and showed my requisition papers to the cop in charge of handing out uniforms.

"Just the extra pips?" he asked, stamping the paperwork.

"The whole lot."

He looked at me again: "Haven't you already been issued with a uniform?"

"Plain clothes. But now I need a service uniform too—so far I've only been issued dress."

He shrugged and turned to the shelves, "What size?" he called over his shoulder.

★

Twenty minutes later I had what I needed and was out of there. He'd even given me a patterned *dederon* shopping bag to put my new uniform in. I reached into the bag and checked the shoulder boards—they had the usual green piping of the *Volkspolizei* rather than the Bordeaux red the RS had inherited from the Stasi. I grinned and checked the left sleeve of the jacket—it had the *Volkspolizei* shield sewn on it.

"Very sloppy" I murmured.

If that cop had been paying attention he would have given me the Bordeaux RS shoulder boards and removed the police shield from the jacket, but he hadn't checked my paperwork—just assumed I was a cop too. That was fine, it suited me and my plans perfectly. For my purposes it would be much better to be seen as a cop than a member of the RS.

17:17

I got off the tram at the planetarium on Prenzlauer Allee. I'd made sure to look around as I boarded, watching who else was getting on, then checking for the same faces when I got off. All clear, no familiar features, so I walked over to the planetarium entrance and spent a few minutes admiring the notice board, then bent down to tie my shoelace, which gave me a chance to look back the way I'd come. Plenty of people were walking up and down the Prenzlauer Allee, but nobody loitering, waiting for me to start moving again.

Walking around the building with a stick of chalk hidden in my hand I discreetly made a mark on the corner, just a short horizontal line at hand height. I carried on through the park, parallel to the railway tracks, on the way towards the Thälmann memorial.

Between the planetarium and the memorial there's a narrow stretch, the path edged in by buildings, and at just that point it curves round to the right. I stood close to the bushes just after the bend—it was a good place to spot a tail, from here I couldn't see the planetarium, which meant that anybody following me wouldn't see me until they reached the bend.

After a few minutes, I was satisfied nobody was behind me and I left another chalk mark on the corner of the swimming baths.

Pushing through the shrubs, I came up behind the huge memorial, a bronze sculpture of Ernst Thälmann, the German Communists' hero, fist raised in front of a red flag carved from stone to look like it was flowing in a strong breeze. The red granite plinth for the ensemble was wide enough to hide a squad of cops behind, but when I walked around, pretending to admire the stonework, I could see I was alone.

All clear, mark on the corner of the plinth, and off again.

A couple of turns around the small pond in the park, and finally, Dmitri was standing there, in civilian clothes.

"Martin, how long do you have? Everything OK?"

"Things have started happening—I need some more information."

"Ah! Martin, you have decided to trust me?"

"I've run out of other choices. Listen, Dmitri, last time we met you mentioned the Stasi taskforce, and you said you'd look to see if there were any links with Maier. Have you had a chance to do that? And were ex-Stasi, or even the KGB involved in the death of Maier?"

"Martin, Martin," Dmitri shook his head, almost sadly. "An Englishman once said to me: It's not the questions that are dangerous, it's the answers—think twice before you ask anything, he said. And I think that was good advice. These OibE operatives are not amateurs, and nor are the KGB. No, someone else killed the Maier politician. But, here, I have something that might help."

He pulled a file from under his coat. The cover was buff coloured, with a red diagonal stripe, some Cyrillic letters and numbers on the front. I opened it, flicked through the papers, my eyes sliding off the Cyrillic letters.

"What does it say?"

"I don't have time now, but it's an internal KGB report on the taskforce that Maier was part of. Let's just say someone from the KGB team sent by Moscow was persuaded to hand it over. Maier was run by an OibE—I don't know whether from here in Berlin or from Moscow, but the OibE is called GÄRTNER, he is leading the group. There is also a list of agents he's been running. I believe one of them panicked and killed Maier, then moved the body to the coal mine."

GÄRTNER—gardener, another agricultural codename to go with Milkmaid, Field and Tractor.

"Why did they panic?" I asked Dmitri. "Was it because Maier was getting too cosy with West Germany?"

"That is what I am thinking too, they had to ensure that Maier didn't get too close to the West. Maybe Maier was too much of a loose cannon, couldn't be trusted any more. Perhaps GÄRTNER didn't intend to have Maier silenced, just wanted him scared enough to do what he was told."

This was at odds with the police investigation's findings—did Fremdiswalde kill Maier because of an argument, or because he was ordered to by the Stasi, or Moscow?

I flicked through the file again, this time a little more slowly. Codenames were written in Latin characters, and I could see now that TRAKTOR came up a few times, along with both FELD and MILCHMÄDCHEN and some new names: BAUM, ZIEGE, SPATEN—tree, goat, spade. This was confirmation that Maier was involved in the Stasi's plans.

"Do you know anything about TRAKTOR?"

"I haven't had a chance to analyse the documents, I just had a quick look and thought that you probably needed it more than I do. But I think TRAKTOR is based in Berlin, he keeps a low profile. BAUM is in Berlin, she's close to TRAKTOR."

"She?"

The files refer to BAUM as a female: *yeye, ona, eu*."—Russian for she, her.

"Do we know anything else about her, or the others?"

"I have my staff working on it, although we do have some other priorities."

I thought of the situation in Moscow, what was happening there made my little adventure look petty.

"Of course, sorry."

"No need to apologise. I think everything is linked. Stay with it Martin, you're on the right track, and your timing is perfect."

"How do you know what I'm up to?"

Dmitri didn't answer, he just pointed at the nylon bag tucked between my feet, the police uniform visible inside.

"I wish I could help you, but I think that if I did it would do more harm than good."

"But there is something you can help me with: can you spare a couple of your people? I need to make sure a friend doesn't get into any trouble."

I gave him the details, and Dmitri nodded, then held out his hand.

"Martin, when we meet again we shall have a drink together, and make proper toasts—this time not to the great leader Stalin."

"How do you ... oh, never mind."

It was time for my next appointment.

18:26

In Friedrichshain park, I stationed myself in the undergrowth at the bottom of the footpath that winds up to the top of the Grosser Bunkerberg, one of the many rubble hills in Berlin—the grass and trees around me were growing on the pulverised bricks, windows and joists of Berlin buildings destroyed during bombing in the Second World War.

I didn't have long to wait, Erika, Laura and Klaus passed my hiding place and went up the hill together. I squatted in the foliage for another five minutes, waiting and watching to see if they had any tails. Once satisfied they were alone, I followed them up the path.

At the summit, I could see Klaus and Laura deep in conversation, Erika was standing off to one side, listening. She saw me climb the last few steps and came to meet me.

"Martin, what's going on?"

On hearing Erika speak, the other two turned to face me.

"Honestly, I don't know what's going on, but Chris Fremdiswalde is dead, allegedly suicide, the bruises tell another story. After I saw his body in the morgue, I decided to take a closer look at what he'd been up to—it seems Maier was both his handler and his lover, and the cops have jumped to the conclusion that he murdered Maier in a fit of passion. Then Dmitri from the KGB thinks there's a Stasi plot to destabilise West Silesia, perhaps the whole of the GDR and it looks like Fremdiswalde and Maier were both involved. And if he's right about this then the Minister is involved too."

"Whoa, back up a bit. Dmitri? KGB? Plot?" asked Klaus.

"Dmitri Alexandrovich, I don't know his last name, he's a captain

169

in the KGB, Nik is in contact with him—I think Dmitri's OK."

The three of them stared at me.

"We know Fremdiswalde did it, the case is closed. The report from the Saxon police arrived this afternoon," said Laura, handing me a large envelope.

It had already been opened, and I slid out a police report on the death of Maier. It was quite thick, full of unnecessary technical particulars that I wasn't in the mood to pore over, but I scanned the summary and leafed through the rest. There wasn't much new in it, just more details and a catalogue of evidence. There was enough to justify closing the case now Fremdiswalde was dead—particularly if no other suspects came to light.

On the 22nd of September, Hans Maier had been at the Nochten open cast lignite mine for an official meeting. After the meeting ended, he said he wanted to inspect the mine by himself and was issued a hard hat and told where it was safe to go.

Shortly after, he was strangled using a length of soft material, most likely a scarf, and his body was found at half past one the next morning, placed across the tracks of the transformer cars at the excavating end of the F60 overburden conveyor gantry. The police guessed that the original intention was that the body should be covered by the spoil dump, but the murder happened at the wrong end of the gantry and, unable to carry Maier's the body 500 metres down into the pit and up the other side to where it could be left to be buried in the spoil ejected by the F60 mining machine on its next pass, the perpetrator had left the body on the rails, presumably in the hope it would be mangled beyond recognition when run over.

There were photographs of the scuffed sand near where the body was found, supposed evidence of the struggle, and further photographs showed two pairs of footprints leading to the scene, but only one set departing.

Fremdiswalde, who had worked at the mine after leaving school, was recognised on his way out of the mine by a works security guard at around 20.30 on the 22nd, which matched the estimate of time of death.

At Maier's flat, the police found the draft of a letter ending his relationship with Fremdiswalde, and it was assumed that Maier had asked Fremdiswalde to meet at the mine in order to finish the affair in person.

The final piece of evidence was a Technical Services report matching skin particles and hair found on and near Maier's body to Fremdiswalde's blood group.

Laura waited until I'd finished flicking through the file, then: "It looks pretty cut and dried to me."

"The Minister will be pleased the case is closed—because he's involved, and he's in danger of being discovered while the case is still live. How else can you explain everything that's been happening over the last few days? This wasn't a murder of passion, it's something much bigger than that!"

"You're still talking about the Minister? How about you give us the facts? OK, let's just assume you're right, how long have you suspected him? Do you think he set those goons on you?" Laura said.

"The suspicion has sort of been growing over the last few days-"

"And you didn't tell us? And what about Bärbel—why isn't she allowed to know about this meeting?"

"I told you about the Minister—several times! I told you he was behaving suspiciously, I told you I was being followed. And as for Bärbel—just think about it, somehow the Minister knew I had my doubts about Maier and the West Silesian situation—how did the Minister know that? And why wasn't Bärbel surprised when the cops —if they were even cops—came to arrest me today? She isn't one of us, she was an official under the old regime and we just inherited her —what do we know about her, really?"

"Martin, are you sure Maier and the Minister were connected?" Klaus interrupted.

I looked at him, held my hands palm outwards, the police report and Dmitri's papers stuffed under my arm.

"I haven't got real evidence yet, but I think the connection between the Minister and Maier goes back to the old times. We were close to the Minister back then and I think our old Stasi files may contain useful information—you did bring them, didn't you?"

We stood for a few moments, all looking at each other, then Laura pulled a couple of folders out of her bag. She handed one to me—it was my Stasi file. I placed it on the low wall surrounding the summit area, then, gesturing the others over, I opened Fremdiswalde's file next to my own. As I flicked through the pages I told them what I'd found out. I explained how Fremdiswalde was codename FELD, part of a taskforce put in place around various departments and institutions before the Autumn Revolution.

"Now they're ready for the counter-revolution—West Silesia is just the beginning. Maier was part of the same taskforce, but he was following his own agenda, got too close to West Germany. He liked the idea of an independent West Silesia, imagined himself at the helm. So he needed to be brought back in line. Except the disciplinary hearing went wrong and he ended up dead in that open-cast mine.

"Dmitri also told me about the links between the taskforce and the Ministry of the Interior—look," I showed them the note in Fremdiswalde's file that showed TRAKTOR to be the same agent as GOTTFRIED. "That's the taskforce agent in the Ministry, I recognised the codename because it crops up in my files too—if we can work out who it is, then we'll have identified the agent in the Ministry."

I leafed through my own file, looking for mention of GOTTFRIED. Erika was the first to join me at the wall, opening her own file. I could hear Laura and Klaus murmuring to each other in the background, but after another short hesitation they joined us, bringing their files too.

"GOTTFRIED is mentioned in a report from September 1983, the human chain for peace between the American and Soviet embassies. GOTTFRIED was present at the action, but left before the participants were taken into detention," said Erika.

"That doesn't help! There were hundreds of us there that day." Klaus snorted.

"Here's another mention: *Situation Report on 1987 Peace Workshop*— that's the one the church tried to ban, look: 'GOTTFRIED made representations to Diocesan *Genaralsuperintendent* Krusche, offering to act as guarantor for the groups involved'."

Far from being an IM determined to impede our work, that entry made GOTTFRIED look like he was on our side. But it also showed he had links with figures high up in the church, which helped to reduce our pool of suspects.

"What about this: *Situation Report on morale of opposition groups after the Zion Church affair.* It says 'GOTTFRIED has begun to discourage groups from using his church'," said Klaus. "It's in my file because I was in one of those groups—and the church they're talking about was where the Minister was pastor."

It added up—the Minister had links to the diocesan *Genaralsuperintendent*, and he was there the day we formed the peace chain between the embassies. I remember him making sure he got his photo taken by Western journalists then leaving just as the police vans turned up.

The four of us stood there, at the top of the Bunkerberg. The leaves of the trees and bushes on the hill around us were turning yellow, bronze and red, whispering in the light wind. Under different circumstances it would have been a pleasant evening, but not when we'd just found out the head of the ministry we worked for was involved in a plot to turn the clock back to the old times.

I'd suspected it, I'd been on the verge of knowing it, but now, suddenly, I didn't want to believe it.

"What are we going to do about this?" Erika asked.

"Whatever we do, we'll have to act fast. Immediately. They're already looking for Martin, they've worked out he knows something is happening." Klaus answered.

"Dmitri also seems to think we need to act soon," I added.

"Can we trust him?"

That was the big question. Dmitri had told me Moscow was running the Minister, who in turn was manipulating the West Silesian situation. Should I believe him? If I believed Moscow were capable of running the Minister, then I could just as well believe they were capable of setting me up—a few operatives overtly observing me, a couple of meetings with a KGB officer briefed to feed me disinformation and I'd be ready to do whatever they wanted me to do. Anything was possible.

"I don't know," I concluded. "But Maier's death only makes sense in the context of what Dmitri told me. If it's all just disinformation—well why would the Russians do that? What would they gain? They've already got their hands full with the coup attempt in Moscow, and what do they care about the future of our country? It all fits together —we have a duty to act." I could see Laura was about to raise an objection but carried on talking, not wanting to give her the chance to interrupt just then. "If we had more time we could investigate further, talk to the Round Tables, but Klaus is right, we have to act now and we can go to the Round Tables afterwards."

I looked around at my colleagues' faces, each of them dimly lit by the last light of the day.

"Erika?" I looked at her, waiting for her answer.

"Yes, let's do it."

I turned to Klaus, he nodded slowly. That left Laura.

"You really think this is the only way?" she asked.

"Yes. I don't like it either, but what else can we do? You got any ideas?"

Laura shook her head. "OK. What's the plan?"

I patted the bag with the police uniform in it. "You're going to like this."

20:02

As it turned out, my colleagues didn't like my plan, but since they couldn't come up with anything better they agreed to go along with it. We made our arrangements, then parted. Now I was waiting for Annette on the bridge that spanned the central slaughter yards and the S-Bahn tracks. It's a long bridge, more of a tunnel on stilts, full of shadows and darkness. Even during the day not much light makes its way through the dirty, frosted glass; standing in the gloom of the city night it was clear why my daughter called this the spooky bridge when she was small.

The echoing clang of footsteps on steel told me someone was coming up the steps from the S-Bahn platform. I was standing further back along the bridge, so couldn't see them yet, but it sounded like more than one pair of feet. When the figures arrived at the top I saw Annette, but she'd brought someone with her—my daughter.

"Katrin, what are you doing here?"

"Hi Papa. Your colleague said you needed help, so I decided to come with Annette."

"What's going on, Martin, what's so important? Katrin said it was really important."

I was a bit put out by my daughter's unexpected arrival, it had knocked me off balance, but before I could think of anything to say the sound of a further pair of footsteps echoed down the bridge. I turned, startled at how close the two men were. Both wore hats pulled low over their eyes. One had a *Lederol* fake leather jacket on, the other a short trench coat, much like mine. They glared at us as they came closer, there was no doubt that we were in their sights.

"Shit-"

"What is it, Martin?" Annette asked, picking up my stress.

As for my daughter, she stared at me, her eyes accusing me of dragging us all back to the past.

As I dithered, unsure what to do—our only choices were down the steps onto the platform, or along to the other exit at the far end of the bridge. But I was worried there would be men in plastic-leather jackets waiting for us there too.

A train ground into the station below us, and I'd almost decided to take my small group down the steps, hope to get on that train, but unsure how to prevent the two men from following us, when I felt someone brush past me. I hadn't heard anyone come up the steps, but here was the Russian NCO that had been driving the jeep the other day.

"Platform's clear, get on the train!" she hissed as she went past, casually swinging a heavy shopping bag as she went.

I grabbed Katrin and Annette and pulled them down the steps to the platform. The last thing I saw before I went around the corner was the Soviet soldier kick one of the men in the crotch while aiming her bag at the other guy's face. We could hear the men's grunts as we ran down the stairs, jumping on the train just as the door buzzer went.

"Martin—did you see what that woman did? Is she anything to do with you—those men, she just attacked them!" Annette was glaring at me as I slumped down to the floor next to the door.

Katrin was looking back at the receding station, lit up in the dark.

"Nobody followed us down to the platform. Right, Papa, you have some explaining to do."

"In a minute! The next stop is Lenin Allee. If there's a train on the other side of the platform we run across and get on it, but we need to be sure we're not being followed. Annette, you check to our right, see if anyone else crosses to the other train. Katrin, check behind us, and I'll look to the left. We need to keep watching until the train pulls out of the station."

Katrin nodded at Annette, who, after some hesitation nodded too. As we drew into the station, I saw with relief that there was indeed a train standing on the other side of the platform. I hauled open the doors before we'd even stopped, jumping down as the command from the platform attendant buzzed through loudspeakers: "Schönefeld: *zurückbleiben!*"

Katrin jumped into the doorway of the other train just as the red lights lit up and the buzzer sounded. She blocked the doors from sliding shut, allowing us to slip in. We were clear—no one had followed us across the platform.

I led the way to some empty seats, and we sat down, Annette and Katrin sitting opposite me, not saying anything, just staring at me, waiting for an explanation.

"Annette, I need your help. There's some stuff I've got to deal with, and I can't do it by myself. I need your contacts, I think some of the squatters could help."

Annette looked suspicious. "What kind of stuff?"

In a low whisper I told her of my suspicions about the Minister, how he was probably connected to the Maier case.

"Are you sure? It's all a bit far-fetched."

"Did you see those two men on the bridge, if it hadn't been for ..." I realised I didn't even know the name of Dmitri's NCO.

"What about them? Two dudes on the way to the station and they were assaulted-"

"They were Stasi." I sighed, and leaned back.

"Come off it! The Stasi was dissolved three years ago!"

"Papa's right. They were Stasi."

Annette looked from Katrin to me, eyes wide. Astonished, and now, at last, a little afraid.

"You better be worth the trouble," she said, not quite under her breath.

★

Annette suggested we head over to the Squatters' Council—they were meeting that night in Friedrichshain and we'd probably get there in time for the beginning. We left the S-Bahn at Frankfurter Allee and walked to one of the Wessi-squats near by where Annette shouted up to the balcony where a couple of punks were chatting and smoking. A key on a piece of string was dropped down to us, and we let ourselves in. The key was hauled back up.

The meeting was in a kitchen on the ground floor, about a dozen young squatters sitting loosely round a table too small for the number of empty beer bottles and fag butts it was expected to hold. A couple of them looked up as we came in.

"Oh shit! Oh man! Who the fuck are you bringing this time?" The question was directed at Annette, but was clearly about me.

"Hey folks." Annette's voice and accent had roughened, she sounded like a young punk herself now, drawling the words out. "This is Martin, he needs our help. He's from the *Republikschutz-*"

"Fuck off! Bull-pig! Stasi pig!" The guy who'd first spoken was on his feet, shouting, pointing his finger at me, but staring at Annette, his spit flecking the front of her anorak.

"Wait," Annette tried to get them to listen, "Wait! Martin's been in the opposition for more than 15 years—he was doing actions when you were all in nappies!"

"Yeah, and now he's part of the institutions! Just look at him in his dirty spy-trenchcoat!"

"Never trust anyone over the age of thirty!"

"Bulls out!"

Pretty much everyone in the room was on their feet, shouting at Annette, only Katrin looked at me.

"Papa, let's go. Come on."

Katrin was pulling me out the door, I grabbed Annette and we went back out onto the street.

There was silence for a couple of minutes, then Annette took my hand, too.

"Sorry. That didn't go as planned."

I was shocked. Is that what we'd worked for, what we'd sacrificed so much for, just so that Westerners could come over here, squat our buildings and insult us? Ever since Rudi Dutschke the fucking Wessis had been telling us we were passive and apolitical, trying to give us lessons on Marx and Lenin, as if we weren't getting enough of that every day from the Party! And now, once we'd thrown out the Stalinists, these Western kids were living here in our Berlin, them and their patronising fucking arrogance. I didn't feel like I had any energy to carry on. Let them sort out this mess if they thought themselves so much better than us!

"Martin? I'm sorry," Annette said again. "I should have thought, the council is meeting in a Wessi-squat tonight."

"I thought the Squatters' Council was for all the squats?" asked Katrin.

"It is, but the local squatters are getting pissed off with the Wessis, so most of them don't go to the meetings if they're being held at a Wessi-squat. But Martin, that punk who spoke at the demo, why don't we try her?"

"I'm not sure talking to Karo about this is such a good idea ..." I tailed off, remembering the last time I'd seen her, huddled in the corner, shaking, probably traumatised.

The three of us were walking slowly back to Frankfurter Allee, Katrin quiet, probably as shocked as I was by the Wessis' vitriol. Annette tried to be encouraging, which just aggravated my feeling of dejection.

"Why not? What's wrong with Karo?"

"Nothing. At least I hope not ... There was a police raid at her place a few days ago. It was pretty bad, and I was there. With the cops, I mean."

"God, Martin, you don't make things easy, do you? Right, where does she live? You two can hang around somewhere and I'll go and talk to her, see if we can sort this mess out."

We walked along Rigaer Strasse, Katrin and I ducking into the *Fischladen* bar while Annette went round the corner to the Thaerstrasse squat.

Food was still being served and Katrin brought us two plates, overflowing with steaming goulash. We both picked at the stew, neither of us saying anything.

All my preparations for the next day, they just weren't going to amount to anything. I had to get hold of my colleagues and call off the action I'd planned against the Stasi taskforce—without more bodies there was no way it could work. But if we didn't do it tomorrow then we may not get another chance. And then what?

I was still deep in my thoughts when Katrin patted my arm. Annette was standing in front of us, her eyes and face hard. She avoided looking at me, speaking only to Katrin.

"Karo wants to talk to you."

Katrin got up and the pair of them left the bar, leaving me behind, brooding over my ruined plan.

"I'm sorry about what I said to you, you know, during the raid on Tuesday."

It was Karo. She was standing in front of my table, looking down at her feet. When she finally looked up I could see a large bruise shading her left eye.

"You're the last person who needs to apologise," I answered. "I should be apologising to you."

"No, it wasn't you, brother. It was the bulls. Katrin made me realise —she said you'd never do that, that you'd do whatever you could to stop it. It made me think again about what happened. And I guess that's what you did—try to stop it, I mean."

Not sure what to say, I looked down at my goulash, cold, untouched.

"Annette says there's something we can do for you."

"It's not for me, it's for all of us," I looked up, meeting Karo's eyes, hope welling in my chest. "Fancy another revolution?"

"Hell, yeah! Any day! Do we get to settle up with the bulls?" Karo grinned at me. I was forgiven.

"I think we might find a way. And there's something else I need too."

"What?" Karo looked at me, her eyes bright.

"I need a place to crash tonight."

Day 10
Friday
1st October 1993

***Moscow:** The Soviet Army has declared support for the President of the Soviet Union, Mikhail Gorbachev. Broadcasting from Moscow's television complex, Marshal of the Soviet Union Gennady Bereskov announced an operation to round up rogue KGB troops in the capital. President Gorbachev is expected to return to Moscow this morning.*

09:47

In 1906 an unemployed cobbler donned a second hand captain's uniform and commanded some soldiers to follow him. He deployed them in an occupation of Köpenick town hall, arresting the mayor and confiscating 3,577 Marks from the council's coffers. His plan was very simple: it relied on the blind obedience of the soldiers he'd rounded up on the street—without his uniform he had no authority, and without that authority he had no chance of stealing the money.

I think I probably felt much the same way the Captain of Köpenick did when he began rounding up his troops. I was pretty nervous, but a uniform is as good as a coat of armour—nobody could tell I was shaking inside.

The military cut of the green jacket and trousers, the shiny shoes, the peaked cap, all straightened my spine and lent me an arrogance I would not normally want. I strode confidently down Mauerstrasse—a Captain of the *Volkspolizei*.

My ragtag troop of punks followed in silence. They'd been busy during the night: I had sworn them in to the service of the Republic, toasting them with beer. Each had a strip of red material tied around their left arm, white letters spelling out *HelferIn des RS*—RS auxiliary. Most of them had daubed flowers, crude representations of peace doves or the national *Swords to Ploughshares* emblem below the letters. Beside me I had Laura, Klaus and Erika, each of us, in our own individual ways, caught up in the drama of the situation.

I marched up the steps and pushed through the main doors of the Ministry of the Interior. Pulling myself up to my full height, adjusting my voice to fit the uniform, I commanded the porter to call the Central Round Table and the Round Tables' Committee for Internal Affairs, requesting they convene immediately here at the Ministry. Behind me, the squatters streamed into the building, weaving past the policemen guarding the doors. I waved an impatient hand at one of the cops who was trying to stem the flow of punks—a curt gesture, slicing the blade of my hand through the air. The guard came to attention, eyes front.

The porter, who had been about to question my order, similarly stiffened and picked up the telephone. Karo was beside me, and I asked her to stay here with the porter, make sure he didn't make any other calls.

Turning to the cops, I ordered them to lock the main doors and accompany me. Erika, Klaus and Laura were still with me, but once the front doors had been locked, they split up, each leading a small crew of punks to seal off the other exits to the building.

I took the two policemen up to the Minister's office—we barged through the door, but the Minister wasn't at his desk. Out again, this time through the next door to the secretary.

"Where's the Minister?" I demanded.

The secretary stopped typing, nonplussed. "He's in his office-"

"Call the Central Command of the Border Police—see that he doesn't cross the border," I snapped at the policeman by my side, telling the other to guard the office, then headed down to the main hall at the bottom of the stairs.

"Looks like the Minister's done a runner—but there's a chance he could be still in the building. Can you form a search party?" I asked a couple of the punks who were still in the porter's office with Karo, they ran off shouting and sliding over the shiny parquet.

Watching the punks disappear around the corner, I wondered what to do next—we hadn't been here five minutes, and already the mission was failing.

When I turned to go back up the stairs, I discovered Laura at my side. She didn't meet my eyes.

"Sorry, Martin, this is my fault. I went into the office this morning, and when Bärbel asked why nobody was in I just said where we were going, I didn't think-"

"Someone needs to phone the chair of the Central Round Table, tell her what's going on, that we need her here, now," I said, trying to hide my anger.

I'd just reached the top of the stairs when the policeman came out of the secretary's office, saluted and reported.

"Border Police have been informed, Comrade Captain!"

"Thank you, comrade *Wachtmeister*. Now go to the personnel archives and get whatever files they have on Minister Hartmann and Hagenow, Evelyn."

I didn't really think the files would contain anything useful, but I wanted to get rid of the policeman, I needed to sit down for a moment, unobserved. And I was curious about Evelyn, why was she on the scene again, and how come she was at the Ministry? I went into the Minister's office, told the cop there to go and stand in the corridor, then sat down at the desk. What now? No Minister, no evidence and the Central Round Table about to descend on us, wanting to know what the hell was going on. It couldn't get much worse. If the Minister had already crossed the border, or come to that, if he was hiding out somewhere in the Republic then we wouldn't find him in time, if ever.

A knock at the door, and the cop came in with the files. I ignored the Minister's file, and idly thumbed through Evelyn's: 1988 in-service training in Moscow, then attachment to the Ministry of the Interior. Before that, she was an administrative worker at the State Opera.

I frowned and flicked back to the beginning of the file. If she was just a cultural administrator, how did she end up getting a prestige posting to Moscow, followed by a position as case handler in a ministry? And if she was a high-flier, why was she serving drinks at a party thrown for the *Bonzen* all those years ago when I first saw her? And why did she come to my factory a few months later, wanting to see the works' Party secretary?

I was looking at a pretty thin legend—Evelyn had been more than some petty IM informant. Reading between the lines it sounded like she'd been put in place in the Opera to spy on Party *Bonzen* when they attended performances, later on liaising with Party bigwigs in the factories, before being transferred into the Ministry at the same time the taskforce was formed around OibE GÄRTNER.

But I was wasting time. I had to push away my reactions to finding out Evelyn was possibly a Stasi sleeper agent, concentrate on finding proof about the Minister's involvement. Because unless I found it, I would be in deep shit. Alternatively, if there were no proof, if I was just plain wrong, well ... same result.

I was mulling over this possibility when there was another knock at the door.

"Comrade *Hauptmann!* The Minister has been stopped at Friedrichstrasse Border Crossing Point. The Minister and a woman, also in the vehicle, have been detained."

"Have them brought to me immediately."

The Friedrichstrasse border crossing wasn't very far away, they'd be here in just a few minutes. In the meantime, we had to search the building for anything that might confirm my suspicions, and it made sense to start in this office. Going to the door, I asked the policeman standing outside to fetch Karo and Laura from downstairs.

While I was waiting for them, I looked around the office. If I were the Minister, where would I hide potentially incriminating material? I opened cupboard doors at random, poking through files, getting more and more frustrated with myself. I was still desperately casting about the office when Karo arrived.

"Karo, we need to search the building for any clues about what the Minister was up to. Do you think you could get your crew to safeguard the archives? We need to make sure that nobody removes anything."

"Sure thing, Martin. But what about the computer?"

I looked around, and, sure enough, in the corner of the room, on its own little table was a grey steel box, beside that a television sitting on top of a smaller steel box. I pushed the big button on the front, and a red light came on, with a green light flickering alongside it. The green light went out, but nothing seemed to be happening on the television set. I shrugged and looked at Karo, who laughed at me.

"Try turning on the monitor—the button's on the left-hand side, underneath. Just wait a moment, I'll fetch Schimmel."

As Karo went out the door, Laura came in. I explained to her what we needed to find, and asked her to organise a search of the secretary's office next door, as well as the secretariat and archive downstairs.

"Worth a try, since we're here, but it's a bit of a long shot."

I turned back to the computer, which didn't seem to be doing much. Just like me.

Karo came in with another punk, presumably Schimmel. Like all the punks here today he was young, with ragged hair and a ripped leather jacket. He took one look at the computer and gave a shriek.

"Cool, a P8000 compact! I wonder if it's the triple processor? And the operating system—Wega!"

I peered over Schimmel's shoulder at the screen: "WEGA login:" it said.

"What's your minister's name?" Schimmel asked.

"Benno Hartmann."

Schimmel typed in the name Hartmann, then: "His date of birth?"

I opened up the Minister's file, and read out his date of birth, Schimmel typed that in too.

"We're in! Believe it or not, the manual says you should use your date of birth as a password and most people are stupid enough do just that ... Right, we're in. What are you after? OK, so let's have a quick look at what files he has in here," he typed a few letters and looked at a long list of gobbledygook. "Any of these file-names look interesting?" he asked over his shoulder.

I peered at the screen, there must have been hundreds of files listed, and with a few strokes of the keys, Schimmel made another screenful appear. He looked at me, and just as Karo had, laughed at my helplessness. A few more quick taps of the keys, and the printer below the table started screeching, paper turning out of the top. Schimmel reached down, tore off a couple of sheets and handed them over.

"Here, that may be easier to read. Just look through the names there, see if anything sticks out."

He was right, it was easier to look at the print-out than the flickering green letters on the screen. I scanned the names—most looked boring: LetterRT or LetterRT2, Rota-17 and the like. I was about to give up again when I spotted ProjGart—short for *Projekt Garten*? And if ProjGart was the garden, maybe OibE GÄRTNER was the head gardener.

"That one, let's look at that."

I watched him type "file: md(0,1600)ProjGart", then a load of random letters and shapes came up on the screen, and the computer beeped a few times.

"Fuck!" He groaned. "It's been hashed somehow ... like a code. It hides the contents of the file," Schimmel tapped away at the keyboard, then: "OK! I've got the programme that does it, but we still need a password. I've already tried his birth date, it's not that. If we can guess the password then we can read the file—it's that straightforward."

It didn't seem that straightforward to me—what would this password be? It had looked so promising for a moment, but maybe it was a waste of time after all. I slumped into the Minister's chair, putting my feet on his desk.

A knock at the door, and one of the cops came in, "Herr Minister Hartmann has arrived, Comrade Captain. Shall I bring him in?"

I didn't much like the idea of being confronted with the Minister. Even though he'd just been caught trying to leave the country, his word would still count for a lot more than mine; in his position I'd probably try to bluff it out, order my arrest, something like that.

But it was time to face him—I'd given up hope of finding any real evidence to back up my suspicions about the Minister. If I spoke to him, perhaps I could shame him into a confession?

"Who was the woman detained with the Minister?" I asked the policeman.

"Fräulein Hagenow, Comrade Captain."

There was just time for one last throw of the dice.

"Schimmel! The password we're looking for, try: *Evelyn*!"

EPILOGUE
Friday
8th October 1993

Görlitz*: Following days of street protests, the West Silesian government has lost a vote of no confidence in the Region's parliament. The vote followed last week's exposure of an alleged plot by former Stasi officers to destabilise the GDR. The West Silesian Round Table has invited representatives of the Central Round Table in Berlin to negotiate terms for the full reintegration of the Region into the GDR.*

Moscow*: Soviet President Gorbachev continues to consolidate his position after surviving the failed coup attempt last week. Elections for both Soviet Parliaments have been announced, and several ministers in Gorbachev's government have been replaced. The Soviet Ministry of the Interior has announced an investigation into the role of the KGB during the crisis.*

11:32

Erika, Klaus, Laura and I sat in an ante-room in the old Communist Party Central Committee building, waiting to be called to the Central Round Table to account for our actions. Dieter was with us—he'd come back from his annual leave to find he'd missed the show, but he wanted to be with us, and we appreciated the gesture. He wasn't just a reassuring presence, he had helped us sort through the aftermath too. The work hadn't stopped with the arrest of the Minister and Evelyn—we'd spent a lot of time analysing both the file that Schimmel had decrypted and the KGB file Dmitri had given us. Along with other papers from the Minister's office we had more than

186

enough information to dismantle the Stasi taskforce.

The encrypted file had turned out to be a running report, written by the Minister for the leader of the taskforce, GÄRTNER—a comprehensive detailing of all his actions during the West Silesian crisis. It started last year with the Minister encouraging the West Silesian League to campaign for autonomy from Saxony, channelling money from a numbered Swiss bank account into the League's party coffers. The plan was to destabilise the GDR with the threat of West Silesian secession, making it possible to recentralise power structures, just as Dmitri had predicted.

But once the West Germans started pouring their own money and technical support into the breakaway Region, the threat of secession became an all too real possibility. That would have bankrupted the GDR, leading inevitably to a full takeover by West Germany.

Maier had spotted an opportunity to feather his own nest, negotiating a power deal—both for political and electrical power—with the West Germans, hoping that with their protection he could outwit the Stasi taskforce he had been part of.

I felt for Chris Fremdiswalde, it couldn't have been easy for him to carry out his orders, to save the plan by silencing his lover. Maybe that's why he botched it so badly, leaving the body on the tracks rather than disposing of it properly.

Meanwhile, an analysis of Dmitri's file provided more general background detail to the beginnings of the operation. As we'd already worked out, the Minister was TRAKTOR. But BAUM wasn't Evelyn as I'd suspected: it was none other than our own secretary Bärbel, who hadn't been seen since the raid on the Ministry. Bärbel, always sitting quietly in the corner, making notes about absolutely everything, and never really noticed by any of us.

But I hadn't been completely wrong about Evelyn, she'd been at the Ministry all along, keeping tabs on the Minister, and on the *Republikschutz*. Her time in Moscow had been spent preparing her to lead the taskforce—Evelyn turned out to be none other than GÄRTNER.

We hadn't yet worked out who ZIEGE and SPATEN were—whoever they were, they were still out there, but finding them was a job for the cops, not for us.

We'd spent a lot of time wrapping up this case, and we'd had lots of discussions about the state of our Republic. We'd had to confront some of the key issues our society faced: the way attitudes in the police force hadn't changed since the days when they took their orders from the Party, the way Chris could be beaten up and die at the hands of prison warders. His death was more than enough proof for me that there were still connections between the current security apparatus and their ex-colleagues who had been in the Stasi.

It was ironic to think how the same police force and prison service currently had custody of Benno Hartmann and Evelyn Hagenow. I was glad it wasn't for us to decide what was to happen to them—that would be a question for the courts. Nevertheless, we couldn't help but think about what kind of punishment they might deserve: prison or exile seemed the most obvious options, but neither seemed particularly palatable. Exile was the way the old regime dealt with those it considered too troublesome; an exclusion from friends, family and familiar landscapes. Prison represented another kind of exile, an exclusion from life without actually having to take that life. A sadistic punishment wrapped up in the language of protecting the population.

"How are things with Annette?" Erika asked me suddenly.

I could have answered. I could have told her I hadn't seen Annette since that Thursday in Rigaer Strasse. That I'd spoken to her just once, on the phone, and she'd asked me not to contact her, that she would call me when the time was right. I could tell Erika that Katrin had suggested she talk to Annette on my behalf, but I'd been too proud to accept the offer of help. But I said nothing.

Erika had already gone back to staring at the opposite wall, her legs and arms crossed, one foot tapping nervously, her question idle, empty, already forgotten.

I thought of my daughter. I'd seen a lot of her this last week. Somehow events had brought us closer. I think Katrin had been glad to play some small part in what happened, it made her feel she'd finally contributed in some way, made up for leaving the country in 1989. I think Karo and her friends had a similar sense of pride. They'd celebrated last Friday after the Minister and Evelyn had been arrested. I'd bought them a few crates of beer, and they'd partied far into the next morning, proud to be a part of this great social experiment of ours.

My thoughts returned to the present, and I restlessly flicked through my copy of the report we had prepared for the Round Table, arguing that ministerial mandates concentrated too much power in too few hands, and were therefore open to abuse. We suggested that a small and accountable team should take responsibility for co-ordinating the work of each ministry instead of individual ministers. Other chapters of the report observed that there was an acute need to democratise the police force, recommending the presence of civilian observers in any potentially controversial operation, to be decided in each case by a standing sub-committee of the local Round Table.

The problem of violence against prisoners was also addressed, and an independent investigation into Chris Fremdiswalde's death called for. We'd discussed the need for re-education efforts in the police and prison service, but the very phrase, with its Stalinist shadows, made us hesitate to include it in the report.

The document had been signed by every single member of the different branches of the *Republikschutz* and an outline of our suggestions had been published in the newspapers.

But now we had to personally account for what we'd done the previous week. Although the files we'd found at the Minister's office were more than enough to vindicate our actions, we were unsure how we'd be received by the Round Table—by detaining a democratically elected member of the government we had seriously exceeded our authority.

The door opened, and the five of us stiffened, wondering whether we were about to be called in. Instead of an usher, a Russian officer walked in—Dmitri. He smiled broadly, arms outstretched, including us all in his welcome.

"Comrades! The naughty comrades! What a brilliant plan, an instructive subversion of authority! But, my friends, don't look so worried, I think all is well!" He considered my anxious face for a moment, "I have given the Central Round Table of the GDR a full report on the activities of GÄRTNER and her team. I explained her links to the KGB faction that attempted to overthrow President Gorbachev last week and I impressed upon them that without your revolutionary vigilance GÄRTNER, and her crew would have destabilised the GDR to the extent that West Germany would have simply taken over policing responsibilities in the interests of keeping order. Now the West Germans will have to find another excuse to interfere in your country."

"But what are you doing here? How did you get to address the Round Table?" I asked.

"My friend, I thought you could use a little help. After all, you very kindly took the minor problem of the OibE at the Ministry off my hands—and that meant that I had enough capacity to take action against the anti-Gorbachev forces here in Germany. As soon as the coup in Moscow failed I was able to round them up and make sure they didn't do any further harm." Dmitri rubbed his flat belly and grinned.

"There's something else, isn't there?"

"Yes, there is." A theatrical pause, then: "You are now looking at the senior liaison officer between the KGB and the government of the GDR. I have requested that you be my contact here in Berlin." A little bow, "I think, *tovarishch*, that you and I will be working together again. But right now, the Round Table is waiting for you." And with a mock salute, Dmitri marched out of the room.

THOUGHTS ARE FREE
Book 2 of the East Berlin Series

Thoughts Are Free

(German, trad.)

Our thoughts are free,
Who may guess them aright?
They pass fleetingly,
Like shades of the night.
No-one can know them,
No hunter can shoot them
With powder and lead:
Our thoughts are free.

I think what I will,
And what gives me pleasure.
It's all very still,
And all in good measure.
My wishes and longings
Let no one be mocking.
It will always be
That thoughts are free.

And if they locked me
In a dark dungeon,
That would clearly be
A labour in vain;
For my own thoughts, they
Tear down the barriers
And the walls that be:
For thoughts are free.

That's why I forever
Cast off all worries,
And nevermore will
Let whims plague me.
For in our own hearts we
Have laughter and fun.
And thereby we see:
That thoughts are free.

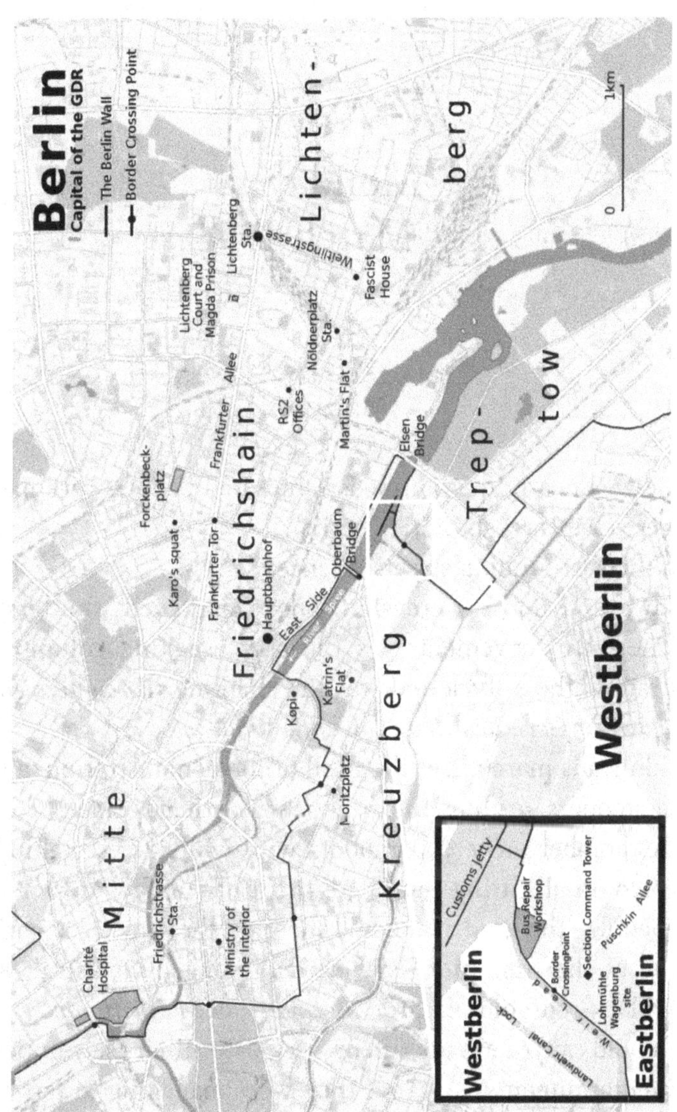

Map of Central Berlin
showing detail of the area around the
Border Crossing Point Puschkin Allee

DAY 1
Monday
14th March 1994

20:11
Martin

The noise was neatly quarantined. A hundred people were marching
—they were chanting, shouting, jeering.

But in the surrounding streets: silence.

Windows and doors were shut. Shops darkened, shutters rolled
down. The only movement was the slow, snaking column of the
demonstrators; the only sound was the chanting: *Foreigners go home!*
German jobs for Germans! Tear down the Wall!

The skinheads marched at the head of the demonstration, a waddle
of goose-steppers leading the pack. Shaven heads, faces contorted
with hate, bomber jackets, paraboots with white laces. Behind them
bullish men in ill-fitting suits. At the back, a few dozen people,
normal people—the kind you could meet on the street, at work or in
the queue at the tram stop—shepherded along by a fistful of skins
carrying black-red-gold placards: *Germany: one Fatherland.*

How could anyone take them seriously—their self-importance,
their stilted arguments? And yet they were managing to tap into the
fears of our time, they were gaining in strength and numbers. Many
people in the GDR were unsettled by current immigration levels—
higher than at any time since the end of the war: Russian Jews fleeing
persecution, Vietnamese and Algerian contract workers stranded by
the shipwreck of the Communist regime, refugees from the Balkan
wars, idealists arriving from other countries, eager to support our

cause. And we needed them all: without their support, the labour shortage would bankrupt the country within days.

And a bankrupt GDR would suit the fascists just fine.

Behind the marchers came half a dozen cops, shields dangling from left hands, helmets clipped to belts.

In the wake of them all came the police lorries. I stood next to the operations commander and his lieutenant on the back of a W50 truck, the tarp pulled back to give us a clear view of the demonstration. A police radio dragged at my shoulder, the earpiece keeping me abreast of the reports being made and the orders being issued.

Concentration anti-fascist repeat anti-fascist demonstrators Jessnerstrasse, crackled the radio. *Concentration Antifa repeat anti-fascist Pettenkoferstrasse.*

"Numbers?" demanded the police lieutenant next to me.

The static stirred, snapping and whistling. We were following the march down Frankfurter Allee and the wide railway bridges over the road ahead of us interfered with radio reception.

"Say again! Say again!" The lieutenant shouted into the microphone, but there was no need. We could see over the heads of the marchers—a black-clad knot of Antifa had run out of a side street on the right. About a dozen of them were wearing motorcycle helmets.

The march in front of us disintegrated. The skins from the back were shoving their way through the ranks of followers who were now casting about themselves, unsure what to do, where to go. A few looked back at the police lines behind, as if seeking advice.

"Squad C into position," sighed the captain behind us. Without hesitation the lieutenant repeated the order into the radio mike, looking over his shoulder to watch the riot cops jump down from their transport.

In front of us a second group of Antifa emerged from a street on the left, running across the central reservation, spearing into the demonstrators, isolating the skins from the other marchers scattered along the roadway. The cops headed towards the skins who were already encircled by punks and squatters.

There was a moment of sudden stillness—the skins stood in the middle of the road, facing outwards in a ragged square, placards ripped off poles to make wooden staves. Around them the anti-fascists, just out of reach. A loose ring of police kettled both groups.

With a shout the action started. The Antifa clumped together and pushed against the skins, who hit back with fists and poles. The police used their truncheons, lashing out without discrimination.

"Disperse them," murmured the captain. He had turned away and was watching the group of fellow travellers being directed by the couple of cops left near the trucks. A few wanted to stay and watch but most seemed relieved, almost happy to be sent home.

"Disperse, disperse!" shouted the lieutenant into the radio microphone, but there was no-one to hear him. The cops in the mêlée didn't have radios. There weren't enough of them and they had no plan. They were pumped up on adrenaline and were reacting only to what was happening around them.

It was a mess.

22:14

Martin

I was in the canteen when the sergeant came to get me. Sitting at a table, all by myself, leaning against the wall and ignoring the cup of coffee and the slice of poppy-seed cake before me. The other tables had been pushed together and cops sat around them, slapping each other on the back and drinking beer.

"Shoulda left them to fight it out! All as bad as each other," laughed one. "But did you see the fascists' faces when the Antifa stormed across the road?"

This country was going through so many changes, yet I still found it hard to work alongside those who had once been against us. Before 1989 the police had played their part, standing shoulder to shoulder with the Party and the Stasi, repressing social and political dissent. But now the Party was no longer in power and an uneasy dance of reconciliation had begun, a wooing between the police and the politicised population. Somehow I'd been caught up in the machinery, assisting the Central Round Table but assigned to the Ministry of the Interior, often working together with cops.

"Comrade Captain Grobe?" A sergeant stood in front of my table, saluting. "We thought you might be interested in something. A detainee we're interviewing. The duty officer suggested you come to see for yourself."

He led me up the stairs and down a long corridor of brown polished lino, institutional green walls broken by heavy, padded doors. He stopped at one of these and pressed the bell set to one side.

While we waited I looked through a grimy window, down to the courtyard. A row of trucks were parked up, in front of them stood a dozen or so green and white liveried police patrol cars. There were no signs of life down there, just concrete, becalmed vehicles and the blank windows opposite. Last time I was here—just a few months ago —the yard had been boiling with movement and exhaust fumes as a squad assembled in preparation for a raid on a squat. It hadn't been a pleasant experience for me, even less so for those who were inside when the doors were kicked in.

Behind me I heard a door open, and I followed the sergeant into the interview room.

A uniformed police lieutenant was sitting behind a large desk— empty except for a phone and intercom device, and a buff file lying in front of him. The lieutenant held a pen, which he laid down on the thick file as he looked up to see who had entered. In front of his desk a table was set end-on, a couple of chairs to either side.

At a nod from the lieutenant we moved into the room. He didn't say anything, and I kept my silence too. It wasn't until I turned to shut the door that I saw the detainee, sitting on a low stool behind the door; his hands pressed on his thighs, his knees drawn up tight to make room for the door that was pushed against his legs. I quickly looked away, but not before taking in the stone-washed jeans, the white t-shirt showing arms sheathed in dark tattoos and the heavily greased short-back-and-sides haircut.

The sergeant went to the lieutenant, leaning over his desk to whisper something. A curt nod from the officer, then he left, opening the door carelessly so that it rebounded off the prisoner's knees. I sat down at the table, and the lieutenant slid a file over to me.

Flicking through it, I could see the first page was a custody record, presumably for whoever was sitting behind the door. After that were a handful of unused statement forms, followed by a few dozen blank pieces of paper. I looked at a virgin, ash-grey sheet, my eyes tracing the splinters of wood in the fibrous paper, then I thumbed back to the custody record, checking the personal data: Andreas Hermann, born Leipzig 1976, detained at the demonstration this evening. An initial charge of rowdy behaviour under paragraph 215 section 1 of the criminal code was being investigated and prepared. I tried to meet the police lieutenant's eye but he was staring at the man on the stool.

"Where were you today at 1600 hours?" he snapped.

The detainee flinched slightly, I wouldn't have noticed if he didn't still have his knees pulled up so tight. The slight jerk of the man's head travelled down his torso and limbs, making his feet tremble. But he gave no answer, continuing to stare at a point somewhere above the lieutenant's shoulder.

"When was the last time you went to Alexanderplatz?"

Again silence, the same stare over the lieutenant's shoulder.

It was a familiar set up. The sterile interview room, the implicit offer of the comfort that a simple chair with a back could provide: a seat at the table versus the reality of the hard stool. The discomfort, the prohibition against leaning against the wall, the indignity of sitting behind the door. Or alternatively the interviewee might be placed in the middle of the room, back to the door, unable to see who was coming in, whether they were bearing a message, choke cuffs or a cosh.

"Do you go to the Alex often? Meet your friends there? Or do you prefer to hang out in Lichtenberg?"

Silence.

How often had I sat in rooms like this? The endless questions, sometimes in relay, one interviewer replacing the next, only the detainee remaining the same, required to answer the same questions, again and again, hour after hour, day after day.

"But you don't live in Berlin-Lichtenberg."

The lack of sleep was worse than the arbitrary beatings. The lack of sleep played with your mind. You no longer knew what time of day it was, whether it was even day or night. You lost track of what you'd said or not said, what you'd meant to say or not say.

"Spend a lot of time there, do you?"

The lack of sleep made you paranoid, unable to trust yourself. It didn't take long, only a couple of days before exhaustion broke you.

"So you stay at a friend's?"

But they couldn't be using those tactics any more? These new times must have put an end to torture?

"Because it's true, isn't it, that you spend quite a bit of time in that part of town?"

I looked at the custody record again, as if it could show me what interrogation methods were planned for this Andreas Hermann.

"How much time do you spend at the premises Weitlingstrasse 122?"

This time there was a reaction. The detainee moved his head, away from the spot above the interviewer's shoulder, slowly sweeping across desk and table, until he was facing me, his hard eyes challenging me.

"Think you're clever, don't you? But we have him," he said, in a slack Berlin drawl, his words whistling through the gap left by missing front teeth. "We know who he is, your *Zecke*, your little informant. And you know what? We know who you are too. You'll be next. No worries, you'll be next." His head tracked back to its original position, facing the wall, above the lieutenant.

I continued watching the detainee, but out of the corner of my eye I could see that the lieutenant hadn't reacted at all.

"How long have you been registered as living at your mother's address?" the policeman asked.

Silence.

Day 2
Tuesday
15th March 1994

At 7 o'clock on Tuesday the 15th of March here are the news headlines from Radio DDR I. Good morning.

Berlin: *The Information Office for Jewish Immigration from the Soviet Union has announced that there will be a further two thousand arrivals in Berlin this week. Temporary accommodation for the newcomers will be made available in the capital and in the Brandenburg Region, including the towns of Potsdam, Oranienburg and Bernau.*

08:32
Martin

Predictably, the morning meeting at the RS2 office was dominated by news that the police were running an IKM. We were part of the investigation into fascist activities in Berlin but the officers of Department K1 at the local *Kripo* hadn't bothered to let us know that they had a mole in the fascist scene. I'd managed to get hold of Laura on the phone last night, while I was still at Marchlewskistrasse police station and she'd immediately swung into action, making an official request for access to the relevant files. If we were going to do our job then we needed to know what was going on. And we wanted to know why we'd been left out of the loop.

"We have to step up the investigation. Your news just confirms that," Erika said. "Nik from RS1 has been helping out but we're still struggling."

I considered my own workload for a moment. I had nothing

particularly urgent on my desk—I'd been working on the information pack for the three referenda coming up next month, but I'd already passed it back upstairs to the Ministry for them to have a look at. It would take the bureaucrats a while to respond. The other biggish case I was dealing with was a historical investigation into a Nazi attack on a punk concert back in 1987, and I was making hardly any progress on that anyway. I agreed to help out with the investigation into current neo-Nazi activities.

I went to another office with Erika and Laura to discuss the case. They'd started working on it last autumn, but had been much hampered by the fact that we had neither a clear remit nor a direct mandate for our work at the *Republikschutz*. We had been set up by the Central Round Table back in 1990, but after the experiences with the Stasi over the last forty years there was no appetite for a formal counter-intelligence service. So they'd given us some offices and a budget and told us to support the Round Tables on any matters of 'national security' that might crop up. Staff had been chosen from the ranks of pre-1989 dissidents—the idea was that since we'd been on the receiving end of the secret police's attention we'd be wary of developing any Stasi-style structures or tactics. Since then the *Republikschutz* had grown, making up three teams: RS1 and RS2 were based here in Berlin and RS3 was in the south of the Republic.

"We haven't got very far over the last few months," Laura admitted. "It's mostly been about mapping structures, tracing activities."

This surprised me, Laura was good at making things happen—she brought organisation and efficiency wherever she went—which had earned her the reputation of being severe. But she wasn't severe, just straightforward and focussed.

Laura pushed a couple of stacks of folders over the desk towards me, each a good thirty centimetres thick.

"What about their connections with the West?" I asked.

"Nothing useful since that first break last September when we got those photos," Erika said. "You know, the ones I showed you—they'll be in that pile somewhere."

Of all my colleagues I was probably the closest to Erika. We understood each other well, often asking one another for an opinion, and last autumn she'd shown me photos taken inside the house in

Weitlingstrasse, right here in Berlin-Lichtenberg. The house had been first squatted then rented by fascists, and the photos showed wide men wearing wide suits, and of piles and piles of propaganda material. We'd immediately suspected a political-ideological diversion directed by the West—not only did some of the men's suits look Western, but in our broken economy it would have been practically impossible to get the materials to make and print that many placards, banners, leaflets, posters and bumper stickers. It was hard not to jump to the conclusion that it had all been smuggled in from the West.

"So if you haven't had any decent leads, what's all this?" I asked, gesturing at the mountain of paperwork.

Laura frowned, but it was Erika who answered.

"The police have been sending us the carbons of any crime reports with a suspected far-right element. Basically we're spending all our time looking at the reports and sending summaries to all the police forces here in the capital and the regions."

"Martin," broke in Laura, keen to get to the point. "We believe—that is, the police believe that the fascists are going to mount some kind of offensive in the run up to the referendum on the Wall. That's why we feel we need to be more proactive."

The fascists were intent on bringing about a union between the two German states. There was no clear or logical reasoning behind this desire, just antagonism towards the progressive society we were building in the GDR, and a raw, Teutonic patriotism. They felt that getting rid of the Wall would be a significant step towards a union with West Germany, and they'd be right. The Wall was a hugely emotive issue, it had caused so much pain for so long that it had been necessary to wait for a few years before opening that debate across the nation: in the media, in workplaces and neighbourhoods. Months of dialogue had followed, just to frame the question that would be asked in the referendum. And now the rising tide of nationalism might sweep away all those patient efforts in just a few weeks.

"So where do we start?"

"I'm going to go through all these reports again, see if anything stands out or whether it's all just random violence," said Laura in a businesslike manner. "Erika's going to talk to an academic at the

Humboldt University about social factors behind the rise in far-right activity."

"The other thing we need to check on is whether any more demonstrations have been registered by far-right organisations," Erika chipped in. "You were there last night, and they've already announced another for Sunday. We need to see what they have planned in other places—try to work out whether there's a pattern to the public appearances. It's not just the demonstrations and violent crime reports we're interested in—we think we should be looking at leafleting, information stalls and other public appearances. It might give us an indication of which areas they'll be concentrating on in the lead up to the referenda."

10:57

Martin

I took one of the piles of files back to my office, but before I made a start I had a few loose ends to tie up.

Top of my list was to interview an ex-cop. In 1987 he'd been posted outside the church building when 30 Nazis gatecrashed a concert. He and his colleagues hadn't lifted a finger to help the punks being beaten up inside. I'd been given the task of going over the paperwork again, seeing if I could find evidence to support rumours that the *Volkspolizei* and the Stasi had had a hand in events that night. I hadn't found anything useful in the Stasi archives, and I'd been stonewalled by all the cops I'd interviewed so far.

It had taken me a while to track down this particular cop because he was no longer a police officer, but was now in the Border Police Service. He was on duty this morning, and I knew where to find him.

I left the office and got on my bike, cycling over the river to Treptow, then turning onto Puschkin Allee. When I reached the border crossing point there was a short queue. A border guard and his sergeant were watching customs officers open up suitcases and the bulky bags of a small group of pensioners heading West. Even though I kept my distance and couldn't really hear what was being said I could see that the officials were being polite and patient, the civilians in turn weren't cowed by the presence of officialdom. They even seemed to be poking fun at the men on duty—the pensioners burst out laughing, while the official checking luggage blushed and carefully closed a suitcase. It was in such minor exchanges that the major changes in our country could be seen. Just four years ago such a scene would have been unimaginable. In those days border crossings were a place of fear and paranoia, subject to continuous surveillance and the arbitrariness of soldiers and state officials. In those days the Wall had been an invisible fact of life, too dreadful to contemplate or acknowledge.

But after we took to the streets in 1989, after we deposed the Communist Party everything had changed.

Finally, the pensioners moved through the gap in the Wall and I showed the border guard my RS identity card before asking where I could find Corporal Giesler.

The guard saluted and directed me to the Section Command Tower, a hundred metres off to one side. Before I could take back my pass the sergeant stepped forward.

"You're the guy who arrested the Minister last year?" he asked, taking my ID off the guard and opening it to check the name there.

I nodded, waiting for him to continue. We stood looking at each other for a long moment.

"I just wanted to say, I admire you, I mean ...." the sergeant stuttered, paused, then carried on: "I mean, what you did. Last year." He held out his hand for me to shake.

The sergeant's enthusiasm surprised me. My relations with the security forces had been less than cordial since the events of last autumn. I nodded again, pasting a smile onto my face, and took my pass back, embarrassed, unsure how to react. But the sergeant still had hold of my hand. I looked at him again. He was young. Acne still scarred his reddened face. Looking uncertain in his oversized uniform he was as at least as flustered as I was. More so.

"Thanks." I pulled my hand from his grasp and started along the cement pathway towards the watchtower. My admirer kept pace with me, not saying anything, but still watching me.

"How are things here?" I asked finally, filling the silence.

We'd come to a stop where the cement slabs of the border crossing met the cobbles of the road. The outer, West-facing wall was behind us now, built along the bank of the weir channel while the line of the *Hinterlandmauer*—the Eastern edge of the death-strip—was still a few metres in front of us. That East-facing wall was no longer there, the death-strip now was alive with colourful wagons and trucks.

The sergeant followed my gaze. "Well, they can be a nuisance."

We looked over to the jigsaw puzzle of wooden and aluminium-sheet wagons, the kind that were usually to be found on building sites to provide workers with a place to have a cup of coffee or shelter from the rain. They'd been fitted out with wood-burners, kitchens and beds and dragged here by trucks and tractors. Stacks of cut wood were left over from winter, lines of washing, empty beer bottles and toys surrounded raised beds of soil, young leafy salad plants and brassicas peeping out. This was a *Wagenburg*, an alternative community, an alternative way of living.

"They jump over the Wall," the lad in uniform said. "Every time we take a ladder away they put up a new one. They don't want to show us their identity cards. I don't understand it—once they climb over the Wall they can't get any further unless they want to get wet." He chuckled and gestured at the deep water on the other side of the Wall. "So they come along the bank to cross the bridge—they pass within a couple of metres of us—and then they have to show their papers at the West Berlin checkpoint anyway. It doesn't make any sense."

I nodded in sympathy. The Wall no longer had any power to imprison us—people felt free to live next to it, to talk about it, to joke about it. Even climb over it. The Wall had always been an economic necessity, but a controversial one. Now it was mutating from a buttress for an illegitimate government to a thin line of protection from the greed of capitalists, a modern day customs barrier. Without the Wall the West Berliners and the West Germans would be over here, buying up our food and consumer goods. Our currency was weak, sold on the black market for as much as ten Eastmarks to one Westmark: our struggling economy couldn't withstand the purchasing power of Westerners buying up our scant stocks. We'd already experienced that, back in November and December of 1989 when the Wall first opened—food shortages throughout East Berlin and along the inner-German border were the result. So we kept the

Wall, and we kept the customs checks on the crossing points.

"You know these people, don't you? They understand you. Can you talk to them?" he asked me.

It was an unusual request. A bold one, but one that suited the times. Instead of submitting an official request for 'administrative co-operation' that would be lost, found again, delayed then queried as it passed through the bureaucratic channels, he had simply asked me, person to person, citizen to citizen.

I shook my head: "I don't know these ones, no."

"But you know some other ..." he looked again towards the *Wagenburg*, "people like this, don't you? You worked with them on that case last year? I read about it in the papers, you were on television, on the news." He wasn't going to let me go that easily.

"I'm here to speak to Corporal Giesler," I said, changing the subject.

The sergeant misinterpreted my unease and stiffened. "*Jawohl*, comrade Captain. Comrade Corporal Giesler is on comms duty. I shall take you to him now."

He turned again, ready to march off to the watchtower, but I put a hand on his arm to stop him.

"What's your name?"

The sergeant half-turned, unsure whether to stand to attention or not. "Staff Sergeant Müller, comrade Captain."

I held out my hand and offered a smile. "How about we drop the formalities? I'm Martin."

Müller relaxed again, he shook my hand. "Rico," he said as his acne burned.

Rico took me up to the observation level of the watchtower. Giesler had stood to attention as soon as we appeared through the hatch at the top of the ladder.

"Nothing to report, comrade Staff Sergeant," he announced when his superior had fully emerged.

"At ease, comrade Corporal. The comrade Captain from RS wishes to speak to you." With a nod to me Rico descended the ladder again.

Giesler continued to stand behind his desk adorned with telephones, radio sets and banks of dead lights. I looked him over, trying to work out the best way to approach him. He was older than me, still muscular, but his skin was grey and saggy. Pale grey eyes glared at me from beneath fine grey eyebrows and a widow's peak. I wondered what had made him change his *Volkspolizei* uniform for that of the Border Police; whether the move had anything to do with the incident I was investigating.

I decided to try the friendly approach.

"As you were, comrade Corporal. I shan't take much of your time. I'm just clearing up some paperwork from the old days, and I wanted to check whether you had anything useful to add."

Giesler sat down again, his eyes never leaving me.

I went to the window and looked down at the wagons and the punks below, and started to speak without turning around. "It's to do with an incident in Prenzlauer Berg on the 17th of October 1987." Although Giesler was behind me I could see his silhouette reflected in the window before me, but there was no shift, no start of recognition.

"Does that date mean anything to you?" I turned around to face him again. "It was the night a church building was attacked by rowdy elements. You were there that night, observing comings and goings. I just need a few details clearing up."

"I'm sure I don't remember, comrade Captain. I can only suggest you look at the report I filed at the time." Giesler was now eyeing the phones—perhaps hoping that one would ring—but beyond that he showed no nervousness.

"It's just a minor detail." I sat down on a chair next to the desk, leaning forward, elbows resting on my thighs. "Did you have orders not to intervene when the fascists attacked the concert-goers?" I asked in a low voice, staring intently at Giesler.

He gazed blankly back at me, waiting a few moments before answering. "I've already said, comrade Captain, that I have no clear recollection of the incident."

I stood up and took hold of the pulley that held open the steel hatch at the top of the ladder, paying out the rope and letting the steel door bang down. There wasn't much space in the watchtower so I was still less than a couple of metres away from Giesler.

"Comrade Corporal—it's just you and me now. Nobody can hear-"

But Giesler had also got up. With just two strides he was out from behind his desk, and standing directly in front of me, the buttons of his uniform blouson grazing my chest.

"With respect, *Captain*," he snarled, "you'd do well to forget about 1987." He edged closer, trying to push me back. "For some of us the old times are still here."

12:13
Karo

"Hi Katrin, it's me."

The buzzer let me in and I went up the tenement stairs. Katrin's door was ajar when I got there.

"Karo!" she gave me a hug and dragged me into the kitchen. She flipped a switch on the coffee percolator and we sat down and started chatting.

"I've not seen you for ages! How's it all going?"

"Full on! Totally full on! You wouldn't believe what I've been up to!" But I stopped because I could tell something was bothering Katrin. "What's up?"

It was about the volunteering she was doing at the AL offices (I tried not to sneer about the fact that Katrin was volunteering at the West Berlin version of the Green party—maybe I did, a little, but she didn't notice so it was OK). Seems that Annette, Martin's ex, is really worried about the far-right *Republikaner* party.

"Annette was telling me that the AL members with seats on the Senate are worried that they'll lose them to the Reps. And if the same happens to the FDP then it looks like other parties could go into coalition with the right-wingers."

"Yeah, we've got the *Volkskammer* elections coming up in the autumn—it's looking like the fash are going to get quite a few votes." It made me really angry to think about this stuff and I got up and started pacing around the kitchen.

"Is Papa involved in any of this? Is he involved in dealing with the far-right?" Katrin was watching me move around her kitchen, even I could see she was worried. I stopped poking around her tea jars and went back to the table.

I had to think for a bit, but I didn't really know what Martin was up to. I shook my head.

"It's just that, I dunno. He's been a bit preoccupied lately. I was wondering whether he was involved in some case, you know, as part of his job. About the Nazis, I mean."

"Dunno. Haven't seen him for a while. But he's alright, isn't he?" I thought about it for a bit. "Martin's always alright."

Katrin just shrugged.

"Look, I tell you what—I'll keep an eye on him and let you know what's going on. I'll go and see him tomorrow, get him to come to a gig with me. A bit of a bop will sort him out!"

I thought it was a great idea but Katrin didn't look so sure.

12:22

Martin

I cycled back to the office, thinking about Giesler. I couldn't work out whether he was frightened or trying to frighten me. Either way, it was clear that I wasn't going to get any information out of him.

I decided not to bother with a full report on the interview, I'd just include him in the list of cops who wouldn't talk to me. That would save some time. In any case I had already decided to try to interview the other side—see if the punks who were at the concert had anything new to say. I'd read the police reports and the samizdat publications of the time, but it seemed possible that the punks would feel more able to speak openly now.

When I walked into the RS2 offices our secretary, Grit, was waiting for me with a telex print.

"Can you sign this?"

I read the message, it had already been initialled by Laura and Erika. It was from the Ministry—we were being told to back off Lichtenberg *Kripo*, stop asking for information about the mole they had in the fascist scene. I went over to Laura's office.

"Do you know what this is about?"

Laura sat back in her chair, a report dangling from one hand, her glasses perched on top of her head. "You've read it haven't you? Well, you know as much as I do."

"But why would they tell us to back off?"

"Martin, why do you have to make everything complicated?

What's it matter, anyway? They probably just need a few days to sort things out—that's going to claim all their attention and they don't want us breathing down their necks. They'll have their reasons."

I signed the chit and gave it back to Grit.

Once back in my office I spent a few minutes trying to find my *To Do* list. It turned up under my chair, sandwiched between sheets of expenses claims that I should have filed back in January. I leafed through my notes, trying to decipher the scratched out and annotated lists. Karo's name was there—*ask if Karo knows anyone who was at concert in 1987*. But since the Nazi demo last night I was beginning to think I should prioritise current Nazi activities, and not those of six and a half years ago.

Looking further down the list I realised that Dmitri was overdue a call. He was an officer in the FSK—the agency that had taken over from the KGB since the coup against Gorbachev—and he was the main liaison between the FSK's Berlin office and the Central Round Table. I was the other side of that equation, representing the GDR's interests. There was rarely much content to our meetings—most of the administrative complexities of hosting the Group of Russian Forces in Germany were handled by other offices at various levels of the government. Dmitri and I represented a high-level and trusted connection, just in case we ever needed it.

I dialled the number for Dmitri's office. The phone lines to the Russian Forces' quarters in Karlshorst were always very crackly, echoes and ghosting voices lingering in the background, as if the listeners had never gone away.

"*Da?*"

"Dmitri Alexandrovich, it's Martin here."

"Martin Ottovich! Always a pleasure to hear from you, my friend! Is it time for us to sup vodka again? So long, such a long time since we last had a chat."

Dmitri sounded a little preoccupied; his voice was warm and friendly but his mind was clearly on other matters. I didn't ask, the old caution was still with me: don't speak too freely on the phone, and watch what you say to the Russians. I trusted Dmitri, he was a good person and a friendship had grown between us, but I didn't trust his outfit, neither the FSK nor any of the other remnants of the occupying army.

"When shall we meet, Martin? No, wait, I will look at my calendar."

I could hear shuffling noises and muttering down the receiver, as if Dmitri was having to shift heavy piles of paper around on his desk to discover his diary. Finally, he picked up the receiver again.

"You know, I am glad you call, there is much to talk about ... But here, I have my calendar. Next week? Is next week good for you Herr Martin Ottovich?"

We agreed to meet a week on Wednesday at his office.

"Martin, we have much to talk about," Dmitri was repeating himself, which was unusual for him. "I shall tell you all next week, but until then be careful, my friend."

DAY 3
Wednesday
16th March 1994

Jüterbog: There has been a further arson attack on accommodation used by Jews fleeing persecution in Russia. Last night a firework was thrown through a window of the asylum-seekers hostel in Jüterbog. A woman and two children were taken to hospital after inhaling smoke. According to the Round Table Committee on Extremist Affairs this is the sixth such attack this year.

09:12
Martin

I finished typing up a report on my lack of progress in the 1987 case and filed away my copy. I took the original and the second carbon into the front office to give to Grit for filing and forwarding to the Ministry of the Interior.

Returning to my desk I started looking through the files on the fascists that Laura had insisted I look at. But my mind kept sliding off and returning to what the young sergeant had asked me to do. Rico, he'd said his name was: Rico Müller. It didn't feel like there was much I could do about his problem, and anyway, it wasn't my responsibility to do anything about it.

But still, I felt some kind of affinity with the border guard. He was engaged enough to try to come up with alternative solutions, to ask me if I could help. Horizontal links—precisely the kind of thing we needed to encourage if we didn't want our revolution to run out of steam, if we didn't want a new elite to appear, organising our society for us, telling us what to do and how to think.

The obvious option would be simply to have a chat with the people in the wagons and trucks. Had Rico already done that? I hadn't thought to ask him. But the punks on the site and Rico were worlds apart—I didn't doubt that both the border guard and the wagoneers had the best interests of our Republic at heart but they would have different ideas of how our nascent utopia should be nursed. Rico saw the world through a filter of orderliness, predictability, clarity. The punks had a more chaotic, spontaneous vision of how society should function.

I had sympathy with both philosophies of life, but right now I had enough on my plate. Like these files detailing recent fascist activities in the capital. It was vicious stuff and it made for depressing reading. Apparently random violence was being meted out by the skins—foreigners and punks were the main targets, but muggings and assaults on pensioners had also increased in areas seeing fascist activity. After a while I stopped reading the detailed case files, concentrating instead on gaining an overview from the situation reports and the tabulated statistics. That didn't make for easy reading either, and I was glad of the distraction when Grit came in.

"The State Prosecutor's office rang, they want to meet up tomorrow," she said as she handed the memo over.

I scanned the chit. Henschel, the prosecutor in charge of the case against Evelyn. What did he want to speak to me about? As far as I was concerned I was finished with that case, I'd played my part and put her behind bars.

17:37

Karo

I'd had a bitch of a day, but it looked like Martin was having an even worse time. He was reading some report but kept turning back to the circulation list clipped to the front. He looked like he wanted to stab his eyes out with his pencil.

"So this is the headquarters of the mysterious *Republikschutz*," I said, kicking a screwed up memo out of the way. "Aren't you going to offer me a coffee, Mr. Bond?"

Martin put his report on top of a million other identical files on his desk. I tried to work out what it was, but all I could see was a pink stripe across the front and VVS stamped in one corner.

"Only joking!" I said hastily when Martin got up and started lumbering over to the kettle. "Don't worry about the coffee, I just came to say hi."

He sat down again, looking at me. So far he hadn't said anything.

"Aren't you pleased to see me?" Maybe Katrin was right, maybe the big man was under the weather.

He grinned at that and I grinned too, just to encourage him a bit. We did that until the smiles wore loose.

"What are you up to these days?" He managed to squeeze a question out.

"Well—you'd be dead proud of me! I'm training to be a Neighbourhood Facilitator. I really like the idea of it, but the course is just dragging on and on and on," I rolled my eyes to show him just how fucking boring it all was.

He grinned again at that, but I could tell he didn't have a clue what I was on about, so I told him about the programme.

"It's like, now we've got all this freedom—we can say what we want and virtually do what we want—well, that means there's more scope for conflict. People are falling out left right and centre, I dunno, about politics, about what colour they're gonna paint their houses, about solidarity work, noisy neighbours," (I made sure to do rabbit ears around *noisy* because I knew it would wind Martin up). "A million things. You know the score."

Martin did know the score, I could see him thinking about it. I always know when he's thinking about the old days because he looks like he's got some brain-disease and I can tell exactly what he's thinking: cops and the Party. Right then he was probably yearning for the days when you couldn't fart without getting written permission in triplicate.

"So, we're setting up a neighbourhood facilitation team. It's a step before the official arbitration process. We help people resolve their arguments, to talk to each other and understand each other's points of view. And we mediate if that's what's needed."

Martin still hadn't said anything, well, not really. I reckoned Katrin was right about her dad. I leaned over Martin's desk, trying to avoid the paper stacked everywhere.

"Listen Martin: you, me—we're going out tonight. We're going to have a laugh. You need brightening up—you look like a squad of soldiers on a wet May Day parade."

18:16
Karo

They were giving Martin the cold shoulder, and I felt guilty about that because I was the one who'd brought him here. We'd done a deal: I take him to the see the local Antifa group, and he comes to the gig afterwards.

"... so he's trying to find out a bit more," I was saying to the lads around the table. "Because they're getting bolder, getting out more, and the demo the other night-"

Bert had been watching Martin the whole time, really staring at him. And now he interrupted me.

"And why the sudden interest in the Nazis? Bit late in the day isn't it? We've been dealing with the shites for years. Now the State's suddenly taking an interest so we're just meant to let them take over?"

"You're right-" Martin tried to answer but Bert cut him off again.

"I know I'm right, but what I don't know," he leaned towards Martin, getting him to lean in too, "is why you're still here!"

"Bert, back off. This is Martin. He's sorted, really." I put my hand on Bert's arm. He was being a macho arse as usual. "Just hear him out, yeah?"

Bert stared at Martin a bit longer, just to get the message across then nodded and leaned back.

"Look, I know the score," Martin said. He was looking around the group now, trying to work out who to talk to. It was obvious he didn't like Bert, and I didn't blame him. But Bert has his uses.

"This is a problem we've been ignoring for far too long. And you're right, you're practically the only ones who have been dealing with it." Martin had gone into making-a-speech mode, but fair play—the Antifa group were giving him a chance. "Now the police have become

215

involved—I know, I know." Martin held his hands up, as if he could ward off the sarcastic laughter. "I'm sceptical too. Look—all my cards on the table—I'm with the *Republikschutz* and if I'm completely honest with you I don't know whether we can trust the cops to do the job right. They should have done it ten years ago and they didn't, but this time round they've got us breathing down their necks."

No-one had told Martin to fuck off yet, so he was doing well.

"The cops reckon the fascists are gearing up to something big, not just the usual casual violence on the streets or at football matches. They've got a plan. And that's why we're involved-"

"Hang on a minute!" Bert was back in the game and was stabbing a hole in the table with his finger to make sure we all knew he was making a point. "Why should we trust you? You say you're from RS, but that's not a democratic organisation! Nobody's ever asked me if I think it's a good idea to have the RS! You know what? I've got better things to do than have chats with someone in a slouch hat and trench-coat." He sat back and crossed his arms.

"I'm not going to piss you around." Martin wasn't ready to give up yet. "I agree, RS isn't democratic. I could say all the usual stuff, that we answer to parliament and to the Round Tables but if you ask me what I think—I'll tell you it's just not enough. Right now, though, it's what we've got. And right now, I need a drink."

Martin left us and pushed his way through to the bar. I had to admire him—that was a pretty cool move. It gave the Antifa a chance to think about what he'd said.

"Can we trust him?" one of them asked eventually.

"Look, Martin's a windbag, but you know what, he's fucking cool. He's genuine, you know, we're all on the same side. You gotta give him a chance."

The lads all looked at each other and did whatever it is they do when they're making a decision, and I caught Martin's eye. He was at the bar, necking a bottle of pilsner. When he came back nobody said anything. They all just looked at him, like it was up to him to make the first move.

"Can I sit down?" he asked.

Nobody answered so Martin just plonked his bottle of beer on the table and sat down.

"Any questions?"

"Yeah." Bert was the first in the queue. "What do you want from us?"

"I need to know how the fash operate. The cops don't do that kind of thing—they see a criminal offence and detain the suspect, they think that's all they need to do. But now even they've twigged that something bigger is happening. I reckon you're the only ones who really understand how the fascists are operating."

"And what's in it for us?" Rex demanded. I like Rex, he's the most human of them all—like he's not just in it to have a fight with the fash. Thinking about it he'd probably be really useless in a fight, he's dead skinny. No muscle.

"Nothing. There's nothing in it for you," Martin answered. They didn't like that, but I had to smile a bit, I could see where Martin was going with this. "Because I reckon you're like me. I reckon you're not doing it for yourselves, but for all of us, for the whole of society. We need to deal with these fascists, and you're the ones who've been doing that for, what? Six, seven years? If we work together maybe we can make more headway."

That was it, I knew I could relax. Martin had won. He knew it too, and took the initiative.

"How about we start over? I'm Martin, I work with the RS, and right now, I'm really worried about the fascists here in our country, specifically in Lichtenberg. I'm hoping you can help me out. I'm hoping you can give me some background information about them— how they're organised, who's in charge, what they're up to?"

"Rex. Just like the beer." Rex offered Martin his hand to shake. He always had to make a joke of it, and yep, he was holding a bottle of Rex beer from Potsdam, the one with the lanky fusilier on the label. "Who you asking about? The skins? Yeah, well, it's not actually them you need to be worrying about. It's the fascist organisations behind them. The skins are just being used by the suits, they're just the boot boys, out for a laugh and a ruck." He took a swig of beer and put it down, dead prissy, dead centre on the beer mat.

"The skins weren't well organised when they started off, not here in Berlin. They just got together for drinking and fighting. *Lichtenberg Front*, then there was the *Movement of the 30th of January*, after that *National Alternative*—that's where it all started in this town. And somewhere along the way they got organised. We don't know when, we didn't work it out until after the cops stormed their squat back in April 1990. It might have been the *Reps* who got them organised—we know there's a group of 800 of them in Marzahn and another 300 members in Lichtenberg. Maybe that's how they made links with the West, through the *Reps*."

The *Reps*: the *Republikaner* party, they were the ones that Katrin was telling me about just yesterday. Martin told me once about how he reckoned they'd been doing counter-revolutionary stuff back in late 1989 and 1990. Now Rex was saying there's over a thousand members here in East Berlin!

"So, there's the skins," Martin checked in. "And in the background there are party members, some from the West, and they've more or less got control of the skinhead scene?"

"Yeah, except it's not that clear cut. Not all skins are fashos, some are just nationalist, some are even red-skins. And a few skins want more than just a scrap, they're into political stuff in a big way. And then you've got the hools, having a ruck after football matches."

"So if we want to stop this cancer we have to get to the party organisation?"

"Yeah," said Rex. "We've tried to find out more, but we've got our hands full, y'know dealing with the skins and the hooligans. It's the same story everywhere: Leipzig, Rostock, Dresden, Jena .... We can't do everything!"

Martin had a think about that while Rex took a swig of beer.

"If we manage to find a way in to the party organisation, if we find anything out, would you be prepared to help?"

"Depends on what you need, Martin. Depends on what you need."

22:47

Martin

Pulsing lights, endless noise.

Drums. Somewhere, hiding behind the pounding beat, was a tune, a melody struggling to escape. A voice, screaming into a microphone and out of the loudspeakers. Harsh, hoarse, no idea what the words were. I struggled through the crowds, brusquely pushing people out of the way. Nobody minded. I was just one of the pogo-ing hordes.

Finally reaching the exit, through the doors, standing on the veranda, looking out into the shadowy gardens of the club. I took a deep breath of fresh night-time air, then, feeling the need for a cigarette I bummed one off a punk slouched by the door. I stared at the packet as he flipped the top open for me: grey and white chequer pattern, below that the stark red typeface, spelling out the name of the brand, *Karo*. The punk grinned at me, revealing yellow and black teeth, and pushed a box of matches into my chest. A knot of party-goers pushed past me to get through the door and I held my cigarette over my head, out of harm's way. One of the new arrivals saw me: Schimmel. Despite his ridiculous punk-name he was a nice guy: he had that unwieldy skinniness that often came with youth, and he was quiet, gentle. The kind of person you could easily overlook. Some kind of computer geek, he was one of the many punks who'd helped me out last autumn.

Before we could greet each other he was being pushed aside. Another punk appeared, raising her hands in the air as she moved round Schimmel and shouted my name. I put the cigarette back between my lips as she came close to give me a big hug. Her arms squeezed my rib cage, making me choke up smoke and nearly lose the cigarette. She stepped back, keeping hold of both my hands as she looked me up and down. A lazy red coloured mohican flopped over one side of her face: Karo.

"Martin! You're still here!" she asked. Not waiting for an answer she ploughed on. "Have you heard the band yet? Ab-So-Fucking-Lutely Amazing!" she said it just like that, audibly capitalising random syllables. "Oh God! I can't believe you actually came to see *Feeling B*—that is just so cool—I thought you'd probably bunk off!"

As soon as she let go of my hands I took the cigarette out of my mouth. The smoke was getting in my eyes.

"Karo, why did you say I had to come?" I asked, shouting to make myself heard over the din leaking through the open doors of the club.

"Come on, Marty, we're missing the band!" She grabbed one hand again, turning and pulling me, back into the stochastic turmoil.

The band was having a break and we were in a scrum around the bar, waiting to get a drink. Karo was already pretty pissed, I wasn't particularly sober either. I should have chosen another time to tell her about Rico. But I didn't, I told her then.

She blew up.

"For fuck's sake, Martin!" She shouted over the din. "What's your problem? Whose side are you on anyway? Why the fuck should they have to show their papers every time they want to cross a bridge? Isn't that the reason we're having a fucking revolution? And what is all this borders shite? It's fucked up! And identity papers? Like, is this still the 'eighties? Borders are shit. Having an ID card is shit. Of course they should fucking jump over the Wall if they want to! If we're serious about a fucking revolution then we should be getting rid of identity cards! We should get rid of the fucking Wall!"

"We need the Wall. If there's no Wall, there's no GDR!"

"Maybe, but the ends never justify the means, do they? We have to start as we mean to carry on," she shouted back.

"What? Even if it means the end of our revolution?"

Karo hesitated for a moment, I could see doubt creep into her eyes, just for a second or two, before it was discarded. She swayed a little, then finding her balance again, she waved her hand in my face.

"Yes," she bawled at me, with the force of conviction deeply held. "Even then!"

Day 4
Thursday
17th March 1994

Berlin: In a ceremony taking place at midday today, parts of Lenin Allee will be renamed Kropotkin Allee. Local Round Tables in Friedrichshain and Prenzlauer Berg settled on the new name earlier this year, but no agreement could be reached in the district of Lichtenberg where the road will continue to be known by the old name. In a separate ceremony to be held next month, Leninplatz at the western end of the road will be renamed Bakuninplatz.

08:26
Martin

My colleagues noticed my hungover as soon as I walked in.

"What happened to you?"

"Late night. Punk concert."

They shared a grin. My connections to the punk scene were a source of amusement for my peers.

But there was something else. My colleagues were sitting in my office, they'd obviously been waiting for me, and all had an expectant air about them. I stood in the doorway wondering what was going on.

"Your turn to get the bread rolls," murmured Klaus with the half-grin he used when something amused him.

I looked around the room, only now taking in the plates and knives that were piled on my desk, along with a tiny kohlrabi, a bowl of lamb's lettuce and a couple of glass jars: five-fruits jam and what looked like some kind of spread.

"Sorry," I murmured as I moved around behind my desk, pushing the plates to one side to make room for my elbows.

"Can we carry on?" asked Laura, snappy at the delay. "We've already started with the agenda—we've finally had notice of who's going to be on the Ministerial Committee."

The Minister of the Interior had been replaced last autumn by a temporary committee, accountable to both the *Volkskammer* national parliament and the Central Round Table. The plan had been to try out the system before extending it to other Ministries. By announcing new committee members both parliament and the Central Round Table were indicating that they thought the experiment a success and worth continuing for the time being.

"The good news is that a couple of good people are going to be on the new committee: Mario Schreiber and Antje Willehardt."

Before 1989 Antje had been involved in the same dissident group as Erika, and she nodded, pleased at having a friend involved. Mario had been active up in Prenzlauer Berg, often to be seen in the *Umweltbibliothek*, but mostly working as an artist, pushing against the tight boundaries the Party had set around free expression.

"Who's the third person?" asked Klaus.

Laura shook her head, "Somebody from the CDU, never heard of him. Dietmar Rosen."

"Dietmar Rosen?" Klaus nodded. "Yeah, calls himself Timo. An old-timer, in the CDU back when it was still a block-party supporting the Communists. Now he's pro-unification."

A compromise appointment then, chosen to appease the authoritarian and pro-West factions in parliament.

"Frau Professor Doktor Weiss is an anthropologist. She co-ordinates a research group focussing on far-right activities."

Nik from RS1 had come over for the meeting, and was listening to what Erika had to say about the prof.

"Professor Weiss has compiled statistics on the acceptance and social standing of skinheads and their ideology. But I think what's interesting to us are the socio-psychological factors at play. Before 1989 some people were right wing because they didn't fit in, they couldn't find their niche in the socialist society, or they weren't prepared to. However, since the revolution started the numbers of young people with links to far-right movements has increased rapidly. Professor Weiss suggested that this has to do with the social upheaval we are experiencing: loss of direction and expectations; behaviour patterns that were previously rewarded—such as obedience and rote-learning—are no longer encouraged. Far-right organisations are offering the personal and social discipline that we used to have under the old system. It's essentially the way the Communist Party worked before: intolerance, structural violence and repression. Many people like to have that clarity."

"So you're saying the kind of person who felt at home in the Party and the FDJ in the old days are now more likely to join a far-right group?" Nik offered as a summary.

Erika didn't answer but flicked through her notes, "There's more: before 1989 the dual perception encouraged by the Party—the way of seeing everything as either right or wrong, black or white; the categorical, top-down determination—that's also the way the fascists want to see the world. They think they're right, and everyone else is wrong. And if you're wrong then you don't have any right to an opinion."

"The discipline thing interests me," I said. "The local Antifa told me that there's a clear hierarchy. Those at the bottom are exploited by a politically sophisticated inner circle. Did your prof say anything about that?"

"Yes—we saw that during the attacks on refugees at Hoyerswerda, as well as Freital, Thiendorf and all the other places. Same in West Germany, in Solingen and Mölln—different society and culture, but same set up. We should find out more about that inner circle—we can be fairly sure that quite a few of them have come over from the West."

Nik went over to the table where the police reports were laid out. He poked around a bit, then came back with a summary of observation reports from the last couple of months. He laid the paperwork on the table before us, pointing first to one page, then another.

"Here, see this: it looks like several groupings met up on this particular weekend at Weitlingstrasse 122, that coincided with visitors from the West. The same thing, on this date." Nik took the report and riffled through the pages again, finding what he was looking for, then turning the file around so we could see it. "Here, on this weekend. It happens several times, always with more people coming and going than is normal, and always with several well known fascists from West Berlin and West Germany, once even from Austria."

"So they're having meetings. The different groups are getting together and talking to known figures from the West," Laura said, thinking aloud.

"Or they're doing some kind of training." Nik added.

"What kind of training are they going to be doing?" I asked. "They don't need to be told how to beat people up. So it would have to be something else ...." In my head I sorted through the alternatives, and only one seemed remotely likely. "Something like political organising, say for the referenda in a couple of weeks, and after that the *Volkskammer* elections."

That was one possibility, but there'd be others. We really needed hard information. We needed the kind of inside information the *Kripo* must be getting from their informant—the information they weren't passing on to us.

11:27

Karo

Today's the day I get to take Frau Kembowski shopping.

Frau Kembowski is ace, she's really old-school, but we all love her. She was in the resistance in Nazi times and ended up in a concentration camp. But because she wasn't in the Communist Party they wouldn't give her a Victims of Fascism Pension.

She lives next door to our squat and has never complained about the noise and the parties, but maybe that's because she's deaf as a nut.

It started out with us just taking her bottles and waste paper to the recycling shop and spending the deposit money on beer. But when we noticed that she can't see very well either, and didn't get out much, we got a rota sorted to take her shopping and to the park and stuff.

"Mind the step Frau Kembowski—it's a bit uneven here!" I shouted at her.

"Oh deary me, haven't they repaired it yet? Things seem to be going from bad to worse in this country of ours ...." she wittered on.

"Yeah, but we don't want the fucking Party back, do we?"

Frau Kembowski tut-tutted loudly but I knew she didn't really mind me swearing. It's a bit of a game we play.

We'd got the shopping sorted and now we were on the way to the post office. When we got to Frankfurter Tor there were a couple of Nazi-skins handing out leaflets and abusing anyone who didn't take one. I knew exactly what would be on that leaflet: *Foreigners go home!* and *Tear down the Wall!* If I'd been on my own I would have gone and told them they could fucking go home themselves, or maybe gone to get some friends to help me make sure they did. The fuckers shouldn't be hanging around here, this was our *Kiez*.

While we were watching, some normal looking people stopped to chat with the skins. Frau Kembowski shook her head when she saw that and toddled off the other way, dragging me by the arm. "Come on deary, we'll go this way shall we?"

So we carried on up the road and I decided I'd deal with the situation later.

When we got to the post office the queue snaked out the door but we just went past all the people, with Frau Kembowski warbling *Veteran coming through!* It's fun queue-jumping with Frau Kembowski.

Once inside I steered Frau Kembowski to a counter where a bloke my age was being served. The other cashiers were dealing with old biddies and I could see they were digging in to spend the day counting their change and checking their savings books while everyone waited for them to get out the way. I barged in at the head of the queue so that we'd be next. The bloke being served had this really weird package. It looked like a hockey stick wound up in brown paper, and he was having real problems trying to pass it over the counter. It was really funny, he nearly swiped the grey withdrawal forms and the scales off the top while the old ladies looked on and tut-tutted.

When it was our turn Frau Kembowski asked for ten stamps for letters, and she had the exact money ready in her hand.

"Have you got the Kropotkin Allee commemoration stamps?" she quavered.

"Kropotkin's sold out already," replied the cashier, and proceeded to ignore us, waving forward the next person in the queue.

"We'll have the old ones then," I said to her in my rock-hard voice.

The cashier sighed (why does everyone in the GDR sigh all the fucking time? It's like it's catching) and poked around in a folder until she found a leaf of stamps with Beardy Marx on them. "Two Marks fifty," she snapped.

Frau Kembowski gave her the money and a really nice smile on top, and that seemed to do the job or else the cashier must have felt guilty because she started rabbiting on to Frau Kembowski.

"You can tell who's still a Party member, you know. They may not have the pin on their lapel any more, but they always ask for old Karl." They shared a smile and I dragged Frau Kembowski back out into the sunshine.

"You know what, young Karo?" Frau Kembowski was breathing heavily, and no wonder, the way she was wrapped up in that thick coat and big hat. "I do believe things are getting better in our country."

By now we were at the curb and had to wait to cross the road.

"Why's that Frau Kembowski?"

"Well, I think that's the first time anyone has ever said anything civil to me in a post office, and I've been around for a while too. Petty officials taking the drudgery of everyday life out on the customers, that's how it's always been. Just plain fucking wrong!" Frau Kembowski cackled.

15:22

Martin

The State Prosecutor, Ottokar Henschel, was waiting for me just inside the doors of the lower courthouse in Lichtenberg. It was another of those massive buildings built in the time of the last Kaiser

—high ceilings and echoing corridors. I went up the steps and in through the doors, holding my hand out. Henschel took it in his insipid grasp for a moment before letting it fall. He marched off, expecting me to follow him. He didn't look very happy.

"The President of the Court, Professor Doktor Kirchherr, wishes to speak with you—he's not satisfied with the standard of evidence," he said over his shoulder as he strode down the stone flagged corridor. "He has a suggestion, but he wouldn't tell me what it was."

I was confused: if I was to meet the judge in charge of the case then why had I been asked to come to the local court rather than the Supreme Court on Littenstrasse? Before I could ask Henschel he was rapping on a heavy oak door. He stood aside, letting me enter first.

The polished stone floor of the corridor gave way to darkened oak parquet in the room. High windows provided enough light to show off the tall ceilings and dark wood. Robing tables stood off to one side of the room, hooks in the panelling above them. But occupying the centre of the room was a large desk, and very much in charge of that desk sat the President of the Divisional Court.

The judge looked up as we came in, but didn't stand to greet me, just nodded sourly, as if everything that was bothering him in his life were my fault. In a sense he might be right: at least some of his problems were down to me. I was the one who had worked out the role ex-Stasi officers were playing in last year's Silesian Crisis, and I'd arrested the two main figures in the plot. Now Kirchherr was in charge of hearing the case against Benno Hartmann and Evelyn Hagenow.

I wasn't sure how to address the judge. President? Your Honour? I settled for a mumbled *comrade*. He took my hand and pressed it, not too hard, but hard enough to show he intended to imprint his status upon me.

"You are Captain Grobe?" he enquired while looking pointedly at Henschel. The prosecutor took the hint, muttered something polite and left the room.

"Captain Grobe, I have a problem and, given the quality of the case that has been made so far in my courtroom, I have little confidence that you will be able to help me. But on the other hand, we must pursue every possible avenue." He rearranged his papers while he spoke, then raised his eyes to meet mine.

He had clear blue eyes which contrasted with the salt and pepper eyebrows bristling above. Those eyes dug into me, as if demanding a confession. I looked away, and, spotting what I was after, took a chair and placed it in front of the desk. I sat down, prissily crossing and re-crossing my legs. When I was finally comfortable, and felt that the judge had waited long enough, I answered him.

"How do you think I can I help, comrade?" I deliberately emphasised the comrade this time, watching for his reaction.

A frown played at the corner of the judge's mouth. "Captain, times have changed. I was a judge in the days of Democratic Centralism, when the Party viewed the judiciary as one of their many executive organs. That is no longer the case: we are no longer the executive of any governing body in this Republic. Nevertheless, I am asked to preside over a hearing in which the case brought before me—clearly of social importance—has certain ...." The judge cleared his throat. "Shall we say certain *deficits*? Allow me, Captain, to be indiscreet. The evidence against Hartmann and Hagenow is—and I'm putting this politely—mostly circumstantial, and flimsy at that. Am I merely to follow popular opinion and instruct the jury to find them guilty?

"Yet these modern times demand something different, do they not? In turn, I fail to see any opportunity for making this a case of restitution. I cannot see how the principles of restorative justice can be applied. What exactly can the accused restore, and to whom?"

Kirchherr paused for a moment, fixing me with his stare again. Before continuing he picked up a stainless steel propelling pencil and examined the point for a moment.

"Captain, if you will allow me a further foray into the intangible— the West Germans have always taken great delight in stating that we do not have, nor ever have had, a *Rechtsstaat* here in the GDR. They say we do not follow the rule of law, that we are not a constitutional state. They ignore the fact that our laws have always been entirely in accordance with our real, existing constitution. And now we take great pains to comply with the laws that have been both democratically informed and formed. But none of this helps me in the peculiar case I have been appointed to oversee."

In a nervous gesture that belied his calm exterior the judge was pressing the button at the top of his pencil to release the lead, then pushing it back in with the palm of his hand. I wondered whether his flowery speech was also a symptom of his agitation, or whether he always talked like this.

"As I have already remarked, the prosecution is failing to present a convincing case. These are no ordinary accusations the court is hearing—they are entirely political. It is a distinctive case, and how, I ask myself, am I to deal with it? I hesitate to use the word *fair*, yet I wonder how we might treat this case *otherwise*, how may we find a *different* way to proceed?"

I could appreciate his problem. We hadn't managed to find any substantial documentary evidence in this case. When it came to prosecuting Mittag, Tisch, Honecker, Mielke and all the other leaders of the Party we had had hard evidence of criminal complicity—in manslaughter, torture and embezzlement. There was no question of trying them as political cases—all had been heavily involved in not only immoral but also criminal activity.

But now, even though both Benno Hartmann and Evelyn Hagenow had almost definitely been involved in at least one murder, we had nothing but circumstantial evidence. All the hard evidence we had gathered pointed only to a minor player who had conveniently turned up dead.

But it wasn't my problem, I felt like I'd done my part. Now it was down to this pompous member of the old system to work out how to deal with the trial.

"I am considering other options," the judge droned on. Having put the pencil down he was rubbing his nose between thumb and forefinger. "Let's say, for the sake of argument, that the case were to be dismissed, subject to the application of certain conditions, and if such conditions were of an, er, *satisfactory* nature ...." He looked at me from under his eyebrows, expecting a response to some question he felt beneath his dignity to actually ask.

I tried to work out exactly what the judge might be suggesting, but he'd already picked up the threads of his disquisition.

"In the case of Hartmann there is little difficulty. He has already requested, in writing, to be released to the West and promises never to return to the GDR. I am satisfied that his promises are sincere.

"Hagenow on the other hand is a different proposition. She has made clear to me that she regards this as her country, and that she believes she not only acted, but intends to continue acting in what she sees as its interests." He paused for a moment, a silent sigh, eyes turned upwards at the ceiling. "I was wondering whether your department might have any suggestions?"

His question absorbed me for the moment. How could my department have any suggestions? The judge saw my confusion, and helped out.

"Let us put it this way: Miss Hagenow seems to believe that she was serving her country, and wishes to continue to do so. She has suggested to me that you and she may be able to work out what she termed 'a deal'. She explained that you may be reluctant, and asked me to mention what she phrased *certain problems in Weitlingstrasse.*" He looked at my startled face for a moment, then nodded in satisfaction.

"What did she mean?" I asked him.

"I don't know. But I can see that it means something to you. So, Captain, what's it to be?"

I had no suggestions, and my immediate reaction was to refuse her this chance. What was she after? Forgiveness? Redemption? But what was happening around the fascist headquarters in Weitlingstrasse was a big issue, big enough that I felt I should talk to my colleagues, in fact we should refer this matter up to the Ministerial Committee.

But first I had a question for the presiding judge.

"What happens if we don't want to do a deal with her, or if we can't?"

For the first time the judge was visibly less than sure of himself. He glanced down, cupping his chin in his hand for a moment before answering:

"I don't know. Within the judiciary we are proud of the fact that we no longer have political prisoners in the GDR. But what are Hagenow and Hartmann if not precisely that? They are being tried for a political crime, treason, if you will, although that is not what it says in the charges. Their guilt is plain, their agitation and intrigue against the revolution cannot be condoned. If I find them guilty they will become prominent political prisoners, yet if I find them not guilty .... I'm sure you see the difficulty. This is why I agreed to investigate a somewhat unorthodox course of action."

I could see his point, but I was damned if Evelyn was going to get off the hook that easily.

Judge Kirchherr was keen for me to talk to Evelyn. In fact State Prosecutor Henschel had already arranged for her to be brought over from the prison next door. Which explained why we were in Lichtenberg rather than at the Supreme Court. I'd been backed into a corner, and I would be meeting Evelyn Hagenow, like it or not.

Evelyn and I had known each other for years. We had never been good friends, but had moved in and out of each other's lives with a regularity which suggested we were close. But last year I'd had her arrested for treason, and she'd been on remand ever since.

I had been left alone in the robing chambers, but didn't have long to wait before I heard a discreet knock on the door.

"Enter."

Evelyn came in, followed by a warden. Her wrists were held in front of her, bound with choke cuffs, and she waited patiently while the guard unclipped the handles and unwound the chain. She didn't say a word the whole time, she just stood there, looking at me.

"Evelyn, please sit down."

She sat down slowly, smoothing the blue tracksuit bottoms over her thighs, then she looked up, her eyes closing for a moment as she slipped into her role. Behind her the guard left the room, gently shutting the door as she went.

"Martin," she started, her voice warming with every word. "I knew you'd come. I knew you'd be the one to see that I can help-"

"What do you want?" I asked. My voice was hard but unsteady. I wasn't ready for this, but you could bet that Evelyn had been preparing this meeting for weeks, if not months.

She didn't answer immediately, she just looked me in the eye for a heartbeat or two.

"I want to help."

I tried not to show any reaction, but I knew that no matter how hard I tried Evelyn knew me well enough to see right through me.

"You know I want to help, otherwise you wouldn't have agreed to see me. And you know that I really can help."

"I wasn't given a choice. The judge just told me to wait here-"

"And of course Martin Grobe always does what he's told, doesn't he? You can tell that to your hat, I know you better. You were intrigued, weren't you? Go on, admit it."

I didn't admit it. I leaned back in my chair and crossed my legs, pretending to admire the fine wooden panelling. I suppose I wasn't very convincing.

"What's it like? Outside, I mean. I know it's sunny, I can see that much through the glass bricks in my cell. But what's it like?" She knew my weak points, she knew exactly what to say.

"You know what it's like outside, they just brought you along the road." I struggled a bit, trying to get off her hook.

"No." Evelyn shook her head. "They brought me here through a tunnel, I haven't been outside, not properly. Not since last September."

I knew she would have been outside, but only in those exercise cells—small rooms with wire mesh instead of a ceiling. An armed guard looking down on you from the catwalk above. If you stopped to look at the sky he'd tell you to keep moving.

It was no way to keep a person, no matter what they may have done.

"It's spring," I said, feebly.

"Oh, silly Martin," laughed Evelyn, "I know that. But what's it *like*? In the parks, the woods, on the streets?"

The laugh was false, an act, but the questions were serious. I decided to humour her.

"It's warm. Very warm. The crocuses finished last week, the daffodils are starting to go brown. The plane trees are budding, you know that sticky, glossy bud they have? I cycled down Puschkin Allee the other day, and the trees are still dark and wintry, but when you look, you can see they're just waiting to burst out. There's willow catkins along the river Spree-"

"So early, it's all so early!" Evelyn laughed again, and this time it sounded real. "Oh Martin, I just want to get out of these buildings, I want to run through the Treptower Park, I want to see all the grass growing, the Prussian garlic pushing through the soil next to the river, is the dog's mercury out, are the cherry trees in blossom? Just imagine, I'd hear the cuckoo and the woodpecker, if we were there early enough in the morning the blackbirds would be singing. If you took me away from here right now we'd go down to the Rummelsburg Lake and we'd look down the river—we could see for miles and miles, we could watch the cormorants and the herons, see the gulls soaring through the blue sky!"

For Evelyn the walls of the court house had disappeared, she could see the woods of the park, the open spaces of the wide river. Her eyes danced with the joy of her vision.

I couldn't meet her eye. I was the one who'd put her in jail, I was the reason she couldn't see the blue skies and the growing spring.

DAY 5
Friday
18th March 1994

Berlin: Striking workers from the Chemical Triangle will today call for hard currency investment in their industry. The workers from various plants in the Leipzig-Halle-Bitterfeld area, who have been on strike for over a fortnight, will hold a demonstration in the capital this morning.

10:27
Martin

There was no morning meeting today—my colleagues were at the Ministry, having a pow-wow with some big cheese. I'd managed to get out of it, arguing that we couldn't leave the office completely unattended. That's why I was here when Nik came calling. I was typing up a report on yesterday's confab with the President of the Court and Evelyn. The judge had asked me to make a choice, but I didn't feel it was a choice for me or my colleagues at RS, it was one for the Ministerial Committee. I was pecking away at the typewriter, wishing I didn't have to write all these reports all the bloody time—pages and pages of them, most of which would probably go straight into the archives without even being read. A peculiarly German disease, I was telling myself, just as Nik tapped on the door frame.

I got out from behind my desk, and plugged in the kettle, placing two cups on the table and started hunting for sugar.

"No need for sugar," said Nik, patting his waistline.

I shrugged, and poured the hot water over the grinds, the warm aroma of coffee filled the office. I passed Nik his cup, and waited for him to tell me why he'd come calling.

"I was on my way over here when I ran into a demonstration on the Unter den Linden. Chemical workers, you know, the strikers." He lifted a few files off the visitor's chair and looked around for somewhere to put them, before giving up and plonking them on top of another pile. "There were lots of them—at least a couple of thousand. But really, what's the point? Who are they demonstrating to?"

The area around Leipzig, Halle and Bitterfeld, usually called the Chemical Triangle, had been devastated by open cast mining and the chemical industry. With the fall of the Party in 1989 this process had been reversed. Several mines had been shut and chemical production had been cut back while the plants were renovated. This came as a relief to the local population—air quality had already improved, the water coming out of their taps was once again safe to drink—but it came at a cost: jobs.

For some workers the only option was to move elsewhere to take up other work. And who wants to do that?

To be fair, they weren't the only ones in such a situation, lots of people were having to relocate as the economy restructured and industry was repurposed to cater for domestic needs rather than the Soviet dominated international market of COMECON. Sometimes this worked well—factories could be refitted and workers retrained. But at other times it was associated with real social upheaval on a regional level, such as in Bitterfeld, Espenhain and Leuna.

While I was thinking about the workers of the Chemical Triangle Nik had gone into the reception area to fetch his briefcase.

"Here's something to cheer us up." He pulled out a paper bag, put it on my desk and ripped the side open, revealing a couple of slices of cake. "I'll brew more coffee, shall I?"

I went into the front office to get plates from the cupboard and when I got back Nik was standing by the bookshelves. He was looking at a little plastic yellow box.

"Is this what I think it might be?" he asked.

"Guess."

"Socialist Work Award?" He opened it up and chuckled, pulling out a cheap alloy medal. "When did you ever earn a Work Medal?"

"I didn't. One of the punks gave it to me last year. Said it had been his mother's. She's dead, but he reckoned that she'd have wanted me to have it." I shrugged. "It would have been rude not to take it."

Nik sat down again, still smiling, and slid a slice of cake onto his plate.

"You know, they impressed me today on their march."

I cocked an eyebrow at him, but Nik was too busy finishing off his second cup of coffee to respond immediately.

"Some skins turned up," he finally carried on. "About twenty or thirty of them. They tried to join the march, but the chemical workers weren't having any of it, they didn't want the skinheads marching with them. Scuffles broke out. The police intervened. They were trying to pull the skins out of the march, after all, the skins had no chance: thirty against two thousand! And instead of being grateful, the skins started bawling about their constitutional rights, freedom of expression, all that stuff. Hypocrites! Then one of them started singing, and as soon as that happened all the skins stopped fighting, they stood in a line and sang. Every last one of them sang."

"They sang?"

Nik shook his head at the memory. "You'd never rate it, really. They just stood there in a line, as if they'd rehearsed it. They sang that old song: *Thoughts Are Free.*"

I sat there at my desk, sipping my coffee and feeling angry.

"Yeah, exactly. That was my reaction too," said Nik, reading my mind.

We both finished our coffees in silence, and between us hung the image of a gang of skinheads standing in the middle of a demonstration, singing a song of revolution and freedom.

"Anyway, what was it you came in for?" I asked eventually. "You seem to be spending more time here than at your own offices."

"I told Laura that I'd come and have a look through some police reports—she said they'd be on her desk."

I watched him go over to Laura's office, then got on with my own work.

COMMUNIST SCUM!

I couldn't see anybody on the street but the red paint was still wet, dripping down the wall of the offices where Martin works. I shrugged and rang the doorbell.

One of Martin's colleagues let me in, some old dude I'd never seen before, about the same age as Martin. I was going to ask him about the paint job but the guy just looked so grey and tired that I didn't bother.

When I knocked on Martin's door he had his irritable face on, as if he was expecting someone else and wasn't too happy about it. But then he saw me and chilled out.

I sat down in front of his desk but felt embarrassed. I'd come here to apologise, but I wasn't much good at that kind of thing.

"Do you want a coffee? Or there's a bit of cake here-"

"Martin, shut up a minute will you?" I was looking at my feet, but told my head to look at Martin. He'd stopped blethering and was waiting for me to say something.

"I wanted to say sorry. Y'know, for shouting at you the other night." I looked at Martin. Now he was examining his feet. Or his desk because his feet were hidden somewhere underneath.

"No, no. I actually agree with you," he said. "And anyway, it was the wrong time to talk to you about something like that."

"I was pissed."

"Yeah. So was I. A bit."

My fingers were doing that knot thing, you know, when they sort of start squeezing each other and you wonder whether they're ever going to come apart again. I stopped doing it.

"But I'm glad you came to the concert. Even if we did argue. Did you enjoy it?"

Martin looked a bit lost for a minute. "Yes, I did," he fibbed, his eyes sliding off over the desk.

"You liar!" I grinned. "Are we OK then?"

"We're OK."

"But what you were talking about—look, I'm against the Wall," I couldn't stop myself blurting it out, and now I'd started I couldn't stop again. "This time round we've got to stop the power structures from becoming established. We don't need things like ID cards, like the Wall. We can't give the state that kind of control over us!"

Martin didn't say anything, and his eyes went glassy.

"Of course," he said after a bit. "The ends shouldn't ever justify the means you said. But if we keep the Wall we can control who comes in, who goes out, what goods are coming in and going out. It's a practical thing, an economic thing. That's the whole point of it. Without that Wall we won't have the chance to do what we need to do to keep our country going."

I heard what he was saying. He was saying that if we got rid of the Wall then the GDR would follow soon after.

"But so long as we have a Wall we can't be free!" I was almost shouting now.

Something moved behind me, a swish of clothes, it was Martin's colleague. He must have come to check what all the shouting was about.

"But if we can't have a GDR without a Wall, and we can't have freedom with the Wall then there's no answer is there, young lady?" the colleague said.

"Who the fuck asked you, anyway?" I snarled at him, and he backed away, giving Martin a look as he went.

"Welcome to real life," I heard him breathe as he went.

"Who the fuck's that?" I asked Martin.

"That's Nik. Leave him alone."

"Nosy twat!"

I took a deep breath, Martin and this Nik had really got on my wick. I needed to calm down.

"Yeah, I know all of that," I told Martin, "What you and your Nik said. But we've got to do what we think is right, haven't we? Give me some credit, will you? It's not like I was born yesterday."

"How about that coffee?" asked Martin, getting up when I nodded. "It's good that you came round, I wanted to ask you a favour."

"Give me the coffee first and I'll think about it. Can I have that bit of cake too?"

Martin

When my colleagues returned I decided to go home. An earworm was playing like a broken record in my head—the tune wouldn't let me go. In these situations I usually just listen to the song, several times over if needs be, and since most earworms that invade my head are from my own music collection, it's just a case of finding the right LP.

But *Thoughts Are Free* wasn't in my collection.

I was in the kitchen, looking out of the window, down to the S-Bahn tracks below. A red signal glared at me from further along the embankment. *Thoughts are free / Who may guess them aright?* How did it go after that?

I left the flat again, down the stairs to the cellar to open the flimsy padlock on the trellis that guarded my corner. I looked around the small cubicle: shelves stacked with boxes, preserving jars, empty beer bottles, an old cuckoo clock. It was the boxes I was interested in, and I moved them around, trying to read the faded pencil scrawled on the sides. Coughing in the dust, I pulled a box down. It was heavy, almost slipping through my fingers. Opening it up, I looked inside. At the very top a big, hardback book: *Vom Sinn unseres Lebens*. Beneath that, school books, exercise books, a pencil box, a wooden ruler. This was the right one. Pulling the books out, glancing at covers and spines before placing them on the floor. There it was. A yellowish-brown cover: *Songs for the JG*. I opened it up, pausing for a moment at the rounded, childish writing on the flyleaf. *Katrin Grobe, 14 years.* Turning to the last page I scanned down the contents list. There it was—flick back through the book until I got to the right page.

> *Our thoughts are free,*
> *Who may guess them aright?*
> *They pass fleetingly,*
> *Like shades in the night.*
> *No-one can know them,*
> *No hunter can shoot them*
> *With powder and lead:*
> *Our thoughts are free.*

Reading the words, my finger tracing the notes up and down the staff, my mind went back to a damp day in the woods. Saxon Switzerland: a holiday, just me and Katrin. Her mother had already gone, it must have been the summer after. We were walking through the woods towards the *Bastei,* one of those fantastical stacks that the wind has carved from soft sandstone. It was raining, a light drizzle that collected and coalesced on the close beech canopy before dripping into the thick mist below. We couldn't see very far, our world was made up of emerald light, pewter beech trunks and the bronze of last year's leaves covering the earth. We walked hand in hand along the path, gradually becoming aware of the singing that seeped through the rain—deep, slow yet joyous. By the time we could make out the words of his song, he was in sight. Standing beside the path, bare-headed, hands behind his back, face raised to the verdant roof above him.

> *I think what I will,*
> *And what gives me pleasure.*
> *It's all very still,*
> *And all in good measure. My wishes and longings*
> *Let no one be mocking.*
> *It will always be*
> *That thoughts are free.*

He was singing for the pleasure of it, for no audience but the surrounding trees. We stood listening as the tune washed around the woods, and it seemed to both chill and warm us.

> *And if they locked me*
> *In a dark dungeon,*
> *That would clearly be*
> *A labour in vain;*
> *For my own thoughts, they*
> *Tear down the barriers*
> *And the walls that be:*
> *For thoughts are free.*

A beautiful song, a dangerous song. A song in the rare land between official acceptance and overt resistance. A song that was uncomfortable for the Marxist-Leninist Workers' Party—the Party that knew best, that couldn't allow its subjects to have their own thoughts. A Party that had to accept the song for its pedigree: revolution, freedom, resistance against imperialism and fascism. A Party that dare not ban such a song outright.

> *That's why I forever*
> *Cast off all worries.*
> *And nevermore will*
> *Let whims plague me.*
> *For in our own hearts we*
> *Have laughter and fun*
> *And thereby we see:*
> *That thoughts are free.*

A song that wound its way through the trees, wound its way into our hearts. A moment apart from a grey world, a moment in the fairy kingdom of the beech forest and the solitary singer in the mist.

11:26

Martin

I rapped on the steel door of the watchtower and a *Grenzer* opened up, only letting me in after I'd shown him my official papers. I climbed up the metal ladder, past the mess level to the darkened observation deck at the top. As I poked my head up through the hatch I saw Rico holding a muttered conversation with a customs officer. They both turned as I came up, and Rico crossed over to me.

"Martin, thanks for coming. We've got something you might find interesting." Rico held out his hand, looking pleased to see me again. "This is my colleague from Customs Administration Service, *Obersekretär* Kalle Reinhardt."

The customs officer, a tall thin fellow, older than Rico but still with youth on his side, had been peering through the north-west windows. He motioned for us to join him, holding out the binoculars for me. I didn't need them—in the gathering dusk I could quite clearly see the small group of punks climbing a ladder, then rolling over the top of the wall, less than 150 metres from the tower.

"Apparently they're on the way to a squat, it's called the Køpi," I told them, "They have concerts there practically every night. It's on Köpenicker Strasse, just the other side of Engeldamm. And there's another trailer site there too."

Although the Køpi and the nearby *Wagenburg*—Schwarzer Kanal— were in the East, the most direct route between here and there was to cross the Wall twice, heading through the last corner of West Berlin. There was no border crossing near the Køpi, so jumping over the Wall at that point was the only option.

"Reports of provocations have been received from that sector too." Rico nodded. "They're climbing over the Wall on Engeldamm."

We observed the punks until the whole of the small group had disappeared over the rounded asbestos tube that topped the whitewashed concrete of the Wall.

"Have you spoken to them about it?"

"The Section Commander is keen to avoid any conflict. He says we've more important things to worry about than a few chaos-mongers."

Kalle exchanged a glance with Rico, something passed between them, a message, a negotiation, some kind of agreement.

"Perhaps you'd be interested in this?" he said, and shinned down the ladder.

Rico and I followed him, and we left the command tower, walking over the sandy grass towards the other side of Puschkin Allee. Once over the road we picked our way across hard-packed earth, hemmed in by abandoned guard-dog kennels, followed by battered cobbles criss-crossed by redundant tram tracks. We entered a door in the side of the bus repair workshop, a semi-derelict red-brick building from the turn of the century. Up several dimly-lit flights of stairs, all the doorways bricked up, until we reached the attic level. From there we went out onto a walkway that crossed the tar-paper roof, about three metres from the edge. The roof sloped down to my right, and I could see the factory lights shining through the saw-tooth skylights. Ahead of us—merely a shadow marring the sparkling reflection of the moon in the river—I could make out the customs pier. But to the left another railing marked the edge of the building which loomed over the weir lead that ran parallel to the Landwehr Canal.

That was the border to West Berlin.

Kalle and Rico were leaning on the railing that edged the catwalk, watching the weir channel.

"We've had a tip-off: watch the bushes on the far bank. If the information is correct then we should see some activity in the next half-hour or so," Kalle whispered to me.

A lazy wind came off the river, blowing across the roof. I pulled my collar up, and zipped my jacket as far as it would go, leaning back against the railing, burrowing my hands into my pockets. But Kalle was right, we didn't have to wait long. Rico tapped me gently on the shoulder and pointed across the channel to Kreuzberg. The moon wasn't yet half full, and clouds nudged past, casting the landscape into shade. Only the cement works and cranes on the riverside could be seen—the buildings and bushes that covered most of the ground in front of us were as murky as the inky ribbon of water below us. Eventually I made out shadows, denser than the background gloom of the bank. They were manhandling something into the water—a rubber dinghy, perhaps a rigid inflatable. Whenever the wind dropped the lapping of oars cut through the dissonance of traffic drifting over from West Berlin.

Kalle headed along the catwalk and we followed him, around to the right and down some steps. From here we could see the customs pier —part of the border defences—and the gap in the piling that extended to the Oberbaum Bridge. Kalle pointed down that way, but I was too busy watching the mouth of the weir lead, waiting for the dinghy to appear, and I didn't notice the speedboat until its buzzing engine caught my attention. Presumably it had come from one of the old harbour buildings on the Kreuzberg side of the river, halfway between here and the bridge, but it dashed up the river towards us, engine whirring loudly, its bow wave breaking on the banks and piles. A swerve to starboard and it disappeared into the mouth of the Landwehr Canal.

I turned away from the river, wanting an explanation of what just happened, but Rico just nodded towards one of our customs boats. It had set off from the pier, and was making way down the river, presumably looking for the place where the speed boat had launched. But Rico wasn't interested in our customs launch, he was now watching the little dinghy, its nose just pushing out of the mouth of the weir. It hung around, allowing its bow to catch the stream, careful not to be drawn out into the river, the oars being used to keep position.

It was a good few minutes before the customs launch came back our way, searchlight stabbing the banks until it focussed on the dinghy. The two figures in the small boat could be clearly seen now, casually paddling backwards, moving further back into the weir lead, back into West Berlin.

The customs boat stayed in the river, its light following the slow progress of the boat until it disappeared under the lee of our building.

"What the hell was all of that?" I asked Kalle and Rico. Kalle looked away, while Rico gave me a grim smile. They went back along the catwalk, leaving me to follow.

"They're testing us, to see how fast we react, what we notice," Kalle told me, looking over his shoulder as he went. "They know their rubber dinghy is very hard to spot on the radar and that we're relying on visual contact from the observation towers on the pier and in the *Osthafen* on the other side of the river—you can't really cover the mouth of the weir from the Oberbaum Bridge. The problem is that the Wall was built to keep people *in*, not smugglers *out*. Our observation positions are facing the wrong way," said Rico, not bothering to whisper any more, assuming there would be no more action this night. "And the speedboat, it went into the Landwehr Canal—and that's a lock mouth. But they wouldn't have gone through the lock, they would have just pulled the boat up the bank in front of the lock gates." He pointed towards the edge of the roof. "The whole width of the weir lead down there is in Kreuzberg. As soon as that dinghy moved beyond the line of the river bank it was in West Berlin."

Back at the Section Command Tower Kalle brewed up some coffee in the mess.

"Anything to report?" Rico asked the *Grenzer* at the signals desk.

"Yes, comrade Sergeant." The soldier at the desk turned the logbook round for Rico to look at.

Rico read the log, his finger tracing each entry.

"Here, look—while they were messing about on the river a third boat crossed from the Kreuzberg side of the canal, dropping off a package further down Lohmühlenstrasse," he said to me before turning his attention back to the *Grenzer*. "Has a signal already been sent to Staff and the GKSi?"

"Yes, comrade Sergeant."

Rico grunted appreciatively. "I better get on with my report too, but first let's have that coffee. Kalle—how long do you need to brew a cuppa?" he shouted down the hatch to the mess below. "I hate nights like this."

We climbed down the ladder to the mess level where Kalle had a pan of water on the electric ring.

"Is Giesler not on duty tonight?"

Rico and Kalle shared a glance, much the same as they had when I'd turned up earlier.

"No, he put in for a transfer after your visit on Tuesday. And now he's gone." Rico shook his head and Kalle busied himself with taking cups out of the locker. "I don't know how he managed to organise the transfer so quickly but good riddance if you ask me. That one had history."

DAY 6
Saturday
19th March 1994

Berlin: *The new General Secretary of the Communist Party, the PDS, will today call on the government to ensure decisive action is taken against the fascist threat facing the country. In a speech this morning Karl Kaminsky will tell his party that only a strong, central leadership can steer the GDR out of the current crisis.*

08:07

Martin

It was past eight when I left home, heading down the still cool streets toward the office. If I hurried I should just about make it in time for the morning meeting.

I hadn't slept well—it had been late by the time I'd got back last night, and then I'd had trouble getting to sleep.

Excuses I told myself. *It's not about how well you slept, you've got a job to do—it's lack of discipline. Faith,* another part of me replied, *not enough faith.*

Perhaps I had too many questions about whether and how I was contributing to our Republic. In the old days it was so easy—easy to imagine a perfect way of organising our society, easy to ignore the real-life problems, the complex logistics of keeping eighteen million people rubbing along.

But the problems didn't end there, the reality was that not all of those eighteen million souls wanted us to succeed, many had radically different ideas of what our country should look like.

Put that way, we had no chance, I thought to myself.

Too much thinking, old son, too much thinking.

By now I'd got to the office, and was examining the new graffiti on the wall outside.

We'd agreed to come in this Saturday morning to catch up on the meeting we'd missed. So far we'd finished the general part and had moved on to the fascist case.

"I saw Nik yesterday," I told the others. "He told me he saw the fascists try to gatecrash the chemical workers' demo. But the chemical workers weren't having any of it, they literally distanced themselves from the skins."

"Speaking of Nik," responded Laura. "He wanted to drop in this morning but he couldn't get here on time. He's had a look at some of the police reports and he's suggesting we let someone he knows have a look at the material. She used to be an agitation and propaganda expert working for the Party, and Nik reckons she can do something he calls 'reverse engineering'. I think it means having a look at what the fascists have been doing publicly, then taking back-bearings and working out what their intentions are."

Nik's idea wasn't bad, such an analysis could be useful, but it didn't sit easily. The Communists were exploiting the current upsurge in fascist activity—they had their propaganda machine running at full tilt—using a law and order strategy, blaming the Round Tables for being soft on the fascists, despite the fact that the current problems of our country were rooted in the years of the Communist dictatorship.

"Is this analyst still a Party member?" I asked. "If she's still close to the Party then we can't just hand over the material—they'll cherry pick the juicy bits to back up their arguments for a firm leadership by the Party of the Proletariat!"

"I don't know, I'll ask Nik about any current connections to the Party." Laura made a note for herself and the meeting moved on.

I told them about the strange water ballet of the two boats last night, and how it didn't seem to make any sense.

"And what's that got to do with us?" asked Laura.

"This thing with the boats seems to be happening regularly, and customs suspect it's related to smuggling. I think it may tie into our theory that the fascists are smuggling their propaganda material in from the West. It seems sensible to follow it up, see if there are any connections."

Erika nodded in agreement, but Laura was frowning. "We haven't got any capacity for that kind of thing."

"Oh, Laura, we're only going through paperwork and observing fascist marches, I think this lead looks quite promising," said Erika, winking at me across the room.

"OK, let's do it. Martin, do you want to follow up on it—you seem to have the contacts already?"

"I'll talk to the Border Police and Customs."

We ticked off the next few points in short order: the fascists had registered another march in Berlin, and several more around the country too; Laura was to liaise with the Ministry—it was nearly a week since we'd found out about the IKM informant and we still hadn't been allowed access to the operational files.

"There is one other thing—about that meeting I had with the State Prosecutor on Thursday. Turns out it wasn't actually the prosecutor that wanted to see me—it was the President of the Court in charge of the case against Evelyn Hagenow and Benno Hartmann. Evelyn wants to do some kind of deal and the judge is keen on the idea." I filled them in on my meeting with the judge and Evelyn.

"But what does she want to do? What's she offering?" asked Laura.

"To penetrate the fascist scene, to be an agent. To gather intelligence that can be used in a criminal investigation against them."

"Stasi tactics," Erika said, almost under her breath.

Laura ignored the interruption. "But the police already have an IKM there, and anyway, they'd recognise her!"

"No, they've been very clever. Think about it: there's not been a single picture of her in the papers or on the telly. They've been hiding her away, almost as if they've been preparing for this."

But it was Erika who asked the big question, the one that had been bothering me since I'd spoken to Evelyn.

"Can we trust her?"

No-one gave an answer. It wasn't up to us to decide whether or not to trust her. Our job was to pass the information upstairs, to the

Ministry. Let them make the decision. We wouldn't be part of executing any plan anyway—that task would fall to the *Kripo*. To all intents and purposes we'd already done our bit. There wouldn't be any more contact with Evelyn, and I was glad of that.

Once everyone had left my office I rang the Customs Administration, asking when I could see the Chief Inspector of Customs. I spoke to a very helpful secretary who offered me an appointment with an underling in three weeks time.

"And what if I just pop round to the Chief Inspector's office on Monday morning?" I asked.

"That would be quite impossible!" I swear there was panic in that secretary's voice. "There won't be anyone available unless you have an appointment, good day." He hung up.

I'd probably do better to have a chat with my new friend in the Border Police. I rang his regimental HQ in Treptow, and once I identified myself they proved far more accommodating.

"Comrade Staff Sergeant Müller is on early shift this week—he will be at the Section Command Tower Puschkin Allee until 1400 hours."

I looked at my watch, I'd better get a move on if I was to catch Rico.

10:54

Karo

"Fucking wankers!" I turned the radio off again.

I only turned it on to get the music events listing on *DT64*. But some fucker had tuned the radio to DDR I and I got the news instead. Communist Party blaming the Round Tables for the fascist disease! Yeah, well, we tried their authoritarianism for forty years—they're the ones who gave us this problem. Bastards seem to reckon that we've already forgotten that we were the ones who chucked them out!

I decided to stop ranting at the empty room and tried to work out why the news had wound me up so much. I guess I was scared that they could still come back, things would be like the old days again, when people like me would be harassed the whole time, locked up now and again, not allowed to work or only given the shittiest jobs.

When people would give up and try to leave the country rather than put up with the hassle.

And the fucking hypocrisy! The PDS pretending they're concerned about the rise of nationalists and authoritarians—jealous more like, because somebody else was using their tactics!

But they were right about one thing, we needed to act against the fash. I'd been ignoring it for too long. It was time to get involved, cos things were only going to get worse.

11:04
Martin

As I'd told Evelyn, the plane trees were budding early. Cycling up Puschkin Allee I could see the folded leaves glistening in the midday sunlight. The sight of them made me stop to look more closely, appreciating the freedom I had to do just that. Dismounting and pushing my bike between the large concrete flower pots that marked the end of the road and the start of the border zone, I kept an eye open for Rico, but the only people to be seen were the trailer residents.

Leaning my bike against the side of the tower, I banged on the steel door, my knocks echoing around the sandy park that was being laid out on the old death-strip. The door creaked open and a guard looked out. He pointed me towards the roof top of the bus garage on the other side of the street, where Rico, Kalle and I had watched the boats last night.

I climbed up the stairs, and went out through the tiny door onto the catwalk, making my way towards the figure looking down at the river. As I got closer I could see it was Rico.

"Hi Martin." He shook my hand before offering me a cigarette. "The duty officer said you might be coming by."

"I've got some questions about the smugglers. I tried talking to the big cheeses at the Customs Administration, but they just fobbed me off. I thought it might be better talking to someone on the ground."

"You want to have a word with Kalle? He's the customs officer in charge of this sector."

250

I shook my head, Rico could probably help just as well. "We think large shipments are coming in from the West, and we're fairly sure they're not coming in through the proper channels. There's a fascist group with huge amounts of printed materials, including banners and placards that obviously haven't been produced over here. So we're wondering how they might have got them across the border."

Rico laughed, almost choking on his cigarette.

"Are you serious?" he asked. "Ever heard the expression about the needle and the haystack? You saw what happened the other night, they're running rings around us—what you're looking for could be coming in at any point along the border. The Wall leaks like a sieve now, and it's only going to get worse. There's not enough Border Police to keep an eye on the whole of the Wall, and the border zone isn't at all secure since we opened up the death strip. Now they're talking about reducing our numbers. And that referendum coming up —if the people vote to get rid of the Wall .... We're going to have to get used to the fact that smuggling is here to stay."

"What kind of things are coming over the Wall in this sector?"

"Well, you know about that lot." Rico nodded over his shoulder, towards the wagons and trucks behind him. "They're probably taking beer over to the West, maybe cigarettes from Poland. They'll flog them over there and bring cannabis back. But that's nothing, there are rumours of more serious stuff coming in. Heroin, crack, and some chemical thing they're calling 'E'. We're trying to move towards intelligence led policing, but look at us, we're not really policemen, are we? We're just soldiers. For years, they told us to shoot anything that moved, now they tell us we need to be intelligent." He chuckled at his own joke.

"But back to your problem. Look, how big are these consignments, a pallet? Two? It could be coming in on a regular lorry—customs can't check every load like they used to. Or somewhere along the green border, round the back of West Berlin or along the inner-German border—bribe a guard to open up a maintenance gate and look the other way for ten minutes."

He paused for a moment to shake his head, tapping ash off the cigarette. Then he pointed at a barge being pushed by a tug, making its way downriver.

"Or what about them. They come in and out, loaded with coal and gravel." We looked down on the barge, its covers were open, showing several dumps of gravel. "All we can do with that lot is poke sticks in it. In the old days we'd have dogs sniffing, checking for the smell of humans, but it's not people smugglers you're after, is it?

"And come to think of it, what about the Baltic coast? You could have a fishing boat come out of Travemünde or anywhere in the West —a launch could just bring the goods ashore. And now Dömitz has been opened up you can bring small boats in from the Elbe, right into the heart of Mecklenburg."

Rico was piling on the options: there were so many ways in and out of our country, a country that just a short time ago had been hermetically sealed against the West. And the way Rico was talking it all sounded pretty obvious, yet in the office I'd imagined that we could somehow narrow down the options, work out the probable entry points for the fascist material. Now it just looked hopeless.

"Don't look so down in the mouth!" Rico clapped me on the shoulder, "there's always a way. Look, I wasn't here in the old days, before 1990, but there's plenty of guys in the ranks who were. We talk, you know, they tell tall tales of what it was like back then, the loneliness of being on guard duty on the border, just hoping that nobody would try to escape on your watch. Because if you saw someone you'd have to shoot them. If you didn't see them, or if you looked the other way, well, your life wouldn't be worth living."

The tug and barge were past us now, but had slowed down and given off a long, low whistle followed by a second, shorter blast.

"But that's not the point. In the old days the Stasi were always sniffing around. They were always watching us, and at the same time, watching everyone who came into the restricted area near the border. They were on the look-out for people planning an escape over the Wall. Now that's what they really mean by intelligence-led policing, isn't it? Things don't change so much, do they?" Rico shrugged. "So, Martin, what I'm trying to say is, if there's a plan to get something across the Wall, there'll be people who know about it. And there's your weak point. The more people who know about a plan, the more chance there is of a leak. Maybe you need to concentrate on that angle?"

In his roundabout way, the young man was telling me that my only chance was to make an effort to find out what the fascists were actually up to, and not just try to second guess their plans in order to catch them at it.

My thoughts returned, once again, to the mole Lichtenberg Kripo had in the Nazi scene. Presumably they were extracting him now the Nazis knew about him, but why weren't we being given access to the intelligence that had already been delivered?

12:32

Karo

"You ready for this?"

I nodded, yeah, ready as I was ever going to be. I'd gone to see the Antifa group as soon as I'd got up this morning. They were doing training and they'd given me a try-out right then.

I was knackered. I'd shown them all my moves, all the judo and karate self-defence stuff I'd learnt over the years. They weren't impressed, but Bert said I could tag along. A few of the lads grumbled, but no-one said anything to me.

17:54

Martin

I'd been back for a few hours and was trying to relax. Freygang was on the record player, but the political lyrics kept bringing my mind back to the chat I'd had with Rico.

Before I could follow my thoughts any further the doorbell rang.

"Hi Katrin!" I gave my daughter a hug in the doorway. I was so pleased to see her I didn't notice how stiff she was.

She pushed past me, into the hallway, not saying a word. Closing the flat door I followed her down to the living room and stood leaning against the door frame, watching her as she fell onto a chair at the table. She didn't make any further movement, and I knew her better than to press her. So I let her be and went into the kitchen to put a pan of water on the stove to make coffee.

"Papa?" she said finally, from the living room.

In the pan small beads of air gathered around the surface of the water, slowly turning to a faint steam. I turned off the gas and went into the living room. Katrin was still sitting at the table, she looked exactly as she had done a few minutes before, but she must have moved because there, lying in front of her was an envelope, torn along the top. A letter. The white paper looked innocent against the colourful oilcloth.

But from where I stood by the door I could feel the cold fingers of a ghost reaching out to me. I took a step towards the table, towards the envelope. My eyes fixed on it, hardly taking in the West German stamp, just concentrating on the writing. It was intimately familiar to me: the swirls, the pressures, the scratches where the pen hadn't quite lifted off the paper to form the next letter of Katrin's name and address. I hadn't seen that writing for years.

The ghostly fingers slowly, tenderly, wrapped themselves around my heart, tightening and freezing me in the winter of their grip.

"It arrived yesterday," Katrin said. "I didn't know what to do. I didn't know whether to tell you, whether to hide it. Throw it away. Burn it."

I sank into the chair opposite Katrin, my eyes fixed on the letter. Questions swirled, but didn't make it as far as my mouth. *Have you read it? Why didn't you tell me as soon as you got it? Why tell me? Why didn't you hide this from me?*

"It's from Mama." The words broke loose, eddying from Katrin's mouth. Her eyes met mine as she said the obvious.

I looked away, away from the letter between us, away from my daughter's face. Up to the corners of the ceiling, grey webs woven with dust, swaying in the current of emotion.

"She asks if I want to have contact. With her. She says that now I'm 21 I'm old enough to understand the world."

My eyes descended again, focussing on Katrin's face, on the tears gathering in the corners of her eyes. A movement further down caught my attention, her hand was edging along the oilcloth, unguided but drawn towards the letter. I moved around the table, pulling my daughter into a hug, her face against my chest, her arms lying limp on the table.

We sat there all evening, silences punctuated by aborted conversations. Katrin had so many questions. So many feelings she couldn't find a place for.

"Why did she go?" she asked me.

I didn't have the answer, even though I'd seen it coming and had been there when it happened. I hadn't been able to stop it.

"She couldn't stand it. She felt that if she stayed there," it was here, here in the GDR, but it was a different country in those days, so I said *there*. "If she'd stayed there, it would have broken her. She wouldn't have survived."

"She didn't even apologise," said Katrin. "In the letter. She didn't make any attempt to explain or defend what she did." Her mother's decision to leave seemed ineffable to my daughter.

That sounded like her, like Katrin's mother. She was strong, she knew herself, she knew her own limits. She'd decide to do something and then she would go ahead and do it, whatever the consequences.

"When did she go?" Katrin had been small, she'd just started school. But when exactly had her mother gone? In what month, on what day had she actually left the country? I didn't know.

Oh, I know when they came to search the flat, I know when and where we were each and every time they stopped us on the street, every time they took my wife into custody, releasing her minutes, hours or days later. I know when they tried to warn her—so often. I know when they came to warn me, waiting for me at work, on the way to the supermarket, outside the house: *Do you think we'll let you all leave? Do you think we'll let you keep the little girl? You can end this, make your wife withdraw her application to leave the GDR. Then you can get on with your lives.*

But I couldn't end it.

I know when they took her away that last time, the last time we saw her. She was dragged away from us, dry eyed, staring at us, fixing us in her memory as we stood in the doorway of our flat, too scared to follow them down the stairs. Katrin was hysterical, screaming, her clenched fists beating on my leg. The neighbour's doors all firmly shut, knowing better than to show any curiosity.

But I don't know when they let her out of prison. I don't know when they put her on a train to the West.

I don't know when she passed from our country to the other side.

Katrin kept her eyes fixed on the mug of coffee in her hands. She hadn't expected an answer, but she needed to ask the questions. The same questions that I had.

22:14

Karo

We were waiting in the bushes, just by the entrance to Nöldnerplatz S-Bahn station. Behind us was the gate to the railway yard, but at this time of night it was shut and locked.

"Isn't this a really stupid place to wait?" I whispered.

"This is the way they always come. Now keep quiet!" one of the hard lads said.

It was really boring, waiting in the darkness for some pissed up fashos to come sneaking into Friedrichshain. The idea was that they always come from the house they've got in Weitlingstrasse, and head this way to find a punk or foreigner to lay into. But only if the victim's alone—because five fascists against two or three punks wouldn't be an equal fight, would it?

"Do you do this every night?"

"No, just weekends. Now shut the fuck up. If they come now they'll hear us gossiping like girls."

I nearly did my karate moves on him, sexist pig. But I told myself I'd deal with him later. Right now I was here to get the fascists before they got us, and I was going to impress the fuck out of these chauvinist dinosaurs!

That's when the sexist pig stuck his elbow into my ribs. I was about to shout at him but then I heard some laughing coming from the subway that goes under the S-Bahn station. Six skins stopped just under the street light, passing a lighter round and sparking up their ciggies.

Ronny was at the front, and he held up his hand: wait.

The fash carried on, heading towards Kaskelstrasse, still laughing about something. As soon as they were under the next railway bridge Ronny's hand dropped, and we left the shadows, running quietly after the skins.

Ronny got there first, his arm went around the throat of the skinhead at the back, his fist smashed into the side of the fash's head. The other Antifa lads were just behind him, and the two groups collided, but there was no way I could see what was going on. There didn't seem to be any room for me to get in there, just a frenzy of shouts and fists. Ronny went down, and I got hold of his arms as paraboots thudded into his sides. But I managed to drag him out, and he was straight up on his feet and back in the middle of things. Just then, one of the skins made a break for it, went past me, so close I could have reached out my arm to touch him. But I didn't. I just stuck my foot out, and he toppled over, his nose ramming the concrete in a cloud of blood. The other skins must have legged it and left their mate to his fate, because my lot had surrounded the fash I'd felled. They were laying into him, big time. Boot after fucking boot was crunching into him.

DAY 7
Sunday
20th March 1994

Berlin: *The parliamentary parties CDU and SPD are asking citizens to vote against the proposed devolution of power in next month's referendum. In a joint statement the parties called the Round Table system a stop-gap solution, and condemned it as both untenable and undemocratic.*

12:42
Martin

I'd slipped into a new ritual: Sunday Mornings. Somehow, during the winter, and without even deciding to, I'd managed to ease off on the work front. I avoided working on Sundays, and I didn't take work home with me at weekends. Maybe it was because I finally realised that no matter how much I do, the revolution will never depend on me alone. For years, I'd been putting myself into this great project—heart, body and soul—and it was killing me. I was near my physical limits, and, after the stress of last autumn, my mental limits too.

Or maybe it had been Katrin, my daughter, nagging me: *there's more to life than this!*

And here I was, doing my Sunday Morning thing. Sitting in my favourite chair, sipping coffee, listening to records, or today, one of the tapes that my daughter had given me. She was introducing me to various funk and acid jazz bands from the English speaking world. She'd tried to excite my interest in this particular album by drawing comparisons with our home-grown Panta Rhei. I was relaxing to a bootleg of Incognito's *100° And Rising*, wondering whether or not it was actually similar to Panta's *Kinder dieser Welt* or *Gib dir selber eine Chance*. I could see why Katrin had made the comparisons, but the British band was bright and Panta Rhei was downbeat, owing more allegiance to classic blues. Perhaps it was because their best work had been before the start of the Revolution, when things were grey, and hope was scarce, manufactured only in small amounts by underground groups meeting clandestinely.

When Incognito bounced their way to *After the Fall* I got out of my chair, and, taking the cassette player with me, headed for the kitchen. I plugged the music in again, and Incognito carried on playing for me. Looking through the cupboards I wondered what to make for the house potluck lunch. We were becoming more and more creative when it came to cooking—the shortages of meat and milk products were making us re-examine our culinary culture—and I decided a mushroom and hazelnut pie would be a nice addition to the communal meal.

14:07

Martin

I pulled my pie out of the oven, satisfied with the golden-brown crust radiating warmth, the rising steam hinting at the gravy within. Wrapping it in a bath towel to keep it warm and to protect my hands, I negotiated the stairwell, heading for the *Kulturbund* rooms next door where the residents of my tenement held Sunday lunches. I was running a bit late, and most people had already started eating. I placed my pie on the side table, next to big bowls of red cabbage and bright vegetables, yeasty dumplings, letscho, a dish of kasha with root vegetables, a big pan of heaven-and-earth, a couple of kinds of sauces, several bowls of spring salads and a massive pot of *Rote Grütze* pudding.

I filled a plate and looked around for a place to sit. At the other end of the table Margrit, who lived a floor above me, gestured to the empty space next to her. I went over, rubbing her shoulder in greeting and sat down. On my other side was Frau Lehne, who was a bit deaf, and in any case preferred to enjoy her food rather than exchange small talk while at table, so I tucked in. The kasha was really good, and my pie lived up to expectations, garnering compliments from the other residents.

Once I'd finished my plate, I sat back, waiting a bit before going up for seconds. Margrit and I started talking, as usual, about our week, and when I mentioned that I'd been at the fascist demonstration she looked off into the distance, absenting herself from the chatter and clinking of cutlery on plates that surrounded us. After a moment she began telling me a story.

"A few years ago, at our factory, we had a Vietnamese woman in our work brigade. I say in our brigade, but she wasn't really. She couldn't speak German, and she never came along to any of the social events. But every day at work, there she was, stretching up to reach the workbench—she was too small for the standard issue stool that we all used. And one day she wasn't there any more. I didn't really notice for, oh, I don't know how long, a few days probably. Then I went to the brigade leader and asked where our colleague was, whether she was ill, whether anyone had gone to see her and check whether she needed anything. The brigade leader just shrugged and said I should talk to the union. So I went to the BGL office and tried to talk to them but they just shrugged and told me the *Fidschis* were none of my concern. This was in summer 1989, when we were all starting to get a bit uppity, so I didn't let the matter rest. I went to another brigade, one that was only Vietnamese contract workers. Problem was, there was only one of them who could speak any German at all. She said the same thing: *No, no. You leave, nothing for you,* was all she would say to me.

"So after work I went round to the hostel, the place where our factory put the contract workers. It was like student halls, only worse, they were really crammed in, triple bunk beds, a couple of a dozen people to each room. I had to blag my way past the security guard, and once I'd made it in, it took me a while before I could find anyone to talk to. So after asking a whole load of people I found this woman who could speak a bit of German. She told me that my colleague had been sent home, back to Vietnam. She was pregnant. That was it: she was pregnant. She was no longer suitable for work in our socialist homeland. All that propaganda about internationalism, about supporting the socialist brother-countries, but there I was in this hostel, men and women not allowed to mix, roll-call at six every morning, no integration with colleagues, no German lessons. Treated like prisoners, cheap labour, that's all they were. That is what the Party's proletarian solidarity looked like!"

I remembered the contract workers from Vietnam, Algeria, Hungary. Some had returned home in 1990, but many had stayed, seeing more opportunity and hope in our revolution than at home.

"I'll never forget her, but you know what I'm really ashamed of? I don't even know that woman's name. I didn't talk to her when she worked with us. In my brigade we all used to have a laugh, we'd all go to the canteen, go bowling together. But she was never there, she'd join her friends in the Vietnamese brigades. I never even asked her name." Margrit was staring at her plate as she talked, using her fork to poke at a few leftover crumbs of pie crust.

"And now when I see what's happening, just a few streets away, I wonder whether it should really be such a surprise to us—if our socialist state was so racist, so lacking in respect for people, whether its own people or those who've come to help us with their labour—is it any surprise we've got this problem now, these racist, fascist bigots, running riot: pissing on people, pissing on our dreams?"

"But what can we do? What do you think we should do?" I asked her.

"Lock the bastards up, throw away the bloody key. It's what they deserve!" I was taken aback by her viciousness, but she hadn't finished. She gave me a half smile. "And yet we both know that's not really the answer, don't we? Why didn't they lock them up back then? I don't know. What do we do with these fascists? They're not the kind of people we can just *talk* to, are they?"

She paused again, obviously thinking, still poking the crumbs, pushing them along with her fork. Shove, shove, from one side to the other, then back again.

"We need a new way to deal with them. It's not like we can hold a referendum on whether to simply abolish racism and fascism. It's not enough to discuss it at the Round Table, talk about why we don't want them." She paused, still thinking about the problem, staring at her plate.

People had started to get pudding, so I got up and spooned *Rote Grütze* into a couple of bowls, taking them back to the table. I took the fork out of Margrit's hand and pushed her plate away, replacing it with a bowl. She was so deep in thought she hardly noticed the exchange.

"But you know what frightens me most about them?" She carried on as if I hadn't been away. "It's not the violence, although that's pretty awful. It's the absolute commitment, the unquestioning belief that they are right. We've seen it before, we've all seen that before, haven't we? But what scares me is that I too once believed. Years ago, when I first started work, I applied to be a Communist Party member candidate. I had the faith, but they didn't want me in the end. *An absence of political maturity* they said, and I'm glad about that now." She looked around for her spoon and picked it up, resting the blade of her hand on the table. "But you know what that means? It means that I could have been like them, unquestioning, unthinking, conforming."

A pause, while we both pondered Margrit's words, then she continued.

"And you know what? I wonder about it now, too. We have a belief system now. Sure, it's widespread, it's humanist, we're not going to beat people up if they don't agree with us. But how are we going to stop people if they're really set on tearing apart our dreams? People like these skinheads, or like those Stasi stooges you arrested last year. What do we do with them?"

I thought about the old *Politbüro*, the grey men who used to rule the country. They felt a humanist duty too, they thought that duty obliged them to issue orders to shoot people who tried to flee the country. They thought that humanist duty bound them to capture and torture those who thought differently.

The way we deal with those who think differently—the troublemakers, the ones who refuse to participate in our dreams— how we deal with them would be the making or breaking of us.

"Karo!" Schimmel was banging on my door, waking me up.

"The fuck? I was asleep, Schimmel!"

Schimmel didn't even stop, he loped across my room and pulled me off the mattress.

"You've got to see this, come on!"

I shook Schimmel off and left him standing there, arms dangling, face bright red, dead excited.

"OK then, what do you want?" I got up and pulled on a pair of jeans, then followed him down the hall.

Schimmel's room was full of junk. Metal and plastic boxes with wires and circuit boards and shit like that just lying around. It didn't make any sense to me, and it didn't look very homely either. He was squatting on the floor, in front of one of these boxes, a television balanced on top.

"Look at this!" he shouted, pointing at some green writing on the black screen in front of him.

I could see a load of Xs, and if I squinted hard enough I could make out the letters WOTAN BBS.

Schimmel typed something and the screen changed to some kind of list. Using the arrow keys Schimmel made the screen change a few more times.

"This is a Bulletin Board System used by the Nazis. Rex asked me to have a look at-"

"Whoa, slow down a bit! What you going on about Schimmel?"

"Look, it's really simple. This is a computer network, it's like ...." Schimmel took his eyes off the screen for a moment, looking round the room, trying to find a way to explain what he was doing. "Like a library, no, a filing cabinet. A message board. You dial in and you can leave stuff here, and see what others have left. Like files, or messages or whatever." Schimmel was still pressing lots of keys and the screen kept changing. A little box on the floor had four or five green lights that kept blinking at me.

"Dial in? You mean on a phone? We don't have a phone!"

Schimmel was concentrating, but he took a moment to grin at me.

"I spliced into the line from that empty shop next door."

He was still stabbing away at the keyboard and I was about to have a go at him for waking me up for no reason when he yelled again.

"Here it is! I lost the connection before. Here, read this!"

I looked over his shoulder at the screen.

"This is the fash?"

"Yeah, I told you, I got the details from Rex. This is where they talk about what they're up to."

"What, so anyone can read it? Not even the fash are that stupid!"

"No, you can't find this unless you've got the phone number. And even then you need a password." Schimmel could tell I didn't know what he was on about so he tried again. "You get your computer to phone their computer, and they can share this." He pointed at the screen, all the information there. "But you can only do that if you know the phone number and have the right name and password."

"OK ...."

"And they write stuff like this." A few more clicks on the keyboard and a new load of type came up on the screen.

"So what's that, a list of their members?"

On the screen was a list of people's names and addresses. I didn't recognise any of them.

"No, I think it's a kind of hit list."

One of the names stuck out because almost all of the addresses were in East Berlin, but this one was a hospital in West Berlin. Schimmel pressed the down arrow and the lines slid up the screen to be replaced by yet more addresses.

"Shit!" Schimmel stopped pressing keys and pointed at the screen. "That's Martin!"

15:17

Martin

After the potluck I decided to give Incognito another go. I'd just pressed the play button when Karo banged on the door.

"Are you missing me?" I stopped when I saw her face. I don't think I've ever seen Karo look so serious. Schimmel stood behind her.

"Martin, you've got to look at this." Karo came right in, and was unreeling a computer print-out on my kitchen table. She jammed her finger onto one of the names. "This is you!"

I turned off the tape player and looked at where Karo was pointing. There was my name, Martin Grobe, and the address of the RS2 offices.

"What is this?"

"It's a list I found on a Bulletin Board used by the Nazis," Schimmel said from behind Karo.

I looked at Karo for a translation.

"It's like a meeting place for fascists, on a computer that they can all get access to."

Schimmel was about to argue with Karo's description, but she waved her hand at him. "It's a hit list—and you're on it!"

I picked up the end of the print-out and started looking through it. There was about twenty pages of names, all printed out in dot matrix, barely legible.

"Why do you think it's a hit list? Even if it is, there are so many names here that it'll take them years before I get to the top." I sat down and crossed my legs. I can't say I wasn't disturbed by seeing my name on this list, but after the events of last autumn I was public property—I'd been in the papers and on the telly. This kind of thing was only to be expected.

I started at the top of the list again, reading more carefully this time. "Look, practically the whole government is on this list, along with *Volkskammer* representatives, Central and local Round Table members—this is the list of a fantasist."

I managed to get Karo and Schimmel to calm down a bit, told them to make a coffee while I carried on looking through the list. "I'm going to pass the list on to *Kripo*," I told them, ignoring the face Karo pulled at the mention of the police. "And I'll take it into work. I'll go through our files, see if anyone on the list has come to grief recently. That way we'll know how seriously to take it."

Karo slumped onto a chair, her fear draining away. "But you're going to take it seriously?" she demanded. She waited for me to nod before going on. "OK, in that case, and since we're here anyway: I'm helping to set up a gig, up in Prenzlauer Berg. In the *Schlaraffenhaus* —it's going to be really cool. You wanna come? Say you will, because then we can keep an eye on you."

In the end I gave in to Karo's pleading and agreed to come to the gig. That's why, a few hours later I caught the tram to Dimitroffstrasse, but outside the police station a group of people had converged, standing around a bloke strumming a guitar and crooning. Somehow he managed to compete not only with the noise made by the band accompanying him, but also with the elevated railway and the trams going past. A small child strutted around in front of the singer, wearing denim dungarees, her hair was cut short at the front, rat tails dragging down the back of her neck. She held a pair of drumsticks and air drummed while the band played out. Meanwhile, the next act waited in the wings: jeans hanging loose around his waist, shirt open over a T-shirt advertising some Western band.

A drunkard stumbled through the crowd, arms paddling—clawing himself along, hands grappling the air.

Oblivious to the impromptu concert, crowds of people swelled around the knot of music lovers, growing and diminishing to the rhythm of the traffic lights controlling the pedestrian crossing.

The person next to me leaned on me in a drunken, friendly way.

"Drink!" he shouted, waving a bottle of vodka at me and smiling. His forehead was shadowed under the peak of a traditional *Heinrichsmütze* cap, but his face lit up periodically in the headlights of cars turning onto Schönhauser Allee.

He produced two glasses, and poured out some vodka, right up to the brim. Parking the bottle in his pocket, he gave me my shot, looked me in the eye, toasted me then necked the liquid.

"*Prosit!*" I swallowed down my vodka too.

"*Prosit!*" he said again, about to turn away, ready to find another recipient for his liquid generosity.

"Where are you from?" I asked him before he went.

"I am of German Democratic Republic," he slurred, but still rolling the Rs, "of G-D-R" He pronounced it the Russian way: *Djay-Day-Err.*

"You're new here? Welcome!"

"This is my home, *Djay-Day-Err.* I am here. Now I am happy and I am safe. And *Prosit!*" He moved on, readying the glasses for a refill.

I was sorting out the loudspeakers in the cellar-bar when Martin got there. A couple of band members were meant to be helping but they were just getting in the way and being generally annoying. So I left them to it and gave Martin a hug.

"Still alive then?" I could smell drink on his breath. "You stink! You started drinking already? Anyway, you're gonna love this, they're an amazing act—you're going to cream yourself!"

"O-kaaay." Martin raised an eyebrow at me.

"No, seriously, man. You. Are. Gonna. Love. The show!" I told the two hippies what to do with the wires and took Martin back up into the yard. "It's jazz. The band that shoulda played tonight, they bailed out. Post folk-punk-metal it was. But these guys offered to plug the gap, and I listened to a demo tape. Fucking. Ace. I mean, even I like them!"

Martin shrugged as if to say he reserved the right to leave at any point.

I punched him on the shoulder.

One of the drummers was a dude with really wide shoulders, red shirt stretched tight over his chest. Forearms like tree trunks. The whole time he was playing he had his eyes fixed on the other drummer. She didn't ever look at the drums, her hands and drumsticks just, like a blur—you literally couldn't see them—just beating away: bum-bum-bummmm. The guy with the trombone though, he was totally focussed on the microphone stand in front of him. He was pushing his hand and the mike right into the bell of his instrument. The double bass player was even more manic, it was really crazy—he was foaming at the mouth, and mumbling something that you couldn't hear over the noise, his eyes roving over all of us in the audience as if he was looking for the bastard who'd nicked the score sheet.

The saxophonist was the last of the group, and he was really chilled. He had this massive ragged beard that matched his wild hair, and he was doing this weird thing with his sax, wailing and screaming at random moments.

The sound they were making had less tune than your typical neo-grindcore punk—it was just a bass throb intertwined with higher notes. Completely undanceable, impossibly fast, no melody to follow. Totally ace. The dance-floor was chokka, everyone had their hands up in the air.

A disembodied voice sang the Internationale: *Völker hört die Signale! Auf zum letzten Gefecht!* It was like some ghost wailing, and I was trying to work out how they did that. There was no tape player, I know because I set up the sound system. Where was that voice coming from? And then I worked it out. The guy with the trombone, he wasn't blowing into the mouthpiece, he was shouting into it! He suddenly switched the lyrics: *The spoils of revolution / Kronstadt, Budapest and Prague / where the spectre of Communism still haunts / still dragging its chains.* It was so ace, the ghostly hand of the past being totally twatted to fuck by this stupidly fast beat.

It made sense, so much sense. I wanted to write it all down, record it, tell everyone I knew how these people had got it, they'd really *got* it!

I tried to tell Martin about it, but he was dancing, really manic. He'd got it, I could tell.

He was pissed, well pissed.

It was good.

02:04

Martin

"Come on Marty! Let's go and see Annette! She'll be pleased to see us!"

It was past midnight. At least, the blurred outlines of the hands on my watch, they were both pointing somewhere near the top. Yeah. Middle of the night.

Annette? Why not? Something niggled, some thought trying to escape my befuddled brain. Something about Annette. I had fences to mend, I had to tell her how much she meant to me, that I'd missed her and was sorry we weren't together any more. She'd be pleased to see me, and I could tell her how I felt. And Karo was with me, we could go dancing, the three of us. In Kreuzberg.

We climbed the steps to the elevated railway, got on the ivory and yellow train that soon rattled into the station and we cheered as it dived down the ramp into the tunnel. We weren't the only party-goers aboard, an accordion started playing at the other end of the carriage, and I swayed around, more or less in time to the music, hanging on to a strap.

"You know that list you gave me? I sent it to K1," I told Karo, shouting above the noise of the accordion.

"K-*fucking*-1?" shouted Karo back. "Do they still exist? Fucking lowest of the fucking low! Fucking Stasi swine."

"No, no, no." I tried to put her right. "They're DVP, they're cops. They're different from the Stasi."

"Fuck off!" was Karo's answer.

We got off less than ten minutes later, at Märkisches Museum, swerving down the road, towards the border crossing point about a kilometre away. Karo still had her bottle of beer to keep her company, but I seemed to have lost mine. Was it still on the U-Bahn?

"I lost my bottle!" I exclaimed to the sleeping streets.

Karo just giggled and wobbled out into the middle of the road.

The border guards at Heinrich-Heine-Strasse stood just outside their hut, arms across their chests.

"Evening, comrades, do you intend crossing into West Berlin?"

Drunk as I was, I could still sense the disapproval, a priggish concern that if we entered the West in such a bibulous state we may sully the good name and standing of the German Democratic Republic.

"I, comrades ..." I started, before fumbling through my shoulder bag, looking for my identity papers, the ones that identified me as a captain of the *Republikschutz*. "My magic papers, magic will get us through," I breathed over to Karo, who giggled again.

But I couldn't find my magic RS identification. I looked over to Karo, who was carefully balancing her beer bottle on the kerb. Did she have my papers? No. But they're not in my bag and not in my pockets. With a sigh, I decided that a bluff would do the job, I just needed to be insouciant enough in the execution.

"My papers, comrade!" With a flourish I produced my blue civilian identity card.

The guard I was addressing looked over to his colleague, raising an eyebrow. The other gave a small shake of the head, and we were let through.

The West Berlin policeman on the other side deliberately looked away as we crossed the white line that delineated West from East, bad from good, rich from poor.

We stood at the huge roundabout of Moritzplatz, wondering which way to go. A cool breeze was blowing against my face, waking me up a bit. An empty cola can clattered along the gutter, and a sheet of newspaper pressed itself against my ankles.

"Where does your Annette live?" asked Karo, looking around, bewildered, paying attention to the edge of the pavement, aware that here in the West, even at this time of night, it didn't do to stand in the middle of the road.

"Too many fucking cars!" she shouted at a passing Volkswagen.

I was beginning to have doubts. I looked at my watch again. It was after two o'clock. I could see it clearly now, I was beginning to sober up. It was quite a walk from here to where Annette lived. My synapses started to connect again, my brain slowly working out that maybe it wasn't such a good idea to call on Annette right now. Or maybe ever again. I'd scared her off last year, when I'd last seen her. My job had scared her off. Maybe she didn't want to see me. No, if she wanted to see me, she'd have been with us tonight. No, no, no. Not a good idea at all.

I turned to Karo, feeling the need to impart this great news to her.

"Karo, Karo, shhh! Listen: you ready? This is veryveryvery*important*."

Karo drew herself up, standing to attention in front of me, wind ruffling her bright red hair. She pressed her thumb to her forehead, palm held straight out in a mock Pioneer salute: *always prepared*.

"I. Don't. Think." I said, enunciating each syllable so, so perfectly, "That. We. Should. Gotosee. Annette."

Karo shrugged and set off down Oranienstrasse, singing U2's *One*. I followed, not for a moment wondering where we were going.

DAY 8
Monday
21ˢᵗ March 1994

Berlin: *The South Friedrichshain Neighbourhood Round Table has repeated requests for dialogue with residents of the* Wagenburg *on the banks of the Spree.*

A spokesperson for the Neighbourhood Round Table stated that there was ongoing conflict with local residents and industry, including the Reichsbahn and the Border Regiment. The Wagenburg *has allegedly refused to meet local stakeholders.*

08:17
Martin

"Jeez, Papa! How old are you?"

I couldn't work out whether Katrin was pissed off or amused. Possibly a bit of both, I decided in the gaps between the hammer blows that were pounding the inside of my head. It was the same banging that caused my skull to swell and made black rings blur my vision. *Old enough,* I thought to myself, *to know how to avoid a hangover.*

"What are you doing here anyway? At least you didn't puke all over my flat."

One of us had been sick last night. I remembered that. We were ringing Katrin's bell, pushing it, holding it in. I was. That was it, I rang the bell while Karo puked all over the pavement.

"Here's some money, go and get some rolls. I'll get the coffee going and try to wake up Karo."

I looked at the coin in the palm of my hand as if I'd never seen Westmarks before: a West German eagle on one side, and some face on the other, maybe a president or a chancellor? I turned it over and over, noticing the words stamped on the edge of the coin: *Unity and Justice and Freedom.* Putting the money in my pocket I went down the stairs and out of the tenement block. A Turkish lady in a head scarf was throwing a bucket of water over Karo's vomit. She caught my eye and shook her head sadly, as if to say *young people today!* I looked down and hurried off.

Karo's vomit wasn't the only refuse on the street, I wandered past a footstool, horsehair stuffing trickling out of a rip in the vinyl covering. A little further on—sprinkled around the trunk of a tree that looked like it probably wouldn't bother with leaves this year—lay empty cigarette packets, a couple of crushed coke cans and a smashed beer bottle. Fag ends and splots of dried chewing gum littered the pavement. The West: so rich, so many things available in the shops, no shortages. But their streets were paved with carcasses of consumption.

A group of punks came towards me. It wasn't until they were almost level that I realised they weren't the young people I had taken them for but were all about my own age. Ragged, saggy leggings, ripped leather vests and jackets, studs and hoops in ears and noses, they came towards me, uncertainly following the drunken pavement, holding tightly onto their bottles of beer.

"YougoddaMarkforme?" one of them slurred in my general direction.

I shrugged my shoulders, bunching my hands in my pockets.

"Krotte, leave 'im be," shouted another punk from the back of the group. "He ain't got no dosh, he's an *Ossi*! Got less'n us, that lot!"

The group laughed harshly, and disappeared into a bar. Curious, I looked in through the open door, peering past the thick cigarette smoke that condensed into the street. Icons, religious reliquaries and statues hung behind the bar, draped with medals and crucifixes on chains. Many of the clientèle looked like they had moved in when the place opened and had never managed to leave again. Going by the patina of ossified dust and nicotine, that must have been a decade or two ago.

I smiled to myself and made my careful way to the bakery. Eyeing the distended golden crust of the rolls in the basket behind the counter I again considered the money I held in my hand.

"How do you get them so crispy and full of air?" I asked the lady behind the counter.

"Are you going to buy anything or did you come over here just to ask stupid questions?" she snapped back in Berliner dialect.

I shrugged and did some mental arithmetic. I had two Marks, so could just about afford six rolls with a bit of change left over. At home, I could get over twenty *Schrippen* for two Eastmarks—or on the black market I could exchange these two Westmarks for twenty Eastmarks and buy two hundred rolls. And at home they were solid affairs, full of bread; not like the crusty air bags that I was looking at now.

I was taking too long for the shop assistant and she'd started serving another customer. I waited patiently for her to turn back to me.

"So, what's it to be? You decided what you can afford?"

I was looking at the glistening layers of the Splitterbrötchen, the dark surface pocked with powdered cinnamon.

"How much are they?" I asked.

"Mark-forty."

One Mark forty. I looked at the two Mark piece in my hand, and dug into my pockets, fishing out my Eastmark change. I easily had about ten Marks worth there.

"We only take proper money—none of your dodgy scrap aluminium!"

The bread rolls were still warm, I could feel the heat through the colourful paper bag. It felt good in my hand, and I had to stop myself from curling my fingers around one of the rolls, squeezing until the crust splintered and the soft dough inside collapsed. They looked so good, these rolls. My mind fixed on that thought, keeping hold of it, past the waves of pressure that were still gripping my head with every footstep. It was all about appearances, how they looked.

Like the punks. They looked so young, but when they got closer, they were my age.

Here in the West things don't always appear as they seem. *Brilliant Martin*, I thought to myself. *With thinking like that you'll soon solve all the problems of the world.* But another thought was trying to make its way through my hangover. The boat the other night, or rather the boats. I hadn't been able to work out what they were up to, what the point of their theatrical manoeuvres could have been. But, the thought persisted, perhaps that was exactly what it was: a piece of theatre, designed to distract us. Even the boat that had slipped across the Landwehr Canal to deliver a small package was a double bluff.

No, a triple bluff—we were meant to believe that the small package was the reason behind the activity on the river Spree. Next time the *Grenzer* would be watching the Landwehr Canal, and maybe the river between Oberbaum Bridge and Elsen Bridge. Customs and Border Guards would be focussing along the canal and the weir lead. Any forces on the Oberbaum Bridge would be looking upstream. Which would leave the downstream sector of the river—towards Schilling Bridge—practically unobserved. And that was a section of the river that had another *Wagenburg* directly on the water's edge: no border guards on the ground there.

When I got back I found the kitchen table laid for two.

"Karo's still asleep," said my daughter. "She's snoring away, so I left her to it."

I nodded, there wasn't much to say, and I was still thinking about my new theory. We sat down and Katrin cut all the bread rolls in half: neat, no crumbs flaking away from the crust, the soft, doughy bread inside not balling up but sliced straight down the middle.

"Papa," Katrin said in that cautious voice she used when she wanted to talk seriously.

I looked up from my bread roll.

"Papa, thanks for the other day. I know it wasn't easy for you."

I shrugged, what are fathers there for? "Have you decided what you're going to do?"

A long pause while Katrin worked out how to reply, carefully considering how to put her words into place.

"I don't know," she finally said. "I wish I did. It's not like I'm thinking about it all the time. But I sit there in my room, I'm meant to be studying, and out of the corner of my eye I'll see her letter. Sitting there, on the edge of my desk. I don't even know what to do with the letter. I don't want to throw it away, not yet. And I don't want to file it away—that way I'll let myself forget about it and I won't ever decide what to do. So for the moment it's sitting there, on the corner of my desk, reminding me that I need to make a decision."

"It's OK, you know," I said, then broke off and started again. "I mean, it's your choice. To write to her. Or not. I won't be upset." I wondered how truthful my words were. How much would it bother me if my daughter wrote to the woman who had abandoned her when she was a small child? Abandoned us, both of us.

It was so long ago, another life, another State, another history. I couldn't be angry at her after all these years, no, not angry. But it still hurt. I understood only too well why she'd gone: the frustration, the feeling of being trapped, the claustrophobia. I'd had those reactions too but we'd each had different ways of dealing with them.

Except that Katrin's mother hadn't really found a way to deal with it—she'd fought her way out of East Germany, like a wild animal trapped in a cage fights to escape, no matter the cost. She'd left behind her family, so desperate was she to get out. Had I forgiven her? The years had softened the hard, sharp edges of pain, but it was still there. A scar on my heart, reminding me of past torment; aching when the weather turned, or when the moon waxed to full.

"Papa, I know it's my choice." She smiled and touched my hand with her long fingers. "I know. But first I have to decide whether I actually want to have contact with her. If I do, then I'll talk to you about it first." Her eyes sought mine, looking for understanding. "I promise. I don't want to cause you any hurt, but right now I don't even know what to think. I've no idea what to do, what the right thing to do might be."

My daughter had been speaking slowly, with lots of gaps. She was thinking aloud. Now there was another pause, a gap in which we both digested the words we'd said and heard. This conversation had been years in the coming, there was no rushing it. It would take a while to reach any conclusion. Love is complicated, how can it be described? How can it be quantified, weighed across the years and the miles and the borders that stood between the pair of us here in

Berlin and the mother that hadn't been a mother for so long?

"Would it have been better if she hadn't contacted you?"

Another pause while Katrin considered her answer.

"Perhaps," she answered finally. "It's like I can feel her, waiting. Somewhere in West Germany. Waiting for an answer." She was staring at our clasped hands, trying to find the right words. "I can feel her hope. Hoping I'll write back, forgive her. But I'm not sure it's me who should be doing any forgiving. She's nothing but an impression from the past, a ghost. It doesn't feel like it's up to me to forgive her. Maybe that's for you—maybe that's your job. I was so young, I hardly remember her. She was always there, but as an absence—I never found a way to talk to you about it because I could see how much she'd hurt you." She placed her hand briefly on my forearm, a light touch, then she was talking again. "What she did, that hurt you. When I look back at that time, I can't remember anything concrete, except that she broke you.

"And every time I think about picking up a pen, writing an answer, every time I do that, I can't. Because it's too complicated. I don't know what to think, what to say. *Hello mum,*" she said, in a slightly ironic tone, quoting her unwritten letter. "*Thanks for sending me a letter after all these years. I'm fine, Papa's fine, hope you're fine. Lots of love, your daughter.* Doesn't really work, does it? There are too many strands binding the past and the future, and it's like I need to cut through them before I can know what I want."

Perhaps I understood, perhaps I knew what Katrin meant. Writing a letter to her mother wasn't just a simple correspondence, an action in the present. It meant dealing with the past but also looking into the future: just a letter or constant contact? Would it stop at letters, or would they meet? What kind of relationship would they have? What kind of relationship *could* they have? When her mother had left, Katrin had been little, a Young Pioneer in a blue neckerchief. Now she was an adult, making her own way in life.

And her mother would be different too—what she went through back then, all the things that might have happened since then, they would have changed her, moulded her. When she put in her application for an exit visa she was ready for the harassment from the state. To some extent I could support her at that stage, even though I didn't agree, I wanted to stay, wanted her to stay too. But when they took her away, from that moment on she was by herself. I have no idea what she'd been through. She would have been in prison. Softened up in Hohenschönhausen, after that Hoheneck. Hell holes that break your spirit. Then they would have released her to the West. She'd never written to tell me what had happened. Or if she had, then the letter had never arrived. All I knew was that one day I'd received a summons. I was required to go to the police station. An anonymous room, an anonymous man sitting behind an empty desk. He informed me of my wife's release, that she was no longer a citizen of the GDR, that she had forfeited the privilege of living in the socialist state. He had meant release from jail, but for her it was a release from a prison that was the size of this country.

"I wish I knew what to do." Katrin was crying now. The tears came suddenly, they shocked me. She hadn't cried last Sunday when we'd talked about this. I hadn't seen her cry since 1989 when she followed in her mother's footsteps, leaving the GDR. In that year she'd grown up, our relationship had equalised: no longer a father and a daughter, the adult providing protection, advice and support to the child, but two adults, there for each other. More than that in fact, Katrin had become, in some ways, the stronger of the pair of us. To see her cry was hard for me. I went round the table, stood next to Katrin's chair and put my arms round her shoulders. She wrapped her arms around me, and we held each other tight.

A slight cough. "Am I interrupting?"

I turned my head to see Karo standing at the door of the kitchen, looking even more dishevelled than usual.

We left Katrin to her breakfast and headed Eastwards. Katrin had insisted that we go, she said she had a lecture, and didn't I have a job to go to anyway? So we left the flat, making our way down the dingy staircase of Katrin's tenement block, spent bulbs in the lamps, nicotine yellow gloss paint on the walls, worn lino on the steps. Along the side-street and into Skalitzer Strasse, following the U-Bahn viaduct where the orange trains rumble over the corroded structure. We were walking in silence, I was thinking about my daughter. She had been embarrassed by her crying, I decided. She was like her mother in that way.

Like her father, too.

But I was glad we were talking to each other. We weren't very good at sharing feelings even though we'd learned that we had to use whatever time we had together. There was no knowing when circumstance would divide us again.

"Martin! Earth calling Martin! Come in all cosmonauts!"

I'd stopped walking, Karo was shouting at me from in front of the checkpoint at the Wall. Before catching up with her I took a look around me. I decided that Kreuzberg wasn't all that great, it looked as run-down and unloved as most of East Berlin.

But Karo was still waiting for me, right next to the Wall that blocked off the western end of the Oberbaum Bridge. A squat guard tower peeked at us, the corrugated iron roof rusting into holes, windows covered by bars. To the right the rail viaduct crossed over the bridge, but the tracks were cut by several fences and a concrete wall.

We ducked through the gate and walked over the bridge, looking downriver towards the East Side *Wagenburg*. I couldn't see it clearly from here, it was just a bit too far away, but I knew it as a stinking place, rubbish piled high between trucks and wagons, people lying around in a drunken or drugged haze. A real contrast to the gardens and washing lines of the Lohmühle.

But my mind was still turning over the events of last Friday night. If the smugglers' main delivery was to be downstream of this bridge then the only feasible landing place would be the East Side: all fences already removed, no wall at the water's edge, no watchtowers between this bridge and the next, the perfect place for smugglers to land.

"Karo, what do you reckon, the East Side *Wagenburg*—good place for smugglers to bring their stuff in?"

Karo stopped and leant against the railing, gazing downriver. "Yeah. Suppose so. Why?"

Karo

I was standing with Martin on the Oberbaum Bridge, just enjoying the morning sunlight when he started on at me about smugglers. Before I knew what had happened he'd dragged me along to the East Side as if I was his personal tour guide.

I don't go there much—it's got a bit of a rep as a lunch-out zone. People who just want to sit around on their arses drinking schnapps all day and not giving a flying fuck about the revolution. Some say that it's because there's a lot of foreigners there, but you know what, everywhere I look I see foreigners, and they're all doing their bit. Except here. On the East Side nobody does fuck all.

We went through the gate and Martin made a bee-line for the edge of the river. It was still really early so none of the locals were up yet, we had the place to ourselves.

"What you looking for?"

"I don't know. Some signs of smuggling. Could be anything."

This smuggling thing was really getting old. I remembered our conversation at the Feeling B concert and decided to leave it—I'd promised Katrin I'd keep any eye on Martin, not argue with him the whole time.

He was mooching about, looking under the wagons, kicking at the piles of tat that were lying around.

"Martin, you can't just poke around like that! People live here."

"Yeah? And what about this," he said, a triumphant grin plastered over his coupon. He'd lifted the corner of a tarp and was staring into a nest of blankets. "You usually expect to find a stash of antique Meissen porcelain somewhere like this?"

"The bastards didn't give me my fix." I looked up from the crate of pottery.

This hippy was watching us. Thin, spotty. Track marks up her bare arms. I thought she was just ranting about something in her own head so I ignored her, but Martin wanted to know what she was blethering on about.

"Every Friday, about a quarter to ten. We get a fix. Good shit. They come and give us good shit." She sat down on the edge of the crate with the Meissen in it. "But I was late last week. I'd gone out, hadn't I, into town. So I didn't get any shit, did I? Bastards."

"Who? Who gives you shit?" Martin didn't have a clue what she was going on about.

"The guys. The men. The suits, y'know?" the hippy looked at Martin as if he was the one who'd lost it.

"So these guys." I decided to help Martin out—we'd be here all day otherwise. "They come and give you dope, good stuff. Always on Friday." The hippy was dead pleased that somebody understood her, she was nodding away like a member of the *Politbüro*. "And they give it to you for free?" She was still nodding.

"Quarter to ten, Likasay. Good shit. Bastards."

A quick look at the ground and I spotted the wheel tracks and the scratches on the concrete edge of the quay. I walked over to an old army tarp covering something big, taller than me, but not too wide. I peered through a rip in the canvas.

"Martin, check this out—fork lift truck!" I pointed at the tracks in the dust. "Every Friday they dole out smack to this lot so they don't notice anything and nobody's gonna believe them even if they do grass them up. Sweet. Then they bring a boat in, use the fork lift truck to shift this lot." I pointed at the pretty pots in the crate. "And you reckon they're delivering stuff as well?"

I thought Martin was going to object about the boat bit—I thought he'd just tell me they couldn't just bring a boat in under the border guards' noses, but he was stroking his chin and nodding slowly. In fact, I reckon he was well impressed with my reasoning.

"Oi!"

Oh fuck. This wasn't good. The hippy had vanished, and two skinheads were standing next to the fork lift truck, each holding a wooden chair leg.

"Martin! Run!"

We legged it. Dodging between the trucks and builder's wagons, trying to give the skins the slip. If I'd been by myself I'd have been straight out of there, but I had Martin in tow. I couldn't leave him behind. I jumped up onto an old flatbed and looked to see where Martin was. He was lagging well behind.

"Martin! Move it! Come on!"

He ran along the side of the trailer, below me, with one of the skins just behind him.

"Fuck you!" I jumped at the skin, landing on his back. He stumbled, dropping to the floor and letting go of his bit of wood.

"Martin—run!" I was on my feet before the skin. I grabbed his stick and without even thinking about it just twatted him on the nose. The skin screamed and dropped down again, landing on his knees, hands to his face. Blood fucking everywhere. I got out of there fast.

I was just behind Martin and the gate in the Wall was dead ahead of us, get to that gate and we'd be on the busy road, we'd be safe. Martin was breathing heavily, clutching his side.

"Come on Martin, come on!"

Just then the other skin darted out from behind a truck. He grabbed Martin by his bag, using it to swing Martin round, down on to the sand. I ran up behind the skin and whacked him, hard as I could. Chair leg to the back of the skin's head. I got hold of Martin's hand and dragged him up, towards the gate. He looked like he was going to argue, but I just pulled him along.

I got us out of there.

That was well close—if I hadn't dealt with those two skins then Martin wouldn't have made it. I don't know whether he got that, he was kind of dazed, and I don't think he would have liked the fact that I'd just twatted those two fuckers. I don't know how I felt about it, you know, after Saturday. That lad, the one on the floor, getting the shit kicked out of him by my mates. Just couldn't get it out of my head. The Antifa group had been on a real high after that, we'd gone to a social centre and everyone had to hear about how fucking heroic we'd been.

I'd left soon after.

And now I'd done it again. It felt kind of different because it was self-defence. But so was Saturday, except we got to them before they could do any damage to any of us.

"You OK?" I asked Martin. He was bending over, trying to catch his breath. We were at the Hauptbahnhof station now, we'd run all the way from the hole in the Wall that leads to the East Side. I had an eye open for the skins, in case they were still coming after us.

"OK. You win. I'm going to take you seriously about this smuggling stuff," I told Martin.

Martin wobbled over to one of the benches. "You want to give me a hand with the smuggling stuff?"

I hadn't said that, I'd just said I was going to take him seriously. Then again, I'd also promised myself I was going to take the whole fascist threat thing seriously too. So, yeah, I could help Martin out.

"You see, the next thing on my list is to have a chat with the people at the Lohmühle *Wagenburg*."

"Martin, what is your problem? What's the Lohmühle got to do with smuggling?" Maybe I was still wigged by what had just happened at the East Side, but I could hear myself getting louder and louder. "How many fucking times do I have to say it? It's like you're not taking me seriously!"

Martin looked a bit shocked, like he hadn't been expecting my reaction, but he should have done cos I'd already told him what I think.

"Look, I know what you're saying, but sometimes there are bigger things going on, we have to look at the bigger picture," he started, but then he backed off a bit. "Like we have to consider how to make it harder for the fascists to smuggle stuff into our country."

"And why are you telling me this?"

"Well, about talking to the Lohmühle people about jumping the Wall ... I was thinking that it might be better if it came from someone a bit more, you know, a bit more like them."

"Like me, you mean?" Now I was really wicked off, I'd expected better from Martin! "Dream on! You can do your own dirty work."

Martin slouched back and looked down. It was like somebody had stuck a pin in him and all the air had come out.

He started rubbing the side of his leg and pulling a face. That's where he must have fallen when the second skinhead grabbed him.

"My bag, damn!"

I laughed at him, we'd just escaped with our lives and Martin was more worried about his bag.

"My shoulder bag, Katrin gave it to me."

Could have been worse, if you ask me. But then I thought about last night, coming through the checkpoint.

"Martin, what was in your bag?"

"Just a hanky, paper, some pens, junk." He scratched his head and thought a bit more, then groaned. "My identity papers."

He didn't seem too bothered, he hadn't cottoned on to it yet, was probably just thinking about the hassle of getting new ID.

"That skinhead has got your *Ausweis*," I told him. "That skin has got your name and address!"

I watched his expression change from irritation to fear.

12:08
Martin

When I finally got to the RS2 office a burly, middle aged fellow passed me on the stairs. He wasn't wearing a uniform, but he was a cop if ever I saw one. Going into the offices I was greeted by unusual levels of activity. Laura was giving Grit a list of things to do, she sounded even more brusque than usual.

"Draft a memo to that effect for the Ministerial Committee, carbon copy to Police Headquarters. Then ring the district police—VPI Lichtenberg. Tell them we want copies of the medical reports, an up to date briefing on what's going on—yes, demand that someone comes down here to give us a full report in person. Then phone the General State Prosecutor's office, I want to know who is going to be in charge tomorrow, and I want to be briefed about what they hope to achieve. Inform them that one of us will be present."

I stood by Laura's elbow, watching our unfortunate secretary make shorthand notes, waiting for Laura to run out of steam. She finally turned to me, frowning.

"Martin, come with me." We made our way over to Erika's office. "Lichtenberg police have finally told us what's going on."

I waved a greeting at Erika, who just blinked in response. She had a police interview record in front of her.

"You've seen the newspapers?"

I shook my head, and took the copy of *Die Andere* that Erika passed over to me. Before I could scan the headlines Laura was talking again.

"Page four, bottom right." Then, exhaling loudly, "It doesn't matter, listen: the IKM we asked about, the informant in the Weitlingstrasse scene. He's dead. When Erika saw the article about a police informer dying in a West Berlin hospital we put two and two together. Lichtenberg K1 has finally condescended to bring us up to speed."

Laura paused for breath, her foot was tapping the lino, making me nervous. I hadn't seen her this way since 1989. Erika had gone back to the interview record she'd been reading when we came in. She seemed absorbed by her task, and she was bothered by what she was reading.

"Yesterday the informant turned up half-dead on the street outside the squat," Laura carried on. She'd taken the newspaper off me and had rolled it up tightly. "He was taken to the hospital in Friedrichshain, in a coma, trauma injuries to the head, severe internal bleeding, collapsed lung—the lot. They moved him to a hospital in West Berlin late last night so that he could get better treatment, but he was found dead this morning. Somebody had turned off his life-support machine-"

"Laura," Erika suddenly broke in. She was looking up from her report, her face drained of colour. One finger was pressed against the paper, marking a paragraph. But Laura wasn't to be stopped.

"The West Berlin police haven't any leads, and they seem determined to treat it as a cock-up by the hospital-"

"Laura! Martin!" Erika tried again, louder.

She was holding out the transcript, trying to get our attention. I took it from her, checking the title at the top. It was the record of the interview with the fascist that had been arrested at the demo last Monday: Andreas Hermann—the interview I had been present at.

"What about it, Erika, what?" Laura was annoyed at being cut off.

"This guy, he threatened the informant last Monday." Erika was looking at me now.

"Yeah, so what? What would you expect him to do?" I asked.

"No, Martin, look: not only did Hermann know about the informant a whole week ago, but he actually threatened the informant. And now he's dead. But Hermann also recognised you, and he threatened you. He said he knew you—that you'd be next!"

I looked at Erika, then at Laura who had taken the transcript off me and was scanning through it, trying to find the relevant part. At first,

I was a bit taken aback, but I put that down to the chase at the East Side, and I got a hold on reality again. I'd been vaguely aware of the threat at the time, but hadn't taken it seriously. By itself it seemed to be just an empty threat, there wasn't really anything to be scared of.

"*You'll be next. No worries, you'll be next,*" read Laura from the transcript. "That's you he's threatening. Why you?"

"I doubt it's anything, just bluster from a violent young man. Bravado, he probably wasn't even involved in the IKM situation. Coincidence." I was trying to calm them down, but the fact that my colleagues were taking it seriously meant that I was re-evaluating the situation too. After all, that threat to the mole had turned out to be far from empty. Maybe it wasn't mere coincidence.

And now I was on some list, and now the skinheads we ran into this morning had my home address.

"Look Martin, we need to take this seriously. Since the Silesian Crisis you've pretty much become the public face of RS—if they think we're investigating them then it stands to reason that you'd be a target—you'd be the first target."

Erika nodded agreement at Laura's words, but I wanted a bit more time to think about it.

"So what's next?" I tried to deflect the conversation back to what the cops were doing. "Presumably K1 or whoever from *Kripo* told you what their next steps will be? They can't just leave things as they are." My ploy seemed to work, at least with Laura.

"They're going to raid the Weitlingstrasse house tomorrow, see if there's any evidence of involvement in the murder of the informant. One of us should be present."

"I'll do it," I offered.

"Well that's going to make you even more of a target—they're sure to recognise you!"

"Yes, but on the other hand, why should we risk anyone else? Right now I'm probably the only person they know in RS." I decided, for the moment, not to tell them about losing my *Ausweis*. "Best limit the faces they know—otherwise they may target you two or Nik as well."

"I'm not happy about this," Erika told me. "I'm not sure any of us should be putting ourselves at risk in this way."

"But we have to, because we don't trust the cops, do we?"

DAY 9
Tuesday
22nd March 1994

Berlin: The Central Round Table has responded to the statement made by the CDU and SPD last Sunday. Round Table member Hanna Krause appealed for calm, saying that discussions around next month's referenda should be measured and based on facts rather than propaganda.

05:54

Martin

I cycled past the fascist squat. All was quiet, no signs of life this early in the morning. It wasn't actually a squat—they'd squatted the building next door but now legitimately rented a whole tenement building from the Housing Association.

I didn't stop but carried on to the next junction and turned left. I locked my bike to a lamppost, blowing on my hands before jamming them under my armpits, trying to warm up my chilled fingers after the dawn cycle ride.

As so often happens when you're waiting, time telescopes and it feels like hours are drifting by. My impatience wasn't helped by the fact that I was nervous; the last raid I'd observed hadn't been pleasant, and quite a few people who had since become friends had been the victims of police violence that day. But, as I told myself in the grey darkness, this time I was less likely to feel any empathy for those who may be on the receiving end of truncheons and fists.

My thoughts were interrupted by a patrol car drawing up across

the junction at the end of my side street. An officer got out, holding a
white and black traffic baton, posting himself in the middle of the
road. This was my cue; I walked back to Weitlingstrasse, waving the
traffic officer away with a flick of my RS identification card, then
went down to the squat. A scrum of uniforms was gathered by the
front door, slowly funnelling in through the narrow gap. By the time I
reached them all but a handful were inside, and I pushed my way in
too. I could hear boots hammering up the stairs, but no swearing, no
shouts of resistance or cries: the only sound was that of the bulls
crashing around. I went into the ground floor flat, which was where
the office was meant to be. A couple of cops stood around, staring at
the empty space. A couple of desks, a few overturned chairs and a
telephone wire hanging from the wall; nothing else to be seen. No
fascists, no electronic equipment, not even a typewriter or a scrap of
paper. I went into the next room: also empty except for a couple of
wooden pallets leaning against the wall.

I stood for a moment, nonplussed, irritated by the echoing
emptiness, then went back out into the hall, running up the stairs,
looking in through open doors at each landing. Cops were standing
around in the empty rooms, chatting and smoking. The only other
occupants of these flats were dust and empty beer bottles.

Our birds had flown.

I went back down to the ground floor, where a sergeant was taking
reports from other cops. Next to them was a low doorway, I stooped
to go through, finding myself on a steep stairway. Feeling around, I
found a light switch and twisted it until a bulb clicked on, lighting up
the stained wooden steps. Careful not to slip, I made my way down to
the cellars, looking into each of the three large, low rooms. These
cellars were also empty except for bits of junk: a few crates of empty
beer bottles, a tattered and ripped black hoody and a few wooden
banner poles in the corner. I walked over to them, crunching across
shards of glass and sandy grit, and kicked the stack of wood. Light-
coloured timber, spruce or pine, about three by three centimetres,
most just over a metre long, but a few were broken in half, jagged
ends sometimes matching the negative impression of a neighbour.
Many of them, particularly the broken pieces, had a reddish-brown
discolouration, splashes that had soaked into the wood, in a few cases

leaving a crusted layer on the surface.

I stood for a moment, looking at the stains. Shuddering, I made my way back up the cellar steps.

"All empty?" I asked the cop standing in the hallway, who was still taking notes while listening to colleagues' reports.

He nodded without looking up from what he was doing, and I went back out onto the street. A police lieutenant was leaning against a green and white Wartburg smoking a cigarette and toying with the microphone of the two-way radio hanging over his shoulder.

"Are you in command of this operation?" I asked, impatiently holding my hand up to ward off a junior cop that looked like he might drag me away from his chief. My gesture must have carried enough authority, because the bull stopped, looking towards the lieutenant for guidance.

"I asked you a question, Lieutenant!"

The lieutenant didn't seem too impressed with my performance, but did at least stand up straight.

"Are you Captain Grobe?" he asked. "I was told to expect you. Yes, I'm in charge here. Lieutenant Steinlein. Anything I can help you with, comrade Captain?"

"Lieutenant, I want to know why this house is empty!"

The officer shrugged, turning towards the sergeant who was heading across the pavement, his notes clutched in his hand. "Better ask the people you were expecting to find."

08:17

Karo

"Schimmel, we've got to do something!"

Schimmel wasn't awake yet. He just sat there, staring into his mug of coffee. I shook his shoulder.

"Schimmel, wake up! This is important, we've got to do something!"

Schimmel managed to look up from his coffee. He might have said something, I don't know, I was too busy pacing around the kitchen. I'd had too much coffee already, and I was pissed off. Pissed off with the two skins yesterday. Pissed off with the computer stuff that

Schimmel had shown me the other day. Pissed off with Martin for not taking it all seriously enough. Pissed off with the Antifa group even though I didn't know exactly why.

And now I was feeling pissed off with myself for not doing more.

08:32

Martin

My colleagues were surprised to see me back so soon.

"They'd cleared out, the place was empty," I told them.

It was pointless speculating about why they would have given up the building they'd been using—the only reasonable explanation was that they'd been tipped off about the raid.

The number of people who'd known about the plans for the raid had been pretty much limited to our team at RS2, and the main police station in the district, VPI Lichtenberg. Obviously we'd be pointing the finger at the cops, and they would be returning the compliment.

"There has to be a leak at VPI Lichtenberg," said Nik. "First of all the fashos find out about the mole, then somebody—presumably the fascists—murder him while he's in a West Berlin hospital, even though nobody other than the Lichtenberg cops knew he was there. Now there's been a tip-off about the raid. The whole thing stinks."

Yes, it stank, but was it so surprising? I almost said that, but held back. Such remarks weren't going to help us decide what to do.

"We've already informed the Ministerial Committee that we're unhappy with the way the VPI Lichtenberg has dealt with the matter of the informant, so we can just update our position with a memo," stated Laura, as ever trying to deal with action points rather than speculation. "I think we need to stay on their case though. We can't just let them do what they did during the Silesian Crisis, it's not good enough to have a narrow investigation and ignore the wider picture. We should get authorisation to be more involved—that way the cops won't be able to complain about us breathing down their necks."

We all agreed with Laura's suggestions, but my mind was on more immediate matters.

"One of us needs to go down to the cop shop and lean on them, I mean this morning, not sometime next week. Right now they'll be trying to work out how to cover their arses, and we need to get to the bottom of this before they have a chance to get their story straight."

"I'm not sure you're the right person to do that," Laura objected. "Maybe someone who is less well known to the security forces would be more acceptable?"

We were just about to get into another argument when Klaus stomped into the office, a deep frown creasing his face. In his hand he had a copy of the *Berliner Zeitung*.

"Have you seen this?" he demanded as he sat down heavily in a chair opposite me, throwing the newspaper onto the desk.

I looked at the article Klaus was pointing out. The chemical workers were saying that several of them had been detained by the police and questioned regarding future plans for their campaign.

I passed the newspaper on to Laura, who scanned the article briefly and gave it to Erika. She shook her head in disbelief.

"Where's it all going to end? This is political policing, just like in the old days," she said quietly. "For three or four years they go round with their tail between their legs, afraid of offending anyone, and now they're growing in confidence again and they go after the chemical workers."

"It's not a police matter," Klaus said, obviously irritated by what he'd read. "And if anything actually needs to be done then we should be the ones doing it, not the cops."

"But it isn't a matter for us either, is it?" was Nik's reply. "The chemical workers aren't posing any economic or political danger to the Republic, they're just exercising their rights."

"Precisely!" Klaus responded. "They're exercising their rights. Their political rights. Just because that's uncomfortable doesn't mean the bulls should get heavy on them."

"But even if the cops are involved it doesn't mean we have to get involved, does it?" Nik shook his head.

"Nik's right," said Erika, so softly that her contribution was nearly lost in the scraping of chairs and rustling of the newspaper. "We're not here to hold the police to account, or interfere in their cases—no matter how worrying they may be. That's a job for the Ministerial Committee."

"But that's exactly what we are doing: holding the cops to account, monitoring their investigation. Why else was Martin at the raid this morning? Why else are we hassling the cops to tell us what they're doing about the dead informant?"

Erika didn't reply to Klaus's questions, she just looked at Nik and me, expecting us to respond. Neither of us did, but Laura had something to say.

"Klaus, listen: Martin's back from the raid already because the squat was empty. We reckon they had a tip-off."

Klaus gave me a hard look, as if he blamed me. He pulled a cigar from his pocket and chewed on the end for a moment or two.

"And the only place they could have got the tip-off would have been VPI Lichtenberg?" It was a question but he said it more as a statement.

None of us felt the need to answer, we just sat there, giving him time to think it through.

"Then we definitely need to go and read them the riot act," he said eventually.

"We can't just mix it all up because we're cross with the Lichtenberg cops!" Laura took the newspaper back off Erika and crumpled it up. "There are different issues going on here: there are questions around the mole and the potential leaks and we need to handle those separately from any concerns we've got about whether or not the cops are getting political again. Maybe we should put some pressure on the cops about the leaks like Klaus said, we're already involved." She tossed the mess of newsprint on to my desk. "But the other issue, well, if the cops are taking political decisions about who they will allow to demonstrate and how people may use their right to freedom of speech then that can only be a result of decisions taken at a high level. Dealing with that isn't our job. But we can't just ignore it either. We can't allow political policing to begin again—the chemical workers aren't breaking any law, at least nothing important. We should ask the Committee to give us oversight powers in the interests of accountability, the same responsibility we had when we sent Martin along to observe the Weitlingstrasse raid."

We thought over Laura's suggestion, there were no objections.

"And if the Committee says no then we should do it anyway!" muttered Klaus.

Somehow I got my colleagues to agree to let me be the one to talk to the cops. It wasn't far to the district police headquarters on Schottstrasse—just over the road from the Lichtenberg courthouse where I'd met Evelyn last week. Unlike most police stations in Berlin it wasn't built in an imposing style, it looked more like an ordinary pre-war tenement block.

The Kripo were based at the back of the building, overlooking a concrete yard. But first I had to get past the front office. While I was waiting for the officer at the front desk to get round to noticing my presence, Lieutenant Steinlein sauntered in, accompanied by several other uniformed officers. He hesitated for a moment when he saw me, then came over, wearing a smile that didn't reach his eyes.

"Comrade Captain Grobe," he said, giving me a relaxed salute.

I glanced over to the duty officer behind the front desk who was still studiously ignoring me, and took Steinlein by the elbow, steering him through the double glass doors that led into the police station proper.

"You're going to take me to the *Kripo* officer responsible for handling the IKM in the squat. When you've done that, I want you to fetch the written orders you received for the raid this morning, plus any other paperwork you have on this matter. Understood, comrade Lieutenant?"

Something in my tone must have warned Steinlein. He just nodded, no attempt to be as cool as was this morning at the raid. He took me straight to a door that looked like all the others on an endless corridor. The plaque on the wall said *Captain Neumann, Kriminalpolizei Department K1.*

Neumann looked up from his desk, irritated, as I opened the door and went into his office without knocking.

"Dismiss, comrade Lieutenant," I said over my shoulder, but Steinlein announced me instead.

"Comrade Captain Neumann! Comrade Captain Grobe from the *Republikschutz* to see you. The comrade Captain wishes to see all written orders regarding the operation this morning."

Neumann looked me in the eye while he countermanded my order and dismissed his subordinate. I looked straight back at the captain for a few moments, then sat down in the chair in front of his desk.

"Comrade Captain, I think we can dispense with the formalities and get down to what matters. You know why I'm here, and I'm sure you are aware that there will be consequences if you refuse to co-operate."

But Neumann wasn't taken in by my bluff, he just sat there, quite calm and collected in his brown corduroy suit, light brown shirt buttoned up to the collar, but minus a tie. A *bonbon*, the Communist Party badge, adorned his button hole.

"And your authority, comrade Captain Grobe?" he asked, holding out his hand for the written authorisation he knew I wouldn't have. I might get it one day—although that was far from certain—but the slow milling of government machinery meant it was impossible for me to have gained authorisation to investigate something that had happened just a few hours ago.

Round one to Neumann.

I leant back in my chair, crossed my legs, breaking Neumann's staring competition for long enough to pick an imaginary speck of lint from my knee, noticing as I did so that I was still wearing my cycle clips. I ignored them. Looking up at Neumann, I started round two.

"Comrade Captain, you know as well as I do that written authority will not have been issued yet, but make no mistake, it will be. And when it is, any early co-operation—or lack thereof—will be noted."

I was putting Neumann in a difficult spot. Although both of us held the same rank, he would be aware that I had the Ministerial Committee's collective ear, whereas he was just one captain among many others on the police force. That gave me the potential for a lot more clout, although he could count on his colleagues to block, hinder, obfuscate and fudge any internal investigations. And whether or not he was responsible for the leaks, or was aware of who may be responsible, he could hardly tell me about it without incurring the wrath of his comrades. He was a member of a militarist organisation with a strong *corps d'ésprit* and a harsh system of informal punishment for those who stepped out of line.

All in all I think it was fair to say that in Neumann's position I would think twice before co-operating.

Neumann lifted the left edge of his lips in a crooked half-smile. The right side of his face was immobile, pinched to a scar that ran down the side of his nose and past the corner of his mouth. Now that we'd stopped the staring contest I was finding it difficult to keep my eyes away from his damaged face. I focussed on his eyes again, waiting for a response.

He leant back in his chair, pulled open a drawer in his desk, removing a packet of cigarettes and a box of matches. Taking out a cigarette, placing it carefully in the left corner of his mouth, he looked up at the ceiling as he struck a match and lit up. He exhaled through the nose, then balanced his cigarette on the edge of a small glass ashtray.

"What is it you want to know?" Pause, "Captain Grobe."

"I wish to speak to the officer who handled the informant in the Weitlingstrasse squat."

"I'm sure that can be arranged. In the meantime, how else can I be of assistance?"

"Do you have any other informants in place in the fascist, hooligan or skinhead scenes here in Lichtenberg?"

"Captain, I can't possibly let you have that kind of information. It's a matter of protocol. And of safety for the putative IKMs, of course."

I considered my position. At some point I would have to start pushing back, but was this the right moment? I decided to give him an easy question, see if he had any intention at all of 'being of assistance' as he had put it.

"What operational procedures did you use to handle the IKM? How often did the handling officer and the IKM meet, how were crash meetings arranged? I want to know about briefings and debriefings, support mechanisms—the lot."

Neumann hesitated for a moment, a tiny delay which he tried to cover by reaching for his cigarette.

"We did everything by the book."

"And what book was that? The one written by the Stasi? The same one written by our Soviet friends, the Chekists? If everything was done by the book then why wasn't the informant given protection at the hospital?"

Another indecisive movement betrayed Neumann's uncertainty. "The handling officer wasn't informed of the IKM's transferral to the hospital in West Berlin."

At last, a break in his stonewalling. I wondered whether Neumann was preparing the ground to deflect the blame that was coming his way.

"Why not?" I demanded, leaning forward in my chair and taking a cigarette from his packet.

"The decision to transfer the IKM was made by the hospital. It has become common in serious cases such as this one—the patient benefits from procedures and equipment that are currently unavailable in the GDR. The hospital informed Police Headquarters in Keibelstrasse, but the night duty officer didn't think to forward the message on to us until the next morning."

He chucked the box of matches over to me—underarm, no force or malice in the throw. I caught them, and lit up my cigarette.

"And the protection detail at the clinic here?" I asked after taking the first puff.

"Two uniformed officers were detailed to protect the IKM while in Friedrichshain. They were from Station 51—Friedenstrasse. They informed their duty officer on return to the police station, but he didn't think to pass the information on to us."

As I thought: arse-covering. Point the finger anywhere that wasn't K1 in Lichtenberg. I didn't want to let Neumann get away with it that easily.

"So, Captain Neumann, let's see if I've got this straight. You have at least one IKM engaged in an extremely volatile operation. You're careless enough to let him get severely beaten, then without your knowledge he is taken out of the country and murdered in West Berlin. Is that a fair interpretation of events?"

"The West Berlin police are at present investigating the case. It would be a mistake to make assumptions about the nature of the death. We are co-operating with the West Berlin police in this matter-"

"Perhaps, comrade, you'd do better to start co-operating with *me*." I stood up and leaned over the desk. "And for a start you can send me a copy of all files relating to this IKM." I walked over to the door, turning back as I opened it. "Have Lieutenant Steinlein bring over the paperwork—I shall expect him by the end of the day."

12:11
Karo

Schimmel and I managed to get everyone in the house together for a meeting. I told them about what had happened yesterday, how Martin and I had narrowly avoided a beating, or worse.

"We've been ignoring this problem for too long. The fash are back in Friedrichshain—not just coming by at night to catch a few stragglers. They were at Frankfurter Tor the other day handing out their hate-propaganda! And now this, what happened to me yesterday. God! We've got to take this seriously!"

"Yeah, Karo, I don't disagree, but we've all got our own projects on the go—like you've got your Brown Coal Coalition and the stuff with global warming and your facilitation course. I'm doing my refugee support. We're all doing our bit. None of us have got time to go hunting Nazis."

12:53
Martin

Things were looking busy when I got back to RS2. Grit was at her desk in the front office, hammering away at an electric typewriter, the carriage pinging and growling back at the end of each line. Through the open office doors I could see and hear that everyone was on the phone. Erika's door was nearest, and I stood on the threshold to her office, listening in to her phone call.

"Yep, urgent. You got it. Thanks, appreciated." She hung up.

"What's going on?"

"After you left we decided that we should follow up whatever contacts we have in the police, see if we could come up with anything about the leaks."

"What? Just phone up people and ask them to tell us which cops like a bit of a gossip?" When Neumann got to hear about this he'd be

296

even more pissed off than he already was.

"Come on, Martin, give us some credit! We're being a bit more subtle than that: asking how many IKMs are on the go across the Republic, how they're handled. General sort of stuff."

I ran my fingers through my hair then shook my head. These testosterone contests with cops never did me any good.

"Sorry. But look, I'm back, maybe I should let you all know about my meeting with K1. My office in ten?"

Erika nodded, and I told Klaus and Laura the same thing. Nik had already made himself at home in my chair and was using the telephone. I held up ten fingers, then motioned towards the kettle. He nodded before going back to his one-sided conversation.

I spooned some coffee into the big glass pot and got five cups out of the cupboard. I pushed a pile of paperwork to one side and ignored the domino effect this had on the rest of my desk.

The kettle started steaming, so I pulled the plug out and poured water into the pot. Everyone was in the room by now. Laura had a sheet of paper with lots of notes on it, the others just sat there and started to slurp their coffees.

I told them about my visit to Neumann, and summarised: "He didn't really tell me anything, but I got the distinct impression that there was something wrong—I don't mean losing an IKM—I mean, like he was out of his depth or something-"

"Oh." A sort of popping noise came from Erika's direction. "I've got a friend who works in *Kripo* Central Co-ordination at Police HQ. When I asked about IKMs she said that officially there aren't any—the experienced handlers have all been discharged from service because they were too close to the Stasi. Basically, there's no-one in the police force with any real experience of running informants."

"What about unofficially? You said officially there were no IKMs. And unofficially?"

"She didn't say, but it sounds like the Ministry is turning a blind eye to the practice."

I'd been idly shovelling up all the files and papers that had cascaded off my desk, trying to persuade them to stay in the general area of my in-tray rather than slide back off onto the floor. Nik helpfully moved his elbows to give me more space, and as he did so a yellow envelope came into view.

"Oh, yes, this came for you by ministry courier. Had to sign for it and everything," he said.

I gave Nik a dirty look, but he didn't notice. The envelope was sealed and had *VS* stamped on it. I slid the short message out.

"They want us to send Evelyn in: undercover operation at the Weitlingstrasse premises." The others looked as astonished as I felt. *"Preparations for operational measures to begin with immediate effect, with a view to said measures being implemented at an early date."*

So the old Ministerial Committee, about to be replaced, were having a last shot at getting into the history books.

There was silence while we digested the news, and I took the opportunity to read the message through again. They wanted evidence for the purposes of criminal prosecutions.

"Well that makes it all a bit final, doesn't it?" I said at last, mostly to break the silence. "Anyone have anything to add?"

Nobody had anything to say, so all in all we weren't that much further.

Except for one thing.

There was no way we were going to allow the *Kripo* to handle Evelyn's operation: they'd either get her killed or lose her.

19:43

Karo

I went to see Antifa Bert. I was pissed off with my housemates and wanted to get another perspective.

"Smuggling," he said after I'd told him about the incident at the East Side yesterday. "So that's why your friend from RS is suddenly interested in the fash?"

He sat there with his chin on his hand, trying to look like some Greek statue.

"And he's right about the fash getting more active. We've been monitoring this for a while, and we reckon they're gearing up for something big. The referenda, then the *Volkskammer* elections. But they might be planning something else entirely, who knows?"

"So what are we going to do about it?" I was pleased that Bert was taking this as seriously as I was.

"What do you mean? We're already doing loads!" Bert was almost shouting. I'd hurt his pride. Bloody men!

"I know you've been doing stuff. But maybe it's gonna take more than that? We need some new ideas!"

Bert shook his head. "Look you were good the other night, we need more people like you. What we're doing works."

But that was the question: was it really working?

"Look Bert—you and the others, you're doing a good job-"

"Too right we're doing a good job. If it hadn't been for us .... We're the ones who pushed the Nazis out of the centre of Berlin. And we have to do more, we need them out of Berlin and out of the country!"

"But they're coming back! What you've been doing worked for a while, but we're seeing more of them on the streets. More people are getting beaten up—more than have been for years."

"Yeah, so there needs to be more people doing the job. You coming again on Friday?"

"Don't you think there's got to be something else we can do? We've got to be strategic about this—take the fight to them." Bert was shaking his head, but I just carried on. "They're leafleting in our neighbourhoods, we need to do the same. They're recruiting young people, we need to get there first. They meet up at the Weitlingstrasse house before they do their hunting, we need to take the fight there— we need to take the fight to them!"

DAY 10
Wednesday
23rd March 1994

Erfurt: Several Russian citizens were injured at a club in Altenburg last night. Early reports indicate that skinheads were involved, but a police spokesperson declined to confirm whether there was a racist-fascist motivation behind the attack.

10:04
Martin

As soon as the morning meeting was over I headed off to see Dmitri in Karlshorst. As I left, Grit passed me a green A4 envelope.

"This arrived from the Ministry."

I had a quick look. They were release forms for Evelyn Hagenow. I was to sign them if and when we decided that Evelyn had been sufficiently prepared for her mission. Until I signed and returned those forms, Evelyn would be staying where she was.

Getting off the tram in Karlshorst I walked through the Russian colony—a town within a town—schools, shops, offices and military bases for the Russian forces and their families. The red star and the letters CA were still to be seen everywhere, but since the breakup of the Soviet Union this area was under the administration of the Russian Federation. On flagpoles the red banner with hammer and sickle had been replaced by the Russian tricolour.

Showing my RS pass to a guard standing outside the door I went into the nondescript pre-war building that housed Dmitri's office. A

Russian non-commissioned officer escorted me up the stairs.

"Martin! Come in, come in and we shall drink a toast!" Dmitri and I had first met during a covert operation, and a bond had grown between us. But now we seemed to be meeting up just to push paper at each other, there was none of the adrenaline and excitement of our first covert meetings. Nevertheless, Dmitri always seemed pleased to see me. He was a large but gentle man with grey hair and a military bearing. About the same age as me, he was usually either cheerfully grinning or else frowning in concentrated thought. To people who didn't know him, his most remarkable feature was a black leather eye patch over his left eye, which, despite his frequent grins, gave him a sinister yet rakish look. I think Dmitri rather liked this image, and that was possibly why he used the patch rather than a less conspicuous glass eye. Perhaps it was for the same reason that he rarely gave a straight answer to a straight question, preferring instead to speak in Sibylline riddles.

"You seem a little pre-occupied today, *tovarishch*," Dmitri said after we'd looked over a few files.

I considered telling him what was on my mind, about the aborted raid, our concerns about the cops, and that my next appointment was with Evelyn, my own personal nemesis. We shouldn't be discussing live cases, and none of this had anything to do with the community of states which had once made up the Soviet Union; it was something I should have left at the door.

"Remember the case last year? The woman who headed up the Stasi task force? She's my next port of call today."

Dmitri grew grave, the joshing grin of a moment ago no longer in evidence.

"I thought that was out of your hands? No longer your responsibility? Evelyn Hagenow, wasn't it? Codename GÄRTNER?" I could see him adding notes to the files he kept in his head. "Where is she now?"

"In Magdalenenstrasse remand prison. I've been ordered to brief her for an undercover operation against a fascist group in Lichtenberg. They're growing in strength, or at the very least they're becoming bolder. There's no longer any doubt that they're a tangible security threat to the future of the Republic." I closed the file I'd been looking at and let if fall onto Dmitri's desk. "But we're in the dark. We need eyes on the ground and we have no-one who can do that kind of thing. The *Kripo* have been worse than useless. That leaves the ex-Stasi. Evelyn has volunteered."

"What is it you are trying to discover?"

"K1 had an IKM in place, but he was beaten and murdered a few days ago-"

"K1? You mean *Kripo*—they had an informant?" Dmitri knew full well that K1 was the shadowy political branch of the police which had once been the link between the Stasi and regular detectives—he was only asking to buy time while he mentally tabulated the information I was giving him.

"Yes, yes. But what we've known for a long time is that they have large amounts of propaganda and agitation materials, presumably brought in from the West. We should assume that they've been receiving financial assistance too. But none of that's new. It's the combination of this material with the recent surge in activity." Dmitri was still frowning, and I wondered what use he would find for this intelligence. "They're far more aggressive on the streets, they're demonstrating regularly, using the current refugee situation to make people scared. Don't tell me you haven't noticed—the target of these activities are often Russians!"

Dmitri's one good eye was intently watching me. Hands folded in his lap, he was a picture of relaxed concentration. But he didn't say anything, just waited for me to continue.

"Is there any intelligence on a link between yours and ours— between the fascists here and Pamyat, Otkasniki, any of the other far-right movements in Russia?"

Dmitri finally responded. He shook his head, then picked up a pencil and started tapping it on a file on his desk. He frowned for a minute or so.

"No, there was nothing flagged as being of interest to the GDR, and there's nothing I've come across. The groups around Shirinovski, the nationalist groups, they're just that: nationalist. They're not looking to support other nationalist movements in what was once the Soviet sphere. If anything they see it as being in their interest to undermine similar groups in other countries, not to support them. I think their main focus at the moment is Russian nationalism and anti-Semitism. They're feeling smug at how successful they've been in forcing so many Jews to leave our country, and they don't care whether they go to Washington, Tel Aviv or Berlin." He thought for a moment longer, tapping the pencil again, then carried on. "No, I don't see a connection there, but I think you're right to be suspicious of the West. You can't expect West Germany to give up so easily—they've wanted to take over East Germany for nearly fifty years—they'll still be doing everything they can to catch the prize."

"So what do you think? Will they be working underground, using the BND intelligence service? Or maybe agitating at a political level?"

"Oh, Martin, you know the answer as well as I do! You're just fishing for information." He dropped the pencil and spread his hands over the desk, palms down, a shrug lifting his shoulders. "You know I'd be the first to give it to you if I had anything at all. But I'm dry. They know where my sympathies lie, and so they keep me dry." Another shrug, the hands gathered back together in prayer. "All I can do is speculate, same as you."

Dmitri picked up the pencil again, playing with it for a moment before getting out a pack of black Russian cigarettes. He offered me one but I shook my head.

"If I were to speculate," he rolled the cigarette between his fingers, the loose paper creasing up as it met his thumbs. "I would say that anyone looking into this matter needs to take great care, yes, to be careful."

He put the cigarette in his mouth and lit it from a desk lighter, drawing in, then breathing out a cloud of dark smoke. "You mention politics," he drew on his cigarette again, speaking as he exhaled. "Have you considered your fifth column: the political parties. So long as you have parties then those involved will be representing a party and not the people. And while you have cross-border party affiliations the Western politicians will be telling their colleagues over here how to think, how to vote-"

"But we can't restrict free political association!"

"No, no, but I like the way your central government and parliament is losing power day by day; I watch with great interest your preparations for a referendum on devolving more power to the Round

Tables." Dmitri drew on his acrid cigarette, exhaling again before continuing. "But the Round Tables offer the politically ambitious much less room for manoeuvre, so the parties resist decentralisation. *Power gathers power*, as they say in Moscow." Again Dmitri spread his hands out over the desk, like the wings of a dove, a peace offering. "And remember how well the West-parties played that particular role when they tried to derail the events of 1989 and 1990?"

Re-unification propaganda—mostly sponsored by the West-CDU—had flooded our country even before the Wall opened in November 1989, and that was the start of the rumours of close links between the West-CDU and the far-right.

"Are you suggesting that the parties, the ones *here*, in the GDR, could be supporting or encouraging the fascists?"

"Political groupings may see supporting unrest as a canny move. Oh, it may not be direct support, but they're not exactly going out of their way to deal with the problem either. It's always been that way—remember the SPD in 1919, the workers' own party involved in liquidating the Workers' Councils? How Minister Noske tolerated, even supported the nationalist *Freikorps* in order to preserve his position in government."

I'd long been uneasy about the way the political parties, particularly the CDU and the SPD, with their close links to the West, had continuously spoken out against the Round Tables and the Works Councils. Now Dmitri was drawing parallels between today's situation and the bloody suppression of the Workers' and Soldiers' Councils at the start of the Weimar Republic.

"That's how it will always be," said Dmitri, thoughtfully tapping ash off his cigarette. "If people are scared they will be susceptible to calls for strong leadership. If people are confused they will demand simple solutions. Just listen to the arguments—every day on the radio, in the newspapers: the central government, all the political parties in the *Volkskammer* are saying you need strong leadership and clear policies to deal with the problems. Doesn't matter if they're talking about the referenda, economic restructuring, or the increasing violence by fascists. But your revolution is in the creative phase: the chaos that follows the usurpation of power. You're working out new systems, new ways of doing things. Trial and error: a painful, slow, frustrating process. Without this creative chaos you can't decentralise, you can't have autonomous districts and neighbourhoods. Such things can't be decreed from above, only built from below. I need only refer you to Vladimir Ilyich and his abortive attempts at harnessing the revolutionary power of 1918. And just look where that took us ....""

Sometimes Dmitri had these periods of eloquent contemplation, he would look into the middle distance, seeing beyond the walls of his office, beyond his past as a KGB officer and his present role in the FSK. Ever since we first met there had been an instinctive trust between us, allowing him to voice unorthodox thoughts. Yet each time he did so I was taken by surprise. Still, I enjoyed his ramblings; they helped me remember that the experiment in our little Republic didn't only affect us, it wasn't just for our sake—it represented something much larger for so many people in the world.

"Dmitri, that's all very well, you're as persuasive as ever. But it doesn't actually help me right now, does it?"

Dmitri smiled, shaking his head at my short-sightedness.

"On the contrary, my friend, I rather think it does. I'm telling you that you need to deal with your fascists before they spread too many seeds of doubt. You can't let them give the centralists the excuse they so badly want. You must defend your revolution—and quickly!"

"Again, it doesn't help me, does it? There's not so much we can do to defend the revolution: there aren't any Chekists any more, and we wouldn't want them even if-"

"Martin!" Dmitri shook his head in bafflement. "How is it, you Germans—a culture that gave us Schiller and Goethe, Heine and Hölderlin—not to mention Kant and Arendt—how is it you need everything clearly spelt out? You must deal with your fascist problem promptly, and in my opinion, you must do so without involving any form of central authority. Work at the grassroots, strengthen the basis, not the centre."

"So, we shouldn't let K1 handle Evelyn—we should do it ourselves, but-"

"Yes." Dmitri smiled again, a different smile, pleased that I'd finally cottoned on. "Controlling the operation of a penetration agent could be the first step. But what about the raw intelligence—how will you analyse it, what will you do with it?"

As always, Dmitri was way ahead of me. My colleagues and I were already thinking about bypassing the *Kripo* when it came to running Evelyn but we hadn't thought about what to do with any information she might pass on. I guess we were just going to stay within the remit given to us by the Ministerial Committee: task Evelyn to find evidence that could be used in a criminal case against key individuals —disrupt fascist activities that way. But that's exactly how they did things in the old days—it hadn't worked. Sending fascists to prison only made them and their groups stronger. Dmitri on the other hand was talking about acting on intelligence, he hadn't mentioned prosecuting individuals at all.

"You think that Evelyn would deliver useful intelligence? What could we do with that?"

"I think Evelyn has much experience in this game, and if there is anything to find then she will find it. And she may even give it to you."

"Things like supply lines? Money trails, information about support from the West?"

"Yes, yes." Dmitri nodded earnestly. "And once you have that information you will have the means to disrupt them. You can involve the local Round Tables, the Works Councils in the Border Police regiments and local *Kripo*. Let them take responsibility for stopping these supply routes. You could help with co-ordinating and networking the efforts to discover and disrupt new routes. But you should let those involved take the decisions on how to deal with the problem. You provide the information and let the organisations at the local level decide how best to use it."

"But Evelyn, I don't know if we can trust her."

"Desperate times, my friend, desperate times," Dmitri commiserated, his eye twinkling mischievously.

"I'm not even sure I can brief her. I mean how does one do something like that?" There was silence for a moment while my thoughts wandered on. Then: "Dmitri, would you do it? I could get you access to the files, and-"

"Martin, Martin, no. I'm flattered." He held his hands up. "But no. This is not my struggle. I have my own worries."

"I'm sorry, it was silly of me-"

"Yes, but you know Martin, that's why I like you. You are a breath of fresh air, a refreshing addition to our little clique of spies. When I go to see the French or the Americans, or even my colleagues in the GRU, it is always poker. Here a card, there a bluff. But with you, we can pretend we are still human, and we can talk as friends."

He gave one of his little giggles, followed by a heavy sigh, a sigh that made me feel inexperienced and feckless. Dmitri often helped me put my own thoughts in order, see events and problems from an operational perspective, but always at the price of reminding me of my amateur status.

"Comrade, as I said, I have my own worries. Things can't continue like this much longer. There's too much pressure at home, things are falling apart—we're needed back there, not here. There are already signs of a preparation for withdrawal from Germany: personnel not being replaced, there's been less servicing of materiel, you know the kind of thing. Things are even more chaotic than usual.

"But, wait." Dmitri shuffled through papers on his desk, coming up with a grey-yellow file, a pink stripe splitting its cover from bottom-left to top-right, a long series of Cyrillic characters and numbers handwritten on one corner. "This is for you, my gift, because you are such a naif in our jungle. In the middle of all this chaos there's a young officer in Dresden, one of ours, FSK/KGB. Keen. Eager to make a splash. Ambitious. You know: the dangerous kind, destined to go far. No, wait!" He held out his hand, preventing me from opening the file. "Don't open it yet! And be careful who you show this to. The rumours are that our young officer has been buying up all the left-over IMs in the Dresden area. All the informants that have been left without the father figure of the Stasi, all those who feel they need to confess, report and inform. He's got them. And in there you have a list of previous IMs that we believe he has been in contact with, also the cadre files of the officer in question—redacted, of course. I don't know what he plans to do with all these informants, but then, that's your problem."

Normally after meeting Dmitri I would feel reassured—he provided me with a solidity that had become rare in my world—but now I felt less than calm. Certainly not the best mood for a meeting with Evelyn. I sat brooding on the U-Bahn, wondering how best to handle her, but as so often before, I came to the conclusion that I couldn't handle her. I could only wait to see how she would handle me.

I reluctantly climbed the steps out of the U-Bahn station and trailed up Magdalenenstrasse. The few tenement blocks soon petered out, replaced by a five metre high wall topped with barbed wire, lights and contact lines. Arriving at the main entrance, I pressed the buzzer, a wicket gate opened and the guard checked my visitor's papers and RS pass. As a second pair of high steel gates creaked open I walked into the courtyard of the prison, taking in the dozens of blind windows that looked down on me. Behind one of those windows Evelyn had her cell, she'd already been here for several months awaiting trial, or as it might turn out, her chance of restitution.

I followed the guard across the narrow courtyard, heading for the administration wing. They gave me the use of an interrogation room. The usual kind of place: one wall lined with *Sprelakart* cupboards, a desk with telephone, lamp, notepad and a two-reel tape recorder. In front of the desk a plain table, set end on, so that the interviewee couldn't get too close.

The interviewee's chair was in the middle of the floor, and I moved it to the table. For this kind of meeting I should have placed both chairs near to each other, with neither table nor desk between them, but I felt the need to keep my psychological distance to Evelyn so I sat down behind the desk.

I didn't have to wait long before there was a knock on the door.

"Come in!"

In a repeat of the procedure last week, Evelyn said nothing until her wrists had been freed and the prison guard had withdrawn from the room. She stood there, looking at me, a slight smile playing at the corner of her lips.

"Martin, I'm glad you've come to see me again." She sat down, angling her head so that she could look up at me, her eyes wide. "It gets so lonely in here-"

"I've been sent by the Ministry," I interrupted. "If it were down to me there'd be no second chance."

But Evelyn had picked up on my uncertainty. She was good at reading me, she was good at reading everyone. And she knew how to use the skill.

"So the dear old Ministry wants my help now that the house in Weitlingstrasse has been abandoned?" She was doing a damn good job at appearing ingenuous.

I don't think I betrayed my surprise that despite being locked up, Evelyn had somehow found out about yesterday's events.

"Oh, Martin! Don't look so shocked. Of course I'll help! Anything for an old friend."

"Why?"

"Martin, you are a sweetie! This is my country too, no matter what you've done to it. What? You think that just because I'm still faithful to my Chekist colleagues that I don't love our GDR? Listen Martin, those fascists," and for a moment her voice was vicious, "they're scum. What they want goes against everything I've ever worked for and everything I've ever believed in. That's what gives me the right to fight them." She sat back in her chair, hands held open, palms towards me. "And I really can't help if I'm stuck in this shit hole, can I?"

I reached down to my briefcase, taking out a file and slowly opening it on the desk. I was using the time to try to regain some composure—she'd only been here for a few minutes and already she had me on the back foot. I needed to find a way to exert some control over the situation.

"I have been instructed by the Ministry to brief you on current events, and request your assistance in this matter-"

"I'll do it." Evelyn's amiable persona had returned.

"I haven't told you what we want you to do yet!"

"Here, let me have a look, it'll be quicker that way." She stood up and reached across the desk to take the file from me, beginning to scan the pages before she'd even sat down again. "After all," she winked at me, "I am a pro!"

I was about to take the file back from her when I realised that she was right. Just as with Dmitri a couple of hours ago, I was meeting with someone who had undergone both extensive training and years of operational experience. I on the other hand was a mere amateur, one still in denial of his role.

It didn't take Evelyn long to leaf through the whole file. She closed it carefully, pushing it back over the table towards me, then leaned back and let out a sigh.

"You don't have much to go on, do you?" she said, more statement than question. "Don't you have any of the backstory? Haven't you found the files? Lichtenberg K1 should have some of them. A few of the more senior and short-sighted comrades thought it might be a good idea to train up some of these fascists, teach them some discipline then get them to report back on what was happening. They got the whole package: paratrooper training, combat exercises, conspirative-operational instruction, the lot. But we lost control of them. That would have been about 1987, 1988. They just passed their new skills on to their Nazi chums."

"No matter," she tapped her head, "I've got the most important stuff in here. I'll do it."

"But I still haven't told you what we want you to do!" I protested again.

"Well I'm doing it anyway. Time to clean up the mess my comrades left behind. When do you want me to go in?"

It was almost as if Evelyn could no longer surprise me—she knew what we wanted from her, and she knew that I wasn't happy about the plan. But she also knew it wasn't up to me, I'd had my orders from the Ministry.

"I have a release order. Once it's been signed you can leave here. But we'll need to prepare you first: a full briefing, set up your team, contact procedures-"

"Martin," quiet, but determined, almost exasperated, "once again: I'm a pro. Give me the use of that phone now, and I'll be ready by tomorrow midday. Just give me whatever files you have. What, this is all you have, isn't it?"

"The cops have more, but we haven't got copies yet-"

"What about related crime reports, who they've been beating up, intimidating? Good, get copies of those to me, I need to know what they'll be gossiping about, sick bastards. Right." She walked around the desk, dragging her chair behind her. Sitting down next to me she pulled the phone over. "I have work to do. As you said: preparations. If I'm going to do this then I'll be doing it my way: I'll arrange my own conspirative meetings, my own cut-outs, my own fall-backs and safety procedures. What?" She pulled a face at me, trying to make me laugh. "Did you think I'd trust those clowns at K1 to set things up?"

She picked up the phone and dialled. "It's GÄRTNER. Get me DAEDALUS." She gave me a business-like look, gesturing with her thumb towards the door.

I picked up my briefcase, and left the room, leaving Evelyn in charge of phone and file.

"Operation WITHERED VINE—it's on again," I heard as I closed the door behind me.

13:14

Karo

It was a bit of a gamble, calling a Squatters' Council. There hadn't been one since last year when it split in two—the Wessis on the one side and the Ossis on the other. But this was something we could all agree on: we were all against the fash.

It felt like we had to think bigger. Yesterday's argument with Bert had shown me that we can't just rely on the Antifa groups to do everything. But right now the meeting was just about boys telling war stories. The usual crap: late night run-ins with skins, near escapes, standing guard outside refugee hostels ...

"Look, we can spend all day yacking about what's been happening. That's not why we're here," I told them. "So let's just stop with the stories! The fash are preparing to take over our country. It's not just the referenda, it's not just about the Volkskammer elections, it's about more and more people getting beaten up, injured. It's about hate and fear spreading. It's got to stop. And the question is: how are we going to stop it?"

Part of me was relieved that Evelyn was ready for her task but I couldn't shake the feeling that I'd been out-manoeuvred. Apart from anything else there were serious trust issues. Evelyn had shown herself to be an active opponent of the changes happening in our country; she wasn't in favour of all this freedom and participation—as far as I could tell she wanted the autocratic rule of the Party back. I only had her word for it that she wanted rid of the fascists as much as we did. But once we let her off the leash who knew what she'd get up to?

When I got back to the office I knocked on Erika's open door. She looked up from her typewriter and gestured me in.

"Martin, you're back. How did it go? Want some tea?"

I shook my head and sat down on the visitor's chair in front of her desk.

"How was it? You don't look too happy."

"Oh, the usual. How did we get into this situation?"

"Look, Martin, we're doing the stuff that nobody else wants to do. It's never going to be easy, and it's good that we ask ourselves difficult questions." She patted my hand. "That's what you're doing right now, isn't it? Asking yourself difficult questions?"

Erika and I had worked together for a few years now, we got on well, we understood each other. She was cautious, sometimes even timid, but when she decided that she could trust someone then she trusted them; she didn't try to second guess them, she was there for them, no matter what.

"What did Evelyn say?" she asked eventually.

"She jumped at the chance. In fact, she completely took over and sent me away. Right now she's arranging it all with some of her old friends in the Firm."

It was obvious that many of those who worked for the Stasi still had some kind of network going, but it was unclear just how far it went, or what they were prepared to do. It was yet another threat that we had no kind of handle on.

"I suppose that's good for us this time around," Erika came up with after a while. "They know what they're doing, and they're probably better resourced than us. We'll just have to deal with any consequences when they happen."

"She also confirmed the historic links between the far-right and the Stasi."

"Interesting. I suppose we'd better inform the Ministry." Erika got up and poured herself some tea.

"There's something else?" Erika sat down again.

"I saw Dmitri. I told him about Evelyn, and he gave me a few ideas."

Erika was watching me over the rim of her cup, waiting for me to continue.

"He thinks we should be aiming higher, that we should get Evelyn to do more than gather evidence to prosecute individuals. He thinks she could get useful information, maybe even enough to smash the fascist movement."

Now that I was saying it out loud it sounded obvious, but Erika didn't respond—she had her cup held up to her lips, but wasn't drinking. She was thinking.

"We have clear instructions to brief Evelyn only for gathering evidence for prosecution-"

"And Dmitri also suggested that if we get anything useful from Evelyn we shouldn't just pass it upstairs. He reckons we should be distributing it to local groups: Round Tables, Works Councils, local police and Border Police companies ...."

"Why?"

"Because it's the right thing to do. Because right now we're sleepwalking into a nightmare—the fascists, the nationalists, the skins, it's getting worse. Taken together it's probably a greater threat than the economic crisis. And what Dmitri got me thinking about is that *we* have a choice. For once, we hold the levers: we can give the intelligence to the Ministry and the politicians and the government, or we give it to the grassroots. If Evelyn does her job we could get enough to smash the far-right. If we give it to the central institutions then the politicians will take the credit. They'll turn it into a convincing argument for a strong centralised government here in Berlin."

Erika put her cup down. "And going by their recent behaviour they'll be using that argument to defeat the referendum on devolving power to the Round Tables."

14:19

Karo

We did it—we agreed to hold a mega-demo on Friday afternoon, at rush hour. There was going to be a massive mobilisation over the next two days. I knew we could make it happen: nearly every squat in East Berlin had a representative at this meeting, and we were going to end early so that we could get moving, talk to absolutely everyone we knew. By the end of tonight everyone in the squatting scene would know about the plan. We'd put the word out to Leipzig, Dresden, Rostock, Erfurt and Jena: it was going to be big. No, it was going to be *mega*.

15:01

Martin

After talking to Erika I put a brief summary of my ideas on the agenda sheet for tomorrow morning's meeting and went back to my office. It had been a long day and I was feeling tired, but I wanted to make a start on preparing Evelyn's briefing. I sat at my desk but I wasn't taking any information in. I decided to take the paperwork home.

It was a good move—I felt better as soon as I left the office. The sky was clouding over, and the day was cooling rapidly. Walking in the fresh air was bringing my grey cells up to operating speed, and I wasn't paying attention to where I was going, just letting my feet do the navigation. Before I was properly aware of it, I was climbing the stairs in my tenement, opening the door to my flat.

I decided to go through the case summaries first, get some perspective on what had been going on, see if it gave me any clues as to what we should get Evelyn to watch out for. Dmitri's suggestion had been simple: gain intelligence that could be used by networks and organisations all over the country, help them to shut down fascist

314

activities in their area.

But what kind of intelligence? I'd already been over most of these files once or twice before, and if there were any clues in there then I should have found it by now.

But I hadn't found anything useful, nor had Laura, Erika or Nik. Nor, presumably had K1. Perhaps I should just give all the files to Evelyn, she'd probably be more able than I to ferret out any useful bits.

It was slow, boring work, and I took frequent breaks—standing up, stretching, making coffee, going to the toilet—but I kept at it, hour after hour.

At about eight o'clock I looked through my notes for the thousandth time, wondering how to rationalise them, group things together so that they'd still make sense tomorrow. But it was useless. I gave up and took Evelyn's file over to my armchair, leaving the rest on the kitchen table.

I was much more familiar with Evelyn's file, having worked extensively on it last autumn. We'd pieced together her Stasi career, but it had been well hidden, not recorded in the usual archives at the Normannenstrasse complex. We still didn't know who else had been on the Stasi task force that Evelyn had led until a few months ago. Evelyn had steadfastly refused to answer any questions on operational processes so we were still very much in the dark. We had codenames but had found no records in the old Stasi files— presumably these codenames had been assigned after the end of 1989 when parts of the Stasi went underground.

Nor had we been able to comprehensively track Evelyn's activities over the years. There was still an unexplained period in 1988. After the Luxemburg Affair she had dropped out of sight here in East Berlin and resurfaced a few months later in Moscow. Her time in Moscow was a closed book—even Dmitri was unable or unwilling to shed any light on it.

Too many riddles, too few answers.

Thinking about Evelyn's association with Moscow made me think of Dmitri again—I hadn't yet looked at the file he'd given me. I got out of my chair and made my way over to the kitchen table where I'd stacked all the files, searching through them until I found the yellowish cardboard folder.

Which was when the phone rang.

"Martin, you asked me to chase up those reports Lieutenant Steinlein was supposed to be bringing round." It was Grit—she was still in the office. "I've just had a phone call—comrade Lieutenant Steinlein was taken to hospital last night—he's been badly beaten by skinheads."

Steinlein. The officer in charge of the raid on the fascist house yesterday. A uniformed police officer beaten up by skins.

A revenge attack.

Shaken by the news I returned to my armchair in the living room. I still had Dmitri's file in my hand. I glanced over the Russian text but it made no sense to me, my eyes merely focussing on the few German words and names there: Дрезден, Котвус and the like, but I had no idea what it all meant. I'd have to give it to Klaus to use his Russian skills on.

I thumbed back to the front. A loose sheet had been inserted, noticeably different from the others: this was the first copy from a typewriter, not the indistinct blue of the carbons in the rest of the file. Intrigued, I scanned the Cyrillic script, wondering whether I could decipher any of it. A few words in the first paragraph looked familiar:

Ул. Вытпинг 122, 1134 Берлин-Лихтенберг

The address of the fascist house in Lichtenberg! Cursing myself for not paying more attention at school I started at the top of the sheet, attempting to understand what was typed there. But beyond the Cyrillic rendering of some of the names we already had there was not much I could understand.

Shutting the file again I considered what this meant. Dmitri had let me ramble on in his office about the operation with Evelyn, he'd told me to my face that he knew nothing about our fascist problem. And then he'd given me a document about the Weitlingstrasse house.

It wasn't an oversight, it wasn't a mistake—Dmitri didn't make a move without first considering all the angles. So he was trying to tell me something, something he couldn't say to me in his office or on the phone. But what?

Day 11
Thursday
24th March 1994

Jena: There were violent scenes last night after football club Dynamo Dresden played away at Carl Zeiss Jena. In a related incident, the Junge Gemeinde Jena, which is active in anti-fascist and refugee support initiatives, was subjected to a sustained attack by hooligans associated with Dynamo. Lieutenant Walther of the VPD Jena stated that negative-hostile groupings had been successfully dispersed following police operations.

05:19
Martin

Little good had come of the telephone since it had been installed a couple of years ago. In the old days I had dreamed of having my own telephone connection, of no longer having to queue at the phone box down the road, no longer relying on friendly neighbours to take a message and leave it on the notepad hanging from my front door. But the reality was that the phone—installed when I began working at RS —was a means of summoning me to work, a way to wake me from slumber, and on not a few occasions, from hangover-induced near-death status.

Today it was an early-morning call.

With the first whirr of the bell I started into wakefulness. My reading material had long slipped out of my hands, loose sheets had sailed over the floor. By the second ring I'd worked out where I was, and with the third long ring I was out of my chair and on my way into the hall.

"Grobe," I said into the receiver, my voice still encrusted with sleep.

"Martin, it's me. Now I do hope I haven't woken you, but I suspect I may have, I *am* sorry, dear Martin."

Evelyn. Not the first time she had woken me with a telephone call, but how had she managed to get access to a phone in the prison?

"I thought you might like to meet up again before I start my little adventure. I don't have much time, so shall we say one hour from now?" She gave me an address in Hellersdorf and rang off before I could argue.

It was a few moments before my brain engaged. I was splashing water on my face in the kitchen sink before I realised that Evelyn was no longer on remand. Somehow she had been released, even without my signature on the necessary forms. I looked at my reflection in the little shaving mirror that I kept next to the soap dish and the *Fit* washing up liquid. The usual grey, stubbly face looked back. No surprise to be seen on that face. Evelyn, for all her adroitness, had definitely lost her power to shock me.

It wasn't until I reached the S-Bahn station at Nöldnerplatz that I looked at my watch. It was just getting light, and that alone should have told me: not yet six o'clock. Once past the shunting yards at Lichtenberg station the train line runs between allotments, parks and back gardens, the only industrial intrusion a hot-water distributor pipe. The train itself was fairly empty, most people travelling the other way.

I changed onto the U-Bahn at Wuhletal, not having to wait long before the train climbed up out of the tunnel. Sitting down on the blue plastic seat I looked out of the window as we dived underground and screeched around a curve, emerging into a cutting before the next station. Above the banks the sun was spearing light beneath the grey clouds drooping in the sky, glinting windows reflected the steel light down into the cutting.

Getting off at Paul-Verner-Strasse, I walked down the main road before checking my map and turning off onto a service road lined by dusty Trabants and a few Ladas and Wartburgs. Reaching a door—one just like all the other doors in all the other concrete-slab flats—I pushed it open and entered the hallway. Ignoring both the ranks of letterboxes in the hall, and the dented steel door of the lift, I climbed the narrow stairs, feet clattering up the terrazzo steps.

On the first floor I knocked at a flat, a confident double tap, followed by two singles. The door was bright yellow, punctuated by a peep-hole in the dead centre, handle and modern lock on the side. A grey cardboard square was pasted next to the doorbell, the inked name faded to illegibility.

The door opened silently on well-oiled hinges, and a silhouette ushered me in. Evelyn. Through the frosted glass of the lobby door behind her I saw the suggestion of a second figure flitting past. But when I went through, the room beyond was empty. A closed door was next to the kitchen-niche in the corner. I went straight over to the smudged windows, checking the main road I had just left. An Ikarus bus started up, its dark orange paintwork shaded further by dirt, the bendy belly concertinaing as it pulled out of the bus-stop, shuddering across the concrete-roadway. Dark, heavy fumes lay in its wake over the grey surface. No-one was in sight, no-one had got off the bus, and the wide road was now empty of moving vehicles. Rain began to spot the glass.

Turning back to face Evelyn I could see she was in the kitchen, boiling water for tea. She hadn't said anything, and I kept my peace, waiting until she was ready to talk. In the meantime I looked around the room. Sparsely but adequately furnished; the sofa deep, doubling up as a bed. The arm chairs matching the beige and brown of both sofa and thin carpet but clashing nastily with the mint-green diamond patterned wallpaper. Orange curtains, pulled back beside the windows, contributed to the impression that the place was furnished with left-overs, that no-one had ever lived here. Opposite the kitchen stood a wall-unit, no knick-knacks ornamenting the shelves, the cabinet doors ajar, showing equally empty insides.

Evelyn brought a couple of cups over to the low glass coffee-table, placing them next to a box of West German chocolates, then went back to the kitchen to fetch the tea-pot. She still hadn't said a word, and this, rather than any nervous tic or twitch, any fidgety movement in Evelyn's manner, told me just how uneasy she was feeling. Normally so ebullient, Evelyn wooed her conversational partners; a black widow of an operative, she graciously drew you into her scrupulously laid web. She seated herself in one of the armchairs, leaning back comfortably, crossing her legs.

"Are you OK?" I asked her as I sat down opposite her, on the sofa.

"How sweet! Yes, dear Martin, I'm fine." She laughed, a tinkling, false laugh.

I poured out the tea, and leaned over the table to hand her a cup. She took it with a smile, and sat back again, carefully sipping her drink.

I didn't ask whether she was ready, I didn't ask why she'd asked—told—me to come here. The answers were obvious: yes, she was ready, she had the support of her ex-Stasi colleagues, and the less I knew about that, the more comfortable I would feel. And she'd asked me to come here to show me, once again, that she wasn't dependent on me for anything, not even to sign the forms to get her out of jail.

But since I was here I decided to make use of my time.

"We didn't get to talk about your mission yesterday." I ignored the face she was pulling. "The Ministry requests that you gather evidence for the purpose of prosecuting individuals associated with groups using the premises Weitlingstrasse 122, with specific reference to any persons of cadre status."

I paused to sip my tea, Evelyn's face was pointed towards the kitchen, looking deliberately bored. She took out a packet of cigarettes—Russian, the same brand that Dmitri smoked—and carefully lit one. She offered me the pack, but I waved it away.

"Oh Martin, still trying to give up? You know it only makes you crotchety-"

"But my colleagues and I are particularly interested in background intelligence," I spoke over her, determined to say my piece. Evelyn had stiffened, her eyes focussed on mine. I finally had her full attention. "We don't just want to know whether and how materials are being smuggled into the GDR, we want intelligence on the groups' background, their make-up, movements. We want patterning data, connections, interests and influences by and on other groups. And we want to know more about the geographic spread. If you can tell us who we need to be concentrating on, here in Berlin and throughout the Republic-"

"Martin! This is why you're so dear to me—you're always good for a surprise! I should have recruited you years ago, if only so that you could have learned the lingo," she said archly. "But I understand, I know what you're talking about."

She leaned forward, smoke leaking from her mouth as she spoke, a low whisper: "But tell me, darling, why should I give you this information. Do you think you're the only game in town?"

"Your network?" I found that I too was speaking in a low voice, not whispering; whispers carry too easily, a murmur, letting the words get lost in the carpet and the curtains.

Evelyn glanced at the closed door, then brought her cup up to her lips, buying time to think.

"And you have the files for me? The police reports?"

I drew the summary reports, the ones I had taken home with me last night, out of my briefcase, laying them on the coffee table.

"Thank you, Martin." Evelyn put her cup down, and pushed the box of chocolates over to me. "Here, would you call that a fair swap? Some friends gave them to me, a get-out-of-jail present. But you know what? I just don't have any appetite right now. You take them."

She mashed her cigarette into the glass ashtray and picked up the files. She spread them out on the table, checking the reference numbers.

"Nothing from October 1987 then?" She didn't even pause to see what effect her question would have on me. "Might be wise to let that one drop. Some bigwig in the scene doesn't want that particular can of worms being opened up."

With that she picked up the files and stood up. She reached the door next to the kitchen niche and turned, looking me in the eyes, a gaze somewhere between disappointment and apology.

"My network, as you call it, will be watching out for me, they'll be in contact with me, providing me with backup. I shall owe my safety, my life to them. What can you offer? What do you have to bargain with?"

The door had opened, as if by itself, but a figure was standing there, dark blue suit, white shirt, no tie. It wasn't so much the suit that I noticed, nor even the man himself, but the way he stood. Knees slightly bent, feet barely in contact with the floor. Shoulders wide, curved forward, his arms slightly bent at the elbows, hands half closed, held just below his stomach.

Evelyn continued in the same easy tone as before: "Please tell the Minister, or the Ministerial Committee or whatever you call it nowadays, tell them that they'll get their evidence."

"And the other information, the intelligence I mentioned?" I stood up as I asked the question. As I moved, so did the suit. As I sat back again, the suit returned to his position in the doorway, both of us marionettes on the same pulley. Behind him I could see a bathtub, the sides lined with cork tiles.

"I think, dear Martin, that it's time to leave, don't you? Goodbye." Evelyn blew me a kiss and the suit stepped aside as she went into the room beyond.

As I stood up, the suit returned to his position. I looked at him, and he looked back. A steady, hard but not malicious look. A step towards the doorway where he was standing, and the hands came up, clenching into fists.

I considered my options, consulted my experiences with the Stasi, with Evelyn, and decided the other doorway—the one that led to the stairwell and the outside world—might be a safer option.

07:49

Martin

I'd gone straight to the office, it was still early: nobody there. But a telex was waiting in the basket: I'd received the summons. And when you receive the summons you don't delay. Frau Demnitz, the senior civil servant responsible for the sundry agencies attached to the Ministry of the Interior enjoyed summoning her minions. She was old school—like many civil servants she had survived the transition that started at the end of 1989. This was apparent in her arrogance and her bureaucratic manner—she blamed you for everything, even the very fact that she had to deal with you. Reports were always too long or too short, illegible, incomprehensible or inconsistent; you were too late or too early; too well-dressed or too informal. And never, ever had you filled in the correct forms in the correct order using the correct stamp. Her endemic criticism wasn't an expression of political belief or values—although we had never talked about politics, so I couldn't be absolutely certain—but her attitude was typical of civil servants in the GDR. Oh, things had improved: officials were softening, bending in the wind of change, but up in the rare heights of the ministries and the organs of central government the situation had remained much as before.

So when you were summoned by Frau Demnitz it was best to go as soon as you could, and if at all possible, sooner.

As I got off the S-Bahn at Friedrichstrasse my thoughts were on Evelyn and the other person with her this morning. To them I was more a hindrance than any help, and they were probably right about that. Reaching Unter den Linden I headed down the side of the Russian Embassy to reach the neo-classical grandeur of the Ministry of the Interior. I passed the policeman standing under the trinity of flags by the main door, and climbed the marble stairs to Frau Demnitz's office.

I wasn't kept waiting but was immediately ushered in. I greeted Frau Demnitz, but she didn't look up as our hands clasped each other in a handshake. She was looking at a flier on her desk. I noticed it because it wasn't the kind of thing one expected to see there—usually her attention was occupied only by manilla files and heavy, dark archive boxes. But this A5 piece of grey paper, badly mimeographed in purple ink, looked like the samizdat newsletters we produced before the revolution.

"Thank you for coming at such short notice comrade Captain Grobe." She sniffed. She was famous for her sniffing, I often had the impression that my presence was somewhat offensive to her. "I presume you have seen this publication, although why you didn't think to inform the Ministry I cannot conceive."

I reached over and turned the piece of paper round so that I could read it. Although it was badly copied, it looked like the original had been laid out and printed from a modern computer. There was even a picture, taking up nearly half the page: a face. I looked more closely, it was hard to make out the features in the blurry, purple ink, but the person in the photograph looked familiar.

Holding the flier at arm's length, trying to decipher the smeared words: STASI SCUM IN YOUR NEIGHBOURHOOD was the title. Below the picture was my name.

I looked up at Frau Demnitz who was watching me with a calculating gaze.

"I see you aren't familiar with this. Well, you can read it at your leisure, but in short it provides some biographical details, including your current occupation as an officer of the *Republikschutz*, and goes on to encourage the reader to," again the sniff, "take action, shall we say, to deal with what they see as a problem."

"Where did this come from?"

"Well, apparently they're pasted up all over your part of town, although someone was kind enough to deliver a copy to the Ministry at some point in the night."

PARRASITES LIKE SO-CALLED 'CAPTAIN' GROBE ARE LIVING OFF YOUR WORK AND LABOUR! NO BETER THAN THE STASI THIS REPUBLIKSCHUTZ SCUM ARE NOTHING BUT SPYS PREYING ON HONEST WORKING GERMANS! I managed to read before Frau Demnitz continued, her voice betraying her distaste at dealing with such material.

"I expect you, comrade Captain, to deal with this situation. We simply can't allow this ordure to bring the Ministry into disrepute. I would be grateful if you could prioritise dealing with this matter."

I looked at her in disbelief. *Bring the Ministry into disrepute*? She couldn't be serious?

"Is it the spelling mistakes that bother you most, Frau Demnitz, or the threatening nature of the message?"

Demnitz didn't answer, she just fixed me with her glare.

"So, let me get this straight, Frau Demnitz: you demand my presence at the Ministry, make me come all the way into town, present me with a leaflet that is calling for physical violence to be done to me, then demand that *I* do something about it?" I was angry now, standing up and leaning over the desk, hands resting either side of her blotter pad. She didn't even flinch.

"Thank you comrade Captain, as ever you have succeeded in summarising the situation in a commendably succinct fashion. Now perhaps you could find your own way out?"

"Tell me, would you have pulled this trick if the new Ministerial

Committee were already in place?"

But she must have pressed a button somewhere because her office door opened, and a young civil servant was standing there, silently but politely inviting me to leave.

I ran down the stairs, my heavy feet sending echoes before me. I pulled open the outside door with a suddenness that caused the policeman standing on the steps to look around, then I stalked off down Mauerstrasse.

As my pace slackened and my pulse slowed I found myself standing at the end of Unter den Linden, looking at the Brandenburg Gate. The Wall glowed white beyond the columns, and over in the West the trees of the Tiergarten were budding, the branches picked out by the early sunlight. Tourists were already passing through the checkpoint, customs and Border Police cursorily checking papers and joking with the Westerners coming over to sightsee in central Berlin. The open space, the calm purpose of the tourists with their cameras and their intent gazes—it was all a million miles away from what was happening in the East Berlin that I knew.

I took the leaflet out of my pocket, but it didn't improve on second reading. Putting it away in my briefcase I found the box of chocolates that Evelyn had given me. Why had she given me chocolates? Had they been tampered with? I checked the cellophane wrapping, but it appeared undamaged. What could Evelyn or her Stasi friends have put in a box of chocolates?

A microphone? Too easy to discover, and why bother?

A transmitter to follow my movements? Again, too bulky to evade detection—I'd discover it as soon as I opened the box.

Poison?

I laughed out loud at the thought, and a policeman who had already been keeping half an eye on me started walking towards me. I continued up Otto-Grotewohl-Strasse, still trying to work it all out.

No, like she said, she just didn't have any appetite right now. Fair enough, given her plans for the day.

The thought of Evelyn going undercover to penetrate a fascist group put my little problems into perspective. Sure, there's a shoddy flier with my picture on it, sure, I've got Frau Demnitz on my case, and yes, I've been considering how to undermine the central government of the GDR. But all of that was a breeze compared to the task Evelyn had volunteered for.

Crossing over Marschall Bridge I paused and looked down at the river Spree. Seeing the barges tied up there, next to the whitewashed concrete slabs of the Wall, I remembered my conversation with Rico the border guard just a few days ago. But it felt like more than a just few days, much more.

By now I was nearly at the Charité, the hospital where Steinlein was being treated for his injuries.

I wondered whether Steinlein might appreciate a box of chocolates.

It took a while to persuade the staff on reception that they could admit to having Steinlein as a patient, and a further few minutes for the police officer on the ward entrance to agree that my RS credentials were bona fide. But eventually I was allowed into the private room where Steinlein lay.

He didn't turn his head when I came in, just continued staring at the ceiling. His face was badly bruised, swelling over his left cheekbone, plasters covering most of the right side of his face. His hair had been shaved in patches to allow stitches to be sewn into the scalp. Two fingers were taped together around a splint, and a drip was attached to the back of his right hand. Beyond that I couldn't get an impression of his injuries: a starched white sheet and hospital blankets were drawn tightly around his chest.

I stood by his bedside and touched my right thumb to my forehead in a Pioneer salute. A stupid gesture, one I was hoping would elicit a smile from Steinlein. But he just stared at me, his eyes flickering briefly in greeting. Gone was his sardonic look, his disrespectful attitude. It wasn't just his body that was bruised and battered, I could see that the Nazi boots had kicked his soul around too.

"Comrade Lieutenant Steinlein, I'm sorry to meet you again in these circumstances."

Again the vague flicker of his eyes. There wasn't much to read into that, and I wasn't sure what to say. Steinlein didn't look like he was about to help out with any conversational openings. We looked at each other for a moment before I remembered the chocolates.

"Here, these are for you. Chocolates. *Mon Cheri*—from the West." I waved them around for a bit, then put them on the visitor's chair next to the bed. "I, er, just wanted to say hello. To say sorry. I mean, sorry that this happened to you. But look, you probably need your rest-"

A slight movement on Steinlein's face, his lips parting slightly, then closing again. The tip of his tongue protruded, moistening his lips, his eyes closing at the pain this tiny movement was causing. Then he looked at me again. Intent, trying to communicate.

I bent over, putting my head nearer to Steinlein's, watching his eyes close and open again. A breath taken, then: "*Angst.*"

That was it. Just one word.

Fear.

10:37

Martin

I couldn't get Steinlein's word out of my head. Sitting on the S-Bahn, travelling back to Lichtenberg, the word echoed around my skull. *Fear.*

The train whined and clacked its way around the curves. Opposite me was a young woman, wearing a sweater with the hood pulled over her head. Her toes pointed inward, her eyes unfocussed, deep in thought.

Of course Steinlein was frightened. The hospital staff wouldn't tell me the extent of his injuries, insisted that since I wasn't family I had no right to know. But it had looked pretty bad. Maybe Steinlein was scared that he'd never recover from his injuries. Perhaps there was some sort of spinal injury. Or brain damage?

Or maybe he was scared for his colleagues. Worried that they would be attacked too.

Or his family.

I took the leaflet out of my pocket, smoothing the crumples and folds as I read it through again. Badly written, badly spelt, badly copied. Everything about it was bad, from the politics to the paper it was written on. Despite that, the laughable quality of the whole thing made it hard to take it seriously.

But Steinlein would probably disagree. And so would the informant who had been killed in a West Berlin hospital. Or the man from Mozambique who had been kicked to death a few weeks ago, or the Russian family that had been spat on in the supermarket, or the Vietnamese family who had once had a shop near Lichtenberg station —boarded up since the windows were smashed back in January.

Or the young woman who'd been urinated on in the S-Bahn a couple of weeks ago. I looked at the passenger opposite me, her skin, darker than mine, her hair beneath the hood dark and glossy. It was someone just like her. The skinhead had just got his dick out and pissed on her, shouted "Gypsy scum!" and got off at the next station.

How had we let it get this far?

11:16

Martin

"I guess it's not so surprising, after all," Laura said, not quite looking at me.

"What do you mean? What's that meant to mean?"

There was a pause while Laura contemplated me, measured, disapproving.

"I just meant, well, you've been putting yourself out there. Poster boy of the RS and all that."

How to answer that? If Laura spent less time in the office and being a bit more pro-active then I wouldn't have to put myself out there so much! I looked around at the others, waiting for them to support me. But Klaus was fiddling with a paper clip, and Erika was avoiding my eyes.

"What I meant to say was, you're the best known member of the RS—I mean, if you're not talking to the Border Police about smugglers you're having meetings with the KGB. You were even on *Aktuelle Kamera*. It stands to reason that sooner or later you'd be a target!"

"*Putting myself out there*," I repeated. "*Poster boy*? I've been doing my job—yes, I've been getting out there, talking to people. Because reading files and fiddling with paper clips isn't ever going to change anything!"

Another pause while I glared at everyone. Only Laura met my eyes —she was glaring right back at me.

"What I think Laura is trying to say," Erika murmured. "She's trying to say that you're good at making contact with people, listening to what they have to say, and using that to get an overview. You're good at seeing the bigger picture. But that perhaps right now, considering what's happened, and what we're planning, perhaps it's a low profile that we need."

I snorted, standing up suddenly, pushing my chair back so that it clanged against the radiator. I needed to move, but Laura was giving me a look, the one that told me she found my behaviour aggressive.

I pulled the chair back in and sat down again, then shoved my feet out, leaned back and stretched my legs. I crossed my arms and looked down at my scuffed, brown shoes.

"So is that it? I've been *a bit too high-profile* for your tastes, have I?"

Nobody answered, and I ventured another look around. They were all watching me—that look that adults use when confronted with a toddler having a tantrum.

Klaus cleared his throat and put the bent paper clip down on my desk.

"Perhaps we should concentrate on the current situation," he said slowly, looking between me and Laura. "Martin is under some kind of threat—we should think about what to do about that."

"Right now I feel like I could use your support, rather than all these accusations!"

Laura rolled her eyes and exhaled, breath hissing between her teeth.

We sat there for a while, avoiding each other's gazes and not saying anything. Uneasy shuffling and scraping of chair legs on the lino.

"Well it must be said that Martin hasn't been respecting the team's decisions." Laura finally broke the silence, voice rising plaintively. "While we've been getting on with the paperwork and the background tasks he's been off gallivanting. Trying to catch smugglers, winding up the *Kripo*, going on raids. It's always like that, it's like he thinks he's Old Shatterhand!"

"You like doing paperwork!"

"Martin, no need to shout." Erika was patting the air in a calming gesture.

"I'm not shouting! But I don't need to take this shit either!" I jumped out of my chair again, and ignoring the surprise on my colleagues' faces I marched out of my office.

Slamming the door behind me helped a bit but it also made Grit jump, so I shut the outer office door more carefully. But I was still pissed off, and I ran down the stairs, fast, aiming for every second step.

Just as I reached the half-landing Nik came up the other way.

"Hi Martin, guess what I've ... Hey! What's up?" he called at my rapidly descending back.

I stopped and took a deep breath. It wasn't Nik's fault, no need to take it out on him.

"I've had a death threat from the fascists and all Laura can do is have a go at me about the way I do my job!"

"Whoah! Hang on, wait. That sounds a bit serious!"

"It is fucking serious. I expected better of them all!" I ignored Nik's puzzled face. "How long have we been working together? And then I get this crap!"

"Martin, I was talking about the death threat. What are you going to do about it?"

"Well seeing as I'm not going to get any help from that lot up there ..." I shook my head, "I don't know."

"Listen, where are you going? Right now?"

I shook my head again. No idea.

"Right, you and me, why don't we go for a walk? Work out what to do?" he asked me, in a calm, patient voice that nearly set me off again.

I was still angry, but Nik meant well, and I appreciated the fact that he was there for me.

"OK." A deep breath. "Thanks Nik."

We left the office and walked in silence, Nik giving me a chance to calm down. It wasn't until we'd reached Pfarrstrasse that he spoke again.

"OK, tell me what's going on."

So I told him. The vague and insubstantial threat from the skinhead who'd been arrested last week, the long list of names that Schimmel had given me, being chased by skins at the East Side, the stupid flier that Demnitz had given me a hard time about, my frustration with my colleagues.

"Look, I'll talk to the others, don't worry about that. Everyone's a bit on edge, we're all a bit concerned that we might have bitten off more than we can chew. Give it a bit of time, let them cool off. You too."

I let Nik woffle on. I wasn't upset or stressed. Maybe the others were, but I certainly wasn't.

"Are you taking all this seriously? Because I think you should." Nik paused for a while, considering something, then he shook his head and continued: "You've heard about last night? In Jena? Really heavy stuff. The Dynamo hools went for an away match with their friends from Zwickau and a few casuals from Lobeda. They were organised, it wasn't just a rampage—they went straight for the JG group. Fireworks, steel bars—the lot. Not really surprising—JG Stadtmitte have been a thorn in the fascists' side since before the revolution started."

I grunted, not really listening, just walking along the road, watching the tips of my shoes as they swung in and out of sight.

"Martin, you have to take this seriously—they've never tried anything this big before. And if Dynamo Dresden have done it then the BFC hools here in Berlin are going to do it too—it's a question of pride for them. And you'll be on the list, won't you? They've already attacked Steinlein, who's to say you won't be next?"

Nik was still talking, we were still walking, but I was still thinking about my colleagues.

"What are you planning on doing? Because you can't just ignore these threats. Martin, are you even listening to me?"

"Well I don't trust the cops to catch whoever's responsible. And I don't trust them to protect me," I snorted.

Nik nodded, agreeing with me.

We carried on walking in silence until we'd nearly reached home.

"Fancy a coffee?"

"Martin ...."

I followed Nik's worried gaze, over to the front door of the house where I have my flat. Red paint, same colour as had been used to daub the walls of the RS2 offices. The swastika was crude, badly drawn, the hooks on the cross bending the wrong way. And it was still wet.

"Fuck ..." I breathed.

"Right, you can't stay here." Nik looked up and down the road before pushing me in through the door to the hallway.

We stood there for a moment, listening. The door creaked shut behind us, slotting back into the frame, the loud click echoing off the high ceiling. Putting a finger to his lips Nik started up the stairs, stopping just before the first bend and signalling that I should follow.

We made it to my flat door. It seemed intact, no signs of damage, no signs of forced entry. The little notebook and pencil still hung from their string—no notes, no threats. Nik put his finger to his lips again, then mimed a key turning in a lock. I gave him my key, and he opened up, peering into the dark hallway of my flat. No noises, nothing to be seen.

We went in.

After scouting through the flat, checking it was empty, Nik came back and closed the front-door, then pulled the bolt across.

"That's it, Martin. You can't stay. Pack some stuff, we have to get you out of here," he whispered.

He followed me into the bedroom, and stood watching me pile some clothes into an old army rucksack.

That's when it hit me. Delayed reaction, I thought glassily as I was pulling clothes out of my cupboard. I could suddenly see the flier that Demnitz had shown me. It was there, clear before my eyes, as if I had it in my hands and was reading it. What Nik had been telling me about, the events in Jena last night. The whole series of demonstrations. The nightly beatings in Lichtenberg, Pankow, Marzahn. The whole ghastly, scary array of actions that the hools, the skins and other bastards had been engaged in.

I was in shock. Not the wide-eyed, panting kind of shock— although I noticed that I was breathing in short gasps, my chest heaving, air bellowing through my throat—but a lost sort of shock, sensory perception reduced, not seeing or hearing very well, not even thinking particularly well. A bled-dry sort of shock.

I slowly finished packing, feeling detached, as if I were watching myself through a thick glass window. "OK, I'll go somewhere, I'll stay out of sight."

"Where can we put you? We need to keep you safe for a few days while we work out what to do."

I nodded again, trying to think clearly. Nik was right, my flat was no longer a place of safety; I couldn't stay here—they obviously knew where I lived. I could go to Katrin's, in West Berlin, but I didn't want to endanger my daughter. Thinking about Katrin made me think of her mother. There was a little hut on a small plot of land, on a lake out to the east, it belonged to the family of Katrin's mother, except they were all gone now. I hadn't been there for years, but I knew where the key was kept, in a little nook under the cover of the well. I could go there.

"Yes, there's a *Datsche* in the woods, the other side of Storkow. It's on a lake. I'll go there."

Nik thought about it for a moment. "OK, that sounds good. Where's your phone?"

I pointed through the door to the hallway, and he went out. I could hear him punching the buttons, then silence as he waited.

"Laura? Listen, I'm at Martin's .... Yes, yes, I know, he told me. Listen, this is important: bring the office Trabant round to Martin's, no, wait, not here. Bring it to the supermarket, leave it on Kernhofer Strasse near the supermarket. Martin's in more danger that we thought, we need the car."

He put the phone down, and gave me a worried smile. "Got everything? Good, let's go." Nik opened the front door and held it open for me before double locking it behind us and giving me the key.

We got to the bottom of the stairs, and we paused in front of the house door.

"Right, we're going to the car, and you're going to go to your *Datsche*. I'll call the cops and get them to put a patrol outside your house. Phone me every evening at 9 o'clock, OK? Find a phone box and ring me to let me know you're OK. I'll tell you when it's safe to come home. Right? Let's go."

We walked out onto the street, past the supermarket and up Kernhofer Strasse until we reached the Trabant. Laura was nowhere to be seen, but the car door wasn't locked, and the keys were on the seat under a blue book of road maps.

"Thanks Nik, but I'm sure we don't need to go to all this effort-"

"Just go, Martin, just go. I'll let you know when it's OK to come back."

I pulled the choke out, opened the fuel cock and turned the key. Pressing the accelerator, I listened to the undulating clatter of the engine racing. Satisfied that it wouldn't die on me, I let up the pressure on the throttle. Giving Nik a brief, nervous smile I pulled out on to the road, heading for the countryside.

DAY 12
Friday
25th March 1994

Berlin: *An anti-fascist demonstration will take place in the capital this afternoon. The call for the demonstration has been supported by over four hundred Works Councils and Round Tables across the country.*

If the fascists march, so will we!

If the fascists fight, so will we! The anti-fascist bloc calls on all residents of the GDR to defend our Republic against racist hate-speech, against fascist and imperialist threats and to demonstrate for a society of solidarity and respect.

No state, no nation, no borders, no capitalism!

The anti-fascist bloc supports the emancipatory struggle for dignity and freedom, we reject the nationalist and capitalist logic of repression!

This means:

We will stop the race-hate and the marches of the fascists in East Berlin and throughout the GDR!

We support the anti-fascist struggle here and everywhere!

We show solidarity with Roma and Sinti and with refugees from Russia and from the wars in the Balkans! We support their struggles and their right to stay!

We are determined to reject, hinder and obstruct the programmes of the political parties which support unification with capitalist West Germany!

Let the city rebel! Collectively organise against political policing!

Organise in the work place, in the neighbourhoods, for the independence of the GDR as the basis of social renewal!

Long live the Round Tables and the Works Councils!

That was when Schimmel flipped.

He totally lost it. He was shaking, foam flecking his mouth, eyes wide—I could see the whites of his eyes, all the way round—and shouting. I couldn't make out the words, it was just white noise, a background to the chanting and slogans coming from both sides of the demo. It was really fucking freaky, and then it got worse. I was standing next to him, looking at him, thinking *what the fuck is going on?* and he just lunged, he just went straight for a gap in the line of cops. They hadn't clocked him until then, but they must have thought he was going to jump them or something, and the line of cops tightened, the batons and shields held towards us, one of them struck out, catching Schimmel on his forearm. He didn't even notice, just kept trying to push through the cops, trying to get to the Nazis beyond. We held him back, it took three of us, he was flailing around, still shouting as we dragged him back into the crowd behind us.

"Becker! Becker you arse, I'm going to fucking get you!"

I could make out bits of what he was shouting now, he was still pointing at the crowd of fashos hiding behind the cops. It was a load of skins, but one of them, standing at the back, was a bit older, early forties, short-back-and-sides, a snide grin on his face. He was staring at Schimmel, egging him on.

I dragged Schimmel back into the crowd, and made sure our affinity group went with us. As soon as we were out of sight of the cops Schimmel collapsed, he just lay on the wet road, crying, shaking.

"We've got to get him out of here, he's flipped!" I said to the others, and we literally picked him up off the floor, and got him out of the demo, out the other side. He was still crying and shivering. Man, he was totally broken.

"What the fuck's going on, Schimmel?" I kept saying to him, but he didn't answer, just moaned.

We got him to the nearest squat, and we put him on a mattress. It was really scary, and I had no idea what to do, I just pushed the rest of our team out of the room, and went to the kitchen. Somebody had already put some water on to boil, and I filled a tea-egg with peppermint leaves, put it in a cup with loads of sugar.

"Is he going to be alright?" somebody asked me.

"How the fuck should I know? Am I his fucking mother?" I poured hot water into the cup, taking it up to Schimmel. Playing mother.

He had got off the mattress and was crouched in the corner, crying, still shaking. I knelt down next to him, put one arm around his shoulders, holding the cup in front of him with my free hand.

"Here's some tea," I said, as calmly as I could.

There was no reaction, it was like he hadn't even noticed I was back. Then suddenly his arm shot out, spilling the hot tea over the floor.

"Fuck's sake Schimmel! You trying to get me burnt?" I shouted, then tried to calm down again. "Fuck's sake," under my breath this time. "Fuck's sake ...."

"Becker," Schimmel moaned, "it was Becker."

"Who's Becker? What you on about?" I asked him, thinking of the Nazi, grinning. How did they know each other, these two?

I went to the door and shouted downstairs for another cup of tea, then went back to Schimmel, put my arm around him, pulled his head onto my shoulder and rocked us both, back and forth, back and forth.

It was ages before I could get any sense out of him. The fresh cup of tea had arrived, and I made him take sips of the hot sweet drink. Then more hugging, rocking, making shushing noises. It started trickling out, strings of words, all knotted up, snarled in memories and emotions, mixed with tears and shivering.

He was 13 when he ran away from home: Lössnitz. Some dump down in Karl-Marx-Stadt district. Edge of the world kind of place, near the uranium mines. No wonder he ran away. He got as far as Berlin before the pigs picked him up. A night in the cells, the next day they took him to a secure home on Stralau. First he was beaten, then he was thrown into solitary for a week. The way he told it, it might have been more than a week—no way of knowing: no light, just a cold brick floor, a musty mattress thrown into his cell in the evening, taken away in the morning, and a bucket to shit in. Dry bread, thin broth, nothing to drink. Shit, he was thirteen! All he did was run away from home, a young punk trying to find somewhere to fit in and they put him in a kids' prison!

But it got worse, it must have done, that's where this Doctor Becker comes in, and Schimmel was shaking and moaning again, the name Becker coming up again and again. I couldn't get any more out of him, fuck, I didn't want to. What did they do to you, Schimmel?

And then this Becker turns up, at a Nazi demo. Not one of the bovver boys, either, he looked neat, a suit, tidy haircut. He looked like someone with a bit of clout.

I was going to get this Becker bastard, whatever he'd done to my friend, whoever he was, I was going to get the fucker.

I left Schimmel at the squat. I didn't feel too good about that, but I reckoned he was going to be OK now, and I really needed a break. The others were looking after him. He's just in shock, I told myself.

Thing is, I'd decided to go to to the meeting at the Lohmühle *Wagenburg*. I'd told Martin I wasn't going to do it, there was no way I was going to talk to them about jumping the Wall. I'd told Martin that I was against all borders, end of. I didn't agree with Martin and his *tactical case* for keeping the Wall, but I wasn't 100% sure he was wrong either, and I wasn't comfortable with the fact that the Nazis wanted to get rid of the Wall too. They wanted to get rid of it for different reasons, I know, but it still didn't feel right. So I'd talk to the Lohmühle people, give them Martin's message. I'd do that for him, but I wouldn't argue the case for him. If he wanted that to happen then he'd have to come down here himself.

I walked down Puschkin Allee as far as the concrete flower pots that were at the end of the road, just before the checkpoint by the bridge to Kreuzberg, then I picked my way through the scrubby wasteland between the road and the camp. I could see a chain of paper-bag lanterns and tea lights in jam jars. Figures showed up black against the flames of a camp fire and on the far side faces wobbled in the smoke. It looked really homely.

They'd already started the meeting, and someone was speaking when I found a space to sit on a half-knackered deck chair. It was still free because it was downwind of the smoky fire.

"Smoke follows beauty," some guy leered at me.

I ignored him, and looked around me, trying to work out who was facilitating, and what people were talking about. It seemed to be the usual stuff—people getting pissed off with each other for things that don't really matter: who's using too much firewood, who's leaving fag butts where the kids play.

Finally, there was a pause in the flow of the discussion and a woman turned to me, asking if I was there for the meeting. She was small, and even though it was getting chilly she was wearing just a vest and some army work trousers. Her bare feet were burrowed in the sand. I was dead embarrassed, and I wondered why the hell I was doing Martin this favour.

"I'm here for a friend, I said I'd ask you about jumping the Wall, you know, because you're not going through the Border Crossing Point." I vaguely waved over my shoulder to the sentry box by the gap in the Wall, maybe a hundred metres away. The people at the meeting behaved themselves: I could see a few of them pull a face, but nobody interrupted me. "Look, I don't agree with him, but this friend of mine asked if I'd have a chat with you about it. See, it seems there's a problem with smuggling going on, and that's going to hurt all of us-"

"Is this about those brew-crew smackheads over on the East Side?" A vague giggle came from somewhere in the dark.

I told them about how Martin reckoned people jumping the Wall was distracting the border guards from concentrating on catching the fash smuggling stuff, and this guy with a Bavarian accent started having a go at me for supporting the system.

"So what if we're going to the Køpi—how's that fucking helping the fash?" he asked, and some idiots nodded along with him.

The thing is, I didn't really know either. I was just here because I was doing Martin a favour, I didn't agree with him, but here I was putting across his opinions. Before I had a chance to answer, the discussion had somehow moved on, and I sat down again, waiting to see which way it would go.

There already seemed to be two sides—a few people were saying that we had to fight the fascists, and that meant we had to sometimes do stuff we didn't want to. The other side were saying that borders and passports were fascist, and you can't fight fascism by giving up your freedom!

I sat there, listening to people getting more and more pissed off with their neighbours. What was the fucking point of coming? I'd just split this group straight down the middle. I sat there feeling sorry for myself. Then I looked over to the person doing the facilitation, she looked younger than me and she was struggling. She was trying to get people to calm down and listen to each other, but they were just ranting away and ignoring her. That made me even more pissed off with everyone. But then I thought about the stuff I'd been practising, this course I'd been doing—the neighbourhood facilitator stuff. Dunno why I didn't think of it before, but I knew how to deal with people having arguments and dissing each other.

I had a quick think, hands over my ears to shut out the ranting, then went over to the facilitator and had a chat with her. She nodded, and we talked for a bit as the meeting fell apart around us. Then she got up, walked over to the middle, right next to the fire, and shouted as loud as she could.

"Shut the fuck up! Shut up for a fucking minute will yous?"

It was ace. Everyone shut the fuck up and looked at this hardcore woman. She was dead small, and really thin, but she shouted so loud that everything just stopped.

"Thank you," she said, in her normal voice. "I'm going to call a break, then we're coming back in ten minutes, and we're going to have a proper discussion. I'm facilitating it, and I'm going to let everyone have their say, and we're all going to *fucking listen to each other!* Anyone got a problem with that?"

Nobody had any problems with that, so she walked out to the edge of the group and I got up out of my broken deckchair again to go and talk to her. Tam, she said her name was. I told her about the ideas I had, and she liked them, so I let her get prepared before the meeting got back together and went over to the watchtower, just a few metres away.

I banged on the door and asked for Rico. He came out, and was a bit gobsmacked to see me standing there. Probably wondered what the fuck a punk was doing banging on the door of his watchtower. It was really funny, this German lad, about the same age as me, with his stupid uniform and his spotty face. But I told him I was a friend of Martin's and about what was going on over in the *Wagenburg* so he agreed to come over. I told him to lose his uniform jacket and cap, so he left them behind, putting a padded blue work jacket on and buttoning it up. He still had his fatigue trousers and boots on, but at least now you couldn't see he was some sort of officer or whatever.

Walking back I could tell he was nervous. He puffed his chest out, and started marching, swinging his arms in time to his strides, but they were short, uneasy strides, and he stayed half a step behind me the whole way. Had to smile to myself.

We got back to the meeting just as it was starting up again, and Tam asked me to speak first.

"Hey, I started off on the wrong foot before. Sorry. I think it's because I've been asked to present something that I don't actually agree with either, so I didn't think it through properly, about how to explain it. But basically, like I said before, you've got people worried about the way you're jumping the Wall here and near the Køpi. But I shouldn't have said it that way, so if we can start again I'd like it if we could let Rico here talk: he's from the Border Police, so perhaps he can explain better than I can what he sees as the problem."

Tam took over then, reminding people that we're not here to just say yes or no to Rico, but to look to see if there are any solutions that work for everyone.

There was a tense silence while people waited to see what Rico had to say. I wasn't the only one feeling unsure about having him here, even though it'd been my idea to bring him over.

Rico began to tell us why he had a problem with people jumping the Wall. He talked a load of tosh about security and order and respect for state borders, and it was dead obvious that people were finding it hard not to get pissed off with him.

But then he started talking about the smugglers. People laughed when he said how the smugglers were taking the piss out of the Border Police. Then he started ranting on about what the smugglers were doing to the economy. There was nothing new there, we knew the score, but it was good to hear it said because it was relevant, it was part of what we were talking about.

When he ran out of steam I spoke again, and talked about how it looked like the smugglers were bringing in stuff for the skins and fash over here. Basically I just said the same as I had before the break but this time people were actually listening to me.

"Do you want to tell us about drugs on the East Side?" I asked the person who'd interrupted me earlier.

"We don't talk to the cops." A head shake.

Yeah, they were right. We don't talk to the cops. People were nodding their heads around the circle, and Rico was getting a few dirty looks. The facilitator stood up and said it was time for another break and would someone put the kettle on.

Rico had got the message, and was about to leave. He looked really sad. A bit pissed off, too, but mainly sad. But before he could go Tam was by his side, asking him to stay until the end of the break. She wanted to ask the group if he could stay for the discussion. He shook his head, but stayed anyway, sitting back down on a log near the fire, nobody looked at him, everyone avoided meeting his eyes.

They got the tea going, and warm cups were passed around, that was dead good because it was getting a bit nippy, and we sat there slurping, waiting for Tam to start the meeting again.

"I'm going to ask if anyone can tell Rico why we jump the Wall rather than go through the Crossing Point, but first I want to check if it's OK for him to stay. Yeah, alright, he's Border Police, but he's already part of the discussion. We've listened to what he has to say and I think he should be allowed to hear from us too. Maybe he can help us find an answer."

There was a lot of grumbling at that, but no-one blocked it, so Rico was allowed to stay, looking a bit nervous and isolated on his log.

The gobby Bavarian kicked it all off with a rant about why it's ideologically purer to use a ladder to climb over a wall than to show your ID to someone in a uniform. Rico was dead intense, listening to what people said, trying to understand them. After a while he put his hand up, like he was at school. Tam nodded at him, and he stood up again.

"But you end up showing your ID cards to the West German official on the other side of the bridge! Is he better than us? He's the class enemy, but you'll show him your *Ausweis*. And I'm on your side but you're not even comfortable with having me at your meeting! Aren't we meant to be working together now? Aren't we meant to be building our new society together?"

"All cops are bastards!" came a shout from the shadows. "Take off your uniform and join us!" someone else said.

I had to smile, it was quite funny, even though I felt sorry for Rico too.

"Why do you hate us so much?" Rico asked. He was being dead genuine, but everyone laughed anyway.

"You serious? You for real?"

"Rico asked a question," Tam intervened again. "Are we going to give him an answer?"

"Where were you in 1989? And before that? When people like us got beaten up, tortured, sent to jail by people like you? People like you set dogs on us, pointed guns at us; you beat us! Come on, you know the score!"

Rico shook his head slowly: "No, I've only been doing this for three years, I'm just doing it before I go to university. And where I come from, up in Mecklenburg, not much happened in 1989, I kind of missed all of that. And I'm sorry if they treated you that way, but you must have been doing something to make them-"

Groans all round, cries of *What planet you from?*

"Look, Rico, maybe this isn't the time to talk about this stuff, but why don't you hang around afterwards and we'll tell you the stories," Tam said. "Is that OK with everyone?"

A few people reluctantly nodded.

"Rico asked something before," Tam continued. "We still haven't given him an answer. He asked why we won't work together with him and his colleagues?"

There were no offers. I didn't have a good answer either. This naive, liberal uniform had asked us why we weren't prepared to work with him. Wasn't it time to think about that question? We went on marches, we hassled our local Round Table, calling them stick-in-the-muds, saying they had to change with the times, listen to what people wanted. Maybe we had to move with the times too?

Maybe he was right, we ought to talk to him. He was answerable to the Round Tables, and we could get involved as much as we wanted to—the Round Tables were open.

But there was too much hurt, too many good reasons not to trust cops. And I don't want a police force—not any kind of police force, whether on the streets or on the borders. So, no: I couldn't co-operate with them.

And I said that to the group, we can't trust cops, and we don't want cops. People whooped when I'd finished.

"Yeah! No borders, no police!" someone shouted, and everyone laughed.

Except for Rico. He didn't laugh, he just looked confused. I was starting to feel sorry for him again. How did he do that to me?

I sat there for a bit, thinking, *What would Martin do? What would Martin say?* and for a while I lost track of the discussion. When I tuned in again it had turned back to rants. People were lining up to have a go at Rico and all he stood for. He looked really miserable, but, fair play, he stuck it out, he was still there, listening, trying to understand. More than could be said about any of us.

The whole thing was falling apart. Again. Maybe it just wasn't possible to have a discussion with a cop, to find agreement?

But Tam stood up again and spoke.

"Look, we're going round in circles. We're not going to get any further if we carry on like this. We have a choice now, and we have to be serious about it. We can stop this discussion and carry on jumping the Wall like before, just ignore what we've heard tonight. Or we can think about whether the stuff about fascist smugglers means we have to do something about it!"

"I'm not working with the cops!" shouted the Bavarian.

"So don't! Make a proposal that doesn't involve the cops!" shot Tam straight back. That shut the gobby twat up. She was fucking ace, that woman!

But Rico just sat there through it all, looking lost. It was like he was still there only because he didn't have the energy to get up and walk away.

"I hate myself for saying this," the person next to me said. "But I gotta say, the cop is right—in just over a week there's the referendum on the Wall. Things have changed, we have a say now. We want to get rid of the Wall, but we can't do that just by ignoring it, or *them.*" A finger pointed at Rico. "We have to talk to people, get involved in the discussions that are happening at the moment. It's time for us to take part and not just moan and blame others when things don't go the way we want them to!"

That was the point I'd thought about before, but still I shook my head. The Bavarian had something to say about it though. "Fuck's sake—we're *punk*!" he shouted. "We're against all of this shit. Punk means *resistance!*"

"Yeah," I shouted back, irritated by his arrogance, "in Bavaria punk is resistance, but what are we meant to be resisting here? If you want to resist then go back to the fucking West! If you want to help build something new then stay and take responsibility!"

By the light of the fire I could see people nodding their heads, but the smug Bavarian just shook his head in disgust.

"We could just open our own Crossing Point," somebody joked.

But Rico looked up at that, and you could tell he was thinking about it, I could hear the gears working.

Someone else took up the idea: "Yeah, there's a Crossing Point here, but we need one on Köpenicker Strasse so we can get to the Køpi and the Schwarzer Kanal!"

"I guess it would be possible," Rico started, he was still thinking about it, trying to work out how realistic it would be. "We'd need to take a proposal to the neighbourhood Round Table, and the Berlin Regional RT too-"

He was interrupted by groans. Doing it that way would take ages while all the old farts in the Round Tables argued about it—by the time we got a decision the referendum might have already decided to get rid of the Wall anyway.

"But we could get it fast-tracked. If you were serious about it, if you agreed to staff it, and we put in a joint proposal together, I mean, all of you and my lot at the regiment and the customs administration-"

He was interrupted by whoops of laughter and hands waving in the air. People thought the whole idea—working together with the Border Police regiment—was really funny. Despite all that had been said before I could tell they loved it.

"But you'd have to agree to do the border controls-" Rico started again, but nobody heard him in all the laughing and shouting.

"I think we may have a decision." Tam smiled over to me and Rico.

Rico grinned—the first smile I'd seen from him—a big, goofy grin on his pockmarked face, teeth glittering in the firelight.

DAY 13
Saturday
26th March 1994

Berlin: *As the country prepares to vote in three referenda next week the Central Round Table has repeated its call for a fair and fact-based debate on the issues. In a statement issued this morning the body said: 'Only by informing ourselves and only after careful consideration and discussion will we be able to help our Republic reach appropriate decisions.'*

The Round Table was responding to statements recently made by the main parliamentary political parties.

06:50
Martin

When I woke up this morning the mist still covered the far bank, a smoky veil hanging in the moisture-laden air. It was a queer feeling, opening my eyes and expecting to see dawn, but being greeted instead by blankness. Everything else: white. Sheer nothingness.

I took the rowing boat out onto the lake, the water rippling away before dissolving into that impossible emptiness. So beautiful, yet—in an atavistic way—terrifying. A canvas of a world, ready to fill with hope and fears. If I were to take my brush, what would I paint on this emptiness? Would I make the same awkward political landscape of Round Tables nudging up against layers of parliaments? Would there be a more elegant way to give people the chance of self-determination? Would there still be the egoists, the oddballs, the power-hungry and those who just wanted to be led? Would there be any people at all? Or just me, the last loner?

After all, we have the system that history has bequeathed us. We can fiddle with the knobs and dials and valves of society, but we are moulded by our pasts. There's no scientifically determinable march through social progression. Each advance has to be fought for, then fought over, again and again, lest it become jaded, corroded, worthless.

Alone in that white mist I'd felt the weight of the world on my shoulders, and my heart lifted when the fog thinned. The fir trees to the left and right materialised, grey, then black, finally their true green darkness showing up against the light tips of fresh growth.

The wind soughed across the water to keep me company on my watch.

07:40

Karo

I ended up spending the night at the Lohmühle, staying in an empty wagon. Only problem was that the person whose wagon it was turned up really early the next morning, still pissed out of his skull. He woke me up by crashing through the door and then falling on top of me. Then he wanted to talk to me, he sat there on the bed, slurring total shite.

So I left.

I wasn't happy about getting up so early, but the low sun was glinting off the shiny buds of the plane-trees on Puschkin Allee and that was nice—it felt good to be out and about. I walked all the way over the bridge to Friedrichshain, and by the time I'd got to Ostkreuz station I'd decided to go and see Martin. He lived quite near by, and I was sure he'd want to hear about the meeting last night—I felt quite proud of what we'd achieved.

So I walked a bit further and went under the railway bridge onto Martin's street.

But when I banged on his door there was no answer. I wrote a message on the notebook that was hanging there: *I came to see you but you were still asleep you lazy git. PS clean up the graffiti on the front of your building—you'll give your neighbourhood a bad rep.*

I stood outside Martin's tenement wondering what to do now. The original plan had been to go home and go back to bed, but I was awake now and buzzing with the memory of last night. I could go and see if Martin was at his office, it was on my way anyway. And it would be just like Martin to go to work on a Saturday. Sad case.

It's not far to walk to the RS office, and I was there in no time. The aluminium and glass door stuck a bit and I had to give it a good push to get past. Why do all offices smell the same? That official floor-wax-and-detergent smell. And soap too—the same grey, hard soap that you get in schools. Not a good smell.

I was still wrinkling my nose when I knocked at the door of the RS office up on the first floor. Laura answered and she must have seen me pulling a face because she didn't look very pleased to see me. Or maybe that was just her usual sour-puss.

"What do you want?"

"Good morning to you, Frau Laura," I answered, all nice and sweet. "Is Martin here?"

"No. He's out of town on important business." I could tell Laura wanted to get rid of me so I tried to think of something else to say, just to piss her off.

But I wasn't quick enough and Laura gave me a curt *Tschüss* and shut the door on me.

I last saw Martin on Wednesday, just a few days ago. It's not like he reports all his movements to me or anything, but he hadn't mentioned any important meetings outside Berlin.

I shrugged and started skipping back down the stairs. Sour Laura wasn't going to spoil *my* day with her bad manners.

When I got to the bottom somebody was trying to push the front door open, but it was jammed again, so I helped out. It opened with a jerk and Erika fell through the gap, almost landing on top of me.

"Hey Erika!" I laughed. "Bit early for drinking isn't it?"

Erika looked sombre. Grey. She always looked a bit worried, but this was different. She didn't even say hello back to me, just sort of nodded and tried to push past me.

This wasn't like her at all. I liked Erika, she was the best of Martin's colleagues. She always said hello and how-are-you, and she listened to the answers too. Something was up.

"Erika? You OK?"

She just nodded again, not stopping.

"Erika, I'm looking for Martin, do you know where he is?"

That stopped her. She'd reached the bottom of the stairs, but now turned round to face me.

"What's up? What's going on, Erika?"

Erika looked up the stairs, then went to the door that was still jammed open and looked outside before answering.

"Karo, it's all gone horribly wrong. I'm really worried about Martin, about all of us-"

"Erika, what is it? Erika?"

"It's the Nazis. They're after Martin. He's had to leave town, he's gone to some *Datsche* out of town. I don't know where it is, somewhere near Storkow? But I'm worried about him. About all of us. We were meant to have a police officer on the door but they haven't sent one yet."

"Shit, you serious? Like, they're *really* after Martin?" I thought of the graffiti on Martin's door—I'd assumed it was just a random tagging, but from what Erika was saying ... "Fucking hell!" I hissed. "I've got to find him."

Erika looked surprised, but didn't ask me why I needed to find Martin.

"A *Datsche* you said? Like in an allotment garden? Out of town? Where? Katrin will know where it is, won't she? Do you have her phone number?"

Erika shook her head.

"Fuck! How do I get hold of Katrin?" My mind was whizzing. My address book was at home, that was nearly as far as Katrin's, and to get to either place would take ages, I'd have to walk loads and get a tram and a bus. "Erika, have you got your bike with you? Can I borrow it?"

Martin was well fucked when we arrived. Not the welcome I'd been expecting after tracking him half way across Brandenburg. The journey had taken us ages. From Katrin's we had to get back to East Berlin, take the S-Bahn all the way to Königs Wusterhausen then change onto a stopping train. After all that there was a hike through the woods from the station. Under different circumstances it could have been quite nice, like in the summer when we have a bit of a party down in the woods by the Müggelsee. You know, get a bit of a camp fire going, couple of crates of beer, bit of a swim. But this was different. Katrin was dead worried and didn't say a word for the whole journey. On the train she sat in the seat opposite me, and there was an empty cigarette packet scrunched up on the floor, I could only see *Cab* written on it, the *inet* bit was lost in a crumple. An empty beer bottle rolled around whenever the train slowed down or sped up or went round a curve. A dark, sticky stain of dry beer was spread between our feet. That's not the kind of thing I'd normally pay attention to, but there wasn't anything else to do was there? Not with Katrin pretending to be mute.

We got off the train and went down the sandy road. At some point the forest just started, a wall of pine trees—it was really dark in there, the road got narrower and sandier and we went down the middle of the track, tripping over tree roots and avoiding deep holes filled with loose sand.

We passed an empty holiday camp, witches' cabins with steep roofs, all standing empty in the woods, waiting for summer—they were well spooky. I pointed them out to Katrin and she just looked around and said *they're not witches' cabins, they're just holiday chalets.*

After that I kept my gob shut.

We walked for miles through those woods. It was dead creepy, no birds, nobody else, just us. And when we got there and I gave Martin a hug I could smell schnapps on his breath. Katrin noticed it too, she was freaked out by that but tried hard not to show it. She held her father by his shoulders for a while, looking into his eyes as if she could read his soul or something. And then she started talking again.

"Papa, what's going on?" she asked him.

Martin just shrugged, looked away from her. As if he was embarrassed or something.

I hate scenes, and I thought this was going to turn into one of those family rows, so I decided to try to lighten the atmosphere.

"Took us ages to get here, Martin, you're totally in the middle of nowhere!"

Martin just turned round, turned his back on us. He was looking out over the water. I'd never seen him like this, well, apart from last week when we crashed at Katrin's. He looked dishevelled, crumpled. He'd definitely slept in his clothes if you ask me. I decided I was being a bit mean, so I didn't say anything—I just thought it in my head. But it still wasn't fair.

So I decided to be a bit more charitable: maybe the smell of schnapps wasn't on his breath, but coming off his clothes? Maybe he drank himself into a stupor last night, and hadn't had time to have a wash and change. Or clean his teeth. Even though it was already past midday.

"Papa?" Katrin touched her dad's elbow, trying to draw him back, find out what was going on.

"It feels like I've failed." Martin still had his back to us, being all dark and mysterious and fucking rude too, if you ask me. He was still looking out over the water.

I gave Katrin a look that said *what the hell?*, and she moved around to stand in front of Martin.

"Failed? How?"

Martin shook his head, looked at Katrin, then turned around a bit so he could see me too, like he'd just realised that we were both there. And then he must have decided to get his shit together because otherwise Katrin was going to lose her rag. He looked around the garden, then extended his arm, pointing to the Hollywood swing.

"Why don't you girls sit down? I'll go and make coffee."

I studiously avoided reacting—Martin wouldn't normally be that crass—he must be in a pretty bad state to call me girl. So Katrin and I shared another look, and Martin bimbled off into the *Datsche*. It was one of those wooden frame and hardboard jobs, with a slanting roof covered in tar paper. Looked like it hadn't been used for a few years:

moss was growing up the outside and the windows were so dusty I couldn't see through them, but I could hear the clattering of pans and cups. We sat down on the swing, looking down the garden to the lake. A beech tree was just coming out in leaf, and it cast a soft green light. Further down the garden, bushes were growing wild, blocking the pathway, but between them I could see a small boat tied up next to the bank.

When Martin came out again he was carrying a tray with three cups of coffee. He looked more human, more like the Martin I knew. He'd made an effort, changed into fresh clothes, washed his face. He didn't smell so much any more either. Just a bit musty, but that was fine. Meant I could look him in the eye again.

"Sorry, haven't got anything to eat," he said as he sat down. "I was just thinking about going to the village *Konsum* when you arrived."

"Papa, are you going to tell us what's going on? Why did you say you've failed?"

He kept shtum for a bit, and then that weird, faraway look—the same one he'd been wearing when we arrived—it came back. He didn't look at us, just stared down the garden. Then he began to speak slowly and irregularly, as if he was in a ket-loop.

"I haven't got the energy for this kind of thing any more. All these years I've been fighting, the whole time, and it never seemed like we'd ever get anywhere—up against the Party, the Stasi. And then the revolution began, and when it was clear that we had won, that the people had won, no more Party, no more Stasi, just the will of the people ... once we got that far I thought I could relax. And I did, just helped out a bit, stayed in the background, doing boring stuff that nobody else wanted to do."

Martin was still staring at the water, as if we weren't there, or maybe he was just pretending we weren't there.

"But that business last year, with the Minister. And then this, the fascists," he continued, still speaking slowly, quietly, as if to himself. "I feel like I have a duty to get involved, to continue defending the revolution, the will of the people ...." He trailed off, and his eyes shifted to mine, daring me to disagree, to argue with him.

He was really starting to freak me out now. He was just staring, not blinking. I swallowed, and thought, *he needs you, just listen to what he has to say.* I just nodded—a smile would have felt a bit stupid right then.

"Look, I can see you're upset-" I started, but he cut me off.

"No, not upset. Not upset. Wrong word. It's a kind of, no .... I feel a kind of *Weltschmerz*."

I wasn't even sure what that meant, but Martin didn't give me any time to ask.

"I have this sense of duty in me, this feeling it's my responsibility. But it costs so much, it's already cost too much. I think it was last year—it was when they started targeting me—it wasn't just that they were following me round, but they'd been in my flat, they'd messed with my things, messed with my head. It was like nothing had changed, like I was back in the bad old days. Too much. All too much. And I don't know how much longer I can keep going, not with all this shit that's happening."

There was this moment of total silence in the garden. None of us said anything. None of us even moved at all. I sat there thinking *shit, shit, shit, what the fuck do I do?*

But it was obvious what I had to do, and you're probably reading this and thinking, course it's fucking obvious. But it wasn't until that moment, just then, that I knew what to do. So I kind of got up a bit so that I could reach over to him and put my arms around my friend. He didn't move, he was really stiff, and his eyes were welling up, and I was nearly welling up too, had to really bite my lip to stop from laughing or crying or both at once.

Katrin knew what to do—no-one had to tell her. She just put her arms around both of us, and we just stood there, hunched over the table and the coffees, all hugging each other for what seemed like hours.

"Come on, let's go and get some stuff from the *Konsum* for dinner," Katrin said at last, and we stopped all the touchy-feely stuff and Katrin and I headed around the side of the *Datsche* towards the lane. I didn't look back at Martin. He needed space. Probably needed to repair his bruised ego or rebuild his emotional wall or whatever.

★

It took us about half an hour to walk to the village and buy some stuff for a salad, some bread and a jar of plum purée from the shop. The woman behind the counter was dead nosy, wanting to know who we were and whether we were on holiday. As if that wasn't enough there was a skinhead in there, buying milk and Katrin had to put her hand on my arm to stop me saying anything. But he clocked me alright, and swore at me as we left the shop. Fucker.

When we got back Martin was looking loads better. He'd put an oil cloth with a flowery pattern over the garden table and laid out plates and cutlery. A fresh pot of coffee was keeping warm on the little candle stove and he sat there, looking nervous, waiting for us.

He'd put some music on the tape player in the hut and noise leaked out of the window. He's always got some music on the go—typical of Martin to take some tapes with him when he left. Normally he listened to some old-school rock or blues from some has-been GDR band but this time it was some stuff I've never heard him play before, something in English. Katrin gives him these tapes, and he's always really chuffed to get them, it's really sweet. Then he plays whatever he's been given, listening to it like she's sending him some message, dead serious like. But his English is a bit shit, so I don't think he knows what he's even listening to half the time. I looked at the cassette insert and worked out what song was playing: *I've been left on the shelf*, about some old dude who pretends not to be sad that he's all by himself, feeding the ducks for company and he's only got his hot water bottle to take to bed. But there's Martin, like, *yeah, Katrin gave me this tape: Jake Thackrey, some Englishman. It's really nice, isn't it?* He didn't even get that Katrin was taking the piss! I was really good and didn't say anything to him about it, just told him it was cute and gave Katrin a sharp look. She did the innocent act and pretended she didn't know what was going on.

Katrin and I sat down at the table in the garden, waiting for Martin to finish getting everything together for our midday meal. A book was splayed out on the table, I picked it up. Erich Fromm, The Fear of Freedom. I glanced over at Katrin, pulling a face: heavy reading. Looking at the page Martin had dog-eared I read a sentence that had been underlined in pencil. Scanning up and down a few paragraphs I could see it was a commentary on policing; or rather crime, how crime is caused by restricted lifestyles, by fear and deprivation and poverty. And how prison is just one more restriction, so can never be an answer to criminality.

"Good book that—borrow it if you want." Martin had come out of the hut, carrying the bread and a bowl of salad.

I shook my head. It looked a bit too heavy for me. I mean, life was a bit too heavy for me right then, I didn't need to add to the burden.

"It's another of those things we have to find an answer for. Prison isn't a solution, it's just another problem."

I didn't respond so we all sat there for a while, chewing away at our rubbery village bread, wondering what to say about Martin's little speech. It was like we were all pretending that the little scene from an hour ago had never even happened.

So I just dived straight in.

"What the fuck's going on, Martin?"

Katrin looked really pissed off, as if she was the only one allowed to be direct with her dad. But Martin started telling us about this demo he'd been 'observing'. It was gross, all these fucking Nazis marching, chanting, and he'd just stood there watching them. I had a bit of a go at him. I shouldn't have, but I couldn't help myself, sometimes he's such a *mensch*, being all reasonable, trying to see all sides of any argument, and it pisses me off because we're in the middle of a fucking revolution! I told him we had to take sides.

"So what should we do about them?" he asked, all reasonable-like.

"Shoot 'em!" I didn't really mean it, just wanted to provoke him a bit, but he was shocked.

"Really?" he asked, taking me seriously, again.

I sighed, then looked him in the eye and shook my head.

"No, but it's my first reaction. It's what they want to do to us." I watched him think about that for a bit. "And you've got to admit, the Antifa have done a lot of good: hitting Nazis keeps them from spreading so fast."

I was right and he had to admit it. If the Antifa weren't prepared to beat the shit out of fascists then the whole situation would be loads worse. The fash just want to attack, kill off anything different: punks, anarchists, foreigners, queers, the disabled. They even had a go at the Central Round Table building once.

I could see Martin thinking about it, his face moving as the thoughts passed behind his eyes. In my head I could almost hear him think: *but we overthrew the Party,* he'd say in that old-fart way of his. *We ended a dictatorship and started a revolution without violence. The only violence came from the security forces.*

He didn't say it, and it's not like he needed to. We all knew that. But even he had to admit that it was kind of ironic that our oh-so-peaceful revolution had led to a gang-war. Fash against Antifa. Yeah, the fascists started it, but you have to admit that it's not like the Antifa aren't up for a scrap, is it? Far too much fucking testosterone in that scene if you ask me.

"But beating Nazis up isn't going to solve the problem," he finally came up with. "It might keep them in check, but we're not going to get rid of them that way. The more violent we are to them, the more violent they are back, so then we have to up the stakes to keep them down. Using that logic we'll end up shooting them, unless they shoot us first."

He looked so self-satisfied, as if he'd been really perceptive. I groaned again. Times like this I wonder why I hang out with Martin. I looked at the beech tree, the one growing in the middle of the path, trying to work up a bit of patience.

"So what do you suggest we do, then, Mr. Clever Clogs?" I asked him.

"In the medium term, well, we know the answer already—some people are doing it. We need to talk to the young skins, people who are getting dragged in. They need to be listened to, made to feel part of our society, our revolution."

"What, you mean we should just tell them they can take part in our revolution, integrate their fascist filth into our society?" I threw back at him, he was really starting to piss me off now.

"No, no, I didn't mean that. I mean, get them before they've really bought into the whole ideology of hate. Or if they're already part of that, get them to start thinking, asking questions. I don't mean we should give them a chance to sow their hatred. I meant we should welcome them as individuals and encourage them to feel respected, just as they should respect others. We need to give them back their sense of self-worth, their place in society, so that they don't feel that hate, so they don't have the need to destroy everything that is different."

The most annoying thing about Martin is that he's usually right. I guess he's been around for so long that he's thought about practically everything there is to think about. Doesn't make it any easier to listen to him being all opinionated though.

"But what about the short term?" I asked him.

"I don't know." He shrugged at me. "You got any ideas?"

Great.

If not even Martin knew what we had to do then we really were fucked!

Katrin had gone inside while Martin and I were arguing, I could hear her clattering around, washing up our plates, tidying up the little hut. I wondered what it was like in there, probably a total tip.

But our little talk had ground to a halt, and Martin just sat there, gawping at the little candle under the coffee pot. And I was just sat there too. Probably gawping into space as well. Thinking about the fash had made me think of Schimmel again. I couldn't get what he'd told me out of my head. The stuff about being abused in the secure homes they'd put him in when he was a kid.

And that was when I realised that I really wanted to tell Martin about it all.

Which made me realise just how much I trusted Martin.

But Martin had his own problems right now. *Fucking ace friend I am*, I thought to myself, *I've got two friends having a really hard time of it and I've got no clue how to help either of them!*

Under normal circumstances I would tell Martin about Schimmel, and he'd know what to do. Then again he'd probably tell me to go to the Reconciliation Commission. Yeah, right, as if I'd do that! I didn't want reconciliation for my friend. I wanted fucking revenge.

I smiled, thinking about what Martin would say to that.

"Something amusing you?" he asked me, the ghost of a smile crossing his lips too.

"Nah." I shook my head. "Just wondering how to deal with this current situation."

"What?"

"You know the fasho-squat on Weitlingstrasse? They've only gone and moved back in again."

Martin was gobsmacked.

"Yeah, seems the cops didn't bother to guard the place after the raid, lazy eejits. And before the District Housing Association could change the locks the place was overrun with Nazis again!"

His face was a picture. It was almost worth it just to see his coupon. But, let's be honest, it was a shit situation.

"So what are we going to do about it?" I asked him.

He just shook his head, as if he didn't want to answer. That just wound me up again.

"I'll tell you what we're going to do," I told him. "We're going to get a bunch of good people together, and we're going to take that house right back off those bastards. We're going to re-socialise it, give it to someone who needs it, like those people who've come from Russia, or the families from Serbia and Croatia."

"We can't do that! It's just too much. Too undemocratic." He was still shaking his head, as if I was suggesting we build a missile or a tank or something.

"Yes we can! Come on, we did it before! That's what direct action is all about!"

"What? Setting ourselves up to be the vanguard of the revolution? No."

"It's not a fucking vanguard! We're stopping the bloody counter-revolution. We're stopping the fascists from being the vanguard of the counter-revolution! The time for talking is gone. We need new impetus in this revolution of ours!"

"Maybe you're right." But he was still shaking his head, like it was on a spring or something. "But I've been wondering whether we even have a consensus in our society-"

"What are you on about now?"

"Well, look, we're trying to set up this independent, grassroots GDR. But does *everyone* actually want it-"

"Course they fucking do!" I interrupted, but he carried on as if I hadn't said anything.

"But back in 1989, all those people marching, they said they wanted the end of Communist rule. But did they say what they wanted to replace it with? Or did we just make assumptions? Did we just think this was our revolution because we'd been resisting for so long, opposing the state, encouraging debate?" He paused for a bit, he had wrinkles on his forehead, as if he'd been thinking too hard. "What I'm trying to say is, back in 1989 and 1990, did we just assume the privilege of influence, use the Round Tables to push our agenda, just because we were there already, because we were already organised?"

I shook my head. He was talking bollocks. It wasn't just him and his cronies, for fuck's sake, there were literally millions of us marching back then—of course we wanted this!

"So these skins and fascists," he was still wittering on, thinking aloud. "Maybe they're not just a small minority, maybe lots of other people feel the same way—*Foreigners Out, Germany for the Germans, Time for Strong Leadership*? Or even *One Germany*? Maybe no-one's interested in all this stuff about solidarity, a progressive society, freedom, fairness, grassroots democracy, respect for one another ...." He tailed off, lost in a pit of thinking inside his head.

"Bollocks! Fucking shitey bollocks, Martin!"

He grinned at my fierceness, but let me continue.

"You know what, you're not the only one who thinks about this shit! Because I think about it too, and so do my friends. And we're out there, on the streets. We hear what people are saying and they say some pretty shit things! Know how many times I've been told that I should be gassed? Just because I'm a punk, just because people don't like the way I look? People spit at me, and I spit right back and give them the finger too. Cos some people have an ugly side. Jealous, scared, bitter, whatever. Fuck, we've all got an ugly side, just some people are more ugly than others. Yeah, and that's gonna come out when they're frightened, and you know what, these are fucking frightening times—hell, even I'm a bit frightened sometimes, and I love all this chaos! Thing is, Martin, just because some people are bitter, twisted shits doesn't mean that we have to give up, does it?" I stared at him, daring him to disagree, daring him to interrupt.

"Know what I think?" I carried on ranting—nothing could stop me now. "You know what? All that shit that the Communists used to spout? Well here's the news: all their talk about scientific socialism was just cronyism, privileges, authoritarianism. And the funny thing is, people knew they were talking shite, and still the propaganda stuck. I reckon people in this country believe in fairness, believe in helping each other out, sharing. Soli-*fucking*-darity. The labels were all bollocks, all a sham, but what those labels should mean, that's what stuck with us."

I sat back, arms crossed, feeling a bit better for having got that off my chest. Except now I felt a bit bad, because Martin was already giving himself a hard time, and now he'd got me ranting at him as well.

I felt something move behind me, a stir of the air, or maybe a faint breath. Looking over my shoulder I could see Katrin had come back out of the hut.

"Come on you two let's go inside, it's getting chilly" Katrin was looking at her dad, dead tender. She looked sad.

We sat together on the train, heading back to Berlin. There wasn't much to say, we were both a bit shocked by Martin's behaviour. At some point, Katrin started talking.

"I think it started last autumn, he's been different since then. I've always thought of him like a bear. A big bear of a man. Large, generous. And quick to anger. But since last year he's been, I don't know, pensive? Thoughtful?"

I only got to know Martin last autumn, so I had nothing to say. I let Katrin do the talking.

"But maybe it goes further back. My mum. Maybe it was when she went …." She shook her head, looking out of the window. There was nothing to see out there, it was already dark. But looking out of the window meant she didn't have to look at me.

She told me about her mum, about how she left the country when Katrin was still young, leaving Martin to look after her. "The personal cost you had to pay for wanting to leave the country …. I often wonder what it cost her. But the thing is, it cost *us* a lot, too. Me and Papa, particularly Papa. It cost him too much."

I put my arm around her, and she snuggled up against me, burying her head in my shoulder, still avoiding eye contact.

"Too much," she repeated. She told me that her mum had written to her, wanted to have contact. I knew there was something going on, something about Katrin writing to her mum—I'd overheard that much on the morning when Martin and I had stayed at hers.

"What are you going to do?"

Katrin glanced up, then hid her face again.

"I don't know," came the muffled reply. "Don't know. I'm curious. But then I think of what happened .... actually I don't really know what happened, I don't know her."

"What about your dad? What are you going to do about him?"

Katrin froze for a moment, as if this were a new thought for her. She shook her head again, still buried in my side.

"Oh, who knows? He's always asking me what I want. But yeah, what about him? I don't know. Perhaps it's time for me to be there for him. For my whole life he's been there for me, looking out for me, always there if I want help or advice. And I just get annoyed by him, lose patience with him. I've been unfair, maybe. But now it looks like he's the one that needs some help."

I stroked Katrin's hair. She was right, it was time for us to be there for him.

DAY 14
Sunday
27th March 1994

Magdeburg: The Sascha Berkmann Brigade at the SKET factory in Magdeburg have written an appeal to mobilise support for widespread anti-fascist action in the GDR. In their statement the brigade call on humanist, anti-fascist and peace-loving citizens and residents to unite in their opposition to the negative-reactionary forces that are attempting to disrupt and destroy the Social Experiment in the GDR.

15:27
Karo

I spent most of Sunday with Schimmel. He was fine, or at least he was pretending to be fine. He didn't mention what had happened on Friday, so I didn't ask him about it either. We just hung out, played music and went up to Forcki park with a few beers. I told him about Martin, not the bit about Martin breaking down, just that the fash were after him and that he'd had to leave town.

By mid-afternoon it had clouded over and was getting chilly so we went back to our squat on Thaerstrasse. When we got there Katrin was waiting for me in my room, huddled against the wall, chewing her bottom lip.

"Papa's gone missing! Karo, he's gone, they've taken him—I don't know where he is!"

I put my hands on her shoulders just as she'd done to her dad yesterday.

"OK, calm down. Tell me what's happened."

"I got the train out to the *Datsche* this morning, but when I got there the place was empty, the door was smashed in, the place was a mess. I went straight back to the village and dialled 110. I said it was the Nazis, that they'd taken Papa. But the dispatcher wouldn't take me seriously, she just told me to go back to the *Datsche* and wait for him there. They weren't going to help so I came here-"

I put my arms around her, held her close until she stopped talking. She was right to be scared about her dad's safety. But what to do? Schimmel was standing in the doorway, he'd heard what Katrin had said, it was like it had woken him up.

"I'll go round to Rigaer, get Antifa Rex, he might have some ideas-"

"Wait! Phone Erika too, Martin's colleague. The number's in my address book—over there."

Schimmel got the address book then stopped, patting his pockets.

"You got twenty Pfennigs for the phone box?"

Erika came straight round, she was here even before Schimmel got back. If she'd looked worried yesterday morning she was positively scared now. Katrin and I were on the bed, next to each other. She'd stopped crying, but I still had my arm around her. I filled Erika in on what I knew and she sat for a while frowning.

"We need to talk to Captain Neumann from K1. He'll know what to do. And if you ask me this is probably his fault too. I'll go and give him a ring, get him to come-"

"No! No cops are coming in here! Ring him if you want, but he's not coming here."

Erika stopped in the doorway, working out how to react, then nodded. "Before I go to the phone box though, maybe I should tell you something. There's someone else who might be able to help." She gave me a look, glanced towards Katrin, then moved her eyes towards the door. She wanted to speak to me without Katrin overhearing.

"No, Erika, tell me now. Come on, we haven't got any time to lose!"

Another of her long pauses. Erika always has to think before she says anything, normally it's annoying but right now I was getting really impatient and was ready to shout at her.

"Evelyn." Erika took a step backwards. "Evelyn could be able to help-"

"For fuck's sake!" I shouted. "What the fuck has that bitch got to do with this? Isn't she locked up in fucking prison?" I think I'd prefer to get help from the cops than from that Stasi sow!

"Karo, it doesn't matter how you feel about Evelyn, I shouldn't have told you anyway. I'm going to the phone box now-"

"Oh no you don't!" I jumped off the bed and grabbed Erika by the elbow. "You've started so you'll finish. How is Evelyn involved?"

"She's gone undercover in the fascist scene. She's got her own support team, from her old Firm. They may be able to locate Martin, and if he's in danger-"

"You're saying the Stasi can help us? Didn't we deal with them last year? Tell me they're not still around!"

Erika stood there, saying nothing.

Great. Not only had Martin probably been kidnapped by the fucking fash, but the only people who could help us were the bloody Stasi, because the cops sure as hell weren't going to be any fucking use.

"So are you going to ask them for help?" I asked Erika.

"Martin was handling Evelyn." She shrugged. "Nobody else knows how to get hold of her."

"And Klaus? Nik? What about Laura, she's always on top of everything, doesn't she know?"

Another shrug.

"Can't find Rex!" Schimmel pushed past Erika, breathing heavily. "But I've sent everyone out to find him or anyone else from the Antifa core-group."

"I'll go and phone Neumann from K1," said Erika, ignoring Schimmel. "He may still have some contacts in the Firm. Don't worry, I won't bring him back here. I'll come back after and tell you how I got on."

"K1? The Firm? What's going on?" demanded Schimmel as Erika went down the hall.

"It's Evelyn. She's back. She may be able to help Martin," I told him.

Schimmel slowly shook his head and came to sit down on the bed with Katrin and me.

"So what are we going to do now?" he asked.

The three of us sat there in silence. Katrin hadn't said anything the whole time Erika was here, and when I looked at her now I could see she was staring into space, a hard, stony look on her face. I put my hand on her knee to reassure her.

"Don't worry. We'll work it out."

Except I didn't sound very convincing, not even to myself.

19:50
Karo

We waited by the telephone box on Forckenbeckplatz. It was dark already, and the occasional car threw its headlights at us, making the railings dial shadows across the park. I leaned against Schimmel, and shivered. I was glad I'd brought him along.

Schimmel was bricking it, but he'd been a total star. After a bit of a think he'd told us about the Stasi man who'd tried to recruit him, back when he'd first been released from the secure home.

"I followed him home once. I don't know why, maybe because it felt like turning the tables. Spying on the spies, you know?"

Schimmel told us all this and then went round to this bloke's house and demanded that he put the word out: we wanted to speak to Evelyn's support team.

"He denied he'd even been in the Stasi," Schimmel reported when he got back. "He pretended he didn't know what I was talking about, so I told him that lives were in danger, that it was about Evelyn Hagenow. He shut up when I mentioned Evelyn's name. He shut up and shut the door on me."

But Schimmel didn't go away. He stayed on the staircase outside the man's flat, hammering on the door. None of the neighbours complained, nobody came to see what the fuss was about. Eventually the man opened up again, he said: *2100 hours. Telephone box. Forckenbeckplatz. One person.* Then he'd banged the door shut again.

And that was it. Easy as that.

Except for Schimmel it hadn't been easy. For him it had meant facing up to the ghosts of his past.

But here he was, waiting in the cold with me. We didn't know what to expect, whether the phone would ring, or a car would arrive. Maybe someone in a leather jacket or a trenchcoat would come along and slip a note into our hands. Thinking about it now it's easy to make it sound like some stupid American spy movie, but I was well scared at the time.

I don't know how long we'd been stood there waiting, watching the cars go past, waiting, waiting. But at some point a Barka van pulled out of a side road and slowly climbed the hill towards us. Schimmel and I both held our silence as the van struggled up the cobbles.

"You were told to come alone." A Saxon voice from behind the steering wheel. "He stays. You get in."

I looked at Schimmel and shrugged. He looked like he was going to try to stop me.

"You're not going by yourself, Karo, who knows what these bastards will do to you!"

The driver revved the engine, and the Barka inched forward before stopping again.

"Your choice, young lady. It's you and your friends who wanted to speak to us, remember?"

I opened the side door and got into the back of the van, it was too dim to see anything, the windows covered by purple polyester curtains. Schimmel made to follow me in, but I held my hand out, stopping him and pulling the door shut on his taut face.

The small engine howled again, and the van drew away, turning right, juddering over the uneven road.

"Sit down." It was a different voice this time, Berlin accent, gravelly from cigarettes. A man was with me in the back of the van.

Enough light from the orange street lamps penetrated the thin curtains to let me see the bench down the side, and I sank onto it, facing the dark figure that was my companion for the ride. I had to grip the edge of the slatted seat to stop myself from sliding off as we went around each corner. Don't ask me how long the journey took—I don't know the answer. At least ten minutes. Maybe half an hour? We sat there in silence, the whining of the engine and the strobe of the passing street lamps the only way to mark time and distance.

There must have been some kind of signal, a knock I didn't hear, a sequence of corners, a change in the quality of the lights outside, who knows? But the shadow stood up, and efficiently pulled a cloth bag over my head. Before I could react the job was done. I clawed the bottom of the cloth, trying to pull it off my face.

"Leave it on." That voice again, calm. "If you take it off then that's the end of the meeting, we'll take you back and you'll never see us again."

A deep breath, trying not to gag on the mustiness of the bag.

The van stopped, and the door was opened. A hand gripped my elbow and I was roughly guided through the low doorway, down the step onto the ground. It was flat and even: concrete or tarmac. The hand on my elbow was removed, then it came back again, perhaps it was a different one.

Across a short stretch, ten paces, no more, then up some steps. Four, five? We were in a corridor, I could tell by the lights and the echoes of our footsteps. Not far before we rounded a corner, and I was pushed onto a chair. I was afraid I would fall, gasping by now, trying to keep a grip on myself. It wasn't easy, not easy at all.

The bag was pulled off my head, and I found myself in a room I'd been in before. Maybe not this exact one, but definitely one like it: a small room, lino, desk, a few chairs. You can find this room in any police station, or in the old days, any Stasi building.

Opposite me was an old man. Grey suit, grey hair combed over the top of his bald head, the smell of *Atoll* deodorant emanating from his armpits. I'd met him before too. Him or one of his many clones.

"Why are you here?" he asked. Pleasant enough, but with just the right dose of menace to make the situation clear to even the most stubborn punk. It probably took years of practice to get it just right.

"Cos I was dragged here!"

"Miss Rengold, I think we should start again, don't you? Why are you here?"

God, some things never change! What do we have to do to get rid of pricks like this? We already started a revolution and they're still here!

"I'm here because I need to get in touch with Evelyn Hagenow."

"Now that wasn't difficult, was it, Miss Rengold?" The prick smiled, wiping his hand over his head, making sure his comb-over was holding.

God, I wanted to punch him! Shout in his smug face, tell him his time was up, his time was over—the future belonged to us, not fucking Stalinists! A swallow, *keep calm Karo*, I told myself, *this is for Martin, and he's going to owe you for this. Big time.*

But Martin already owed me big time, I'd already saved his arse more than once! Another deep breath.

"You know my name already, so who are you?" I asked, civilly enough.

"Why do you wish to speak to comrade Hagenow?" the prick demanded, as if I hadn't spoken.

This was hard work. I didn't know what was worse, being kidnapped off the streets, or having to deal with Mr. Prick.

"Martin Grobe's gone missing. We think the fascists have got him. We know they were after him, and he left town to get away from them, but now he's gone missing and the place where he was staying has been trashed."

"Miss Rengold, or may I call you Karoline? Well, Karoline, I think you need to tell us how you know about comrade Hagenow, and exactly what it is you want of her."

"I was told about the operation, about Evelyn going undercover. They told me after Martin went missing."

"They? Please do try to be precise. Who are *they*?"

"His colleagues. At RS." I didn't want to tell the Prick anything, but if he could help Martin ....

"I see. Not too difficult is it now? And perhaps you can tell me why you wish to speak to comrade Hagenow?"

"We're hoping she can find Martin. If the fash have him then who knows what they'll do to him-"

"We? Who is this *we*? Who thinks comrade Hagenow might be able to help?"

"His colleagues. And friends."

The prick made a note, then nodded to himself.

"His colleagues. I see, how moving. We'll be in touch, Karoline."

This time I screamed when the bag went over my head, trying to lash out at whoever was behind me. A sharp jab to the kidneys and I went over, retching and moaning on the floor. I couldn't see it, but I definitely felt the prick's smile as I was bundled along the corridor, dragged down the steps, back to the van.

DAY 15
Monday
28th March 1994

Berlin: *Far-right groups have registered demonstrations in each of the Regional capitals for this evening. Counter-demonstrations have also been announced under the motto "We are the people!"*

02:17
Martin

What can I tell you?

I blacked out, I must have done. I remember being hit. The ears, they aimed for the ears: once, twice, once again. After that, nothing. It must have been a blackout. There's no other way of describing it. If I try to concentrate on that moment, remember when I was next conscious, the memories just skitter away, and all I can see are crowds of people. We're standing shoulder to shoulder in the streets, candles lighting hands and faces. Standing, waiting. The fear, *that* fear again. Men in green uniforms and white helmets running towards us, shields raised, truncheons raised, running, running, running towards us; running away from them. The silence, no noise. Was it because they hit me on the ears? Or did we not scream and shout in our terror? Being hit, back of the head, a truncheon, a fist. On the floor, boot to the stomach, dragged along the road, by the hair, screaming. Yes, there was noise, they were screaming at us, swearing at us, threatening us. Lifted, thrown onto a lorry, kicked again, move, move, move avoid the boots, avoid the fists, move back, further into the truck. Movement, truck rumbling, shouting get off, get down, get out. Down the steps, stumbling, falling onto the backs of others, Katrin, where's Katrin? Is she safe, is she in a hole like this? Down the steps, face the wall, legs spread, arms up, hands on head, shouting, shouting, fall over, boot to the back of the head, stand up, stand up, screaming, shouting can't stand must lie still can't move stop just stop please stop.

Please.

A fever? Concussion? My mind delivering false memories to cover the confusion, the blankness, the blackout? 1989. So long ago, so recent. Whatever you want to call it I saw a different future that day, in the cellar. We were there, with our candles, every night, we went out, we faced down the dogs and the pigs of the Party. They beat us and we didn't back down. But bit by bit the Party did: they crumbled. They were leaderless, they had no plan, no scientific socialism to guide them any more. Grasping at straws, they take their cues from the West. Propaganda flooding the country, *Deutschland einig Vaterland*, the promises, the Deutsche Mark: whatever you want to buy, you buy it with your Westmarks. Work: we'll have all the work we want—well paid, good clean jobs, short hours, long holidays. Join the West, West is best, *test the West*. Let them tell us what to do and they'll see us right. They promise the Earth. Currency union, the Westmark comes, destroying industry, jobs, communities in its wake. And soon after that, the coup de grace for our all our hopes: unification with West Germany.

Feverish hallucination? A dream?

Nightmare, more like. Another universe. One I wouldn't want to be in.

09:32

Karo

Katrin was still in my room. She'd been really quiet since yesterday, but I guess I hadn't said much either. There wasn't much to say. I didn't want to tell her about my trip to see the Stasi and what else was there to talk about?

We spent the night lying next to each other, just holding each other. Exactly like last Sunday. It was becoming a habit.

But now it was morning and I was in the kitchen, Schimmel was making a pot of coffee, and Antifa Bert and Antifa Rex were at the table.

"Look guys, it's really straightforward. The fash are organising demos all over the country. We've been mobilising for counter-demos, and after last Friday I reckon we can get enough people-"

Bert had been nodding to everything I'd said so far, but now he broke in. "Precisely. We need to outnumber them, make it clear to everyone that there's a vast majority of people who don't agree with the Nazis and who aren't going to let them spread their poison."

"No!" I banged my cup down on the table. "We need to take it to them. Mass demonstrations aren't going to do the job, we need lots of small groups. While they're busy marching down Frankfurter Allee and Unter den Linden or wherever, we need to be hitting all the different places they hang out—including Weitlingstrasse! When they come back they'll have been evicted. Game over. Martin is probably in one of those places—he's in danger!"

"And that's why we can't do that—it's too dodgy. They'll fight back, it'll get nasty. You're talking about putting normal people without any experience into a dangerous situation!"

09:33

Martin

They were holding me by the shoulders. I was sitting on the cement floor, a skinhead either side of me, and another one standing behind me, holding my head, making me look at a figure in the shadows. It was the size of a person, the approximate shape of a person. But it was lying on the floor in a way that looked like no human body. Arms and legs were bent in an attitude that no person could achieve. Not without broken bones.

"Don't worry, *Zecke*. He's probably dead already." The skinhead behind me had a slow, deliberate way of speaking. There was no sense of emotion in how he talked. "But we need you to give us a hand."

My head was released from the tight grip, and the skin holding my right shoulder let go, but grabbed my hand instead, holding it up. The speaker came into sight, dressed much the same as the others: stonewashed jeans, a t-shirt and denim jacket, shorn head. He was wiping something on his t-shirt, a gun. He held the barrel through the material and placed the grip in my hand. I tried to make a fist to stop him, but the skin holding my wrist squeezed a pressure point. My hand went limp and the pistol was placed inside it.

My index finger was forced into the trigger guard, my arm extended, gun pointing at the body, and with a sharp strike on my knuckle they made me squeeze the trigger.

09:40

Karo

"Karo's right." Rex poured another cup of coffee for himself. "It's time to take the fight to them. *This* feels like the right time. People will join in. People are pissed off, and they're scared. The attacks all over the place, the way the fash are mobilising for the referenda next week —people can't ignore them any more. And that's our chance."

"It's this afternoon we're talking about! We've left it too late." Bert wasn't about to give in.

"It's not. We can still do it." Schimmel spoke up for the first time. "This is what we've got phone trees for. We can reach nearly every Antifa group in the country in a matter of hours. And we'll get Martin's colleagues to start sending telexes to the Round Tables and Works Councils that are likely to be up for it—like the Berkmann Brigade at SKET. We've already started the mobilisation, the people are coming already—we just need to redirect them."

Bert shook his head. "It's not going to work."

17:02

Martin

The strip-light quivered into life.

I started to move my hand up to my eyes, shielding them from the glare. The dull ache in my chest changed to a sharp pain. Without instructions from my brain my movements were slowing down. A gasp, heard as from someone else's throat, a scrape as a door opened.

372

Instinct demanded that I turn my head, look towards the door, see who was coming into the room. Slowly I turned onto my side, ribs stabbing into my lungs, panting in pain. I lay there waiting until I could breathe again, waiting for the burning in my side to recede. More aches began to make themselves known. Left knee: throbbing. Right eye: swollen, restricting vision. Right ear: nagging pain, dampness.

Enough.

I moved my concentration away from my body, towards my situation. A cellar. In a Nazi house. Weitlingstrasse maybe. Perhaps they've moved me somewhere else. Perhaps I was no longer even in Berlin.

Another scraping noise: a boot against grit. I lifted my head, turning it slightly, ignoring new messages of pain coming from my neck. A pair of para-boots, soles worn on the inside edges. Toe caps scuffed, marked with dark stains. White laces, above them white socks. Then the turn ups of stone-washed jeans, cut tight. My eyes carried on up the body. Green bomber jacket hanging open over white Lonsdale t-shirt. Above all of that, the head. Hair shorn, a fringe around the neck and face. A face I recognised. Blue eyes, pointed chin. But I didn't recognise the hardness to the eyes, the determined set to the chin, making it appear more prominent. But it was still her: Evelyn.

I gasped her name as she advanced, she checked over her shoulder, nobody behind her, then hissed at me: "Shut it!"

She put her hand over my mouth, with the other she pushed my head back on to the floor. Thoughts whirred through my mind: *Why? What does she want? Revenge?*

I struggled, feeble, muscles aching. I could feel my energy slipping away. My lungs fought for breath. A fight I lost as I slipped back out of consciousness.

There were already loads of people at Lichtenberg station, and more kept arriving every time a U-Bahn train rolled in. The fash were starting their march a couple of stops away, down the road at Frankfurter Tor, and they must have wondered where our counter-demo was. Well, we were here, and we were going to take back their precious fucking Weitlingstrasse 122.

Schimmel was pushing his way through the crowds, ducking under banners, looking around, trying to find me.

"Hard to say how many," he panted, out of breath. "But there's definitely someone in the house—it's not empty. We need to be careful."

We'd wait a bit longer, see how many more people came. The more the better, because Bert was right—it could get dangerous.

17:09

Martin

A pulling on my wrists, constant, nagging. I still couldn't breathe, my throat scratching, making me want to cough, but coughing would hurt too much. My shoulders ached. I opened my eyes, Evelyn was above me, she was holding my arms, pulling me up, making me sit up.

"Where were you? Evelyn, where were you?"

Evelyn looked down, breathing heavily.

"Saxony. I got word and came back to get you, you fool. Now shut it." She looked up, talking to someone else. "Let's get him up the stairs before they find us."

Hands grasped my wrists, my ankles, my back was scraped against steps as I was carried up the stairs. My eyes closed, it was too much.

The bang of a door, shouting. I'm lowered onto the floor, none too gently. Forcing open my eyes: two skins, shouting, pushing Evelyn around, punching her in the belly. There was another man there, another skin, the one who'd had hold of my feet, he was trying to pull the others away from Evelyn. She was screaming at them, spittle flecking her lips, her eyes wide in fear and hate. I turned over, and got to my knees, crawling away, into the corner. The screaming had stopped, I could hear grunts and whimpering.

"That's enough! We don't want to kill them. Not yet." A strong Berlin accent, sounding disinterested.

I propped myself up against a wall. The two skins were standing over Evelyn, she was lying on the floor, not moving. The other guy, the one who had been helping her, was slumped against the wall. Close enough that I could see the blood flowing from his nose, his eyes tight shut. But he was breathing. One of the fascists aimed another kick at Evelyn. Right in the stomach. She whimpered again, but didn't move.

"Lock 'em in the storage room, the boss will know what to do with them when he gets back."

The other skin grunted, grabbing Evelyn under the arms and dragging her towards a doorway. He returned for Evelyn's friend. His colleague stood there, watching while the work was done. Finally, they came for me.

"Awake are you? Too soft on you, were we?" This time both skins took hold, pulling me up by the arms, then pushing me into the same room as Evelyn and the other guy.

I stumbled as they let go, nearly falling onto a pile of placards. Leaning against the wall, I watched as the door was slammed shut.

17:10
Karo

We were about forty or fifty people now, plus Rex and the Friedrichshain Antifa group. There was no way of knowing how many people had turned up at the other meeting places, but there were enough of us here to take over a nearly empty house. I was about to say that when Schimmel and this kid who should have been at school dashed up to me and Rex.

"It's all kicking off at Frankfurter Tor—a bunch of people turned up for the counter-demo, they didn't hear about the change of plan. They're getting their heads kicked in! We've got and help them out!"

A few people had heard what Schimmel had said and were already moving towards the U-Bahn entrance.

"Wait!" I yelled, but nobody took any notice. "Schimmel, get them to wait just two secs will you? Rex, do you reckon your lot can deal with what's happening at Frankfurter Tor?"

"Yeah, get everyone to stay here, we'll sort it." Rex was already on his way. "We'll be back in thirty."

"Wait here! Wait! Everything is under control!" I bawled.

The crowd was already breaking up.

17:11
Martin

I staggered over to Evelyn, then sank down next to her. I shook her arm, but there was no reaction. I put my fingers on her wrist, her pulse was slow, much too slow. Running my hands over her body, checking for blood, they came away dry. Didn't mean there wasn't any internal bleeding or broken bones though.

Turning to the man lying next to Evelyn I did the same thing. Similar results, except for his nose and the fact that his pulse was stronger. There was movement beneath his eyelids. I slapped his cheeks gently, he groaned, his eyes twitched.

Good, that counted as progress. They were both alive.

I sat between Evelyn and the stranger and looked around the room: the pile of placards that I'd nearly fallen onto, several boxes of leaflets, another box with what looked like black, white and red striped armbands. On the other side of the room was a neat stack of torches, the kind that the FDJ used to have for their torch-lit parades past the tribune on which the *Bonzen* stood smiling down at us.

Uncalled for, a child's song came into my head: *Am Kindertag, beim Fackelzug, da darf ich auch mitgehn*—'on Children's Day, on the torch-lit parade, I'll go with the others'.

Shaking my head, trying to clear it, I stood up again to look at the window. A normal window, but the kind that doesn't open. I was sure we were on the ground floor, but the frosted glass meant I couldn't tell how far the drop from the window sill to ground would be.

Turning my attention back to my fellow prisoners, I slapped each gently on the cheeks again, hoping for a reaction. The man stirred, groaned, his eyes trying to focus.

"Are you OK?" I asked him. The man just stared at me, his eyes unfocussed. "Listen, can you get up?"

Obediently, he stood up. He winced in pain, but he managed it.

Standing up, he didn't look in bad shape. He looked much fitter than I felt. That was good enough for me.

"Do you smoke? Have you got any matches?"

The man just stared at me, not understanding what I wanted. I patted down his pockets, finding a soft-pack of *Juwel* cigarettes. Tucked inside was a brass cigarette lighter. Perfect.

"Listen, get Evelyn on her feet, we need her awake," I told the man, speaking slowly, trying to get through to him.

I hobbled across to the boxes of leaflets and pulled out handfuls of the paper, scrunching them into a big pile on the floor. I tugged at the stack of torches, trying to drag them into the centre of the room. They toppled over with an echoing clatter. The man's scared eyes fixed on the door, listening for any sounds from the other side.

A pause, nothing happened, nobody came. I carried on dragging the torches over to the pile of leaflets, laying them around and over the paper, keeping a couple back.

Exhausted for the moment, I sagged down to the floor again, holding my side and trying to ignore the pain of breathing. The man was holding Evelyn up, he still didn't look particularly aware of his surroundings, but he was doing a good job. Evelyn's head was lolling, but her eyes were open. More progress.

Back onto my feet, trying not to breathe too deeply, I made my way around the pile of paper and torches on the floor. I picked up a couple of the placards and tore the hardboard messages off the poles, letting the black-red-gold propaganda fall onto the pile already spilling across the floor.

A moment to gather myself, then back to the man. I gave him one of the poles and looked him in the eye.

"We have two chances," I told him, still speaking slowly, checking to see whether he understood me. He nodded in a vague but committed way, the way a drunk would. "If we can't get out that way," I pointed at the window, "then we have to shout and make noise. When they come to see what's going on ..." I shook the pole I was holding in my right fist, and for good measure picked up a torch with my left hand.

He nodded. He didn't ask any questions, like how do we get Evelyn out of the window? Or how do we manage to get past whoever comes to find out what's going on.

It was a crap plan, but in his concussed state he didn't realise it.

Another pause for thought, the song still going around in my head. *Ich zünde mein Laternchen an, das leuchtet hell im Dunkeln dann. Am Kindertag, beim Fackelzug könnt ihr es alle sehn.* 'I light my little lantern, so it glows in the dark. On Children's Day, at the torchlit parade, you'll see it then.'

I used the brass lighter to light one of the torches, thrusting it into the pile of placards and leaflets. Another torch caught fire, and a few leaflets started curling brown at the edges before bursting into a blue and green flame. I watched for a few seconds. The fire was going well, dark smoke was gathering into a fine column, mushrooming out below the ceiling. Already the wooden poles of the placards were starting to catch fire here and there, adding to the smoke.

It was time. With one of the poles I smashed the window, quickly knocking the remaining shards of glass out of the frame.

"Get her through the window! Now! Come on!"

The man heaved Evelyn up onto his shoulder in a fireman's lift. He was strong, and that's what we needed.

The smoke was filling the room, flowing and ebbing. I was choking, each cough a stab in my side.

Evelyn was through the window, the man had lifted her onto the sill and she managed to get through by herself. He was climbing after her. I was right behind him, He reached back through the window, holding his hands out to me, waiting to help me through.

"Fuck's sake!" Swearing, coming from behind me.

I looked over my shoulder, the door was open, and in the cross draught the fire climbed higher, the leaflets and placards flaming upwards.

"Get the sand buckets!" Behind the flames and smoke a figure impotently waved at the heat. Other skins came, forearms over faces, trying to push through the blaze. "They're fucking escaping!"

We'd just managed to get everyone to calm down, but some tosser was arguing with me, the kind that talks shit and never actually does anything.

"Look, it's under control—we've got our own mission here!" I told him. "And if you don't like it then why don't you go to Frankfurter Tor and help out there?"

Schimmel was doing a better job, he and a few other people from the squat were going around, telling people what was happening, why we were delaying the march down Weitlingstrasse.

Ignoring the argumentative tosser I looked around, it was going to be OK, people had calmed down, and somebody had brought a guitar out and a group was sitting in the middle of the road, singing *Give Peace A Chance.*

Bloody hippies, can't take them anywhere.

I was keeping an eye on the station, waiting for Bert and Rex and the others to come back, and that's why I was first to notice the skins come up the steps from the U-Bahn. There were about ten of them, and they looked like they fancied their chances against forty assorted hippies, grandmas and punks.

Using a placard I shovelled against the heat, pushing the burning torches and leaflets towards the door, towards the skins.

"Martin! Come on!" Evelyn was shouting from the window. The smell of scorching hair, the hot tingling of eyebrows sizzling, pushing a bit further, pushing the fascists back out of the room. The placard ignited, flames running up the pole towards my hands.

Chucking the burning pole towards the doorway I twisted round and stepped over to the window. Evelyn's colleague was reaching in, he grabbed my forearms, dragged me over the sill. The window frame pressed into my ribs but I didn't feel the pain. I was panicking, trying to get out. I fell down the outside wall of the building, but strong hands held me up. With an arm around my shoulder I was half pushed, half carried down the road. I didn't look round, but behind us I could hear the drumming of boots on the pavement, almost feel the ground shivering beneath my legs.

"Get the fuckers!"

They sounded close, too close.

I was only holding the others back. I willed power into my legs and tried to shrug Evelyn and her colleague off, but they held fast, dragging me on.

17:21

Karo

Everyone had seen the skins by now, but they were just standing around like a load of muppets. If I didn't act soon then we'd lose this battle before we even started it. I had to buy time for the Antifa to get back here.

But how?

"Right everyone, just like the plan." Schimmel was by my side again—he'd climbed up on a railing so that everyone could see him. "Move down Weitlingstrasse, nice and slow. Don't worry about the skins, we're gonna deal with them."

Like how the fuck are we gonna deal with them? The fash were standing just outside the station entrance, taking their time, enjoying the smell of fear.

"OK, you get the people away," he said to me. "I'll stay here and ..." But Schimmel didn't finish his sentence. The fash were watching him, he was marked.

"Like fuck you will! Anyway I'm staying," I told him.

We shared a scared grin as the people around us melted away, moving down Weitlingstrasse in one big block.

"C'mon Bert, c'mon Rex—we need you!"

17:22

Martin

"Shit! It's like 1989 again! Martin, we're going to need your help." Evelyn's voice was calm, almost slow. But it carried a brittleness that made me try to look over my shoulder, catch sight of our pursuers.

"No, the other way." Evelyn turned my head with her free hand, lifting my chin so I could see the mob blocking the road ahead.

I sank down to the pavement. I'd failed. We were sandwiched between two gangs of skins.

"Martin!" Evelyn's voice was more urgent now, "Martin, come on, help us out. Just one last time." Evelyn was crouched down next to me, why wasn't she running? She could make it without me, she'd get through somehow. I turned my head, looking back down the road, wondering how long we had, how many seconds before boots and fists smashed into us.

17:22

Karo

It wasn't Bert, or Rex, or any of the Antifa crowd that came—it was Erika.

She appeared behind the fascists, and she'd brought a whole bunch of very angry looking refugees with her. They just surrounded the skins, disarmed them, just like that. Erika had gone to the refugee hostel near the station, told them what was happening, and brought them all here: Russian Jews, Roma, Sinti, Croatians, Serbians, Montenegrins. They'd all been on the receiving end of fascist violence. For them it was payback time.

Behind us the original crowd were still marching down the street. There were more of them now, local residents had come out and were marching too. I wanted to go and join them. But first I gave Erika a hug.

"You rock!"

Erika blushed and looked away, but before she could say anything Rex ran out of the station.

"Karo! Message from your neighbour, Frau Kembowski! I saw her

381

go into the U-Bahn, she says she's going on the march over in Berlin-Biesdorf!"

Frau Kembowski? Going up against the Nazis in Biesdorf? "Is anyone with her? She's not going by herself?"

He nodded, and I knew what I had to do, I had to go and be with Frau Kembowski. But I wanted to take the Weitlingstrasse house. I was standing there dithering, not knowing which way to go.

"You go to your neighbour. I'll help out here." Erika gently pushed me towards the station.

17:23

Martin

Four skins, ten, twenty yards away. Behind them, smoke was billowing out of the house on the corner, flames licked the window frames, glass littered the pavement. But the skins stood there, not making a move. They weren't staring at us, but past us, towards the big group on our other side. I looked the other way, focussing for the first time on the larger group.

They were people.

Ordinary people.

And they looked very pissed off.

They were nearly upon us, most were concentrating on the skins, but a few were glaring at Evelyn and her friend.

"Martin, tell them!" Evelyn was no longer calm, she was frightened. She shook my shoulder as about twenty people surrounded us. They were young, old, men, women, punks and workers—there was no common feature, other than determination.

"Call an ambulance." Evelyn had stood up again, she spoke with authority. "This man needs an ambulance. We rescued him."

A figure from the back of the group split off and ran across the road to a shop, I could see him through the window, talking to the shopkeeper. The rest of them stood around, staring at us. They didn't do anything, just held us with their eyes.

"Martin, if you don't say something soon then it's going to get nasty," Evelyn hissed into my ear. "They think we're skins."

"These people." My voice croaked, I struggled up, and Evelyn held my arm, supporting me as I stood there. My throat was raw and what sounds came were rasping out of my mouth. "These two rescued me. They're not skins. They're in disguise ...." I looked to see what was happening behind us. About twenty people were surrounding the skins, a further group was standing at the end of the street, waiting for anyone fleeing the burning house. Evelyn's words from a minute ago penetrated the smoke that still fogged my mind: *It's like 1989 again.*

My head dropped until my chin was on my chest, I was exhausted, I had no more to give.

17:39
Karo

We got off the U-Bahn and ran down the road, Rex seemed to know where he was going. Turning off into an alley, it was obvious that we'd arrived. A crowd of people swelled out of a gap between some garages. We pushed our way through until we were standing in the forgotten garden of a ramshackle old villa. There must have been about a hundred people, and they'd made space for about half a dozen skins whose eyes darted around, trying to find a way through the mob.

"What's happening?" Rex asked.

"We cornered them, in their nest, and now they're trying to fly!" A middle aged woman in a pinny laughed. "Fly, little birds, run little rabbits!"

I was trying to spot Frau Kembowski—what was she thinking of, coming here, she'd be crushed by the crowd! Standing on tiptoes, craning my neck, scanning the crowds, but no sign of her, she was too little, she'd be hidden by all the people around her.

There was a sudden hush, and my eyes switched to the front. One of the skins had a knife, he was holding it out, threatening the people closest to him. The blade was already red, he'd already slashed someone. *Shit,* what to do? This was going to turn nasty. I grabbed Rex by the arm and pushed my way through the crowd.

There she was! Frau Kembowski was standing in front of the Nazi with the knife.

383

"I'm Frau Kembowski," she said. "I lived here in Biesdorf for sixty years. I know you, and you know me." She stared at the skinhead until his arm dropped.

I pushed through and stood by Frau Kembowski's side. Her hand clasped mine, it was shaking, but she stood there, as tall as she could.

"I know you, and I knew your father and your mother. Ashamed they'd be, ashamed of you. And so are we. We've all had enough." Frau Kembowski was pointing at each of the skins in turn, using her stick. "Young men, listen to me: you've got a choice, either you bugger off and leave Biesdorf—no, make that: you leave Berlin. Or you stay, you make amends. Your choice. You want to stay, you come to the Round Table. Tonight at eight."

Frau Kembowski shook her head in disgust, then reached forward and took the knife off the skin.

"Come on, young Karo," she whispered to me. "Time for us to go."

I tried to fix the skins with a stare, but they were all looking at their feet, and Frau Kembowski was pulling me back into the crowd.

"Run hares, run like rabbits! We'll catch you!" The crowd was chanting, but they made way for the skins who legged it, shitting themselves all the way.

17:42

Martin

"Goodbye, dear Martin, I doubt we'll meet again."

I opened my eyes. A blue light lunged at me, swept on, came back

"It's a shame, really. We never did get together, did we?" Evelyn whispered. She was holding my hand, her face was close to mine. I felt something soft touch my lips, pressing on them, the smell of *Florena* hand cream. It wasn't unpleasant, but it didn't feel right either.

A kiss.

"Come on, get him to hospital—we haven't got all night!"

The last thing I saw before my stretcher was loaded into the ambulance was Evelyn's silent friend.

"*Dmitriy Alexandrovich peredayet privet,*" he said as he lifted his hand in a clenched fist salute: greetings from Dmitri Alexandrovich.

384

DAYS 16–20
Tuesday 29th March
to Saturday 2nd April 1994

Berlin: Across the Republic celebrations are being held after yesterday's extraordinary events. Last night, in spontaneous demonstrations across the Republic, communities took over buildings used by right-wing groups and parties. The events have been compared to the Monday demonstrations of 1989.

Martin

For the first day in hospital I had refused all visits, knowing that K1 would be the first in the queue. I wanted to wait until I had a clear head before they tackled me.

"Could you describe the one they called the boss?"

"Comrade Captain Neumann, I've told you twice already. I know how this works, but I've given you descriptions, and now I'm feeling tired. It's time you went." I reached for the button that would summon the nurse.

It was true, I was tired, but Neumann was also taking an unhealthy interest in getting an exact timeline of my imprisonment.

I'd decided not to tell him about the gun. The whole thing had been a set up—they'd been trying to frame me for murder, or maybe they had intended to blackmail me at some point in the future. I knew how to deal with such Stasi tricks: just tell everyone. And I would, but I'd start with my colleagues, and not with K1.

And with any luck it might not come to that. The gun was probably still in the building when it went up in flames, burning off my prints. The powder residue on my hands had long since been removed by careful nurses treating my burns. My burnt and sooty clothes had already been disposed of.

"Just one more thing, then I'll go. A body was found on the premises. It was another of our IKMs," Neumann continued. At this stage I wasn't particularly surprised that he'd had another informant in there, but I wasn't particularly interested any more either. "He died before the fire, shot several times. Can you tell me anything about that? Did you hear any shots?"

I was saved from answering by an efficient nurse who ushered the policeman out.

Karo

I went to see Martin again today. They wouldn't let me in yesterday, even when I told them we were best mates. I guess he must have been in a serious state.

"Yay—my favourite old fart! Look, I've brought you some oranges."

"Yay—my favourite punk." Martin was trying to be witty but he didn't have the energy.

He looked pretty done in. Eyebrows burnt off, hair singed, burns on his hands and arms, bandages around his chest and a nasty cough.

"You look like shit," I told him.

"So what have you been up to?"

"What? You don't know? I saved your ass, man!" I said in a cowboy drawl. "While you were lounging around in your luxury cellar we were kicking off—big-style."

Martin propped himself up on a million pillows while I told him what we'd been doing, hassling the Stasi, the demos, getting people sorted, kicking the fash out. He looked impressed.

"So now Antifa groups are working with Neighbourhood and District Round Tables." I took one of Martin's oranges and started peeling it. Little green things they were, Cuban. "They're doing the debriefing—loads of the skins are talking, saying they didn't actually want to be Nazis, they just got dragged into it. I don't believe the fuckers for a minute, but Rex said that they're getting loads of info, they're tracking down the people who were pulling all the strings—

the suits. Fuckers."

I started on another orange, offering one to Martin, but he shook his head.

"And you know that house you set fire to? Totally burnt down. The fire brigade turned up, but they just stood there and watched it burn." I grinned.

I could see Martin was getting tired so I told him I'd see him the next day.

Outside in the corridor I bumped into Erika.

"Erika!" I gave her a hug and she gave me a squeeze back. That was nice, it felt like we were a team now.

"Karo, I'm glad I bumped into you. I wanted to ask you about giving us a hand with investigating the Nazi structures."

"You'd be better off talking to the Antifa—that's Rex's department."

"Yeah, I know, but I thought it would be good to work with you. You'd be our link to the Antifa and the other grassroots groups around the country—we need some help with keeping in touch with them all."

I thought about it. It sounded a bit boring, but kind of cool as well. "Martin's good at that kind of thing—why can't he do it?"

Erika looked down the corridor, towards the ward where Martin was. "I think he needs a break, don't you?"

"He needs more than a break—you should have seen him at the *Datsche*!"

Erika nodded. She knew what I meant.

"Laura's sorted it out with the Ministry. He's going to get paid leave."

"Laura? Would I have to work with her? And that Nik too?"

"Give them a chance. We've all been a bit stressed lately."

"OK, I'll think about it. But on one condition." There was a promise I'd made to myself, and working with RS could help me with that. "There's one particular Nazi I need to track down—it's a personal score I need to settle."

"OK, but nothing illegal."

I just laughed.

The next time I went to see Martin I bumped into Rico, the cute Border Guard. We had a quick chat near the entrance. He was dead embarrassed, blushing and stammering, poor sap.

"Martin says you're going to tidy up the East Side."

It's not the way I'd have put it myself, but yep, I'd had a chat with some of the *Wagenburgs* in Berlin and they were going to go and sort out the East Side—both the site and the people. All part of the new job at RS I told him, breathing on my nails and polishing them on my chest.

"I know that Customs *Obersekretär* Reinhardt wants to investigate the smuggling that's been going on there"

I was confused for a moment, and then I worked out who he was talking about. "Kalle? Yeah, all sorted. I'm seeing him about it this afternoon, we're going to go and have a look."

Rico blushed again.

REFERENDUM DAY
Sunday
3rd April 1994

Berlin: *Polling stations have been busy throughout the Republic as citizens and residents vote in the triple referendum. Voting closes at 10 o'clock this evening.*

Dresden: *The State Prosecutor for Saxony, Dr. Harry Kern, will announce immunity from prosecution for those involved in the events of last Monday. Criminal proceedings will only be opened at the specific request of a Neighbourhood or District Round Table, he said. The Central Round Table in Berlin has welcomed the statement, commenting that it will give communities the room to implement local accountability processes against offenders. Similar statements are expected to be made by State Prosecution Offices in the other Regions.*

13:29

Martin

I didn't have far to go—the local polling station was just next door in the *Kulturbund* rooms. But in my mind I had a much longer journey to make. I hobbled down the stairs, putting my bad leg down first, then gingerly hopping after it. My stick tapped each time I winced down another step.

It was my first full day at home. I'd insisted on leaving the hospital, I couldn't stand lying around on the overheated ward. I wanted to be at home, responsible for looking after myself, not having my food wheeled in and a nurse tutting at me whenever I asked to be let out. They'd been worried about my burns and my head, wanted to keep me in longer.

Bottom step, pause, breathe deeply to settle the pain, then down the hall, past the letter boxes.

I turned sideways to haul open the heavy front door, standing on my good leg and using the stick for balance. Then a few steps down the street, into the next building.

I stood in the entrance of the *Kulturbund* centre. To my right was the polling station, and on the other side was the hall where we held our communal Sunday lunch. I could hear voices, laughter coming from the hall, human warmth emanating through the half-open door. I decided I could use some of that warmth. I would eat before I voted.

I went over to the food table, looking at the dishes that my neighbours had brought. Picking up a plate I hesitated for a moment, unsure where to put my stick while I served myself.

"Here, you can give me that." It was Margrit, smiling at me, laughing at my clumsiness.

But before I could give her my stick she'd stepped forward and enveloped me in a hug. I gasped and Margrit stepped back sharply.

"Sorry! Oh, Martin, you look terrible—are you in a lot of pain?" She stroked a burnt eyebrow with her forefinger.

I shook my head and eased myself out of her clasp.

"If I go and sit down would you bring me a plate of food?"

I tapped over to the nearest table, and lowered myself into a seat, stretching out my dodgy leg, trying not to look too much like the invalid I obviously was. As soon as I'd got myself settled more neighbours came over, clapping me on the shoulder, shaking my hand. It was kindly meant, and in a way I appreciated it, but I was embarrassed all the same.

Margrit came over with my plate.

"What a week! I'm so proud of all of us." She gave me a serious look, "I'm so proud of you."

I muttered something and started eating my food.

"I was at EKL, sitting at my workbench, minding my own business. And then the word went around—we're dealing with the fascists. The whole factory marched out, and I had the same feeling as I did that night, in Leipzig. Back then we were worried about the Chinese Solution. Remember, they brought in the army, we thought they were going to shoot us." Margrit's eyes were seeing the past, she was part of her story. "But still we marched."

Her eyes sought out mine, needing to share the fear and the strength and the determination of that time. "And last Monday was just like that."

She paused, putting her hand on my sleeve. I wasn't eating now, just listening to her. I'd heard the story already. Everyone who'd come to visit me at hospital, colleagues and friends alike, they'd all told me. Karo had come every day, and she'd told me every day. It was the same story, everyone had the same story, but different. Different for each person, each *Kiez*, each neighbourhood, each town and each village.

She shook her head again, astounded at how easy it had been. When the word went out about the demonstrations, when the Weitlingstrasse squat went up in flames something snapped. People said *enough*. They went out there and raided the places the fascists meet: the flats and factories, meeting places, everywhere. There were a few injuries, rumour of a death down in Saxony. But people gave the fascists a choice: go, or stay and make amends to the community.

Margrit was jubilant, still on a high after experiencing once again the power of the people, the ability to make change happen. But her face grew suddenly serious. "But that was the easy part. Now the hard work begins." She looked towards the window, at the town outside. "There's a lot of tidying up to do, isn't there?"

Standing in the booth I studied the slip of paper on the table.

"1. Should the existing installations along the State Border with the Federal Republic of Germany and between West Berlin and Berlin, Capital of the GDR, as well as between West Berlin and the Region Brandenburg be retained, including the maintenance of forward barrier-elements, metal lattice-fencing, observation and command-towers?"

I picked up the pencil and put my cross in the *yes* box.

"2. Should the *Volkskammer* be mandated to approve the Round Table (Constitutional Amendment) 1994 Bill?"

Another vote for *yes*, anchoring the role of the Round Tables and the Works Councils into our democratic institutions, with a clear timetable for further devolution of power away from the *Volkskammer* and the six regional parliaments, giving more say to Round Tables at every level.

So far, so good. Next came the question on the Police (Constitutional Amendment) 1994 Bill. We were asked whether we thought Paragraph 96, article 15 of our constitution should be changed to explicitly forbid the establishment of counter-espionage bodies. If I put my cross in the *yes* box I would be voting myself out of a job.

I thought of all the arguments I'd heard. I remembered all the pain caused by secret police and intelligence agencies in the past, the anti-democratic nature of their work. I thought of all the good we'd done at the *Republikschutz*. Was it possible to have an agency that defended its people from outside threats without itself becoming a threat to the people's power? If that were possible, if there were any example of how to do it differently then my colleagues and I were that example. But we'd had little power, even fewer resources. What we'd achieved had been more through luck than intelligence.

I wielded the pencil, the tip almost grazing the paper as it wandered between the three boxes: *Yes. No. Re-open Discussion.*

In order to be democratic the organs of a state need to be accountable. But by the very nature of the work it was practically impossible to make counter-espionage agencies open and accountable, at least not in real time. I'd been thinking for weeks about this problem, about accountability. The secrecy surrounding the work. The complicated and political nature of it all. The real risks and danger involved. All these factors militated against accountability to anything but a closed committee with long-term membership. But by its nature such a committee would become corrupted, seduced by the cloak and dagger games of the spies.

There were no answers. We could only experiment, that was what the GDR was all about: experimentation.

I pressed the pencil to the paper, and with a hard, quick movement I voted myself out of a job.

Spectre At The Feast

Book 3 of the East Berlin Series

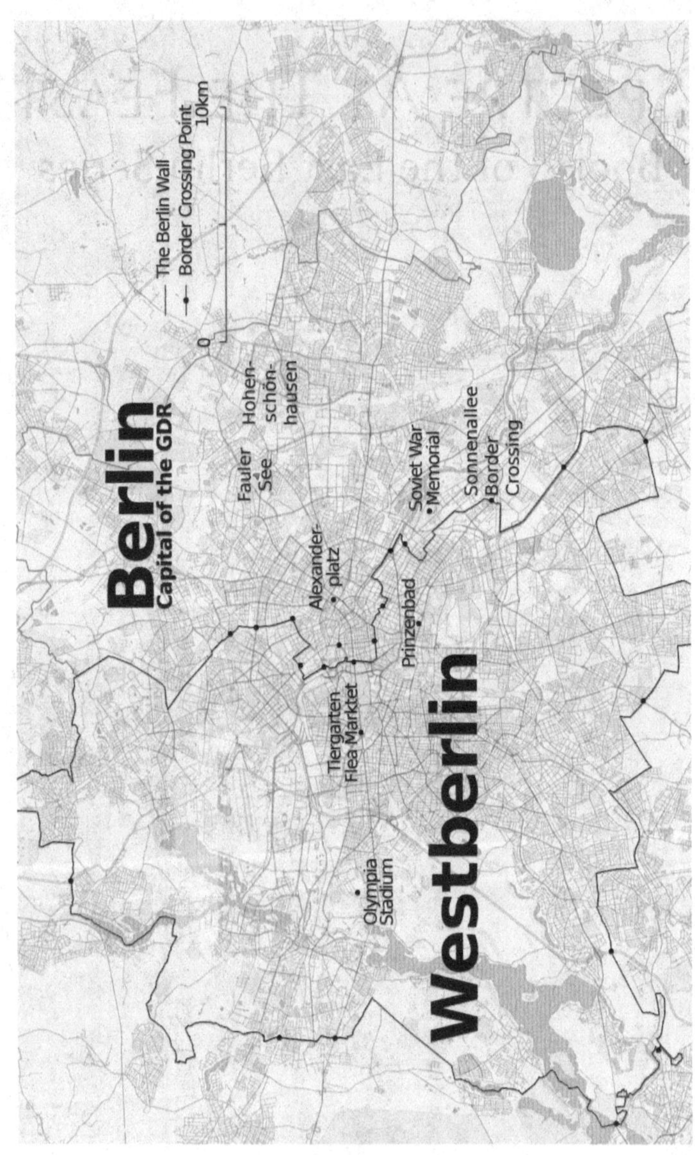

Berlin showing West Berlin and
Berlin, Capital of the GDR

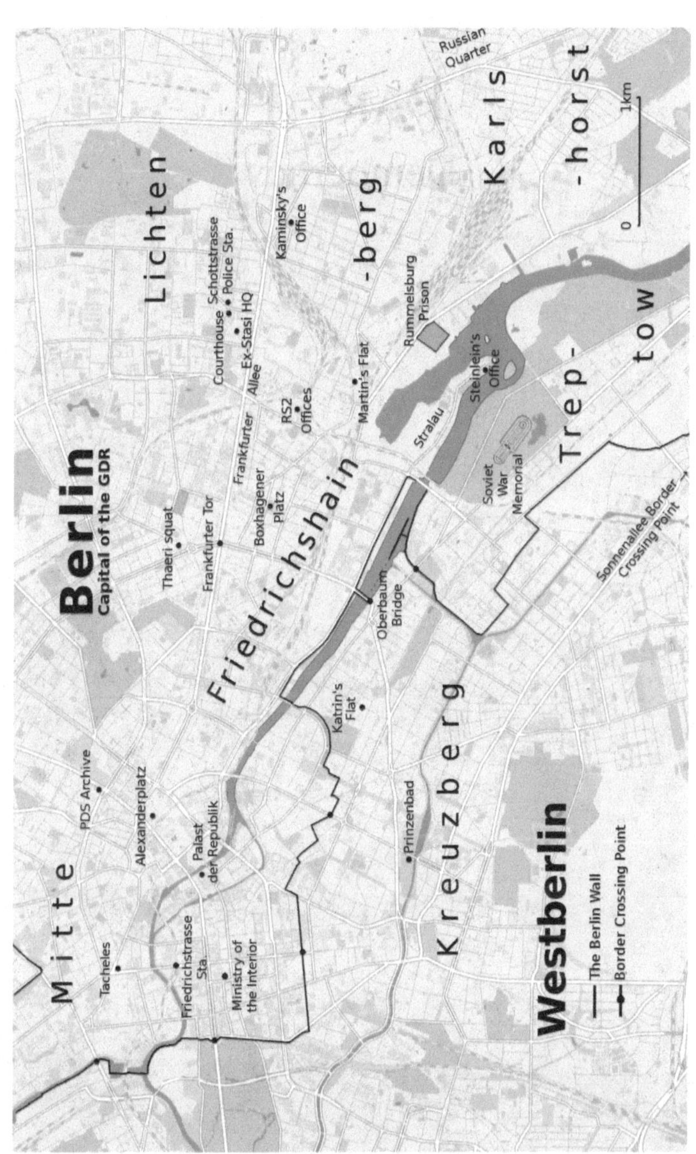

Central Berlin

PART 1
Democracy

DAY 1
Sunday
12th June 1994

Kaminsky stood on scaffolding at the end of Alexanderplatz, one arm raised, fist clenched, saluting the crowds below. He stared out at thousands of faces, at hundreds of placards and banners, flags and flaming torches.

The crowd chanted. *Kaminsky Kaminsky Kaminsky.*

But Kaminsky stood above them all, stock still, fist raised, saying not a word.

The crowd hushed itself, the shouts and chants dying back, murmuring to a standstill.

Only when he had absolute silence did Kaminsky lower his arm and step up to the microphones and cameras.

The government is weak.

The government has lost its way.

They even held a referendum to ask us what to do, but they're still unsure: parliament and Round Tables are bickering.

Our government is paralysed.

But we, the people, we are making history. Right now, all of us here are making history.

And more than ever, in this historical time we need a capable leader. A leader to steer a steady course for our Republic. We need a leader with strength, a leader of ability and moral fibre.

It is time to end the political corruption—but the establishment doesn't recognise this.

It is time to renew our democratic system—but the establishment won't do this.

It is time for real leadership—but the establishment can't provide this!

Again the chant *Kaminsky Kaminsky Kaminsky* swept through the crowd. Kaminsky himself stood back, let the wave of words break on the stage and surge around.

Look at the Resurgence: just a few weeks ago the government of this country was unable to deal with violence and criminality from skinheads and far-right extremists. The establishment showed itself unable to act.

We, the people, took matters into our own hands.

We, the people, cleared up the mess they couldn't handle.

We, the people, exposed the weakness of the elite!

It is time for us, the people, to take back control.

It is time for us, the people, to take back power.

Because we are the people!

Kaminsky stood back, his fist raised again, smiling and acknowledging the chants of the crowd.

We are the people! We are the people! We are the people!

20:13

Karo

I don't think anyone saw us.

My mate Schimmel was on the street corner, keeping a lookout while I decorated the window with red paint. I'd only got as far as RACIST SCUM before I was overcome by the sour taste of anger that rippled up my throat. *Fuck it.* With the heel of my boot I kicked a cobble loose and levered it out.

I took a few steps back, turned, and lobbed the stone.

The window of Kaminsky's office cracked, the glass hanging for a moment before sliding down, shattering as it went. Schimmel twisted around, shock splashed over his face. I grabbed his hand as I legged past him.

At the U-Bahn station we jumped down the steps as a train pulled in and I sat down, laughing at the dismay on my friend's coupon.

"That wasn't the deal!" he said.

"You feeling sorry for Kaminsky?"

Schimmel didn't answer, and I stopped grinning. It was no fun any more, not with my friend looking so pissed off all the time.

"Oh, come on." I tried again. "He deserves more than a smashed window!"

"He does. But what about sticking to agreements?"

"Fuck off!"

The train was pulling into the next station. As I stepped onto the platform my anger and frustration felt like a kick in the back.

20:46

Martin

The police lieutenant limped into my flat on a Sunday evening. He wasn't in uniform and I was just about naïve enough to assume this might be a social visit: *just passing, thought I'd pop in.*

"They let you out?" I asked as I held the door open.

"Had to argue with the surgeon." Steinlein's stick tapped over my painted floorboards.

I offered my visitor the comfy seat, but he preferred the hard kitchen chair at the table. I was about to offer him coffee too, but he lit a cigarette and started to speak.

"I know you're still on leave but I was hoping you could help me with a case. It's sensitive."

The shift in his voice warned me even before his words reached me. This was work. This was police work. I got up, carefully pushed my chair back under the table and stood by the door, pointing out into the hallway.

"You want a cup of coffee, you're welcome. But if you want to get me involved in something ... You know why I'm still on leave? It's not because of this," I touched my bruised panda eyes, the eyebrows that were still growing back, "nor because of this," I pointed at my left knee. "They say it's because I need a rest." I tapped the side of my head. "I think I've had enough of *sensitive,* don't you, comrade Lieutenant?"

"When the fascists attacked me, when I was in hospital, you were the only one to come to visit." Steinlein was still sitting there, hands clasped over the top of his walking stick.

"Doesn't make me responsible for you."

399

"Think about it. Call me when you're ready to talk." Steinlein got to his feet, holding on to the table for support, then tapped his way back into the hall, as slowly as he'd come in. By the time he was at the door, curiosity had got the better of me.

A curiosity I thought long gone. A curiosity I should have known better than to allow myself.

"What is it? What's so bloody *sensitive*?"

With one hand on the latch Steinlein half turned to meet my gaze. "They want to kill Kaminsky."

DAY 2
Monday
13th June 1994

First of all, let me thank you for inviting me onto the programme this morning. I like the radio, yes, it's true, I also like speaking on the radio —I think it's a democratic medium. Everyone has a radio, it's a good way to get the people's message out.

This morning I want to talk about the Round Tables. As you know, I'm an elected member of the Volkskammer, so I get around the ministries a lot. I see a lot of messengers from the Round Tables. We're not talking about one or two, but scores of them. These Round Table lackeys make vexatious queries, and they expect our government ministers to take time to deal with them.

They behave as though they were part of our democratically elected government.

But the Round Tables aren't elected. They're not even mentioned in the constitution. They are lobbies. Lobbies for unelected and unelectable busybodies.

These Round Tables, these lobbies, they're interfering in the serious business of running the country.

And what about Hanna Krause, the chair of the Central Round Table? She claims she can solve the problems of our country. But how can she solve any problems if she spends all her time sitting in meetings?

Let's be clear: Hanna Krause and her absurd knitting circles can't even solve their own problems, never mind the country's.

Karo

First thing this morning I knocked on Schimmel's door. I needed to talk about last night, but I also I wanted to talk to someone about Kaminsky. Schimmel's cool, we've known each other for years, from way back before the revolution started in 1989. We've had loads of fun together, the pair of us opened up the *Thaeri*, our squat near Frankfurter Tor, and we've been living there ever since.

Schimmel was still in bed, I crouched down on the floor in front of him and tried out a smile.

"You were right, I should have kept to our plan."

Schimmel didn't respond, his face stayed blank.

"But you gotta admit, it was the right thing to do?"

Again no reaction from my friend. I swivelled around on my heels, and sat down on the floor, back resting against the side of the bed.

"Can I have the old Schimmel back?" I asked his room.

I looked over my shoulder, Schimmel still hadn't reacted.

"Sorry," I said, feeling useless. I'd been trying to make a joke, but … ach, what was with all the thinking? I'm no good at that. I turned around again, kneeling on the floor, my elbows on the bed, my face close to Schimmel's. "Look, Schimmel, what can I do? You can't let this Becker take over your life, you've got to deal with it. Come on, talk to me!"

In one quick movement Schimmel sat up, leaning against the wall, but still avoiding my eye. We both stayed like that for what seemed like ages, then in another quick movement he got up, pulling on jeans and a t-shirt.

"What can I do?" I asked him again.

Schimmel was buckling his belt, but he stopped, just long enough to shrug.

I felt like screaming at him, but instead I stood up, calmly as I could, and stood in front of him.

"Schimmel, I wasn't joking: I want my friend back. I want the Schimmel I used to have. To get pissed with you, to dance to loud music with you. I want you to tell me boring shit about computers and to teach me how to pick locks and and and … Whatever Becker did to you, we need to deal with it. I'm here, I want to help."

I got a nod for my efforts, but I wasn't complaining—right now that counted as progress.

"Can we talk about it?" I dunno, maybe I was pressing too hard, but it felt like I had to get Schimmel to talk. "How about tonight? We'll take some beers to the graveyard on Boxhagener Strasse. It's quiet there, nobody will bother us. We can have a chat."

Schimmel moved around me, heading towards the hall, but he stopped at the door. "Thanks, Karo," he said.

That was it. I didn't get a yes or a no. What was *Thanks* meant to mean?

After my pathetic attempts at getting through to Schimmel this morning I went to work. Sitting in the office and hassling people is nowhere near top of my list of things I like to do, in fact, it's not on the list at all. But that was my job today, and going by the reactions I was getting I reckon the people I was phoning didn't have me on their lists of good things either.

"It's Karo from RS2 in Berlin, I'm trying to get hold of someone from Antifa Weimar ... No I've been trying to get hold of someone, anyone, for the last week, is there no-one around? OK, yeah, please. No, no, don't phone me back! I'll wait. Just go and get her."

I doodled on the desk blotter as the person in Weimar went to see if they could find someone from the local Antifa group. Down the line I could hear loads of banging doors and heavy steps. Eventually the phone was picked up at the other end.

"Yeah?" said a voice.

"Who am I talking to?"

"Who's asking?" The voice didn't sound particularly suspicious, it was just routine.

"This is Karo from RS2 in Berlin-"

"Yeah, Bert told me about you. What do you want?" A bit warmer now, but still not like she was pleased to speak to me or anything.

For what felt like the millionth time today, I explained what I was trying to find out: whether local Antifa groups were working with the Round Tables on the accountability processes for the skinheads, how that was going etc etc et cete*fucking*ra.

"We haven't had much time for that kind of thing," the voice from Weimar said. "All the Thuringian fash and hools are working with Kaminsky's lot now. There's been loads of pro-Kaminsky demos and stuff like that, but whenever anyone objects the hools kick off, scaring off anyone who might say anything against Kaminsky. *Defending democracy* they're calling it. Basically we're just trying to protect counter-demos from Kaminsky's thugs. We're back to where we were before we all got together to kick the skinheads out. It's pretty scary; we could really do with a hand down here."

"It's happening everywhere and we've got to do something about it!"

They were so lame, I could predict exactly how they would react. Klaus, smoking his foul cigar and chewing on his sad moustache; Erika, keeping shtumm while she thought things through; and Laura —don't get me started on Laura, tutting and giving me her disapproving looks. Grit was there too, but she never says anything, she's *just* the secretary. What a group, what a hierarchy!

"Karo, you know how things stand," Laura began the inevitable lecture. "The *Republikschutz* is being wound up. We have one final job, and that is our only concern right now."

Blah blah blah, I thought viciously, trying not to say anything out loud. She was right, she was always right, but it was just the way she said things: she ate five lemons every morning for breakfast, I was dead sure of it.

Our only concern (according to Laura) was to co-ordinate the debriefing of skinheads and fascists. A lot of them were wanting to turn over a new leaf right now, all dead keen to prove how socially acceptable they were after they got their collective arse kicked during the Resurgence last March. That was absolutely ace, the way people just walked out of work and ganged up on the skins. But now we were dealing with the bureaucratic aftermath. Basically, for us, said Laura, that meant lots of phone calls and boring meetings with committees like the Commission for Truth and Reconciliation.

Except that's not what it was like any more. It had all changed sometime last week, maybe even the week before. All of a sudden the skins weren't that keen to be accepted back into society, they were more interested in playing bovva boys for Kaminsky and his mates.

The room had gone quiet and I realised that Laura had finished. Everyone was looking at me, waiting for a response.

"But he's dangerous!" I didn't know what response was expected, but I knew what I had to say about the situation. "We can't just ignore him! Kaminsky is out to destroy everything we've achieved since 1989! The way he's blocking the constitutional amendment on the Round Tables—he's threatening the Round Tables, and he's got that sick fixation on Hanna Krause, it's dead creepy. And then there's the fash; he's supporting the fash, they're doing their thing again-"

"Karo." This time it was Erika, I like Erika, so I let her interrupt me. "I don't think anyone disagrees with you. But we can't do anything about it. We can't take on any new cases, we don't have the mandate any more. It's a job for the police now."

I snorted but didn't say anything, just kept my eyes fixed on the papers in front of me, letting the meeting drone on around me.

I was still sitting there, arms crossed over my chest, staring at the desk in front of me when Erika touched my shoulder. Everyone else had left, the meeting must have ended, just me and Erika in the room.

She sat down next to me, doing that thinking thing she always does.

"Kaminsky worries me," she said after a while. She was still frowning, still deep in thought. "He's finding ways to tap into people's fears, promising them security at a time when there isn't any to be had. He's creating scapegoats, directing people's fear and anger."

"Like Hanna Krause? OK, I get it that he doesn't like the Round Tables, but does he have to personally attack the chair of the Central Round Table? The way he objectifies her, the other day he called her a *prattling woman ...*"

"I've known Hanna Krause for years, she's strong, she can take it."

"It's not about whether she can take it—she shouldn't have to!"

"We put up with far worse in the past. But you're right, she shouldn't have to put up with Kaminsky's slurs, and I don't know why she does. I reckon she knows what she's doing, she's probably got some plan up her sleeve."

There wasn't much to say to that.

"I went to one of his rallies," Erika continued. I looked up in surprise and she nodded. "I was curious to see his appeal-"

"How could you? Kaminsky is scum! A racist, sexist, nationalist bigot!" Erika nodded again, but I'd only just started my rant. "And we have to do something-"

"Yes, yes. You said that before, and we agree with you. But the *Republikschutz* isn't the right organ for that task. Look, Martin always said we were stronger when we acted as individuals. He felt that his work at RS was too bound up in rules, regulations, protocol. He felt like it tied his hands and made him unable to act. Whereas when we act in our capacity as responsible citizens ..."

"You think we should keep an eye on Kaminsky, but not in any kind of official way?"

"Somebody needs to do it. And if it can't be RS ..."

Erika was right, RS wasn't the right tool for this job. I'd have to take my concerns elsewhere.

15:27
Karo

I left early that day. It didn't count as bunking off because I don't have fixed hours at the *Republikschutz*—I'm just helping out while Martin's on sick leave. But it felt like I was sneaking out, and Grit gave me a wink as I edged out of the office.

As soon as I got home I checked whether Schimmel was in, and, to be honest, I was a bit relieved when I couldn't find him. The usual aceness of living with Schimmel had turned into something else, in fact it kind of felt like I was living with his ghost. It started back in March: we were on a demo when he just lost it. He saw a face from the past, from when he was in the borstal or something, and it made him seriously flip. Knowing why he's changed doesn't really help though—like last night, just a simple change of plan and he totally freaks out on me. It's hard to deal with.

So I went to see Antifa Bert. It's not like he's number 2 on my list or anything, it's just I knew where to find him: sitting in the back bar of the *Schreina*.

"Anything going on?" I nodded towards the CB that Bert was monitoring just in case any alarm calls from other squats and social centres came in.

"Nah, been quiet since the Resurgence. I reckon we can get rid of all this tat."

"Rumours are, the skins have started supporting Kaminsky."

"Re-educating them, isn't he? Doing a good job too, from what I hear." Bert fiddled with the CB kit for a bit, ignoring me while I did a sceptical face. But then he must have felt the need to justify what he'd just said. "Kaminsky's a socialist, he's got nothing in common with the fash."

"Yeah, but the way he goes on about *common sense* and stuff like that, that we need to use common sense when it comes to deciding who we let into our country, he goes on about needing to control immigration—that kind of stuff, it's all a bit-"

"Give the man a break! He's casting his net wide, trying to get people involved. It'll all come together."

Now Bert was in a huff. I hadn't expected this, but I knew what he was like when he was in a mood. There was no point trying to talk to him right now. Probably hungover or something.

16:39
Karo

I still felt the need to talk to someone about Kaminsky (and I guess about Schimmel too) but wasn't sure who. Normally I'd talk to Martin but it didn't feel fair to pile all this stuff on him when he was on sick leave.

So I decided to talk to his daughter, Katrin. I'd only known her since last autumn, same as Martin, but I really liked both of them. Martin could be hard work but Katrin and I got along really well, and it felt like we'd got close back in March when the fash were targeting her dad and the shit was really hitting the fan. We'd seen each other a lot back then, but not so much lately—too busy with work. Now I was in West Berlin, ringing her doorbell, hoping she'd be in.

Katrin opened the door, and when she saw me on the stairs she gave me a lovely big smile and opened her arms for a hug. That felt good, just what I needed after the last few days.

"You got time for a visitor?"

"For you, always. Come in, I've got cake."

I followed her into the kitchen, and helped myself to a bottle of *Apfelschorle* from her fridge.

"Just as bad here as where I've come from," I nodded towards the kitchen table.

Pieces of paper were everywhere, and a tiny tape recorder lay on top. I picked it up—it was a bit longer than my hand, thick as a well-made sandwich. I was going to try out the buttons but Katrin took it off me.

"Don't—you'll lose my place. I've got to transcribe all these interviews for my dissertation, it's so boring, people just say the most banal things."

"I know all about people talking shite, at least I don't have to write it all down!"

Katrin smiled, but I didn't want the conversation to head towards work so I changed tack. "What you listening to?" It was something poppy, but kind of nice too. The singer had a terrific voice.

"Everything But The Girl, new album came out today. Do you want me to change it? Something heavier?" Katrin had given me the tea pot and two mugs, and was carrying a couple of slices of *Linzer Torte* into the living room.

I told her the music was fine and we sat together on the couch. It was nice and cool in her flat, she had the windows closed and the curtains drawn, keeping the heat out. It was cosy.

We talked a bit, and I told her about Schimmel, and she listened. She was a good listener, didn't interrupt, just sat there and paid attention. After a while I'd said everything there was to say.

"What about you?" she asked.

I gave her a whaddyatalkingabout face.

"Well it can't be easy on you either, seeing your friend like that."

"I'm fine."

"You're fine?" Katrin laughed at me. "You say me and my dad clam up when it comes to talking about feelings but you're just as bad!"

I slouched down a bit further on the sofa and crossed my arms.

"Karo, I'm just trying to help. I'm sorry I laughed at you."

I ignored her for a moment or two, but couldn't ignore the fact that she was right—this whole thing about Schimmel was stressing me out.

"It's like I can't get through to him. I'm beating myself up about it because it feels like I'm not doing enough, or not doing the right things. And that hurts. We've known each other for years, Schimmel and me. He's my best friend, he was my first proper friend. Now all of a sudden it's like he's not there any more. It used to be so good, we got up to all kinds of stuff, we put up with loads of hassle from the cops and the Stasi but we never let it get us down."

"Was it bad for you, back then?"

"Just the usual." I thought back to a few years ago, when the *Volkspolizei* would patrol Berlin, looking for punks to hassle. *We'll have to ask you to accompany us to the station. We need to verify your identity.* Like ten times a week, more if there was some state celebration coming up. They'd beat us up on Alex, or on the way home, pretty much all the time. "Just constant harassment. It's not like we'd ever have admitted it but I guess it did wear us down." God, I was glad those days were over! "What about you?"

"Wasn't too bad. The thing I'll never forgive them for is the way they made me leave school at 16. I really wanted to go to university, but there was never any chance of that happening."

"Was that why you left the country?"

"No." Katrin hesitated, her eyes fixed on the cup of tea between her hands. "They asked me to spy on my dad. That was the last straw, that's when I knew I had to get out. So we went to Hungary, me and this boy. We got out that way. I'll never forget the date: twenty-seventh of September 1989."

"Did you tell Martin? About what the Stasi asked you to do?"

"I should have done, I should have shouted it from the rooftops. I know that now, but I didn't then. I left instead. Hardest thing I've ever done."

I put my hand over Katrin's.

"Thing is, those same bastards are still around." I could hear the tension in Katrin's voice, winding itself up, tighter and tighter. "And it's like they've still got it in for my dad. That thing with Evelyn last year, and you can bet they were behind the fascist stuff in spring. They're definitely helping Kaminsky, right now. They're never going to give up, not until they're back in power. Will we never get rid of them?"

"Is that why you're still in the West?"

Katrin lifted her cup of tea to her lips, shaking my hand off. She sipped, then lowered the cup again.

"There's no way I can be in the same country as those Stasi bastards."

"What do you know about this Becker guy?" After a long silence Katrin had started talking about Schimmel again. "Are you sure he's responsible for how Schimmel is now?"

I didn't know the answer to that. Wish I did. I told Katrin I was going to find that out: along with who he was, what he'd done, where to find him.

"Is that wise? You might rake up more than Schimmel can handle."

I thought about that for a while, but it was obvious that the only way to go was through Becker, and it was already weeks and weeks ago that I'd promised myself that I'd find that man and do bad things to him. I mean, it was the whole reason I'd agreed to work with RS in the first place, I thought being in the *Republikschutz* would help me find him. But I'd been sidetracked into meetings and other stuff like all this shit around Kaminsky. I'd lost sight of my main mission.

So it was time to stop saying I was going to track that bastard down and actually start doing it. Talking with Katrin had helped me see that I really, really needed to get my shit together. I needed to get on Becker's case.

"Katrin, I've gotta go, I'm meant to be meeting up with Schimmel. Look, thanks for the chat." I gave her a peck on the cheek. "I'm glad we talked. It helped."

"Do you want to come round sometime, dinner maybe?"

"Dinner? Ooh, how bourgeois!" But then I saw Katrin's face, and that made me shut my stupid gob. "I mean, yeah, sounds great. Tell you what, I'll bring you a tape—broaden your musical horizons a bit!"

I was a bit surprised, but actually really glad that Schimmel was up for that chat I'd suggested. It was getting late and the streets were quiet. It was still hot but it felt a bit fresher under the trees in the graveyard. We found a bench at the back where no-one was going to bother us or look all shocked just because we had a few drinks with us.

I opened the beers and handed one to Schimmel, then tapped my own bottle against his. "*Prosit*".

We sat there for a while not saying much. I'd already thought about how to play this and I'd decided I was going to have to take it slow and be dead patient. That was fine, we had enough beer for a long sesh.

But Schimmel didn't look like he was going to say anything. So I decided to kick it off: "Do you want to talk about it?"

Schimmel shook his head. *Great start, well done Karo.*

"OK, I'll start talking, yeah? Look, the way I see it, everything was fine until that demo in March. You saw this guy Becker, he was hanging out with the Nazis, and you flipped out and haven't been the same since." Schimmel hadn't objected so far, so I carried on. "Is Becker from the borstal? The one they put you in back in '88? Did something happen?"

Schimmel shook his head again. I took a pull of my beer, giving him time to say something.

"Not the borstal. He was the boss at the *Durchgangsheim*." The temporary secure unit for juvenile delinquents.

Schimmel hadn't touched his beer yet.

"The night we met, at the Erlöser Church, was that the day they let you out?" Still no reaction from Schimmel. "You know, I thought you were really sorted."

I got half a grin for that and Schimmel finally lifted the bottle to his lips. "Really? I was well fucked. Didn't know whether to be happy I was free or scared because I had the Stasi on my back, trying to recruit me."

"You did the right thing."

"I was shitting myself."

We smiled at that. Memories. It had been a good day when I met Schimmel, I was glad we'd met. Schimmel was necking his beer, letting the alcohol flow down his throat without swallowing. He was working up to something.

"I was thirteen when they put me in the hard room," he said finally. "I must have been about 43 when they let me out." He'd pulled his knees up into his chest and was staring at the ground.

"What's the hard room?" I asked.

Schimmel shook his head. "On the first day I didn't get any food. After that I got dry bread and thin soup." He was still talking to his knees, the beer bottle held loosely in one hand. "The bread was so hard that I had to put it in the soup. It soaked up all the liquid and all I had left was bread," his words were coming in spurts and stammers. But I didn't push, I just waited, let him talk in his own time, to the rhythm of his memories.

"There was no window in the room, not even a bulb. In the evening they opened the door and I was blinded by the light from outside. They put down a bowl of soup and threw the bread on the floor. There'd be two of them, the other one used to throw a smelly mattress in and then they closed the door on me."

I sat there, next to Schimmel, not knowing what to say, what to do. I wanted to put my arms around him, but was frightened he would stop talking. All this time and he'd never said anything about this. Nothing at all.

"One day, when they threw the mattress at me, it landed on top of the bowl. The soup spilt over the floor. They just laughed, said it served me right for being careless. I tried to lick the soup off the floorboards, but it had soaked into the dust and between the cracks. I cried for hours. I cried until the morning when they took the mattress and the bowl away."

I couldn't hold back any more, this was my friend. I put my arms round him. He was shivering.

"So what are we going to do?" I asked after a while, but Schimmel had gone quiet again. All this pain, this State had fucked up so many of us. And the people who had done this to us, they had names and addresses. "Schimmel, we can't let them get away with this," I was trying to tread carefully, unsure how to say what I was thinking. "If you tell me what you know about Becker, I'll track him down. It should be dead easy for me to do that, now I'm working at RS-"

But it was the wrong thing to say, Schimmel just closed down again. In fact, he put the bottle of beer on the floor, dead carefully, just by his feet. Then he stood up and walked away.

"Schimmel!"

He didn't turn around, but I think he said: *It's my problem*, something like that.

"Schimmel!"

But he'd gone, he was already round the corner, behind the trees.

"Fucking Becker!" I threw my bottle at a headstone. "What did you do to my mate, you shit!" The bottle smashed as it hit, beer spraying over the granite. It made a good noise but didn't make me feel any better.

DAY 3
Tuesday
14th June 1994

We value those who have come to the GDR. We value those who contribute to our economy and our society. But the crucial issue is that it has to be the government that makes decisions about people coming in.

That is a difference between what I stand for and what the Round Tables want. It is very simple, when I look at the issues facing us, I consider the issue, I set out my plan, and I stick to it. It's called leadership.

Hanna Krause and her talking shops can't provide leadership. Only a strong government provides leadership.

We need a strong government—a strong government will give us steady employment. A strong government will give us consumer goods. And a strong government will give us back the respect of the world that we deserve.

08:05
Karo

"Erika, I'm quitting."

I'd thought about it a lot, and it was definitely the right thing to do. Talking to Katrin had made me think about it, and the scene last night in the graveyard had just confirmed my decision. I felt a bit bad about it though, Erika had asked me to help out at RS, and even though it was dead boring I guess the work I was doing was important.

"When?" asked Erika.

OK, I wasn't expecting wailing and gnashing of teeth, but Erika's reaction was a bit disappointing.

"Thanks a bunch, there was me thinking I'd been making myself indispensable."

I must have looked miserable because Erika put her arms around me. She had coffee breath but I didn't shy away; she was being nice.

"You are. You're doing brilliant liaison work with the Antifa groups around the country—that's the kind of thing we really need help with." She saw me rolling my eyes and responded: "It's true! But it's obvious you're not happy here, nor with the way we work."

"Thing is," what Erika had just said made me feel warm, it was good to get compliments—but I also had a favour to ask. "I want to quit, but I don't. See what I mean?"

Erika pulled her confused face. Which is kind of like her normal face, but I knew how to tell the difference by now.

"Remember when you offered me this job and I said I had a mission, and being in RS would help with that?" I still wasn't sure whether I should tell Erika this, but decided to go for it anyway. "A friend of mine, he was in borstal. Back before 1989. And he was in the *Durchgangsheim* here in Berlin. Something happened to him. *Someone* happened to him. Whatever it was, it wasn't nice. It was a member of staff—I'm going to track him down, make sure he pays for what he's done."

"What are you going to do?"

"That's up to my friend. I'm just here to find the man."

Erika had a good think about that, and I left her in peace while she got it all straight in her head.

"One of the staff? Party member?"

"Must have been. And it looks like he got involved in the fascist scene, after '89."

"But if you quit your job here ..."

"I won't have my RS identification any more, and I won't be able to access all the archives and records and stuff. So I'm thinking, I could quit, but not tell anyone. I'll just do this one thing then I'll quit officially, hand in my ID-"

"Karo, that's not the way it works." Erika didn't sound too pleased. "Let's talk to the others-"

"No way! There's no way Laura is going to let me do that kind of moonlighting, and Klaus isn't going to agree to it either!"

Somehow Erika persuaded me to take it to the meeting. It was my own fault, I shouldn't have mentioned it to her. But here I was, trying to explain to Laura and Klaus what I wanted. Grit was there too, but as usual she wasn't saying anything, just taking notes. Except she wasn't even doing that because I'd asked for this bit to be off the record.

"Highly irregular, young lady," said Laura, pretty much as I'd expected her to, but then she totally veered off-course. "What are you going to do with this man when you find him?"

I hesitated, I wanted to beat the shit out of him. But that wasn't really my decision, it was up to Schimmel.

"If this person were to be part of a restorative justice process then I'd have no objections to your trying to find him on work time," Laura continued.

I had to think about that. Could I give any guarantees? But before I had a chance to make any promises Klaus had decided it was his turn.

"You say this man you're trying to find was involved in the fascist scene? At decision-making level?" he tapped an unlit cigar on the tabletop for a moment or two, maybe he was giving me a chance to answer, but once again, before I could say anything he jumped in. "If it is the case that this Becker fellow is a cadre-level Nazi then personally I'd regard the task of finding him and bringing him to justice as being within Karo's remit here at RS."

OK, this wasn't what I'd been expecting. I looked at my colleagues. Laura still had her beady eye on me while Klaus was chewing his cigar and looking up at the ceiling. Erika gave me a wink, and I had to try really hard not to giggle. But this was good, this was totally good. Basically I just had to agree not to beat Becker up. Or let anyone else do it. Still wasn't sure about that bit, but probably best to keep quiet for the moment.

"Shall we say two weeks? We can review the decision then," said Laura, still super-serious, but somehow looking a bit more human. Klaus just carried on chewing his cigar.

I looked around the table, I had the go-ahead from everyone.

Except Grit. Nobody ever asked the secretary what she thought. I don't know why I did, I mean it could have gone badly, she might have disagreed. But I asked her anyway.

"I think you should go for it," she said.

10:14
Martin

When Karo rang the doorbell I was sitting in my favourite chair, smoking a cigarette and thinking about Steinlein. The Jonathan Blues Band were in the background, playing *Little Peter*.

"You been hiding?" she asked as she stomped into my flat.

"Speak for yourself."

"Yeah, sorry, Martin, been really busy. But you could at least pretend to be pleased to see me!"

"Coffee?" I offered, but Karo was already in the kitchen, filling a glass from the tap. As she gulped the water down I headed back to my chair.

Now Karo was poking around the kitchen. "Got any beer?" She was counting the empties behind the door.

"In the fridge. Bring me one too."

Karo came back into the living room, opening the bottle with her teeth

"Are you OK, Marty?"

"Why?"

"You always have a go at me when I take the top off with my teeth. Some remark about cracking them or chipping the enamel. You're smoking a cigarette even though you supposedly gave up last year. Plus it's not even midday and you're having a beer with me. See why I'm worried?"

I took a bottle off her and looked out the window. Maybe it had been a mistake to let Karo in, sometimes it took a lot of energy just to have a basic conversation with her.

"This is the bit where you tell me I shouldn't be worried."

Instead of answering her I clinked my bottle against hers, *Prosit!*

"What's on your mind?"

"Are you going to stop hassling me or do I have to throw you out?"

Karo slumped down in the chair opposite me, all the energy suddenly draining out of her. "Hassling mates into spilling their guts is becoming a habit. Sorry."

"RS?" I guessed.

Karo hesitated, working out whether I could deal with whatever she might say, then she blurted it all out anyway: "It sucks. It's like, I thought I could be doing something useful there, but you just get, like literally, trapped by this lurking *bureauctopus*."

Her neologism made me laugh, and I got a cautious smile in return. "Drowning in paperwork?" I asked her.

She picked at the label on her beer bottle for a beat or two, then: "You going to tell me what's happening in your world?"

It was an obvious subject-changer, but I let her have it.

"Haven't you heard? I'm on sick leave."

"Yes." She gave me an exaggerated sigh that she probably thought suitably ironic. "I did hear something about that. But what are you doing—and please don't tell me you're sitting around all day listening to depressing '70s music and smoking like a Russian panzer!"

"Oh, I'm keeping busy."

"Martin, I'm going to be straight up with you because you're a mate: you look like shit. I mean, look out the window—the sun's blazing down, has been for weeks. Everyone's got sunburn. But you? You look like you've been living in Siberia."

"Been doing a bit of thinking."

"Kaminsky? Yeah, call me psychic if you want but that arsehole is on everyone's minds." She paused for a moment, then: "You're not going all Hamlet on me are you?" She looked pleased at her cultural reference.

"Who'd be my Ophelia?"

Karo looked blank for a moment, then a smile creased her face. "She's the one who went and drowned herself? Couldn't take any more of Hamlet being a misery-guts?"

Things lightened up a bit after that and we managed to get a bit of a conversation going. We talked about Kaminsky, and I suggested he was more Macbeth than Hamlet, but Karo didn't get the comparison.

"It's the whole referendum thing." I mashed out my cigarette. "People voted to wind up RS—that doesn't bother me, that's what I voted for, too. But the vote on the Wall, the way it's split straight down the middle—how can we move on from that?"

"Yeah, but people also voted to give the Round Tables some proper power," Karo said, still trying to cheer me up.

"Kaminsky and his party are blocking that. He just turned up, came out of nowhere." I replied. "As a country we were dealing with the problems, we got to grips with the skinheads and hooligans, but then we get Kaminsky, putting the brakes on devolution. He's like a ghost from the past: centralisation, crude nationalism, casual racism. It's like we've learned nothing, we're back to square one."

Karo had gone silent, as if talking about this stuff bored her. Except I knew it didn't. I knew she was as worried about all of this as I was.

"We're lacking passion." I told her, knowing I was going on a bit but unable to stop. "In the old days the Party gave us passion: love of the fatherland, a quasi-religious belief in Marxism-Leninism. But now we just appeal to people's rationality. It's not enough." I lit another cigarette, wondering where my words were taking me. "Where are the flags to identify with? Why aren't we celebrating what we've achieved? We don't do any of that. We just talk. We talk in meetings at work, we come home and have more meetings with the residents of our block. Then we go to our local Round Tables and talk some more. Talk, talk, talk. No passion. What kind of revolution is this with no singing and dancing? Is it any wonder so many are falling for Kaminsky's spectacle?"

"Shit, Martin, I was meant to be cheering you up and I've just got you all wound up about Kaminsky instead."

"I was already wound up before you came. But being pissed off isn't going to change anything. Never has."

11:55

Martin

Lieutenant Steinlein had found himself an office far from the curtain twitchers at his police station: a small set of buildings sat right at the end of the Stralau peninsular, beyond the cemetery and opposite the last boatyard. The oxidised sign on the gate said *Transport Pool of the Council of Ministers of the GDR*, but Steinlein hadn't been able to find any record of the property in the Council's records. He'd finally gone to the archives at the old Stasi HQ, and found it in a file covered by four years' worth of dust. Like so many others, this building had been forgotten.

"It was used by the Stasi. From here they kept an eye on the barge traffic heading to West Berlin," he said as he struggled with the lock.

The key finally turned and Steinlein pushed the door open. Stale heat escaped from the building, making me feel woozy. I regretted the beer I'd shared with Karo earlier.

I peered into the building, four years' worth of dust coated every surface here too.

"Those prints are mine." Steinlein pointed to the footprints tracking through the grime and mouse droppings. "I've been here a few times."

We went through a hallway, empty except for a dented weapons safe, the doors hanging open and the racks empty. A cardboard box sat on the shelf and I picked it up, tipping a long, slender bullet onto my palm. I turned the brass casing between my fingers, thinking how lucky we'd been in 1989—if it hadn't been for Gorbachev our revolution would have ended in a bloodbath.

I dropped the bullet into the box and put it back on the shelf. Steinlein watched me, his face without expression.

"I've been using one of the rooms upstairs," he said, limping towards the staircase.

I watched him edge up the stairs, favouring his left leg. When I'd first met him, during a police raid on a fascist squat, he'd been insouciant, almost to the point of insubordination. Now his earlier insolence had been replaced by a sober determination. I followed him to the first floor and into a room adorned with framed portraits of Honecker and Mielke. A big window overlooked the river, I could see from the Island of Youth right up to the *Weisse Flotte* moorings near the S-Bahn station. A dozen barges rested against pilings directly in front of us. It was a good view. Calming.

I opened a window, hoping to let out some of the heat and dust. Outside, the trees of Treptower Park were reflected in the slow flow of the river. The slight breeze came into the room, stirring dust.

"There are more desks and chairs in the other rooms, we'll set you up with somewhere to work from."

His attitude irritated me, I didn't like him assuming I'd do the job.

Grey archive boxes were stacked on the floor next to the window and files were spread across the table's surface. Steinlein shifted through the paperwork until he found what he wanted: an ordinary file, light coloured cardboard, a classification code pencilled on the front.

"Doctor Karl Kaminsky, recently elected to the Executive Committee of the PDS, the successor of the Communist SED party. Currently causing so much unrest in our Republic."

I took the cadre file and sat down.

"If you want my help you'll have to be completely open with me," I told him. It sounded trite but I was tired of being taken for a ride by members and ex-members of the security apparatus. "Why do you need my help, and why have you brought all these files here?"

Steinlein brushed his hair from his forehead, fixing his eyes on the portrait of Mielke hanging on the wall.

"Based on available intelligence and taking account of further political-operational indications that have been gained from operationally relevant contacts, we may anticipate that plans are being made to assassinate Kaminsky-"

"Why me? Why work from here and not the police station?"

"Operational information has been received from an individual with habitual residence in the Operational Area," Steinlein continued without pausing, ignoring my questions

"I don't want a bloody report—just tell me what the hell is going on!"

Silence for a few seconds, then Steinlein exhaled, his back loosened and he turned to face me.

"There's a plot to kill Kaminsky, and I think police officers may be involved. I don't know who to trust, that's why I came to you. Will you help?"

"Make me a coffee, will you?"

I poked through the files while Steinlein boiled water on an electric plate. What the police lieutenant had said was serious, beyond serious. But I really didn't want to know, I'd done my bit, so many times, so many years. Doing my bit had broken me. Steinlein would have to find someone else to help him.

"I can't help," I called over to the policeman.

Steinlein measured out coffee grounds and poured boiling water into mugs. He limped back to the table with a mug in each hand, taking care not to spill any of the hot liquid.

"I know," he said when he got to the table. He put the mugs down. "But I don't know who else to trust. There's only you."

"How do you know whether you can trust me? Frankly, only a fool would." I got up, leaving the coffee on the table.

"Comrade Captain Grobe, when I was in hospital, you visited me and-"

"That's what you said the other day. So what, we were both beaten up by skinheads—doesn't make us best friends." I was already halfway to the door, keen to get out of this dusty sauna before I changed my mind.

"You impressed Neumann." Steinlein's superior officer, a hard-case in the political police department, K1.

"Neumann doesn't impress me," I called back.

"You've never been in the Party. You're capable. You have the necessary rank to lead this investigation. And you're not on active duty. No-one else fits the criteria." Steinlein stood up, facing me, his eyes trying to catch mine. "But most of all: you care. You care about our Republic. You care about what's happening to the GDR. And if you just stop for a moment, if you think for a moment, you'll know that right now the country is teetering on the edge—the referenda in April exposed the splits in our Republic. You know that if Kaminsky is assassinated then the whole country will tear itself apart."

Steinlein sat down again. "Think about it then tell me again that you won't help."

We stared at each other. He seemed to think he'd said enough, that I was a hungry fish ready to bite.

"You know something?" I broke the silence. "My shrink, I've only seen her once, but she says one of my symptoms is a lack of trust. She says I need to trust more. But I'm finding it hard to trust you right now. So will you cut the woffle and tell me why we're still talking?"

"You want it straight? Read this. It's not official, you'll see why. I haven't opened the usual criminal proceedings files because it's just been me working at this—read it, you'll see for yourself."

He gave me the folder he'd searched out before. The first sheet was an index of contents, usual stuff. The second sheet was an Information Report. Steinlein had detailed the steps leading up to this meeting. There weren't many, and they weren't convincing. It all boiled down to an anonymous tip-off: Kaminsky's life was in danger. Collateral material: zilch.

I shut the file and looked at Steinlein. He stared straight back, not even blinking.

"It's not much to go on, I know. But in the past I've had tip-offs from a source, good tip-offs. I think this is from the same person. On Saturday I took a delivery: internal Party documents. It was this new source, proving their value. I've been able to compare the material to some internal Situation and Development Reports. It all checks out." Steinlein was still staring at me, talking rapidly. "The Party has done some assessments for just this scenario; the Party actually believes an assassination attempt may happen."

"Fine, pass it on to the police, let K1 handle it—it's a political case."

"I had hoped someone with your background would understand—K1 is still too close to the Party. Before 1990 every single officer in K1 was a loyal member."

I must have looked confused, because Steinlein had to spell it out: "It's an internal threat. Someone or some faction within the Party wants to kill their own General Secretary."

12:03
Karo

It was totally out of order, the way the Party were hanging on to all these massive buildings. If it had been up to me they'd all be squats by now. Or theatres. Something like that anyway. I stood on the corner of Wilhelm-Pieck-Strasse and Prenzlauer Allee and looked up at the imposing columns that flanked the doors of *Haus der Einheit*. It looked dead posh, even with all the rendering falling off and the hardboard covering the broken windows.

I went into the lobby, it was all marble and big staircases, meant to make you feel that small. But it didn't work on me. Well, only a bit, and I made sure it didn't show. I spent a bit of time trying to work out which floor the archive was on, but all I could see on the big board at the bottom of the stairs was something called *Verbundarchiv*, and that didn't sound right.

"Can I help you, miss?" said a chalky voice.

It was some Party lackey, wearing a brown dust coat over his faded suit. But it wasn't that that bothered me, it was the *miss*.

What century did he think we were in?

"Party Archive?" I asked.

"Are you after the pre-1990 files or more recent, miss?"

He had me there. I hadn't thought they might be split up like that, but I guess it made sense. I decided to deal with the more recent stuff first, I might find an up-to-date address and it would be interesting to see whether Becker had left the Party before getting involved with the Nazis.

I followed the caretaker's instructions, going up the marble steps and getting lost in the maze of corridors. Upstairs it was a bit less grand, at least in the bits I was wandering around in right now. Just the usual cracked lino, washed-out gloss paint and dust.

I found the right floor at last. A babushka guarded a desk placed across the corridor. She ignored me for a bit—the usual game: see who gives up first. But I wasn't going to play that game today, because I was a State Official.

"I've come to check personnel records."

Without looking up from her magazine the babushka slid a brown piece of paper over to me. I had a quick read through the form, it all looked pretty straightforward.

"Pen?"

"Supply your own," she said, still not bothering to look up from her magazine.

"Could you lend me a pen please?" Nice as pie, I couldn't do it any nicer than that. But there was no answer.

I went back down to the lobby, wishing I had a ball of string with me so that I could find my way back, but in the end it was OK because I found some back stairs that went straight down to the corridor behind the main entrance.

Mr Brown Dust Coat was still there, and seemed happy to lend me his pencil, so I filled in the form while he talked at me about the heatwave. When I'd filled in the easy bits I headed back upstairs, taking the pencil with me. It was only a chewed stump, he probably wouldn't miss it.

The babushka took the form from me, and still flicking through her stupid romance magazine, she laid it on her desk, picked up the stamp and was about to plonk it in the little round circle printed there for the purpose when she finally decided to check what I'd written.

"*Name of person requesting access*: not filled in," she read out aloud. "*File Reference: not known. Dept./Type of File: Cadre Records. Name of Person: Becker.*" She was merciless, reading out every single bit of the form, even those bits I didn't fill in because I didn't know how to or because the questions were stupid.

It was only when she'd finished that she looked at me for the first time. She got a bit of a shock, I don't think she was expecting a punk to be standing in front of her precious desk.

"Is this some kind of joke?" She asked, obviously torn between wanting to carry on with her magazine, and wondering what the hell I was doing there.

"On the contrary, citizen. Here is my authorisation, please bring me the file I requested." I showed her my RS pass, but she didn't seem interested.

"I'm phoning security." She had already picked up the heavy receiver of an old black phone.

I put a finger on the cradle to cut off the call.

"Citizen, I have already told you what I require, and I have shown you my authorisation. Will you do your job or do I have to do it for you?"

"Miss, if you know what's good for you then you'll leave right now. Your authorisation won't get you very far in this building, you've no right to access post-1990 files, those are for internal use only."

Fuck, she could be right—I hadn't thought of that, the Party archives would no longer be a state matter. I might just have overstepped the mark, just a weeny bit.

I grabbed the search form from her hand and got out of there before she could make that telephone call.

I was in the kitchen when the doorbell rang. Jürgen Kerth carried on singing as I opened the door to Steinlein.

"Have you thought about it?"

"Give me a chance—we only talked a couple of hours ago." I went back into the kitchen, leaving the door open for Steinlein to come in if he chose to. I could hear his cane tapping across the floor, drowning out Kerth's *He junge Mutti*. "Actually, I've been enjoying not thinking about it." I went through to the living room and took the needle off the record. I hated doing that, but I didn't want Steinlein spoiling the reggae-meets-blues of one of Kerth's best tracks.

When I got back to the kitchen Steinlein was leaning against a cabinet. Sweat glistened on his forehead and his eyes were receding into his skull. I reached past him, took a glass from the shelf and returned to the sink to fill it with water.

"Normally I wouldn't be wasting my time on this," he said. "But as I said before, this source has never been wrong-"

"*If* it's the same source."

"We should assume it is." Steinlein's fingers were tapping on the kitchen unit, making it hard for me to concentrate on what he was saying. "This is too big to get wrong. Think about the timing—the country's like a tinderbox. The referendum on the Wall last April divided the country, the *Volkskammer* is dragging its feet on the constitutional amendments and then there are the elections coming up in the autumn. There's no way of telling whether the pro-unification parties will have a majority, or whether the Communists will gain power again."

I didn't answer Steinlein, he still had a long way to go if he wanted to convince me.

"Will you help me out, just for a few days? If we don't manage to substantiate the threats in that time then I'll leave you in peace. Deal?"

He looked so tired and desperate that I gave him the glass of water. That and my word that he'd have my help for a few days.

I went back into the living room and the police officer followed me.

"There's been another contact from the source." Steinlein told me as he eased himself down to a hard chair. "It confirms my initial assessment that they're based in the Operational Area. Maybe that's why they're shy. They say they want to be handled by you only, and first contact is to be a brush past."

Handled by me? A brush past? In West Berlin? It was all too far-fetched for my taste. I shook my head, this wasn't what I had in mind when I agreed to help out.

"There was a message waiting for me when I got back to the police station so I came here immediately. The source has specifically asked for you."

"Why me?" I asked, trying to stall him. "Why do they want me?"

"People know you by reputation. They've seen you on the television, in the newspapers. They know what you did during the Silesian affair, and what happened to you in March. People trust you." Steinlein pulled back his sleeve and turned his wrist to check his watch. "The problem is, they want the brush past to happen this afternoon. In fact, if you leave now you might just be in time."

I crossed over to the westbound platform at Friedrichstrasse station and boarded the S-Bahn just as the signal sounded and the doors ground shut. As always, I looked down at the Wall as we passed over it, then the still waters of the Humboldt Harbour, bright under the high sun. Recently I'd been to West Berlin a lot, visiting my daughter or on some liaison matter, but the other half of the city still didn't feel like home, not the way East Berlin did.

The train slowed as it entered Lehrter Stadt station and stood for a while as we changed drivers. Watching the drivers exchange a handshake and a few words I thought about what it meant to cross the Wall. In East Berlin I knew the people, the streets, I knew the rules. But West Berlin was a foreign country. Same language, similar streets, but a different system. It made me nervous at the best of times, but now I was in the West on an operation my previous anxieties were being put into perspective.

I swallowed my fear and a couple of stops later I got off.

Down at street level I walked along the wide boulevard, heading for the flea market. *Right-hand middle aisle*, I whispered to myself, *Brass goods*. I made my way through the stalls, many selling memorabilia from my own country: military and MfS uniforms, Party books, medals. Other stalls sold items that were still used in many households over in the East, but had here gained an attractive patina of antiquity: meat grinders, mangles, desk pencil sharpeners, fruit juice pans. I pushed through the sweating crowds, keeping an eye open for the brass goods stall. Once there I stood still, pretending to admire the horse brasses, milk jugs and jewellery boxes while the mass of punters edged around me on their hunt for bargains and souvenirs.

I was wondering how long I'd have to stand there, looking at overpriced tat that I neither wanted nor could afford, when I was shunted into the other people looking at the stall. I staggered, and some *Wessi* pushed me back, muttering about clumsy *Ossis*. I regained my balance and my hand went to my trouser pocket, checking my wallet was still there. It was, but my hand also found a piece of folded paper. I pulled it out, not looking at it, just feeling it between thumb and fingers—it was just a scrap, folded over a few times. I pushed it deeper into my pocket and made my way out of the melee.

At the edge of the flea market I paused, glancing back. No way of knowing who had given me the note. Was it the oaf who had barged into me, or had somebody already slipped it into my pocket before that? I pulled the note out, not opening it up, just looking at it. Grey, recycled paper, lined like schoolkids use, and now blotted with damp marks from my sweaty fingers.

I had my prize, first mission successfully completed. I could return home.

At Bellevue station half a dozen West Berlin police officers boarded. They passed slowly down the train asking to see identity papers. They didn't ask everyone, just those of us from the East. I showed them my PM 12, which caused some frowning and nose wrinkling.

"Why do you only have temporary documents?"

"My *Ausweis* was stolen a few weeks ago, I haven't been issued with a new one yet."

The policeman went to confer with a colleague, one with more stars on his epaulettes. He took my PM 12 with him. They stood discussing the issue for a few moments, long enough for the train to pull into Lehrter Stadt station, last stop before the Wall. The police officers got off the train, all except the one with my papers. He was still flicking through the few pages, pretending to look for something. His colleagues were standing on the platform, smoking and watching us through the carriage windows. Up and down the carriage the passengers were pretending not to stare. I ignored the contempt in the eyes of Westerners irritated by the hold-up, I blocked out the sympathy and fear of those from the East, old memories too close to the surface.

"Are you a police officer?" he demanded. "Or a member of the security organs of the GDR?"

I shook my head, mentally double checking that I'd thought to leave my RS pass at home.

Another flick through my PM 12, a stare at the photograph, comparing it to my face, the young policeman trying to make the decision: take me off the train for questioning, or let me go. A glance out of the window at his impatient colleagues and without another word he thrust my papers at me and left the train.

The red signal next to the door lit up, the two-tone bell rang. The doors grated shut between me and the West Berlin cops. I started breathing again as the train accelerated, whining out of the station, over the harbour basin, over the Wall, back home to the East.

15:55

Martin

Once I'd changed trains at Friedrichstrasse I unfolded the note. Small, neat capitals were written in blue ballpoint pen:

VME/E/1059/89

That was it, just a series of numbers and letters. Looked like a file reference, and I knew where I could find plenty of files that had been catalogued that way. If I was quick I could get there before they shut.

Half an hour later I was in the reading room of the Normannenstrasse complex where the Stasi used to have their headquarters. The archivist had gone off to the stacks holding the search form on which I'd entered the reference from the note along with a few made-up numbers.

After ten minutes the archivist returned, shaking her head. "I'll need more time for some of these files, about half are missing, some aren't even referenced. I'll check them against the central indexes, but here's the ones I've got so far."

She piled a good forty or fifty centimetres of files onto my reading desk then wheeled her trolley away.

I was the only person in the reading room, no-one there to observe what I was doing, so I went straight to the file I was here for. The first four or five pages were details of sources, action plans, all the usual Stasi procedures. The seventh page was a letter, addressed to General Mielke, the head of the Stasi. It was typed on German State Theatre letter-paper, and informed Mielke of an artists' resolution condemning the violent behaviour of the security organs during the fortieth anniversary of the Republic in October 1989.

I turned to the last sheet. It was the final page of the minutes for the meeting where the artists' resolution had been agreed. This was just history—was I on a wild goose chase? Fighting off resignation, I flicked through the file again, looking for pages that seemed out of place. And there they were, same kind of paper, but the text from a different typewriter. I scanned these pages: minutes of various meetings, no names of participants, no circulation list, just summaries of what had been said. The language was different, more formal, and the subject of the discussions was identified only as *Zielperson*, target. There were no clear indications about who that target might be, just enough hints to keep me interested.

I extracted these extra pages, folding them into my jacket pocket before putting the file in the middle of the pile on the desk. I opened another folder at random and left it there. Time to get back to Stralau and have a good look at what I'd found, but first I wanted to know who had last accessed that file. I left the reading room and went to the archivist's office. No-one answered my knock so I let myself in, quietly shutting the door behind me. The room was tiny, barely enough space for the desk, chair and filing cabinet that filled it. My search request lay in a tray on the desk. On the shelves below I found the forms for previous days, neatly filed away in ring-binders.

Ticking through the pages, I scanned file references, looking for my file. I'd checked the last seven days and was about to open another binder when I heard a door click shut, somewhere further down the corridor. My ears tensed to the approaching noises: feet slapping along the linoleum, the sounds growing sharper and louder. The door shivered as the handle was depressed. There was nowhere to hide in the small office, no cupboards, no corners. My eyes fell to the floor, still searching for possibilities as the door began to open.

I slipped behind the door, wondering whether I was doing the right thing, whether I should just pull my RS pass and start making demands. The door stopped, and I heard voices, first a low mumble, and then the higher pitch of the archivist: "Wait in the reading room, I'll bring them over."

The door opened further and an arm reached in, depositing a search form in the tray on the desk. The arm withdrew again, the door pulled closed behind it. The slapping footsteps faded as the archivist went back to the stacks.

Before leaving, I had a look at the new search form. The name meant nothing to me: DVP Sergeant Heubach. I copied my own search onto a new form, omitting the reference to the file I'd just looked at, and swapped it for the original. I headed out, making sure not to bump into the archivist or Sergeant Heubach.

17:28

Martin

Once back at the Stralau office I had a good look at the papers I'd found: extracts from at least three different sets of minutes and a situation report. The cover pages from each file were missing, so I had to guess at their chronological order, but I reckoned the first in the sequence was to do with a discussion about whether Kaminsky should be nominated to the Executive Committee of the Party. He was never mentioned by name, but the context was enough for me to be fairly sure they were talking about him. The meeting had concerns that Kaminsky was a loose cannon: his politics were unclear, but he was a good speaker, and he was gaining support among the Party's grassroots. According to the dense prose I was scanning, the main reason Kaminsky was allowed to join the Executive Committee was that he was deemed too dangerous to leave on the outside. The hope was that by giving him more responsibility he would somehow become more manageable.

I turned to the next set of minutes. Once again the meeting was of a small group of senior Party members. Within weeks of Kaminsky joining the Party's executive this group was regretting the decision. There was talk of encouraging him to step down, and if he wouldn't take a hint then the group would make use of compromising material to force his hand.

I looked at the situation report next. It was written by some kind of Party intelligence or analytics department, and documented the rising popularity of Kaminsky. His appeal among various demographics was tabulated by Party membership (pre- and post-1989), employment categories and geographic area. Kaminsky seemed to enjoy strong support among those who'd left the Party in 1989 and 1990, mainly in the south and east of Saxony, and to a lesser extent in Saxony-Anhalt and eastern Thuringia.

The final set of minutes were the most interesting. It was a short document, less than one side. Kaminsky was threatening to set up his own political movement, and to take the Party's members with him. The *Bonzen* in the Party weren't prepared to allow that to happen and it sounded like they were ready to play hard ball: *The committee needs to consider what measures are at their disposal in order to achieve long-term disciplinary effects on the subject.*

18:13

Karo

"You again?"

"Yeah, well, I was just passing."

"Passing West Berlin?" Katrin laughed and held the door open.

"I really messed up today, I think I might be in trouble," I told her.

Katrin was great, she listened to me blether on about my major fuck-up in the Party archives, and then she pointed out that since RS is being wound up anyway there's nothing really bad that can happen.

I wish I could be more like her, she was just so calm and she brought me back down and spotted the important bits straight off, showed me I'd been tying myself up in knots over nothing.

"Something else is bothering you, isn't it?" she asked after we'd sorted out the non-problem of my visit to the archives.

I didn't answer, but went into the kitchen to get some water. Katrin leaned against the door as I let the tap run cold and filled a glass.

"Is it about your friend?"

I took a sip and nodded, still not looking at Katrin. She came over and put her arms around me.

"He told me some really awful stuff last night. He talked about it a bit and then left me bawling away in a graveyard," I mumbled into her shoulder.

Katrin took the glass off me and manoeuvred me into the living room. With soft hands she pressed me onto the couch.

"Want to talk about it?"

I shook my head. What Schimmel had told me was personal, I wouldn't go blabbing about it.

But then Katrin took a different tack: "Do you identify with him, with whatever it is that happened to him?"

Her question confused me, I'd never experienced anything half as bad as what Schimmel told me about last night. I shook my head.

"But you're quite similar to him, aren't you?" She saw my face and rephrased the question. "You said Schimmel left home when he was still a kid, and from what you've said in the past I kind of got the impression that the same thing happened to you."

"It's not the same!" I jumped up and faced Katrin. "Schimmel grew up in the middle of nowhere and ran away from home at thirteen. He spent years in a borstal because of that!"

"It's OK if you don't want to talk about it, I was just wondering ..." Katrin had her hands out, inviting me back onto the couch.

"I was sixteen when I left home so there was nothing they could do about it." I sat down again, but leant forward, elbows on my knees. I couldn't see Katrin, but could feel her right next to me. "Anyway, it was my dad. He chucked me out. Only good thing he ever did. Said I was a disgrace."

"You weren't happy at home?"

A bitter laugh. "Happy? How could I be, with that bastard sniping at me all the time. Nothing was ever good enough for him. I remember one time I brought home a report card from school, I'd got a 1 or 2 in every subject except Russian. I'd only managed a 3, but I was dead proud of it, because I really struggled in Russian. Know what he said? Know what the bastard said? *Won't get very far with these grades.* You can imagine how I felt." I held my hand out, the tip of my index finger and thumb almost touching. "That small."

Katrin leaned forward, trying to see my face. I ignored her.

"Nothing was ever good enough for him. Whatever I did, no matter how hard I tried, it didn't mean shit, just another reason to make snide remarks. So after a lifetime of trying to please him I just gave up. I didn't bother trying any more. I said *Fuck you* to him and his bullying, and I said *Fuck you* to the rest of the world, too."

"Is that when you left home?"

"I went with a friend to a punk concert at the *KvU*. Everyone there was screaming *Fuck you*, loud as they could. For the first time ever it felt like I belonged. I didn't need anyone to love me or care about what I did. I didn't need anyone to tell me I'd done well, because I was shouting *Fuck you* as loud as I could."

This time I let Katrin put her arms round me and we both flopped back against the cushions. It felt good to be held. It felt safe. But even though it felt good I couldn't help but be envious of Katrin, having Martin as a dad.

"Maybe that's why I like Martin, maybe he's the dad I never had, he accepts me," I told her.

"He likes you, he thinks you're great."

"But I push him away all the time. I'm mean to him. Sarcastic. I don't want to be but it's like my own dad is in here," I banged my chest with a closed fist. "He's inside me, making me push away the people I like. I'm not very good at people being nice to me, and you and Martin have never been anything but totally nice to me. Ever since I met Martin he's respected me, no matter how stupid or resentful I've been."

Katrin turned my face towards her, palms against my chin, fingers up my cheeks. Her skin smelt of roses. "I like you. And you won't ever push me away, no matter how hard you try."

We stayed like that for a moment, looking into each other's eyes, but then I got embarrassed and eased myself out of her clasp. I stood up and fished a cassette out of my rucksack.

"Here, I made you a mix-tape."

Katrin took it off me, turning it round to look at the picture I'd drawn for the insert. "Punk?"

"No. Well yes, a bit. But not really—you're gonna like it, there's nothing heavy, no Schleimkeim or anything like that, but there's some Fall, and a bit of PJ and the first track is ace, it's by Stereolab, and I taped some KLF and Feeling B and ..." I was babbling. I tailed off, coming over all embarrassed again, but Katrin pretended not to notice.

She hugged the cassette to her chest. "I've got one for you too." She reached behind her and picked up a tape. "Everything But The Girl— their new album. It's what we were listening to yesterday."

I took the tape off her and made a move for the hi-fi, but Katrin shot across the room, trying to get there before me.

"Mix-tape first!"

I grabbed her by the shoulder, turning her onto her back and climbing over her, reaching out for the tape deck. She put her arms around me, dragging me down and giggling as I collapsed onto her. We were rolling round the floor like a couple of toddlers, laughing the whole time.

"Ssshh, the neighbours!" There was a knocking, it sounded like someone had taken off their shoe and was banging it on the wall, telling us to shut the fuck up, but that just made us laugh even harder. With a sudden wriggle Katrin slid out from under me, reaching out and slotting my mix tape into the machine.

"Sneaky!" We were both still sprawled across the floor, our faces almost touching. I was hyper-aware of her warm breath tickling my nose, of her eyes looking into mine. I didn't think about it, I just moved my head closer. She didn't move away from me, she waited, mouth slightly open, expectant.

My hand sought hers, but it found her thigh first, and with another giggle Katrin wormed away, landing on the couch. She pulled her feet up, hugging her knees while she squirmed her bottom into the corner, leaning against the armrest.

The guitars of Stereolab's *French Disko* had kicked in now, with the vocals gliding up behind, and I moved over to sit next to Katrin. There was silence for a bit while we pretended to listen to the lyrics from opposite ends of the couch.

I could feel Katrin's eyes on me, but I looked off into a corner where some tie-dyed material was hanging on the wall.

"I'm not like that. You do know that, don't you?" Katrin had unfolded her legs a little, she was still at one end of the couch, but her feet were on the cushions next to my thighs. It was like heat was beaming out of her toes, I could feel it through my jeans.

"Is anyone?" I laughed and put my fingers over Katrin's toes. They wiggled a bit, but didn't move away, so I started massaging them, rubbing each in turn.

"But are *you*?" Katrin still had her gaze fixed on me, I was watching my hands knead her feet.

"Who needs labels?"

Katrin's toes wiggled again.

18:44

Martin

Steinlein's tall frame filled the doorway, his stick slanted away from his body, pointing the way towards his desk.

He stood for a few moments, looking not towards me or the papers I'd found in the Stasi archives, but out of the window, at the park on the other side of the river.

I placed the minutes on Steinlein's desk and thought about what I'd read. We would have to check the material's provenance—if the papers were authentic then they'd corroborate Steinlein's theory that the Party was plotting to get rid of Kaminsky. That seemed barely believable, but verifying the intelligence would be a first step towards preventing an assassination. My thoughts were interrupted by Steinlein clearing his throat.

"Any trouble over there?" he asked as he stepped towards his desk.

"West German cops were doing ID checks. They didn't like my temporary *Ausweis*."

"And?"

"No problems. But there's no way I'm going over there again."

Steinlein didn't seem concerned, he was too busy following his own thoughts. "Did you see the source? Did you recognise him?"

I shook my head.

"Shame," said Steinlein, but he'd already started reading.

"Those minutes seem to support your theory."

Instead of answering, Steinlein just gave a grunt. He was holding a sheet of paper up to the light. "Did you see this?" He put the paper back on the desk, his finger poised over an area of text.

I moved in to see what he was pointing at, and as I did so his finger moved closer to the paper. He was indicating nothing but the gap between two lines. I couldn't see anything unusual, the lines were regularly spaced, except the alignment of the letter e was slightly out of sync with other characters, edging up into the white space that so interested Steinlein.

"Hold it to the light," he said.

I took the sheet and held it up. And there, just where Steinlein had indicated, were faint pencil markings.

Tacheles 0905. 2nd window main staircase. Poster.

"Looks like you'll be collecting some post in the morning."

"Why are you doing this?" I asked him.

He looked up, not understanding.

"Why are you handling the case in this way? Unofficially, from here?"

"I've told you, I'm concerned about potential police involvement in the plot against Kaminsky."

"But it could still be handled internally. You could talk to your superior. Who do you report to anyway, is it Captain Neumann?"

"I don't know who's involved, it could be anyone-"

"What's in it for you? Do you actually care what happens to Kaminsky or is this just about preventing a crime?"

Steinlein didn't respond for a moment or two, considering how to answer. "What he says makes a lot of sense."

He had stopped reading, he was waiting for my reaction.

"You support him?" I hadn't even considered that Steinlein might find Kaminsky and his policies acceptable.

"I'm a policeman, not a politician—my job is to protect the people of the GDR. I don't get involved in politics."

How could any even half-way intelligent person support Kaminsky? Wasn't it obvious that he was just on a power trip, that he didn't really have the best interests of the country at heart?

"You have to admit this country's an absolute mess. Kaminsky's right when he says we need strong leadership, we're never going to get anywhere with the Round Tables interfering all the time. Any influence from outside the government and the *Volkskammer* is undemocratic."

"Do you seriously believe that Kaminsky will be good for the GDR?" I asked him.

"He has the support of the people, who am I to question that?"

Kaminsky wanted to roll back everything we had achieved since 1989, and Steinlein was basically telling me he agreed with that. I was shocked by the realisation that the policeman and I wanted such different things for our country.

I physically took a step back from him, then turned and left the building.

DAY 4
Wednesday
15th June 1994

I'm doing something different, and I have your support to do that. Yet there are also doubters, nay-sayers who don't like what's happening: the reactionaries, saboteurs, anti-social elements and anti-democrats—the ones who can't accept the will of the people.

They may not accept the situation, but I accept them.

I tolerate them and their outdated attitudes because I know that the people of the GDR will overcome this irresponsible resistance.

But I can't accept state agencies interfering in democratic processes. I've been informed that there has been an attempt to access my cadre files in the Party archive. Not an attempt by one of those meddling journalists— no, it is far more serious than that.

This attempt to gain illegal access to the Party archive was by a member of a government agency.

Not just any government agency, but the Republikschutz itself.

Agencies like the RS are undermining our country. The RS may claim to uphold democracy but they are unaccountable, secretive and dangerous.

That is why the people voted to wind up the RS. Yet here we are, more than ten weeks after the referendum, and the RS are still going about their dubious business.

This is not acceptable. Let me be clear: the RS is not democratic. It is a danger to our democracy and we cannot allow it to continue to defy the will of the people.

Martin

Steinlein had said it himself: if Kaminsky were assassinated this country would rip itself apart. Steinlein and I wanted not just different things for our country, what we wanted was incompatible. Yet despite our opposing political views, neither of us wanted the GDR to descend into chaos.

That's why, just after half-past eight this morning, I caught the S-Bahn to Friedrichstrasse. Despite the early hour the roads and pavements around the station were hot, the tram tracks shimmered into the distance.

I'd deal with Steinlein later, I decided. First we had to prevent Kaminsky from being assassinated. Once we'd done that I'd take them both down.

My destination wasn't far: a half-ruin just at the beginning of Oranienburger Strasse. Tacheles, they called it. I'd never been there but I'd heard about it, even seen it on a culture programme on Western TV. A group of artists had squatted the building in 1990, just before it was due to be demolished. They did emergency repairs and moved in, using the building as ateliers and exhibition space, as well as the inevitable political meetings.

The main entrance was shrouded in wooden scaffolding, a wide staircase led off the foyer. As the note said, there was a poster taped to the window on the second half-landing. There was nobody about, still too early for the artists.

I clasped my cigarette between my lips, squinting through the smoke as I eased the tape off the bottom left-hand corner of the poster. I pushed my fingers underneath the paper and felt around until I snagged a small square of paper. I slid it out. Another look up and down the stairs, then I was off, back onto the street.

I walked a few blocks before ducking into a cellar doorway, wondering whether I should have suggested to Steinlein that he come along too, hang back and try to spot the source. But I knew what his response would have been: *It's about trust*, he would say. But that was my problem, I didn't see any reason to trust our so-called source, and I had serious doubts about my partner too.

I unfolded the note, same paper, same neat printed letters as last time: *Prinzenstrasse open-air swimming pool 12:30. Bring 400 DM*

Prinzenstrasse was the same road as Heinrich-Heine-Strasse, the name changed when you crossed into West Berlin. I was fairly sure the open-air baths were right at the far end, by the Landwehr canal, but I could do with checking a map, not to mention finding 400 Westmarks. I phoned Steinlein from a phone box.

"I told you not to contact me!"

"It's OK, I gave the switchboard a false name. Listen, the source wants 400 DM. He wants to meet in Kreuzberg just after midday." I listened to the static on the line, waiting for Steinlein's answer.

"Meet me. Warschauer Platz, eleven-thirty." Steinlein's words were chased down the line by the click of his phone being hung up.

When I got back to my flat there was a message on the notebook that hung on the door. *Not seen you in ages* (underlined twice) *let's have beer and a catch up!* There was no signature, but I recognised the scrawl as Karo's.

I tore the message off the pad and went inside. Beer and a catch-up, even though she'd only been here the other day? She probably wanted to talk about whatever was happening at RS. But right now I didn't have time, I had work to do.

The phone rang while I was in the kitchen pulling a towel off the clothes horse. I ignored it, going instead into my bedroom to find swimming trunks. I was in too much of a rush and in no mood to talk to whoever was on the other end.

The phone was still ringing as I left the flat.

09:11

Karo

That was probably the worst experience of my life. I mean, morning meetings are *always* awful, but this one ... After what had happened yesterday I knew Laura would have a go at me but it was Klaus who was really laying it on thick.

"I didn't know! How was I supposed to know? It's not like I asked for Kaminsky's files!"

"No, but he's been on the news claiming you were. We're doing you a favour here, letting you work on your own case—and this is how you repay us? A little bit of discretion is all that we asked for, but what do-"

"Nobody said nothing about discretion!"

There was a gap in all the ranting and shouting, which is where Erika stepped in. "Clearly Karo didn't realise she was overstepping the mark. Perhaps we should look to ourselves, ask whether we failed in our responsibilities—such as making sure that Karo knows what she can and can't do?"

I was well relieved when Erika said that, she was letting me off the hook. But then she turned to me and I held my breath, nervous about what she'd say next.

"And as for you, Karo, I take it you've realised the need for discretion?" She waited until I gave a reluctant nod. "And that if you're not one hundred percent sure about anything—anything at all —that you come and talk to one of us?" A hard look was on her face.

"OK."

"So shall we regard this episode as closed?" Erika asked the meeting.

"How can we?" Klaus still wasn't happy. "There's all sorts of fallout we can expect from this mess."

I wanted to stomp out, leave them to their stupid messes, but I didn't want to piss them off any more than I already had done. I needed to keep my RS pass for a bit longer. So I sat there while they droned on about potentially sensitive scenarios and stuff—on and on, worrying about things that probably would never even happen. It all sounded like a load of paranoid bollocks to me. But then again, they had a good idea of what to expect from our fucked up political system.

As soon as I got out of the meeting I gave Martin a ring, I needed to let off steam about his colleagues. I let the phone ring for ages and ages but he didn't answer, even though he must have been at home. I mean where else would he be if not at home? I slammed the receiver down.

"Typical Martin, not there when I need him. I'm always there for him, but the first time I actually need him-" I was talking out loud, like some batty old dame, but broke off when I saw Erika standing in the doorway to my—Martin's—office.

"Who are you grumbling about now?"

"You. Who else?" I answered. But I was still thinking of Martin and what I'd told Katrin yesterday, about pushing people away. I wanted to do things differently from now on, which is why I'd already been to his flat this morning, y'know, just to say hi. But he'd been out. Or asleep. I left a message, I thought he would have phoned me back by now.

Erika came right into the office. "I just wanted to check in with you, ask if there's anything I can do to help?"

"What with?"

"Becker. It was his files you wanted to see at the archive, wasn't it?"

I nodded glumly. It felt like the whole world knew I'd failed on that score.

"If you'd talked to us first we would have told you about the difficulties with accessing the Party archives." I crossed my arms, mentally preparing myself for another lecture, but Erika had other ideas. "So now you need to be a bit more subtle and you'll have to cover your tracks better. Look, this Becker—you say he was director of the juvenile temporary secure home? Well there will be files at the Ministry for People's Education, so you can start there. If I were you I'd start by asking general questions about similar institutions, get them to bring a whole load of files to look through. Take your time, circle in, look at all the staff, starting from before Becker was working there-"

"And make it look like I'm not actually interested in Becker in particular? Erika, you're a genius!"

Karo

Before leaving for the Ministry for People's Education I gave Martin another ring, but still no answer. I didn't waste too much time on wondering where he might be—I had my own mission right now, and I was prepared: I had a plan and I had a pen.

I showed my RS pass at the main desk of the ministry, went down to the archive in the basement and asked for a Search Request Form. Feeling proud of myself for being so oblique I asked for staff lists for all the Special Homes, *Durchgangsheime* and Borstals in the districts of Berlin, Frankfurt and Potsdam. Under Reason For Search I put *restitution claims*. That sounded dry enough, I reckoned.

I had to wait for about ten minutes before the archivist creaked in, pushing a squealing trolley. She had about a thousand files, all boxed up in heavy, grey cartons. So much for being oblique, it was going to take me all day to find what I needed! I waited for the creaky lady to disappear again before getting a bottle of beer out of my rucksack. I hadn't even got the top off when I heard a clucking from behind me.

"Just what do you think you are doing, young lady? This is an archive, not a bar. Either you put that away or you leave!" She carried on rattling away about what the world's coming to and who'd have thought. I put the bloody bottle away, and opened the first box, and after a vicious stare the archivist crept away again. She'd probably gone to spy on me from her cubbyhole.

It took me a while to find the file for the *Durchgangsheim* here in Berlin, but the good news was that the archivist had been too lazy to sort out just the files I'd requested and had actually brought every single staff-related file, including the cadre files. So I found Becker and all his details in no time at all: Andreas Becker, deputy-director from October 1987 until the end of 1988, just over a year. On paper, he had impressive qualifications: study in Köthen, then awarded a doctorate by the College of Education in Potsdam. Later on he became a member of the Academy of Pedagogical Sciences and the Institution for Pedagogical Psychology.

A big fish, in other words.

I unclipped his photograph and slipped it into my pocket then made some notes about his qualifications and stuff. There was loads of boring stuff in there, like how he volunteered to help the police and the FDJ when he was a student, stuff like that, and I nearly didn't bother copying that down. In the end I decided to. There was no up-to-date address or telephone number, but it was still a good start.

I flicked through the other files for a bit, but I had what I needed. I stacked the archive boxes back on the trolley and left.

11:29
Martin

Most of Warschauer Platz is behind the boundary wall of the Narva lightbulb works. The little that remains open to the public lies between canyons of factory buildings and the derelict U-Bahn station. From down here I could see neither the capped brickwork of the nearby Oberbaum bridge nor Berlin's first high-rise building, the Narva Tower, just a few metres away. In fact, from down here I could see only sooty walls and the solitary figure of Steinlein halfway down the Platz. Instead of a greeting he pressed an envelope into my hand.

"Here's the money. Whatever information the source gives you, bring it straight back. Hide it well so it's not found at the border."

"Hello to you, too."

"This is not the time for jokes, Martin." Steinlein was looking around the whole time, keeping an eye on any passers-by. "I don't know what you're playing at, but walking out while we're in the middle of a conversation isn't something I take kindly to."

"Look, I'm sorry about last night-"

"When you get to your rendezvous wait for the source to come to you. Relax, don't pay too much attention to your surroundings. Let the source play it the way he wants to. If you get a chance to speak to him then tell him we need more information, that we can pay. We need anything he has on Kaminsky, anything at all. Got that?"

"He? You said *he*. Is the informant male?"

"Figure of speech, we don't know. Now get going. I'll be at the Stralau office from three o'clock, I'll wait for you there."

★

Under normal circumstances I would have been at the Prinzenstrasse baths in plenty of time, but as soon as I reached the border crossing at Oberbaum bridge I could tell that these weren't normal circumstances.

"Bit of a wait at the other end," the young border policeman told me as I passed his post at the Eastern end of the bridge.

"What's going on?" A queue snaked back towards us, there seemed to be some hold up at the gate in the Wall at the far end.

"West Berlin police are checking everybody's documents, they've taken some people away for questioning."

"Why? Who are they questioning?"

The guard shrugged, he didn't know and he didn't really care.

I remembered the police officers on the S-Bahn yesterday, the way one of them had been suspicious of my temporary *Ausweis*. Perhaps this wasn't the best day to head into West Berlin, but I didn't have any choice if I wanted to meet the source.

I joined the end of the queue, just a dozen or so people in front of me, so hopefully this wouldn't take too long.

But ten minutes later we were still no further. We stood under the midday sun, and I looked over the parapet at the river below, thinking about the swimming trunks in my shoulder bag. The grey water flowed past, ochre foam collecting by the banks.

"Did you come for the view or are you in the queue?" A Berlin voice behind me demanded.

I looked up, the line in front of me was moving again. Now there was just a couple of people between me and the Wall. We shuffled forwards, and finally I was through the gate and over the white line that marked the border. But we weren't finished with queueing, we were hemmed in by crowd control fences which led us round to the left where a couple of policemen stood. Behind them was a hut, I'd never noticed it before, but the grey paint that peeled from its wooden sides told me it had always been there.

The West Berlin police officers were carefully checking everyone's papers, just as they had done on the train. I held out my temporary *Ausweis*, it was taken off me and each page was carefully examined.

"Holger?" The policeman held my *Ausweis* up for his colleague to check, but Holger nodded.

"Bitte sehr. Der nächste!"

And that was it. I was through.

I hurried along the road towards the U-Bahn station, climbing the steps to the platform and jumping on the train just as the bell rang.

I looked at my watch, I was already late for my meeting.

12:57

Martin

I got off the U-Bahn at Prinzenstrasse and jogged through the traffic to the entrance of the swimming pool. Join the end of another queue, hand over my precious Westmarks, through the turnstile and I was in the open-air baths. I stood just inside, not sure where to go or what to do next. For the last few hours I'd been focussing on getting here on time. But here I was, half an hour late. No welcoming committee, nobody waiting, no-one holding a sign with my name on it.

Not knowing what else to do, I did the obvious. I changed into my trunks, left my clothes and bag in a locker and followed the path to the pools.

A group of Turkish lads were kicking a football around a grassy area dotted with trees, but most people were either in the water or sunbathing. I found a bit of shade and sat down, looking at the hundreds of people, wondering whether the source was among them, watching me. I put my straw hat on the grass and discreetly slipped the envelope of money under it.

I had my watch with me, and I checked my wrist often, marking each minute as it idled by. Part of me couldn't see the point in hanging around any longer, I'd arrived late and the source had probably long gone by the time I'd sat down on the grass. The only thing I was going to get here was heatstroke.

Ten minutes passed, then fifteen. How long should I wait?

Sometime after two o'clock I gave up. I'd been there for more than enough time for contact to be made, it clearly wasn't going to happen. I took another look around, trying to spot anyone by themselves, anyone looking shifty in any way, but could see only couples and families. Apart from me, nobody was by themselves.

It wasn't until I stood up that I noticed the plastic carrier bag next to my hat. It hadn't been there when I sat down, and it certainly wasn't mine—a bright red bag from the Kaisers supermarket chain. I looked around, but there was no-one nearby, no-one to whom it could belong. I picked up my hat, the envelope underneath was missing. My contact hadn't missed me, he'd just been discreet.

"Come with us."

The two men were waiting outside the changing rooms when I came out. They were police, that much was clear from their manner and their clothes—they weren't wearing uniforms, but they might as well have been. The only thing wrong was that they had spoken English, not German. I couldn't be totally sure I'd understood exactly what they'd said, but their purpose was clear.

"Who are you?" I managed in English.

"Come with us, all will be explained." The voice was polite, but the way the two men stepped closer to me left me in no doubt what I was expected to do.

13:21
Karo

After the dusty boredom of the archive I decided to drop in on Katrin on the way home. No biggie if she wasn't there, I just thought it would be nice to say hi.

I got some hassle off the West Berlin cop standing at the border crossing. It wasn't anything major, nothing I've not dealt with a million times before, but since when did they hassle us going *into* West Berlin? Anyway, it was all good in the end, because I bumped into Katrin in her tenement entryway just as I was coming back down the stairs. I'd already been up to her flat but there had been no answer, because here she was, walking in off the street.

"Karo, oh!"

"I was just passing ..."

"Yeah, sure. Nice surprise."

"It's fine if you're busy, y'know if you've got stuff to do ..."

Katrin took hold of my hand, the gesture timid—it was well cute,

448

and we went up the stairs to her flat. We went in and I curled up on her sofa, hoping she'd come and snuggle up with me, but she called through the door as she went into the kitchen.

"I'm making a pot of tea—want some?"

I followed her into the kitchen where she was standing by the kettle, staring into space.

I watched her for a minute before asking if she was OK.

Katrin started, as if she hadn't realised I was standing next to her, then turned to me, putting her hands on my hips and drawing me close. I lifted my head so she could kiss me but she was staring into space again, somewhere over my shoulder.

"What's up, Katrin?"

No answer.

"Is it about yesterday, about what we did? Because if-"

Katrin gave me a smile, it was a really nice smile, except it didn't quite reach her eyes. "Just got a lot on my mind, that's all. Everything's fine."

I wasn't sure what to do. I thought Katrin was happy about what had happened between us, I mean, it was lovely. We had fun, it felt good. Maybe it was because I ran off so early? Maybe I should have stayed longer?

"Because if this is about yesterday-"

Katrin stroked my head, the bit on the side where the hair is cut really short. "I like the spikiness," she said. "It tickles my hand."

I switched the kettle off and took her hands in mine, pulling her gently into the living room, towards the sofa. Our eyes locked and her smile came back, a real one this time. That amazing Katrin smile.

14:12

Martin

I've no idea where I was taken. I was in the car for quite a while, half an hour, probably longer, sandwiched in the back between the two men. It gave me some time to consider my position.

They knew my name. They looked like cops, they sounded like cops and wore their clothes like cops. But they weren't cops, not West Berlin cops. They were Brits or Amis, which meant intelligence services. Whatever was happening to me right now was because of the Kaisers bag.

But on the other hand there had been no attempt to take it off me yet, it was still in my satchel.

The men had refused to identify themselves, in fact, there had been no further interaction once they'd persuaded me to go along with them. I'd considered shouting, making a scene, hoping the crowd of West Berliners at the baths would notice, perhaps even try to help. But the men's use of English had thrown me, and frankly, I hadn't fancied my chances.

The car stopped and the two men got out. One held the door open.

"Mr. Grobe, this way please."

I followed the two men down a concrete path, between green lawns and low brick buildings. Going by the general shabbiness of the complex I decided my captors were British rather than American. I clutched my bag all the tighter and considered my situation. We were on a British military base, which I found preferable to a West Berlin police station—I was more optimistic that I wouldn't simply disappear here. But there were no guarantees.

"I demand to speak to Major Clarie," I said, hoping my liaison partner in British Defence Intelligence could intervene. But my guards didn't react to my demands, they just continued to herd me along the concrete path.

We entered one of the whitewashed buildings and in my agitation I tripped over the step, dropping my satchel and nearly falling to the floor. One of the guards rescued the bag but neither of them offered me a hand. Round a corner in the corridor then I was shoved into a room. I turned around as the metal door banged shut behind me.

Drab walls and a low ceiling pressed in upon me. Instead of a window there was a narrow sheet of metal up in a corner, a series of holes allowing air into my cell. A plastic mat lay on a concrete bed, and a bucket stood in the corner.

This wasn't so different from the cells the Stasi had kept me in. There was nothing I could do but wait. Wait and think.

I didn't want to outstay my welcome and left quite soon. I loved being with Katrin and I was kinda optimistic that the feeling was mutual. But a voice inside me was still telling me not too push too hard, too fast. I was going to give her a bit of space, I wasn't going to rush her. It was all going to be worth it.

You know that warm feeling you get when you think of a particular person and your stomach goes up and down as if it's the lift of the Television Tower? That's how it was for me that night. I was pushing my bike up Warschauer Strasse, literally miles away, thinking about nothing but Katrin, but Kaminsky brought me back down to earth sharpish. It wasn't literally him, just his fuckwit followers. They were marching down Frankfurter Allee, towards Alexanderplatz, holding a demo with their pathetic banners and torches. As well as the usual red flags they had all sorts of vomit-inducing slogans:

Stop the Asylum Flood!
Jobs for Germans!
Expel the Elite!
Real Democracy Now!

I mean, seriously, who believes this crap? How stupid do you have to be to fall for this shite?

But there was something like a thousand people on the march, and all of them eager to swallow Kaminsky's smooth turds of propaganda.

And the worst thing was the chanting: *Kaminsky Kaminsky Kaminsky*, like he was some Messiah, the answer to all our problems!

But then, just when I thought it couldn't get any worse, it did. I instinctively edged back behind the crowd of onlookers: what I was seeing shouldn't have been a shock, but hearing rumours, and reports on the telephone about what's happening somewhere like Weimar—that's not the same as seeing it on the streets of your home town.

A block of skinheads was bringing up the rear of the demo. Skinny stonewash jeans, green bomber jackets, shaven heads, the full works. Except they were wearing black, red and yellow armbands, and most of them were carrying the old GDR flag—the one that wasn't used any more, the one with the hammer and compass in the middle. They were waving them around and smirking at passers-by. Swaggering about, right arms jabbing the air, thinking they owned Berlin.

Made me want to vomit.

22:39

Karo

I was sitting on the floor, listening to a tape of Paranoia, the hardest music I had. Seeing the skins and Kaminsky's marchers together had really put a downer on my day, made me see everything in a negative way. Not only was I pissed off about the idiots and the fash, but I'd started obsessing about Katrin: had she been a bit off with me, was it all OK? What about that weird smile? I dunno, when I first got there it was like she was pulling away, which was strange. It was like I'd overstepped some mark. It was dead confusing and I didn't feel good, so I turned my music right up. Loud. Trying to drown out my thoughts.

But even over the noise I could hear shouting. It was coming from outside, or was it downstairs? Someone was banging on my door. Bourgeois fucks probably wanted me to turn the music down.

"Leave me alone!" I yelled, but whoever was at the door was too stupid to understand.

I threw the door open. "Just leave me alone, yeah?"

It was Sam from upstairs, and he looked well scared. "Karo, it's the fash!" He legged off down the hallway.

I looked out the window, and there they were, a mob of skins heading up Thaerstrasse. Coming for us.

I ran down the stairs after Sam. Housemates were at the front door, pushing whatever they could find against it: beds, cupboards, bits of wood. I looked in the ground floor flat, the shutters had been let down, and mattresses were being pushed against the windows. Into the kitchen, Schimmel was there, on the CB, trying to get a response.

"Thaeri, this is Thaeri. We need help. Fascist attack! Help! Is anyone there? Anyone?"

Shit, no-one was monitoring the radios. We thought we'd dealt with the fash, we'd relaxed—and now we were going to pay the price.

"Help! This is Thaeri—anyone? Please!"

Schimmel was sweating, his eyes were wide open and he was frantically twisting knobs.

"Help! Fash attack! Help! This is Thaeri, anyone receiving?"

There was a stir, a voice hissing over the little speaker. That wasn't the main Friedrichshain station at the *Schreina*, it was from further away, maybe it wasn't even meant for us.

Schimmel calmed down a bit when he heard the voice, he fiddled with some dials, still talking into the mike. "Thaeri, this is Thaeri. Help, we need help, over."

"Kastanien, this is Kastanien. Thaeri do you read?"

Kastanien? That was all the way up in Prenzlauer Berg. The signal was indistinct, crackling and popping, but after Schimmel's fiddling we could just about make it out.

"Kastanien this is Thaeri. We read you. Fascist attack. Friedrichshain station not responding. Can you help? Over."

"Already on our way, hold tight!"

"Shit, Schimmel,why isn't anyone monitoring our station?"

The first stones were already hitting the house, from the kitchen we could hear them rattling off the shutters, the glass splintering behind the mattresses.

"Prenzlauer Berg will be here soon, and they'll wake Friedrichshain up. I'll keep trying."

I left Schimmel at the radio and ran back to the front of the building. In the hall, there was a stream of people heading up the stairs, carrying crates and buckets of bottles, coal, cobblestones, anything they could lay their hands on.

"C'mon Karo, let's show the pricks what we're made of!"

We ran up the stairs: four landings, then a ladder to the roof. Five storeys below us about fifty skins were bunched up in front of our house. They had some kind of battering ram with them and were trying to break the door down.

"Fuck, there's more!" Sam was pointing at another bunch of skins that were marching up the road. They were carrying black, red and yellow flags with the hammer and compass in the centre.

Kaminsky's gang.

DAY 5
Thursday
16th June 1994

We've all heard the news today, we know about the long queues on the border, the strict controls by the West Berlin and West German authorities. We've heard the West German Chancellor appeal for calm, and we've heard their excuses for closing the inner-German border.

They say they need to ensure the integrity of their borders. They talk about civil unrest in the GDR.

This is the talk of diplomats.

I am not a diplomat. I see a spade, I call it a spade; you know where you are with me.

So when I see our country in crisis, when I see our country brought to its knees by an incompetent leadership, I point the finger.

I point the finger at our weak government.

I point the finger at the unelected, anti-democratic Round Tables led by Hanna Krause. I point the finger at the saboteurs, the Round Tables interfering in the day to day running of our country.

I point my finger and I say: enough!

10:37

Karo

It wasn't too bad. Not too much damage, thanks to the other squatters. They'd turned up just after Kaminsky's mob, coming from the other end of the street. The skins had taken one look and legged it. Sad fucks.

But at the meeting in the kitchen the next morning people were well pissed off. They were looking for someone to blame.

"It's your fault they targeted us!"

Everyone was staring at me. I didn't know if what they said was true or not, but what I did know was that some dick had sprayed *Republikschutz = Stasi pigs* on our door. And I was the only one who had anything to do with the RS.

"It's not my fault! They probably came for us because we're that bit further away from the other squats!"

"Yeah, well, they may be the fucking fash, but maybe they're right for once!"

"What the fuck? What are you talking about? Have you got any fucking idea what we do at RS? It's nothing like-"

"No better than the cops. You need to get your priorities straight, Karo."

"You know what, fuck the lot of you! At least I'm trying to do something for the revolution, not just sitting around feeling radical because I smoke spliff and drink beer all day!"

Fuck their stupid meeting, fuck their stupid collective house. I'd had enough. I went to my room and stuffed some clothes into a rucksack. No idea where I was going but I definitely wasn't going to stay here with these pseudo-punks.

When I picked up my bag and turned to the door Schimmel was there.

"Don't go, Karo. They're just scared, they don't mean it."

"Yeah well, nobody talks to me like that. Fuck the lot of them!"

"Karo, I've got to talk to you. About Becker."

I didn't say anything, just waited for Schimmel to say what he had to say.

"Look, Karo, I really appreciate it, what you're doing. But ..."

"What? Just say it, Schimmel!"

"It's ... it's my problem. I know why you've done it, but can you just leave it? It's me, I'm the one who's got to deal with it."

"You think I'm interfering? Is that it?"

I pushed past Schimmel and left the *Thaeri*. It'd been my home for nearly five years and now I was going. Fucking great week this was turning out to be!

★

I guess I wasn't that much different from all my housemates. I was pissed off and scared and I wanted to take it out on someone. When I left *Thaeri* I went round to the *Schreina* bar.

Antifa Bert was there, as I'd expected, but the door was locked and I had to knock to be let in. When Bert opened up I was fair, I didn't lay into him immediately. I gave him a chance.

"Hi Bert. Just wondering, who was monitoring the CB last night?"

At least he had enough self-awareness to look embarrassed.

"Karo, look, I'm sorry, I had to go out—it was just for a few minutes." That was a first, I'd never heard Bert apologise to anyone for anything. But this time he'd fucked up. Big time.

"So you heard about what happened then? Didn't see you coming to help."

"Someone had to stay here, keep an eye on the radios, just in case, you know ..."

"And wasn't it you who said we could stop monitoring the radios? We don't need to worry about the skins any more, you said, because your friend Kaminsky's tamed them. Well guess what—a load of Kaminsky's lads were there last night!"

"No, can't be. That wouldn't have happened. Couldn't have been them, someone else, stirring up trouble-"

"Fuck's sake, Bert, I saw the same fucking mob at Kaminsky's demo earlier on!"

He was still shaking his head, didn't want to believe it.

"You need to get your priorities straight, Bert." I admit I stole that line from my housemates. *Ex*-housemates. "Because if you don't sort yourself out then I for one won't want to work with you!"

"Fuck you, Karo, you sanctimonious shit! At least I'm not working for the cops!"

12:01

Karo

After the shit morning I'd just had I jumped at the chance of meeting up with Katrin—she was exactly the person I needed right then. She'd left a message for me at work, saying she could miss a lecture, did we want to meet up? It was the first time she'd suggested we do something—until now it had been me doing all the running.

"I'm so glad you're here," I told her.

We were lying on the grass in Treptower Park, Katrin's t-shirt had ridden up, leaving her belly bare to the sunlight. Her skin was literally glowing and all I wanted to do was snuggle up to her, kiss that golden tummy.

"No worries. I heard about the new border controls and decided I should come over. It's easier for me to cross the Wall—they're not hassling Westerners."

"Are you a *Wessi* now?" I'd aimed for teasing, but Katrin just shrugged and turned her head to one side. I tried a different tone: "I'm glad you made a bit of time for us."

"Well don't get used to it, It's not often I have cancelled lectures," Katrin mumbled.

"But I *want* to get used to this!" My hand edged up Katrin's flank.

Somehow that didn't please her—she flinched, just a teeny bit, but I could feel it.

"What's up?"

Katrin was now sitting up, she was looking off into the distance, her hair curtaining her face. "It's just, well, you know I don't have much time. I need to get a move on with my studies, I have to fit in a few more seminars ..."

"That's OK, I can work around that. Whenever you want me-"

"Karo," Katrin turned to look at me. She was using a serious voice, her face told me she was determined to say whatever it was she had to say. "Look, I don't think, you know, at the moment ..."

"You don't want to see me any more? Is that was this is?"

"Oh, Karo, don't go off on one, I'm just trying to-"

"I'm not going off on one!"

There was no response. I was glaring around the park, but still watching her out of the corner of my eye. She was picking random pieces of grass and stripping them, looking worried. My mind was churning, trying to come up with explanations for her behaviour.

"You said you'd be there, that you'd be there for me!"

"Karo, I am! I'm right here."

"It doesn't feel like it at the moment, it feels like you're saying you don't want to see me any more-"

"I'm just saying I think we should take this a bit more slowly."

I didn't answer, just grabbed my stuff and headed off.

"Karo, wait!"

But I didn't wait, Katrin had made clear what she wanted, and it wasn't me.

10:39
Martin

I don't know what time it was when they came, so little light filtered through the holes in the steel window that I couldn't say whether it was still early or already midday.

The door banged open to reveal two men. I don't think they were the same ones as before, but they could have been: same build, same clothing, same silence. One had an unlit cigarette in his hand.

"Can I have some water?"

They didn't answer, just stood by the door, one to either side of the frame. I got the hint and walked out of the cell, following one of the men down the corridor while the other brought up the rear.

I was ushered into a room. This one had a window, a table and two chairs. I sat myself on one of the chairs, turning to ask again for water. But the men had gone and the door was shut.

This place also felt familiar, it stood in for all the interrogation rooms I've ever been in. I knew the drill. They'd keep me waiting here for a while, then someone would come in, probably holding a cup of tea or some other beverage, and they'd be only too willing to get me a drink, but first a quick chat ...

Even though I knew how it worked I couldn't stop thinking about my dry throat. They'd kept me in a hot cell overnight and not given me anything to drink. My head was throbbing, as bad as any hangover. I sucked my teeth, trying to muster some saliva but nothing came.

The door opened again and a soldier appeared. British Army fatigues. Some kind of junior officer, just the one set of pips.

"Good morning, my name is Sanders." He shook my hand and gave me an absent smile.

"I'd like some water." We were speaking German, which made me

458

feel a little more confident.

"What? Oh, of course. Certainly."

The captain set a pile of files down, then went back to the door. He opened it a fraction and, in English, ordered a bottle of water.

"Now where were we?" The officer sat down opposite me and busied himself with looking through his files. He had a pair of half-moon glasses perched on the end of his nose, he was squinting through them as he turned the pages.

"I'm not going to answer any questions until you give me something to drink."

He looked up, his wide eyebrows raised, making his forehead crinkle.

"You've kept me in a cell overnight with nothing to drink, and you haven't told me why I'm being held."

"I say, old chap, we can't have that! But, rest assured, the water is on its way. And when we're done here I'll find out who's responsible for this fiasco. You have my word on that."

"If it's all the same to you, I'd rather wait until the water gets here."

"Gosh, I'm awfully sorry about all of this. I quite understand your position, yes." Sanders closed the files, placing his glasses on top and clasping his hands in front of his belly, making him look just like a pastor at confirmation classes.

"I can only apologise, Mr ... er ..." Sanders moved his glasses and had a quick look at the first page of file in front of him. He was very quick about it, too quick, as if the files were empty. "I'm terribly sorry, I don't know your name."

"Grobe," I told him. "It says so in my *Ausweis*, which is in the bag you took off me yesterday."

"Well, Herr Grobe, there seems to have been some mix up, and if it were down to me I'd order you a taxi right away. Unfortunately for us, sir, once the army gets hold of you then there's all sorts of paperwork to wade through ... As I said, I can only apologise."

"So why are you holding me?"

"Well, yes, that's one of the things we need to get to the bottom of. I'm afraid I'll need your assistance in that matter. Just a few straightforward questions: what you're doing here in West Berlin, what exactly happened at the Prinzenbad, you know the kind of thing."

"I've already told you: not until I get some water."

Sanders' eyes flickered over my face.

"And once you get your glass of water, will you talk to us?"

I didn't bother answering, I put all my energy into staring back at this army officer.

He slipped a hand under the table, he made it look fairly natural, the way he slid his palm along the edge of the wood. But I was familiar with the gesture. A button had been pressed.

The door opened, and one of the guards came in. He set a bottle of water and a glass down in front of me.

"There we go," Sanders was wittering on in the background.

I reached for the water, already anticipating the hiss as I twisted the cap, the beads of carbon dioxide swimming up to the surface, the liquid pouring over my tongue, loosening my tight throat. Just as my hand closed around the bottle it was swiped out of my grasp. It skidded across the table, toppling over the edge and smashing on the floor.

I looked at the guard who had knocked the bottle, but he was standing to attention. Sanders moved towards the door.

"All yours, Sergeant," he said.

Sanders left the room and the sergeant took his seat. He leaned back, one hand stroking a tidy moustache under a nose that hooked to the right. Behind me I could feel the presence of another soldier.

"What were you doing in Kreuzberg yesterday?"

I didn't answer. In these situations it's much easier to keep absolutely quiet than try to stick to some kind of formula like 'no comment'. Once you open your mouth it's hard to shut it again—much better to keep it shut in the first place. It's something I should have remembered while Sanders was still here.

"Hard guy, are we? Well if you're that hard then you'll have heard about the Allied Occupation Rights. We're in Berlin, which is still under the administration of the Four Powers. And you Germans," the sergeant leaned in, his fingers dimpling the files left behind by Sanders, his face moving towards mine. "You Germans have no rights. Not a sodding one. We can keep you here for as long as we want, we can give you water or tea or bloody whisky if we choose. Or we can decide you get nothing. Entirely up to us." A smirk crept towards his moustache. "You. Have. No. Sodding. Rights. Capito?"

The whole charade wasn't impressing me. I'd been through worse. In the old days it was the Stasi, a few months ago the skinheads. The Stasi and the skins had told me they weren't ever going to let me go either, yet somehow I'd got through it all and out the other end.

I just wished he'd shut up and give me something to drink.

12:37

Karo

I wanted to go home, but I didn't have a home to go to. A small but loud part of me had hoped I could move in with Katrin, even though the idea was absurd. Even if she'd wanted me the border controls were too unpredictable to be commuting across the Wall every day.

But I couldn't stay here in the park surrounded by happy people doing happy people things in the sun. And I didn't want to cycle around aimlessly. I didn't want to do anything, I just wanted Katrin, but Katrin had rejected me, despite all her promises, despite the way I'd opened up to her, something I've never done with anyone else.

In the end I decided to go and see Martin, he was easy company and he was close to Katrin. It was as if by being with Martin I could somehow still be near Katrin, even though I knew it would hurt.

Romantic bullshit, I know, but that's what I was feeling right then.

So I went over to Martin's, and he wasn't there. I stood outside his door, fighting back tears, wondering what to do. I grabbed the pencil and the pad of paper that hung off his doorframe and wrote "FUCK YOU!!!!"

I ended up going back to the RS offices. There was nowhere else to go. I just sat in the stuffy office, drinking coffee, wondering what to do.

It didn't take long for Erika to come nosing round.

"Laura was looking for you before, but you'd gone out-"

"Yeah, had other stuff on, is that alright with you?"

Erika came in, holding both her hands up, palms out.

"I was just making conversation," she said.

"Yeah, well, next time you could try *Hi!* or even *How are you?*"

"So, Karo, *how are you?*"

I was blinking back tears by now and Erika came bustling over, she put her arms around me. It was what I needed, but it didn't help either because now I really was crying.

I told her about the fash attack last night, and the meeting at the *Thaeri* this morning. I didn't tell her about Schimmel giving me the brush off, or about breaking up with Katrin, if you can even call it breaking up because we never even had time to properly get together in the first place but now it was over before she'd even given us a chance ...

When the crying jag slowed Erika got up and made me another coffee.

"What about a pastry, or a bit of cake? I can pop down to the bakery-"

I shook my head. Coffee was enough right now.

"Where are you going to stay?"

"Dunno. I could go to one of the other squats, I suppose. But I need my own space, need a bit of time away from all that."

Erika nodded, cupping her hands around her coffee like you do on a cold day. There was a long silence.

"Look, Karo, you won't exactly have your own space, but if you want, then you can stay at mine for a bit. You'll be on the couch and-" She didn't manage to finish because I was giving her a big, tight hug.

11:30

Martin

The sergeant kept on and on at me. The same questions, again and again. *Why did you come to West Berlin? What were you doing yesterday? Who are you? Who did you meet at the swimming baths?*

I concentrated on the scarred the edge of the worn table, not even looking up when my interrogator slammed his palms down in front of me. *Don't say anything, concentrate on that mark on the table.* Even without the sergeant shouting in my ear I would have found it hard to concentrate, the dehydration was making me feel light-headed.

My interrogator was now marching around the room, moving a

little closer to me with every circuit. At first, it was a whisper of air when he passed, now his foot caught my chair leg every circuit or so, sending a jolt through my body. Soon his hand would glance off my shoulder, or the back of my head. Casual, definitely-not-on-purpose, but calculated to crack my composure.

Not that I was composed. My tongue filled my mouth, my brain was pushing against the inside of my skull, and my eyes were no longer able to focus on the table.

"Clarie." It was involuntary, like a prayer uttered at the moment of death.

My interrogator stopped his pacing. The silence was louder than all the shouting, the smacking of the table, the stomping around.

"What?"

I didn't answer. I wasn't even sure about what I'd just said, whether I'd even said it aloud.

The sergeant consulted his watch then went back to his side of the table, his hands sliding along the edge of the wood until his fingers caught on the button.

The liquid washed into my mouth, the bubbles of carbon-dioxide burning my cracked tongue. I drained the glass, the thirst smothering my body's need to breathe. The glass landed back on the table, my grip easing away, my chest heaving as my lungs sucked in air.

"*Noch eins.*"

The guard poured more water into the glass, watching impassively as I drank. Shorter sips this time, allowing the liquid to trickle into every corner of my mouth before it slid down my raw throat.

"Martin!" Clarie's voice. I didn't look up, still concentrating on the water. "Get out, you moron! And leave the bloody bottle where it is."

The guard scuttled off and Major Clarie set the bottle of water back down on the table, next to me.

"I came as soon as I heard, how long have these buffoons had you in their tawdry mitts? Appalling, absolutely appalling, I can't apologise enough."

"More water."

Clarie opened the door. "Water, get some more water. Bring a crate of the damned stuff. And tea!"

I was feeling more human now, my head still throbbed, but my tongue was already shrinking to its normal size. I could only put Clarie off for a few more minutes, I had to use what time I had to get some answers ready.

"Right, let's get all this ironed out." Clarie was speaking his own brand of German: plum-in-the-throat accent, strange idioms: *Das werden wir gleich ausgebügelt kriegen.*

A crate of water bottles arrived, and a pot of tea with two cups and saucers, sugar and milk. How did they brew tea so quickly? Did they have it on tap, like the Russians with their samovars?

Clarie ignored the soldier who brought the drinks, using the time to look me over.

"Play mother, shall I?" He'd lost me: *Mutter spielen*? What was he talking about?

"Martin, you must accept my apologies," he said as he poured tea into the cups. "Seems to have been a bit of a mix up, actually."

"If you wanted to talk then all you had to do was give me a ring." I was feeling safer now, I allowed myself some indignation.

"Yes, well, it's a little more delicate than that, as I'm sure you'll appreciate. Sugar? Yes, you'll take a bit of sugar." I watched the major stir three teaspoons into my tea, followed by milk. "You see, your reasons for being at that swimming pool, not entirely above board, what?"

My mind went back to the Kaisers bag the source had been left by my side. Why would the Brits be interested in it?

"You see, we were expecting someone else. My men couldn't show you their accreditation because of the Americans. We can't afford to upset the Cousins, can we now?" Kreuzberg is in the American zone, so presumably Major Clarie had no business kidnapping East Germans there.

"So what do you want?"

"A person of interest. We were actually following him—not you. Although I must say we seem to have lost track of his-nibs, anyway, it seems his-nibs made a pass at you in the baths. Naturally that aroused the curiosity of my men. Good men, by the way, the best. A tad enthusiastic, now and again." Clarie took a sip of his tea. "Rather unfortunate that no-one realised it was you we had in the bag, so to say." Clarie chuckled but continued talking when I didn't join in. "You really should have asked for me earlier, could have had this all sorted out in a jiffy."

"What's your interest?"

"Same as yours, I imagine." Clarie was looking over the rim of his teacup. "Your contact—I'm told he's a good pal of Dr. Kaminsky."

They gave me my bag back and the use of a driver. I couldn't tell whether my driver was one of the goons who had arrested me, he looked similar, but didn't they all?

We drove for quite a while in the unmarked car, heading first back to Kreuzberg, then taking one of the main roads that led out of Hermannplatz. After that I was in parts of Berlin I'd never seen. I asked which Border Crossing Point I was being taken to.

"Sonnenallee, sir. Much quieter than the border posts in the city centre. Easier to make sure you won't be checked so thoroughly there."

Not being thoroughly checked sounded good to me, I'd rather avoid the attentions of the West Berlin police.

Traffic had thinned by now, other than a row of double-decker yellow buses we were the only vehicle on the road. We turned off onto a side street and parked outside some concrete flats that would have looked at home on either side of the Wall.

"Just go through the checkpoint, after that it's another three hundred metres to the bus stop. Good luck, sir."

I got out of the car, and looked back at the main road we'd just turned off. A long, brown hut presumably housed West Berlin customs and police. In front of that, next to a gap in the Wall, a solitary West Berlin policeman leaned on a railing. A watchtower presided over the crossing point.

I walked up to the cop, trying to look natural, trying not to think of the border controls on the S-Bahn last Tuesday.

The policeman had straightened up at my approach, moving away from the railing and into the middle of the road.

"*Ihren Ausweis, bitte.*"

I handed over my papers, and the cop flicked through them, not really paying attention.

"Going home?" he asked.

I wasn't sure whether he was trying to make small talk, or whether the question was the prelude for yet another interrogation. Either way, I was too nervous to answer, so I nodded.

The policeman handed my papers back to me and waved me on. A few paces later, I was through the gap in the Wall, and the East Berlin border guard was giving me a lazy salute. But I hadn't quite made it yet—this was one of the original crossing points, built before the Wall opened up: I had to pass through five gates and walls in the compound. Cars that were making the journey from East to West had a two-hundred metre slalom to negotiate, zig-zagging around bollards and staggered openings between intermediary walls.

There was no challenge as I passed the final barracks, the final watchtower and the final gate.

I was home. I was back in East Berlin.

13:10

Karo

I left soon after that cup of coffee with Erika. There was no point being in the office, and I'd decided to go round to Martin's again: I felt guilty about that nasty note I'd left. It hadn't been fair—it wasn't his fault that he'd not been at home when I needed him. I shouldn't take my shit out on him.

When I got to Martin's I checked the notebook. The page I'd written on had been torn out, but I could still trace the words FUCK YOU!!!! scored into the surface of the next sheet. I pressed Martin's bell, wondering how he'd react when he saw me.

I got a bit of a shock when he opened up. He looked like shit. His clothes were crumpled and there was a gross, sour smell coming off him.

"Karo."

"Well don't sound sooo pleased to see me!" Then again, considering the note I'd left him earlier ... I took a step back, both in my head and in real life. "I'm sorry about the note-"

"What do you want?" Martin was still standing in the doorway, he hadn't invited me in.

466

"You OK, Martin? You look even worse than last time I saw you."

"Bit tired, Karo. Maybe another time?"

"If there's anything you need …"

"I'll let you know." Martin shut the door.

OK, I got it, Martin was pissed off with me because I'd left him a note saying *fuck you*. Or was there something else? I mean, how many times have I left him messages this last week, and did he ever get back to me? What was going on? Had he heard about my trip to the Party archives? Or about me and Katrin?

Whatever was bothering Martin, he didn't look good. He looked like he'd been sleeping in his clothes, he smelled like he hadn't washed for days, and I definitely got a whiff of schnapps on his breath.

I wasn't the only one needing a bit of help.

14:07

Martin

After I got rid of Karo I had a shower and thought about going to bed for a bit, catch up on some sleep. But I knew I'd lie there, wondering what was in that Kaisers carrier bag. I still hadn't looked, until now I hadn't even had the energy to be curious, but maybe it was time to open up the bag, see if there was anything useful.

When I got to the Stralau office I spread the contents of the plastic bag over my desk. Lots of documents to do with Kaminsky's rally on Saturday: situation reports, summaries, assessments, developmental reports, departmental reports, information for the ministerial committee, for *Volkspolizei* departmental heads. I had a pile of paper about ten centimetres high, all recording concerns, worries, fears for Kaminsky's well-being on the day, along with plans of how to keep him safe. I had no way of knowing if this was the usual bureaucratic headless-chicken act, whether this level of concern was normal or represented a heightened state of alert. I needed Steinlein's expertise.

In the absence of my partner I tried to summarise for myself what I had here. A collection of police reports, all concentrating on Kaminsky and his big rally. Public order planning, plans for the deployment of the Red Cross, public transport logistics and all the other things that need to be organised for a mass mobilisation.

Other documents focussed on assessing and providing for potential risks to the safety of the speakers before, during and after the rally.

Looking at the circulation lists attached to the front of these documents I could see that most of them had also been distributed to Kaminsky's office. Other names that came up regularly were the President of the *Volkspolizei*, the police minister, the Committee of the Ministry of Internal Affairs, and Captain Neumann of Lichtenberg K1.

But what I found most significant was the fact that our source had provided only files relating to the rally in Treptower Park. Why no information on other appearances on Kaminsky's barnstorming tour? He'd been travelling the country, holding rallies and demonstrations regularly. This rally in Treptower Park was planned to be the biggest one, marking the end of Kaminsky's first stage of campaigning before the *Volkskammer* elections, but that didn't explain why I'd only been given the files for this one event.

Our source was telling us that the assassination attempt on Kaminsky would happen in just two days.

15:14
Martin

I heard the front door slam shut, followed by Steinlein's cane drumming up the stairs.

"Where were you? I waited all night!" He stood in the doorway, jaw clenched, hands on hips, playing the disciplinarian father.

I held out a few sheets from the papers I'd brought back from West Berlin and Steinlein closed in for a look. Jamming his cane under his elbow, he took the proffered sheets. "What happened?"

"British intelligence pulled me in. Kept me overnight."

"British intelligence?" Steinlein's eyes were buried deep below his brow, darkness directed at me. "What did you tell them?"

"They were following the person who had this bag," I gestured to the carrier bag, still half full of reports. "When he passed it to me the Brits decided they'd like a chat."

"What did you tell them? Did they see these?" Steinlein's cane swung into the pile of papers, flattening them against the desk.

"A few hours of interrogation. Nothing too bad, just the kind of thing you've probably done yourself a few times. I didn't tell them anything."

"And the files?"

"Of course they've looked at the bloody files, what do you think?"

"You should have stopped them!" Steinlein's cane swooped again and the papers flitted through the air, spilling over the floor.

I left him to his tantrum and went over to the kitchen-niche. While the water was boiling I watched Steinlein awkwardly stoop down, using the head of his cane to gather in the loose leaves.

"Is this what the source gave you? This is dynamite!" Steinlein had regained a measure of his former calm, but he was still gripping the walking stick so tightly that his knuckles were white. "What did he say? Did he tell you anything useful?"

"He didn't say anything—I didn't see him."

Steinlein was hardly listening, he was sitting at the desk now, carefully turning over each sheet, scanning the text as he went. "This is an impressive haul."

"Any theories on how he managed to get hold of these files?"

"Heaven knows, but it's pretty extensive." Steinlein pushed his chair back and stretched, a sheet of paper in one hand. "Look, there's another note from our source: *Use Tacheles dead drop to contact.* At least now we know how to get hold of him."

I looked at the writing Steinlein had found—same as last time, vague pencil marks between the lines of a report. How did Steinlein find these messages?

"I've got some more good news," he said, his voice softening still further, the ghost of a smile beginning to tease his lips. "The officer responsible for securing the outer perimeter of Kaminsky's next rally has fallen ill, I'm taking over his squad. I'll be on the inside, I'll have access to collateral and can corroborate at least some of this material. Might even give us a clue who our informant is."

"Why are you a cop?"

Steinlein stopped rustling through the reports, the sudden change of subject confusing him.

"What do you mean?"

"Just curious. I still don't understand why you're doing all this." I looked around the office, taking in the scope of the investigation that Steinlein had kicked off. But it was really the same question that I had asked the other night: was Steinlein doing this for Kaminsky, or because preventing crime was his job?

"I told you, I'm a police officer. This is what I do."

"But why?"

Steinlein took a roll of parchment paper from his bag and limped over to the wall. He unrolled the sheet, tacking the upper corners to the wall. It was a blueprint of the area around the Soviet War Memorial in Treptower Park.

I waited patiently as he smoothed the plans out and tacked a bottom corner down. Eventually he spoke, his back still turned to me.

"My father was a builder, he headed up the construction and maintenance brigade on an LPG farm in the Uckermark. The whole brigade had this racket going, they'd steal building materials and sell it on to people building their *Datsche* and weekend cottages."

"And that bothered you?"

"At home he was a real stickler for discipline. He'd get drunk every Saturday night then come home and beat me and my brother for the week's transgressions. Once he beat us for scrumping apples from a neighbour's tree. Kids are sensitive to hypocrisy and injustice, and when he beat me that time it was like a switch had flicked. I hit him back." Steinlein pushed the last drawing pin in.

"And that's why you became a cop?"

"I told the Party Organisation at the farm about my father's activities." Steinlein took a step back to admire his handiwork. "Nothing happened—he was too well-connected. There might have been an internal Party disciplinary hearing, but if so then nothing came of it. It's no surprise the Party collapsed in 1989; it was high time for change. Internal renewal.

"Anyway, when I informed on my father he made me leave home. I signed up for three years in the army, after that: officer career path in the *Volkspolizei*."

Steinlein limped back to the desk and sat down. He didn't say anything else, just concentrated on his file.

★

We were looking through the paperwork again, comparing notes. It bothered me that we didn't know who the source was.

"The person who gave me this bag is connected to Kaminsky. That's why British Defence Intelligence were interested in him." My words made Steinlein pause, his brow was furrowed, the eyes receding again under his stern brow. "I've been thinking about it all afternoon, I reckon our source-"

"Why are British intelligence interested in Kaminsky?" he interrupted.

"Clarie said he has to take a professional interest in what happens in East Berlin." I answered. "Called it his back-yard. Said it's his job to know if anyone's rocking the boat, and if so, how hard."

Steinlein pulled out a pack of f6 cigarettes and lit one, looking up at the ceiling as he exhaled the first puff. "How does he know our source is connected to Kaminsky?"

"He didn't say. But who is our source? Is Clarie right about the Kaminsky connection? We should check out Kaminsky's staff and supporters—it's someone with access to the Stasi archives, that'll help narrow it down-"

"There's not enough time for all that." Steinlein waved a hand, dismissing the suggestion. "The rally is on Saturday and there are hundreds of people on his personal staff alone. Add all the Party apparatchiks he might be connected to ... What about your British major? Why don't we just ask him?"

"Clarie knows, but he won't tell me, not unless we can trade something, some intelligence he'd be interested in. That's the way he works."

Steinlein passed me the pack of cigarettes and his lighter.

"We haven't got anything for your Englishman, have we?" he asked while tapping the tip of his cigarette against the side of an aluminium ashtray. "Can we not persuade him it's in his interest to help us?"

Steinlein's questions had given me a new idea: Dmitri. "I could ask my FSK liaison. If Captain Pozdniakov knows anything he'll tell us."

"It's like talking to a brick wall!" Steinlein stabbed out his cigarette. "How many times do I have to say it? We can't let anyone know what we're doing here. No-one!"

"I don't see the problem, if Clarie knows about it then surely we can talk to the Friends-"

"The Friends? Talking to the Friends went out of fashion with *Perestroika*! We can't trust the Russians, they're too close to the Party!" Steinlein went to the window, leaning his forehead against the glass. "There's no way you're talking to your Russian. There's too much at stake, and that's final!"

16:48
Martin

As I entered the office, Dmitri hastily shut the file on his desk, turning it over so the front cover wasn't visible. He looked up and a smile split his face when he saw it was me.

"Martin Ottovich! Good, good that you are here my friend—you are looking better. Recovering from your adventures, I am glad to see."

Except I wasn't looking better, I knew that. I was knackered and strung out. Dmitri came out from behind his desk and gave me a slap on the shoulder. Turning to a filing cabinet he retrieved a bottle of vodka and two glasses.

Before he could place the glasses on his desk there was a knock and his assistant came halfway into the room, speaking in a low voice, speaking in Russian.

Dmitri turned to me, his face grave. "My friend, do you know you were followed here?" He saw my reaction and asked. "What is your reason to visit today?"

"Kaminsky. We were wondering whether you-"

Dmitri put the glasses and bottle down then reached for the door handle. "Martin, leave at once. If anyone asks, say you came to visit me, to drink a toast for old time's sake. Tell them I was not here when you came. So you leave without seeing me." The Russian officer opened the door wide, the remarkable force of his personality was distilled into that one action, impelling me into the corridor. "1800 hours. Be at the Fauler See in Weissensee—you know it? There's a bench at the east side of the lake. Wait no more than fifteen minutes. Now go!"

My watch told me it was exactly six. I was on the bench in the woods that surround the stagnant puddle they call the Fauler See. There was nobody around, nothing to be heard in the still heat of the afternoon. For ten minutes I watched the vague reflections of the still reeds on the scummy water. It was hard not to doze off in the sharp scent of the pines.

I heard wheezing and the rustle of dederon long before the old man stumbled into view, leaning heavily on a crutch. He slumped down next to me, and, still gasping for breath, pushed a filterless cigarette between his lips. He lit up and inhaled deeply.

I wondered whether the old man had been sent by Dmitri. If he wasn't one of Dmitri's then I was in trouble—he looked like a talker and while he was here my contact wouldn't approach. But I was wrong, the man sitting next to me didn't say a word, just sucked heavily on his cigarette. When his cigarette was exhausted, he pulled out another and lit up, dropping the packet on the bench between us as he began to cough. He hawked up a mouthful of tanned phlegm, spitting onto the marshy ground, and in the same moment flicked the packet of cigarettes towards me. Without thinking, I placed my hand over it as the smoker got up. He nodded to me and dragged himself off down the path, cigarette dangling from his lips.

I waited until he was out of sight before leaving the bench. It was now a quarter past six, I'd been here for exactly fifteen minutes.

The path meandered around trees and bushes and I waited until I was between two bends before checking the cigarette packet. It had been emptied of cigarettes, but nestling between lining and carton was a cigarette paper, the kind used for rolling tobacco. I took it out and unfolded it, squinting to read the cramped handwriting.

70 → Zingsterstr
Alight Ribnitzer Str
S-Bahn 1st carriage → H-schönh
Steps to bridge
58, 2nd carriage → M-E-Platz

I headed out of the woods, back into the baked fetor of civilisation, jogging the last few metres to meet the tram that was already shuffling around the corner.

I boarded and stamped my ticket, casting an eye over the other passengers. The smoker had passed me a dry cleaning list, a zig-zag course through Berlin that would hopefully show up any tail I might have. Dmitri would have one of his spooks shadowing me, keeping an eye out for any other followers—all I had to do was play the game, work through the list until I got to the menswear department of the Centrum store on Alexanderplatz.

Fifteen minutes later I got off and walked down the canyon of new-build flats, using plate glass shop windows and the side mirrors of parked cars to keep an eye on anyone coming up behind. The few people who had got off the tram with me were quickly swallowed up in the concrete labyrinth of Hohenschönhausen.

Even though I knew Dmitri would have people watching my back I was sensitive to my surroundings. As I stopped to buy an unnecessary ticket at the station, a man in a white shirt with a sparse purple paisley pattern, dark blue corduroy trousers and straw hat walked past me. I pushed my 20 Pfennig coin into the machine and watched the man go up the steps to the platform, unable to shake a feeling of familiarity.

I took my ticket and followed the man up to the platform. He was walking up and down, a lit cigarette cupped in his hand.

The train whined in and I got in the first carriage. The man in the paisley shirt flipped his cigarette into the gap between train and platform edge and entered through the same door. Our eyes met as he looked around for a seat, and instead of glancing away I held his eyes for the half-second or so before he moved his gaze.

I kept Paisley Shirt in my sights, watching his reflection in the window, wondering whether he'd try to stop me leaving the train. I could feel sweat trickling down the back of my neck, sliding under my collar, making it damp. The windows were open, the wheels clacked loudly along the track, a beat that gave rhythm to my thoughts. I had to get away from this man. I had to lose him when I got off at the next stop. He was young, wiry, he could easily outrun me. Did Dmitri have anyone nearby, had they already picked up my trail? Could I rely on them to take out Paisley Shirt?

Using the reflections in the window I checked the other occupants of the carriage, hoping I would recognise somebody as being associated with Dmitri. I could see two young women at the end of the carriage, laughing at the antics of a small child in a pushchair. No help to be expected from that direction, I was on my own.

The next station was already drawing near, the train slowing, the sound of the wheels deepening and slackening. I had to time my next movements exactly, if I were even a couple of seconds out, my plan would fail. In my head I measured the distance to the doors, calculated how long it would take to unpeel myself from the sticky vinyl seat. We were on one of the new red and grey S-Bahn trains, doors operated by push-button. Once the doors were closed they couldn't be hauled open again. That was my chance.

I stayed in my seat as we pulled into the next station. Adrenaline pumped through my body, I had to make a real effort to remain where I was, peering through the dusty window. The platform was empty, and the tannoys almost immediately crackled, coughing commands to stay back: *Zurückbleiben*. On the train the red light glowed, the signal sounded *Tu-tüüü-tu*.

I jumped up, jamming my hand between the closing doors, pushing against them, slipping through the gap.

"*Zurückbleiben!*" the tannoys yelled as I landed on the platform. I turned, facing the train. Paisley shirt was no longer in his seat, he was pinned against a partition, his arm pulled high up his back by one of the women.

As the train pulled out of the station the mother met my eye. She winked.

A tram, then another S-Bahn took me to Alexanderplatz station. It was hotter in the centre of the city, and I was glad to enter the relative cool of the Centrum department store. I climbed the steps to the fourth floor, checking for any tail at each landing, then pretended to admire the meagre offerings in the men's department.

After a minute or so a member of staff announced the store was closing. He came closer, as if to flush out any errant shoppers from between the aisles.

Even though menswear was empty he whispered, using the corner of his mouth to mutter the words as he sidled past, *Emergency exit, then stairs to roof.*

I followed the signs to the fire exit, first up some concrete steps, then climbing a rusty steel ladder, before pushing at the steel hatch above. It opened easily, and I climbed out, lowering the hatch back into place.

"Martin, glad you could make it!" Dmitri was standing behind the hatch, looking comfortable despite the heat. He was no longer in uniform but wore East German clothes: light shirt, grey trousers and brown closed sandals. A warm breeze made its way across the open rooftop. There was no shelter up here, it was obvious we were alone.

"So, you've been caught up in the Kaminsky situation? What's the interest?"

"There's a plot to assassinate Kaminsky, we're trying to find out more. We have a source, we don't know who it is, but British Defence Intelligence might."

"Assassinate Kaminsky?" Dmitri chuckled. "Are you not tempted to let them get on with it? No, no, a small joke. I understand your concern. So, DIS are interested in your informant? Are they aware that he is working for you?" Dmitri's one good eye was dancing, he was having his fun with me, for all the seriousness of the matter. "Maybe your informant is actually working for the Queen, perhaps the product comes directly from Major Clarie?"

I considered this for a moment. It seemed possible, but not likely. Why would the British want to feed us information? Or disinformation? The whole situation simply felt improbable, and that was perhaps why I was feeling so lost.

"You'd better give me the whole story, my friend. Start at the beginning."

I told Dmitri what I knew. There wasn't much to tell; for me it had all begun less than a week ago. Dmitri listened without interrupting, but I could see he was making his usual mental notes.

"So you are working with Lieutenant Steinlein. The name is

familiar, who is he exactly? And why are you not working with your team at RS?"

"Steinlein is uniformed *Volkspolizei*, but he's seconded to the political policing unit, K1. He was hospitalised by the fascists a few days before they got hold of me."

"Let me guess—he used this fact to build a bridge to you? Something you have in common, being attacked by skinheads?" Dmitri smiled as I nodded my head. "And your colleagues at RS?"

"Steinlein is insisting on secrecy. He says he doesn't know who to trust."

"Does he suggest your colleagues may be part of this plot?"

"He suspects the Ministry and the police. He seems very worried, sees a conspiracy wherever he looks."

"Does he know we are meeting? No? Very good. Tell me, are no alarm bells ringing in that head of yours?" Dmitri lit one of his black cigarettes. "No, of course not, ever the trusting Martin."

"I haven't any energy for alarm bells. I haven't the energy to deal with this shit, not today, not ever," I replied. "Kaminsky wants to destroy what we've created. And right now he's succeeding. Everything we stand for, everything we ever fought for—if Kaminsky has his way, all that effort will have been wasted."

Dmitri let me ramble, pulling on his cigarette, looking up at the Television Tower that loured over the railway station opposite.

"Somehow, back in 1989, the revolution started, the Party fell, people wanted change, and together we made that change happen.

"But now I'm wondering whether people really *wanted* change. Because as soon as Kaminsky crawls out of the ruins of the Party … it's like he's the answer to everyone's prayers."

Dmitri didn't answer immediately, instead leading me to the edge of the roof. Seven storeys below us, Alexanderplatz was crowded with shoppers, ants negotiating their way around each other, dividing and clumping together again.

"Martin, you're tired. But are you not also apprehensive about the future? For years you've been thinking about all of this, imagining and discussing different ways of organising society. Yet still you're afraid. How do you think all of those people down there feel? They want to be reassured, they want to know what's going to happen next. As a nation you're feeling your way. You want people to be responsible for their own lives and communities, but is that what *they* want? They've always been told what to do. They've always known what was acceptable and what would bring them trouble and grief. Why shouldn't they want a return to simpler times? Times when they felt they had control over at least the immediate aspects of their lives.

"With your revolution you are offering people freedom. Freedom to take on the responsibility for running society. Freedom to negotiate with their co-workers, their neighbours, their city, their country. They are able to take part in the constant dialogue that is freedom at a societal level. But when there's a fair dialogue no-one knows the outcome, there is no way of predicting the results. Not knowing how things will turn out is scary. Don't underestimate the power of fear. And don't underestimate the power held by those who say they can take fear away."

The smoke from Dmitri's cigarette hung in the air between us as we watched at the masses below. "Freedom is change," he said to the shimmering skyline. "Freedom is danger. Freedom is insecurity." Dmitri dropped his cigarette onto the cement roof, carefully grinding it out with his sandal. "Not everyone wants that. To them Kaminsky offers simple answers, a return to simpler times. He offers to remove the burdens of thinking and doing. He offers a return to the old days."

DAY 6
Friday
17th June 1994

Over the last few days many people have come up to me in the street, they're upset, angry about the delays at the border. They're asking me: do I condemn West Germany for causing these problems?

Let me be completely clear about this: nobody condemns the West German border controls as strongly as I.

The West Germans can talk all they like about 'continued unrest'. They can prattle on about 'protecting' their borders—but at the end of the day it is normal people who are suffering.

It's people like you and me, people like your family, your friends and your workmates. We are the ones suffering from these new controls imposed by the West.

But when it comes to trade, it's business as usual. When it comes to Bonzen crossing the border, it's business as usual. The political elite have no trouble with crossing into West Berlin—for them the borders remain open.

But if you or I want to visit friends or family in the West we are treated very differently. We have to put up with strict border controls: long waits, searches and questioning.

Can we expect the government to do anything about this?

Of course not.

Karo

Erika dragged me into the office with her this morning, which meant I got there ultra-early, like before I was even properly awake. When Laura saw me she was absolutely merciless.

"Since we're all here can we start our meeting?"

So basically I wasn't all there for the morning meeting. I don't think they talked about anything important, it sounded like updates and divvying up tasks. Afterwards I was heading back to my own office for a snooze when Laura stopped me.

"Any luck in your efforts to track down Dr. Becker?"

"I've got an address for him, but that's from 1988. I tried phoning but the line was dead. I guess he doesn't live there any more."

"A lot of people have moved around since the start of the revolution. Have you checked the address registration files at the police station? Although, that may be a little direct—you don't want to set too many alarm bells ringing, do you? But, chin up, I may have something of use."

Brilliant! Knowing Laura she'll have some kind of secret index, compiled by hand using old Stasi files and informants' reports! I followed her into the front office, starting to feel a bit hopeful again.

"Grit, could you pass me the telephone directory for Berlin, please?" Laura asked the secretary.

"A *phone* book?"

"Don't sound so puzzled—your Dr. Becker is likely to have a phone, a man with his connections."

She was right. I took the phone book from Grit and headed back to my office.

Once there I opened the book at B and scanned through until I got to Becker. There was no Dr. Becker, just lots of Beckers with their initials. In fact about thirty Beckers with the initial A were listed. Thirty! What was I meant to do, phone every single one of them up? *Excuse me, sorry to bother you, but are you the bastard who hurt my friend about five years ago?*

Erika came in, saw me with my head in my hands and said: "Phone book no good then?"

"Are you checking up on me again?"

"Yes." She said it in such a matter of fact way that I couldn't feel pissed off with her. She knew things weren't going too well in my life right now, apart from obviously being homeless, but she didn't push me to tell her anything. She just made sure I knew she was available if I did want to talk. I appreciated that.

She went over to Martin's desk and poked around a bit. "It's always surprised me how messy Martin is."

"Yeah, he's got some Neues Deutschland over there—from 1987! Ancient!"

Erika found the Party newspapers and laughed at the headlines. "Look at this: *Farmers keep their word and deliver bumper crop*—that's the headline! They didn't believe in giving us any real news back then. *Greetings to the Democratic People's Party of Afghanistan. The Central Committee wishes the 2nd National Conference every success.*"

Erika was flicking through the paper, laughing at the stuffy stories when suddenly she stopped her rustling and giggling.

"Karo, you should take a look at this."

I peered over her shoulder at the article she'd found.

New deputy director for youth facility. Scanning through all the ridiculous titles and empty phrases that clogged up the first paragraph, I got to the interesting bit: *The Ministry for People's Education has appointed Herr Dr. Andreas Becker, resident in Strausberg, as new deputy director of the Berlin* Durchgangsheim.

"That's him, that's the fucker!" I double-checked my notes, yes, October 1987.

"So now you know that he used to live in Strausberg. Maybe he moved back later?"

"Grit!" I shouted through the open office door. "Have we got the phone book for the Frankfurt District?"

"Ask at the post office."

I had to queue for what felt like hours at the post office, stuck in a huddle of sweaty, smelly Berliners. If anything makes you want to stop believing in humanity then it's queuing in a government department during a heat wave.

Most people were discussing the rumours about Hanna Krause, the chair of the Central Round Table. She was going to be at Kaminsky's rally the next day. Nobody knew what was going on, whether there'd been some kind of deal. Whatever it was, it must be mega, just look at the way Kaminsky had been slagging Hanna Krause off, saying she was hysterical and calling the Round Tables *knitting circles of saboteurs* (he obviously doesn't realise just how dangerous knitting circles can be).

It just didn't make any sense, didn't tie in with the stories Erika had told me about what Hanna used to get up to in the old days. People were coming up with fantastic conspiracy theories: *Kaminsky and Krause have fallen in love,* or *Krause's sold the Round Tables out.*

Listening to all that sick gossip put me in an even worse mood and when I finally got to the head of the queue the clerk behind the counter was really snotty with me. She sighed and complained about having to get off her arse to fetch the phone book.

"You know, you could just leave them out here in front. That way you could sit on your comfy seat all day long and not have to get up for people like me."

She gave me a look like she thought I was crazy. "These books are the property of the German Post, we can't just leave them lying around."

Honestly, sometimes I think these civil servants haven't even heard we're in the middle of a revolution.

The clerk came back and passed the Frankfurt district phone book over. "Move aside so that I can deal with other customers, and don't be too long about it."

I took the book to the tables they provide for you to fill in your withdrawal slips and customs declaration forms and stuff, and riffled through the pages until I got to the Beckers. I groaned, once again there was no Dr. Becker but there were about fifteen different A. Beckers. Great. I turned over a withdrawal slip and started to copy out the addresses and phone numbers, but sweat dripped off my forehead and splotched onto the rough paper. The damp patch kept growing, and was added to by another drop of sweat.

"Fuck it!" I said under my breath, and, checking nobody was watching, I tore out the page of Beckers and left the phone book on the table.

Back outside I considered my options. I could go back to the office, work through all these Beckers, try to eliminate them one by one, or I could do something less boring. The something less boring option was more than appealing right now—I was finding it hard to concentrate, every time I tried to do something my mind kept sliding off, towards Katrin or Schimmel or the *Thaeri*, or all of them bundled up together in a hard ball that sat in my stomach. I just ended up feeling sorry for myself, and that made me feel like a right sad case.

But I had a mission, and right now that mission was the only way I was managing to keep it together.

10:56
Karo

It felt like I'd spent the whole day getting hold of this list of phone numbers for A. Becker, but really it hadn't got me any further in my search. Then again, it hadn't really taken a whole day, it wasn't even midday and I'd done loads of other stuff too, like going up to the old Stasi HQ to look in the files there. I'd taken a list of made-up names so that it wouldn't be so obvious I was looking for that bastard Becker. Surprisingly, I drew a blank, which meant I had to spend a whole hour pretending to be interested in the records of these random people I'd never heard of. It was that bloody bureauctopus again: paperwork expanding to fill available sanity.

I was standing at the side of Frankfurter Allee, waiting for a gap in the traffic, when I had a thought. If Becker was involved in some fascist organisation then it was possible the police would have up-to-date files on him. I turned around and headed up the hill, towards Schottstrasse, the central police station in Lichtenberg. It was on the

483

way up there that I remembered my horrendous experience at the Party archives on Tuesday. I decided to check in with Erika before I went barging in.

I found a phone box on Roedeliusplatz and dialled the RS number. "Erika, what would you say if I went to talk to the cops about Becker? I could say I was chasing Nazis."

There was the inevitable silence on the other end of the line while Erika thought about it.

"You'd need a good reason, but if you can think of one then why not? Tell them you're cross-referencing intelligence from a debriefing, make it from somewhere far away, the Mecklenburg coast or deepest Saxony."

"Yeah, and I could throw several names at them, not just Becker's." I was on top of this, I knew how to play this game now.

"Sounds good to me. But Karo?"

"Yeee-es?"

"Don't rub anyone up the wrong way. And if you meet a cop called Neumann, be careful. He's a nasty piece of work."

Neumann? I knew that name, Martin had mentioned him once. "Is he the one in political policing?"

"Yeah, K1. So if you're asking about Nazis then you'll probably run into him or one of his colleagues."

Oh, fun. Not only was I *voluntarily* going into a cop shop, but I was going to have to deal with fucking K1.

You know that feeling you get when a policeman looks at you, the feeling that you've done something wrong—even if you haven't? Well, that feeling is ten times worse when you actually go into a police station. It's that smell of disinfected fear—like at the dentist, but it's less physical, kind of deeper. Maybe you're a goody-two-shoes and have always seen the police as your friend and helper, maybe you didn't experience the police before 1989. But if you did, then you'll know what I'm talking about when I say I had *that* feeling.

I stood for absolutely ages at the front desk, while some jobsworth in a uniform pecked away at an electric typewriter.

"Oy! Some of us have got lives to get on with!" I shouted through the closed reception window.

The uniform hardly looked up, he'd clocked that I was a punk and was deliberately ignoring me.

I rapped on the partition, and pushed my RS pass up against the glass. "RS! Get your arse over here!"

Uniform got all interested all of a sudden. He scratched his head a bit then waddled over.

"You're from the RS?" He thought I was lying, I could tell he was thinking about booking me for impersonation.

"New times, everything's changing. Now tell me where to find Captain Neumann."

I followed the uniform's instructions, through doors and down corridors, and there he was: *Captain Neumann, Kriminalpolizei Department K1.* I knocked on the door next to the fancy name plate and went straight in.

Neumann turned out to be some kind of militarist doll come alive, complete with macho scar running down one side of his face. He was a bit surprised by a punk turning up in his office, I could tell because he raised an eyebrow half a millimetre.

"Captain Neumann, I'm Karo Rengold from RS2." I held my hand out. Not something I normally do for cops, and definitely not one from K1, but I wanted something from this bull and being polite was the easiest way to play it.

"Did we have an appointment, Fräulein Rengold?"

"It's *Frau* Rengold actually." God, what is it with these cops, don't they know it's the 1990s? "And no, we don't have an appointment, but don't worry—I'll be gone before you know it." I sat on a chair and plonked the list of names in front of him, the one I'd just used at the Stasi archive. "These are the names of people who may have had contact with the fascist house on Weitlingstrasse. I want to see their files."

Neumann picked up the list and read through the names. There was no eyebrow flickering this time, he was signalling that he'd never seen these names before.

"That can be arranged, Frau Rengold. When do you want them by?"

"As soon as possible. I was hoping to get a look at the first few right now."

Finally—a proper reaction! Neumann's mouth curved upwards, but just on one side. It was a dagger of a smile, a gloating curl of the lips. Not the kind of reaction I was aiming for.

"That won't be possible. As you may have heard there's a rally tomorrow, called by the General-Secretary of the PDS. We've got our hands a little full at the moment."

That was a crap excuse, and I told him so. The rally was in Treptow, but Schottstrasse was in the Lichtenberg district.

"Treptow police have requested our assistance in view of credible threats that have been made to the life of Dr. Kaminsky."

"OK, Monday then?" There was not a lot else I could say, the man had already said no.

"Monday then, Fräulein Rengold," he said as he handed me my list.

11:00

Martin

The Treptower Park meadows were full of sunbathers, walkers and volleyball players enjoying the sunshine. I pushed my bike through a line of trees and then through the fence into the Soviet War Memorial arena. Leaving my bike on the cobbled drive I walked up to the hunched figure of Mother Homeland, surrounded by weeping birches. Circling the statue I made sure I had the place to myself—I'd seen no signs of a tail this morning, but yesterday's meeting with Dmitri had made me careful. That's one reason I'd cycled here this morning: not only was it the quickest way to get here, but it's hard to follow someone on a bike—too fast to shadow on foot, too slow to track in a vehicle.

But I was all alone, there weren't even any workers setting up for tomorrow's rally, just an army field kitchen trailer abandoned by the entrance arch.

Before me hung the dipped flags of red granite. As I walked up the slope, the figure of the Red Army soldier rose out of the close horizon, stark against the leached sky, sword in one hand, child on the other arm, swastika trampled underfoot. However much things had changed in our land, this place continued to have a strong hold on the nation's collective imagination; the arena was built with a language of power and subjugation. And that was precisely why Kaminsky had chosen the Soviet War Memorial for his final rally.

Standing between the granite flags, above the field of white sarcophagi and the bronze soldier, I tried to imagine how it would be the next day, thousands of Kaminsky supporters filling the arena. If I were here, amongst his followers, how would I take out Kaminsky? What would be the best angle of attack? On the day itself he would be standing on the barrow at the far end, before the plinth on which the twelve metre high bronze soldier stood. Kaminsky would be looking straight at where I was standing now. He'd be high above the masses, anyone trying to get to him would first have to climb the steps, dodging police and Party toughs.

There would only be one way to kill Kaminsky—to use a gun.

From the edge of the site I could see through the fence to the park beyond. There were very few places with an unobstructed line of sight towards the plinth. Post a police officer at each of those points and there could be no danger from that angle.

That meant, to get a clear shot, the assassin would have to come into the arena itself. Anyone in this area could shoot Kaminsky.

But would they get away afterwards?

I climbed the barrow to the Red Soldier's plinth. Built into the stonework was a crypt, a mosaic lined sanctuary. There was nowhere there to hide, but what about explosives? Instinctively I shrugged away the idea—too unfocussed: there would be no way to guarantee Kaminsky's death. I wandered around the outside of the plinth, looking closely at the joints in the stonework. The stained limestone showed no signs of tampering, no fresh scratches or crumbling edges. Turning around, looking out over the arena before me I thought of the hundreds of places where explosives could be hidden. The cenotaphs were hollow, or what about under the lawns? But these options were no good if Kaminsky were the target, they could only harm the crowd.

Perhaps that was the aim? A terrorist attack on a large gathering of people, designed to cause indiscriminate injury, the senselessness creating widespread fear.

The GDR had been lucky, we'd never yet been the target of a

terrorist operation. But in places where attacks had happened there had always been a tightening of the reins, a new package of 'law and order' measures, tying the population down, winding back the clock on civil liberties and human rights. That would suit Kaminsky just fine, it would strengthen his arguments for strong leadership. A scapegoat would be found—a refugee, or maybe some well-known political figure, one who was progressive, one who opposed Kaminsky and his policies.

My musings raised a new question: what if Kaminsky, far from being the intended target, what if he were the intended beneficiary of the attack?

Speculation. Absurd speculation. Even my cynical friend Dmitri hadn't voiced any concerns about the possibility of an attack. Steinlein was the only one who believed in an assassination plot, and his fears were based only on uncorroborated material from an unknown source.

I was finished here. There was nothing to see, nothing to do, no evidence of a conspiracy. I'd given Steinlein the help I'd promised and I'd paid a heavy price for my generosity. I'd tell Steinlein I was quitting, then go home and get some rest.

I was about to set off down the steps when I heard the jangling of a chain and the creak of rusty hinges. The sound came from behind me, from the back of the arena. I moved around the side of the stone plinth, expecting to see a workforce arriving to set up the infrastructure for the rally. Instead, I saw a *Volkspolizei* patrol car, the boot open. Two police officers heaved a wooden box out, and, stumbling under the weight, carried it through the gates.

The cops didn't see me, they were concentrating on the chest they were carefully lowering to the ground. One pulled away a section of the stone panelling below the fence. It moved easily, revealing a void in the stonework. They slotted the box into the space, and levered the stonework back into position.

When the policemen had shut the gates and driven off I went to where they had hidden the box. The low wall was engraved with quotes from Stalin, and in places it was in a poor state, the cement crumbling under the pressure of swelling tree roots. I pulled at the stone flag, feeling it loosen. Another tug, and it came away, crunching onto the gravel at my feet.

And behind it sat an olive-green ammunition box. Pulling the box out a little, I used my penknife to lever the wooden lid off. I pulled the greaseproof paper aside to reveal a clutch of smoke grenades and ten Makarov hand pistols.

The sun was already high, heat stabbing through the foliage overhanging the fence. I checked my watch, it was nearly 12 o'clock, I was supposed to meet Steinlein in half an hour.

As I walked back to my bike I considered what I'd found. I'd put the box back in the hole, I wasn't happy about leaving the arms there, but they were too heavy to carry, and I couldn't see any other solution.

I'd been tempted by the idea that Kaminsky was a terrorist but the arms cache told a different story, one more compatible with Steinlein's theory that Kaminsky was the target. But why would they need so many pistols? And what were the smoke grenades for?

I was back on Stralau within twenty minutes, arriving before Steinlein. While I waited for him I had another look at the blueprint of the Soviet War Memorial. I was marking the site of the cache when I heard my partner's stick tapping up the stairs.

"I bring news!" Steinlein was now in the room. "The chair of the Central Round Table is going to be at the rally tomorrow—she'll be up there with Kaminsky."

Steinlein's information surprised me: time and again Hanna Krause had been publicly humiliated by Kaminsky, what had happened to make her agree to stand alongside him? But I couldn't let myself be sidetracked, I told Steinlein about the cache.

"This is it!" Steinlein was actually excited, it was the closest I'd ever seen him to being happy. "This confirms what I've been saying all along-"

"But why do they need all those guns? What are they planning?"

"A kidnapping," the policeman answered immediately. "It *looks* like a kidnapping, but it can't be."

"But if it is a kidnapping-"

"It isn't. That's against all the evidence—a kidnapping is too messy, too unpredictable. Only an amateur would try to kidnap Kaminsky in the middle of a rally."

"Assassination or kidnapping—it doesn't matter. The two of us won't be able to stop either of those things. It's time to hand it over to the experts, get Unit 9 involved. There's more than enough evidence-"

"No!" Steinlein moved closer, his eyes widening. "We can't trust Unit 9—we have to find another way."

"There is no other way! Be realistic, we have to go to the Ministry and tell them what we've found out. Let them deal with it."

"Are you even listening to what I'm saying?" Steinlein was leaning closer, both hands on his walking stick. "If we go to the Ministry then the other side will get wind of it. We can't take that chance. They'll postpone their plans and next time we may not hear about it in time. Going to the Ministry isn't the way forward, I've got this under control!"

I shook my head, there was no way Steinlein had this under control.

"There are ten pistols in that box." I was trying to be reasonable, put the facts before Steinlein one last time. "And there's smoke grenades. There's going to be at least ten people involved in the kidnapping, or the assassination, or whatever it is. Ten people! There's no way you and I can stop ten of them!"

"It's under control. It's too late to mess with the plan!"

I didn't like what was happening, Steinlein was genuinely angry, even more so than yesterday—his face red, the knuckles over his cane white, his other hand was a fist, held just in front of my chest.

"The plan? What plan?" I asked, swallowing my own temper.

Steinlein hesitated, but his cane carried on shaking. "*Our* plan: we agreed we'd look into this together, that we wouldn't tell anyone-"

"I agreed to help you look into it, and I have. But now I'm saying this is too big for two invalids to handle!"

"I've got this under control—trust me!"

But I didn't trust Steinlein. I agreed with him that the Party and the police were still close—particularly elite squads like Unit 9. But I was beginning to ask myself why Steinlein was so resistant to making our investigation official.

Martin

The Ministry appeared to be populated entirely by nervous civil servants, all intent on palliating stress by means of dashing around and appearing indispensable. It took me half an hour to parley my way through the over-excited masses and reach a member of the Ministerial Committee. When I finally entered Timo Rosen's office he was arguing with Hanna Krause, the chair of the Central Round Table.

"After all the names he's called you, all the times he-" Timo broke off when he saw me by the door. "What is it?"

I looked uncertainly from Hanna to Rosen. He was standing in the middle of the office, red-faced, while Hanna sat drinking tea in a comfy chair.

"Comrade Minister, my name is Martin Grobe from RS-"

"Martin! Come in, I haven't seen you since ..." Hanna had got out of her chair and was coming to meet me, holding her hands out. "It must have been 1990? Can it really be four years?"

Rosen remained where he was, arms crossed and mouth set as he watched the reunion.

I explained why I'd come, and after listening for a few minutes, Rosen pressed a button on his intercom. "Get the boys from Glinkastrasse over here."

"And if you needed yet another reason not to do this ..." he told Hanna.

"Politics isn't always pure and simple, you know that better than anyone, Timo." Hanna answered. "Lots of people have put their trust in Kaminsky, it's our job to listen to them."

Rosen ignored Hanna's answer, slotting a pair of reading glasses over the bridge of his nose and looking at the leaked reports I'd brought.

"I'll leave you two to it," Hanna said, patting me on the arm. "We should get together soon, bring Laura and Erika. Let's get this horrible rally business out of the way first and then I want to hear your thoughts on how we can get the referendum result on the Round Tables implemented."

Hanna left just as a lieutenant from Unit 9 was announced. He saluted and immediately began sifting through the material I'd brought.

"What do you think, comrade Lieutenant Ziegler?" asked Rosen.

"Hard to say, comrade Minister. There's something fishy here but there's nothing concrete, if you see what I mean."

"And what about the arms cache, is that not concrete enough for you?" Rosen and Ziegler shifted their gaze to me. One shocked, the other dispassionate yet attentive.

"What arms cache would that be, comrade Captain?" asked Ziegler.

I described the box I'd found behind the stone slabs, and the policeman reached for the telephone, swiftly despatching a squad to pick it up.

"Anything else you'd care to share, comrade Captain? Because now would be a really good time."

I spent the afternoon at the table with several Unit 9 officers, answering questions as fully as I could without mentioning Steinlein. The elite police squad sifting through the plans had immediately recognised the significance of the material I'd brought. Ziegler spent much of the time leaning against the wall, listening to what we were discussing. He was behind me but I could feel his eyes on my back, he didn't bother to look away when I turned around, content for me to know that I was under scrutiny.

"Are you telling us everything, comrade Captain?" he asked at one point.

"I don't think I've forgotten anything."

His eyes rested on mine, trying to ferret out whatever secret I was keeping from him.

"Why didn't you come to us earlier?"

"As I said, I wasn't convinced that this was a serious threat."

"Someone passes you the security plans for Dr. Kaminsky's rally and you don't consider it to be serious?"

He was right, he was definitely right. Why hadn't I come sooner? I'd allowed my own doubts to cloud my judgement, allowed Steinlein to lull me into complacency, ignored my instinct and experience.

It was obvious the lieutenant wasn't satisfied, but it wasn't his place to question me. For the time being he could only work with the material I had delivered.

The police unit drew up their plans and got Minister Rosen to sign the paperwork. They would provide a close protection detail for Kaminsky, some wearing standard issue *Volkspolizei* uniforms, others in plain clothes, mixing in with stewards and invited guests.

"Make sure you don't get this wrong. It's bad enough that Kaminsky's at risk, but now the Chair of the Central Round Table has taken it into her head to be there as well ..."

Rosen was fretting.

21:27

Martin

Steinlein waited for me at the top of the stairs, both hands clenching the top of his walking stick.

"Where have you been?"

I moved past him into our office. "At the Ministry, talking to Unit 9."

He stared at me for a few moments, eyes narrowed almost to slits. "Well, we might as well pack up now, that's it—it's all over."

"Unit 9 are going to provide close protection to Kaminsky. They're taking the threat seriously. And Minister Rosen is on the case, he'll be receiving hourly reports and will be in constant contact during the event."

"Dietmar Rosen? Just another hack, covering his own back!"

"Our informant gave us detailed plans. It was my duty to pass on that information."

"Perhaps. Maybe you're right. At least now they can't act surprised when it happens, not now they know RS is involved." Steinlein's voice was muted, but then his head snapped up. "Did you mention me?"

I shook my head and Steinlein relaxed.

"My name didn't come up at all?"

"No. I told them I was acting on my own initiative. They think I was following up a tip-off."

"Good, good." Steinlein seemed to gain energy again. "Good work."

He got up from the chair and headed for the stairs. "I better get back to the station, still lots to do, meetings and briefings. I'll meet you in Treptow in the morning. I'll be there from 0600 hours, doing a sweep of the park with my squad."

That went better than expected. I breathed a sigh of relief and was about to sit in the chair just vacated by Steinlein before I realised there wasn't anything else to do. We'd done all we could, and tomorrow we would find out if it had been enough.

"Can you give me a lift?" I shouted down the stairs.

"I can drop you off at Ostkreuz."

21:46
Karo

I needed to be doing something, and tracking down Becker was all I had left. I was so close to him, I could feel it in my belly; I wanted to go somewhere he'd been, get a feel for him. Hippy shit, I know, but that's how I felt.

I cycled down the main road on Stralau. The bottle plant stank, but it was nothing compared to the oily smell coming from the asphalt factory and the pukeworthy maltiness hanging around the feed mill. I wasn't exactly sure where the *Durchgangsheim* was but Erika had told me it was a big red-brick building on the left.

There it was, past the factories. Just two storeys and a lower ground floor, bars on the windows and doors.

Behind me there was banging and smells of burnt metal coming from a boatyard, but the red brick building before me was dead. A kind of shadow hung over it, even though the sun was still high, shining directly on it, lighting up every cracked brick, every line of soot and every splash of dirt on the windows. All the curtains were drawn so I couldn't see in. I rattled the main door then walked to the side but there was a high wall topped with broken glass blocking my way. I went back to the front and tried to peer through the thin curtains. All I could see were dusty cobwebs.

I could break in, there was nobody around, and more than enough noise was coming from the boatyard to cover the sound of breaking glass.

Except I'd just be chasing ghosts.

That was when I saw the Lada, it went straight past me and I could see Martin in the passenger seat. I was about to wave when I saw the person driving. Something about him made me stop. I don't know why, I didn't recognise him—or I did, but I couldn't place him. He looked familiar, but not in a good way.

As the car disappeared around the curve I just stood there, wondering what Martin was doing here, and why the person driving the Lada was giving me the heebie-jeebies.

DAY 7
Saturday
18th June 1994

Today I come to Berlin. Today I will stand at the Soviet War Memorial, that monument to the sacrifices of our Soviet brothers in the Great Patriotic War against Fascism. Because today we are in the middle of a new struggle, a struggle against the anti-democratic forces ranged against us: the saboteurs, the nay-sayers, the anti-social elements.

Today I meet the people of the Capital of the GDR, and I will listen, just as I have listened to all the people who came to see me in each and every city and town of this Republic.

Some say that my journey around our country has been the tour of a narcissist. But all who come to my gatherings know to expect such egregious lies from the elite. The people who come to my gatherings know that it's not about me, it's about them. They have chosen me, and I have listened to their worries and their concerns.

Today my journey ends. After this interview, I will leave this studio and I will go and speak to the biggest assembly of all. People from all over the Republic, right now, are making their way to Berlin to be with me.

Because today I will listen once again. And then I will go back to the seat of government, and I will act.

Kaminsky made his way through the crowd, flanked by flunkies and stewards. Others went before their leader, holding the old GDR flag and forging a path through the sweating sea of fanatics. The chants were all around them: *Kaminsky Kaminsky Kaminsky.*

I was near the back, on the west side, but I could see Kaminsky clearly enough: crisp, unbothered by the limp humidity trapped in the arena. Along with thousands of others I watched him leave the sump of supporters, climbing up the steps of the barrow. He moved purposefully towards the open gate of the crypt in the pedestal of the bronze soldier. In his arms he held a large wreath, a black, red and yellow ribbon plaited between the foliage. He placed it just inside the chamber. The stewards hushed the crowd, and for a moment, while Kaminsky bowed his head, a whole *Volk* was silent.

Kaminsky slowly turned around. He surveyed the still masses assembled in the heat below, then he raised a fist, unleashing a clamour that rolled through the arena, rumbling forward until it washed against the low hill.

Kaminsky Kaminsky Kaminsky!

A warm breeze drifted up the river, setting trees rustling, cheering Kaminsky on.

But Kaminsky stood, his fist still in the air.

Kaminsky waited as the chants tumbled over his supporters.

Starting from the front, edging back through the crowd, an expectant silence fell. Kaminsky stepped up to the microphones. The wind had brought up steel clouds, roiling through the sky and pooling Kaminsky in a grey light. He was savouring the moment, the power he had to command his legions of followers.

"Today," his voice warm, intimate, letting the microphones do their work. "Today is *our* day!"

Again the crowd erupted, and Kaminsky stepped back, allowing the people to shout their approval.

"Today is our day. We've come a long way, we've taken a hard road together, and here we are—the people!" Another lull, the sound of the cheers still lapping the arena.

"But this is not the end of our road. This is only the beginning! *We haven't even started!*"

The radio unit slung from my shoulder crackled in the charged air. I raised the tiny speaker to my ear. *All units report.* I kept tally as each unit gave their status, starting from the centre and radiating out until Steinlein announced: *Berta 7, keine besonderen Vorkommnisse.* So far, so good.

Kaminsky was still speaking, the people around me intent, focussed on this one man. He was projecting his voice now, the loudspeakers struggling against the agitation of the trees. The breeze was freshening, loosening the close air, a storm was coming.

"No longer will we be treated as second class citizens!

"No longer will we let the politicians and the bureaucrats do as they please! We, the people, are on the march! We the people are dealing with the problems the elite don't care about. It's time for common sense. *Our* common sense will prevail!"

Kaminsky held out his arms, his hands pushing back the adulation of his followers. *Kaminsky Kaminsky!* Beneath the trembling throb of a hundred thousand voices I could feel the susurrance of the approaching storm.

"And common sense is breaking out—we are already winning! Beside me today is someone we all know. Yes, it's someone with whom we've had our disagreements, and that makes it all the more significant that she's chosen to be with us.

"My friends, citizens of the GDR, I give you the chair of the Central Round Table, Hanna Krause!" The rustle of the trees became a roar, perfectly matching the pitch of Kaminsky's voice.

And that was when the lightning struck. It came before the rain, a clean spike of light, slicing the air, striking the bronze soldier—the smell of carbon and ozone cauterising the festivities. Kaminsky and the other speakers on the plinth fell, separating like twigs and leaves shaken from the trees around us. Even at this distance, even in the iron light of the clouds I see the mouths opening to scream. But one figure didn't scream, one figure didn't stand to flee down the steps. Only one figure remained lying at the feet of the Soviet soldier.

The heavy rain fell as waves of thunder crashed in.

PART 2
Guerilla Politics

Day 7
Saturday
18th June 1994

Berlin: *There have been reports of casualties after a terrorist attack at a rally in Treptower Park. Early indications are of at least one death after shots were fired at an event called by the General Secretary of the PDS, Dr. Kaminsky. Further injuries were sustained during the evacuation of the site. Ambulances are attending the scene.*

13:17
Martin

A hand was on my arm, pulling me. Steinlein.

A last look towards the *Bonzen* coming down from the plinth—Unit 9 officers had surrounded Kaminsky and were shuffling him away, other officers knelt by the fallen body. The radio set was squawking, static from the storm threatening to submerge the words: *Ambulance required, repeat ambulance required.*

Steinlein had hold of me, he was thrusting his way through the panic, his uniform making people give way even as they struggled to escape. Under the triumphal arch, onto the road. The rain was falling heavily now—bloated drops that stuck to the cobblestones, filling the gutters and flowing over the curb. A uniformed policeman opened the door of a black Volga, an absurd, drenched salute as I was pushed in. Steinlein took the wheel, blue lights scratching the soused air. He pulled into the road, sluicing through the escaping masses, away from the rally and the body of my old friend Hanna Krause.

DAY 8
Sunday
19th June 1994

Berlin: The death of Hanna Krause has been confirmed. Frau Krause, chair of the Central Round Table of the GDR, died in the Charité Clinic early this morning after being wounded at Dr. Kaminsky's rally yesterday. Police are pursuing several lines of enquiry, but are currently focussing on the possibility that Dr. Kaminsky himself was the intended target.

04:41

Martin

From my chair I watched the morning sky lift from flat grey to washed-out blue. There was no music playing, the turntable stood still, the pickup arm rested on its cradle. A cigarette smouldered between my fingers, a couple of bottles of schnapps lay empty on the floor beside me.

Hanna Krause was dead.

Kaminsky should have taken the bullet.

I hadn't stopped it from happening, I had to live with that.

Hanna had been one of us, one of the opposition. She'd been with us in the old days, putting her life and her family on the line, fighting injustice, desperate for change.

There were no tears in me. There was no sadness. Only rage. Furious, impotent rage.

From the rally, Steinlein and I had headed straight to our little office on Stralau. We'd cleaned the place thoroughly, taken away

501

every scrap of paper, every pen and pencil. We'd wiped down every surface, removed every fingerprint and trace of occupancy. When we were done there was nothing left to mark our investigation, not even footprints in the dust.

I came home and drank a bottle of schnapps. I sat through the night, hating myself for not preventing Hanna's death.

11:56
Martin

They came for me at midday. There was no knock, just a kick to the door. Steinlein brought them, Steinlein took me away.

13:55
Martin

"Let's take it from the top, we need to get our story straight."

Steinlein was sweating, he'd put his uniform cap on the table and undone the top few buttons of his blouson. Now he was holding a pen, ready to write down whatever I said.

We were in an interview room, both of us sitting at the table. I was still drunk, still trying to understand what had happened. Hanna Krause had been shot. Despite Unit 9, despite all the material we'd uncovered. Despite everything.

I sat up straight, trying to sober up, to order my thoughts. But the memory of the lightning flash, her figure falling, the realisation that she would never get up again ... How long had I known Hanna? Ten years? Now she was gone. Why her? Why not Kaminsky? Why always the good people?

Steinlein was right, we needed to get our story straight. The twin reel tape recorder on the table was still, this was between me and Steinlein's pen.

"Everything?" I asked, still trying to stop my brain from replaying those moments at the Soviet War Memorial. I waited for Steinlein to nod. Everything.

"I'm on leave from the *Republikschutz*, and you approached me—when was it? Just over a week ago." I was trying to breathe properly.

Steady, regular breaths. I watched the lieutenant's face closely, searching for a clue as to what to include, what to leave out.

But Steinlein hadn't reacted, his pen hadn't touched paper.

"I received an anonymous tip-off a week ago," I tried again. Steinlein's pen started scratching at the rough greyness of the form, taking down what I was saying.

I gave him an account, edited him out, took responsibility for everything we'd done together. At the end I was shivering, I was thinking about Krause, about Kaminsky's lucky escape, about the whole bloody mess. About our failure.

Steinlein left the room, closing the door behind him. I sat in the chair, indifferent to my fate.

It was another ten minutes before the lock clicked open.

"Comrade Captain, would you accompany us?" a constable requested, politely enough, but with that hint of steel that police officers must practice.

He led the way, a police recruit taking up the rear of our convoy as we went along corridors and down stairs to the custody area. A sergeant stood behind the desk, ready to receive his new guest.

"Martin Grobe, presented for detention," the constable announced.

At a signal from the sergeant the constable pulled my left arm behind my back. I bent over in pain, my head hitting the desk. The recruit emptied my pockets and the sergeant documented my belongings.

"Reason for detention?"

"Criminal Code paragraphs 112 and 99."

The desk sergeant wrote down the paragraph numbers, murmuring to himself as he did so: "Murder. Terrorism."

DAY 9
Monday
20th June 1994

Aktuelle Kamera: Tell me about your bill to disband the Round Tables —does the timing have anything to do with what happened at the weekend?

Kaminsky: The appalling murder of Hanna Krause was an attack on us all. The tragic events of Saturday have changed politics in this country forever. It was a terrorist attack, and this country will never give in to terror. Nevertheless, we need to respond, and to respond quickly. I am calling for a full investigation into what happened. Those responsible will be made to pay for their mistakes.

But let's be clear about this, the outrage happened because this incompetent government allowed it to. We have a weak government and the source of that weakness is the Round Tables.

The Round Tables have no legal status, yet these unelected groups are telling our government what it should do.

Aktuelle Kamera: You say the Round Tables have no legal standing, but in April the country voted in a referendum to change the constitution in order to give the Round Tables and the Workers' Councils more power.

Kaminsky: Yes, they did. And this is an excellent example of political manipulation. That referendum should have never been held. Why? To answer that we need to look at who called for the referendum, and who came up with the questions. It was the Round Tables themselves! Nowhere in our constitution does it say that the Round Tables can call referenda. The democratically elected representatives of the people, sitting in the Volkskammer, opposed this referendum. They had good reason to, and they explained their reasons very clearly in parliament—it wasn't just my party—the CDU and the SPD also opposed the referendum. All the major parties opposed the referendum, but they were outmanoeuvred by the self-selected and self-serving Round Tables —a group of people more interested in their own public profile than in the democracy we fought so long and hard for. These conditions lead to anarchy and to the violence we saw on Saturday.

Aktuelle Kamera: Do you and your party accept the result of the referendum?

Kaminsky: A small group of individuals are seeking personal power—individuals who are neither able nor willing to put themselves forward as candidates in a democratic election. There isn't another country in the world that would put up with such shenanigans. Groups of people are gathering together in living rooms and village halls with the sole aim of putting pressure on our democratic institutions. The so-called Central Round Table presumes to interfere in government business. Our democratically elected government is at the beck and call of a shadowy, unaccountable cabal.

That isn't democracy, it's guerilla politics.

Aktuelle Kamera: The Round Tables say they are open to all, are transparent and accountable. They talk about safeguards such as shadowing, regular rotation and powers of immediate recall by any of the lower levels. Do you accept that this is just a different way of doing democracy?

Kaminsky: I was elected by the people, and my job as a member of the Volkskammer is to uphold the constitution, to guard it to the best of my abilities. And while I remain a democratically elected member of parliament, I shall continue to do just that.

07:00

Karo

Erika had domesticated me. Here I was, we'd only just had breakfast and I was doing the dishes before we went to work. Obviously not the way I'd choose to spend my mornings, but Erika was putting me up so I had to show willing.

"What do you want on your sandwiches?" she asked.

"Don't care."

There was a silence for a bit, just the clattering of dishes and the news on the radio spreading fear and unease. We were both still shocked by Hanna's death. It felt like something had ended and something much worse was about to begin. It felt like the whole country was holding its breath, wondering what would come next.

Kaminsky knew this. He was whipping up the fear levels, talking about the state's failure, the need for strong measures against saboteurs and terrorists.

I rinsed the glasses.

"Erika—were you ever followed, in the old days, I mean?"

"We all were. Surely everyone who was politically active was followed. Weren't you?"

I thought about it. Looking back it was clear that I had been, but usually just a police car or uniformed officers, trying to make me feel uncomfortable. This was different.

"It's just, I've been having this strange feeling, you know, like I'm not alone. Probably just being paranoid."

Erika went over to the radio and turned the volume up. Right up.

"Why did you do that?" I asked.

Erika stared at the radio in surprise. "Oh, habit I suppose. Tell me more about this feeling."

"It's probably nothing. Just on edge after Saturday."

"How long have you had this feeling?" Erika wasn't letting this one go, even though I was now totally sure I was just being paranoid. Talking about it was making me feel stupid.

"Since Friday afternoon."

"Since you asked Captain Neumann about Becker?"

Put it that way and it sounded less stupid. Still paranoid though. "But that sort of thing doesn't happen any more-"

"It happened to Martin last autumn."

"Yeah, but that was when he was chasing some Stasi dudes who still hadn't got the fact that the old days are over."

"I'm not so certain the old days are over," replied Erika.

We had a plan. Like all the best plans, Erika said, it's simple. I was to leave for work first, and Erika was to watch at the window. She even had this home-made periscope thing so she wouldn't be seen.

"How long have you had that?" There was me thinking I was paranoid but having a periscope was on a whole other level.

"Years. Made it with my daughter when she was little." She examined the periscope, the dark cardboard had scribbles of coloured pencil all over it.

"You have a daughter?" Shit, I didn't even know this basic fact about Erika's life!

"Jenni. I don't see her so often any more, she's studying engineering in Ilmenau." Erika was fiddling with the periscope. "Shall we see if this trick still works?"

I left the building, didn't look around but went straight to the bakery (my turn to get the bread rolls for the office second breakfast). The whole time I was trying to be dead nonchalant, deliberately not keeping an eye out for anybody I might have seen once too often, not listening out for the scrape of a shoe on concrete, just making my merry whistling way to the bakery, then on to work.

Erika was already at the office by the time I got there, she must have overtaken me while I was buying the bread.

"Well?"

"You're right. You're being followed."

"This isn't happening, it can't be true! Why would they want to follow me? Who would want to follow me?"

"I didn't get a good look, but she looked familiar, like I knew her, but didn't. It'll come to me." Erika bustled around, unpacking the rolls, putting them on a plate. "I think we should assume this is to do with Becker. Tell me again, what happened when you saw Captain Neumann on Friday."

"He said they were too busy, come back on Monday—which is today."

"Nothing else? Did he say why they were too busy?"

"Because of the rally. So I asked him what he had to do with that because it's in a completely different district, and he said that Treptow had asked for administrative assistance because there was some kind of threat to Kaminsky."

"A threat?"

I shrugged my shoulders. What did she expect? Did she think I'd just walk into the cop shop and start interrogating the hardest hard-ass bull I could find?

"Have you checked the Stasi archive for any mentions of Becker?"

"He's clean. I couldn't even find any reports *about* him, never mind *by* him."

"Nothing? Nothing at all? How thorough were you?"

I was getting a bit antsy now. It was like Erika was checking I was doing my job properly. Not that it was my job. Nor any of her business either.

"I just did the usual F16 search, the person index."

"So you didn't check for reports about him?"

"Erika, will you back off! I did the checks, alright?"

"Karo, calm down. You're being followed, and we're trying to work out who by. Being defensive isn't helping."

"I'm not being defensive!"

"So did you check anything beyond the F16 cards?"

I shook my head, and Erika finally backed off. I watched her sit down and stare out of the window. Her eyes were blank, she was thinking.

"What other names did you give Neumann?" Erika was back with us.

I pulled out the sheet of paper, it was still in my pocket, and I smoothed it out a bit before handing it over.

"Let's take this to the morning meeting," she said.

"What exactly did Neumann say about threats to Kaminsky?" Klaus had the same question as Erika.

"He just said that Lichtenberg police were helping Treptow out with some threat." They were all being super-serious about the fact that I may or may not have a stalker. It was dead embarrassing and made me feel patronised.

"Look, I can take care of myself, there's no need to be so worried about it."

"Last year, Martin told us he was being followed and we didn't take him seriously. That was a mistake," Erika replied. Laura and Klaus nodded, both looking anywhere but at Erika and me.

Klaus moved the subject back a step, maybe he'd noticed I was feeling uncomfortable, but he was probably still focussed on the information I had about the rally.

"I don't like what Neumann said. We haven't been told anything about this threat, but we should have been—that's what RS is there for."

"We are being wound up, a few more weeks and there won't be any RS any more."

"Still, a matter of courtesy, if nothing else. And anyway there may be some kind of link between Karo being tailed and what happened on Saturday." Klaus wasn't letting this go.

"I'm going to see Antje at the Ministry later, I'll talk to her about it," Erika offered.

Klaus nodded, stroking his lame moustache.

The deal was that I wasn't to go *anywhere* alone. I was *always* to be accompanied by a responsible adult, aka my RS colleagues.

So that meant I got to come to the Ministry with Erika, and in return she got to join me on my visit to Neumann. It all felt way over the top, but I kind of liked the idea of not having to face Neumann alone. He gave me the creeps.

"We need to work out what the threat level is. Why are they following you? Is it to find out what you're up to, to intimidate you, or something worse?"

I didn't like the sound of the something-worse option but didn't really want to think about it either.

"Why can't I just go to the cops, tell them I've got a stalker?" I didn't want to ask the cops for help with anything, but that's what they're there for, and if they can't even deal with something like this …

"Seriously, Karo? Right now the cops are going to be running around in circles trying to work out what to do about last Saturday. And anyway, we're wondering whether Neumann *ordered* the tail, so I'd say that rules out going to the police."

Great, that made me feel really stupid. Thanks, Erika. Still, it was interesting that Erika and the others seemed to trust the bulls even less than I did. I hadn't realised they were that critical, particularly since they work with the cops so much. But here was Erika making me feel bourgeois and naïve.

"So who's Antje?" I asked.

"She's one of the three members on the Ministerial Committee. She and I are old friends—we used to do stuff together in our Women's group, back in 1988 and 1989. She went into politics at the start of the revolution, joined *Neues Forum* just before I got roped into RS."

But Antje didn't seem very friendly when we got to the Ministry. We were kept waiting in some meeting room by a hardcore secretary, and then when Antje came in she looked really stressed.

"Erika, didn't my secretary phone to cancel? I don't have time-"

But Erika just stood up and pulled a chair out. "Antje, sit down. Karo, go and sort out some coffee." Erika was dead confident, I hadn't seen her like this before.

I hung around in the doorway for a moment, looking at Antje, a tall woman with a really cool hairstyle (she had it done up in this ironic grey bun at the back of her head). She sat down and let out a weird, squeaky gasp. "I'm sorry Erika, it's all gone crazy. Kaminsky has called a special session in the *Volkskammer*, I've been summoned ..."

I went out to the nasty secretary and told her to bring three coffees, and pastries too. The secretary gave me a stern look, as if she'd caught me lying, but she pressed a button on her oversized telephone and passed on the request.

When I went back into the room Antje was still talking, but she broke off when she saw me.

"It's OK, this is Karo. She's our newest recruit. You can trust her."

Antje held out her hand and gave me a polite smile, but immediately turned back to Erika.

"Kaminsky has tabled a motion to suspend the Round Tables. He says the referendum result can't be allowed to stand, not after this act of terrorism. He's already got a law and order bill prepared, and he's demanding the Round Tables be completely closed down."

"He can't do that! The people won't let him!" I blurted out, then turned bright red.

"I'm sorry, Karo is it? I think he may manage to do exactly that. The legislation mandated by the referendum hasn't been enacted yet, the *Volkskammer* can simply refuse to vote it through. And as for the people," Antje breathed out heavily, "until a few weeks ago, I might have agreed with you. But it's like the word *Volk* has changed its meaning. Just a short while ago it meant everyone in the country, but now it seems much of the population supports Kaminsky and his new definitions."

The secretary came in with a tray which she slid onto the table. Cups and a coffee pot, but no pastries.

"I told you to bring cake!" I hissed at her, but she ignored me.

"Was there any prior intelligence on the attack at the rally?" asked Erika.

Antje looked up in surprise. "Your colleague, Martin Grobe, he turned up on Friday with a sackful of material."

"Martin?"

OK, that was weird. One: Martin was meant to be on leave. Two: if Martin had found anything suspicious then he would have talked to us. And three: well, I couldn't think of a number three, but that didn't make it any the less disturbing.

"Martin didn't mention any of this," I told Antje, but she just shrugged, she didn't seem interested. "We want to be involved. In the investigation, I mean."

"In an oversight capacity," added Erika. "We thought it wise, considering the Party connections."

Antje thought for a moment, then went over to a telephone in the corner of the room. "I'll check in with Timo and Mario."

While Antje was talking to the other members of the Ministerial Committee, Erika squidged her face up at me. "Why do we want to be involved?" she whispered.

"Because it's our job! I bet Klaus really wants to do it, and I thought we could maybe, I don't know, *do* something."

"Do something? Do what exactly?"

Erika really wasn't getting this, but I couldn't find the words to explain myself. We had to stop Kaminsky, and maybe this would give us a way to do that. Although, thinking about it more, it probably wouldn't help and would just create more work. OK, maybe it was a shit idea, but it was too late now. Still, nice of Erika to back me up.

"Timo and Mario are fine with you participating—in principle. We'll have to be careful about the parameters of your activities, particularly considering Kaminsky's dislike of your department. In the meantime I've asked the Police Minister to send someone up to brief you."

Antje stood by her chair while she finished off her coffee.

"Right, back to the grindstone. I'll make-"

The door burst open, and a man crashed in. It was one of those grey men that seem to breed in government offices, except he was more red than grey. His face was flushed and he was panting as if he'd just run up all the stairs in the whole ministry.

"Frau *Ministerin* Willehardt, there's a problem." But he stopped when he saw me and Erika.

"What is it Herr Winkler? Don't worry, these are colleagues from RS."

But Winkler just went even redder. I was starting to enjoy my trip to the Ministry.

"Come, on, spit it out!" Antje wasn't a patient woman. She turned to us and said: "Herr Winkler is the Police Minister."

Winkler spluttered a bit more, then spat it out. "RS can't possibly be involved in any investigation."

Antje fixed him with this awesome glare that would make even Laura look cuddly. The Police Minister didn't stand a chance.

"The suspect," he stammered. "The person being held for the attempted assassination, it's an RS officer called Martin Grobe."

10:45
Karo

Erika and I legged it all the way to the station, and then spent the whole journey wishing we could be there already. The Police Minister had said that Martin was up before the judge this morning, it wasn't the proper court case, just a remand hearing. But the first rule of prisoner support is to make sure the prisoner knows they're not alone.

We reckoned that because we were colleagues of Martin there'd be no way they'd let us into the courtroom, so we came up with a plan. I thought it was good enough, Erika was a bit worried it might backfire, but I calmed her down. I'd make it work.

When we got off the train I headed into the little supermarket that used to be just for the Stasi and got myself a couple of small bottles of beer. I took the cap off one, then ran after Erika. I caught up with her just as she was going through the door of the court house, shoving past her and disappearing down a corridor. It didn't take long for a court officer to try to head me off. I pretended to be pissed, not walking straight, and then: trip and pour beer all over the officer's shirt, dodge him as he swears and makes a grab for me. Behind me I could hear Erika tut-tutting loudly and ordering the other court officers to call the police. That was enough, I was out of there. But before I went I smashed the second bottle of beer against the wall.

I got through the doors and shot off down the road, the officer puffing and panting, but left way behind. A look over my shoulder, and I could see Erika at the doors, gesticulating and ordering another load of court officers around. They all gathered at the entrance, keeping an eye on me, and Erika wasn't challenged as she slipped away up the stairs. Result.

After all that excitement I went back to the office and waited for Erika on the street outside. I didn't have to wait long, maybe twenty minutes or so, just enough time to regret having chucked that second bottle of beer instead of bringing it back to drink.

"Did you talk to Martin?" I asked when she turned up.

Erika shook her head. "No, but he saw me, he knows we're looking out for him. Come on, we should let the others know what's going on."

As soon as we were in the office, Erika rounded everyone up and told them what was going on.

"He's being accused of murder, terrorism and committing crimes while in state service. Considering the severity of the accusations the judge has agreed to remand him."

There was silence around the table, everyone was completely gobsmacked. It wasn't like anyone believed Martin would do anything like that, no, the question was how had Martin got caught up in all this. Even by his standards this was a real mess.

"We need a plan of action." Laura had already shifted into getting-things-done mode. "We have to get Martin out of prison, the longer they hold him, the more watertight they'll be able to make their case.

Only by getting him out can we help Martin prove he's been framed. First thing to do is to find out what evidence they have against him-"

"The evidence they've *made up*, don't you mean?" I interrupted, but Laura ignored me.

"Then we can work out how to get the charges against him dropped. While that's happening we should make a timeline of what Martin's been doing the last few weeks. We need to do that now, before his trail goes cold—hopefully we can turn up some useful alibis. Once we know exactly what's happening we can start a publicity campaign. That's enough for the next twenty-four hours. Let's meet tomorrow morning to do some proper planning once we know more. Everyone agreed?"

We all nodded, Laura was spot on, as usual.

"I suggest that Erika and I start talking to the Ministry of the Interior and the Ministry of Justice, try to squeeze some information out of them and make arrangements to meet Martin. Klaus and Karo, why don't you start plotting Martin's movements?"

I was impressed by the way my RS colleagues had swung into action. I'd expected them to have a big discussion and to argue about whether or not they were allowed to do this kind of thing. But as it was, within a few minutes we had a plan, and a pile of work to go with it. Klaus and I had a quick confab and he headed off to talk to Martin's neighbours, local shops, that kind of thing. I was to contact Dmitri, and somehow I'd agreed to talk to Katrin. OK, somebody had to talk to her, I was the obvious person, and it would have sounded really crap if I'd refused to go and see her about her dad being arrested. So I agreed and regretted it even before the words were out of my mouth.

15:25

Karo

The conscript in front of the metal gate stopped pacing and stood in my way, feet wide apart, hands on his hips. He was about the same age as me, maybe even younger, but he had a uniform on and a gun slung over his shoulder so he thought he was well hard.

"*Stoi!*"

I never paid much attention in Russian classes at school, but everyone knew that *stoi* meant stop. And it wasn't like I could do anything but *stoi* anyway, there was a locked gate in front of me, for fuck's sake.

"I've got an appointment, can you open up?"

Now I was standing there with my legs wide and hands on hips too (bloody testosterone, it's like it's infectious). I was in a rush and not in a mood to be held up by a kid with a gun.

The Russian guard just shook his head and gave me a load of verbal Cyrillic.

"I have an appointment, let me in," I said really slowly, trying not to get angry. I waved my hands at the gate and the building behind it.

The guard said another bunch of stuff and waved his hands in my face, trying to get me to move back.

"Captain Dmitri," I tried.

I wasn't sure that Dmitri was a captain, and I didn't know his surname, but thought it was worth a try. I hadn't expected this kind of difficulty, after all, getting the appointment had been easy—I'd just phoned the number in Martin's contacts book from his desk drawer. The secretary had been really friendly once I'd said I was from RS, and when I said it was urgent he'd assured me I could come round whenever I wanted.

But now it looked like they weren't going to let me in.

"Dmitri, KGB." I was about to lose my rag, almost shouting at the kid in the uniform. I tried to think of my Russian lessons at school, but all I could come up with was the alphabet. "Kah-djay-bay." At least, that sounded right. Ish. "Dmitri, Captain!"

I could tell the guard was getting even more frustrated than I was, I was worried he was going to get physical on me, but suddenly he stood to attention as the gate clanged open behind him.

Some other soldier, probably an officer, came through the partly opened gate. He ignored the guard, who was still standing, chest out, head back, looking like a dummy in a shop window.

The officer guy didn't say anything, just held his hand out as if he wanted me to give him something. I wasn't sure whether it was a bribe he was after, but if it was then he'd have to make do with my RS pass.

"Who?" he asked, in German.

"Captain Dmitri, kah-djay-bay."

The officer nodded and walked off, back through the gate, still holding my RS papers. I followed him and nobody stopped me so I reckoned I was getting somewhere.

I didn't get very far, though. The officer stopped at the guard hut, a little box made of corrugated metal, and spoke to the soldier inside. A phone call was made, more rapid Russian that made no sense to me, and the officer handed me my pass back, indicating with a curled forefinger that I should follow him.

Martin had told me good things about Dmitri—he clearly admired the Russian. But when I finally met him (which was after what felt like days of winding through a maze of corridors and rooms) I got a completely different impression. This bloke obviously took great care over his appearance. His uniform would have made my mother happy. It was spotless, pressed, and he was still wearing his tunic even though it was well over 30 degrees outside. But it wasn't his dapper appearance that made me dislike him, it was his show-off eyepatch. It said *look at me, hero of the KGB*. And once he'd opened his gob it didn't get any better, it just confirmed my initial impressions.

"Ah! You are the famous Karo! Our mutual friend Martin has told me much about you. You are most welcome, and I am glad we meet at last."

He just really wound me up, the language sounding warm, but actually it was all about himself, the accent so clipped and exact, yeuch!

"But how is dear Martin? I hear he is still on leave. I wish to go and see him, but ..." he waved his arms around, taking in his office, and the whole building, the whole Russian quarter, as if to say he was so *frightfully* busy that he couldn't *possibly* find the time to go and see his *best* pal.

"Yeah, well, maybe you should have gone to see him while you had the chance."

Dmitri leaned back in his chair, one hand holding the other in front of his belly. He was doing the same eyebrow trick as Neumann.

"Oh, for God's sake! Martin has been arrested. They think he was involved in that thing on Saturday."

Now I had Dmitri's attention, there was a definite eyebrow flicker.

"Can you help him?" I asked.

"As an officer of the Russian forces in Germany I regret I'm not in a position to offer assistance. It is not our place to interfere in the internal affairs of our host country-"

"Firstly," I held up a finger, "you are not an officer of the Russian forces—or do you think I don't know what those blue flashes on your uniform mean?" I held up another finger. "Secondly. I'm not asking you to interfere, just tell us if you know what Martin was up to these last few weeks."

"Thirdly ..." And I ran out of steam. I was going to have to stop doing this first-second-third thing, but then I thought of something. "Thirdly, Martin considers you to be a friend. So maybe you better return the fucking compliment and see if you can't see your way to helping him out!"

"I see you know our friend Martin well." Dmitri gave me a crocodile smile. He got up and moved over to a filing cabinet, taking out a bottle of vodka and a couple of glasses. "Why don't you take a seat? You'll forgive my caution, it is become a second nature over the years. But, please, please sit down. Let us drink a toast—it's customary to seal a new friendship-"

"I don't want fucking vodka." I really did want vodka, a whole bottle would do nicely, but I wasn't going to give him the satisfaction.

Dmitri paused, then let the bottle and glasses disappear back into the filing cabinet. He came back to the desk and sat down opposite me. "Now Martin. Yes, he came to see me ..." Dmitri ruffled a few pages in his desk diary, but I was dead sure that he didn't really need to check. "On Thursday. He said he was trying to stop Kaminsky from being assassinated-"

"Kaminsky?"

"He said he was working with the policeman Steinlein."

Steinlein. Now I heard the name I knew him. He was the person I saw in the car with Martin last Friday—it was like I could see his smug face right now. He'd been in the papers, the fash had beaten him up, and he and Martin were in the magazines. Headlines: *Heroes of the Resurgence.*

"And why was Martin working with Steinlein?"

Dmitri angled forward across his desk, and in a voice so low I had to lean over to catch what he said: "I asked him that exact question. And his reply? Steinlein wanted their little project to remain secret, not even the colleagues in RS should know."

"So Steinlein knows what Martin was up to?"

"More than that, the whole project started with Steinlein."

"Steinlein was in on it? Has he been arrested too? Kaminsky is going to crucify them!"

"No, no. I don't think that is likely. Kaminsky is clever, he knows he has had his impact."

"You mean Kaminsky planned this whole thing—that it was staged?"

"I don't know, but I certainly believe it was more than staged, young lady. After all, they shot someone. But perhaps our first concern should be how to get Martin off the hook."

I got out of my chair and headed for the door. I'd heard enough; it wasn't the *young lady* bit, it was Dmitri himself. I knew his type, sit there and talk while others do the work. I had the information I needed.

"Are you always this *grosskotzig*?" I asked when I got to the door.

"*Grosskotzig*?" Dmitri looked puzzled, it probably wasn't very often he came across an unfamiliar German word.

I had to think for a moment before I could come up with an explanation he'd understand. "Pretentious and arrogant."

Dmitri laughed. The whole thing was just a joke to him.

21:29

Martin

I heard the key scrape in the lock and got up to stand at the back of my cell, already well schooled in the protocol of prison. But when the door opened it wasn't a grey uniformed warder who came in—it was Karl Kaminsky.

He looked less imposing up close, smaller than on the television or at his rallies. Despite the Western suit and sleek hair he looked like a real person.

I stayed at the back of the cell. I had no desire to take his hand, to greet him. Nor did I want to sit down on the stool again—I preferred to remain standing, to meet Kaminsky at eye-level.

Kaminsky gave my cell the once-over, then allowed his gaze to settle back on me.

"So, this is the man who wanted to kill me. I'm surprised you had it in you. So close, and yet so far away." His hand fluttered in the air, Hanna's soul leaving her body.

"Do you believe in anything?" I don't know where that came from —all the things I could say to him yet my mouth opens and a question like that spills out.

"Believe? What do you mean by believe, old man?" It was intended as an insult—Kaminsky and I were of the same age. "I'll tell you what I *couldn't* believe. I couldn't believe how easy you made it for me. You did everything I needed. I ought to thank you."

"Why me?"

"Why you? Why anyone? I needed a fall guy, and Captain Grobe was my *Schlemiel*. A perfect fit for the job. You did well, you created a masterpiece of confusion. And to make it all the more perfect, Captain Grobe is no mere van der Lubbe—he's a guardian of the establishment. I've no need to set the Reichstag on fire when I can use you to saw the legs off the Round Tables."

Kaminsky chuckled, amused by his own words. But the smile soon dropped from his face. "You asked whether I believe? Don't you know I am the deliverer of our nation? I shall bring peace and prosperity to our GDR. I tell the people: trust me, put your faith in me, give me your power and you won't have to worry about anything. I love my country. I love the achievements of the last forty years and I'm not alone in that. There's a *Volk* out there, desperate to trust me."

Seeing that I was no longer paying any attention to what he was saying, Kaminsky headed to the door.

"You're history," I told him as he turned. "You're a ghost walking in the daylight."

"How poetic—the spectre of Communism! But I think you'll find you're the one who's a ghost. The slaughtered innocent haunting *our* party." Kaminsky paused at the door. "Face it Grobe, I've won. I'd already won before you even realised you were in the game."

DAY 10
Tuesday
21st June 1994

Berlin: A suspect has been detained in the case of the murder of Hanna Krause. Police sources have indicated to Radio DDR I that the person is known to Berlin Kripo and is a member of a state agency.

08:00
Karo

I got really frustrated at the morning meeting: everyone was being so negative, and although I was desperate to tell everyone about my visit to Dmitri, I had to wait ages before it was my turn.

Klaus had nothing useful to report, Martin's neighbours hadn't noticed anything—nobody had even seen me, despite the fact I'd called round nearly every day last week.

Erika and Laura said that Martin's solicitor was sorting out a visiting order so that we could go and see him, and they had brought a pile of paperwork, but they were concentrating on the one file lying open before them.

"The police seem to think that Martin shot Hanna Krause by mistake, that he was aiming for Kaminsky," said Laura. "Their theory is that he was at the rally, he shot Hanna during the storm, and then passed the firearm to an accomplice. They haven't found any gun, neither at the scene, nor at his flat."

"So, have I got this straight?" Klaus reached over to take the file from Erika. "They are saying that Martin was in the middle of the rally, he took out a gun and shot Krause, nobody tried to stop him, nobody tried to hold him, not one of the tens of thousands of people there even saw him do it?"

"Bollocks, absolute bollocks! They're trying to frame him!" I blurted out, but nobody responded. Klaus was skimming the file and Erika was looking through the pile before her.

"The police have also said ..." she paused while she pulled out a piece of paper. "They said they can show the whole thing was planned. The ministry hasn't seen that evidence yet so Antje hasn't been able to tell us what it is. She's not convinced by the case against Martin but can't come out publicly until we have something concrete to prove the cops are making it all up."

"What about publicity and protests?" I asked.

"It's a bit delicate, don't you think?" Laura said. "This could seriously damage the image of the GDR—an officer of the RS being accused of terrorism. Whether or not Martin is released he'll be associated with this assassination attempt."

"But it's going to come out sooner or later anyway. We've got to do everything we can to get Martin out! Or are you worried that he may have done it? Seriously, none of you can believe that our Martin shot someone?"

"Of course we don't think Martin did it but we can't openly support him until we have hard evidence," answered Erika. "We're in the same boat as Antje."

"So you're more interested in being good RS officers than in saving Martin? Fuck RS! It's being wound up anyway, what have we got to lose? Or maybe you're looking forward to being transferred to the police? Do you think all this might damage your chances in department K1?"

"Karo, that's not how it is, as you well know!" Laura retorted. "We're doing everything we can to help Martin, and if you want to be part of that effort then you'd better pipe down and stop making ridiculous accusations."

"OK, but I don't want to rule out protests in support of Martin. I want that to be an option."

"Fine. Shall we work out what to do next?"

"We still don't know what Martin was up to these last few weeks, we need to find that out first." said Klaus.

"Hang on. I've got something useful: Dmitri said that Martin was investigating a plot to shoot Kaminsky, he was working with that cop Steinlein, the one who got beaten up by the fash in March. And I saw them together, on Stralau, they were driving from the far end of the peninsular towards town. It was the night before the rally."

There was a suitable silence while everyone digested the news.

"OK, we should check that out—the whole Steinlein angle is our priority. We have to try to talk to him," said Erika.

"We need to be discreet about it. Steinlein won't want to be seen talking to us," said Laura. "I'll approach him when he's off duty."

"We'll do a bit of digging, if we can find out what Steinlein and Martin were doing together it may help you prepare your approach," agreed Erika. "Karo, do you want to do that with me?"

I nodded, but Laura had already chipped in with her next point: "I'm meeting Martin's solicitor this morning. I'll ask about the new evidence and try to have the remand order revoked."

"And what about publicity, and getting some protests happening?" I knew I wasn't making myself popular by banging on about this but I didn't want it to be forgotten.

"I think we should hold off for the moment, if for no other reason than to protect Martin. He may still be released before his arrest becomes public knowledge," said Laura. "How about we put it on the agenda to discuss tomorrow?"

Everyone agreed to that, except me.

"OK," I caved in. "But if that arsehole Kaminsky starts making political capital out of Martin's arrest then I'm going to make it my main mission to organise some demos."

09:17

Karo

"So this is where you saw them?"

I'd already told her twice and now Erika was asking me again. We were standing in front of the *Durchgangsheim*, Erika had a map in her hands.

"And they came from there?" she asked, pointing right.

"Erika, how many times? I was standing here, they came round

522

that corner in a car." I took the map off her. "Why don't we just go and have a look what's round that bend?"

I had a look at the map, and saw why Erika was so confused. There wasn't anything much around the corner: a church, three shipyards, a few houses, a couple of other buildings and what looked like a park.

"Well, they won't have been at the shipyards, will they? So let's concentrate on those other buildings."

"Why have they got it in for Martin?" I wondered aloud while we walked towards the end of the peninsular.

"Bad luck, I guess. Martin always manages to be in the wrong place at the wrong time. But he'd probably say it's the other way round: that he's always in the right place."

I tried to grin at Erika's crap attempt at humour. "But this all seems so, I don't know, kinda random."

We'd passed the church and graveyard and the last residential house.

"Maybe it is random. But Kaminsky needs a scapegoat. He's been winding the whole country up for weeks, you know how tense it's become. Now he needs a trigger to make that tension spill over into action."

"So you think Kaminsky could have planned this?" Erika's theory reminded me of what Dmitri had said. Kaminsky was a real piece of shit, but would he gamble everything on something so risky?

"Framing Martin benefits Kaminsky," she replied.

We'd left the last boatyard behind, the clanging of hammers and the ring of tools faded. Calm descended—birds twittering, children playing—I could even hear the lapping of the river against the pilings. The kids that I'd heard were outside a building with lots of large windows. A woman, just a bit older than me, was keeping an eye on them.

"What's this place?" I asked her, trying to look friendly.

"We call it the Blue House. And what do we call yous?"

"We're looking for two men who were in this area last week." Erika showed the woman her RS pass.

The woman laughed. "Well, if yous are looking for men hanging around ye've come to the right place! Blue House is where us bargees hole up while we wait to go through West Berlin." She gestured at a couple of freighters that were moored up nearby, and then at another dozen or so on the far side of the peninsular. "We've been held up these last few weeks because the *Wessis* are playing silly buggers with the border checks. And afore you ask we can't get down the River Oder because water levels are low. So we're stuck hanging around here, just like the old days."

Erika poked a couple of photos under her nose, probably to shut her up.

"Who are they?"

"Have you ever seen either of these men?"

"That one's a cop!" the woman stabbed her finger at Steinlein's mugshot. "I saw him once in uniform, lots of silver and gold pips weighing down his shoulders. But usually he was just wearing normal clothes-"

"When did you see him?"

"I dunno, when did we arrive? Must have been Thursday, yeah, Thursday because Willi was bringing his lighters over from the power station. I was stood here watching them come alongside when I saw that cop. Limping, had a cane. But as for that other one ..." She shook her head.

"Anyone here who might have seen this person?" Erika shuffled Martin's picture to the top.

"You'll be after asking old Henning. Goes to church twice a day, and wanders up and down the road when he's not on his knees. That's his boat, there, the push tug, keeps it nice and tidy, does our Henning-"

"Could you fetch Henning for us?"

Erika was being so patient, I would have totally lost it by now if I'd been asking the questions. But the woman was already heading into the Blue House, still talking: "You mind and keep an eye on those kids for me ..."

As soon as she was out of earshot I grabbed Erika's arm, shaking her with excitement.

"We're finally getting somewhere, we know Steinlein was here last Thursday!" I said to her.

"Don't get your hopes up too soon, we'll need a lot more than this to get Martin out. And until we do, we haven't got any hope of stopping Kaminsky."

Before I got totally depressed by Erika's über-realism this Henning guy appeared. He wasn't that old, maybe the same age as Martin or Erika, so definitely not quite ancient. He lumbered to a halt in front of us, and stood, waiting patiently for something to happen. At least it didn't look like he was going to blether on and on like the last person.

"We're wondering if anyone here saw either of these two men," said Erika holding out the photos of Martin and Steinlein.

"Aye."

"Which one?"

"That one first." He pointed at Martin's picture. "Looked beat up. Black eyes, bit of a limp. Thursday it were. Then the second one come out about ten minutes later. He had a limp too, worse than the other."

"Where?"

The man walked a few paces until he had a clear view down the road and pointed.

"That building there?" Erika asked.

The man nodded, waiting patiently for further questions.

"What were they doing in there?"

"How would I know a thing like that? Plenty of shouting, mind. Could hear them cussing and blinding from the road." Henning shook his head in disgust.

"Did you see either of them before Thursday?"

"Just that once. But if you ask Paule, he were here since the Monday of last week."

"Can we speak to Paule?"

"Ha! Only if yous are psychic."

Psychic? The way he said it made me think of sinking boats and drowning sailors, or maybe Steinlein ran amok with his service weapon. But it was more prosaic than that.

"Our Paule and his crew: long gone. Set off yesterday, they did. Tekkin' a load up to Eberswalde."

Erika got on the smoky Ikarus bus to the S-Bahn station. She'd be in Oranienburg in just over an hour, hopefully she'd manage to catch up with Paule's barge and get a statement from him. It definitely looked like Dmitri was right: Martin and Steinlein had been up to something. Which meant Steinlein should know what Martin was doing last week.

Steinlein was the key to this whole thing. But what part had he played? He was based out of Schottstrasse police station, same as Neumann, and that was where they'd charged Martin—was Steinlein involved in framing our friend?

I crossed the road to look at the weird little building that the bargee had pointed out. It was half pre-fab concrete, half old-build. Two rusty gates closed off the drive, one of the gateposts had a sign: *Council of Ministers of the GDR*. Weeds were growing through the concrete slabs of the driveway.

But the thing that I noticed was that some of the weeds were crushed, as if they'd been driven over.

I tried the gate, expecting it to be all creaky and squeally, but it swung open soundlessly. I had a look around: three doors, I checked the locks on each. I looked through the dusty window of the first door, I could see a hall and a flight of stairs. On one side was a metal cupboard, the doors hanging open, revealing empty shelves. There was nothing else to see. A look through the windows told me all the other rooms on the ground floor were just as empty, just some of those gormless portraits of Erich Honecker which suggested the building hadn't been used for over four years. But the crushed weeds told a different tale.

I was cycling away, heading towards Ostkreuz, trying to solve the riddle of the crushed grass when two cops waved to me from the side of the road. I looked around, no-one else about, they were definitely flagging me down.

I pulled into the kerb and put my hand into my pocket, reaching for my RS pass.

"What are you doing here, miss?" asked one.

"State business," I answered, showing them my RS pass.

The one that had spoken took my pass, looked at it then gave it back to me. As soon as I'd pulled the pass on them their arrogance had given way to confusion.

They took a few steps back and held a short, worried conference.

"Our apologies, miss, we've received reports of suspicious activity ... person answering your description." The cop touched his fingers to the peak of his cap, and I cycled on.

At the next corner I looked over my shoulder. One of the cops was holding his radio mike to his mouth, the other was staring after me.

14:19
Karo

"No grounds to detain them," the border guard said to the punk.

The border guard was Rico, and the punk was Tam. The punk lived on the *Lohmühle* trailer site just beyond the watchtower. I'd first met both of them in March when Tam was facilitating a meeting at which Rico was a reluctant participant. Now they were both looking through the gap in the Wall, watching two figures waiting to be cleared for entry by West Berlin police.

"Who you talking about?" I asked them.

"That's Giesler. Used to be a border guard under my command. Martin wanted to talk to him a few months back—that's when he and I first met."

"And the skin with him," added Tam, "used to be in my school. Steffen Huber. Nobody liked him, he never really fitted in. First of all he was a total communist, ultra-enthusiastic about being in the FDJ. Then he really got into all the militarist training crap with the GST. After 1989 he got involved with the skins. Feels a bit weird, seeing him again."

I looked across the bridge towards West Berlin, the two figures were heading towards Schlesisches Tor.

"Why did Martin want to talk to Giesler?"

"Gang of skinheads attacked a punk concert about six years ago. Giesler was a policeman at the time, and Martin wanted to ask a few questions. Doubt he got very far though," Rico answered.

Martin must have been interested in the attack at the Zion Church in 1987, which explained the old newspapers in his office. It was ancient history. Famous, but still ancient. What is it about Martin, he's always digging up the past as if he thinks the present isn't already hard enough.

I was about to suggest we head over to the watchtower for a cup of coffee when a car pulled out of the little petrol station just over the border, thirty of forty metres inside West Berlin. As the car swung onto the road I could clearly see the driver.

"Fucking hell—that's Becker!" It was definitely him, I recognised him from the photo in his personnel files. I grabbed Rico's field glasses and focussed on the car. It stopped to pick up Giesler and Huber, then drove on. "Been looking for that man for months." I returned Rico's binoculars.

"And it looks like he knows our friend Giesler. Did you get the make and licence?"

"Er, it was red wasn't it?" I tried.

"Volkswagen Polo, West Berlin plates. Here, I'll write the number down for you." Rico scribbled in his pocketbook and tore the page out.

I crossed into West Berlin, for some reason the border checks had been relaxed and I didn't have to wait long before the cop on the other side of Wall waved me on. My task was to go and see Katrin, tell her about her dad. I guess I had to reassure her somehow that it was going to be OK (even though right now everything was the complete opposite of OK) and the closer I got to Katrin's flat the more I wished it wasn't me having to tell her. I wanted to see her, I really did, but was nervous about it, too. And I definitely wasn't looking forward to telling her about what was happening.

Maybe that was why I took the long way round and ended up cycling through Lausitzer Platz, which was a good thing. Because, there, parked by the church was a red Polo. There was a good chance that it wasn't the same one, I mean, have you seen the number of little red cars in West Berlin? I carried on to the next corner then got off my bike and tried to find the piece of paper Rico had given me. I squinted around the corner, yep, that was the car, sitting empty. What do I do now? I looked across the square, lots of people, sitting at tables outside cafés, cycling around, walking around. Becker and the others might even be somewhere close, on their way back to the car.

I decided I needed some camouflage. If I'd been in my half of town I would have just ordered a coffee at a café, but there was no chance of that over here in the West, I couldn't afford the prices. So I just sat down in the shade of a building and asked passers-by for spare change—it's what punks do most of the time over here—I fitted in perfectly.

I got a load of abuse and a few coins, and was just starting to think I might be able to afford that coffee after all when Becker came back to his car, followed by the skin, Huber. They were about twenty or thirty metres away, close enough to see clearly, but not close enough to hear what they said.

Huber stood behind Becker, who opened the car door and reached in to grab something. It was an envelope, one of those rough grey ones we use over in the East. It was folded over lengthwise and when Huber took it, he folded it again before sticking it in his pocket.

Becker got into the car and started the engine. I had a choice— follow Becker in the car or Huber who was now crossing the square on foot? I decided to go after Huber—I wanted Becker badly, but I didn't rate my chances of keeping up with him. Easier to follow someone who was on foot.

I unlocked my bike and went after Huber. He just loped along, not particularly bothered about anything at all. He crossed Skalitzer Strasse on a red light and the cars all beeped at him, but he just carried on. By the time I'd managed to cross he'd disappeared. I guessed he'd gone into Görli park, but when I went through the gates I saw I had no chance—everywhere I looked there were masses of people: hippies lounging around smoking pot, punks with ghetto blasters and Turkish families setting up barbecues. The place was packed. Literally packed. I'd lost the skinhead.

I was pissed off with myself, why hadn't I just run across the road instead of waiting for a gap in the traffic? Then again, I was in West Berlin for a reason, and I guess right now that was more of a priority than looking for Huber. And anyway, was it so surprising that Becker knew this skin? Becker was involved with the Nazis, and so was Huber. The only surprising bit was this Giesler that Rico said used to be a border guard. I'd mention it to Martin once we'd got him out of the nick.

I walked to Katrin's, still thinking about Huber. It was time to forget about Becker and the others, and start trying to work out how to tell Katrin about her dad. I rang her bell, and waited for ages but no-one answered. Maybe she wasn't in? I felt hopeful and despondent all at once. I rang the bell again and waited for even longer but finally I had to admit it.

Katrin wasn't home.

16:16
Karo

Some kind of wake was going on back at the offices, everyone was talking in low voices, passing round pieces of paper as if they were death notices.

"How are we getting on?" I decided a cheery note was in order.

But nobody reacted. I sat down at the table and took the evening newspaper that Klaus handed me.

"*Kaminsky in bid to abolish Round Tables*," I read the headline out loud. Now I knew why everyone was so down. It looked like Kaminsky was serious about wresting power from the Round Tables, and if he succeeded then it would be the end of the new-GDR, the end of direct grassroots involvement in running our country. It would stop our slow revolution dead.

Before I could react Klaus handed me a bundle of files and photographs.

"What's all this stuff?"

"Martin's solicitor got access to the initial evidence," Klaus replied.

They were statements by witnesses who saw Martin in an unstable state just outside the Soviet Memorial, immediately after Hanna Krause was shot.

"What's all that about? They're saying Martin was off his head? Do we believe that?" I asked

Nobody answered, so I looked at the next sheet. It was an analysis of fingerprints found on a Makarov pistol. Result: they were Martin's. Results of ballistic analysis of said Makarov: the pistol had been used in the murder of a police informant in April.

OK, this was getting unreal. I couldn't imagine Martin with a gun,

530

never mind shooting anyone! Just not his style. Feeling queasy, I looked at the next load of papers. It was another mix of statements and photographs. I read the top statement, it was making out that Martin had contact with foreign agencies, subtext: Martin was a traitor.

"For fuck's sake! This can't be happening! There is no way, just no fucking way ..."

"Have a look at the photographs," Laura said.

I shuffled through them. Martin getting out of a Western car in front of some concrete flats; Martin shaking hands with a British army officer; a series of snaps showing Martin wearing shades and swimming trunks, looking the other way while a person approaches and picks up an envelope that's lying on the grass next to Martin. The camera's focus had remained on Martin, and the figure was blurred.

I was about to make some stupid comment about the photos when the envelope caught my eye. I couldn't be exactly sure—the photo was black and white, but it definitely looked like a grey envelope. It was A4, and looking at the next photo I could see the person who had taken the envelope was folding it lengthwise.

It was the way the envelope was being folded that had caught my attention. Becker gave Huber a grey envelope, just a couple of hours ago. Same size, same colour, folded lengthwise—not the way you or I would fold an A4 envelope, along the long side to make an A5 size. It was a standard, grey A4 envelope like millions of others. It couldn't really be the same envelope, despite the weird folding.

But the blurry figure photographed with Martin, I knew who that was. "That's Becker!"

I looked more closely at the other photos in the series, yep I was sure of it. I jumped up and went into my office, bringing Becker's file and photo back. I passed it around, and my colleagues compared Becker's portrait with the unclear figure in the photos.

"How can you tell? This figure in the photo with Martin is completely blurred, it's as if the photographer did it deliberately," said Klaus.

"I know it's him, I've seen him in real life, I followed him this afternoon. That's definitely him in the photo!" I quickly reported what had happened in Kreuzberg, how I'd seen Becker, Giesler and the skinhead Huber.

While I was speaking Laura went to the chalkboard. She wrote the three names and linked them with lines.

"We know that Martin has had contact with Steinlein recently—we've got two independent witnesses, plus Karo has confirmed it." She added Steinlein's name to the board. "Now we know he had contact with someone who may be Becker-"

"Not *may be*, it's deffo him! It's obviously him in the photo!"

"OK, let's assume for the time being that it's him. Now, if we believe the dates and times they say these photographs were taken then all of these meetings took place last week." Laura drew an arrow from Becker's name and wrote Martin next it. "We also know that Martin had contact with Steinlein several times last week." She wrote Steinlein and joined him to Martin with another line. "What do we need to find out?" she asked the room at large.

"What was Martin doing with Steinlein, did he know Becker, and did he know Becker was there? From the photo we can't tell whether he's deliberately looking away or whether he's completely unaware of Becker's presence," said Klaus.

"What about if we try to find out what Steinlein was doing on the days Martin met Becker—around the times the photos were taken?" suggested Erika.

"And why did Becker take that envelope from Martin, what was in it?"

"And is it the same envelope that Becker gave to Huber?"

"Where were the photographs taken, and by whom?"

They carried on coming up with questions and ideas while I looked through my notes on Becker. I couldn't see any links. Steinlein was a cop, always had been as far as I knew. Becker had worked for the Ministry of People's Education up to 1988, and sometime around or after 1989 he got involved with the fascists. I told the others what I was thinking.

"Go further back, where did Becker do his national service?"

I leafed through my scribbles again, wishing I'd been more systematic. My notes were all over the place, my thoughts, bits of stuff that Schimmel had told me, scrawls I'd added when I was in the

Ministry for People's Education archive. And then, there it was: "Becker was a *Volkspolizei* auxiliary when he was a student in Köthen."

"Anything else? Who did he work with, what dates?" Klaus was already reaching for the phone.

I gave Klaus the dates, and we all sat waiting while he spoke to someone at Köthen police station. A few minutes later he hung up, a rare smile appearing under his moustache.

"Don't you just love these small towns where nothing ever happens? Can you believe it, the desk sergeant actually remembered Becker from twenty years ago? Apparently he was usually attached to work with a certain sergeant Neumann, who transferred to Berlin *Kripo* in 1977."

Klaus crossed over to the board, added Neumann, and drew a line from Neumann to Becker, and from Neumann to Steinlein.

"And there we have the missing piece of the puzzle," he announced.

We stared at the chalkboard, trying to get our heads round this new development. Martin was working with Steinlein. Steinlein answered to Neumann, who knew Becker. And I'd seen Becker hanging out with Giesler and the skin Huber.

"Who's heading up the investigation into Martin?" I didn't really need to ask, I could already guess.

"Neumann." Klaus went to the board again and drew a thick line between Neumann and Martin. Now a messy web linked almost every name to each of the others.

I stood in front of the board, looking at all the lines. This was good, we had opened up a whole new way at looking at what was happening. I wanted to kiss and hug my colleagues—we were finally getting somewhere. But before I could get too smug about it all I noticed Klaus frowning over the disclosure papers. The way he was pulling a face made me want to scream at him—we were finally getting somewhere but he was about to go all negative on us.

"Something's not right, it doesn't feel right." He had an outline map of the Soviet War Memorial on top of the other papers, his thumb was pressed against the barrow with the statue of the soldier on, his forefinger was pressed on the first oblong of grass. "Is that fifty metres? Would you say that's about fifty metres?"

I shrugged, but Laura was peering over Klaus' shoulder, her eyes measuring the distance between his thumb and finger.

"Makarov," said Klaus. "Great weapon. Simple, reliable, cheap to produce." Klaus was looking around, expecting us to take an interest in his gun fetish. "I trained with it during national service. Only problem with the Makarov is that it's not a precise weapon. Fifty metres, any more than that and you can't be sure of hitting your target."

"So?" I couldn't see what Klaus' point was, but he seemed excited about it.

"So, if Hanna Krause was shot by a Makarov then the shooter would have been standing in one of the first few rows of the crowd. I can't imagine anyone using a Makarov from further back." Klaus was staring at the map, finger pressed against where he imagined the assassin standing. "But it makes no sense—those first few rows would be where Kaminsky's biggest fans and his security were standing. If you fired a gun in Kaminsky's direction while you were in the middle of that lot—you wouldn't get out alive."

DAY 11
Wednesday
22nd June 1994

Berlin: The suspect in the case of the murder of Hanna Krause has been named. Unofficial sources have identified the alleged shooter as Martin Grobe, known for his activities as an officer of the controversial Republikschutz counter-intelligence agency.

Earlier today, Dr. Kaminsky, Member of the Volkskammer and General-Secretary of the PDS repeated his calls for an immediate dissolution of the RS: "The Central Round Table has no control over their own agency —it's out of control and, tragically, on Saturday Hanna Krause paid the price."

08:07
Karo

At the meeting this morning we checked on progress, and I talked about last night—it had gone really well, and I was dead chuffed about it. I told my colleagues about how, after leaving the office last night, I'd gone back to my own scene.

The first thing I did was go and see my best mate, although when I got there Schimmel didn't seem that pleased to see me. Trying to mend fences, I said sorry. Again.

"You told me to back off and I didn't. I should have listened to what you were saying."

Schimmel was sitting on the floor, staring into space. I wasn't even sure he'd heard me apologise. "You go delving into my life, digging up my personal shit," he said. "It doesn't matter to you whether or not I'm OK with that. But if anyone ever asks you about your past you go ape. It's not on."

It was a rant, but it came out all mechanical, the whole time he was speaking he stared across the room. It was dead weird, and it made me feel really uncomfortable. Maybe it was just because he was right and I was finding it hard to face up to that fact.

"This is for you. Peace offering?" I gave him an envelope, one of those grey ones that had got Martin into trouble.

"What's in it?" Schimmel took the envelope, but didn't open it.

"It's what I've found out about Becker. There's a photo in there, and some biographical details. But I haven't managed to get hold of an up-to-date address."

Schimmel just shrugged and put the envelope on top of one of the computers that clutter up his room.

"I've kept a copy because we might need it to help Martin." I told him.

"Martin? What's he got to do with it?"

I told my friend what was happening to Martin, I thought he might be shocked, but he was more pissed off.

"How long have you known about this? And you're only just telling me now? Martin's a mate, which is more than can be said about you!" He lurched to his feet and ran down the stairs to the central kitchen. As I followed I could hear the gonging of the cymbal that hangs over the sink.

My ex-housemates began dribbling in. "What's up? What's the alarm?"

Schimmel told them about Martin. "We were there when he raided the Ministry of the Interior last year, and you know about when the fascists kidnapped him and we kicked their arses. Well, Martin needs our help again. The bastards are framing him for shooting Hanna Krause. He's on remand and nobody knows about it!"

They were making all the right noises so I just sat at the back and listened. They were talking about doing a demo outside the prison. Definitely sounded like a good start to me.

"C'mon you," said Schimmel after a while. He grabbed my hand and dragged me out of the kitchen. "Let's go and spread the word!"

We spent the evening going round all the squatted social centres to tell people about the demo. It was good to be with Schimmel again, and it was doing him good too—that evening was the first time for ages that I'd seen him actually look really alive.

"We need to speak to Martin, find out where he was standing at the rally," Erika said. "He might have seen something."

"I'll contact the solicitor again, find out how she's getting on with the visiting order," answered Laura.

It went on like that for ages, everyone coming up with things we needed to find out, do or discuss.

At some point I managed to escape and headed over to West Berlin. Rico wasn't on duty, but I got a salute as I passed through the border checkpoint.

I'd phoned Katrin, made sure she would be at home when I got there. Talk about uncomfortable—that was probably the worse phone call I've ever had—and all the worse for having Erika and the others in the same room.

So you can imagine how nervous I was when I rang Katrin's bell. I hadn't told her what I wanted to see her about, just that it was really urgent and really important—she probably thought I was planning to dump my heart at her feet and beg her to give me a chance.

But when I told her about Martin she went quiet.

"What are you doing about it?"

I told her everything. That we were working on getting enough evidence to free Martin, that we were worried that if we didn't manage to do it soon then the other side would make up enough stuff for at least some of the charges stick.

"Who's the other side?"

"We don't know." I watched Katrin, she was dead still and her face was hard. "But we're pretty sure some cops are involved. A Lieutenant Steinlein and his superior, Captain Neumann. Probably others too."

"Cops? Some cops are framing my dad? That's insane! Why can't you just live in a normal country like the rest of us?" Katrin was really screwing herself up over this, and fair play, it was about her dad.

"And why are you only telling me now? Two whole days you've

known about this! Why didn't you tell me as soon as you found out?" Katrin stopped pacing around, she stood there, hands on hips, storms of emotion marching across her face.

"That's my fault, I ..." I couldn't find a way to say it—my reasons for not hanging around yesterday, not waiting for Katrin to come home, not even phoning, they seemed so petty and useless now: because I was too embarrassed, heartbroken, proud.

Crap. Really crap reasons.

"Pick up the phone, that's all you had to do. Pick up the phone." Katrin had turned around, she was facing the other way. "I want you to go."

"We wanted to ask you, about getting word out, you know, in the newspapers, the radio—get it into the Western media-"

"Fine."

"We were thinking you might have some contacts, you know, through the work you do with AL?"

"I said, *fine*."

"What about the details? I need to-"

"I'll get them from RS. Just go."

I should have gone straight back to RS but I wanted a bit of time to think. Katrin was really upset, she had a right to be, I should have phoned her the moment I found out about Martin. I felt shit.

Again.

So far, this week was turning out to be even worse than last week. I didn't want to hang around the streets of Berlin, feeling sorry for myself, but I didn't want to go back to the office either. I just wasn't cut out for all the paperwork, the phone calls and working through all the bureaucracy. It was all necessary if we were going to get Martin out, but it didn't feel like *me*.

What I did last night, being with a gang of punks, getting fired up about injustice, being there when demos are organised, going on protests—that's what I do best, that's me.

Still, you do what you've got to do, and Martin's a friend, it's my job to help him. Solidarity. Right now that meant I should stop brooding and get back to RS.

While I was doing all this heavy thinking I'd been wandering the streets of Kreuzberg. I'd got as far as the Kotti. There were millions of people about, just like there always are, but one of them was a skinhead, patiently waiting for the traffic lights to change.

The skin was Steffen Huber.

Huber crossed the road and went straight past me, heading up Skalitzer Strasse. I followed him, watching him sway from one side of the pavement to the other, passers-by nervously dodging out of his way. What to do? I wanted to confront him, try to find out what was going on, but dealing with a pissed up skinhead didn't sound like such a great idea.

I followed him as far as Lausitzer Platz, just round the corner from where Katrin lives, and watched him go into a kebab shop. Maybe this was my chance after all.

I reckoned I had three minutes. I legged it to Katrin's and kept my finger on her bell until she buzzed me in.

"Katrin. Sorry, really, really sorry, but I need to borrow your tape recorder thingy. Just for ten minutes, quick! It's for Martin." I was puffing and panting from running and I must have looked desperate because Katrin didn't argue. She just got the recorder.

"Can you lend me five marks as well?"

She gave me the dosh, still without a word, her face tight. Before I'd even turned to go back down the stairs she'd shut her front door.

I ran back to the kebab shop. Huber was still in there, watching his döner being put together. I waited on the street, catching my breath and trying to look inconspicuous. I looked around, checking that nobody was paying too much attention, but in Berlin nobody really cares what you do or what you look like. Except, perhaps, for that woman in the red top on the other side of the square. When I first looked in her direction she'd been staring into the plate glass of an empty shop window. Didn't really notice her until it struck me how odd it was to spend so much time looking at an empty shop. I looked again, but she'd gone.

I was still trying to process it when Huber came out.

"Steffen, great to see you!"

Huber looked like he was about to tell me to fuck off, but I didn't give him time to do that.

"Listen, mate," I moved closer and lowered my voice, trying to come across all conspirational. "You did great work—absolutely fucking ace. Let me shake you by the hand."

He was looking confused now, unsure whether to punch me or to offer me his hand. His pupils were like black holes and he had a really bad case of red-eye. So not drunk, more stoned. Or both. This was perfect, almost too perfect.

"You know what, I'm going to buy you a beer. Least I can do after all you've done for the movement."

Huber puffed his chest out and stood up straight, not noticing his kebab was dripping on his boots. "Well, you know, it was nothing." Huber wasn't just beginning to relax, he was about to burst with self-satisfaction.

"I want to hear all about it—let's get that drink, come on." I took him to a bar with benches outside. "I'll go and sort the beers, you plonk yourself down there."

I poked my head through the door and signalled to the barman that I wanted two beers, then I clicked on Katrin's tape recorder and put it back in my pocket before heading to the table where Huber was waiting for me. The confused look had returned—his coupon was a picture—like he was trying to work out a difficult sum in his head.

"Who are you?" he asked.

I lowered my voice again. "I'm in disguise—I'm not really a punk."

Huber nodded, a smile of relief climbing onto his face. "Wow, undercover! That's so cool," he whispered, as if he'd never heard of anything so amazing.

I was starting to enjoy myself, but a voice in my head was warning me not to push it too far. The barman brought the beers and I waited until he'd disappeared before I spoke again.

"You celebrating? Too right, after what went down on Saturday." I didn't know if he'd been at Kaminsky's rally, but it was worth a try.

"It was amazing! I was up a tree, two hundred meters, there was a storm." He smacked a fist into the palm of his hand. "*Bam!* Piece of piss hitting that bitch." He smiled to himself and took a sip of beer. "Took her out, *no problemo*, same moment as the lightning struck. It was amazing."

Shit, I hadn't seen that one coming! This was way heavier than expected.

"No hassle from the cops?"

"Nah, the Corporal sorted out those losers!"

"Corporal? You mean Becker?"

Huber stared at me for a moment, the pride on his spotty face turning into something else, something like suspicion.

"The Corporal! *Everyone* knows the Corporal." He looked at his half eaten kebab, then back at me.

Oh shit, think fast! "I meant Giesler, yeah, Giesler," I tried, but it was too late. I'd fucked up.

Huber was still staring at his kebab as if it would tell him what to do. While he was waiting for an answer I got up, pushed my beer over to his side of the table and nabbed his glass.

"Listen mate, been a total honour, but got to head off ... you know, bit of a mission. Say hi to the Corporal for me!"

I headed off sharpish, pouring the beer into the gutter and putting Huber's glass into a paper bag.

13:53

Karo

I was buzzing when I got back to RS, but I had to be patient. Laura was on the phone and everyone shushed me when I tried to tell them what I'd just found out.

Laura finally got off the phone, a curl of a smile on her face, like a trout that's just been hooked.

"Two of us can go to see Martin this afternoon. There's a visiting order waiting in the director's office."

"We can go and see Martin? That's ace, c'mon, that's really brilliant!" But the others didn't share my enthusiasm.

So I told them all to pin their ears back and listen while I played them the tape of Huber's confession. I was almost as proud as the skin had been. Everyone heard Huber pretty much admitting that he'd shot Hanna Krause. Trouble is they didn't look as excited as I felt.

"What's the problem? Hanna Krause was taken out by this low-life who says he was up a tree, two hundred metres away. Look," I pulled the paper bag out of my rucksack, "I even got his fingerprints. This is evidence, this is going to get Martin off the hook!"

"It does confirm our suspicions that Hanna wasn't shot with a Makarov, the confession and the prints, however, can't be used," said Laura.

"What you talking about? This is pure gold! We know who did it and how he did it!" This wasn't exactly the celebratory atmosphere I'd been expecting.

"Karo, you made a secret recording and obtained prints of someone in West Berlin—a foreign country. Even if you'd done it over here it wouldn't be admissible—you're not a sworn in RS officer. What you've got there is hearsay, nothing more."

Did they always have to piss over everything I did?

My consolation prize was to go with Erika to see Martin. Before we went into the prison we stood in front of the scary gate, about five metres high and made of grey metal.

"I always hoped I'd never have to go in here," I told Erika.

"And I hoped I'd never have to come back," she replied.

I reckon she'd won that round. I wanted to ask her when she'd been inside, what it was like, but it wasn't the right time. Anyway, it was kind of hard to talk—drums, whistles and fireworks were going off all around us—it was dead loud. The Friedrichshain and Lichtenberg massives were out in force, all to show solidarity with our Martin. The banners were a bit rubbish but at least there were loads of them: *Set Martin Free*, that kind of thing. But the crappiest was probably: *Martin Grobe: People's Martyr*.

"You ready?" I asked Erika, but she was already on her way to the sentry box where a nervous screw was keeping an eye on the demo.

"You can't come in, not while that lot's here," he was telling her, and he started to look even more nervous when he saw me coming.

"I am Lieutenant Lang, and this is my colleague Frau Rengold. We are expected by the director." Erika was doing that determined thing again, the same as when we were at the ministry the other day.

"I'm sorry comrade Lieutenant, I have my orders-"

"Then use that phone of yours to get new orders!"

The guard used the internal phone, muttering something into it and waiting for a reply. Eventually he hung up.

"Someone is coming."

Erika didn't look very happy about that, but decided not to argue the toss. We waited a few more minutes before the grey gates scraped open. Five or six screws came out, truncheons at the ready, and they formed a line between us and the demonstrators.

My mates saw what was happening and must have thought we were being kettled because they surged forward to rescue us. I waved them back, and Erika and I disappeared through the gap in the gate.

On the other side a more senior screw was waiting for us.

"Comrade Lieutenant, Colleague Rengold, would you follow me?"

All this formal shit was getting boring, but Erika was already following the senior dude up some steps into a building.

We went up to the first floor and along a corridor to a door, helpfully marked *Direktor*. But before we could go in, another senior dude with even more silver on his shoulders came along.

"Comrade Lieutenant, the Director apologises that he isn't able to see you personally, but-"

"That's fine," said Erika in a tone sharp enough to cut through all this crap. "We only need the visiting order to see Captain Grobe."

"I'm afraid that won't be possible, you understand-"

"No, we *don't* understand! The visiting order, if you please comrade *Obermeister*!"

"Because of the current situation StVE Rummelsburg is in lockdown, it is impossible to visit any of the detainees." This *Obermeister* was hardcore, he'd just carried on as if Erika hadn't spoken.

"There's a handful of kids out there and you're in lockdown?" Erika sounded dead contemptuous, I was so impressed I didn't pull her up on calling my mates *kids*.

"Correct, comrade Lieutenant."

It went back and forth like that, and Erika was dead scary, but this dude wasn't budging a millimetre. The oberscrew accompanied us back downstairs and into the yard between the two sets of gates. There was the gate we'd come in through, and I guess the other went into the prison. There was even a watchtower and a load of screws holding truncheons. Unless somebody opened that second gate we had no chance of getting to see Martin. Even I had to admit defeat.

"Inform the Director that the Ministerial Committee will hear of this, comrade *Obermeister*," was Erika's parting shot as we were let back onto the street.

"Did you notice something in there?" asked Erika before all the punks came to ask us what was going on.

"They were dead jumpy?"

"Not just that, didn't you hear the noises from inside? Metal plates and cups being banged against bars—the prisoners know about the demonstration out here, they can hear it."

15:22
Karo

"What did Martin say? Did you get the information we need?" Laura demanded as we walked through the door.

"There was a noise demonstration going on outside, they used that as an excuse not to let us in," Erika replied.

"A demonstration? Outside the prison? Irresponsible!"

"It's not like they knew we were on our way to see Martin!" I snapped, stung by Laura's criticism. "We agreed it was time to make some noise—remember? So you're totally out of order saying my mates are irresponsible!"

"Stop it you two!" Erika shunted me away before Laura and I could get into a real argument. "Laura, take it easy—we're all getting a bit tired and stressed. And as for you, miss," Erika turned to me. "Stop winding Laura up. No, no," she made shushing motions with her hands, stopping me from answering back.

Which was the moment Klaus chose to come in. He went straight to the radio and turned it on.

After widespread unrest throughout the country the emergency bill proposed by the General-Secretary of the PDS, Dr. Karl Kaminsky, has been brought forward. The Volkskammer *will debate the bill to abolish the Round Tables and Workers' Councils on Friday. Dr. Kaminsky said in an interview earlier-*

"Fucking ace!" I shouted as Klaus switched off the news again. "There's so much protest going on that Kaminsky has had to change his plans! That's incredible!" I was really excited, but Laura just pulled a face.

"Perhaps you weren't listening properly, young lady. It means we have less than two days to get Martin released and to stop Kaminsky."

23:44

Martin

It was late when the hatch in the door rattled open. The cell light had been switched on, and darkness curtained the glass bricks in the outside wall.

I stood at the back of the cell, waiting for whoever it was to come through the door. I hadn't been let out for exercise today, so hadn't had spoken to any of the other prisoners. It was frustrating not knowing what was going on outside—I'd heard the noise of a demonstration but I didn't know what it was about.

When the door finally opened it revealed not the grey uniform of a prison warder, but *Volkspolizei* green. Steinlein eased into the cell, glancing behind himself as he did so. He threw a bundle of clothes onto the bed and held a finger to his lips.

"I've come to get you out. Put those on," he whispered. He saw my hesitation and pointed to the clothes on the bed. "Come on, we don't have much time!"

"I can't just leave."

"You can. If you ever want to get out of here then now is the time."

I looked at Steinlein, standing by the door, listening for the footsteps of the guard. Could I trust him? I'd trusted him this far and look where that had got me. But he'd come to get me, I couldn't afford not to go with him.

I pulled off my prison clothes and climbed into the civvies Steinlein had brought.

"How are you going to get me past the guards?"

"No time to explain, pull the hat lower. Now come on."

Day 12
Thursday
23rd June 1994

Berlin: The border between West Berlin and the Capital of the GDR has now been completely closed to all traffic. The West Berlin Senate announced the measures this morning, expressing concerns about continued civil unrest in the Capital of the GDR.

10:30

Karo

Even though it was early the main kitchen at *Thaeri* was packed. It felt like the whole of Friedrichshain was there, and most of Prenzlauer Berg and Mitte too. People were feeling good about getting it together yesterday, pulling off a noise demo at the prison. Now they were talking about a march.

"What's the latest, Karo?"

I told them that we still hadn't been allowed to speak to Martin, and that we were worried about Kaminsky's next move.

"Listen, Karo, no disrespect, and I know you're involved in this RS stuff, and so is Martin. But Martin's a good guy, heart in the right place—you know what I'm saying? So if he's in the can then I'll do my bit to get him out. But the Round Tables? Are they really that great? It's just a load of old men talking. There's no space for any of us there! What have the Round Tables ever done for us?"

"Have you ever been to one?" I asked. "Have you ever actually contributed? At any level? You ever checked out the Neighbourhood Round Table? Maybe it is full of old men talking, but if they're the only ones who bother turning up then what do you expect? The tools are only as good as the people using them!"

"Yeah, but it's not really our scene, is it?" someone else offered.

"Fuck's sake! What do you mean it's not our scene? This is where you live, and you say the neighbourhood RT isn't your scene? Four years we've been at this, four years! It's no wonder people are saying that it's not working! If not even people like us can be bothered to get involved then it's not going to fucking work, is it?"

"Easy Karo, we do our bit! Look at all that stuff that went down in spring, we dealt with the fash, didn't we? Without us none of that would've happened."

"It's not enough! How can that be enough? We're not just needed when something really major goes wrong. It's not enough to just turn up whenever there's a sexy action or a fuck-off demo being planned!" I realised I was shouting, but by now I didn't care. "If we don't think the Round Tables are doing the right things then we need to get involved and not just fucking moan about it."

"You know what Karo, again, no disrespect, but maybe you've been hanging out with that lot from the RS too much. Institutionalised, that's what you sound like."

"Fuck you, fuck the lot of you!" I left them to it, lazy fucking shits. It was like they *wanted* Kaminsky to centralise all the power again so that they could blame somebody else when things got worse.

I stood on the doorstep, feeling absolutely fucked off. *Deep breath, Karo* I told myself, *deep breath.* I needed to stick to the script. Twenty-four hours to get Martin out and stop Kaminsky from trashing everything we've achieved since 1989. I was about to get on my bike when I heard the door open behind me. I turned around, ready to take a bite out of whoever it was. But it was Tam.

"Do you remember back in March, when you came to that meeting at the *Lohmühle?*" she said. "We decided to open up a new border crossing. You weren't sure about working with the local Round Table either. None of us that night thought it would work. Except Rico, maybe." Tam broke off to give me a shy smile. "But we did it, and it's working out. It's hard work dealing with all these other people when the only thing you've got in common is that you happen to live in the same neighbourhood. But it can work."

"Yeah, well, we don't have to worry about that for much longer, Kaminsky will have got rid of the Round Tables by this time tomorrow."

"The point I was trying to make is that all this is scary. It's scary to take responsibility, to open yourself up to other people. Maybe it's just," Tam looked over her shoulder to where the front door of *Thaeri* still stood open, "maybe they're more scared than lazy."

"So why don't you go and talk to them about it? No point telling me, is there?" I was being mean now, but I was still pissed off by my ex-housemates and all the other losers who think they're so radical but can't actually be arsed doing anything about it.

"What's your next step?" Tam asked.

"I want to get some demos and stuff happening tomorrow, outside the Palace of the Republic while the debate is going on. Let parliament know that we're not going to give up our Round Tables and Workers' Councils without a fight."

"OK, leave it with me. I know everyone from *Wagenburg Lohmühle* will be up for that. I'll talk to the Alt-Treptow neighbourhood Round Table, see if we can spread the word that way too. Don't worry, we'll get it sorted."

I got on my bike and cycled down the hill, feeling better after the chat with Tam, and maybe that's why I wasn't paying enough attention. Before I'd even noticed what was happening I had a cop car on my left and a Barkas van behind me. The car at my side accelerated and pulled across the roadway in front of me. I was pulled off my bike and shoved into the back of the van. Bastards didn't even let me lock my bike up.

11:07

Karo

The van stopped and I was pulled out of the back. They'd put handcuffs on me and, unable to steady myself, I nearly fell to the ground as I was dragged down the steps.

Watch out, you pigs! I wasn't stupid enough to say it aloud, but I definitely shouted it inside my head.

I had a cop on either side of me, they were deliberately trying to hurt me, one shoving me, the other pulling me by the wrists. I tried to keep my cool, tried to keep breathing. They just wanted me to kick off, they wanted me to scream and try to escape, any excuse to get their batons out and lay into me. Fucking pigs.

They shoved and dragged me into the police station. I recognised it, I'd been here before: Marchlewskistrasse. This lot thought they were well hard, the cocks o' Berlin. They had something to prove, and I was determined not to let them use me to prove themselves on.

I'd spent the time in the back of the van doing some thinking. There was too much at stake, I couldn't afford to let them keep hold of me—I had to get out, and fast.

We'd reached the custody officer, sitting all comfortable behind his desk. One of the cops had shifted his grip, he now held my arm, thumb jabbing painfully into my armpit, his knuckles resting against my left breast. He was deliberately moving his fingers back and forth and he was getting off on rubbing against me. I was going to get this fucker, I was going to memorise his face and track him down.

"Name and reason for detention?" demanded the custody sergeant. He hadn't even looked up, just had a pen in his hand, ready to fill in the form.

"Rengold, Karoline. Detained in execution of an arrest warrant," said the perv on my left.

"Authority issuing warrant?" asked the sergeant, bored.

Perv and his copper mate exchanged a look. They didn't have the details, someone else had requested the pick up.

This was it. Deep breath, keep calm. Don't protest, sound authoritative. I straightened my spine, making myself as tall as I could. I looked at the top of the custody sergeant's head and willed him to look up. "There is no warrant, comrade Sergeant."

The sergeant looked up, then did a double take when he clocked my appearance—my punk outfit didn't match the voice I'd just used on him.

"Contact Captain Neumann from Lichtenberg K1 to confirm. And in the meantime take these cuffs off, I need the toilet," I said, still using the voice.

The sergeant looked from one of my guards to the other, his eyes demanding answers. Perv had taken his hand off me and had shifted away slightly, as if disowning me.

"The signal came from Lichtenberg, comrade Sergeant," said the other cop, not sounding too sure of himself.

"Escort Miss Rengold to the toilet," the sergeant barked.

Perv stood to one side, watching as his colleague released my wrists and took me down a corridor. Behind me I heard the sergeant pick up the phone.

Prisoners have buckets in their cells, and since I didn't have a cell yet I was taken to the staff toilets. I had no plan, no idea what to do next —but I'd bought myself a few minutes and hoped that I'd think of something.

"Be quick about it," my guard ordered, unwilling to give up his authority over me.

As I walked into the toilets my heart leapt. I was in the female locker room, the toilets themselves were through another doorway. I tried the first locker, civvy clothes, magazines, hairbrush. On to the next one, traffic cop uniform, that'd do. I pulled on the white blouson, the uncomfortable green skirt and the stupid, stiff white hat. Into the toilets, check in the mirror, push my hair under the cap. Now it looked like I had a skinhead, but that was better than a red mohican.

I pulled open the window, it wasn't barred because it let out into the inner yard and not the street outside. Fine, poke my head out, no-one in sight. Hopefully nobody was looking out of any of the windows either. One leg over the sill, then the next. Jump down to the concrete a metre or so below, then march over to the gate. *March* I told myself, don't slouch, don't run. Look like you're a cop, think like a cop. *Be a cop.*

12:57

Karo

"Maybe we've made a bit of progress in getting Martin out, but we're not even close to stopping Kaminsky," I was having a go at my RS colleagues again. "We haven't even got a proper plan yet! Oh, sorry, no. We have a plan: get Martin out and that will somehow magically be enough to stop Kaminsky. Super. Brilliant. Fan*fucking*tastic."

"The two are related, as you are well aware." Maybe I was giving them a hard time, but Laura could give as good as she got. "And as you also know, we thought we had a few weeks to deal with the situation."

"So, Kaminsky moved the goalposts. And now it looks like he's after us. Didn't you see me march in here wearing a copper's uniform? Didn't you hear me tell you I'd just escaped from police custody? We have to act. Like now—so what are we waiting for?"

"Karo's right," said Erika. "We need to adjust our plans. They're coming for us, we have to act now, before they arrest us all. We need something concrete against Kaminsky, something that will discredit him, show how he's been manipulating the situation to make sure his bill is passed."

Klaus and Laura were giving each other meaningful looks, it was like they blamed me for the situation we were in.

"I don't think they'll try to arrest us here, at least not yet, but no-one should leave this office alone. We always go around in pairs. Anyone not in this office should check in every hour. That way if one of us is arrested we'll know and can try to do something about it." Erika had taken over, she had a plan. "Laura, can you contact Antje and see about getting Karo's arrest warrant revoked? And check whether warrants have been issued for the rest of us. Then you and Klaus can carry on working on Martin's release, or at least get us a visit. Karo and I will dig a bit deeper, work on these possible connections between Kaminsky, Becker and Giesler."

"What about the skinhead? He practically admitted he shot Hanna," I was still proud that I'd found Huber.

"If we had more time we could work on that angle, but we don't have much to go on," Klaus joined in the conversation. "Kaminsky is our priority now, and there's no obvious link between Kaminsky and Huber. I think we need to let Steffen Huber go for the moment, he's a small cog and he's holed up in West Berlin where we can't reach him anyway. We'll pass his name to the prosecutor once we've dealt with Kaminsky."

Now we were starting to get somewhere—still too much talking, but at least we were making some solid plans. But it all came to a grinding halt when Grit poked her head round the door.

"Just had a call from *Ministerin* Willehardt's secretary, it's bad news. I passed on Klaus's query about where Martin was standing at the rally, and whether he was close enough to have used a Makarov on Kaminsky and the others. Apparently the *Ministerin* asked the police for clarification and it took them over a day to get back to her. Now they're saying there was a mistake in the autopsy report, that she was killed by a ..." Grit checked her notes, "a soft nose 7.62×54 mm. They've found the casing of a bullet of that type with Martin's prints on it."

"Dragunov rifle," Klaus whispered.

"There's more: Martin's escaped, just heard it on the radio. He's on the run."

"Come on, it's not all bad news! They're obviously fabricating evidence against him, I mean, it's so bleeding obvious, first it was a pistol, now it's a rifle. They can't even get their own story straight. And now Martin's escaped—that's ace! First I get away from the cops and now Martin has too—go Martin!" This was exciting, this was the best news all week!

Except the others weren't excited. They looked pretty flabbergasted. Everyone's eyes and mouths were so wide open that they all looked like goldfish. Except Erika, who was holding her hand in front of her mouth, and goldfish don't have hands.

"Karo," said Laura after a moment. She used that patronising tone of voice that made me boil, "This is very bad news. This is going to make it easier for them—the focus now is going to be on Martin, they've got evidence against him, but if he's gone underground then he can't help us to prove he's been framed."

"Is this a bad time?" A quiet voice came from behind Grit.

Schimmel edged around the door, one hand clamped to the frame, the other fidgeting with the zip of his hoodie.

"We're rather busy at the moment-" started Laura, but Erika interrupted.

"Is it important, Schimmel?" she asked him, but from his face it was obvious that it was important.

"It's OK, I've got this, you carry on." I took Schimmel into my office, sat him down and listened to what he had to say.

"I looked at that stuff in the envelope, your research on Becker. I didn't want to look, but it felt stupid ignoring it. Is Becker," Schimmel swallowed, his eyes met mine for a second, then he looked down at his feet. "Is Becker really involved in framing Martin?"

"We're pretty sure he is." I was looking towards the door, wanting to get back to the others, but Schimmel needed to talk.

"Karo, you've been telling me for months that I need to move on, and I've just been a total pain in the arse, haven't I?"

"And you kept telling me to back off, but I didn't. Sorry."

Schimmel gave me a smile for that, then his head dropped down again. He was trying to work up the courage to say something difficult.

"You're right Karo, I need to move on. There's other stuff I need to be doing, and Becker's already fucked up my life once, I'm not going to let him do it again." Schimmel's face moved up until his eyes met mine. "If we get Martin out, if we stop Kaminsky, if we save the Round Tables and all of that—then Becker's lost hasn't he?"

"Haven't you heard? Martin's on the run, he broke out last night. Now it's all or nothing. We need to clear Martin's name and stop Kaminsky from destroying the Round Tables."

Schimmel did the same goldfish impression as the others. "I want to do my bit, I need to do my bit. Tell me what to do."

"Can you ring some Round Tables and Workers' Councils, see whether they're doing anything about Kaminsky's bill? If they're not, put them in touch with the nearest Round Table that is. We've got to mobilise them all, even if they just have a big meeting or something, it's got to be better than letting Kaminsky stomp all over them."

"I can do that." Schimmel actually sounded excited. "What about Martin?"

"I don't know. We've only just found out about it. Listen, make a start and I'll be back in a bit."

"What do I tell them—shall I say I'm from RS?"

I hesitated—I should have asked the others, but fuck it, we didn't have time for stupid questions like that. "Tell them you're ringing from RS."

★

553

I went back to Erika's office. She was adding names and arrows to a big piece of paper on the wall.

"What's going on?" I asked her.

"We're making a list of people Martin might contact. He's going to need help, so the chances are he'll get in touch with someone."

"Be serious! We've already done all this names and arrows and lines shit, and it didn't help. Let's just *do* something. I mean, if Martin's going to get hold of us then he will, a list of names on your wall isn't going to change that, is it?"

"What do you have in mind?" Klaus asked.

"I think we need to be a bit more radical."

"Ye-es." Erika said. I could see they were getting a bit jumpy, preparing themselves in case I came up with something *too* radical.

"OK, the only workable theory we've got is the one linking Becker and Giesler with Neumann and Steinlein. But we can't chase up the Becker-Giesler-Huber bit of the equation without Martin's help. So if we can't talk to Martin then we should go back to where it all started."

"What do you mean?" Klaus was leaning forward now, elbows on the table.

"Look, the way I see it, Steinlein and Neumann are cops. They probably produce nearly as much paperwork as we do, and an operation like this with Steinlein working in the field and Neumann behind his desk, I'm guessing they've sent about a hundred memos to each other."

"Well that's for the public prosecutor-" said Laura but I ignored her.

"Here's the plan: we break into Neumann's office."

I sat down, wondering how they'd react. To their credit they didn't just say no, they sat there and looked at each other and had a think.

"I know you're going to say no." I couldn't bear the silence any longer. "If anyone's got another plan then I'm all ears, but at least think about-"

"OK," said Laura.

"OK? Did you just say OK?"

"I said OK. Let's hear more about this plan of yours, but you'd better make sure it's a good one."

Karo

The three of us were standing in the bushes outside the church on Roedeliusplatz, and even at this distance we could hear the demo outside Magdalenenstrasse prison.

"C'mon you lazy gits!" I murmured. The cops were taking their time—the demo had been going on for at least ten minutes already but not a single squad had left Schottstrasse police station.

"Here they come," Erika sounded excited, and who could blame her? "And another lot—three lorries. Great, the police station should be practically empty."

We waited for the trucks to disappear, one down the hill to the Magda prison, the others heading west to Rathaus Lichtenberg where the local Round Table was demonstrating against Kaminsky's bill.

"They were tooled up, did you see them?" asked Schimmel. "They're ready for a fight."

Nobody answered, I think we were all trying hard not to think about what might be happening at the demos. The only thing we could do was to carry out our plan. And so far it was working: we'd organised the demo outside Magda prison and roped our mates into coming along. The Round Table demo outside Lichtenberg Town Hall was lucky coincidence.

"OK, Laura's here, she's going in. Now it's our turn."

We legged across the road, trying not to trip over the buckets and mops we were carrying. I had to giggle at the sight of Schimmel, wearing a dress and a nylon pinny, a scarf covering his spiky hair. His lean body and face had an androgynous quality; he suited his disguise. Erika and I had the same get-up, but somehow I didn't find it half as funny.

We entered the police station, moving with self-assurance past the front desk where Laura was playing a bothersome neighbour complaining about the noise from the demo down the road. She was giving the desk officer a hard time, not letting him get a word in edgeways. I think she was enjoying her role.

I guided my cleaning posse through the glass doors towards the back of the building where the *Kripo* had their offices. The whole place felt deserted, the *Kripo* had long since gone home, and the uniformed officers were out hassling demonstrators. I was whistling, starting to relax, actually looking forward to the task ahead. Down one corridor, through a door on to the next. Except a cop was there, coming towards us. A shove in my back, and I realised I'd stopped dead. I'd stopped whistling too, shock rooting me to the scuffed lino. Another shove, and my limbs mobilised. The three of us shuffled past the cop, who didn't even register our presence. A door swung shut behind us and he was gone.

"Fuck!" I breathed.

"C'mon, no big surprise," whispered Schimmel in my ear. "Just a cop in a cop shop. But be careful, we may find a typewriter in one of the offices—they can be really scary!"

I appreciated Schimmel's attempt to bolster my confidence, and just a few paces later I stopped outside Neumann's office. "This is us, time to do your magic."

Schimmel took a wallet out of his pocket, opening it up to take a couple of picks out as he dropped to his knees. Erika and I went to either end of the corridor to keep an eye open for any intruders.

I stood there, holding a mop across my body, listening to my pulse booming in my ears. It was so loud that I was sure I wouldn't hear anyone approaching. I was there for ages, concentrating on the door at the end of the next corridor, hoping no-one would come, wondering what I'd say if they did.

"Psst!" Schimmel had cracked the lock, and Erika and I scurried into Neumann's office. We shut the door behind us and let our eyes take everything in. The desk with a glass ashtray on it, a lamp, a blotter. Window opposite us, floor to ceiling cupboards covering one wall, Party and *Volkspolizei* pennants and certificates on the other.

Schimmel closed the curtains and turned the light on, then moved back to the door, gazing at us expectantly.

"You take the drawers, I'll do the cupboards," suggested Erika.

I tried the first drawer, locked. I gestured Schimmel over and he got to work while I took his place next to the door. It was a small office and there wasn't anywhere else to stand.

Erika had a cupboard open, revealing a rack of uniforms and a set of shelves full of ring-binders. She was patting down the pockets of a uniform jacket when I heard footsteps in the corridor outside. I flipped the light off and held my breath.

I could hear the tapping of feet on lino and the grumble of two men talking. The noises grew louder and clearer as they approached, punctuated by the rattle of door handles.

With a single stride I reached Erika, her shadowy form just visible in the dim light leaking through the threadbare curtains. I pushed her into the cupboard, pulling the doors shut as I followed her in. The last thing I saw through the narrowing gap was Schimmel disappearing into the knee hole of the desk.

The cupboard was tiny. Every time I breathed in I could feel the door shudder outwards a fraction. I tried not to let the dust tickle my nose, or to let the smell of Erika's perfume scratch at the back of my throat.

"The Captain's left his door open—that's not like him." The two voices were in the office now, they'd switched the light on and must have been standing less than a metre away from us. I had to press my face into one of Neumann's uniforms to stop myself from giggling with nervousness. Stale smoke and body odour filled my nostrils. I was going to gag.

"You sure it was here that you saw the cleaning ladies?" The voice droned on, but the door had shut now. The lock clicked and the footsteps receded.

Schimmel was back on his knees, working on getting the door unlocked again. Every so often I could hear a scratching noise and an almost silent *shit!*

While he did that, Erika and I were hard at work, but we were getting nowhere. Nothing interesting, just admin crap like duty rosters and sheaves of impenetrable statistics.

"Woot! I got it!" The lock finally clicked and Schimmel got up and swung the office door open. "Ta-da!"

"Oh fuck!" I said it under my breath, but Schimmel heard me. His eyes swivelled in my direction, not understanding what my problem was.

My problem was standing in the doorway, just behind Schimmel.

My problem was a cop named Steinlein.

Karo

"You've got to be kidding!"

"Not now, Karo," snapped Erika. She was getting to be as catty as Laura.

I wasn't happy about being brought to this flat in Hohenschönhausen. In fact, the only reason I was here was because Steinlein had threatened to arrest me and bring me here in cuffs if I refused. I wished he had just let me go, like he had Schimmel.

"*Dobryi vyechyer.*"

"You too, Dmitri." Erika stood erect, breathing easily, refusing to return Dmitri's oily smile. She wasn't going to take any shit off this suave KGB officer. "What's going on?" She was looking at Dmitri but the question was meant for Steinlein.

"The comrade Captain would like to help you."

"You're going to help us? How?" I demanded of Dmitri. "You got some secret plans up your secret sleeves?"

"I'd like nothing more than to help." Dmitri turned his greasy smile on me. "But I'm sure you know there's not much I can do. What would you like me to do? Shall I surround the *Volkskammer* with Alpha Group troops? This is not Russia, and I am not Boris Nikolayevich Yeltsin."

"So what's the point of you?"

I was being rude, but Erika didn't stop me, so I reckoned she was as unhappy about the situation as I was. Then again she may have been distracted by the arrival of yet another person.

"Who's that?" I asked, but nobody answered.

I didn't know her, how could I? I'd never seen her in my life, but it felt as if I should know her, and that I should dislike her. She was attractive in a conventional sense, and she knew it. She was the kind of person that would think nothing of using her forget-me-not eyes and her killer smile to get whatever she was after.

"Karo," another smile from Dmitri, "allow me to introduce an old friend: Evelyn Hagenow."

★

"You must be Karo?" It wasn't a question, it was a statement, smiled at me by Evelyn.

I threw her the most vicious look I had.

"You're the one who came to ask my comrades for help when Martin went missing last March?" Another statement. "How brave of you. That's what real friends are for, and I do hope we will also be friends. After all, we have someone in common." She still hadn't switched off the smile, and it was irritating the fuck out of me.

"What do you want?" Erika's voice made it plain what she thought about Evelyn.

"And you're Erika?" The smile hadn't diminished a single watt, she was still beaming away. We were all at a diplomatic reception and she was the gracious hostess. "Martin told me so much about you, he has a great deal of respect for you."

"Perhaps you could get to the point?" Erika's tone was as icy as Evelyn's was false.

Evelyn wasn't at all flustered by the animosity we were chucking her way, she just danced around the room, wafting her perfume around, picking up ornaments and putting them back, trailing her hands over Dmitri and Steinlein when she swept past them. Evelyn was making sure she was the centre of attention, and I was busy wrinkling my nose at the transparency of her act when a thought struck me.

"Have you been following me?"

Evelyn floated over to the table, focussing on me. She was still smiling, but her eyes were no longer doing that flirty thing. "You were very helpful."

"What do you mean?"

But Evelyn's gaze had flicked towards Erika and her eyes softened again. "I have something for you. Or Martin. Yes, let's say it's for Martin, because once again it's about our dear friend." She took a file out of her handbag and placed it on the coffee table.

I stepped forward, reaching across the table, but Evelyn saw me coming, she placed her fingers on the grey folder and shook her head.

"Patience. You'll get the file, but first, let's be civilised. Please, sit down. We'll have a little chat."

Erika sat on the sofa opposite Evelyn and I sat next to her. Dmitri remained standing and Steinlein had moved over to the window. He had pushed the mint-green curtains apart to keep an eye on the road, but was actually taking more of an interest in what was going on in the room.

"Where have you been since March?" Erika broke the ice.

"Oh, here and there, working on a case. Truth be told, being on the run wasn't as much fun as I thought it would be. But I kept myself busy, had a few agents that needed looking after."

"You've been running agents? Here in the GDR?" Erika's voice had cooled even further, it was now well below freezing.

Evelyn gave one of her smiles and held up a hand. "Yes, here in the GDR. But hear me out before you jump to conclusions." She gave Erika a chance to nod. "I've been after Kaminsky for a long time. Operation WITHERED VINE was the reason I was so keen to help out earlier this year when you had your little problem with the fascists."

"Always helping, that's you, isn't it, you Stasi sow!" How could I not call her out on her fucking hypocrisy?

Evelyn shifted her attention from Erika back to me, a searchlight on full beam swept along the sofa.

"I had my own agenda, it's true. But I'm sure we agree on what we think about the fascists." The spotlight shifted back to Erika. "Kaminsky and the far-right have been in bed together for a long time—it's not just a recent thing."

"What's in it for the far-right?" Erika was hooked, but I was still sceptical.

"Power. What else is there?" Evelyn was no longer smiling, she was serious, her eyes narrowing in concentration. "Kaminsky did a deal with the leaders of all the larger far-right parties and groups. If they help him into power then he'll give them positions in his government."

"What kind of help?"

"Well, I assume even you amateurs know about the skins stewarding Kaminsky's marches and rallies, intimidating counter-demonstrators, that sort of thing?"

"We don't have to take this shit," I told Erika, but she just nodded at Evelyn, letting her know she should continue.

"It goes further, much further than oppressing the proles.

Kaminsky climbed the Party ladder by bullying and threatening anyone who might oppose him. And guess who did the threatening part? Once Kaminsky gets his bill passed and disbands the Round Tables he'll move on to the next target: the other political parties. He's got dirt on all the major CDU and SPD politicians and he can terrify the smaller parties and the grassroots with his skinhead shock troops. By election-time in October Kaminsky will be the only one still standing."

Evelyn was painting a much bleaker picture than any of us had even begun to imagine: in the space of a few months Kaminsky intended to take our country back to a pseudo-democracy with all the strings in his hands.

"Some senior figures in the Party tried to stop Kaminsky, there was some talk of special operative measures, but they didn't even have the balls to come up with a proper plan, never mind carry it out. And anyway, the Party likes the idea of being back in power."

"Wait!" Steinlein had stopped even pretending to peer through the curtains and was now standing next to Evelyn. "Are you saying the Party never meant to assassinate Kaminsky? What about the attempt on his life at the rally?"

"That was Kaminsky's plan—a fascist cell carried it out. He got rid of a major opponent, and now he's playing the martyr card and blaming the government for their inability to keep the peace."

All the colour had drained out of Steinlein's face. He slumped onto a chair next to Evelyn and she placed a hand on his knee.

"Oh, sweetie. Bit of a shock, isn't it? There's never a good time to find out you've been played, is there? You and Martin did everything exactly as Kaminsky planned."

I wanted to ask Steinlein what he and Martin had been up to, but Erika put her hand on my arm, silencing me.

"Do you know where Martin is?"

Instead of answering, Evelyn turned to Steinlein who had now slumped even further down the couch.

"I tried to get him out last night. I failed," he mumbled. "I got away but they caught Martin. He's still in custody, they'll have him in solitary."

I had a million questions, but Erika's hand was still on my arm, and she tightened her grip briefly, telling me to hold my tongue.

"Why was Hanna at the rally?" she asked.

"Blackmail. Before 1989, Hanna's son was an informant for our lot," answered Evelyn. "He reported on the peace movement for years. Kaminsky found out and told Krause that he'd make sure everyone found out about her son's involvement with the Firm unless she endorsed Kaminsky at the rally. An impossible situation—whatever she did she'd lose her credibility. I suppose she hoped to at least save her son from being outed."

"And I presume you have evidence of Kaminsky and the fascists working together?"

"It's all here," Evelyn said, tapping her long fingers on her Get Out Of Jail Free card. "I must say young Karo was very helpful, it's thanks to her that we found out about Becker and Huber. We did a bit of digging and we're satisfied there's enough evidence for a prosecution."

"So you were following me?" I was getting really pissed off now, half rising from the sofa, but Erika still had her hand on my arm and pulled me back down.

Meanwhile, Steinlein was watching what was happening with greedy eyes, his gaze constantly flicking back to the file on the table.

"You can have the file, but first we need to negotiate. If the authorities get their hands on me I'll end up in prison again." Evelyn fixed her baby-blues on Erika. "I need a new identity, new papers. Sort that out and I'll go into retirement, make a new life far from Berlin. Would Thuringia be far enough for you? Or maybe the Baltic coast?"

"Why don't you get your friends in the KGB to give you a new identity, you can go and live in Russia!" Her demands were making me even angrier.

"You know, young Karo, I think you and I have a lot in common. Why are you still in the GDR? Why haven't you left? You could go West: Spain, France, America—world's your oyster. But you're still here. Why? Because you want to make a difference. You belong here, in the GDR. Just as I do—I belong, and I won't go into exile, not to Russia, nor anywhere else."

"You can't be trusted," I threw back. "If we let you stay in the GDR you'll just carry on working to overthrow this grassroots democracy we're building."

Evelyn did her false laugh again, looking around at the men, checking for their approval. "Yes, I'll carry on working against the fascists, but to be honest, they're a spent force. If Kaminsky weren't supporting them they'd have splintered and disbanded by now. As for your Round Tables, if Kaminsky doesn't manage to get his bill through tomorrow then they'll be unstoppable. As dear Dmitri never tires of saying," she beamed in his direction, "decentralisation is the best defence against power grabs from the likes of me and my Chekist friends."

"You know we can't provide you with a new identity." Erika said as Dmitri bowed his head in acknowledgement of Evelyn's words.

"Naturally. However, you do know the right people," Evelyn shifted her attention back to Erika and Dmitri was left in the shadows again. "You know people who can organise a new life for me."

Erika nodded, thinking about Evelyn's offer. After a while she turned to Dmitri.

"Have you seen this file? Does it have what we need?"

"I've seen it." Dmitri held his hands out, embracing the whole room, grateful to be at the centre of it all, if just for a moment. "There are one or two gaps, a few empty spaces on the stage, that's to be expected in a case like this. But there's enough in there: photographs, phone records and transcripts. Kaminsky is canny enough not to trust the fascists, but foolish enough to have made written contracts with them. That file will save Martin, and quite probably your country too. Take the offer, it is the right time—Martin wouldn't hesitate for a single moment and I urge you to do the same."

More silence while Erika thought about this. I didn't know what to say, I didn't know whether accepting Evelyn's bargain would be the right the thing to do. Could we trust her? Should we put our faith in Dmitri's judgement?

But Erika had already made a decision.

"It's a deal," she said.

DAY 13
Friday
24th June 1994

Berlin: The Volkskammer will today debate Dr. Kaminsky's bill to dissolve the Round Tables. The bill will face a rough passage through parliament after documents were leaked alleging co-operation between Dr. Kaminsky and far-right parties.

Round Tables and Worker's Councils throughout the GDR have responded with calls for mass meetings and demonstrations.

Berlin: Martin Grobe, the suspect in the Krause shooting, has escaped from prison. Grobe's absence was discovered by staff at Rummelsburg prison yesterday morning. The former Republikschutz officer was on remand for the murder of Hanna Krause, the Chair of the Central Round Table.

08:56
Martin

The hatch in the door clanged open and a guard peered in.

"Back against the wall!" he commanded.

But I stayed on my bed, hands behind my head, listening to the radio. I thought the news of a general strike was far more interesting than anything the guard could offer. But I was wrong.

"Accused 592744, you are being transferred." The guard marched into my cell.

"Why?" I was sitting up now, wondering what they were planning to do with me.

"We can no longer guarantee your safety in this institution. Now get up!"

"Where are you taking me?"

Instead of answering the guard pulled me to my feet and wound choke cuffs around my wrists. He prodded me down the echoing corridors, closed cell doors to either side, barred gate at the end. We were buzzed through the gate and I was taken out of the cell block and into the yard.

Inmates were coming out of the next block and being marched to assembly work in the workshops on the other side of the prison.

"Hey!" I shouted, "I'm Martin Grobe, they're taking-" I didn't get any further because I was on my knees in pain as the guard twisted the cuffs tight around my wrists.

A couple of prisoners saw what was happening, and word spread through the work party. They ignored the warders, moving as one towards me. After that, I was hardly aware of what was happening around me, bile was rising in my throat, fighting with the air that was screaming out of my lungs as the cuffs were twisted tighter. I would have fallen over, but the chain around my wrists was pulling me upright. My stomach heaved and the pain in my wrists eased, I must have vomited and collapsed full length on the concrete because the next thing I knew, another prisoner was helping me sit up. My vision cleared and my hearing returned, a klaxon was wailing, my guard sat on the floor, his own choke cuffs bound his wrists, tying them tight behind his back. Other guards sat close to him, all surrounded by prisoners.

"You're Martin Grobe? They said you'd escaped."

My breathing was heavy and ragged, my wrists burned, pain shot up my arms when I moved my fingers. A part of my brain nagged me to get a grip, to work out what was happening.

I stood up, glad of the hand given by a burly man with a tattooed skull. I looked down at my former guard, he was being held now, kneeling on the floor, two prisoners grasping a shoulder each, waiting for me to kick him, hit him, do whatever I wanted to him.

"Let him go."

The two prisoners shrugged and released the guard.

"We've got this far without spilling blood." My breath was ragged, my words came in spurts. "We shouldn't start now just because the old order is fighting back." The other prisoners were grumbling. "Remember Bautzen? We can do that here, now!"

"Bautzen?"

"We all know what happened in Bautzen prison four years ago, we know how they took over the jail, set up a Prisoners' Council. Isn't it time we did that here?" I looked around at the work party, they were all listening to me, the warders unattended. "Out there, beyond these walls, Kaminsky is trying to destroy the Round Tables and the Workers' Councils. So what better answer than to set up our own Prisoners' Council? This is our first step towards freedom. Who's with me? Let's see some hands!"

There was no need to take hands, the prisoners were ready.

09:01

Karo

As soon as Antje appeared I went to the secretary's office, just as Erika and I had planned.

"Frau *Ministerin* Willehardt asks not to be disturbed."

It was a different secretary from last time, a nicer one who assured me she'd hold all appointments.

That was easier than expected, and satisfied with my success I went back to Antje's office, pausing only to collect the daily papers from a side table.

"I can see the urgency," Antje was telling Erika. "But this goes way beyond my powers-"

"Nobody will question you. Have you seen the newspapers this morning? History is on our side." Erika interrupted.

"I have responsibilities, there's no way I could do this and still carry on as minister. I'd have to resign, all my work ... it would be for nothing."

"This is probably the most important thing you'll ever do. Take a step back—see the bigger picture."

Antje was standing behind her desk, running her fingers through her hair. Erika took the newspapers off me and spread them out before her. Kaminsky's duplicity had made the headlines in all the papers except for the Party's own Neues Deutschland and Junge Welt.

Kaminsky link to fascist murder plot was the Berliner Zeitung's offering, while Die Anderen announced a general strike and called Kaminsky a nazi puppet. In the leader they accused him of complicity in the murder of Hanna Krause: *Dr Kaminsky may not have pulled the trigger, but Hanna's blood still indelibly stains his hands.* It had been a busy night for us, but we'd done our work well. The contents of Evelyn's dossier had been made public, along with the details of the murder of Hanna Krause.

Erika put Katrin's tiny cassette on top of the newspapers. "This is a taped confession by the young fascist who shot Hanna. The case against Martin is crumbling. By releasing him you'll be sending a clear message that Kaminsky is no longer pulling the strings. Releasing Martin gives us all a chance to save the Round Tables."

"You're sure Martin hasn't escaped?"

"Martin's still in custody. And when he walks out of Rummelsburg prison the world will see how the police and prison service have conspired with Kaminsky."

Antje picked up a newspaper and scanned the headlines.

"What's the government here for?" Erika asked her.

"To ensure law and order," Antje replied mechanically, taking another newspaper. "To make the best decisions on behalf of the people."

"Have you forgotten all our years in the *Frauengruppe*, hounded by the Party and the Stasi?" Erika took the newspaper away from Antje, forcing the minister to meet her gaze. "You're here to do the people's will. The will as decided at the grassroots. In April the people voted for devolution of power to community Round Table level. Today the Round Tables are calling for a general strike." Erika held her hand out and I gave her the unsigned order to release Martin. She placed it on the desk, in front of Antje and gave her a pen. "We need you."

I managed to hold myself back until we got out of the Ministry, but when we hit the street I gave Erika a hug.

"We did it!" I shouted.

"Don't yell in my ear!" Erika pulled me away from the entrance and the cop who was stationed there. "Come on, there's still plenty of work to do."

"Don't be such a killjoy, I know we've got work to do, but can't we just be pleased that we're getting somewhere?"

"Let's see how far we get first."

We started walking towards the State Prosecutor's office, the streets around us were empty—it was weird, literally nobody about, just us. It stayed that way until we got to the Opera and cut through to Unter den Linden. Now we could hear shouting, chanting. And sirens. A line of cops wearing helmets and holding shields blocked Marx-Engels-Brücke.

"You got your RS pass with you?" Erika looked nervous.

She already had her pass in her hand. I pulled mine out and the pair of us marched up to the squad commander, showing our passes and demanding to be let through.

"Your funeral," The cop said, shrugging. He wasn't too concerned about our funeral.

We filtered between the police lines and crossed the bridge onto the island that is home to the seat of the *Volkskammer*, the Palace of the Republic. About ten thousand people were there, most with placards or banners: *No Return to the Dictatorship of the Party!* and *Let The Grassroots Grow!*

The energy in the demo was amazing. Inside the Palace, the *Volkskammer* was sitting, debating whether these people here should be allowed to continue running their own neighbourhoods. The so-called democrats sitting in there were trying to roll back the progress of the last four years. They couldn't be allowed to do that, we wouldn't allow them to do that.

"We have to get a move on, we haven't any time to waste." Erika was pulling me through the crowds by my arm.

I trailed behind her, looking around, feeling inspired by everyone there. Erika had already reached Liebknechtbrücke, the bridge that leads to Alexanderplatz, but her way was barred by a line of riot cops. She held her RS pass out and demanded to be let through, but the cops were doing that no-hear-no-see-no-speak trick they're so good at.

"Constable, I am on State business. Let me through immediately!"

I was directly behind her, but still didn't really see what happened next—the cops sort of shuffled their shields, and all of a sudden Erika was on the floor.

"Fuck's sake! Do you know who this is?" I shouted.

But the cops were back in automaton mode. I pulled Erika out of their reach and helped her up. She had a cut above her eye, I dabbed it with my hankie.

"Listen, you fucking idiots," I was facing up to the cops, "this is Lieutenant Lang of the *Republikschutz*, and you're going to let us through-"

But Erika had hold of my arm, pulling me back. I tried to drag myself out of her grasp and she stumbled. The sudden release made me stagger the other way, just as a truncheon whistled through the space I'd just moved out of. It was so quick I didn't even see which cop was holding it.

I quickly backed up a couple of paces, but now people were pressing in behind us—some demonstrators had seen what was happening and had come to help out. They had their arms linked and were chanting *Keine Gewalt!*—no violence.

Erika stood facing the protestors, her arms outstretched.

"It's OK, it's OK. We're here to show the *Volkskammer* that they can't ignore us, so let's do that, let's go back to the main entrance of the Palace of the Republic!"

It did the job, our new friends ebbed away, leaving space in front of the police lines. Erika took my arm and pulled me with her. This time I let her.

We went back to Marx-Engels-Brücke, the way we'd come in, but when we got there the officer that had let us in was nowhere to be seen. Erika didn't hesitate though, she just pulled out her RS pass again, holding it at arm's length and marching towards the ranked cops. I saw the shields move sideways, making a gap just in front of Erika and I grabbed her shoulder, jerking her backwards just as the cop in front lifted his arm, truncheon ready to hammer down.

We stumbled back into the crowd, I was still holding onto Erika.

"You OK?" she asked me.

"Am I OK? You're asking if I'm OK? You nearly got your head split open—Erika, you're even harder than I thought!"

But Erika was already trying to find a way through the crowd. "We have to get through, let's try the Rathausbrücke on the other side of the Palace of the Republic."

"We can't go! These cops are just waiting to kick off!"

The crowd was getting restless, shouts chorused up and down the square, some pissed up idiots were taunting the line of cops behind us.

"Karo, you stay if you think it's important. I'm going to get Martin's release order to the State Prosecutor, we haven't got any time to waste and Martin's my priority."

Shit, she was right. I felt dead bad about leaving the demo, solidarity and all, but this time we had a different mission.

We pushed past the Palace of the Republic, down to the other end of Marx-Engels-Platz. But our way was blocked by yet another line of cops, keeping us kettled in front of the Palace.

"Do you reckon they'll let us through this time?" Erika asked, but the answer was obvious.

"There's less of them here," I said. "They're not so close together. If I create a diversion you might be able to run through one of the gaps."

At least it was a plan. Sometimes it worked, mostly it didn't, and when it didn't whoever was trying to jump through the police lines got a good kicking. But I couldn't think of anything else to do, apart from trying to mobilise the demonstration—and that was just a recipe for cracked heads and broken ribs.

"We can try to get into the Palace, then we can make some calls, get someone to fetch us out of here."

"Erika, that plan's as shit as mine. They're not letting anyone inside—didn't you see the cops barricading the foyer?"

Erika was facing the cops, she was thinking, her eyes taking in the gaps in the line, how they widened and narrowed as the bulls shifted nervously from foot to foot.

"I'll get a few people here to help," she said eventually. "We'll do the diversion thing and you can jump through. You can run faster than me, you've got a much better chance."

But it was already too late: three olive-green lorries were driving on to the bridge in front of us. Men wearing fatigues were jumping out of the back.

"Here come reinforcements," muttered Erika.

Martin

When I tried to walk my legs collapsed under me. I was helped up again, and I staggered over to the boiler house where the prisoners were gathering. Some had gone off to release those still locked in their cells, and the warders were being ushered out of the main gate. A couple of men had climbed the water tower and were hanging a bedsheet daubed with boot polish: *Under New Management.*

It wasn't long before I was surrounded by hundreds. We sat in groups with others from our cell blocks, and within a few minutes spokes from each block had been selected and were sitting in the middle, putting together a list of what we needed to talk about and what we needed to do.

It wasn't long before they asked me to speak.

"My name is Martin Grobe, you may have heard of me. Perhaps you saw me in the newspapers last year, or heard about me on the radio. I helped to stop a plot by ex-Stasi officers. And I was there a few weeks ago when the population of our country united to stand against skinhead thugs and fascists. I'm on remand for the murder of Hanna Krause. If any of you are in any doubt, let me tell you this: I did not shoot her."

"We're all innocent here!" some wit shouted to applause and laughter.

"Hanna was my friend." The chuckling died out. "I knew and worked with her for years. I can't say the same about Kaminsky—he stands for everything I never want to see again. But even if I'd had a gun in my hand last Saturday, even if I'd had the opportunity, I wouldn't have killed him. Kaminsky and the Party need a way to make us afraid, they're trying to make us want the security that they're promising. I'm here because they need a scapegoat. I'm here so they can point to me and say: *You can't trust anyone!*"

There were mumbles of agreement coming from the prisoners around me, I waited until I had their attention again.

"Remember Lenin? *Trust is good, control is better.* Today the country decides whether we want control or trust. Today the country decides: representative democracy controlled by the elite and the politicians; or grassroots democracy working through Round Tables and Councils just like the one we're starting here?

"Out there, the country is on general strike. Out there, the people—not Kaminsky's People—but the people of the GDR, the people who live and work and play in the GDR, the people who came here from other places and the people who were born here—they are all deciding for themselves whether they want the Party back, or whether they want to carry on this experiment that we started in 1989.

"It's time for us to choose, too. Are we with them? Are we with the people of the GDR? Are we on strike?"

09:42

Karo

The men in fatigues fell into columns and rapidly marched over the bridge to relieve the regular police units. It was scary how efficient they were; it took less than a minute to replace the lines. The cops were initially a bit unsure what to do, but a non-com took them in hand and marched them off towards Alexanderplatz.

"You notice anything?" Erika asked.

Only a million things, like how scary those lads looked. How fucking confident and efficient they were.

"Look," Erika insisted, like I wasn't already looking. "They're not carrying shields, they're not armed: no guns, not even truncheons."

Shit, how had I *not* noticed that? What I did notice, though, was one of the trucks moving over the bridge. The line of uniforms opened to let it drive through.

"And, look at their epaulettes. The corps colours."

I didn't know what corps colours were, and anyway, I had my eyes glued to that truck. The hatch in the roof of the cab was opening.

"That isn't the *Volkspolizei*, that's-"

"It's Rico!"

Rico the border guard had stood up in the hatch, megaphone in hand.

"*Achtung! Achtung!* This is *not* the police. I repeat, this is *not the police*." The amplified sound of Rico's voice bounced off the Palace,

572

sending shock waves through the demonstration. Everyone was looking at Rico, daunted at the sight of army trucks at the demo. "Do not be alarmed. We are here to guarantee your democratic rights. We have relieved the police of their duties and you are free to stay or to leave as you choose. I repeat: you are free to stay, or to leave."

A file of border guards was now making its way through the crowd, heading for the entrance to the Palace of the Republic.

"Please allow my comrades through. They are going to the Palace of the Republic to enable an orderly and safe withdrawal of police forces."

"They've got nothing to fear from us!" someone shouted.

But Rico didn't answer, because I was scrambling up into the cab of his truck.

"Is this a mutiny?" I asked as I squeezed past him through the hatch.

Climbing onto the roof of the cab I gave Rico a hug, and the crowd yelled its approval, then I took the megaphone.

"*Kaminsky out! Wir sind das Volk!*" I shouted.

The crowd shouted right back, so loud I had to put my hands over my ears. I was just raising the megaphone to my lips again when I saw Erika below, hands on her hips, doing a Laura face.

"Karo, come down here this instant!"

I laughed at her, and Erika's face lifted into a smile. I slid down off the roof, Rico holding my arms as I hung over the windscreen. I landed on the ground, and had to push my way through the crowd gathering around the truck, cheering and hugging the border guards. By the time I got to Erika, she was talking to Rico. He was listening carefully, finger crooked below his lip.

"Get into the back of the truck, we'll take you—you won't make it by yourself. Public transport is on strike, the police have set up checkpoints. There are marches and demos all over Berlin."

Rico got into the cab and we clambered into the back along with a few border guards.

It took only a few minutes to get to the Court on Littenstrasse, and Erika climbed over the tailgate to go into the building. Rico came into the back of the truck and talked for a bit to the radio operator. I sat and waited, listening to the noises and chants of another demonstration, just round the corner on Alexanderplatz.

A few minutes later Erika reappeared.

"Got it!" She handed me an envelope before clambering up into the back of the truck.

I opened the envelope and looked at the letter from the General State Prosecutor.

"Have you seen how many stamps are on this piece of paper?" I asked Erika.

"Five," she answered, and looked like she was going to tell me what they all were and why they were there.

But I'd stopped listening, I was about to burst with excitement—I was on the back of an army truck (no, make that a mutineering army truck) and I was holding the piece of paper that would get Martin out of the clink.

And once Martin was out of jail we'd sort Kaminsky and his shitty plans.

10:20

Martin

They wanted to elect me as a representative, but I said no. Some weren't very happy about that and started arguing with me.

"If you want a figurehead then I'm the wrong one to choose. Not interested. The only ones interested in that kind of thing are people like Kaminsky."

It was the wrong thing to say, and the spokescouncil descended into arguments, but finally things began to settle down, and more immediate issues were considered.

"We need to get ourselves sorted," a grey haired prisoner said. "Any moment now the screws are going to come in here looking for revenge."

But it was already too late: one of the lookouts up the water tower was pointing towards the front gate. "Screws on the march!"

I'd found my feet again and was able to follow everyone else around the corner to see what was happening.

A squad of warders, wearing helmets, carrying shields and truncheons, had come through the steel door at the entrance and were waiting to go through the first of two gates in the wire fence. Their visors were down, it was hard to see their faces, but you could tell that they were spoiling for a fight.

A buzzer sounded, and the first gate slid open.

The warders marched up to the second gate, drumming truncheons on shields as they came.

10:27
Karo

A police checkpoint blocked the main road near the Hauptbahnhof, so we turned left, heading into Friedrichshain. It was so eerie, the streets were completely empty—apart from the cops we hadn't seen a soul since Alexanderplatz. But that all changed as we turned off at Franz-Mehring-Platz. If the empty streets had been weird, then this was even weirder. Sitting on the grass, on kitchen chairs or standing around, everyone was facing the middle of the square where several people were having some kind of discussion. More people were leaning over the balconies of the tower blocks surrounding the square. Before I could make anything else out we'd swung around the corner and the Neues Deutschland printing works blocked the view.

"That was unexpected," I said to Erika, but she was lost in her own thoughts.

We crossed Warschauer Strasse—normally full of bikes, people, shoppers—now it was just empty. But when Boxhagener Platz hove into view we could see another gathering—hundreds of people sitting there while five or six figures stood in the middle discussing. As I watched, an old lady got off her chair, went to one of the standing figures, tapped her on the shoulder and then took her place. The woman who had been talking went and sat down.

The truck ground on, and as we drew near to the RS offices Rico rapped on the back window of the cab, and held up four fingers.

One of border guards put a clunky pair of headphones on and leaned over the radio, playing around with it for a moment or two.

"Berta zwo Berta zwo Berta zwo. This is Anton eins, over."

The radio crackled a bit, then: "Berta zwo receiving, over."

"Anton eins, execute orders zero-four, over."

"Berta zwo, zero four received, out."

A couple of minutes after the cryptic message we were passing under the railway bridges near Rummelsburg station when I saw another olive-green truck coming from the right.

"Hey guys, are they on our side?"

Instead of answering, the sparky pushed the tarp further back and waved. The truck behind us flashed its headlights, and the hatch in its cab roof clanged open. A dude in a Hawaiian shirt popped up, heaving a massive camera onto his shoulder. He was pointing it in our direction.

"What the fuck?"

"West TV, they've come to join the fun." The sparky smiled.

"But the border's closed!"

"We brought them over on a customs launch. They climbed out of a window in Kreuzberg, a customs boat was waiting for them on the river below."

OK, this was a bit much. Here was this platoon or regiment or whatever it was, just turning up and turfing out the cops, and now the customs boats and stuff. What was going on?

"Did Rico organise all of this? Are you all, like, under his command or something?"

The border guards in the back of the truck with us had a laugh about that, and Erika began to pay attention.

"The Soldiers' Council of the Border Regiment 33 had a meeting this morning. We're on strike."

"You call this being on strike?"

"Yeah, fun isn't it?"

Fuck me, I think this classed as another revolution!

We pulled up in front of the prison, and Erika climbed out. She stalked over to the sentry, looking dead imposing. I scrambled down after her, but the guy in the Hawaiian shirt and his camera beat me to it. He shoved the camera right into the sentry's face and the poor git had Erika on one side and this massive camera on the other. He didn't know what to do. He lifted the telephone and made his report: *There are representatives from the General State Prosecutor's office here.*

We went through the big steel door, into that scary bit by the administration building—high gates blocking the way forward and back, a sentry box and a watchtower spying on us. Shouting could be heard from inside the prison, even louder than the noise demo the other day. Erika was already half way up the front steps of the admin block, and I was about to run after her when I heard someone shouting my name.

"Karo! Karo, wait!"

It was weird, my mind must have been addled—too much sun or excitement or something—I could swear it was Katrin's voice. Hawaiian-shirt dude and his sound crew were trying to manoeuvre all their tat through the gate, and squeezing through the middle of them all was Katrin.

She ran up and hugged me. I nearly dissolved into a puddle, but I took a step back before I lost it.

"Karo, I've got an apology to make-"

"What the fuck are you doing here? Listen, Katrin, not a good time, really not-"

"I know, I know, I came with the TV crew. Now go—go and do what you need to do—I'll be here, waiting for you."

I hesitated for a moment, not knowing whether to hug her or apologise or just walk way.

I turned to look for Erika, but she was already out of sight, so I decided to go up the watchtower, see what was happening on the other side of the prison walls. I climbed up the ladder, the TV crew just behind me. The three wardens at the top tried to bar my way when they saw me coming up.

"Stand aside, I'm from the General State Prosecutor's office!" I waved my RS pass at them, making sure to move it around enough so they couldn't get a good look.

Looking out of the window I couldn't believe my eyes—it was a full scale revolt down there! A load of tooled up wardens were trying to get through the last fence, they looked like they were ready for business. Prisoners were trying to chain the gate shut, but the bastard screws were ramming truncheons through the fence to stop them.

"Call the guards back, tell them to fall back!" I ordered the nearest screw.

He hesitated, looking down at what was happening below, then at me, then at the TV camera.

"I'm only going to say this once more, and if you don't do it then I will make sure the General State Prosecutor herself hears about this."

The guard's finger moved towards a switch, he pressed it and leaned over the microphone: "Tactical Unit stand down. Tactical Unit stand down."

Wow! I couldn't believe I just made that happen! I could definitely get used to ordering people around. I watched as the riot-screws dribbled away from the inner compound—they looked really pissed off, even I could tell that might be a problem. I went to the window on the other side of the tower, the side that looked down on the space outside the admin block, and shoved it open.

"Rico, you need to get up here!"

Back at the control panel. I pressed the switch and bent over the mike: "This is Round Table Task Force One," I made that bit up but it sounded good—all the prisoners were cheering and waving. "Is Martin Grobe with you? We're looking for Martin Grobe."

The mass of uniformed prisoners was moving, someone was being pushed towards the front, and there he was: Martin, looking up at the tower. He had his hands cupped in front of his mouth and was shouting something, but no way could I hear anything through all that cheering.

I pressed the button again. "Martin, wait there, don't go anywhere!"

Rico had reached us now, so I asked him to send a couple of his men up, "Make sure these clowns don't try anything stupid."

Rico did some hand signals through the window and all of a sudden there were too many people in the tower. Rico and I went back down the ladder, taking the TV crew with us.

I told Rico I was worried about the screws in the yard, they were psyched up, ready to fight and we needed to make sure we outnumbered them. "Can you get more of your colleagues?"

Rico shook his head. "It'll take at least twenty minutes, maybe thirty." He headed over to the lorry where the sparky was fiddling with his radio, and I looked around for Katrin. She was being interviewed by the telly people, but I dragged her away from them.

"Katrin, your dad's OK, I've just seen him. We're going to get him out of there any moment now."

Katrin was fighting back tears, and I was welling up too, but I couldn't afford to lose it, not today, not now.

I was saved by Rico.

"There'll be forty men here soon."

"No guns?"

"No guns." He confirmed.

I looked around the yard, there was too much going on, a DDR TV crew had turned up and were filming as well, some screws were standing around, unsure what to do. The outer gate was still open, and when I peered through the gap I could see a police patrol car outside. Leaning on the door, smoking, was Steinlein. He took the ciggie out of his mouth and gave me a smile, like he was happy to see his best mate. I ignored him, wishing he would go away.

But something was nagging at the back of my head, I was missing something: Erika.

I looked at my watch, and wondered what was taking her so long. She'd been in the admin block for at least ten minutes, and that made me jumpy. I grabbed a couple of Rico's border guards and went up the steps. We were just about to go through the doors when a buzzer sounded. Looking over my shoulder I could see the inner gate opening, tooled up screws were streaming through.

I watched them march through the gate, not able to move, not able to make the decision: grab Katrin and leg it out the main gate, away from these scary, radge fuckers; or try to find Erika, make sure she succeeded in getting Martin free.

"Katrin! Get out! Go now, go!" I screamed over my shoulder as I ran up the steps into the admin block. Up the stairs to the first floor, but more screws were coming the other way, a couple tried to grab me, but the border guards overtook me, batting the screws down the stairs. More wardens were clattering up behind us.

"Hold them off—long as you can!" I shouted above the sound of the klaxon.

I could hear yells and scuffling as I ran up the last few steps, I charged down the corridor and shouldered open the door to the director's office.

"Call your men off!" I shouted into the room.

"As I was explaining to Lieutenant Lang," the director ignored my demand—the supercilious bastard didn't even bother looking at me —"releasing a prisoner is out of the question at the present time. As you can see the whole institution is in lockdown-"

"Listen, Mr. Director." I leaned over his desk, putting my face in front of his. "First of all you're going to get your men to stop being macho idiots. Then you're going to hand over Martin Grobe. I don't care whether you're in lockdown or in fucking meltdown!"

"I think it's time you left. Comrade Lieutenant, perhaps you could take your young colleague with you?"

"We're not going until we've got Martin!" I was shouting at him now. I really, really wanted to punch the arrogant shit.

In fact, I might have punched him, but I was distracted by another voice: calm, pedantic, infuriating, "Thank you, Frau Rengold."

It was Steinlein. He must have followed us up here. I was about to tell him to mind his own business when he addressed the director.

"It's time to let Grobe go, Director. You may phone Captain Neumann if you wish to confirm the order."

Suddenly it was a completely different guy behind the desk, he'd turned into an obsequious shit.

"Certainly, comrade Lieutenant. One moment." He was already reaching for the phone, ready to pass on the order to release Martin.

Erika was ushering me towards the door. As we passed Steinlein she gave him a long, hard look.

Martin showed his wrists to the TV crew, and they zoomed in on the bracelets of livid contusions. Gross. After all the hugs and excitement we stood around, wondering what the hell to do next. We'd been concentrating so much on getting Martin out of the prison that we hadn't really had a chance to plan any further.

We withdrew to the edge of the road in front of the prison where Rico marshalled his men onto the trucks and the telly crews were trying to persuade the prison guards to give interviews.

Steinlein was back by his squad car, smoking, when Martin shook his hand. "I hear your bluff was what got me out?"

"Might be wise not to stay here too long—they may still change their minds."

We piled into the back of one of Rico's trucks and headed towards Friedrichshain, Steinlein following in his police car. Martin was at the end of the bench with Katrin next to him. I sat on the other side of her, our hands sort of touching. She didn't pull away, and nor did I. In fact, her fingers closed around mine and I squeezed back. My heart was beating so fast it felt like I was going to pop.

Ten minutes later we were at Boxhagener Platz. We helped Martin down from the back of the truck and sat at the edge of the big group of people we'd driven past earlier. There must have been a few thousand people there, and despite the PA we could hardly make out what was being said. Every so often one of the speakers was replaced by another person who'd been waiting.

"What's going on?" Martin asked someone sitting on the grass nearby.

"Neighbourhood Round Table. We had to hold it in the square because so many people wanted to participate. Kaminsky's plans have backfired, the Round Tables are more popular than ever—there are mass meetings being held all over the country!"

The guy's enthusiasm was all a bit too much for me and I wandered off, leaving Martin to natter with his new friend. Steinlein sat in his cop car, making everyone feel uncomfortable just by being there and Erika had disappeared into the crowd, I could see her chatting with someone. I wanted a moment for myself—too much had happened and I needed a chance to catch up.

Katrin saw me move away and jumped up to run after me. We stood facing each other, just a few centimetres apart, neither of us sure what to say.

"I'm glad you came," I managed after a bit.

Katrin just nodded, her eyes not quite meeting mine.

"Well, this is awkward ..." I went for humorous, but it didn't work.

In fact things just got even more awkward because Schimmel bounced up. I hadn't seen him this happy for yonks, and most of me smiled to see him like this, but a big part of me just wanted him to go away and leave me and Katrin to our scary, stiff non-conversation. Didn't he have any tact? Couldn't he see Katrin and I were trying to talk?

"Come on you two! This is amazing, this is the best day ever! You got Martin out!"

"It's just the start—we're not even halfway there yet."

"You're having me on?" Schimmel stopped his bouncing and examined Katrin and me. "No, you've really not heard, have you? The Volkskammer voted against Kaminsky!" Schimmel's mouth widened into a smile. "And guess what? *Neues Forum* reintroduced the bill to devolve power to the Round Tables—the other parties were so scared of being tarred with the same brush as Kaminsky that they just nodded it through—the Round Tables are here to stay!"

"You're kidding? Really—we won?" I was jumping up and down, this was it, we'd done it, we'd seen off Kaminsky!

Schimmel and I grabbed Katrin, and it all turned into a group hug. I felt like shouting, like running around and setting off fireworks.

"I missed you." Katrin's voice was muffled, her head pressed against mine.

I let go of Schimmel, and he must have had more tact than I'd given him credit for because he went over to Martin. It was just Katrin and me—the whole of Boxhagener Platz, the whole of Friedrichshain had faded away. I had my hands on Katrin's shoulders, she was looking at the ground.

"I know it's not cool to say that I missed you, but I did," she mumbled.

I was hastily wiping tears away with the back of my hand.

"Can I have a hug?" She looked up, her face red.

I put my arms around her, not saying a word, just burying myself in her hair.

"If I come home, will you be willing to give it a go? I mean, give me a go?" Katrin asked, her lips tickling my ear.

"Home? Here?" I moved my head back so I could see her. It was all that I wanted, but it was too much to take in.

"It's time to come back to East Berlin. You're right, there so much work to do, I want to do it with you. Will you ... can we do that? Can you give me-"

I hugged Katrin, hard. With all my strength I pulled her into me. My tears wet her hair.

Martin

It was such a relief, a relief to allow myself to feel optimistic again, to feel that we might be getting somewhere. The people here on Boxhagener Platz were really involved in their local Round Table, they were participating, *owning* it. For years I'd been waiting for this, hoping for this, but instead I'd watched the chances for our participatory democracy dwindle as people struggled to survive the everyday battles of their lives, leaving decisions to the career politicians.

But here they were, brought together to save something that was on the verge of dissolution. And not just here, but everywhere in the country.

Katrin and Karo were off to one side, hugging each other and looking happy. Schimmel was giving me a detailed account of the proceedings in the *Volkskammer* this morning. I was glad to have them all with me—they were excited, proud even—I could feel the enthusiasm coming off them. Enthusiasm was a good thing to have— after all, it was going to be up to them and their generation to shape our country.

My deliberations were interrupted by a hand on my shoulder. It was Steinlein.

"I've been monitoring the radio—there's a police squad coming to arrest you," he said, his hand gripping my shoulder painfully.

"Here? How do they know I'm here?"

"We need to go, come on. I'll take you somewhere safe."

"I have to let Katrin know-"

"No time, come on, we have to go, right now!" Steinlein still had hold of my shoulder and was pulling me towards his police car.

"Schimmel—tell Katrin!" I shouted as Steinlein pushed me into the passenger seat.

"I'm going to put these on you." He held a pair of handcuffs. "If we're stopped then I can say I'm taking you in. OK?"

I nodded, my mind numb, working too slowly to keep up with events. The cuffs clicked around my wrists and Steinlein put the Lada into gear.

"I'll take you to my allotment, once we're there we can work out what to do next."

I nodded again, not really taking in what Steinlein was saying. He twisted the volume knob on the police radio, listening to the staccato messages as he drove the car south. We went over the river and passed under the S-Bahn tracks near Baumschulenweg station, a few minutes after that we pulled up outside an allotment colony.

I got out to open the gate, feeling awkward with my cuffed hands, and Steinlein drove through, parking a few metres down the sandy track.

When I caught up with him, the policeman was still sitting in the driver's seat, his eyes red-rimmed, hands on the steering wheel, arms stiff. The radio was chattering, static almost drowning out the words.

"Somebody saw us," he told the windscreen. "They've put out an alert for both of us, we have to change vehicles."

Steinlein jerked into action, sliding out of the police car and looking around the lane. A Trabant was parked a few metres away, bright sunlight glaring off the windscreen. Steinlein tried the passenger door, it was unlocked. He held it open for me to get in.

I hesitated, threads of doubt beginning to unfurl down my spine.

"Get in!" Steinlein ordered, practically shoving me into the car. He slapped the door shut and swung around to the driver's side, pulling off his cap and uniform blouson as he went.

I tried to grab the door handle, wanting to get back out, but my manacled hands were making me clumsy

"I wouldn't do that if I were you." It wasn't Steinlein, it was another voice, one I knew well. Smooth, but dangerous, a shiv dipped in honey. My spine seized under the pressure of a gun barrel.

"Evelyn."

"Clever boy. Couldn't go without saying goodbye, could I?" Evelyn replied.

Steinlein had got the Trabant started, and the engine howled as we pulled out of the allotments and onto the road.

"What do you mean, goodbye?"

"Time to go. You're my ticket out of here, dear heart."

Ignoring the dead metal of the gun I twisted around, trying to catch sight of my nemesis in the back seat.

"My work here is done, and I couldn't have done it without you—you've been an immense help." She laughed at my blank face. "We needed to get rid of Kaminsky."

"You knew about the plot? You set me up?"

"Sorry, my dear. If there'd been any other way … As it is, Lieutenant Steinlein here was our agent—we knew of Kaminsky's every move. But I do hope your brief stay in jail wasn't *too* horrendous."

"You should have left me there."

"Now, now, don't be bitter. Don't forget, you also wanted to get rid of Kaminsky. Now we've assigned that populist dreck to the dustbin of history the Party can get on with the real job of sorting out the mess your counter-revolution is causing. Kaminsky was just the warm up act, now it's time for the Party to really start its comeback."

"Fuck you!"

Steinlein wasn't participating in the pleasantries, he was concentrating on the road, hammering the Trabant.

"Oh, and if you get the chance, please do thank your colleagues for the small but significant roles they played."

"My colleagues?"

"Oh wake up, dear Martin. Yes, the amateur spies from RS, not to forget that bumptious fool, Dmitri Alexandrovich. Couldn't have done it without them, although I suspect they won't be too pleased when they hear that. I spun them a little line, told them I wanted to stay here. They seemed to trust me after that, the darlings."

The engine screeched as Steinlein shifted gear and with a vicious yank of the wheel we turned into Sonnenallee. I was thrown against the door as the car skeetered around the corner, another howl of the engine as Steinlein stamped on the accelerator. The little Trabant was galloping towards the border crossing, the guard barracks and the tall spotlights loomed larger as we careered up the road.

"The border?"

"Do *try* to keep up darling, I've already told you—you're my ticket out of here."

"Don't say a fucking word," Steinlein muttered as a border guard waved us to a halt.

"Papers please." The guard saluted.

Evelyn's gun had slipped down from my neck, now pressing into my left side, Steinlein's body hiding it from anyone outside the car. Steinlein himself hadn't reacted, he was still hunched over the steering wheel, revving the engine and peering through the dirty windscreen.

Evelyn reached forward and passed her papers through the driver's open window. The guard checked the *Ausweis*, took a closer look at Evelyn and stepped back, his eyes widening in surprise.

"Yes sweetheart, I'm Evelyn Hagenow, and I'm on your most-wanted list. But you're going to let us through, and you're going to radio your comrades to tell them not to stop us." Evelyn moved the gun forwards, allowing the guard to see it. "Because if we aren't allowed into West Berlin then comrade Captain Martin Grobe here, national treasure that he is, will have made his final journey."

Steinlein lifted his foot off the clutch, and the car jumped forward, curving through the gateway in the first wall, tyres slipping on the cracked concrete.

The second wall of the checkpoint was looming, the gap looked impossibly narrow.

"Stop! Let me out!" I was panicking, my chained hands struggling to find the door handle.

We slalomed around bollards, through the next wall, my hands were braced against the dashboard. I could no longer feel the gun barrel pressing into my body, Evelyn needed both hands to hang on. Steinlein shifted down two gears, the engine screamed and the wheels left the road as the Trabant bucked through the narrow gap. Another wall bore down on us, just metres ahead, Steinlein heaved the steering wheel to the right, his shoulder jutting into mine as he forced the car around. His knee went down as his foot slammed onto the accelerator again, through another gap, around chicanes. The last wall was before us, a border guard jumped out of the way as the car lined up for the final opening. Another few metres and we'd be in West Berlin.

Giving up on the door handle, I pulled my fingers into fists and slammed the metal handcuffs into Steinlein's wrist, knocking his hand off the steering wheel. Grabbing the wheel, I dragged it towards me, sending the car off to the right. The wheels bumped over a curb, a wing crumpled against a bollard and the Trabant rebounded, two wheels no longer in contact with the road. We hung there for an eternity, breath held, Steinlein meeting my eyes, his hate melding our fates together.

The car glissaded back to earth, spinning into the concrete wall. The windscreen crazed into opacity, the engine died.

"You'll never win." My voice was as pitted as the windscreen, my neck tense, expecting a bullet. "You may try to escape, you may try to stop us." Border guards surrounded the car, each levelling a machine pistol. Steinlein's door was torn open, rough hands grabbed him, pulling him out, other hands plucked Evelyn from the back seat. "We are the people, the people of the GDR, with all our dreams and hopes and convictions. With all our colours and histories and cultures."

But there was nobody to hear me, Steinlein and Evelyn had been taken away.

"We are the people, and we will always win," I said, wondering who I was trying to persuade.

HISTORICAL NOTE
The Point of Divergence

Historically minded readers will have noticed the point in time at which the narrative presented in Stealing the Future forks from reality. It is true that on the 4th of November 1989 there was the largest independent demonstration in the history of the GDR, but the For Our Country statement talked about by Martin and Margrit at the communal lunch on Sunday didn't actually make an appearance until the 28th of November 1989, when it was almost overshadowed (at least in Western accounts) by Helmut Kohl's '10 Point Plan' for German re-unification.

In Stealing the Future, however, both the Statement and the 10 Point Plan are launched on the same day as the mass demonstration—five days before the fall of the Wall.

This slight change to history resulted, at least in Martin's world, in increased awareness of West Germany's plans for a hasty annexation of the GDR, and in turn, of the issues that were considered in the For Our Country Statement.

The result: a continued existence for the GDR, and the grand social experiment that forms the backdrop to this book and its sequels.

More information about the point of divergence and the For Our Country Statement can be found on the author's website: www.maxhertzberg.co.uk

PREVIEW
OF
COLD ISLAND

Meet Boris

The car floundered through mud, sleet tracing the beam of the headlights. At the end of the track, a woman watched, rucksack slung over one shoulder, thin cords of rain twisting down her face and tunnelling below the collar of her parka.

She'd spent the last few days shivering in the ramshackle bothy up on the moors, subsisting on Marmite sandwiches and rainwater heated over a primus stove. A shelf of foxed books had provided the only entertainment—she'd found Animal Farm there, a book which had been censored in the East Germany of her childhood, and had thus attained an almost mythological status in her mind, but which hadn't come her way before.

She'd also used the time to cut her hair, but never satisfied with the end result, had sheared off more and more until all that was left was a short bob. Her head felt light, she could walk more easily. By hacking off her locks she had lightened the touch the land had on her. A bottle of brown dye completed the styling and, looking in the mirror, she realised that now she had lost ten inches of hair she would have to grow a new self-identity.

Her hair had been buried on the moor, just a hundred yards from the bothy. She'd checked each window before leaving, careful to avoid any approaching ramblers or estate workers, but in the sleety rain there was little chance of encountering another human in the empty uplands. So with a rusty spade she sliced into the thin layer of soil, striking rock within inches. She scalped a tussock, burying her past in the earth of England.

When she got back, she changed into dry clothes and stood by the window, staring out into the emptiness. The radio she carried around with her chirruped, a burst of static, then: *ETA twenty minutes.* A final look out of the window—dusk was falling and it was already dark inside the hut—then she packed Animal Farm, her sleeping bag, the scissors and the empty bottle of dye.

When the car stopped, she put her rucksack on the back seat and climbed into the front.

"Good night for it," said the driver with a welcoming smile. "I'm Boris."

As the car started back down the track and onto the road, the woman held out her hand for Boris to shake, but before he'd taken his own hand off the steering wheel she'd had second thoughts. She pulled back, wiped the dampness from her forehead and looked out at the blackness beyond the windscreen.

"I'm Mara," she told him when they reached the gate at the end of the track.

Boris didn't reply immediately, his focus was on the night outside, counting darkened buildings and fluorescing traffic signs.

"We're coming up to a main road," he said eventually. "I'm going to pull over so you can get down in the footwell in the back and I'll cover you with a blanket."

Mara looked at him in surprise, the glow from the dashboard lit ruddy cheeks, a face built for laughter, but now so sober.

"We don't need a fugitive sitting up front when we hit civilisation."

"Welcome to the Den, I'm Boris," said the person with a mass of messy dreadlocks tied up at the back of her head.

"Boris?" Mara was confused. She looked over her shoulder to where Boris, the Boris that had brought her, stood in the doorway.

"We're all Boris here." The one with the dreads laughed. "If it helps, you can call me DJane Boris and the other one, he's Transport Boris."

"Everyone calls me TB," the first Boris chipped in.

"Should I be Boris, too?" Mara wondered.

"You can be whatever you want to be." DJane Boris pulled her further into the bungalow.

"I'm Mara, thanks for your help-"

"C'mon, enough of the introductions. You must be starving? Let's sort you out with some food."

DJane and TB disappeared down a long hallway, assorted coats, scarves and gloves on pegs down one side, a closed door opposite.

The smell of cooking spices drifted down the corridor and Mara felt her eyes moisten. To be in the warmth, hot food waiting, friendly company—these were the basic comforts of life that she'd not expected to miss so much.

Mara followed DJane Boris to the kitchen and stood in the doorway, watching as TB began rolling out flat circles of dough. DJane Boris stirred a huge pot on the range.

"Can I help with anything?" Mara asked.

"Sit yourself down—you've got a visitor." DJane pointed a wooden spoon towards a table behind the door. In the flickering light of a single candle, a face watched Mara.

She sat down opposite the face and stared at it. "What are you doing here?"

"I once knew a girl," the face said. "She was great, real fun to be around. That girl was good for me-"

"Beth, what are you doing here?"

"She was German. Just like you."

"I don't need to hear this." Mara's voice hardened.

"It was a long time ago, feels like centuries. Actually, now I think of it, it *was* last century when I met this girl. 1994. She was called Mara."

"Will you shut up? It's not story time!" Mara looked over her shoulder at the Borises, but they were politely busying themselves at the stove.

1994

Whenever Mara thought back to her first days in this country, when she allowed the fingers of her mind to scoop through the arid sands of memory, she would settle on that first meeting with Beth, cheeks bright with daubed spirals, a third eye glowing in the centre of her forehead, smudged after eight hours in the cells. It was the grin that was so remarkable, a lopsided smile that drew attention away from the face painting and the D-lock strung around her neck.

Beth was wearing the grin when she saw Mara waiting. They'd seen each other at the road protest site, but never actually spoken.

"How do, lass?" asked Beth in what might have been a comedy Lancashire accent, but which in this small town passed for normal.

Mara pushed herself off the wall and held out her hand for a shake. Beth eyed it suspiciously for a moment before throwing her arms around the other woman.

"Thanks for waiting for me, it's horrible in there, you've no idea how nice it is to see a friendly face! Have you got my key?"

Mara took the key out of her pocket and handed it over. Once Beth had released the lock she hooked her arm through Mara's and started marching down the road, towards the camp. "What's up? Cat got yer tongue?"

Mara wasn't sure how to answer, she was still confused by so much in this country, still getting to grips with how people interacted here.

"I'm gasping for a cuppa, hope they've got the kettle on the fire. What's been happening anyway? Did I miss anything?"

"Cops came on site last night. Said they were looking for a runaway teenager." Mara stumbled over the words, glottal stops slicing her sentences. "We told them to fuck off."

"You're the kraut?" Beth stopped and scrutinised the other woman, as if appearance alone could betray nationality. "You are, aren't you? You're the one everyone has been talking about." Beth shifted gear again, pulling Mara with her, subject of foreignness effectively closed. "Let's pop into Sainsbury's, I could do with using a proper loo."

It was their first conversation, Beth rabbiting on, enjoying the high of being released after a night in the cells. Something clicked between them that day. In the years to come Mara would wonder whether the pair of them realised at the time that neither had shown her true face, or whether the realisation came much later. Beth had less confidence than she pretended, she smothered her insecurities with words; Mara felt handicapped by her poor English, which forced her into a passivity which back home she wouldn't have allowed herself.

Mara waited outside the toilets, hoping nobody would challenge her presence. She knew she didn't fit into the antiseptic white and orange of the supermarket—she was marked as alien by the smell of woodsmoke that clung to her stripy top that was grey with dirt, by her hair matted with twigs and last year's leaves. And by Beth's D-lock cradled in the crook of her elbow.

But she needn't have worried, the local residents were supportive. They gossiped about the 'eco-warriors' and brought food and building materials to the camp under the trees. A woman bustled past, arguing with a trolley that was dragging her off to the side. As the shopping trolley made a lunge at Mara's legs the woman gave her a wink and a ten pound note while her husband looked on, face dark with parsimony.

When Beth came out of the toilets the relief showed on Mara's face.

"What's up?"

Mara showed her the tenner and told her what had happened.

"Nice one!" Beth snatched the money and headed towards the aisles. "Come on, let's grab some White Lightning—could do with a drink after being banged up all day!"

When they got back to the camp, Beth shinned up the ladder set against the wall of a cottage. Mara hadn't been in the building before, it had always seemed so busy and she'd preferred to stay in a bender in the woods on the other side of the lane. Now she followed Beth through the first floor window and into the dusk of the unlit rooms.

The floorboards had been taken up, and while Beth danced over the joists, Mara had to take a moment to let her eyes adjust.

The window she'd just come through was the only one that hadn't been boarded up and she was backlit by the setting sun. The pink rays of day's end shone on the walls, picking out bright paintings and slogans but leaving what remained of the floor in shadow.

"Are you coming?" Beth shouted from deep inside the cottage.

Mara picked her way over the joists and loose boards, stopping in the doorway to think about a chalked message she found on the wall. *No rules, just respect!*

The floorboards in the hall were still intact, as was the light fitting in which a dim bulb burnt. Through another doorway to where Beth was sparking up. She turned as Mara entered, throwing back her head and expelling a lungful of aromatic smoke. She held the spliff out to Mara, her eyes glinting like snowflakes in moonlight.

"Come on, chill a bit."

Mara accepted the spliff, taking a puff while she squatted down. Beth took the D-lock and placed it on the floor next to a boy with a tufty beard and weedy hair to match. He watched the spliff jealously, impatient for his turn, his fingers rubbing in anticipation.

Mara made him wait a few more seconds, holding the burning tip in front of her, listening to the seeds crackling. She finally handed it over and turned to Beth, who was grimacing at the acidity of the cheap cider.

"What did you get nicked for?"

"Locked on to a JCB." Beth laughed and passed the bottle of cider to Mara. "First of all the driver was all, like, yeah fine, time for a break anyway. Got his newspaper out and had a gawp at page three. So we had a conversation about objectification and patriarchy, but he wasn't enjoying that so he fetched the foreman." Beth got the spliff back and took a hit before continuing. "Foreman was shitting himself, didn't know what to do. So he goes over to the portacabin and radios the pigs. Took them nearly an hour to work out that they didn't have to cut the lock off me. All they had to do was unscrew the bumper!"

"Did they charge you with anything?"

Beth eyed Mara for a moment, pinching the spliff between forefinger and thumb, then she shoved it in her direction.

"Nah, it was just breach of the peace. Hot bit?"

Mara shook her head and the joint, now just a smouldering roach, went back to Tufty.

The bailiffs and cops arrived the next morning. They ignored the benders in the woods and surrounded the cottage, arms linked to prevent anyone from getting into or out of the fortified squat. Mara prowled the edge of the cordon, ignoring cops and greedy cameras, scouting for a gap between the men with their yellow vests and plastic helmets. She knew it was a waste of time, the ladder had been drawn up, barbed wire and a mattress closed off the window she'd climbed through the night before. Even if she got through the line of sheriff's men she'd never manage to get into the house.

Mara crossed the road and looked back at the cottage. From down here she could see Beth lying along the ridge of the roof, her arms and hands buried under the tiles. It looked like she was locked on; they'd need bolt croppers, maybe something even more heavy-duty to get her off. Mara wanted to be up there with her, she wanted to be the support team for her new friend.

She turned back to the woods, through the gap in the wall where Tufty sat, arms linked with a few others, vaguely planning to prevent any machinery from coming in to the woods.

A tableau, Mara thought, lines drawn, immobile. Activists in the house and on the roof; police and bailiffs encircling the building. But the impasse was only temporary—a clanking grumble could be heard from down the road and the forces of law and order bubbled out to take control of the narrow lane.

"Get up the trees! There's trees still unprotected!" Tufty was shouting, spittle flecked his bum-fluff beard and his eyes were pleading with Mara, please save a tree.

Keeping a wary eye on the police cordon that had grown and solidified just a few feet away, Mara vaulted over the line of hippies and ran to the nearest mature tree. She struggled up the wide trunk, snapping off twigs as she went, adrenaline lifting her from the ground and into the boughs.

She lay along a branch no thicker than her thigh, just out of reach of the ground, feeling her heart bass-lining through the wood.

As her pulse slowed she lifted her cheek from the smooth bark, sparing a glance for the police. They were pressing themselves into the hedge as an excavator lumbered around the corner, tracks clawing the tarmac as it swivelled to make the sharp curve. Clouds of greasy smoke burped from a pipe and coated the guard of honour. She waited uneasily, watching the human in the barred cab, waiting to see which levers would be pulled. Right for the house, left for the under-defended woodland.

The beast drew closer, the creaking of its yellow limbs growing distinct against the ceaseless roar of its iron heart.

Left or right?

Mara held her breath, focussed on the driver. There were people in the house, they couldn't knock it down, not with everyone in there?

The beast lumbered closer, drawing level with the gateway to the woods, the boiler-suited Tactical Support cops crowded the row of cross-legged protestors.

A grinding, the pitch of the clanking rising, the excavator shuddering as the tracks slowed and halted. The puppet master pulled a lever, pushed another, the body of the beast swung round to the right, its arm rising high and deliberately lowering into the roof of an outbuilding, the bucket delved without discernable effort through the tiles, shattering slate into dark shivers that skittered to the ground. A wall collapsed, brickwork powdering under the force of the yellow arm.

To the beat of the heavy engine, the crashing snares of the collapsing building and the cries of the protesters, Mara pulled herself up against the tree trunk. Her tree was linked to others by fine strands of blue rope and a few feet further up a palette had been lashed to branches. Ignoring the throbbing of her heart, louder than any yellow machine, Mara hugged the tree, feeling for branches with her feet, climbing one limb, then another, not looking down, concentrating on the bark an inch before her face, edging towards the platform above.

"Mara! Are you up there?"

Mara's head peeked over the edge of the platform before retreating again, tortoise like, behind the lip of the pallet.

"Chuck us a rope!"

A timid hand appeared, feeding a coil of blue polyprop over the edge. The end of the rope wound its way lazily through the air, rippling its tail as it fell. Beth tested it with a couple of sharp tugs, then pulled herself up, gripping the knots between feet and knees.

"What you doing up here?" Beth asked as her head appeared alongside the palette. Her grin slipped as she took in the sight of Mara, lying on her tummy, white face pressed against the coarse boards, fingers gripping the edge of the flimsy structure.

"Oh dear, how are we going to get you down?"